GHOST
WARRIOR

GHOST WARRIOR

Lucia St. Clair Robson

TOR®

A TOM DOHERTY ASSOCIATES BOOK
NEW YORK

This is a work of fiction. All the characters and events portrayed in this book are either products of the author's imagination or are used fictitiously.

GHOST WARRIOR

Copyright © 2002 by Lucia St. Clair Robson

www.luciastclairrobson.com

Map by Ellisa Mitchell

A Tor Book
Published by Tom Doherty Associates, LLC
175 Fifth Avenue
New York, NY 10010

www.tor.com

Tor® is a registered trademark of Tom Doherty Associates, LLC.

ISBN: 0-812-57609-8
Library of Congress Catalog Card Number: 2001058612

First edition: May 2002
First mass market edition: May 2003

Printed in the United States of America

0 9 8 7 6 5 4 3 2 1

This book is dedicated to Jeanne Hazard Savage Robson. If everyone had her wisdom, her humor, her capacity for love, and her understanding of how to be a parent and a friend, the world would be an infinitely better place.

Thank you, Mom. I love you.

Acknowledgments

My first thanks go to author Jeanne Williams for introducing me to Lozen and Victorio, and for persistently suggesting I write about them. I want to give special thanks to Nochita of Dragoon, Arizona. He told me stories that made Lozen's spirit come alive.

Gunsmith David Eccles shared his encyclopedic knowledge of weapons. If I've managed to get the gun references wrong, that isn't David's fault. Eric Smith helped me solve a problem with shotguns.

Author and historian Candy Moulton told me how to change a wheel on a loaded wagon in the middle of a desert. Celeste Coffee of Groesbeck, Texas, and novelist Mike Blakely answered questions about horses. Frank Moorman introduced me to the work of Keith Basso, whose studies of the Apache's use of language provided a glimpse into their worldview. Vivian Waters knows all about the interior of the human body and filled me in on the effects of lead bullets on it.

Myrtle Marks, Glenda Marks, and Domikki Marks of Jackie's Kitchen in Mt. Vernon, Alabama, not only served up some fine catfish and coleslaw, but they also told me how to find Mt. Vernon barracks, the army post where Geronimo's people were held and where Lozen died. My old friend Shizuko Osaki McLaughlin went with me on explorations of Apache country. My brother, Buddy Robson, unraveled computer knots for me.

I owe heartfelt gratitude to my agent, Virginia Barber, and to Joseph Brendan Vallely. Their insights were a tremendous help.

Finally, thanks to my editor, Robert Gleason, for his encouragement, enthusiasm, and confidence.

My sister is my right hand. Strong as a man, braver than most, and cunning in strategy, Lozen is a shield to her people.

—Victorio

Why is it that the Apaches want to die—that they carry their lives on their fingernails? They roam over the hills and plains and want the heavens to fall on them.

—Cochise

The Apaches are the tigers of the human species.

—Gen. George Crook

Author's Note

The Ndee avoided using a person's given name, even when speaking of them in the third person. When they had to refer to someone, they used terms of kinship or nicknames. The nicknames were usually humorous and unflattering and not spoken in the person's presence.

The People often went by Spanish names, as well as the ones they chose or that were chosen for them; and they changed those names from time to time. When someone died, that person's name was no longer spoken. If it was the same word as a common object or animal, the Ndee made up new terms for those rather than risk calling up the ghost of the one deceased. For this reason, some names or their translations have been lost.

Some people were known by one or more names to their own people, but by different ones to the Mexicans and Americans. Cochise, for instance, was called Cheis by the Ndee.

To avoid adding more confusion to a situation already difficult for those not familiar with it, I have people refer to individuals by their given names, although rarely calling them that to their faces.

PART ONE
1850
Child

How the Pale Eyes Got Guns

Long ago, they say, White Painted Woman and her son, Killer of Enemies, were the only human beings on earth. White Painted Woman wanted another child, so she prayed a lot. One day while she was praying a spirit told her to take off all her clothes and lie on her back in the rain. The water entered that place—you know the one I mean—and she had a second son. She called him Child of the Water.

When Yusen, Life Giver, decided to put people on earth he wanted two kinds. He set out a gun and a bow and arrows on the ground, and he called to Killer of Enemies and Child of the Water. He told them to pick which one they wanted. Killer of Enemies was a big coward, but he was the older brother, so he got to choose first. He took the gun and left Child of the Water with the bow and arrow. The followers of Killer of Enemies became Pindah, the Pale Eyes people. Child of the Water became the leader of us Indians.

Killer of Enemies was not only cowardly, but he wasn't very smart, either. I heard that he almost chose the bow and arrows. If he had done that, we would have had the guns first. What do you think of that?

Chapter 1

HOOFBEATS OVERHEAD

Sister didn't know she had horse magic, but her older brother Morning Star did. That was why he brought her to the fiesta in the Mexican town of Janos, even though his friends didn't approve. Broken Foot was forty and lame besides. He didn't care much about appearances anymore, but Cousin and He Who Yawns were twenty-four. They cared a great deal. They ignored Sister, but they had the look of men who had stepped in something smelly and couldn't get it off their moccasins.

The hems of their best breechclouts reached their knees in front and the middle of the calves behind. The big silver disks called *conchos* decorated their wide leather belts. Their high moccasins were thickly beaded, and the upturned strip of leather on each toe was painted red. Their black hair hung loose, swaying against the backs of their thighs as they walked. Turquoise earrings dangled from the holes in their lobes. They had intended to impress everyone in Janos today, but here they were with a girl-child trailing them.

The boys resented Sister, too. When she left them guarding the horses on the outskirts of town, they had pelted her with acorns. Morning Star was sure they would pay for it later. They always did.

Probably the women who stayed in the camp upriver were yammering about her. Among the Ndee, thirteen-year-old girls did not associate with boys and men. Where his little sister was concerned, Morning Star never cared what people said. That was just as well, because she had been giving them something to talk about since she took her first tottering steps out of the cradleboard. She showed no signs of changing.

This was the first time she had seen a Mexican fiesta. As she strode through the plaza she seemed unperturbed by the noise and unimpressed by the goods laid out around her. She wore a fringed doeskin tunic over the leather skirt whose uneven hem reached below the tops of her high moccasins. She had slung her bow and fox-skin quiver across her back. A few strings of glass beads and a small bag of *hodenten*, the sacred cattail pollen, hung around her neck.

She had a child's mouth, with a full upper lip that curved like a double-arced bow, but someone much older looked out from her dark eyes. She had skin the deep reddish brown of the rocky bones of the mountains where her people lived. This morning she had fidgeted while Morning Star's young wife, She Moves Like Water, had combed her knee-length hair with a bundle of stiff grass. She had twisted it into a shiny black coil and secured it at the nape of Sister's neck with the curved piece of rawhide that marked her as an unmarried maiden. She Moves Like Water had tried to give Sister advice on proper behavior, but Morning Star knew she was wasting her time.

"Hola, amigos." A trio of mounted Mexicans cantered toward the four Ndee men. One of them handed Morning Star a gourd filled with pulque, but Morning Star passed it to Cousin.

Morning Star and half the men would stay sober today so they could look out for the drunk ones, but he would have refused the pulque, anyway. He did not drink when Mexicans were around. As he walked through Janos, Morning Star watched the crowds of Mexicans and Ndee men mingling to drink and to gamble. He scanned the flat roofs of the low adobe buildings, looking for the barrel of a musket. When a string of firecrackers exploded, he put a hand on the haft of his knife and looked around for Sister.

The villagers of Janos had invited the Ndee to hold council and to receive presents, even though they believed their Apache guests quite capable of murdering them. And even when they themselves would have murdered their guests if it seemed advantageous. The Mexicans and the Ndee had warred for so long that the stories passed down about it did not have a beginning. No one believed they would have an end, either.

The Ndee maintained an uneasy peace with the people of Janos in order to trade dried meat, hides, and the horses, mules, and cattle they stole from the neighboring state of Sonora. In exchange the Mexicans gave them knives, beads, blankets, and corn. The sorcery of alcohol, though, could change friendship to emnity with the flight of an insult or the flash of a knife blade.

Morning Star was relieved when they passed the last thatched hut on the outskirts of the village. On the open stretch of desert beyond, the horses milled in the corral of mesquite branches woven between uprights.

"Cimarrones," Sister murmured. Wild ones.

The mustangs were wild, all right, and the Mexicans and the Ndee flapped blankets at them and poked them with poles to make them wilder. Morning Star saw no fear in his sister's eyes, and he didn't expect to. Oblivious of the noise around her, she stood at the fence and assessed the horses.

"That one." She pointed her nose at a chunky pony the color of dried blood. He had a long neck, a large head, and crafty eyes. His delicate ears pricked forward, as though he were analyzing the situation. His wide nostrils indicated good wind.

Morning Star went to talk to the jefe, the Mexican in charge, a short man wearing straw sandals and a clean white cotton shirt and trousers. He carried a stout oak club and a coil of rope into the corral.

He shook out a loop in his rope as he stood in the eye of that storm of hooves, teeth, and tempers. With a flick of his wrist he threw the loop over the ears of Sister's selection and pulled it tight. Men ran to help him haul the horse out of the corral. They looked like a stew at a full boil, surging this way and that while the pony bucked and thrashed. Finally they secured his legs, slipped a rope over his lower jaw, and buckled a wide strap, a surcingle, around his middle. They snubbed him, trembling and wild eyed, to one of the posts set in a line and went back for another horse.

Sister held out some sugar in the palm of her hand and murmured to him. He eyed her with suspicion.

"Is that the one you're going to ride?" Cousin asked Morning Star.

"No."

Ndee usually waited for others to explain themselves if and when they wanted to, but this was different. This involved wagering.

"Which one are you going to ride?" inquired He Who Yawns.

"None of them."

Broken Foot didn't ask any questions. He watched the horse stretch out his neck and snatch the sugar from Sister's palm. He watched her take pollen from the bag around her neck and make a cross with it on his forehead. He saw her blow into the pony's nostrils; then he limped off to place a wager on him.

"Your sister will ride for you?" Cousin obviously thought Morning Star had turned foolish.

"Yes." Morning Star went off to place his own bet.

The heaps of wagered objects grew higher. The Ndee shed their necklaces, their silver armbands, and their *concho* belts. They threw down saddles, bridles, and blankets and everything else of any value. They weren't only betting on the winning horse. They were wagering on which riders would still be clinging to their mounts' backs at the end of the race and who would be dead, alive, or badly hurt.

Roping the other ten horses took most of the afternoon and a week's worth of sweat and swearing. By the time all the animals stood tethered in a line, the jefe's pants and shirt were no longer white and Sister was running her hands along the rust-colored horse, murmuring to soothe him. She draped her arms over his back and stood on a rock so she could lie across him. He sidestepped and looked back at her with bulging eyes, but he didn't try to bolt.

"*Listos, muchachos,*" shouted the mustache. "*A caballo.*" The men holding the mustangs took a firmer grip while the riders did their best to climb aboard. Sister hiked her skirt up under her belt. She took a running start and jumped. She scrambled into a sitting position, picked up the rope that would serve as a rein, clamped her legs against his sides, and waited. A shudder passed along his spine. Sister understood why. She must have felt like a young cougar landing on him. He roached his back, gathered his feet like the stems in a handful of wildflowers, and awaited developments.

The trumpet blasted. There was a moment of stillness while the mustangs devised their strategies. The horse next to Sister promptly laid down and rolled over. The rest took off bucking and twisting, scattering onlookers or running over them.

Sister's pony and two others ran for the tall pole at the finish as though a pack of wolves snapped at their heels. Sister pulled ahead and was about to stand up on his back to show off when a shot rang out. The pony stumbled. His nose hit the ground, and his momentum carried his hindquarters up and over his head and Sister's. Sister somersaulted, landed on her feet, and ran a few steps to regain her balance.

The pony's hooves jerked, and his eyeballs rolled up. Sister squatted and ran her fingers over his chest until she found the bullet hole. None of the Ndee here possessed one of the fire sticks that spat balls of black metal. A Mexican had done this.

"Someone must have bet on one of the other two horses," Morning Star said.

Sister was outraged. "I would have won."

"Don't let them see that they've angered you. That gives them power over you. You can't change what's past, but you can learn from it. What have you learned today?"

"That I cannot trust Mexicans."

"You can never trust Mexicans."

————

SISTER GLARED AT NA'TANH, CORN FLOWER, SPRAWLED ON his stomach in a curdled puddle of half-digested beans and bad booze. If she put the chile powder into his breechclout now, he probably wouldn't even notice it. He looked dead, but he snored like a bear. He had made himself stupid with pulque, a brew that smelled worse than old moccasins.

She kicked the sole of his very old moccasin with the pointed toe of her own, but he only grunted. She bounced a stone off his bare buttock, taut as a drumhead. That made her feel better, but he seemed none the worse for it.

Whooping and weaving in their saddles, the drunken ones had left Janos the night before surrounded by those who had stayed sober. Morning Star had pulled her up to ride in front of him, and she had slept with her cheek resting on his war pony's mane and her arms around the horse's neck.

When they arrived in camp, most of the drinkers had slid from their horses and staggered off to fall asleep. Some of them had brought pulque home and shared it with their wives. Many of the sober ones decided to make up for lost time. The party had lasted until dawn.

Like Corn Flower, some of them hadn't made the effort to return to Janos for the second day of talks and trading. Sister's father had been one of those. When she passed his brush shelter, she heard him snoring.

He had never stopped mourning his wife, killed and scalped by Mexican bounty hunters when Sister was an infant. Morning Star had given horses, blankets, and saddles to this shaman and that one in the hope that they would cure his father's grief. Sister prayed every day, asking the all powerful spirit, Life Giver, to cure him.

Whenever women brewed a batch of *tiswin* from the sap of the mescal plant and announced a party, her father was the first to arrive and the last to leave. Sister would wait while he danced with the other revelers. Women whom she'd always known to be chaste would stagger off into the bushes with him. Sister's cheeks would burn as she listened to the laughter and the rustling from the darkness. In the pale light of many dawns she had helped her father home.

Sister couldn't stay sad this morning, though. The sky arched intensely blue. Butterflies floated in the palo verde trees crowding the dry streambed of the arroyo. Doves wooed in the mesquite trees. Women called softly from one family's cluster of brush-thatched shelters to another as they ground corn and mended moccasins.

When Sister reached a stand of mesquite trees, she laid out the rawhide loop of the tumpline. She began gathering limbs and placing them in one end of it. As she wandered farther away in search of firewood, she saw a barrel cactus on the sunny wall of the arroyo. Last fall's shiny yellow fruit grew in a whorl around its top.

She slid down the slope at the shallow mouth of the gully and walked downhill. The arroyo narrowed; the walls closed in overhead and sliced the bright strip of sunshine thinner. The overhanging rim threw a deep shade that cooled the air.

She reached up and picked one of the fruits. She squatted at the bottom of the cleft and rested her arms on her knees while she savored the tart juice and the crunch of the tiny black seeds packed inside.

A puff of cold wind startled her. It didn't belong here in the middle of the summer. It stirred the wisps of hair around her face. Its chill started a prickling at the nape of her neck. A roar filled her skull, a babble of voices. She stood up and raised her chin, her mouth partly open, her eyes closed.

She raised her arms to shoulder height, her palms cupped upward, as she had seen *di-yin*, holy men, do. She held them there and waited for the Wind Spirit to speak to her. When it did, the voice-that-wasn't-a-voice resonated in the bones of her face like the flutter of leaves in the cottonwood. She turned slowly until dread stopped her as surely as a stone cliff. She faced into the approaching evil and imagined Ghost Owl swooping toward her, come to steal her soul. Chills chased along her spine; her heart raced.

When the rumbling started she thought it was the Wind Spirit again, but then the ground began to tremble. Dirt fell from the arroyo's rim onto her shoulders and outstretched arms. The rumble fragmented into the beat of hooves. She opened her eyes as the first horse reached the edge of the gorge and leaped it. More followed. She saw the tensed muscles of their foam-flecked legs and the wide cinches under their taut bellies as they passed overhead. Drops of their sweat fell on her. She saw the clumsy wooden stirrups, each containing a dusty black boot.

Mexican soldiers. Lancers probably. She counted fifty or sixty at least. Not many warriors had remained in camp, and they were as sick as her father and Corn Flower.

When the last soldier had leaped the gully and the thunder of hooves receded, Sister tried to scramble up the steep side, impelled by the need to warn her brother's wife, her father, and the others. The soles of her moccasins slipped on the gravelly slope, and she slid to the bottom, sand driven to the quick under her fingernails.

She sat with her knees drawn up to make herself as small as possible. She twined her fingers together to keep them from shaking. Already the soldiers were shooting. They laughed and shouted. Sister heard the clatter of an iron lancehead striking rock and bouncing. She heard the screams of the women and children.

She fought back the fear rising in her throat. Fear was a distraction, and she had to be able to think and act. Her brother had told her that as soon as she was old enough to understand the words.

She could tell by the scattering of hooves and the rustle of bushes that they were chasing their prey through the undergrowth. She heard a horse approaching the arroyo, searching the thick brush for survivors. Sister crawled backward on her belly among the cactus and creosote bushes, the thorns catching at her skin and clothes and hair. The rocks scraped her elbows and knees, but she didn't feel it. When she could go no farther in the narrow cleft, she found a coyote den dug into the wall. She breathed a quick prayer of thanks to Life Giver, though she would rather have been beholden to any creature but a coyote. Coyotes were trouble—always had been, always would be.

She poked a yucca stem into the hole to dislodge any

rattlesnakes that might be there; then she wriggled in feetfirst.
When her toes hit the back of the den, her head and shoulders
were still exposed. She grabbed a broken piece of dried ocatillo stem shaped like half a cylinder and perforated where
the thorns had been seated. She lay her left cheek on the
warm ground, cupped the ocatillo stem around her nose and
mouth and scooped the sand over her head. Then she buried
her arms and hands in it.

As the sound of the hooves grew louder, she wondered if
she had covered enough of her black hair. The horse stopped
just above her. Sand cascaded down the slope and onto her
head. She could feel the soldier's eyes searching the bushes
and the shadows under the arroyo's walls. She waited for a
lead ball from his musket to drill through her skull. She
wondered if she would feel the solid heat of it. She wondered
if, when she died, she would see her mother in the Happy Land.

She heard the soldier ride away, but she stayed motionless.
She breathed through the holes in the cactus stem while the
silence from the camp lengthened and the sun climbed up
the slope of the sky, hovered at the peak, and started down
the other side. She lay there until the light in the arroyo
dimmed. She didn't flinch when a rattlesnake slithered over
her arm.

She murmured to him as Morning Star and her grandmother had taught her. "Ostin, Old Man, I have troubles
enough. Don't bother me or give me snake sickness."

When he moved on, she wriggled out of the hole, shook
sand from her hair, and brushed it out of her ears and eyes.
Her throat ached, and her lips stuck together when she tried
to moisten them.

Sister peered over the rim of the arroyo. The sky had
turned pink, but it pooled bloodred at the western rim of the
world. Shadows crawled farther out from the rocks and trees
and bushes as though ambushing the day. A wind moaned
sorrowfully. Smoke still rose from the remains of the shelters.

Sister knew the route to the site where her people had
hidden food supplies, water jugs, weapons, and utensils. All

the children over the age of five knew they should make their way there in case of an attack. She also knew she should leave immediately. Even if the soldiers didn't come back, the souls of those they had killed would be restless. Sister imagined them flapping like wounded birds around the campsite, confused by their sudden change in form and frightened about the long journey ahead of them.

Supernatural creatures scuttled around at night, eager to bewitch the unwary. And Ghost Owl soared about in search of souls to steal. No one traveled after dark unless necessity gave them no choice.

Sister wriggled through the bushes on her stomach, as silent as the shadows lengthening along the stony ground. She lay motionless under a bush, ear to the ground, listening for the faint vibration of boots or hooves before moving to the next bit of cover.

With a prayer to the helpful spirits, she took ashes from the campfire and rubbed them on her face and hands to ward off ghosts. The ashes were still warm. An old woman and a young one had thrown themselves across three small girls in an attempt to shield them, but the soldiers had shot them all and taken their scalps. In the last of the day's light Sister recognized the mother, wife, and daughters of He Who Yawns.

Those were the first bodies she used for cover, and soon she had more of them than she needed. Most of the dead had been scalped, with bloody holes where their right ears had been. To collect on the government's bounty, the Mexican lancers had condemned the Ndee's spirits to wander eternity mutilated. That was as bad as the killing itself.

Sister crawled on her stomach until she reached the charred ruins of her father's shelter. He lay on his back in front of it. He still clutched his bow with an arrow nocked, but a Mexican dragoon had driven a lance through his chest and pinned him to the ground. His head was turned toward her, his face on a level with hers. His eyes were open, and she thought he might open his mouth and demand that she pull the lance out of him so he could get up.

Her father's blankets would be useful in the cold mountain nights to come, but Sister did not touch them. She did not untie the knife sheath from his belt or pry the bow and arrow from his fingers. To take anything that belonged to a dead person might lure the spirit back and cause it to cling to her.

She entered a dry gulley and followed it to the camp of her grandmother and She Moves Like Water. She did not find either of them there. They might be lying dead in the bushes, hidden by the night shadows, or the Mexicans might have captured them to sell as slaves.

Sister retrieved her blanket from the ashes of her shelter. Fire had charred the edges of it, but it was usable. Still lying on her stomach and with a wary eye on everything around her, she rolled it tightly. She took spare moccasin laces out of one of the pouches hanging from her belt and knotted them together. She tied each end of the roll with the long cord. She put the cord over her head and adjusted the blanket roll so it rode in a diagonal across her back.

Panic swept through her. Was everyone dead? Had the Mexicans of Janos ambushed her brother and the other men? Was she alone, many long days' journey from the valley to the north, the one her people called home?

She slid to the bottom of the gully where she felt safe enough to move at a crouch. Feeling her way, she found the small spring that had supplied water to the camp. She drank enough to wet her throat and ease the thirst. Keeping her head below the gulley's rim she followed it down the mountainside, moving like a wisp of smoke through the darkness.

By the time she reached the bottom of the mountain, the night air had cooled considerably. Ahead of her stretched the valley leading to the Janos River and the thicket of vines, cactus, and willows where those who had survived would meet. She could run there in a short time, but she couldn't risk that. Soldiers might be waiting in the darkness for her to blunder into them.

She slid on her stomach over the edge of the gully and started out, pulling herself forward with her arms and pushing with her legs. In camp, Creep and Freeze was a game all the children played. Now she knew why.

Chapter 2

"THE RAVELLED SLEAVE OF CARE"

Rafe Collins and Absalom Jones stood at the bar that ran along the far end of Doña Yolanda's cantina, La Luz. Horses, Texans, and a billiard table filled the center of the room. Campaigns with these Texans and others just as rambunctious had battered the table. It boasted a marble base that had required most of the population of Mesilla to lift it off the freight wagon and carry it into the cantina, but whenever a horse backed into it, the heavy red silk cord tassels at the corners swayed.

The Texans were playing billiards on horseback. Each player in turn took his outside foot from the stirrup and slid down so his cue stick was level with the table. If their game had rules, they weren't evident to the casual observer. Whenever one sank a ball, he celebrated with a Comanche war whoop that made dread dance a Virginia reel up and down Rafe's spine.

They were raising a lot of ruckus, but there was too much tobacco juice on the dirt floor for them to raise a lot of dust. Rafe was glad about that. He'd hauled a load of salt beef and flour from El Paso the night before, and since he made the forty-mile trip as fast as his mules could travel, he'd breathed enough dust already. Rafe knew better than to dawdle between El Paso and Mesilla. Apaches found dawdlers easy pickings.

Rafe considered searching out a bar infested with fewer Texans, but he liked La Luz. Besides, most places had a clientele as rowdy as this one. The war between the United States and Mexico had officially ended in February of 1848, more than two and a half years ago. The settlement of Mesilla had sprung up in the disputed strip of land between Texas, New Mexico, and northern Mexico. The rule of law had not yet taken up residence.

Rafe caught Doña Yolanda's eye and held up two strong, scarred fingers, tanned by years in the sun to the color of old whiskey. The same sun had bleached his blond hair almost white. After a life spent staring into its glare, he narrowed his light green eyes out of habit, giving him a thoughtful look. The sun had nothing to do with his long legs, slender waist, big hands, powerful arms, and broad shoulders. His parents and the handling of an indeterminate number of mules were responsible for those. Countless tussles with adversity made him look older than his twenty years.

"Two more shots of Taos Lightning, gentle lady." He watched Doña Yolanda select a slender bottle from among the dowdier soldiers on the back bar. She filled two small glasses.

The bottle's label proclaimed it to be Taos Lightning, but Rafe doubted that it was the real thing. The whiskey's manufacturer had been slaughtered in the Pueblo uprising in 1847, though there were many who claimed that his spirits, if not his spirit, lived on.

"That ol' Meskin is fixin' to shoot hisself with a hoe," Absalom Jones observed.

Absalom's accent proclaimed North Carolina roots, but Rafe didn't ask. One didn't inquire into a man's origins here. Absalom had mentioned that he was headed for California, but that didn't set him apart from the thousands of others headed for the newly discovered goldfields there.

Rafe glanced over Absalom's shoulder. A fog of tobacco smoke obscured the view, but sure enough, Miguel Sanchez stood in the doorway with the butt of a wooden hoe handle in his mouth. Rafe had seen this drama before.

"It ain't loaded." Rafe took his extra shot of whiskey from the bar and carried it to the man.

He held out the glass. Sanchez studied it over the end of the handle. The whiskey's amber silk glowed seductively in the lantern light. Rafe waited until Sanchez realized he could not drink the whiskey while his mouth was occupied by the non-business end of a hoe. He set the hoe against the wall and accepted Rafe's gift with a gracious nod of his white-haired head and a smile that gave a tonsil-view unobstructed by front teeth.

"Dios le bendiga, señor," he said. May God bless you.

"Same to you, old man." Rafe said it in Spanish; then he nodded politely and returned to the bar.

"Apaches." He tapped his temple with the scarred, callused tips of his fingers. "They unsettled his reason."

"How's that?" Absalom asked.

"Sanchez was hoeing his corn when a bunch of brunets rose up around him. They'd stuck corn leaves in their hair and blended with the crop. Mexicans swear Apaches have mastered invisibility, and I reckon they might be right."

"What happened?"

"One of them stabbed Sanchez with his own machete. Knocked out his front teeth and punched on through the back of his neck. Sanchez executed a passable possum imitation, but he expected them to finish what they had well begun."

"And they didn't?"

Rafe shook his head. "Apaches are capricious critters." He took a sip of the whiskey. "Sanchez ain't been right in the head since."

It was a long speech for him. It left him feeling out of breath and foolish for having used up so much air in the making of it, but he squandered a little more. "How old would you say he is?"

Absalom studied the man. "Sixty or seventy."

"He's shy of forty. The fright turned his hair white as a boiled linen shirt."

"I'm surprised the savages left him his scalp."

"Apaches don't lift hair, which is odd considering their own scalps bring a hundred pesos each on the other side of the border."

"Their hair?"

"The Mexican authorities have put a bounty on it."

Rafe drained his glass and set it on the bar. Doña Yolanda filled it. She allowed a few drops of whiskey to slosh over the sides. Such extravagance was rare for her, but she had fixed her attention on the Texans. They bore watching even in sober circumstances, although in Doña Yolanda's experience, sober and circumstances were mutually exclusive terms where Texans were concerned.

These Texans didn't disappoint her. One of them, mounted on a nervous gray, drew his old navy Colt revolver. He aimed it at the six ball cowering in front of the four ball near the far pocket. Doña Yolanda laid the barrel of her shotgun along the high bar, its muzzle pointed at him. Rafe and Absalom moved apart to give her a clear field of fire.

If the Texans hadn't been as free with their money as they were with their mischief, she wouldn't have tolerated them. She allowed horse billiards in La Luz, but she forbade pistol billiards. She likewise frowned on their shooting at the cockroaches.

"Párate, pendejo," she barked.

The Texan looked up, astonished by her crankiness and deeply hurt by her referring to him as a pubic hair.

"No pistolas." She repeated it loudly and slowly in English. "No pistols."

"But ma' am . . ."

"No pistolas." Doña Yolanda waved the musket's muzzle at the line of holes in the adobe wall behind the billiard table. They were a souvenir of the first, last, and only game of pistol billiards Texans had played in La Luz.

"Yes, ma'am."

The Texan returned his Colt to the waistband at the back of his filthy canvas trousers. He shifted the wad of tobacco in his mouth and spat onto the dirt floor.

With her forefinger Doña Yolanda separated out a strand of hair over her ear and pulled it from the bun nesting at the nape of her neck. She stretched it taut so Rafe and Absalom could see the silver streak, like a moonbeam in the lustrous midnight of her hair.

"Tejanos . . ." She leaned forward. Rafe translated her

Spanish for Absalom. "Texans are devils sent by God to turn us gray," she said. "They and the Apaches drive us early to our graves." She tucked the end of the lock back in place.

Rafe didn't mention that he was a Texan himself. He also didn't mention that he had been with Gen. Winfield Scott's forces when they stormed Chapultepec castle in September of 1847 and won the war. He was the sweat-soaked, powder-blackened, sixteen-year-old soldier who had lowered the Mexican flag flying above the fortress and raised the colors of the Voltiguer Regiment. He hadn't kept count of how many Mexicans he had sent early to their graves that day, and he didn't want to think about it now. He didn't object to killing if the situation required it, but he took no pride or pleasure in it.

A stout individual appeared at Rafe's elbow. So much hair sprouted on his face and stuck up above his buttoned collar that he looked as though he were wearing a bearskin under his red flannel shirt. He smelled as though the bear hide hadn't been properly tanned.

He made a run at the Spanish pronunciation of *general*. It sounded like *Hen-or-Al*.

"The Hen-or-Al is looking for you, Collins."

"Which general would that be, Jim?" Rafe had noticed that when the war ended, every former Mexican soldier above the rank of corporal promoted himself to colonel at the very least, and often to general.

"Armijo. He's bivouacked at the inn on the square."

"Manuel Armijo? I heard he'd fled to Mexico with his tail between his fat legs."

When Jim shrugged, the thick fringe of hair around his collar meshed with that of his beard making it seem as though his head were sinking into a brush pile. "He's headed for Chihuahua with the *conducta*."

Rafe was surprised that he hadn't heard the clamor of the *conducta*, the annual wagon train pulling into town on its way south. The solid wooden wheels of the Mexican oxcarts alone made enough racket to raise the dead. But then, the Texans had been making plenty of racket themselves.

"I suppose he intends to sell guns to the Apaches," Rafe said.

"That would be my guess."

"Did he say what he wants of me?"

"Naw. The Hen-or-Al always did keep dark."

Rafe finished his Taos Lightning. He laid down a silver peso, picked up his wide-brimmed, dirt-colored felt hat from the bar, and nodded farewell to Doña Yolanda and Absalom.

As Rafe left, Miguel Sanchez dodged into the milling press of billiard players so he could shovel up a pile of fresh horse manure. Doña Yolanda paid him a centavo for each warm deposit he removed. The work suited him.

La Luz's cantina was as close to a cornfield or a grassy prairie as Miguel intended to get. Fields and prairies had a way of sprouting Apaches, but then, so did rocks, arroyos, cacti, creosote bushes, and bare desert floor. Cantinas had yet to produce any, though, so Miguel Sanchez had decided to live out his remaining days here. He might have been crazy, but he was no fool.

NIGHT SHADOWS WERE DRAPING THEMSELVES OVER ME-silla's ragged edges and dangling from the protruding butt ends of the roof beams of the swaybacked adobe houses when Rafe left the cantina. He dodged into a doorway to avoid an ox-drawn wagon that almost scraped the houses on each side of the alley. Mesilla's main plaza wasn't far away. Nothing was far from anything else in Mesilla. The settlement sat at about the halfway point on the six-hundred-mile route that began in Santa Fe. It crossed the contentious new border with Mexico at El Paso del Norte and wound its perilous way to the city of Chihuahua.

The wagon train had been making the trip for at least two centuries. Even the poor went along carrying their woolen weavings on their backs or loaded onto burros so they could trade them for chocolate, silver, and silk. The ratio of soon-to-be-married men would be high. Mexican men traditionally made the journey to bring back Apache women as slaves, wedding gifts for their brides-to-be.

Wagons and draft animals, pack mules, drivers, and exasperation filled the square. Mesilla had become a favored spot for resting the animals and repairing the vehicles, for stocking up on supplies, and for getting drunk and renting love. Already the sound of guitars and singing in the various cantinas mingled with the babel of the drivers' oaths sworn in several languages and the braying and lowing and cracking of whips in the square. The rattle of wagon chains and the shriek of axles added to the din. The perimeter of adobe buildings concentrated the noise and amplified it.

Everyone carried a pistol or two, a long piece, a sword or machete, and a knife, the bigger the better. The mounted men added holster pistols, rifles, and shotguns slung from their saddles. Rafe knew they probably carried other knives and pistols hidden in boots or under the striped cotton blankets that covered them from neck to thigh.

Rafe detoured around a Mexican oxcart whose driver was disputing the right-of-way with a Missouri teamster on the high seat of a Studebaker wagon. Several arrows stuck from the side of the Studebaker. While the two drivers occupied themselves discussing each other's lineage in Spanish and Missourian, Rafe grasped the arrow close to where the iron head was embedded in the wood. He pushed against the side of the wagon with his thumb and wiggled the shaft until he dislodged it.

He could tell by the red, black, and yellow stripes painted on the shaft that an Apache had made it. He broke the arrow in half and tossed it away. Rafe already had a large collection of Apache arrows, limited to those that Apaches had shot at him personally.

Two Mexicans stood guard over the covered freight wagon parked in front of the inn. They wore the usual blankets and tight leather pantaloons that flared below the knees. The lacing on the sides allowed the white cotton drawers underneath to show through.

Painted on the side of the wagon was a rendering of the

Virgin Mary with a complexion that suggested jaundice. A swarm of cherubim buzzed around her head. Their expressions were probably intended to be pious, but they looked constipated instead.

Strings of what resembled dried figs hung along the wagon's sides. They were dark brown and shriveled. Rafe knew they were General Armijo's collection of Apache ears. When Armijo had occupied the governor's palace in Santa Fe, he had adorned his office with them. Now he carried them with him. Rumor said that he left them on display even while he was distributing guns from the tailgate of the wagon to possible relatives of the ears' former owners.

During the long hours Rafe spent driving his own wagon, he entertained himself with Shakespeare. He could quote hundreds of passages. The one that occurred to him as he looked at the strings of dried relics was, "Friends, Romans, countrymen, lend me your ears." But the line that seemed most apt in Mark Anthony's funeral speech for Caesar was, "The evil that men do lives after them."

Armijo probably sold the guns in Chihuahua with the understanding that the Apaches would use them only on the inhabitants of the neighboring Mexican state of Sonora. After all, the Indians stole Sonoran cattle, horses, and mules and sold them to the grateful citizens of Chihuahua. The Apaches were as adept as Armijo when it came to playing factions against each other.

Rafe found General Armijo seated on a bench in the corner of the inn's front room. In the dim light he loomed like an outcrop of rock that had gone soft. He wore a white shirt that could shelter a small family. His belly hung in folds over the waistband of white pantaloons stretched taut across his thighs. The straps of his leather sandals sank into the flesh of his stubby feet like harnesses on an overfed pair of piglets.

An Indian woman crouched in the opposite corner. She was a slave most likely and Apache by the look of her, though she wore a Mexican skirt and white tunic blouse, and her hair was neatly plaited in a single braid long enough for her to sit on. If looks could kill, Armijo would have been attracting even more flies than he already was. She was lovely and young, probably not more than fourteen, and Rafe didn't have to guess what use the general made of her.

You'd best not allow a knife anywhere near her, General, Rafe thought. She will find your gullet under all that suet and divide it in two for you.

Rafe thought it a good thing that Armijo had been both governor and commanding general when Stephen Watts Kearny and his ragtag army entered Santa Fe five years ago and claimed the province for the United States. Armijo had capitulated so fast that the occupation had been bloodless. The bloodletting came a year later when the Pueblo Indians rose up and slaughtered every American man, woman, and child they could find in the town. Rafe suspected that Armijo had been behind that. During his tenure as provincial governor he had been behind most of what was greedy, venal, murderous, and dastardly in New Mexico.

Manuel Armijo smiled broadly when he saw Rafe. "Mr. Collins! What a pleasure." His English had improved since the Americans took over.

"No."

"You are not Señor Rafe Collins?" He had a booming, jovial voice. When he smiled, his small black eyes disappeared into the rolls of fat around them like currants into bread dough.

"The answer is no."

"But you do not yet know my proposition."

"Doesn't matter. The answer is no."

"They say you're the only one who has carried goods between here and El Paso without losing a side of bacon or a grain of corn to the savages."

"Just lucky, I guess."

"My driver has fallen ill from an excess of Pass whiskey. I would say he is more driven than driving." Armijo might have winked, but since the flesh of this face almost obscured his eyes, Rafe couldn't be sure. "I'll pay you two hundred and fifty dollars to take my lead wagon to Chihuahua—and bring it back, of course."

What Rafe had in mind to say was, "I'll do it when there's enough frost in hell to kill snap beans." What he said instead was, "No."

Rafe turned and left, although putting his back to Armijo made him uneasy. He had heard the stories. Armijo was the winner in a walk when it came to vindictiveness.

Night had fallen with a thud by the time Rafe reached the wagon yard behind the hostler's shop. Horses, mules, burros, and oxen and vehicles of all persuasions had filled the trampled field since he'd tethered his mules that afternoon. As he approached his old Packard wagon, he realized that Absalom was sitting with his back against the front wheel. He passed a bottle to the man sitting with him.

In the darkness the second man seemed to have misplaced his face. The space between the wide brim of his floppy straw hat and the ragged shirt collar was blank except for the startling round whites of a pair of eyes. Then Rafe walked close enough to see that he was a Negro.

Absalom stood hastily and dusted the seat of his trousers with his hat. "Is this your wagon, Rafe?"

"It is."

"I didn't think the owner would be back tonight." He looked toward Mesilla and the sounds of celebration. "Loud, ain't it?" He grinned. "Those boys do murder sleep."

Rafe smiled at the discovery of someone who could quote Shakespeare.

"We were fixin' to bed down with our horses." Absalom nodded to the three animals hobbled nearby. He waved his hand to include his companion. "This is my man, Caesar."

The black man stood up. He took off his hat and held it in front of his chest. "Pleased to meet ya, massa, suh."

"Likewise."

Rafe watched the two of them collect their blankets and lay them under another wagon. He thought it odd that Absalom would be sharing a bottle with a slave. Southerners would dine with hogs, drink with their horses, kiss their coon hounds on the mouth, bed down with cattle, and dance a reel with a hairy, two-hundred-pound fur trapper, but they were fastidious about doing anything that might suggest social contact with a son of Africa.

Rafe had learned early in his twenty years not to pry into other men's business. He also knew that the racket from Mesilla would become more contentious and punctuated with gunfire. He pulled his blankets from the wagon's leather boot and laid them under it. Before he rolled up in them, he took a cloth packet from his pocket. He unwrapped the beeswax inside, pulled off two pieces of it, and stuffed one into each ear.

The army hadn't needed to teach Rafe to shoot. Any boy growing up in Comanche country could hit what he aimed at. It hadn't been able to make him obedient, except when survival demanded it; but a young West Point lieutenant had taught him to read. A captain had lent him tattered copies of *Hamlet*, *Macbeth*, and *Julius Caesar*. He had sat spellbound in the rowdy audience of soldiers while the officers performed *Othello*, *As You Like It*, and others.

He drifted off to dreams with the Bard in his head. "Innocent sleep / sleep that knits up the ravelled sleave of care."

Chapter 3

REAR GUARD

The coyote hustled, nose to the ground, following a jackrabbit's scent through the desert darkness. When he heard the soft, bubbling cry of a quail, he veered toward it. Saliva flooded the coyote's mouth at the prospect of tearing into the quail's succulent flesh. He could almost feel the feathers tickling his nose, the tantalizing flutter of wings against his face before it went limp in his jaws. With muzzle down and bony hindquarters and banner of a tail up, he put one paw out, eased over it, and set another. The muscles of his shoulders and haunches bunched to pounce.

"*Ba'ts'osé,* Brother Coyote . . ." The voice came from a rounded lump next to a large creosote bush. Twin reflections of the full moon shone in the dark eyes that looked out from it. "I have troubles enough," the mound said. "Play your tricks on another."

The mound stirred as Sister shifted under her blanket to relieve a cramp in her leg. By the moon's bright light she thought she could see chagrin flash in the coyote's eyes when he realized she was not a quail. He turned and sauntered back to the jackrabbit's spoor.

Sister had spoken Coyote's name aloud deliberately. Speaking someone's name put great weight to the request, but that might have been a mistake. Old Man Coyote was a trickster. Sister wondered if evil consequences would follow her talking to him.

Coyote was responsible for death. Back when the earth was new and animals spoke like people, Coyote had thrown a stone into water. He had declared that if it sank, all living things would experience a sleep from which they would not awaken on this earth. The stone sank, and people and animals and plants had been dying ever since.

Sister wondered if death and the Mexicans had taken everyone she knew. She imagined walking north alone. She imagined arriving at her village and finding her grandmother and the other old ones dead, too.

She withdrew deeper into the cave of her blanket and stared out at the expanse of thicket along the river. Night and the pale moonlight had changed the landscape and made it menacing. Thorny mimosa vines wove the willow, acacia, and cactus into an impenetrable wall. She walked along it, but she could not find the narrow trail made by wild pigs and deer passing through it on their way to the water. She could not even find the stubby cylinder of gray rock standing near the path.

Her brother had pointed it out. "It looks like Mouse's penis."

Sister had laughed. Everyone knew the story of Coyote trading his big penis for Mouse's small one so he could woo a beautiful woman.

Now the rock was gone. Maybe Trickster Coyote had taken it the way he had taken Mouse's penis. Sister took a long, deep breath to still the panic rising in her. In her life she had experienced danger. She was familiar with death, with hunger and thirst, bone chilling cold, and intense heat, but she had never lived alone.

She gave the quail cry again, and this time she heard an answer from the thicket. It would probably have fooled another quail, but she recognized it as her brother's. He had taught her to make the cry, after all.

It sounded again, and she walked along the shadowy wall of vines and bushes, following it. She found the path and crawled into it, relieved to have the thorny branches close in around her. Soldiers on horseback could not follow her here. Even Ghost Owl would not likely risk becoming entangled in the thicket's treacherous embrace.

She stood up in the clearing.

"Enjuh," Morning Star said. "It is good."

She wrapped her arms around his waist and felt the strength of him encircling her. She held on as if he were a log floating in a flood. She inhaled his aura of smoke and sweat, tobacco and horses. She felt the sharp pressure of the hawk-bone amulet that hung around his neck.

"I was afraid they had killed you," she murmured.

"Soldiers from Sonora attacked the camp. The people of Janos say they knew nothing about it."

"Our father is gone."

"We must not speak of him again." He stood back and pushed her tangled hair away from her face, something he hadn't done since she was a small child in need of comfort. "If we mention those who have left, we call them back and hinder them in their journey."

Women and children emerged singly or in small groups from the bushes, but Morning Star waited for one who had yet to come. The boy, Talks A Lot, arrived to tell him the men were gathering for a council and Skinny, the band's leader, wanted him there.

"Tell him I'll come soon."

When She Moves Like Water finally appeared, she was carrying a sleeping child on her back. "This is Little Squint's daughter," she said. "A soldier's horse stepped on her arm and broke it."

The girl whimpered when Sister lifted her and held her against her chest. Sister laced her fingers to form a seat for her, and the child laid her head on Sister's shoulder, her broken arm dangling at her side.

Morning Star enfolded She Moves Like Water in an embrace so passionate that Sister knew Skinny and the rest of the men in council would grow impatient before it ended. She turned away, unable to bear the sight.

Sister wanted to rejoice in her brother's happiness. She wanted to like the woman who had displaced her in his affections. She wanted to admire She Moves Like Water's beauty and grace, two qualities she was sure she would never have herself, but all she could manage was a false courtesy.

Sister went off in search of Little Squint, walking among

those looking for lost relatives and friends. People spoke in hushed voices. The women and children were scratched and bruised. Many were bloody. The children lay exhausted where they fell. In the chill night air, they cupped together for warmth and shared what blankets they had. Broken Foot's wife, Her Eyes Open, distributed food and water jugs from the cache of them hidden in a crevice under a heap of boulders.

Sister found Little Squint huddled in her blanket. She rocked back and forth, desperate to grieve out loud for her lost child, but knowing she dared not.

"*Ta'hinaa*, she lives." Sister put the girl in her mother's outstretched arms. "Ask Her Eyes Open to mend her bone."

Little Squint was so grateful she blurted the words that were used only in extreme circumstances. "*Na'ahensih*, I thank you."

Sister was weary all the way through, but she went looking for the kin of those she knew the soldiers had killed. The news that she had gone among the dead traveled faster than she did. Some people avoided her, as though the ghosts clung to her like smoke, as though she were the killer and not merely the messenger. In a way, she was. As long as they didn't know for sure, they could believe that their loved ones had been captured or they had only been delayed reaching here.

They could hope that the missing ones would appear days, weeks, even months or years later. That had happened before. The missing were not dead until Little Sister said so. She felt like Ghost Owl, spreading dark wings of grief.

In her sad wake she left orphaned children staring into a darkness that wouldn't dissipate with the sun's rise. Women sawed off their long hair with their knives. They pulled their blankets over their heads and rocked silently back and forth, shaken by grief.

The last one she found was He Who Yawns, on his way to the council.

He spoke to her first. "They say you walked among the dead."

"Yes. Your people have left on their journey."

"The Mexicans killed all of them?"

"Yes."

His mother, his young wife, and his three daughters lay dead and mutilated. No one had lost more than He Who Yawns.

She returned to where She Moves Like Water slept wrapped in her blanket. She unrolled her own blanket next to her. She fell asleep to the low drone of voices as the men argued whether to take revenge now or wait until later.

She woke when Morning Star shook her shoulder. "We are going home," he said in a low voice.

Sister could tell by the moon glowing through the trees that dawn would not come for quite a while. She draped her blanket over her shoulder and joined the line, walking next to her brother. As one of the youngest warriors, he guarded the rear of the march.

She expected to see Nah-tanh, Corn Flower, glaring at her. He always followed Morning Star around, hoping for the privilege of being sent on some errand, or for the honor of leading his favorite pony to the pasture. He had not returned, and Sister knew the Mexicans must have taken him. Fourteen-year-old He Steals Love followed them instead, his handsome young face alert for any indication that Morning Star had a favor to ask of him.

As they walked, in a voice almost inaudible, Morning Star told Sister what had happened in council. The young men, led by He Who Yawns, had wanted to take revenge on the soldiers immediately, but Skinny, Broken Foot, and Morning Star had prevailed. When they were not burdened with wounded women and children, they would perform the dance called To Take Death From An Enemy, and leave on the war trail.

Sister passed He Who Yawns standing beside the trail. The scowl on his square, homely face looked as permanent as the wind-chiseled crevices in the face of an outcrop of basalt. He spoke to no one. She glanced back and saw him fall into line and lag until he was no longer visible in the darkness.

The healthy ones helped the wounded as the weary column started north in the darkness. No one spoke, but Sister could sense the presence of the people around her, like moving shadows. She could hear the prolonged sigh of their footsteps.

The men had turned their ponies loose. On a journey like this, horses would be a liability. They left tracks. They made noise. They had to forage. The men could steal more horses later.

Sister remembered the route. By the time the sun rose, they would climb up into the first of the ragged peaks. They would travel for two days and three nights along the high ridges, stopping only so some could sleep briefly while others kept watch.

The Ndee men raided often into Mexico. They knew the location of every spring and water tank. They knew the safest places to camp and where the women had hidden food, utensils, and blankets. They would look for medicinal plants along the way, and they would treat the wounded. They would wear out their moccasins long before they reached home.

Sister considered telling her brother about the spirit that had warned her of the soldiers' coming, but maybe he wouldn't believe her. She didn't believe it herself. Why would the spirits speak to a child—and a girl child, at that?

Maybe she should call the Wind Spirit back and politely refuse its gift. People had been known to do that. Magical powers came at a price. The ones who held them must always be at the service of those who asked favors of them or expected extraordinary feats from them. She decided not to tell even her brother.

SISTER AND THE PEOPLE OF HER BAND REACHED THE PRAIRIE to the south of their village as the sun was rising. The plain was the holiest and most beautiful of all the beautiful places in The People's country. There White Painted Woman had taught Sister's ancestors the ceremony that gave the gift of blessing to girls and brought them into womanhood.

Sister's bare feet were raw and bloody from walking, but she wanted to dance with joy when she saw the peaks rising ahead of her—Old Man, Round Nose, Big Breast, and the long sinuous ridge called Sleeping Woman.

Sister could tell the time of day and the season of the year by the mountains. They glowed with the color of pale sand at dawn, then took on a greenish tinge. The green darkened and shifted to a pinkish brown, deepening to the color of tobacco. As the angle of light changed the mountain's colors, it altered the shadows that Sleeping Woman wore. It shrank them and shifted them into long tatters around her contours and crevices.

When they reached the old camping spot where Sister was born, she lay down so her brother could roll her in the four directions. The custom reminded her that she had come from this earth and she was part of it.

"Respect the Earth," her brother often said, "And it will always take care of you."

The women pulled the stones from the opening of the shallow cave near the collection of *kuugha*, domed lodges, that made up their *guuta*, their village. They divided up the blankets, wickerwork water jugs, and burden baskets, the grind stones, kettles, and dried venison, parched corn, mescal, and acorn meal, and the dried fruit they had hidden there.

They found their camp as they had left it. The huge cottonwoods lined the narrow stream that raced noisily along over rocks even in the summertime. For as long as anyone could remember, Sister's band of Red Paints had lived in this canyon. High rock walls protected it; deep green cedars and pines, walnut and ash trees shaded it. The two pools known as Warm Springs lay not far away.

Sister raced through the tall grass where the ponies grazed, and she pelted across the dance ground. The old people who had stayed behind laid down their mending and the sticks with which they were weeding the small corn patches. They stood to watch the weary procession that trailed behind Sister.

Sister started shouting when she passed the hide-covered tipis and the brush-covered lodges and arbors of She Moves Like Water.

"Shiwoyé. Grandmother."

Her grandmother put aside the cradleboard she was making. She stood and held out her arms. Sister ran into them. "You have come." Grandmother's voice broke with joy and grief.

The boys standing watch had seen the procession approaching. They had told the old ones that the number of people returning was much smaller than those who had left. Grandmother had waited all day while anxiety pecked at her like magpies at a horse's sore back.

Others put their arms around the old ones who had stayed behind to look after the lodges. They held them close in a silent greeting. Smoke hung over the village for days as people set fire to the belongings of those who had died. They had to burn so many lodges that they moved the village. But even there, the women's wails of grief sounded from the forest each evening at sunset.

MORNING STAR AND COUSIN RAN BAREFOOT IN A ROCKING lope behind the two horses they had stolen from the pickets of some Pale Eyes wagon drivers. Morning Star looked back over his shoulder at the cloud billowing up and outward from the desert floor. It disgorged a pair of men on horseback, their forms blurred by the dust. The fine powder had coated the horses. It had permeated the riders' canvas trousers and cotton shirts, heavy boots and wide-brimmed felt hats. As they drew closer, they seemed to materialize from the cloud itself. Finally they solidified into flesh and bone, canvas, leather, felt, and a goatee.

Morning Star and Cousin reached the thicket bordering the rock-strewn creek. They flapped their arms to send the ponies veering down a narrow track through the bushes to join those few that they had been able to steal on this raid. The herd boys, Talks A Lot, Ears So Big, He Steals Love, and Flies In His Stew, guarded them.

A mother bear with a cub had made this raid harder for Cousin. He had been lying on his stomach drinking at a spring when the bear snagged his moccasin and tried to drag him away as though he were a fat trout. Cousin objected. In the tussle the bear tore the left side of his face before he drove the knife through her eye and into the brain. He made a necklace of the claws and teeth that had disfigured him.

Blood still stained the teeth and claws. Cousin's face was still swollen and raked with raw, red slashes. In the fight he had gained something more valuable than a necklace. Killing her had given him Bear Power. Bear Power was unpredictable, though, and those who had it were unpredictable, too. Bear power could make a person act insanely. Already people had begun to treat Cousin with a wary respect, and when he wasn't around, they called him Loco, Crazy.

The two men stood at ease in front of the snarl of stunted willows, cactus, and interlacing vines. Loco lifted his torn eyelid so he could see out of it.

"Two white men are chasing us," Morning Star told the thicket. "One of them is black."

"Black?" the thicket asked.

"Maybe that one was left too long in the sun when he was a baby," Loco added for the thicket's edification. "He's as black as that mule steak your wife let fall into the flames."

"If you don't like my wife's cooking, why do you show up whenever the meal's ready?" the thicket retorted. "How far away are they?"

"They're coming into range now," Morning Star said.

The thicket quivered and rustled, and Broken Foot, Skinny, and the fifteen other men in the party stepped out of it. They brandished their lances and bows and commenced whooping.

The pursuers reined to a stiff-legged halt that sent up a shower of dirt. The horses reared and plunged as the two men scrambled off. The black man's foot caught in the stirrup, and he hopped around, trying to free it, while the horse circled and kicked. Both men tangled themselves and their weapons in the reins when they put their arms through them to keep their mounts from running away.

"I think they mean to shoot each other," Loco observed.

"The white white man needs an extra mule to carry that big gun," said Broken Foot.

Morning Star chuckled. "They're either brave or stupid."

"I would say stupid," said Loco. "All Pale Eyes are stupid."

"I think their guns misfired."

Loco began to leap up and down and shout. "You Pale Eyes are such bunglers you can't find your arse holes with your nose-picking fingers."

"I'll bet you've shit into those trousers of yours," shouted Skinny. He turned and lifted the tail of his breechclout, to give them a clear view of his bony rump.

Loco, Broken Foot, Morning Star, and everyone else turned around too, presenting their attackers with a long row of bare, brown backsides. They beat a tattoo on them, and hooted and shouted insults.

When the two men realized that their guns weren't going to fire, they chased their horses in circles at the ends of the reins. The black man clambered aboard first and held the other's big shotgun so he could vault into his, bypassing the stirrups. As the two rode off, clinging to their horses' necks and with their own rear ends bouncing, Morning Star and the others let fly a shower of arrows gauged to fall just short.

When the dust cloud had swallowed the two men again and whirled them off to a safer place, the Red Paint men trotted out to collect the arrows. Then they sauntered to the small horse herd that Morning Star and Loco had increased by two. Morning Star gestured to He Steals Love to bring his new pony.

The horse was a compact little stallion, the yellow dun color of a smoked hide. He had big restless ears, sly eyes, long legs, and a short body. Morning Star decided to call him Coyote.

Morning Star mounted and rode laughing after his friends. He Steals Love and the other herd boys trotted behind him.

Chapter 4

PANDORA IN A BOX

Rafe hooked a leg over the pommel of the Mexican saddle on his big roan gelding, cocked his old Hall rifle, laid it across his thigh, and watched the pack of men approach. They were heading south, toward the border most likely. God help any poor Mexicans they found. Any Indians they found would have to help themselves.

Rafe glanced to heaven, where a raiding band of Comanches in west Texas had sent his own mother and father when he was fifteen. He thanked God for constructing him with yellow hair. Comanches preferred scalps with yellow hair attached, but not these men. He curled his finger around the trigger, reassured by the hard, smooth curve of it.

The bounty hunters carried enough weapons to outfit a group containing twice their numbers. Bundles of scalps, salted and stretched on hoops, dangled from the lead rider's saddle. The horse's bridle looked as though it were made of braided black horsehair, but Rafe had seen it up close before. The human teeth dangling from it as decoration reinforced his belief that the hair hadn't come from horses.

Rafe was acquainted with the tightly strung, greasy-haired, undersize individual who occupied the saddle on the lead horse. He had crossed paths with John Joel Glanton and his rabble of bounty killers before. He knew, for instance, that Glanton had once been a preacher, and that he referred to the scalps as "golden fleeces."

Attrition ran high in Glanton's crowd. They'd been known to scalp injured members of their own company on the principle of "Waste not, want not," but today the gang consisted of a familiar bunch of cutthroats. Rafe recognized two former

Texas Rangers, a runaway Negro slave, an Irishman, a French Canadian, a Comanche, two Mexicans, and a Delaware Indian. A few of the men were strangers to Rafe, and they didn't look completely at ease in the company they were keeping. They were probably gold rushers who thought to earn some quick cash in the scalp trade.

Instead of their usual leather britches and hunting shirts lacquered black with grease and blood and dirt, they wore breechclouts and moccasins. A few of them carried bows and quivers slung across their backs, which meant the rumors were true. Glanton had killed so many Indians that his quarry had become wary and difficult to find. Dressed as Apaches, he and his men were now attacking Mexican villages.

The rumor was that after they murdered the inhabitants—men, women, and children—they filled the cattle with arrows to make it look like an Indian raid. Rafe knew that Apaches didn't scalp their enemies, but most Mexicans—Americans, too—believed they did. Glanton's crowd collected on the Mexican scalps in the governors' offices of Chihuahua and Sonora. Glanton was a pragmatic man, and black hair was black hair. The authorities wouldn't know the difference.

When they got close enough for Rafe to smell them, which was well beyond rifle range, Rafe raised a hand that was more a warning that they advance no farther than a greeting.

"Good day to you, John," he said.

"Rafe." Glanton reached two fingers up to the place where a brim would be if he were wearing a hat. "Seen any 'Patch around here?" He spoke with a cultured North Carolina accent.

"Can't say as I have."

"Well, keep your hair under your hat."

"I will endeavor to do that." Rafe watched until they had ridden out of sight around a bend in the river before he kicked his mule into motion.

When he reached his camp, he wanted to strip naked, wade into the muddy water of the river, and wash the stench of Glanton's rabble off his skin. Instead, he stood with arms folded across his chest and listened to the report of his three

Mexican drovers. Apaches had stolen two of the horses from the picket line, and Señor Absalom and his big Negro had gone after them. Rafe was about to set out to find Absalom and Caesar when they saved him the trouble. Their horses were lathered and blowing.

When the two men dismounted, they walked with a distinct wobble. Caesar led the horses off to rub them down and feed them.

"I see you didn't recover the ponies or take the scalps you bought that blunderbuss to hunt." Rafe nodded at Absalom's big shotgun. Absalom had had one barrel rifled in order to bring down much bigger game than quail.

"We were fortunate to escape with our lives."

"I don't doubt it."

Absalom started to give details, but the arrival of a few wagons interrupted him. All of them were loaded, but the lead one rode lower on its front springs than the others.

"Damnation," Rafe muttered.

"Someone you know?"

"General Armijo."

John Glanton, Apache horse thieves, and Manuel Armijo all on the same day, Rafe thought. The devil must be in a particularly meddlesome mood.

Armijo pulled up, axles shrieking. The color was flaking off the Virgin Mary and her mob of cherubim painted on the wagon's side. They looked as though leprosy had been added to their afflictions of jaundice and constipation. Three Apache women and a teenaged boy, their wrists tied behind their backs, walked behind. The ropes around their necks tethered them to the wagon's tailgate. They glared from behind the dark bangs that fell in front of their eyes.

Some carpenter had strengthened the wagon seat with extra boards, but still it sagged under Armijo's weight.

"Señor Collins, what a pleasure to encounter you here. We will camp with you tonight." Armijo spread his arms to include his little caravan, though the arms' bulk prevented them from ever lying flat against his body, anyway. "As you can see, we reached Chihuahua in safety, thanks be to God, and have returned. On the way back I bought some servants for my wife." He gestured to the ragged and filthy women and the boy behind the wagon. "General Carasco captured them at their camp outside Janos."

Three of Armijo's men helped him climb down from the seat, giving Rafe an unwelcome view of the man's backside.

It was an arse, Rafe thought, that was big enough to be declared a Mexican state.

Armijo was wheezing like a leather bellows when he finally made landfall. He jerked a chain, and the same young Apache woman Rafe had seen with him three months earlier in Mesilla climbed out of the wagon. She was still beautiful. She still looked lethal.

When she jumped down, she landed on one foot. The other foot and ankle were swollen and bruised a dark purple, and she could put no weight on it. The ankle was obviously broken and must have hurt like the very dickens, but Rafe could see no indication of pain in her eyes. Only hatred smoldered there, a hot and well-tended fire.

The chain was fastened to a shackle around her undamaged ankle. Armijo looped the other end to a spoke of the wagon wheel and fastened it in place with a large iron lock. He put the key into the pouch hanging from his belt.

Armijo nodded to the swollen ankle. "She tried to escape again, so I have ensured that she will not make another attempt."

"For the love of God." Rafe turned on his heel and walked away.

"Will we be moving to another campsite?" Absalom asked.

"It's too late for that, but we'll hitch the wagons and drive upriver a bit. I don't like the smell of this place."

RAFE AND ABSALOM SAT BY THE FIRE. CAESAR MENDED A bridle at a discreet distance. Since Rafe found them sharing a bottle in the wagon yard in Mesilla, he had never seen them give any indication that they were other than a Southern planter and his loyal slave. At five feet eleven inches, Rafe had always thought of himself as a tall man, and strong enough to make a six-mule team sit up and take notice. Caesar dwarfed him in every physical dimension. He worked hard, said little, and never complained.

Absalom held up two pairs of moccasins. The soles and the leather patches used to mend them had worn through. The knee-high tops were scarred. Four parallel gashes ran diagonally on one of the left moccasins, about midway between the ankle and knee. From the size of them Rafe would have bet that a bear had left them there.

"We found these hanging over a low branch where our horses were tethered before the Apaches stole them."

Rafe took the one with the claw marks. He ran his fingers over the deep grooves and imagined the encounter that had put them there. He noted the neat stitching, the way the strip of leather from the sole had been brought up and sewn in place to reinforce the toe. The style was Apache, and peculiar to the bands around here, the ones who called themselves Red Paints. He wondered, briefly, what the moccasin's previous owner was like.

"Why were they left there?" Absalom asked.

"They're a message," Rafe said. "The Apaches are saying, 'We walked until our moccasins wore out. Now we have your horses, and you can walk.' "

"You know," Absalom said. "I had every intention of shooting those two thieves today and taking their scalps as souvenirs. When that horde of fifty or sixty Apaches stepped out of the bushes, I'll tell you. Rafe, I pissed myself. They could have skinned and salted us both, yet there they all were, jumping around like cockroaches in a hot skillet. They preferred to have their joke and spare our lives."

"There's no telling what an Apache will do. They'll steal stock from everybody, and they'll kill anybody tries to stop 'em, but their blood feud is with the Mexicans."

Absalom took a drink of whiskey from his tin mug and stared into the fire. The two men sat in a lengthening silence that Rafe found far more comfortable than talk.

"I suppose you're wondering about Caesar," Absalom said finally.

"No, I'm not."

"His mother was in charge of the nursery at the big house on my family's plantation. We grew up together, Caesar and I. When we were young, we fished and picked berries together. We raided the watermelon field in the summertime. I taught him to read."

Rafe made no comment, in hopes that Absalom would not turn loose any more information. He had found that personal histories almost always contained troubles. People didn't confess good news or virtues. Rafe had troubles enough of his own. He didn't need to weigh down his heart's springs with anyone else's. Besides, the histories of most men out here included crimes and derelictions that could prove dangerous to know.

"My ma died when I was a sprat, and Caesar's mammy raised me. When she was dying of a fever, a year or so back, I promised her that I would set Caesar free. My father passed on not long after, and as the inheritor of his estate I found myself in a position to make good on my promise." He glanced at the spot where Caesar had been sitting.

"I thought about taking him north, but slave-catchers are on the lookout for runaways. The laws are designed to prevent a colored person from leaving the South for any reason. We thought perhaps they would accuse me of slave theft as a ruse to throw me in jail and sell Caesar down the river to the rice plantations." Absalom threw a few more limbs onto the fire. "We decided to slide sideways, joining the Argonauts in search of gold. We wouldn't be suspected, heading west instead of north. We reckoned to ride clear to California. Since slavery is not allowed there, Caesar can be a free man whether he finds gold or not. When I see him safely set up, I shall return home and marry the beauty who waits for me."

Absalom reached into the inner pocket of his vest and pulled out a miniature portrait in a double frame clasped shut to form a box. He opened it and held it up. Rafe studied it in the fire's light.

He felt uneasy, staring at another man's betrothed, but he couldn't help himself. The sight of her, blond hair falling in ringlets around the narrow oval of her face, set up a longing in him. It reminded him that there were riches in the world that had nothing to do with gold or silver; but obtaining them was next to impossible and fraught with its own peril.

"That's an admirable undertaking." Rafe kept his voice noncommittal, although when Absalom put the portrait away he wanted to ask if he could look at it a while longer.

"When we finish this delivery to the Santa Rita mines with you, we'll have enough money to continue our trip." Absalom took another sip of whiskey. Whiskey might set free the demons in some men, but for Absalom it was apparently the key to opening his heart and letting out angels of good deeds. "I have some money hidden away, but that's to stake Caesar when he gets to California."

Rafe raised his tin mug of whiskey. "To the success of your enterprise." But he had his doubts.

With few exceptions, this territory was populated by men like John Glanton, scoundrels of every race and nationality who had only one thing in common. They had committed murder, rape, theft, arson, blasphemy, loitering, and every other conceivable misdemeanor. Some of them came to New Mexico Territory to enjoy a system of justice even more lackadaisical than the one in Texas. For others, San Francisco's Committee of Vigilance had made life too precarious and liberty too uncertain, so they had drifted east and washed up here. Rafe would not have wagered a centavo that a pampered Southern fop and an inexperienced slave could avoid the snares laid by man and nature between here and California.

To end the conversation, Rafe rolled up in his blanket near the fire. With his saddle for a pillow he went to sleep.

He awoke with a start and sat bolt upright with his pistol cocked and leveled at the shouts and oaths coming from Armijo's camp. Rafe threw back his blankets and pulled on his boots. He kept his pistol in one hand and picked up his rifle in the other. He approached Armijo's wagons warily. Absalom and Caesar followed.

"The gen'ral's lookin' sour as buttermilk," observed Absalom.

Armijo waved his arms and screamed. His fury had pumped so much blood to his pockmarked face that it reminded Rafe of the pomegranates in Mesilla's marketplace. The shackle that had held the young Apache woman lay empty next to the wagon wheel.

"*¡Carajo!*" Armijo screamed. "*Maldita puta india.*"

"He's all in a fester, ain't he?" Absalom added the obvious. "What do you suppose happened?"

"Looks like that Apache woman vamoosed."

Armijo rounded on them, suspicion flashing in his beady eyes. "Have you seen her, Collins?"

"Can't say as I have."

Armijo waved both hands at his men and shouted in Spanish. "You misbegotten piles of goat shit, saddle up and scour the hills. She can't have gotten far."

Rafe chuckled as he watched Armijo waddle off to direct the search. He looked around at a landscape cut by steep ravines and littered with boulders. It was a country of stunted cedars and creosote bushes, cacti, and rank growths of Mother Nature's malice. It would be sure death to most crippled travelers, but not to an Apache. Broken ankle or not, Rafe was certain no one would find this one.

Rafe glanced up at the sun rising above the mountains to the east. "Let's hitch the teams and go, or we won't make Santa Rita by nightfall."

While Absalom and Caesar brought the mules and positioned them between the traces, Rafe lowered the tailgate of the first wagon and checked the load. The barrels of flour and salt beef stood lashed in place, but he noticed that the large crate of horse shoes and iron ingots near the tailgate had shifted slightly. Forgetting that it would be too heavy for him to move alone, he started to push it back in place. Caesar materialized at his elbow.

"I'll take care of that for ya, suh." But Caesar was too late.

When Rafe shoved the trunk, it moved. He also noticed that someone had pried the lid up slightly on one end, leaving a narrow opening.

"What's the problem?" Absalom asked.

"Someone's stolen shoes out of this crate." Rafe climbed onto the wagon bed, took the crowbar from its leather loops along the side, pried the lid up, and stared down into the box. "I'll be damned."

Folded inside the crate and staring up at him through the tangles of her hair was Armijo's Apache slave.

"Did you tuck her away in here, Absalom?"

"I swear on God Almighty's Holy Bible, I didn't."

Rafe studied her warily, as though expecting her to pop out, knife in hand, like a death-dispensing jack-in-the-box.

"I've heard of Apaches getting things out of locked places, but never nailing themselves into one." Rafe turned in time to catch a glance pass from Absalom to Caesar. He stared through narrowed green eyes at Caesar. "Did you do this?"

Caesar suddenly forgot the English language. Mouth half-open, eyes wide and blank, he looked down at Rafe in total noncomprehension.

"You shouldn't have done it, Caesar," Absalom said.

Caesar recovered his ability to speak. "I couldn't leave her there, Massa Ab'slom."

"How did he get the shackles off?" Rafe asked.

"We're both good at picking locks with a wire. When we were kids, we used to get into the brandy supply my father kept shut up in a trunk."

"I would have set the others free, too, Massa, but the Mek'scans stood guard over 'em all night."

"I'm sorry for any trouble we have caused you, Rafe." Absalom picked up his saddle. "We'll forfeit our pay for this run and be on our way. We'll take her with us on our spare mule."

"She'll make catfish bait of you at the first opportunity."

"Beggin' your pardon, suh," said Caesar with uncustomary boldness, "But no, suh, no she won't."

"So, you're now an expert on Apaches, are you?"

"No, suh, I ain't."

"Where are the shoes and the pig iron that were in the crate?"

"I hid 'em behind the barrels, suh."

Rafe climbed onto the wagon bed and looked. Horseshoes were stacked in every crevice around the sides and back of the wagon bed.

"By God, man, you're as devious as any Apache."

Rafe didn't want Absalom to go. He knew Shakespeare, and they had passed the hours lining out the Bard. Besides that, having Caesar along was like employing three men, all of whom actually put in a full day's labor.

"I need you and Caesar to finish the trip. We'll hide her under the canvas, but she rides in your wagon. And if she strangles you with your own suspenders, it's your fault."

"Can you tell her that?"

"¿Habla Español?" Rafe asked.

She said nothing, but she had been Armijo's captive, so Rafe figured she had picked up some of the language.

"Usted va con nosotros. Estará segura." He turned to Absalom. "I told her she could go with us and that she'd be safe." Rafe sighed. "We'll figure out what to do with her when we reach Santa Rita. Some of her people will probably be there."

"They'll take her in then."

"Maybe."

"But she's an Apache."

"With them it's hard to say. I can't keep all the bands straight, and half the time they seem to be at war with each other."

Rafe shook his head. In his years in this country he had seen just about every variety of human being, mostly those roosting at the lower end of the social order. For sheer cussedness, wind, and eccentricity, though, the Apaches had every other race whipped.

"I figure to call her Pandora." Caesar grinned, and Rafe saw the light of a keen intelligence in his eyes. Maybe he had underrated him. Maybe he and Absalom would make it to California after all.

He also realized that Caesar's eyes were the same dark hazel as Absalom's. He hadn't noticed it before.

"Do you know who Pandora was?" Rafe asked.

"Yes, suh. Back in the old days the Greeks' god, Zeus, he was jealous 'cause Prometheus done give fire to humans. Zeus made a woman out of clay, and he blew the breath o' life into her. Then he sent her down to earth with a little box. Prometheus' brother, he got curious about dat box, no matter that Prometheus warned him not to look inside. He opened it, and evil come swarmin' out. He set loose all the sorrows that devil us now."

"One thing remained in the box," added Absalom.

Rafe knew what that one thing was. "Hope," he said. "What remained was that sly, old deceiver, hope."

He wondered what troubles this Pandora would unleash.

Chapter 5

INDIAN GIVING

Sister and Talks A Lot carried a cowhide so stiff that when a gust caught it, it blew them backward a few steps. They collided with Ears So Big and Flies In His Stew, who followed them. Sister and Talks A Lot maneuvered the hide edgewise into the wind and continued climbing.

Sister had scraped the flesh from the inside of it and soaked it in water for three days. Instead of pegging it down to stretch it, she had left it to shrink in the summer sun while the women lectured her on the error of tanning it that way.

Sister knew she should be tending the cookfire and helping She Moves Like Water prepare the venison stew that would feed visitors. The people of Sister's Warm Springs band had camped near Red Sleeves' village in the mountains overlooking the old copper mine at Santa Rita. Talks A Lot, Flies In His Stew, and Ears So Big had planned to spend the day watching the men play hoop-and-pole until they saw Sister set off toward the cliff with her hide.

They knew her well. Whatever she planned to do would likely be interesting, maybe dangerous, and almost certainly unusual. But if the other boys found out they had gone off with a girl, the ridicule would dog them for a long time, so they had loped away in another direction and circled around.

When they reached the top of the ridge, the wind snapped the tattered blanket around Sister's legs and whipped her shoulder-length hair into her face. To show her grief for her father's death she had cut her hair and made her blanket into a poncho. It would replace her doeskin tunic and skirt for the customary time of mourning.

Sister led the way to an old mine shaft gouged into the

side of the cliff. Talks A Lot looked down at the steep spill
of gravel that covered the side of the mountain and fanned
out like a delta onto the valley far below. Talks A Lot
guessed what Sister had in mind. It was a frightening prospect, but he couldn't back out now. He beckoned to Ears So
Big and Flies In His Stew.

"You can watch," he said to Sister.

He tugged at the hide, but she held on. He tried to shove
her to the edge of the rock shelf to force her to let go, but
she braced her legs and gave him her flintiest stare. He knew
how strong she was. When they were about eight, she had
wrestled him to a state of immobility that he still heard sly
comments about. He also knew she would rather be flung off
the cliff than give in. He let go and glowered at her.

"Four will fit." Sister was gracious in victory.

She sat down and hooked her feet into two of the straps
she had sewn on the front. Talks A Lot sat next to her. Ears
So Big and Flies In His Stew positioned themselves behind.
The riders each stuck a foot out and shoved. The cowhide
scraped forward until it teetered on the edge; then it dropped
as though the ground had fallen away from under it. The
world tilted. Sister stared into a golden abyss of sunlight.

The children careened, shrieking and laughing down the
slope in a rumble like an avalanche. As the hide rocked and
pitched, they leaned from side to side to keep from flipping
over. Sometimes it took to the air, landing again with a
kidney-jolting thud. The dislodged gravel tumbled and
chuckled beside it like Mountain's children. The valley floor
rushed up at them. The hide hit the bottom of the slope,
leveled abruptly, and sped out onto the overflow of gravel.
Sister's sixteen-year-old cross-cousin, He Makes Them
Laugh, was waiting for her.

He was small, slender, and strong. He had acquired an old
wool vest with brass buttons on the front. He had hung two
of the buttons from the holes in his earlobes. He had knotted
cords through the button holes and tied bird skulls and lizards
to them. Six dead rats dangled from a thong passed through

their mouth. They looked as though they were clinging to it with their teeth.

"The Pale Eyes leave their garbage everywhere, and the rats swarm over it." He lifted one by the tail. "Look how fat they are. They'll make a lot of grease in the stew."

He wrinkled his long nose, stuck his upper teeth out over his lower lip, and did a scuttling little dance, chanting a rat song he made up on the spot. The boys laughed as they rubbed their bruised tailbones.

"Cousin, your brother's wife wants you," he said when he finished.

Sister felt suddenly ashamed. A child was beginning to make a bulge in She Moves Like Water's belly. She vomited every morning. She always had work to do, and she needed Sister's help.

The hide had cost Sister a lot of work, and she wanted to take it with her. If she left it here, the boys would wear it out. She thought of how many times her brother had told her that a leader gave his people whatever he had that they needed. She remembered what Grandmother told her, "Whatever you give away comes back. It might not be anything you can see, but it will come back." She slid the hide toward Ears So Big; then she and He Makes Them Laugh started at a lope back to camp.

Sister's cousin always had a good-natured disregard for the opinion of others, but even if he cared what people thought, he could still keep company with her. He was the son of her mother's brother, which made him Sister's cross-cousin. Cross-cousins could never marry each other, and so they were not bound by the same constraints as others.

When Sister reached her brother's wife's cluster of lodges and arbors. She Moves Like Water kept her voice low when she scolded.

"Have you been going around with those boys again? People will say bad things about you. You'll disgrace the family."

"Granddaughter," Grandmother called from the cooking arbor. "Grind more cornmeal. We have a guest."

When Sister saw the guest, she understood why She Moves Like Water did not want to start a loud argument. Cheis was the leader of the Tall Cliffs People. His name meant "Oak," in the sense of an oak tree's strength and endurance. He was tall, and Sister had to admit he was as handsome as her own brother. He was a man people expected would provide for them and protect them.

He had brought his people to hold council with the Red Paint men about avenging the massacre at Janos. He was almost twice as old as Morning Star, who was twenty-four, and he should have been with the older men at the fire of his wife's father, Red Sleeves. Instead, he had settled down here and offered tobacco to Morning Star, Loco, and Broken Foot. He had been discussing horses ever since.

One reason he kept away from Red Sleeves' camp was that his woman's mother, Red Sleeves' third wife, was there. Cheis never spoke her name. Instead, he used the title for a wife's mother, She Who Has Become Old. Avoiding contact with one's wife's mother was the respectable way to behave. Today it was also prudent because Red Sleeves' third wife was not happy, and when she wasn't happy no one was.

Red Sleeves had captured her on a raid when she was a beautiful thirteen-year-old. That she was Mexican wouldn't have mattered if she had accepted her position as the least important wife. But being third, or even second, wasn't in her nature. The resentment of Red Sleeves' first two wives had simmered for forty years.

Earlier that day, She Who Has Become Old had fallen asleep with her hair draped over a boulder to dry. Someone had worked the spiny seeds of the come-along bush into it. Her Mexican slaves had spent all afternoon combing them out. Everyone heard about it. Wife number one or wife number two had probably done it, but few of the women liked her, so the choice of pranksters was large. Cheis had reason to avoid Red Sleeves' camp, all right.

"People say that your little sister is good with horses." Cheis smiled in Sister's direction.

Sister felt her cheeks grow hot at the attention. She bent her head over the grind stone.

"She has horse magic," Broken Foot said.

"You should have seen her ride in Janos," added Loco.

While Loco told the story of the wild horse race, Sister scooped the cornmeal into a gourd bowl. She worked deer grease into it and added dried gooseberries, piñon meal, and water. She patted handfuls of the stiff dough into flat cakes and laid them on the stone in the coals.

"Will you make a charm for my horse, little sister?" Cheis asked.

Sister glanced at her brother. He raised one eyebrow, maybe as surprised as she was that Cheis would ask a favor from a child. Sister started to answer when a woman's voice sounded from the darkness. A boy's yelp followed it.

"Get out of my way, you little lizard."

Consternation passed so quickly over Cheis's face that Sister only thought she saw it. He stood abruptly and almost broke into a trot so he would be out of sight when She Who Has Become Old appeared.

THE SUN WAS POISED TO SET when RAFE, ABSALOM, AND Caesar reached the Santa Rita mines. Until its abandonment thirteen years earlier, the Santa Rita had been a Mexican outpost. After the United States' victory over Mexico three years ago, the territory changed hands, and a few dozen Americans had arrived to dig for the silver recently found there.

They gave the impression that working for silver rather than taking it at gunpoint was a new proposition for them. The Mexicans they had hired were mostly outlaws from the states of Sonora and Chihuahua. They, too, looked capable of slitting a man's throat for the gold in his teeth. Rafe kept his pistols ready whenever he came here.

A rattler slithered from among rocks and headed for a nearby mine shaft. Its dappled pattern of light and dark looked like sunlight and shadows on water as it flowed into the darkness.

Absalom nodded at the pole notched along its twenty-five-foot length. "Is that what the peons used to climb to the surface?"

"Nope. Apache slaves. They worked on their knees in holes as black as a scalp hunter's heart. They broke up the rock with picks, put the chunks in those bags, and carried them out on their backs."

"I imagine even Apaches fell off them now and then."

"Hell yes. Didn't matter, though." Rafe started the wagon forward again. He raised his voice so Absalom could hear him over the rattle of the trace chains, the complaints of the axles, and the miners' dogs, barking and howling like the chorus of a Greek tragedy. "The mine owners could always buy more Apache slaves in Chihuahua City. They still can, for that matter."

Rafe stopped at the blacksmith shop. "Rogers," he called.

A hulking lad appeared from the back of the shed. He wore a greasy leather apron over a pair of wool trousers with the cuffs rolled up. Sweat-damp spikes of coarse brown hair stood up like a dry stand of yucca above the red bandana tied around his head. He didn't look older than twenty.

"Did ya bring a nip of the critter, mate?"

"I have no whiskey to sell."

"Did ya bring the horseshoes then, an' the pig?"

"The shoes and the iron are in the wagon. Tell José to unhitch the teams and give them grain."

"Let the nigger do it."

"He has business to attend to." Rafe nodded to Caesar.

Caesar rode alongside the wagon, lifted the canvas off Pandora, and helped her settle in behind him.

"Bloody hell." Shadrach Rogers spat a stream of tobacco. "We ain't plagued with enough savages around here, but what you've got to import more, and niggers besides."

"I'll be back soon. Get that wagon unloaded." Rafe mounted the big roan he called Red and flicked the reins.

Absalom fell in beside him, on a gray, and Rafe motioned for Caesar to ride next to him, too."

"Where does he hail from?" Absalom asked when they'd left him behind.

"English by way of Australia."

"One of the prisoners there, then?"

"I suppose."

"How did he get here?"

"He didn't say."

Absalom glanced at the rotting wooden frame of a crude ore crusher. "Did the Mexicans ever turn a profit here?" ·

"They hauled out twenty thousand mule loads of copper ingots a year for the mint in Chihuahua City. A mule load is a hundred and fifty pounds. You can cipher the sum."

"Why did they abandon it?"

Lordy, Rafe thought. The man is filled to the brim with *why*.

"Apaches started causing death and destruction on a perpetual-motion basis."

"Why's that?"

"About thirteen years ago scalp hunters befriended an old Red Paint chief named Juan José. His men got the chief and his people drunk—then he pulled the canvas off a cannon loaded with nails and scrap iron. He lit the fuse with his cigar, so I heard, and mowed them down, wheat, chaff, and weevils." Rafe stared glumly between his horse's ears. "It wasn't just an evil act, it was a stupid one. The old man's successor was a firebrand named Mangas Coloradas. He escaped the postprandial entertainment. Mangas is probably the shrewdest leader the Apaches have ever had, and the largest."

"Doesn't Mangas Coloradas mean Red Sleeves?"

"Yep. He left no one alive here to pull a trick like that again."

Hearsay held that Red Sleeves took his name from a scarlet shirt he once had owned, but Rafe thought otherwise. He imagined the chief's sleeves scarlet with the blood of both the guilty and the innocent.

Rafe looked around at the Americans, their own sleeves

rolled up, digging and hammering and hewing. "Looks like old Red Sleeves has decided to let bygones be bygones."

Rafe, Absalom, and Caesar, with Pandora riding behind him, followed a trail up into the mountain overlooking the mines. Stands of cedars scented the air. Streams cascaded between the willows and cottonwoods at the bottoms of shallow canyons. Birds sang. Rafe was always struck by the difference between the scenery in the mountains and the desert below, as though Heaven and Hell were within sight of each other.

In a meadow of sweet grama grass, fifty or sixty ponies grazed. They had burrs in their tails and skepticism in their eyes, and if a coyote had run under them, he would hardly have cleared their bellies. They would have looked just as at home in a Mexican corral, which was probably where they came from.

"Do you see your two horses?" Rafe asked.

"Nope. I reckon the chief has them up one of those red sleeves of his," said Absalom.

Rafe could see why Red Sleeves refused to leave this place, even though white men had despoiled the valley below. In a grove of cedars stood the clusters of hide-covered tipis, arbors, and domed brush shelters. Naked children raced back and forth. Smoke and the smell of roasting horse meat snagged in the branches above. Rafe looked for Pandora's reaction, but she would have made a formidable poker player.

The women gave them sideways glances. The men stood or squatted in groups and smoked cigarillos. They looked as though they were engaged in what Texans called swapping lies. They ignored the three men, but the children gathered in clumps to watch them approach.

Caesar turned to help Pandora off the horse, but she had already slipped down. Without a backward glance, she limped to the nearest group of women tending a cook fire. They acted as though she had just come back from the river with water.

"You didn't expect gratitude, did you, Caesar?" Rafe asked.

"I di'nt do it for the thanks, suh."

"Should we explain how we came to have the woman?" asked Absalom.

"They'll get the story from her."

An individual rose from the fog of smoke surrounding the nearest group of men, and he kept on rising."

"Good lord," Absalom murmured. "He must top six and a half feet."

"Speak of the devil," Rafe answered.

"Is that Red Sleeves?"

"I suppose so."

Each item in Red Sleeve's inventory exceeded specifications, from his bowed legs and long muscular torso to a forehead broad enough to lay out a poker hand were it horizontal. His nose and nostrils resembled the prow of a ship going downwind with the sails unfurled. His mouth looked capable of swallowing a prairie chicken, leaving only the claws to pick his teeth with. Age was beginning to leave its tracks in the leathery surface of his face. Rafe guessed he'd weathered sixty years at least.

"Hermano," Red Sleeves said. *"¿Tienes tabaco?"*

Rafe pulled a braid of tobacco from his pocket, cut it in two, and handed him half.

"¿Y fósforos?"

"Unos pocos. A few." Rafe always kept a few friction matches separated from his supply of them so anyone asking wouldn't know how many he had. Apaches were always begging matches, and they didn't need them. They could strike a light with two sticks and a pinch of dried grass almost as fast as he could pull a match from his pocket. With flint, steel, and dried moss they could produce fire as fast as with a match.

"¿Tiene usted pelo de búfalo?" Rafe asked.

Red Sleeves stood silent for the briefest of moments, just long enough to betray curiosity about why the Pale Eyes wanted buffalo fur.

He held up a hand, a signal to stay put. He gestured to one of the women who ducked into a lodge and came out with a large sack. Red Sleeves brought it to Rafe.

An Apache child of twelve or thirteen moved closer for a better view. Her shaggy black hair and the Mexican blanket she wore as a poncho made distinguishing her sex difficult, but Rafe had a feeling she was a girl. She had an angular grace about her. The poncho reached only to her knees, exposing bony calves covered with scratches and scars. Even barefoot she moved with ease across ground so rough and thorny Rafe winced at the thought of walking shoeless on it.

When she got closer, Rafe could see that she wasn't interested in him or Absalom or Caesar. She studied Rafe's big roan with the look of someone who intended to either make an offer or help herself to him.

"Don't let it cross your thieving little mind, sprat," Rafe said cordially. But he couldn't blame her for coveting Red.

Red came from thoroughbred and Percheron stock. He stood two hands above the average American horse and twice that much taller than the Mexican ponies the Apaches rode. He had a generous forehead, slender muzzle, wide nostrils, a dark mane, and tail. In his youth he had held the position of near wheelhorse of the first artillery piece. Red knew it was a post of honor, and he always behaved accordingly.

He had a skinful of courage, a skullful of savvy, and a sense of humor. Rafe hoped no one ever played the bugle call for an artillery charge, though. Red would take off like cannon shot.

The Apache girl diverted her attention from Red long enough to stare up at Rafe. He saw sagacity in her wide, dark eyes, as though someone much older were using her as a disguise. He half expected her to say something in a voice that would sound nothing like a child's. She held his gaze long enough to let him know that he didn't intimidate her. Then she strode off to join the women at the cook fire.

"There's a hoyden if ever I saw one," said Absalom. "Brown as pan gravy, sassy as a jaybird, and full of the dickens."

"We'll take turns guarding the horses tonight." Rafe knew the gleam of the horse-acquiring itch when he saw it.

Absalom nodded toward the Apache men. "I wonder if the two scoundrels who lifted our horses are among that mob."

"Wouldn't you recognize them?"

"I was preoccupied at the time, Rafe. And picking one Indian out of a crowd is like trying to identify a particular crow in the flock."

"Maybe if they turned around," suggested Caesar. "We would recognize their bottom halves."

Rafe and Absalom laughed as they rode away.

"What's in that poke Red Sleeves gave you?" Absalom asked.

"Buffalo hair."

"Are there buffalo in these parts?" Absalom looked eager to hunt them.

"Naw. They must have traded with the Lipan Apaches farther east."

"What are you going to do with the fur?"

Rafe wanted to tell Absalom that he asked too many questions for someone who desired to reach California alive. To say that would be too much like giving advice, and Rafe considered advice just another sort of meddling.

"I'm going to knit some stockings."

Rafe, Absalom, and Caesar rounded a bend in the trail. They did not see the girl throw her arms around Pandora and hold her close for a long time. They didn't hear the two of them crying from happiness.

Chapter 6

COYOTE KEEPS IT UNDER HIS HAT

Night had fallen by the time Rafe settled up with the blacksmith. Rafe gave Absalom and Caesar their share of the silver pesos as they sat near the fire, scooping up eggs and beans with leathery tortillas. When he finished eating, Rafe rooted to the bottom of his pack and took out a pair of carding combs. Then he sorted through the sack of bison fur. He was pleased to see that someone had picked most of the burs, twigs, and larger specimens of life from it.

He teased out a clump of fur, laid it onto one of the combs, and pulled the other one across it. He stroked the carding combs back and forth until the fibers lined up among the iron teeth. He peeled the hair off in a fluffy cylinder and laid it on his bandana. He pulled out another handful and repeated the process.

Absalom began cleaning his rifle with vinegar and sacking. Caesar took out a stack of calico squares with a needle and black thread stuck through it. He took off his shirt that was already a patchwork in the same calico print. The calico patches might have come from any old castoff, but Rafe noted the reverence with which Caesar handled them. Maybe the cloth had been a frock, the only good one a slave woman might own. Maybe it was the only thing she could leave her son when she died.

Caesar laid the torn tail of the shirt across his thigh and positioned one of the calico patches under it. When he picked up the needle, it disappeared in his big hand. He turned under the raw edges of the tear as he worked and laid down a neat bird-track of stitches.

When the pile of carded fur glowed like a golden cloud

in the fire's light, Rafe took out a peeled willow stick sharpened at both ends, with a four-inch disk set a quarter of the way up the shaft. He moistened the wool and wound it onto the upper end of the spindle. He laid the shaft across his thigh with the point of the short end resting on the ground. With his free hand he tugged at the hair, stretching it gently as with the palm of his hand he rolled the spindle along his thigh to his knee. He slid it to the top of his leg to start the process again. When most of the first strand had wound itself onto the spindle, he worked another clump into the tail end of it. Spinning never failed to soothe him.

"Where did you learn to do that?" Absalom asked.

"A Navajo taught me."

Rafe didn't add that the Navajo had been a velvet-voiced woman and that the year he had spent with her had been the happiest of his life. That year defined contentment for him, a concept with which he would otherwise have been unfamiliar. His memories of her included her spinning, always spinning. With a small weighted drop spindle and a bowl of carded wool, she spun while walking. The yarn would lengthen like spider's silk at the ends of her fingers.

She had died in his arms, killed between sunup and sundown by the cholera that the gold rushers hauled west along with their iron stoves and millstones, their pianofortes, family portraits, and the good china. He didn't mention to Absalom that he had wept when he saw the light in her eyes extinguished like a candle, or that for months afterward when he lay at night in his blankets, tears angled across his cheeks until they dampened the pale hair curled around his ears. Even now, almost two years later, sorrow as unavoidable as a desert sandstorm swept over him from time to time.

She didn't tell him her real name. Indians had odd notions about the power of names. But in the dark, when he whispered in her ear, he called her Dream Weaver. To tease her he had sometimes called her Spider Woman, the holy being who gave the knowledge of weaving to her people. To honor Spider Woman, she always left a hole in the middle of each blanket she made, like the hole at the center of a spider's web.

He had one of her blankets with him still. When he saw the hole, it reminded him of her absence. The spindle had belonged to her, and when he held it he imagined the warmth of her small brown hand.

She hadn't taught him to knit, though. In Texas when he was young, he and his sister would gather snagged clumps of buffalo hair from the bushes. His mother had taught him to make stockings from them.

"Aren't stockings of buffalo wool on the rough side?" asked Absalom.

"Yep."

Rough but substantial, he thought. These might last long enough to keep my feet warm until a bullet or an arrow or a rattler sends me to the place where warm stockings aren't necessary. Given the prevailing moral wind in this territory, that might not be so long from now.

A full moon and a sky spangled with stars supplied almost enough light for Rafe to see his work without the campfire. The Apaches' fires twinkled on the mountainside above them. A cool breeze carried the sound of their laughter, flurries of it at first, then gusts, then finally a full-out gale.

"Do you suppose they're laughing about that joke they played on Caesar and me?" Absalom asked. "Them presenting their posteriors for our inspection and making off with our mounts to boot."

"Maybe so," Rafe said. "Apaches do like a joke."

A HUNDRED OR MORE PEOPLE FROM SKINNY'S AND RED Sleeves' bands gathered at Broken Foot's fire to hear his stories. The warriors sat in front, then the apprentice boys, and finally the women and children. Sister sat with her arm around her cousin, the one called Dazsii, Stands Alone. She pressed against her, as though to make up for the two years she hadn't been able to touch her or see her, as though to keep her from being stolen again.

Stands Alone stared toward the fire, but Sister had the feeling she wasn't hearing the stories. Sister had told her that she had found the bodies of Stands Alone's mother and sister at Janos. Stands Alone's father had died from the bite of a rattlesnake several months earlier.

Grandmother had bound up Stands Alone's broken ankle and sung over it. Sister and Grandmother had made room for her in their brush shelter. Tonight she would share her blankets with her as she had when they were children.

In the cleared space near the fire, Morning Star and Loco were telling the story of the white man and the black white man who had chased them to recover their two stolen horses. Morning Star poured water onto the front of his breechclout, as though he had urinated on himself, and everyone laughed. He grunted as he pretended to lift a heavy shotgun to his shoulder. The laughter grew louder when he and Loco bumped into each other and waved their pretend weapons and stared at them when they refused to fire.

They chased their phantom ponies in circles while people doubled over. Weak with laughter, the children clung to each other. The women put their hands over their mouths and giggled behind them.

Cousin and Morning Star pretended to fling themselves onto the horses' backs. They fell off, rolled in the dust, got up, and tried again. With their arms wrapped around the invisible ponies' necks, they galloped into the darkness, weaving from side to side.

When the uproar finally died down, Broken Foot limped to the center of the circle. He had invited them all here tonight, and he and his wife would give presents to those who stayed until he finished his stories. People came not so much for the presents but because he was a good storyteller.

"Long time ago, Trickster Coyote saw some miners, some diggers coming. They rode fine horses, and they led mules piled with good things. Coyote knew about Pale Eyes, so he made a plan."

From somewhere among the boys came the sound of a voice. Broken Foot peered into the darkness. "You," he pointed his nose at Talks A Lot. "My wife's brother couldn't come tonight, but he promised me tobacco. Go to his camp on the other side of the ravine and get it for me."

Talks A Lot stood up and raced away. Everyone else laughed. They knew that Broken Foot's wife's brother would send the boy to someone else for the tobacco. That person would guess what was happening and would pass him farther along. Talks A Lot would return footsore and exhausted the next morning, and he might think twice about interrupting the next time.

Broken Foot continued. "Old Man Coyote defecated by the side of the trail. He took off his hat and put it over the turds. He waited for those Pale Eyes diggers to pass by.

" 'What do you have under your hat?' they asked.

" 'A magical bird, all brightly colored,' Coyote answered. 'He can answer any question I ask him.'

" 'Can that bird tell you where to find money?' they asked.

" 'Sure.'

" 'Show him to us.'

" 'Only the one who owns him can talk to him.'

"That really got the diggers excited. They put their heads together again.

" 'Sell him to us,' the diggers said.

" 'No. He's worth too much.'

" 'We'll give you our horses and our mules and everything.' "

Coyote pretended to consider the offer. " 'All right,' he said. 'But I've had this bird a long time. He likes me a lot. If you let him out before I've gone far away, he'll fly after me.'

" 'All right,' the diggers said.

" 'When I come to that last ridge over there, I'll wave to you. Then you lift the hat just a little bit and reach under it and grab him and hold him so he can't fly away.'

"The diggers waited until Coyote rode far away. When he waved to them, they reached under that hat, and they grabbed real hard. They grabbed so hard they squeezed that brown stuff right out between their fingers. Those Pale Eyes were so mad. Even today they try to kill Coyote whenever they see him." To fool Coyote into thinking he wasn't talking about him, Broken Foot added the usual deception, "I'm talking about fruits and flowers and other good things."

The sun was still a few hours from rising when people went off to their shelters. Sister and Stands Alone whispered as they always had. Sister was about to tell her cousin who was courting whom these days when she heard a faint roaring inside her skull. It grew louder.

"Enemies," she whispered. She shook Grandmother. "Enemies are coming."

She ducked through the low opening. Stands Alone and Grandmother followed her. Embers winked from the fire circles. Starlight illuminated the shelters. From a nearby shelter she heard Loco snoring like Old Ugly Buttocks the Bear.

Sister held her palms up. She looked toward the stars and turned slowly. When she faced east, the spirit stopped her.

She ran to She Moves Like Water's shelter.

"Someone bad is coming!" She kept her voice low. One didn't shout and attract enemies.

Morning Star grabbed his lance and bow and quiver.

"Come back," She Moves Like Water called after him. "She's just a child."

"She sees what we cannot." Morning Star didn't stop to wonder how his sister knew that enemies were coming, and he wasn't surprised that she knew. He found her shivering, her eyes wild and staring.

"From which direction?" he asked.

She pointed toward the east and the boulders where a few sentries kept watch. Morning Star ran from lodge to lodge calling softly to the men inside. They were emerging from the shelters when the first shots rang out. The shadowy horsemen swept down from the rocks, firing as they came. Children screamed, and the women took what possessions they could. They rolled them into their blankets, grabbed their babies, and ran. The light of a burning lean-to illuminated the Red Paint men as they darted from cover to cover.

They kept up a steady fire with their bows and arrows so the women and children could escape.

Sister was collecting water jugs when she heard the hoofbeats and saw a horseman galloping toward her. Morning Star leveled his bow and swiveled, following the horse's course. He fired and the rider jerked and pitched sideways. His boot caught in the stirrup, and the horse passed Sister, dragging his rider by the heel.

Sister saw Grandmother and She Moves Like Water disappear into the ravine. She found her cousin Stands Alone limping through the confusion. She put her arm around her waist and helped her down the slope, too. Sister pulled brush over the two of them; then they waited.

THE GUNFIRE WOKE RAFE. HE LISTENED UNTIL HE LOCATED the source, the Apache encampment on the mountain.

"What do you suppose that is?" asked Absalom.

Rafe slid back into his blankets and fluffed up his saddle. "It's probably a *tiswin* celebration that got out of hand. Most of them do."

"Tiswin?"

"A nasty brew they make from fermented mescal."

Caesar picked up his old firelock pistol and started off.

Absalom called after him. "You can't help Pandora this time."

"Got to try, don't I." It wasn't a question.

Caesar untied his horse from the picket line and rode up the trail into the green defiles of the mountain. He dismounted before he reached the Apache camp and crept forward. Men moved about in the glow of the burning shelters. When Caesar saw they were not Apaches, he stepped into the light.

The scalp hunters were too busy ransacking the lodges to notice him. One of them stooped to carve a circle around the crown of the head of the body sprawled on the ground. He put a foot on the nape of the corpse's neck and yanked. The skin came off with a sucking sound. By the light of burning brush shelters Caesar recognized the individual who held up the long hank of black hair. He was Shadrach Rogers, the blacksmith's apprentice.

Caesar jumped at the sound of the voice behind him.

"Who in hell are you?"

Caesar held his hands out from his sides to show he meant no harm.

"Turn around slowly."

Caesar pivoted on his heels to face a small man whose eyes were hidden in the curved shadow of a wide-brimmed hat. He held an old caplock rifle, cocked and leveled at Caesar's chest.

"What are you doin' here, nigger?" The man's North Carolina accent started up an old, chaotic fear in Caesar.

It brought back childhood memories of packs of men with voices such as his, of baying bloodhounds, galloping hooves, and the pop of musket-fire in the night. It reminded him of flaring torchlight and white men standing at ease, laughing over the mutilated body of the man Caesar had called father. It reminded him of his young mother weeping.

"I come to see what the shootin' was 'bout, massa."

"You needn't meddle in other folks' business." John Glanton surveyed Caesar's solid, six-foot-three-inch frame, the thick muscles of his arms, the breadth of his shoulders. He nodded to the scalped corpse. "The Comanch there cashed in. We're short a man. Are you looking for work?"

"Suh, I's headin' for California with my massa."

Glanton braced the butt of his rifle on the ground, covered the muzzle with his hands, and leaned his chin on them. Caesar thought it would be a boon to humanity if the gun were to go off and take the man's brains with it.

Glanton surveyed the burning camp and the absence of dead Apaches. "We been off chasing 'Patch through the bushes like quail." He sounded peeved. "We was all set to murder them in their beds. Somethin' spooked 'em, though, and we had to ride in and try to catch 'em on the run."

Caesar didn't offer his sympathies for the failure of the

man's enterprise. He put two fingers to the brim of his hat, turned, and went to collect his horse.

He wondered where Pandora and her people had gone. He thought of them hiding in the mountains in the cold of the night. He could easily imagine what they were feeling. He breathed a short prayer for them. He asked God to give them a safe haven, even though they were heathens, but safe havens seemed in as short supply here as where he came from.

Chapter 7

HER FUTURE IS IN THE CARDS

The next time Rafe visited the Santa Rita mines he was alone. Absalom and Caesar had left for California in early November almost three months ago. Rafe wondered if they had gotten through the mountains before the snows. He didn't like the thought of them as a main course for fellow travelers, like the misfortunate souls in George Donner's group.

Here in the high country of southwest New Mexico Territory snow had halted the survey of the new border with Mexico. It piled in three-foot drifts against the sides of John Cremony's big tent. Inside, Rafe sat knitting on an empty powder keg. He shared the heat from the iron stove with Cremony of the United States Boundary Commission, Cremony's two mastiff dogs, and his employee, José Valdez.

Hundreds of Apaches had come for talks with the Americans of the Boundary Commission. Warriors sauntered about like lords of the manor, but John Cremony placed his confidence in the goodwill of chief Red Sleeves. He also trusted in God, José, the mastiffs, four six-shooters, a Whitney percussion rifle, a double-barreled shot gun, a machete, two bowie knives, and the shiny, Smith-Jennings .54 caliber repeating rife that the United States government had issued to the commission. Cremony figured he and José could fire twenty-eight shots without reloading.

Rafe inspected the new Smith-Jennings. "The government finally bought repeating rifles," he said. "So why did you seal the breech and turn it into a single-shot muzzle loader?"

"Damned bureaucrats," grumbled Cremony. "It requires a newfangled cartridge that doesn't carry enough powder.

They call it a 'rocket ball,' but it's a fizzle, if you ask me. As a single shot, with the new sight, it'll knock a crow out of a tree at three hundred yards."

Rafe leaned the rifle against the center pole and ducked to avoid the cluster of cartridge belts and powder horns hanging there.

"A Major Heintzelman passed through here," Cremony said. "He told me the Yuma Indians killed someone named Glanton."

"John Glanton?"

"Yes. Who is he?"

"A scalp hunter."

"Well, it seems the lad was killing off the competition for ferry service across the Colorado River. What with the gold rushers passing through, the ferry has proved lucrative."

"He was probably taking Yuma scalps for the Mexican bounty, too."

"The Yumas came in unarmed to his camp. They brought firewood and built a blaze with the branches pointing out from the center. Everybody sat down for whiskey and philosophy, and when the branches burned down to the size of clubs, the Yumas grabbed them and attacked. The fire had hardened the ends into fine weapons."

Rafe was dubious. A man as evil as Glanton couldn't be killed that easily.

The dogs' hackles rose along their backs. José reached for the carbine and laid it across his thighs. Rafe's hand went to his pistol. John Cremony relit his pipe and settled deeper into the camp chair.

"A month ago," he said, "I had hardly finished setting up my tent when a villainous-looking set of Apaches showed up, wanting tobacco. They've been on the prowl ever since."

"They watch you from up there." Rafe nodded toward the wooded clefts and crags of the nearest peak.

"They beg, but I think begging is not their foremost objective."

"They're after information," said Rafe. "The number of arms, men and horses, amount of ammunition. They're asessing the morale here, the discipline, and the plunder to be taken at the least risk. Every time you scratch your arse, they know about it."

"I suspected as much."

"Habla del diablo," muttered José Valdez. "Speak of the devil."

Brown fingers as stout as tent pegs pulled back the edge of the front flap. Red Sleeves and five or six Apaches filed in after him, along with a few Navajos. Rafe wondered what they were doing here.

The two dogs set up a steady duet of growling until Cremony ordered them to cease. The Apaches carried no weapons, and Rafe couldn't see where they would hide anything larger than a toothpick. In spite of the deep snow, all of them except Red Sleeves wore the usual cloth headbands, breechclouts, and high moccasins. Some of them wore cotton Mexican blankets over their shoulders or wrapped around their waists, but more as decoration than as cover.

Red Sleeves had on the uniform of a United States Army officer. In the two days since the head of the Boundary Commission had presented it to him, the old chief had made some modifications. Rafe didn't blame him for cutting away the front half of the black leather shoes. Red Sleeves' case-hardened toes hung so far out from the holes that it was plain he could never have worn them otherwise.

One gold-fringed epaulette dangled on a thong around his neck. The other was sewn at rear of the coat where it hung like a docked tail. Another man wore two of the brass army buttons as earrings. Red Sleeves must have wagered and lost them at cards. A second man wore the uniform's once-white canvas shoulder strap across his bare chest. He had already hung an assortment of amulets and pouches from it.

Red Sleeves grinned and stretched out his right hand. John Cremony reached up from his camp chair and allowed it to engulf his.

Cremony gestured to each of the Apaches in turn. "You know Red Sleeves. May I present Delgadito, Skinny, chief of the Warm Springs band." He waved a hand at the three

Navajos. "I don't know those bucks, but that broad-shouldered fellow by the door is Cochise, chief of the Chiricahuas to the west of here.

Rafe had heard of Cochise. Even men who hated Apaches admitted Cochise was tolerably good looking. They understated the case.

"They tell me he's known as Cheis by his people," said Cremony. "The shorter one who resembles him is his younger brother."

Cochise turned to face them. His black eyes were bright and opaque at the same time. Apache eyes always made Rafe uneasy. They sank, dark as wells, into those high-cheeked brown faces. They took everything in and let nothing out. Cochise was muscular and taller than average. The look in Red Sleeves' eyes struck Rafe as shrewd. Cochise's expression was wise. Rafe appreciated the difference.

If one could choose one's enemies, Rafe thought, these men would be worthy candidates for the job. Rafe doubted the government could keep them as friends for long. The role of enemy suited them better.

Rafe picked up his knitting where he had left off.

"What are you making?" Red Sleeves asked in Spanish.

"A sock."

"What is a sock?"

Rafe braced the toe of one boot against the heel of the other and pried it off. He held up a foot clad in one of the lumpy, bison wool stockings he had already completed. Red Sleeves tugged the sock away from Rafe's ankle and rubbed it between his thumb and fingers. He pinched Rafe's toes, maybe to see if Rafe had the standard number of them. Embarrassed by the fact that the stocking was perfuming the tent, Rafe pulled his boot back on.

"Pata Peluda." Red Sleeves laid a hand on Rafe's shoulder as though conferring a knighthood. Rafe knew that from now on he would be called Pata Peluda, Spanish for "Hairy Foot," by any Apache who approached within hailing range. He hoped none got that close.

Red Sleeves had a request to make of John Cremony. José

Valdez helped him with the more complicated Spanish.

"We want you to explain to us what your *nantan*, your chief, says in council tomorrow."

"I can tell you now that he will invite you to go to Washington to visit your Great Father. He will tell you to stop raiding, and to live in peace. He'll advise you to cultivate the soil and to raise your own horses and mules, rather than stealing them from the Mexicans."

The crackle of wood in the stove and the dogs' growls punctuated the silence in the tent while Red Sleeves thought about that.

Finally he said, "I am too old to raise corn. If the young people want to dig in the soil, that's for them to decide. And as for killing Mexicans, are we to stand with our arms folded while they murder our women and children as they did at Janos?"

"The Mexicans were once our enemies, too, but now we are friends. You, too, can be friends with them."

"The Americans are a brave and clever people," Red Sleeves said. "I want to be friends with them, but never with the Mexicans." He turned and ducked through the tent door, and the others filed after him. The air in the tent resonated with the backwash of their departure.

"Well," John Cremony looked pleased. "With old Red Sleeves on our side, our problems with ambuscades and horse thievery are solved. If anyone can keep the young bucks in line, he can." He saw the look on Rafe's face. "Don't you think so?"

"With the Apaches, it's every man for himself. Red Sleeves can only try to influence their opinion."

Rafe started to say that he wasn't sure Red Sleeves wanted an alliance, in spite of his bunkum about eternal friendship. He decided to wait until he could eavesdrop on those Navajos some more.

SISTER KNEW THAT HAIRY FOOT'S BIG ROAN WOULD WIN even though he faced the opposite direction, and Hairy Foot sat with one leg hooked over the pommel. Hairy Foot seemed to doze through the uproar of betting, but Sister saw the muscles of the roan's shoulders and hindquarters quiver, and his ears twitch.

Talks A Lot and Flies In His Stew sidled up next to Sister. Talks A Lot stared straight ahead, as though he didn't notice her.

"Which horse do you think will win?" he muttered.

"Hairy Foot's red."

Flies In His Stew snorted. "He might win if they move the finish line back there."

Talks A Lot turned his head slightly so Sister could see his shadow of a smile. He had bet on the roan.

The Bluecoat in charge raised a pistol over his head. Still Hairy Foot sat with his eyes closed and his leg up. Sister began to worry. She had wagered her new moccasins on him. They were the first pair she had sewn by herself, and she didn't want to lose them.

The pistol shot rang out, and Hairy Foot swung his leg down, shoved his boots in the stirrups, and held on. The big roan whirled. While still turning, he bunched his hooves and soared. Sister's heart took flight with him. When he landed, his long legs devoured the ground in such huge strides that he overtook the rest of the field as though they stood still. Sister fell in love with him.

She ignored the footraces and the wrestling matches among the Ndee, the Mexicans, and the Americans who had come for the council. When Hairy Foot led the big red horse away, she knew he was heading for his camp at the base of the butte by the river.

She walked through the Pale Eyes' settlement, making her way around the broken machinery and the rotting timbers. Her people called the Santa Rita mines The Place Where They Cry because for generations the Mexicans had forced Ndee captives to dig here. Their tears had saturated this ground. Their cries of pain and grief had seeped into the rocks. Sometimes when the wind blew around the stony promontories The People could hear them crying still.

The diggers had left foothills of rubble. They had trampled the grass. They had cut down the trees. The ore crushers caused Sister the most dread. A mule walked in an endless circle, pushing the long pole tied to his harness. The heavy stone attached to other end of it ground the earth's bones to powder with a crunch and shriek that raised bumps on the skin of her arms. The sound symbolized the Pale Eyes' incessant digging, hammering, sawing, chopping, and building.

This was winter, the season of Ghost Face. Sensible people took life easier in winter. During the cold nights sensible people gathered to dance, but these men had no women to dance with. In winter sensible people told stories about Old Man Snake, Ugly Buttocks the Bear, and Trickster Coyote, but the Pale Eyes here had no children to listen to their stories. Maybe they had no stories, and if they had, what kind would such men tell?

Sister climbed through the cactus and scrub cedars growing among the boulders of the butte. When she reached the outcrop that provided the best view of the meadow below, she inched out to a large rock at the edge of the drop-off to the valley. Below her, the big roan's coat gleamed like new copper in the dappled sunlight.

Sister scanned the trees, bushes, and boulders around the pasture, assessing the hiding places, the best approaches. She felt a twinge of reproach about wanting to steal from someone who had returned her cousin to her. Stands Alone said that Hairy Foot was different from the other Pale Eyes. He had sense. He kept his word.

Still, this wasn't just any horse.

She imagined riding him to Mexico on a horse-stealing raid with her brother. She felt the powerful surge of him under her and the blur of the ground rushing past her, carrying her away from any enemy who might pursue her.

When a voice said, "*Ugashe*, go away," she jumped and lost her footing. The loose rock gave way under her. Her forward momentum stopped abruptly, and she hung, suspended, before the hand that had caught the back of her tunic hauled her to solid ground. She turned, expecting to see

Talks A Lot or Ears So Big, He Steals Love, or Flies In His
Stew. Instead she stared into Hairy Foot's iridescent green
eyes.

"Ugashe," he said again.

She straightened her leather tunic and raised her chin. She
brushed past him and stomped away, trying not to slide on
the loose gravel of the slope and lose what little dignity she
had left. She wanted to turn around and ask him, in Spanish,
if she could ride his horse, but she didn't know the words
she would need. He wouldn't permit it, anyway. He would
throw rocks at her like the other Pale Eyes did.

SISTER SAUNTERED OVER TO JOIN THE BOYS AS THEY MOVED
up to compete at archery, and she felt everyone's eyes on
her. She wished she could retreat and stand with the women
and girls, but she couldn't quit now. Talks A Lot and his
friends glared at her. She was going to embarrass them again.
Talks A Lot was about to shove her away when an older boy
from Red Sleeves' band swaggered toward her. His own people called him Angry for good reason.

"Ugashe," he shouted at Sister. "Get away from here."

As one, Talks A Lot and his friends moved in front of
her. Sister was an annoyance, but she was their annoyance.
Angry lost the staring contest and stalked away.

Hairy Foot stuck a playing card onto a tree fifty paces
away. Sister waited until the last of the boys had fired and
retrieved his arrow from the card. She walked over to Hairy
Foot as though she had never seen him before.

"Por favor." She held out her hand.

He gave her the deck and watched her shuffle through it.
Holding the cards, she could feel the essence of the strange
smelling, pale-eyed men who had handled them. The hair on
the nape of her neck stirred as she felt their spirits travel
through her fingers and up her arm, like the tingle she got
when she hit her elbow on a rock.

She chose the card with five black arrow heads. One was
in the center and the others arranged around it like the four

directions of the wind. She glanced up at Hairy Foot with a look that wasn't so much request as complicity. He gave a solemn nod of consent.

She pulled the torn card off the twig and replaced it with the new one. She returned to where the boys stood but kept walking to take up a position twenty paces behind them. Any of the boys could have hit the card from here, but they hadn't thought of it. They would be angry with her for doing it, but they were usually angry with her, anyway.

Her arrow landed in the middle of the center figure on the card. She placed the next four in the shapes around it, going from west to east. The Pale Eyes cheered when she finished, and she looked at them in surprise. Hitting the card was easy and not worth any fuss. The Mexicans and the Americans crowded around her, though.

"*Muy lozana.*" A Mexican reached out to pat her on the shoulder.

"*Eres lozana,*" shouted another.

The rest began to chant *lozana.*

Sister dodged through the crowd and joined the women and girls watching from one side.

"Now you have a Mexican name," said She Moves Like Water.

"What does it mean, Grandmother?"

Grandmother would know. When she was young, Mexicans had captured her and held her for three years before she escaped.

"*Lozana* means 'sprightly' or 'spirited.'" Grandmother opened one side of her blanket and draped it around her so they shared its warmth. "It's a good name."

Sister said it softly to herself, pronouncing it her own way. "*Lozen.*"

Calling people by their real names was disrespectful if they were alive and dangerous if they were dead. This was a name she could use without fear of consequences. Lozen.

RAFE WATCHED HER FROM THE CORNER OF HIS EYE. THE Mexicans were right. She was spirited. She also had a larcenous heart and good taste in horseflesh. He couldn't identify the young woman with her. Her face was shrouded by her blanket, but he thought she might be Pandora.

John Cremony walked over to stand with Rafe and watch the contests. "Things are going well, wouldn't you say?"

"For the time being."

Cremony nodded toward a group of men walking past. They wore loincloths, loose cotton shirts, moccasins, and cloth headbands, but their long hair was tied into a club at the napes of their necks. "I'm not familiar with those Apaches."

"That would be because they're Navajos."

"Navajo territory lies more than two hundred miles to the northwest. What would bring them here?"

"Red Sleeves invited them. He married off one of his daughters to a Navajo chief." The Navajo didn't know Rafe understood more than a little of their language. "Red Sleeves sent runners to tell the Navajos we have strong horses and mules, and heaps of goods. Sounds like the old chief is gathering allies to comb the pestiferous white men out of his hair."

"But he just agreed to keep the peace."

Rafe shrugged. "They were assessing how strong the defenses are here. They were discussing whether to launch a direct attack or be content with small raids and ambuscades."

"I'll be damned."

"The good news is that the Navajos decided the slim pickings here weren't worth the whole passle of them making that long trip."

As they walked toward John Cremony's tent, the blacksmith's assistant, Rogers, reeled toward them. He had draped his arm around a young man whose smile covered most of his thin face. Rafe could tell they both had been drinking.

"Looky here." The young man set the tooth-size gold nugget in the palm of his hand and rolled it back and forth with one grubby finger. "I found it in the water off yonder." He pointed up toward the canyon carved by the stream that passed near Red Sleeves' village.

If Red Sleeves thinks he has troubles with white men now, Rafe thought, they are about to get much worse.

LOZEN STARTED FOR THE STREAM AT TWILIGHT WITH A wicker jug in a tumpline on her back. She almost tripped over the young Pale Eyes sprawled near the water. He was the apprentice of the white man who worked in fire and iron.

He lay where he shouldn't have, so close to Red Sleeves' village. Lozen set the water jug on the ground. When she squatted at his side, she could smell the whiskey. She lifted the lower edge of his filthy wool coat, gripped the pistol butt, and eased it out of the waist of his trousers. She stuck the gun into her belt. She took the man's big knife from its sheath and put it next to the pistol.

Lozen eased the tongue of the cartridge belt out of the metal buckle and tugged it loose; then she considered how get it out from under his waist. No clever plan occurred to her, so she braced her feet against his side and shoved, pulling on the belt as he rolled over. He grunted and stopped snoring, but he didn't wake up.

She threw the bandolier over her shoulder, adjusted the water jug on her back, and stooped to collect the iron basin. She walked away at a leisurely pace. When she came to the river, she braced the jug between rocks in the streambed with its mouth facing into the current. While it filled she untied the small leather pouch hanging from the bandolier. It held bits of yellow rock. She upended it, spilling the contents into the water.

She watched them scatter downstream like glittering gnats.

Chapter 8

WASHINGTON SAYS...

While Skinny waited for his turn at hoop-and-pole, he chanted his prayer for success.

The wind will turn your pole.
The wind will make mine fly true.
This time I will win everything.
Later I will win again.

The mountain spirits called the Gaan had handed down the instructions and the sacred symbolism of hoop-and-pole. No women were allowed near the field where the men played the game from morning until night. Its religous origins didn't stop them from laughing and joking, though. While Skinny was preoccupied with his prayer, some of them cackled over the fact that he couldn't sit down.

Not long after the solemn council with the Pale Eyes, the temptation to steal the Santa Rita miners' horses and cattle had grown too strong to resist. Skinny, Morning Star, Loco, and thirty other men had made off with fifty cows. Hairy Foot, John Cremony, and twenty Bluecoats had given chase.

Certain that he was out of rifle range, Skinny had turned his back, lifted his breechclout, slapped his rear end, and taunted the Bluecoats. Cremony had handed his new rifle to Hairy Foot. Hairy Foot's shot had plowed a furrow diagonally across Skinny's buttock. The warriors and the Bluecoats stopped shooting and laughed like coyotes as Skinny sprinted up the mountain with his hands clasping his wound. To make matters worse, the Bluecoats had recovered the cattle.

Red Sleeves and Loco each balanced a long pole upright

in the palm of his right hand and steadied it with his left.
They waited for Broken Foot to roll a willow hoop toward
the furrow in the dry grass piled at the north end of the
playing field. He swung his arm, releasing the hoop at the
top of its arc. It rolled across the pine needles laid down to
make the surface slippery. Loco and Red Sleeves lowered
their poles and chased the hoop. As it entered the cleft in the
pile of hay, they threw the poles along the ground after it,
trying to slide them under the hoop as it fell.

Everyone gathered around to inspect the nine notches on
the butt of each pole and the beads on the hoop's thong
spoke. Broken Foot began the complicated process of tabu-
lating the score.

"Here comes your horse again," said He Who Yawns.

Morning Star watched his pony approach at a diligent canter. The dun had an innocent look, as though convinced that
Morning Star had called him.

"The herd boys are lazy," grumbled He Who Yawns.
"They play cards all day and let the horses run where they
will."

"Coyote sits back on his tether and breaks it," Morning
Star said. "My sister has seen him do it. And he chews
through hobbles."

"He's a coyote, all right," added Broken Foot. "He came
into my wife's camp yesterday and ate her meal cakes."

The horse that Morning Star had stolen from Hairy Foot's
two friends had a sharp, slender muzzle and roguish eyes. His
long, loose-jointed legs tapered to oversize hooves giving him
a clumsy, shuffling walk that rolled into smooth, light-footed
flight when he galloped. He was coyote colored, with a dark
brown mane and tail and stripe running along his backbone.
Like Old Man Coyote he favored the ladies, and he wooed the
mares with enthusiasm. He acted as though he accepted Morning Star's authority because doing so amused him.

Broken Foot declared Loco the winner, and Red Sleeves
shrugged out of his blue coat and handed it to him. He had
already lost the last two buttons, so Loco wore the coat open
and hanging loose over his breechclout. Since the Pale Eyes

had distributed presents to the Red Paint leaders several days ago, the new blankets and calico, the mirrors, knives, and shirts had flowed like a river among the winners and losers at hoop-and-pole. All Red Sleeves had left of his splendid suit of clothes was the fringed, gold epaulet dangling from the back of his belt.

Red Sleeves took up his pole again, ready to recoup his losses, but He Who Yawns raised himself onto the balls of his feet so he could murmur into his ear. Red Sleeves looked up at the sun, just disappearing behind the peak to the west. He glanced regretfully at the coat, whose sleeves Loco was rolling up so they didn't hang past his fingertips.

Red Sleeves sighed. He Who Yawns was right. At tonight's council they would plan the raid into Sonora to avenge the massacre of their women and children at Janos. By the time they finished the meal that Red Sleeves's wives were preparing and gathered at the council fire, the night would be well along.

Everyone knew that the revenge scout preoccupied He Who Yawns. Even though he wasn't a member of the Red Paint Chiricahuas, Red Sleeves had sent him to invite allies to this council. He had traveled across the Pale Eyes' new imaginary line between here and Mexico, and climbed the steep track to the stronghold of Long Neck and his Enemy People. He had ridden to Cheis's Tall Cliffs People in their aerie among the crags and spectral stone columns on the western side of Doubtful Pass. He had visited Skinny's· band at Warm Springs. Wherever he went he spoke of little else but revenge.

He had married Alope at seventeen, younger than most, and he had loved her and their three small daughters with all the fervor of youth. No one had lost more to the Mexican lancers at Janos than He Who Yawns. Even though he was young and inexperienced, and he lacked the tact and generosity that would make him a great leader, Red Sleeves had decided to place him in charge of the raid. Now Red Sleeves would have to persuade the other warriors to agree with his decision about He Who Yawns, but in his thirty years as chief he could count on one hand the times his men had refused to do that, and he would have fingers left over.

RED SLEEVES GAVE CHEIS THE HONOR OF BEGINNING THE council by smoking to the four sacred directions. Cheis rubbed his tobacco pouch between his thumb and fingers to show it was empty. He looked at his younger brother, Co-yundado, who sat farther down in the ranks of warriors. In Spanish *coyundado* meant "tied to a yoke," but in naming Cheis's brother that, the Chiricahua meant the ox himself.

Cheis's strength was of the tall, supple variety, swaying almost imperceptibly, like an oak, to accomodate the vicissitudes of life. His brother Ox was powerful, too, but built low to the ground. He took more than the usual amount of time to consider every question, which gave him a reputation for being slow to act. Cheis relied on him for advice, though, and rarely went anywhere without him.

Ox unrolled of top of his moccasin and retrieved the small leather sack he had folded into it. Before he opened it he fingered the contents. Amusement and chagrin flitted across his round face too quickly for anyone to see except those who knew him well. Cheis's impassive expression never shifted as he watched his brother.

The rest waited while Ox wrapped the thick fingers of one hand around the sack to hide the angular, untobacco-like bulge in it, and reached in with the other. He poked around and pulled out a pinch of tobacco. He closed the sack, replaced it in his moccasin cuff, and rolled the tobacco in a sumac leaf.

He handed the cigarillo to Cheis, who accepted it solemnly. No one gave any sign that they knew what had happened, but most of them had heard of the wanderings of the rooster feet. The story circulating among the nightly fires was that when Cheis was thirteen, he put a rooster's foot into seven-year-old Ox's gourd of stew. Instead of making a fuss, Ox had acted as though it weren't there. When Cheis went on his first scout as an apprentice, he had found the foot in his water sack. It and its sucessors had been passing between them ever since, in a blanket roll, in a moccasin, under a saddle, or tied to a war cap along with the feathers, and with never any indication that it existed.

After the opening ritual, Red Sleeves started the discussion. The Americans intrigued, puzzled, and irritated everyone. If the Ndee complied with the Americans' demands, they would not be able to avenge the massacre at Janos. That was unthinkable.

"Wah-sin-ton says this. Wah-sin-ton says that." Morning Star looked around the council fire. "Who is this Wah-sin-ton?"

"Maybe he's the Pale Eyes' most powerful chief," Red Sleeves said.

"The Pale Eyes want our leaders to ride many days to visit this fellow, Wah-sin-ton. Why doesn't Wah-sin-ton come to us instead?"

"Maybe he's too old," said Loco. "Maybe his joints ache when he camps anywhere but in his own lodge."

"Why won't the Americans give us guns and powder and ammunition to kill Mexicans?" Loco said. "The Mexicans are their enemies, too. We're not asking them to fight the Mexicans for us. We'll kill the treacherous coyotes ourselves."

"We don't need their guns," said He Who Yawns. "When we use bows, we do not have to depend on the Pale Eyes for powder and bullets."

Cheis and Ox, Morning Star, and Broken Foot had faces that fell easily into smiles. He Who Yawns did not. His eyes glowed like coals from under an overhanging brow. His sharp nose, wide mouth, and thong-thin lips gave him a look of ferocity that was almost perpetual.

"The Americans and the Mexicans fought for two years." Red Sleeves fell silent and stared off into the past, something he did more often these days. "We've seen the ground strewn with their rotting dead. The coyotes and the buzzards grew fat during that war. In all our years of making war with the Mexicans, I doubt we killed as many of them as the Americans did."

Something else was bothering all of them. Broken Foot

spoke of it first. "Are we children that the American colonel should tell us what we can and cannot do in our own country? We have always gone to Mexico for horses and slaves. Mexico is our second home."

Red Sleeves turned to a compact individual dressed in the white shirt and loose white cotton trousers of a Mexican farmer. Juan Mirez had taken off the breechclout and moccasins he had worn since Red Sleeves had captured him in Mexico at age nine. On the pretense of looking for mules to buy, he would find out where the soldiers had taken the captives.

"Do you have everything you need, my son?" Red Sleeves asked him.

"Yes, Uncle."

Since Red Sleeves had recommended He Who Yawns as the leader of the biggest war raid anyone could remember, he had become even more overbearing than usual. He recounted again the perfidy of Mexicans soldiers and the warriors' obligation to the spirits of those murdered at Janos.

He committed the most basic discourtesy. He talked so much that he didn't allow others to make their own pictures in their heads. By leaving nothing to the imagination, he demanded that they see it exactly as he did. A good speaker said only enough to encourage the listeners to open up their thinking and travel in their minds to the place being spoken of, to see the events there for themselves.

"I have war magic." He announced it as if they hadn't heard it before. "That night by the river, after the Mexicans had slain my mother, my woman, and my children, the spirits promised that bullets could never kill me."

"Did they give you the power to stop bullets from killing the rest of us?" Broken Foot said it in a voice too low for He Who Yawns to hear, but the men around him chuckled softly.

While He Who Yawns talked, Morning Star let his mind wander. He thought about that invisible line undulating across mountains and deserts and rivers, the line the Mexicans were not supposed to cross. The People considered this an advantage. Mexican lancers could not chase the raiding parties across it.

Morning Star didn't agree. The Pale Eyes who called themselves American had taken a vast territory that the Mexicans considered theirs. If the Americans took land from the Mexicans, would they try to take land from The People, too?

At first The People had thought that the Pale Eyes with their rods and strings were playing a game, like hoop-and-pole, only this game required a field as big as The People's entire country. When they learned the real purpose of the chains and the poles and the far-seeing tubes, they had laughed uproariously around their fires at night. The Pale Eyes thought they could measure mountains and deserts and rivers the way a woman measured a buckskin to see if she could cut a shirt front or a moccasin top out of it.

Morning Star didn't laugh. He remembered watching with his sister from a ridge as a company of Mexican soldiers rode up the valley below. They had stopped at the ford in the stream, conferred, and then headed back the way they came. Morning Star told Lozen that the boundary lay there.

"How can they witch a wall from the air?" she had asked. He had looked solemnly at her. "They urinate in a line like Brother Wolf when he marks his hunting lands. When the Mexicans reach it, they smell the urine and turn away." She had exploded into that wild, infectious laugh of hers.

Lozen. What to do about the child who was no longer a child? She was supposed to be helping She Moves Like Water and her sister, Corn Stalk, prepare for the ceremony that would mark her as a woman. Instead she was sneaking off with the boys and begging him to let her serve as his apprentice on his horse-stealing raids.

After the ceremony of White Painted Woman, his little sister would be free to marry. She would spend her days in the company of women. She would bear children and raise them. She would care for grandchildren when her own daughters went on raids with their husbands. The thought should have made him happy, but it didn't. She had horse magic and the power of far-sight and who knew what other gifts. He couldn't shake the feeling that the spirits had other plans for her.

Chapter 9

SUN RUMBLES INSIDE IT

Since before Lozen was born she had heard her grandmother singing. Her brother said their mother sounded like Grandmother. Lozen wished she could have known her mother for as long as her brother had. When the Hair Takers attacked her people at the Death Feast, Morning Star had grabbed Sister's cradleboard and run with it, but he had not been able to save their mother.

When Grandmother sang, Lozen closed her eyes and pretended the voice was her mother's. When she was younger, Lozen had wakened each morning to the sound of her Grandmother's song, a greeting to the day and to Yusen, Life Giver. Each morning she had reached out and felt the warmth of the blankets where her grandmother had lain beside her.

Lozen grew taller and Grandmother grew smaller with the years until now Lozen could look down and see the individual gray strands of hair growing from her grandmother's brown scalp. Grandmother laughed and said that the rain and the sun had shrunk her like the Mexicans' cotton cloth.

Time had eroded a crisscross pattern of wrinkles in her cheeks. The bones of her skull formed large hollows around her eyes, leaving her sparse gray eyebrows perched at the apex, and giving her the look of a startled owl. She had the biggest ears and the kindest eyes of anyone Lozen knew. Her eyes were framed by the heavy lids above them and the pouches of skin underneath. When she smiled, the folds and gullies of her face shifted into a look of impish joy. Around her wrinkled neck she wore thirty or forty necklaces of shiny seeds and glass beads. Blue stones dangled from earlobes that looked like a pair of tree fungi.

Grandmother was a *di-yin,* a shaman. Women with sadness in their eyes came to her fire to ask her to sing away an illness, or sing back a straying husband. Some came smiling, their palms caressing their swollen bellies, and asked her to sing a cradle into being and welcome a new baby into the world. Those were Grandmother's favorite sings.

This time She Moves Like Water had brought her the traditional four presents of tobacco, yellow pollen, a well-tanned buckskin, and a black-handled knife. She asked her to make a *tsoch,* a cradleboard for her three-day-old daughter. She Moves Like Water had held out her arm, and Grandmother had used a buckskin thong to measure from the crook of her elbow to her closed fist. She Moves Like Water could hold a cradle this wide comfortably when she nursed her daughter.

At dawn this morning, Lozen and Stands Alone went with Grandmother to collect the materials. Both of them knew that White Painted Woman had given the instructions for cradle-making back at the beginning of time, but Grandmother always explained them again.

"The materials must be gathered and assembled in one day," she said. "Pine is easy to cut and shape for the frame, but it attracts lightning. Black locust will make the child grow straight and strong."

Grandmother sang while she cut locust for the frame, a willow branch for the canopy hoop, cedar for the footrest. She sang while she gathered absorbent moss to pack around the baby and yucca stems for the back slats. While they were at it, the three of them cut strips of willow bark to grind into a powder that would soothe rashes. They collected cottonwood down to stuff the baby's pillow.

Stands Alone helped Lozen hoist the loaded basket onto her back, and they followed Grandmother back to their family's camp. Next to the arbor Grandmother stirred up the fire she would use to shape the locust and willow into the frame and canopy. Stands Alone laid out cowhides for Grandmother to sit on while she worked.

Lozen arranged the materials in the necessary pattern and

order. She went into the lodge and searched through Grandmother's storage pouches until she found the bags of bird
bones, shiny pebbles, and bits of lightning-struck wood to
hang from the canopy's rim as protection against lightning
and illness.

Grandmother began by rolling tobacco into a dried leaf
and smoking to the four directions. She asked Life Giver to
send his power through her hands so the cradleboard would
give health and long life to its tiny occupant. When Grandmother used the gifts the spirits had given her, she radiated
a serene confidence.

Time, hard work, and old injuries had swelled Grandmother's knuckles and bent her fingers at rigid right angles
to her hands, and she needed more assistance these days than
in the past. With the knife She Moves Like Water had
brought, Lozen helped Grandmother scrape the yucca stems
smooth for the back slats. Grandmother fastened them so that
everything fit together tightly to make a cradle that was
strong and graceful. As she shaped the frame into an elon-
gated oval, bent the willow into its graceful curve for the
canopy, and lashed the back slats into place, she sang the
most beautiful song of the hundreds she knew.

Good, like long life it moves back and forth.
By means of White Water under it, it is made.
By means of Rainbow curved over it, it is made.
Lightning dances alongside it, they say.
Good, like long life the cradle is made.
Sun rumbles inside it, they say.

When she wasn't singing one of the cradle-making songs,
she repeated the refrain that would create a special bond with
her great granddaughter. She had sung it while she made
Lozen's cradle fourteen years ago and Lozen's mother's forty
years before that.

"Look at her, this pretty little one. She calls me Granny.
She calls me Granny. Look at her." She had made so many

cradles that most of the children called her Granny, and so did their parents.

She let Lozen stain the buckskin with the sacred yellow pollen and taught her the words to sing while she did it. Lozen made a line of holes in it with her bone awl and held it in place while Grandmother laced it tightly around the canopy and frame. Then Lozen helped her attach the buckskin pieces that would lace in a zigzag, like lightning, up the front to wrap around Daughter and hold her in place. With fine stitches Grandmother sewed the buckskin sides on in two sets so that the top half could be left open in hot weather.

She worked more slowly than she had in the past. Lozen worried that she might not finish by dusk, but the sun was just setting when Grandmother attached the rawhide tumpline to the sides and cut the half moon in the leather covering of the canopy to signify that the occupant was a girl. She tucked a packet of sacred pollen and gray sage into an inner pocket for added protection against lightning. Into the other pocket she put a small, turtle-shaped bag with a piece of Daughter's umbilical cord and a slice of fragrant *osha* root to keep away colds and sore throat.

She stood it against the arbor's corner pole, and she and Lozen sat back on their heels to look at it. Its lines were graceful and practical. The yellow pollen gave it a cheerful look, like solid sunshine. Lozen thought of the last two lines of Grandmother's song. "Good, like long life the cradle is made. / Sun rumbles inside it, they say."

With the tips of her fingers, Lozen set the dangling bird bones and pebbles to swaying and clicking together softly as though having a private conversation. She opened the front flaps and felt the soft padding of leather. She smiled up at Grandmother. Sensing enemies at a distance was good magic to have, but Grandmother's gifts were better.

SINCE HE MARRIED SHE MOVES LIKE WATER, MORNING Star had come to understand why the old men cheerfully turned their responsibilities as leaders over to the younger

ones. He understood why they seemed content to stay home
by their fires while their grandchildren crawled over them
like puppies and younger men rode away to steal ponies,
captives, and glory. Sometimes he thought he would be
happy to spend most of his days watching his woman move
about her camp as slender and supple as a willow withe, as
graceful as a hawk in flight.

Now he watched her take her best doeskin skirt and tunic
top from their parfleche and shake the creases out to the
music of the tin cones that formed a thick fringe all over
them. It was the same costume she had worn at her ceremony
of White Painted Woman. Morning Star had come to Warm
Springs to attend the feast and to visit Cousin before he became known as Loco. He had seen She Moves Like Water
often when he visited here, but she had been a child then.

He had fallen in love with her when he saw her emerge
from the tall tipi of oak saplings. After she had run four times
to show her strength and agility, he had joined the line of
people waiting for her blessing. When he kneeled and felt
the butterfly brush of her fingers making a cross of pollen
on his forehead, he had felt as though he were tumbling head
over heels down a steep, grassy slope.

He had summoned the courage to approach her when the
dancing began. He remembered the gentle pressure of her
head on his shoulder and the warmth of her breath on his
neck during that first dance. He remembered moving in time
with her, circling to the rhythm of the drums, like their own
hearts beating. He remembered feeling light-headed with joy
and longing and surprise.

Most of the unmarried men of the Warm Springs band
had courted her, but none as single-mindedly as he did. He
had helped her cultivate the cornfield, and he had cut firewood
for baking the mescal she and the other women harvested. He
had waited by the trail for her to pass, and she had spoken
shyly with him, always observing propriety by having a friend
nearby and keeping bushes between her and him.

When she kept the haunch of venison and the tanned hide
he left at the door of her lodge, he knew she would marry

him. His sister and grandmother had packed the family's belongings onto a few mules, and the three of them left their home in the Mogollon Mountains to the west. She Moves Like Water and her mother and younger sister raised a tipi of hides for the couple near their encampment and built a domed lodge for Sister and Grandmother. Morning Star's family had always had relatives among the Red Paints of the Warm Springs band, and they had visited often. Lozen already knew the children here and, he remembered with a wry smile, had fought with most of the boys at one time or another.

As night approached, Morning Star dressed for the dancing. She Moves Like Water had laid out his best breechclout and moccasins, his war cap decorated with eagle and turkey feathers, and the cartridge belt Lozen had taken from the drunken Pale Eyes and given to him. The belt's original owner would not have recognized it. Lozen had rubbed it with pollen, giving a golden burnish to the leather. She had beaded the edges and decorated them with a fringe of metal cones. She had added cowrie shells and pieces of the Pale Eyes' green glass.

She Moves Like Water set out the fringed and beaded parfleche, but she didn't open it. Inside it Morning Star kept his bags of pollen, his war amulets, and his *izze-kloth*, the medicine cord.

Medicine cords were worn on the war trail and during the Fierce Dance, like the one they would hold tonight. Only a shaman with great influence could make a cord that had Enemies-Against power. Broken Foot had assembled this one of four twisted rawhide thongs that he had painted, each a different color—red, yellow, black, and white. He had woven eagle down, beads, shells, petrified wood, an eaglet's claw, bits of lightning-struck wood and the sacred blue stone into them.

Each item carried its own special power. The blue stone would make his bow and his pistol shoot accurately. The wood protected him from lightning. Other items would ensure that no bullet could harm him and would keep him from getting lost. Morning Star lifted it reverently, said a prayer, and put it over his head. He settled it across his chest from his right shoulder to his left hip and fastened his bags of pollen to it.

He sat cross-legged on the hides spread across the lodge's floor. She Moves Like Water knelt behind him and combed the snarls from his hair. His hair was so long that she had to comb it in sections, starting with the ends.

"Maybe you will find a woman in Mexico," she murmured. "One who will satisfy you and will work hard."

The touch of her hands in his hair and on his neck sent thrills through him. They had not coupled since the baby began to make her presence known by a bulge under She Moves Like Water's skirt. Nor would they be able to for several more years, until Daughter stopped nursing.

Coupling led to pregnancy, and pregnancy interrupted the flow of milk to the first baby. Besides that, caring for two small ones while cooking, tanning hides, sewing, harvesting, preparing food for winter, hauling wood and water, and making baskets and water jugs imposed an unreasonable burden on their mother. People scorned a man who got his woman with child too soon, but no one condemned him if he took a second wife or slept with a Mexican slave.

"I would go with you if I could," she said.

The deepening darkness seemed to separate them from the rest of the world. They had not slept apart for more than seven or eight days, and this was the first war raid since then. She Moves Like Water would never admit to being afraid for him, but she was. He was stronger and handsomer than any man she knew, but he was more than that. He had magic of his own. It drew people to him and made them like him and trust him. He had the power to make She Moves Like Water love him more than life itself.

Morning Star picked Daughter up from her nest of rabbit skins.

"I've talked to my sister," he said. "She knows she must help you and do whatever you tell her."

"The time of her feast is coming."

Morning Star knew that a girl's ceremony of White Painted Woman influenced how people regarded her family. Doing everything right, and generously, was making She Moves Like Water anxious. "I'll bring back horses to trade for the things we'll need. It will be the best feast anyone has seen since your own."

"Lozen hasn't said so, but I know she wants Stands Alone to celebrate with her."

"We can gather enough for both of them."

"For their dresses we'll need ten deer hides with no blemishes or holes in them."

She Moves Like Water's sister's new husband called from outside. "Brother-in-law, the singers and the drummers are gathering. *Nantan* wants you to enter the dance first."

"Tell him I'm coming."

"Skinny wants you to lead? Why didn't he appoint an older man?"

"I don't know." He handed Daughter to her and touched his medicine cord with one hand. "I should have asked Broken Foot to include a charm to keep me from tripping over the end of my breechclout while I dance."

She Moves Like Water leaned close, intoxicating him with her smoky aroma. She lowered her voice.

"Watch over my sister's husband." She didn't have to remind him that this was Corn Stalk's man's first time on the war trail, and that he tended to be rash and heedless.

Morning Star put his arms around his wife and his daughter and held them to him. Then he pushed aside the hide door and emerged into the dusk, tying on his war cap as he went. The tin cones that Lozen had sewn onto the bandolier jingled as he went to join the men, all of them dressed in their best, looking fierce and capable and ready to dance up the sun.

Chapter 10

SHADOW WARRIOR

The warriors danced away into the night beyond the bubble of the fire's light. The drummers and singers stopped abruptly, leaving the rhythmic music of the tin cones on the men's clothes jingling in the darkness. The sound grew fainter until it became inaudible, leaving the women, the children, and the old people in a vortex of silence.

During the Fierce Dance the boys had maintained their usual ferment of mischief on the perimeter. They jostled and insulted each other, they dropped thistles into breechclouts. They threw pebbles at the girls who disdained to notice them. Once the men's dance ended, the undercurrent of noise continued among the boys, but they came alert, too. Social dances would follow the Fierce Dance. They always did. Not to hold a social dance after a war dance invited disaster in battle. Even on the war trail the warriors followed the custom, with half of them taking the women's part.

Dancing was embarrassing enough, but dancing with a girl was a more frightening prospect than war. Those who had seen at least twelve harvests had reached the age when they realized that girls had the power to cause them extreme mortification. They also knew that someday they would live in intimacy with those mystifying and dangerous creatures who glanced like hungry panthers at them from the other side of the fire.

Skinny announced the first dance. The singers and drummers refreshed themselves with drinks of *tiswin* and took their positions again. The boys pulled up their moccasins, smoothed their hair, and adjusted their necklaces and belts. Comments passed back and forth in undertones.

"You fart when you hop around out there."

"Your breechclout will fall off."

"You dance like a pregnant badger."

"My cross-cousin says she hates you."

The women always asked the men to dance, but the boys knew they'd increase their chances if they lurked in the girls' vicinity. A valiant few ventured into enemy territory. To reach them the boys had to dodge the older women.

"Be careful with those girls, you boys," Her Eyes Open called out. "They have teeth down there, you know. They'll bite your little mouse penises off if you try anything."

Talks A Lot, Flies In His Stew, and Ears So Big had discussed that teeth threat while they gambled away the afternoons at the horse pasture. They had tried to cajole information from the older boys, but they had received no reliable answers. They decided that a second set of teeth was unlikely, but with girls, anything was possible.

As for the girls, they proved that a great deal can be said without speaking. They signaled with fleeting looks, with casual waves of a hand, the toss of a head, or cock of a hip.

Neither Lozen nor Stands Alone were inclined to play the game.

"He Who Steals Love has been watching you," Stands Alone said.

"Why?"

"Why do you think?"

"He's too old for me."

"I know five women who want to marry him."

"Then let them."

"Here come three of them now."

Tall Girl, She Sneezes, and Knot walked by with their arms linked.

She Sneezes spoke loudly enough for Stands Alone to hear. "Who wants to marry an Already Used Woman?" The other two laughed.

"Only a very fat man would want her," Knot said.

"A fat man with too many ears."

"*Besdacada*, knife-and-awl." Stands Alone hissed the

worst insult in her people's language. "Smell this!" She extended her fist with her thumb wedged between the first and second fingers and flung it open in the obscene gesture.

"Ignore them, Sister." But Lozen knew how difficult that was.

Not only had Manuel Armijo kept Stands Alone for his personal use, but since her family had died at Janos, she had no one to prepare the feast of White Painted Woman for her. She was old enough to be a woman, but she had not gone through the ritual that would give her a woman's status. Lozen decided that she and Stands Alone would have the ceremony together or not at all.

Flies In His Stew caught Lozen's eye as he approached, but she raised her hand in a small gesture that said she would not ask him. She would not dance until someone asked Stands Alone.

He Makes Them Laugh sauntered over. No war amulets hung from the fringed cotton shawl he wore tied at a slant across his chest. He did not carry the scratching stick and the drinking tube that apprentices took on the war trail. Instead of arrows, peeled sticks carved and painted with silly faces poked from the top of his quiver.

Lozen was fond of her unambitious cross-cousin. She was almost amused by the fact that she wanted to go on the war trail but couldn't, and he could but didn't want to. He said that people could be brave for a little while, but they were dead for a long time.

"Aren't you going to Mexico with the men?" she asked.

"Someone has to stay behind and protect you women." He glanced at Stands Alone. She looked away, suddenly shy. He wasn't her cross-cousin, and talking freely with him wasn't proper.

"Will you dance with me?" He wasn't supposed to ask her, but he specialized in doing what he wasn't supposed to do.

Without looking at him, Stands Alone started for the circle of couples. He caught up with her and leaned down to say something in her ear. She threw her head back and laughed.

Lozen hadn't heard her laugh like that since before the Mexicans captured her.

From the corner of her eye Lozen saw He Steals Love start in her direction. She turned away and walked to where Talks A Lot stood. She poked his shoulder hard with her finger and headed for the dance ground. He followed, looking everywhere but at her.

Talks A Lot had dressed for the war trail. This would be his first raid as an apprentice, and it was the biggest anyone could remember. He had haunted Broken Foot's camp for weeks, running any errand, doing any chore, and giving him his family's best pony in exchange for the war cap Broken Foot had sung over for him.

He had even asked Lozen for a charm that would help him see enemies at a distance. Lozen had chosen creatures with good eyesight and had made him an amulet out of hawk down, a vertebrae from the mountain lion whose pelt was now a quiver for her brother's arrows, and a turquoise bead. She had prayed to her spirits and asked them to bless it, but she told Talks A Lot she couldn't guarantee anything. He had given her a fine deer hide for it, the first of the ten she would need to make the ceremonial dresses for herself and Stands Alone.

Talks A Lot danced well, but Lozen could tell he was thinking about the coming revenge raid. She envied him.

THE SUN HADN'T RISEN, BUT A PALE RIBBON OF LIGHT LAY along the horizon. The dark figures of the warriors and their women moved silently about, their slhouettes barely visible against that faint glow. Now and then Lozen heard a jingle of metal or clatter of cowrie shells as the men dressed and collected their equipment.

"We're leaving the horses behind so our enemies will have less of a trail to follow if they come after us." Morning Star was making a quick repair to his moccasin while Lozen packed the last of the parched corn, the dried venison, and juniper berries. "Ride Coyote often or he'll become ill tempered."

"How could we tell if he becomes more ill tempered?" She Moves Like Water spoke softly from the other side of the lodge where she nursed Daughter. "He's so surly already."

Morning Star went on with the instructions to Lozen, although he knew she knew all of it already. "Don't scatter the wood from its pile, or you'll bring the warriors bad luck. When you eat, keep the bones piled in one place, or we shall become separated on the trail."

He stuck into his belt the old pistol that Lozen had taken from the drunken blacksmith's apprentice. Morning Star was one of the few who had a gun. He had used up the powder and bullets she had stolen, but maybe he would find some to steal on the way.

When he left the lodge, She Moves Like Water followed him outside, the baby still at her breast. "May we live to see each other again," she said softly.

Lozen hurried to keep up as Morning Star strode to the outcrop of rocks called They See Them Off. The warriors and apprentices there had painted the broad, reddish-brown stripe like a mask across their faces. Skinny surprised Lozen by turning to her.

"The men want you to pray for them and ask your spirits if enemies are near."

Everyone watched as Lozen traced a cross of pollen in her left palm. She lifted her hands, palms up, and held them over her head.

"Life Giver, hear me," she chanted. "Guide the men on the trail. Let nothing delay their journey. When they meet with the enemy, make their arrows fly true and turn aside the bullets of the evil ones. Bring all of them back safely to us. Cover them with honor."

An eddy of morning wind stirred the wisps of hair around her face and blew the golden flecks of pollen into her eyebrows. She turned slowly; then she shivered and opened her eyes.

"There is no one nearby to hinder you."

The men started off single file down the steep trail in the cliff face. The women returned to their fires, to their sleepy, hungry children, and their day's work. Lozen waited to catch sight of the war party when it reached the plain below.

The men would join Red Sleeves' warriors, then travel west to meet those of Cheis's band. They would turn south and find Long Neck's warriors from the band called the Enemy People. He Who Yawns would bring the men from his own small band known as the In Front At Behind People. The force would then head for the Sonoran town called Arizpe.

In his journey south, the Mexican captive, Juan Mirez, had joined a mule train traveling the wind-scoured passes and deep gorges of the Sierra Madres. Muleteers went all over northern Mexico. They knew what was what and who was where. They said that some of the Janos captives were being kept as slaves in Arizpe. Juan returned with the news. Now he was part of the expedition to take revenge.

A pebble from the ledge above hit the ground near Lozen and rattled down the slope. She slid behind a boulder and waited for Stands Alone to pass before she tossed a stone at her.

Stands Alone whirled around. She had put on the clothes she had worn when the three Pale Eyes men returned her—a full skirt of cotton cloth and a white tunic belted with a red sash. Instead of moccasins she wore straw sandals. A gourd of water hung at her waist.

"Where are you going?" Lozen asked.

"Juan Mirez told me he met El Gordo coming back from Sonora. The old carrion eater is headed for Mesilla."

"You said he always travels with guards. How will you kill him?"

"Life Giver will show me a way. Don't tell your brother's wife where I've gone until it's too late for anyone to come after me."

Manuel Armijo. El Gordo. He was a wily one. He was like the fat rat that ate the cornmeal every winter. El Gordo was eating Stands Alone's chance for happiness. She would not feel like a woman of The People again until she killed him. If Stands Alone returned safely, she and Lozen would celebrate the ceremony of White Painted Woman together.

"May we live to see each other again," Lozen said.

Lozen watched Stands Alone grow smaller as she descended the trail at a fast walk. She pulled the wooden plug from the opening of her gourd canteen and poured a little water into a deposit of red clay. Lozen dipped her fingers into the mud. She closed her eyes and smeared it across the upper part of her face to form the red stripe that distinguished the Red Paint warriors.

She looked out over the narrow valley that pointed southwest like the head of a lance. Ground fog pooled there, clinging to the base of the mountains that sloped into it. The lavender peaks rising beyond those surrounding the valley lay at the end of a three-day march. The vastness of the country exhilarated her. For her, the horizon was just another destination. She saw it all with a hawk's eye. She wanted to spread her arms, step off the edge, and soar out over the green slopes. Broken Foot said that his Goose magic let him do that, though never when anyone was watching. Maybe he was teasing her and maybe not.

She saw the men far below, moving through the mist. They entered a stand of cedars and disappeared.

"*Yalan,*" she murmured. Good-bye.

THIS WAS THE BEGINNING OF THE SUMMER SEASON CALLED Thick With Fruit. Trays of boiled locust pods, sumac berries, and yucca fruits pounded and glazed in their own juice were stacked under a brush arbor and ready to be set out again in the morning sun to dry. Everywhere in camp burden baskets leaned against each other. They were filled with mesquite beans, sunflower seeds, juniper berries, and the glossy seeds of the grama grass.

Women roasted piñon nuts by tossing them with live coals on trays woven of green yucca leaves. Before He Makes

Them Laugh took up his sentry position above the camp, he left the ribs of a deer and a stomach full of blood. Grandmother had added wild onions and chili peppers to the paunch, and it was now cooking over the coals.

Lozen sat between She Moves Like Water and her sister, Corn Stalk, and passed them each a cake of mescal flour sweetened with sumac berries.

"My mother and I went to the lodge of Her Eyes Open at dawn this morning," said She Moves Like Water. "She accepted our gift of an eagle feather and a blue prayer stone. She will sponsor Stands Alone for the ceremony of White Painted Woman."

Lozen was elated. It was a act of overwhelming generosity. Preparing for one feast took months of work. A second one would impose an almost impossible burden on Lozen's family.

"I'll haul all the wood and water and tan the hides, Sister," Lozen said. "I'll grind the mescal meal and hoe the corn and weave the baskets and trays. I'll cook and mend and watch Daughter."

She Moves Like Water laughed. "You're usually making arrowheads and tending the horses. Did you look down there and see that you have a girl's thing and not a boy's?"

"I don't know." Lozen pretended to look under her own skirt. "What does a boy's thing look like?"

Corn Stalk giggled around the hide she was chewing for Lozen's ceremonial dress.

Grandmother stood in the fire's light, and all the women came to attention. Grandmother was a good storyteller.

"A young woman was so beautiful," she said, "that all the young men wanted to marry her. She told them, 'After a while, if you all show me your penises, I'll marry the man with the smallest one.' Old Man Coyote, he went to Mouse and offered him a present in return for exchanging penises."

As Grandmother told the story, Lozen looked up at the sky, thrown over the world like a black robe beaded with light. She realized that she liked not having the men around. The women could sit closer to the warmth of the fire when men weren't occupying the best seats. The women were merrier when they were alone, and more mischievous. Definitely more mischievous. Lozen ducked to avoid the prickly pear fruits that some of them were tossing at each other.

Grandmother went on with the story in spite of the giggling. "After all the young men lined up, the young woman said, 'Coyote has the smallest penis. I'll marry him.' But then Mouse appeared dragging Coyote's huge penis after him. Dust and burs covered Coyote's penis. Cactus spines stuck to it from being pulled across the ground. Everyone poked it with sticks and wanted to know why it was so big. 'Because it belongs to Coyote,' Mouse said. The girl laughed and said she would never marry anyone with such a large penis. It would get stuck inside her. It would hurt her. Old Man Coyote got so mad, he fastened his own penis back on; then he killed that mouse." Then to fool Coyote, Grandmother added, "I'm talking about fruit and flowers.

"Old Man Coyote is a trickster," said Grandmother. "And men have learned to be like him. Even if Coyote offers you something good, don't take it."

Amid the laughter and the cries of "Wah, wah, wah," a tremor started in Lozen's chest. A roar vibrated her skull and rang in her ears. Her heart began to race. She stood abruptly.

"We have to go."

Without question or argument, Grandmother began herding the children together, making sure they each had a blanket and food.

"Don't spoil the fun," Tall Girl called out.

"We have to go. Now. Everyone." Lozen helped She Moves Like Water settle her daughter's cradleboard on her back.

"The boys will tell us if an enemy comes," Tall Girl said. "We're not following a crazy girl into the mountains at night."

Her Eyes Open grabbed Tall Girl by the elbow and hauled her up like a half-filled burden basket. She shoved her forward so hard that Tall Girl stumbled and almost fell. Her

Eyes Open only had to give She Sneezes and Knot the look. They hustled after the others.

"What about the food?" asked Squint Eyes.

"Leave it."

Lozen searched the campsite, looking into every shelter for any child who might be sleeping; then she trotted after the silent procession. What if she couldn't get them away in time? What if she were wrong about enemies approaching?

She picked up a straggling girl and carried her at a run to her mother, who was searching for her but didn't dare call out. She returned to the rear of the column. With an arrow nocked she followed the others until they entered the boulder-strewn underbrush. She knew that Grandmother, Her Eyes Open, and the other older women would see that everyone reached the cave that was their hiding place.

Lozen climbed the slope to the lookouts' post on a high ledge. He Makes Them Laugh was waiting for her. Two small boys, the other sentries, slept curled together on a blanket. They sat up and looked apologetic.

"What happened?" murmured He Makes Them Laugh.

"Enemies are coming from the south."

"Mexicans?"

"I don't know."

He Makes Them Laugh primed and loaded the ancient musket that Skinny had left with him. They didn't have to wait long. Holding torches over their heads, thirty horsemen thundered into the camp below. They set the brush shelters ablaze as they rode. By the light of the burning lodges and arbors, Lozen could see them pitching baskets of seeds and nuts into the flames. Some wheeled their mounts, trampling the women's belongings. Some of them urinated on the trays of drying fruit. Lozen could hear their laughter.

"Pale Eyes diggers," Lozen breathed. "From Santa Rita."

He Makes Them Laugh turned to look at her. "The old ones are right about you, Cousin."

He smiled at the boys who huddled against the rock wall. "Now, warriors, we'll play a game of Creep and Freeze. We'll leave those Pale Eyes far behind us."

Chapter 11

SAINTS PRESERVE US

Rafe couldn't remember when he'd been in the presence of so many women of his own race. He was surrounded by two of them, to be exact, and one of them was big enough to divide and create a third. Sarah Bowman was six feet tall, and her heap of cayenne-red hair increased her altitude. During the war with Mexico she had worked as a laundress and cook, and the soldiers had nicknamed her The Great Western.

Since the war, her legend had gathered steam. Strong men and unruly ones said she was the roughest fighter on the Mexican border. The Indians believed she was supernatural. The Mexicans were only slightly more afraid of God and the devil than of her.

He had met her a year before because of her inflatable rubber bathing tub. The longing for a hot bath and a warm woman had lured him to her hotel in the teeming Texas border settlement that people were starting to call El Paso.

In El Paso she had seemed completely at ease among the hordes of gold rushers, sharps, and opportunists who thronged the settlement on their way west. She looked equally at ease now, playing euchre by firelight in a tree-choked canyon, deep in Apache country. The noisiest things around were her talkative old mule, Jake, the stream chuckling in the darkness nearby, and laughter from the bivouac of the army escort.

Western had sold her share in the hotel in El Paso and packed her chattel into the wagon now parked next to Rafe's. She said she was going to meet her husband, Albert Bowman, who was helping with the construction of Camp Webster, the new army post near the Santa Rita mines. She always referred to Albert as The Sergeant. Rafe had met The Sergeant, and he recognized the bright gleam of gold fever in the man's eyes. Rafe figured Albert would lead The Great Western a merry chase, but then she was used to that. She had followed the army to hell and back for more than a dozen years.

The second American woman in the party, and Rafe's partner at euchre, was Anna Maria Morris. Mrs. Morris was on her way to join her husband. Major Morris had taken command of Camp Webster, hence the company of soldiers as escort. Mrs. Morris held her cards with her arms around the Negro baby who slept in her lap. The child belonged to Mrs. Morris's slave, Louisa, who was grinding corn for the morning's bread.

The Great Western's friend, Cruz, was crooning a lullaby in Spanish to her six-year-old daughter and the four youngest of the five towheaded sisters who traveled with Western. The girls in their long calico skirts lay on top of their blankets like fallen blossoms.

The fifth and oldest sister, Nancy, was Sarah's partner at euchre. In fact, Rafe found himself in the company of an entire flock of female beings. It was an unprecedented occurrence that made him think he might be happy, for the moment, anyway. The country's founders had promised life, liberty, and the pursuit of happiness, but Rafe had been too busy holding on to the first two to chase the third.

Sarah Bowman raised her head and sniffed the breeze. "I pray that skunk ain't planning to pay us a social call."

Rafe, too, had noticed the odor getting stronger. "Does your mule eat skunks as well as rattlesnakes?"

"If he was hungry enough, I reckon."

Sarah had laid out three tricks and declared trump when five Mexicans arrived with flat-brimmed straw hats in hand. They stood in the mysterious country at the firelight's border, where any sort of supernatural occurrence was possible. Four of them stared at Sarah Bowman as though she were the answer to their prayers.

Sarah spoke to the fifth one in Spanish. "What do they want, Juan?"

Her driver and cohort, Juan Duran, shrugged. "They're worried about the general."

"Armijo?"

"Yes."

Rafe sighed and glanced toward the pale gray oblong, like a storm cloud stalled near the stream. It was the filthy canvas cover of Armijo's old trading wagon. Armijo was all the plagues of Egypt in one loose bale. Wherever he went, trouble followed.

"The general went to relieve himself, and he has not returned."

"Then go fetch him," Sarah said. "He's probably drunk."

"They are afraid of Apaches, Western," Juan answered in English.

"Then pray tell," Mrs. Morris asked, "why don't they ask the soldiers for help? Ten armed men sit in bivouac not three hundred yards from here."

Juan shrugged again.

Rafe wasn't surprised that the Mexicans hadn't gone to the soldiers. Mexicans were accustomed to American soldiers as enemies, not as allies. But he was almost annoyed that they had come to The Great Western for help instead of to him. People had a habit of turning to him when they wanted someone to put a hand into the fire to save their bacon. And there was danger enough to go around. For the past six months Apaches had been ambushing wagon trains and stealing cattle and horses, too. They were up to some serious mischief. So much for old Red Sleeves' promises of eternal friendship with his American brothers.

Sarah stood and straightened her skirts. She took a flaming mesquite limb from the fire to use as a torch. "Which way did he head?"

Rafe had had his pair of Johnson army-issue flintlock pistols converted to percussion. He bit off the end of a paper cartridge, shoved it into the muzzle, and rammed it home. He half cocked the gun, and with his thumb he pressed a percussion cap onto the nipple. He did the same for the second pistol. With Armijo's men crowding close behind them, Sarah and Rafe set out in the direction the general had taken. The smell of skunk grew stronger.

They found the general toppled forward, his naked buttocks pointed toward heaven like the voluptuously curved prow of an overturned whaleboat. His white cotton trousers hung in folds around his ankles and feet. Rafe put his boot on the man's hip and pushed him onto his side. He tried to stand between the body and Sarah.

"Why don't you go back to camp, Mrs. Bowman," Rafe said. "You shouldn't have to see this."

"In the war I saw sights as bad as can be, Mr. Collins." Sarah bent over and held the torch close. She crossed herself. "Saints preserve us." She pulled one of the pistols from her belt and looked around. "If they'd been Apaches, Jake would've warned me."

"Jake?"

"My mule. He can smell Injuns a long ways off."

"The skunk," Rafe said.

"They covered their own scent with it?"

"Probably."

"Clever devils, ain't they?"

"You could say so."

Blood still pulsed in a slow trickle from the neat slice that started at one ear and curved under Armijo's three-tiered stack of chins to the other ear. That he had any blood left was amazing, considering the amount of it that formed a lake around him. His eyes bulged. Two bloody patches marked the former location of his ears. His severed genitals protruded from his mouth. Aside from the fact that his penis and testicles had migrated north, something else was strange about them.

"What is that?" Sarah asked.

Rafe squatted for a better look. Millipedes crawled up from under his shirt collar and into his hair. "It's a padlock."

"A padlock? On his peter?"

"Yes."

"Why?"

Rafe shrugged, but he knew.

This padlock had held the young Apache woman captive, the one Caesar, Absalom, and he had stolen away from Armijo. He wondered where Pandora had hidden herself. He wondered how long she had been watching them. He wondered if she was watching them now.

"AY, DIOS." THE SERGEANT CROSSED HIMSELF AND TRIED not to flinch when thunder crashed almost simultaneously with the flash of lightning, looking and sounding for all the world like an explosion of a wagonload of dynamite. It wouldn't do for the eight privates on guard duty to see him rattled, but the roar almost deafened him. The lightning restored color to a night that was as black as the depths of a cave.

For an instant he could see the eagles on the brass buttons of his men's blue wool uniform jackets. He could see the patches on the jackets, too. The uniforms had fought through the final desperate year of the war with the gringos. Life had not been easy for them since then.

A blast of wind stormed across Arizpe's central plaza, bending the apricot trees almost to the ground. A large limb on the nearby mahogany cracked, crashed to the ground, bounced, and quivered. The rain started as suddenly as a dam breaking. The sergeant pulled open the jail's flimsy mesquite-wood door, and he and the soldiers crowded into the guardroom. Torrents hit the tile roof, creating a steady rumble inside the adobe room. Lightning pulsed through the high, barred window. The sergeant lit an oil lamp with an ember from the banked cooking fire.

He lay down on a straw mattress in a front corner. His men set out a monte bank and a deck of cards on a blanket in the center of the floor. They lit their cigarillos and settled down to gamble.

The sergeant was just starting to doze when he heard a rasping sound. It was an insignificant noise compared to the crashes of thunder and the wailing of the wind, but it was

clearer, more penetrating, and more terrifying than both of
them. It sounded like metal, a gun barrel maybe, rubbing
against the rough outer surface of the jail's adobe wall. No
one in his right mind would be outside on a night like this.
The noise was followed by the call of a nighthawk. Unlikely
one of those would be abroad now, either.

"Be quiet," the sergeant said. The men stared at him.

He half sat up, supporting himself on one elbow, but he
heard nothing more. One of the Apaches in the cell behind
the guardroom began chanting, probably to let his countrymen outside know where the prisoners were. A second man
took up the chant, then the boys. The women started that
demented cry that reminded the sergeant of damned souls
with their *cojónes* pinched in the hinges of hell's gates. The
soldiers began loading their ancient Brown Bess muskets, but
their fingers shook so badly they spilled most of the priming
powder.

"Apaches," the sergeant said.

"But the wall . . . ," protested one of his men.

The sergeant gave him a pitying glance. He was newly
arrived from Mexico City. He didn't know that the high wall
around Arizpe meant nothing. He didn't know that Apaches
drifted through walls like ghosts. They blew over them like
an evil wind. They scuttled across them like scorpions. They
slithered under them like rattlesnakes.

A closer, more insistent rumble echoed the thunder. Someone was pounding on the door with what sounded like a large
rock. The Apache prisoners began calling to their friends
outside. The sergeant knew that no one in the town would
come to his aid, not even his fellow soldiers, asleep in their
barracks.

He wondered if he would live to see his wife and five
children again. His men stared at him while he tried to think
over the drumming of blood in his temples, over the cater-
wauling from the cells, the thunder, and the relentless pounding.

"We'll let the prisoners go," he said finally.

"Are you mad?" Mexico City blurted.

The sergeant took the ring of keys from its peg on the wall and headed for the cells. "Open the door a crack when I say so, but for the love of God, not before then or we are all dead men."

"Our orders . . . ," Mexico City said.

"To hell with our orders." The sergeant unlocked the two cell doors. The prisoners—two men, six women, and three boys—filed out.

In a single line, with the men leading, the women in the middle and the boys at the rear, they ambled toward the front door. They didn't seem concerned that it was bolted shut. When they had almost reached it, the sergeant said, "Open it now."

Mexico City did as he was told. Without a backward glance, the prisoners slipped through and out into the raging night. Mexico City slammed the door and slid the bar across it.

When the soldiers' hands stopped shaking, they rolled new cigarillos and went back to their monte game. The thunder grumbled away to strike terror elsewhere. The rain slowed to a patter.

The sergeant lay back down. He would see his wife and little ones after all. He breathed a prayer of thanks to God and the Virgin Mary. While he was at it, he thanked Jesus and every saint he could think of, particularly San Geronimo Emilian, Saint Jerome, a soldier saved by the intercession of the Blessed Virgin. He wasn't as famous as the other Saint Jerome, but the soldiers considered him their own. They would celebrate his feast in a few days, on the twentieth of July.

The rest of the garrison could organize an expedition in the morning, if God and the *comandante* willed it, and chase down the accursed Apaches. The sergeant didn't know that the army wouldn't have to chase these particular Apaches.

"DIOS Y SAN GERONIMO ME DEFIENDAN." THE SERGEANT crossed himself as he and his men walked toward more

Apache warriors than he had ever seen together in his life. He estimated that two hundred of them had gathered in the cottonwood grove by the river, twice as many as the number of soldiers in Arizpe. He tugged his high, stiff collar away from the rash that covered his neck where the coarse cloth rubbed.

He held the white flag higher. The *comandante* had instructed him and his men to leave their muskets behind to show their peaceful intentions. The *comandante* should have led this company, but he said that since the sergeant had released the Apache prisoners yesterday, their kin would be better disposed to talk to him. The real reason, as everyone knew, was that the *comandante* was a coward.

Morning Star, Broken Foot, He Who Yawns, and the others watched the eight soldiers approach. He Who Yawns turned to the boy standing next to him. Cornflower had grown at least a hand in his year as a captive. During that time a mule had kicked him in the face, breaking his nose. The Mexicans had named him Chato, Flat Nose. Already his friends among the apprentices had started calling him Chato, too.

"What do you know about them?" He Who Yawns asked.

"They were with the soldiers who attacked us at Janos."

"It wouldn't matter if they weren't," He Who Yawns muttered.

"They come to hold council," said Morning Star.

He Who Yawns flicked his hand, as though shooing away a horsefly. "I know what the white cloth means."

He and seven of his warriors walked foward to meet the soldiers. When they were within range, He Who Yawns called out, "*Natseed*, kill." He and his men unslung their bows, nocked arrows, and fired.

As the soldiers fell, He Who Yawns slashed, clubbed, and speared the wounded. He dipped the white cloth in the sergeant's blood and returned waving it over his head.

"We have no chance of fighting the soldiers if they hide behind their wall," he shouted. "This will bring them out of the city," He grinned in Morning Star's direction. "We do not need anyone's sister to tell us where the enemy is."

Morning Star ignored him. He Who Yawns might be in charge of this war party, but Morning Star didn't have to like him.

He Who Yawns had declined to go with him and the ten others to rescue the captives. If they hadn't gotten their people released, the Mexicans would most likely have killed them when they realized that an Apache army had camped outside their town. Morning Star had the feeling that vengeance meant more to He Who Yawns than the lives of the captives. Morning Star also suspected that he had been too afraid of last night's lightning to leave the cave where he and his men had sheltered. His magic only warded off bullets. Lightning was a powerful source of magic, too, but also of death and insanity. Only a fool would not fear it, but a man should still do what was right.

The night's hard rain had washed the dust off everything. The damp ground steamed in the hot summer sun, and so did the warm blood pooled around the bodies of the eight Mexican soldiers. The vapor reminded Morning Star of ghosts, the spirits of the murdered Mexicans.

As flies began to buzz around the soldiers' bodies, Morning Star went to find Swimmer, his wife's sister's young husband. For months Swimmer had talked about this raid. Today he would have the chance to prove himself.

Morning Star had fought in skirmishes. He had ambushed mule trains and swooped out of the rising sun to steal horses from pastures and corrals. He had never stood in sight of an army as it marched toward him. None of them had.

He Who Yawns positioned the warriors among the cottonwoods, with the river at their backs. With only trees and bushes for cover, and an enemy that knew exactly where they were, Morning Star felt exposed and vulnerable and stupid. He Who Yawns said this was the strategy his spirits had given him, and so here they all were.

Morning Star braided his long hair and stuck it into his belt. He checked the string of twisted sinew on his bow and ran his fingers over the amulets woven into his medicine cord. The other men fidgeted, too, all except Swimmer. Taut as a bowstring, with only his eyes shifting, scanning the broken country ahead for the enemy, he leaned into the prospect of battle.

They saw the infantry first, followed by the cavalry, iron rings rattling on the bridles of their horses and bells jingling on the saddle skirts. Their lances, held upright, looked like a forest of saplings as the riders adanced.

"Bullets can't touch me," He Who Yawns shouted. "Follow me."

He pulled his knife and raced across the open ground. Morning Star and the others shot their arrows in a high arc above him, and when they landed, some of the foot soldiers fell. At the second volley of arrows the Mexicans scattered for cover, and gunfire started popping from every bush and tree.

He Who Yawns ran so fast he almost knocked over the first infantryman. He slashed at the man's throat, and a rush of blood covered him. He grabbed the musket from his victim's hand before he hit the ground. He lifted off the bullet pouch and the powder horn. Holding them high he ran back and tossed them to one of his men; then he turned and headed into the fray again.

He fought wildly, untouched by bullets and lances. He charged one soldier after another, overwhelming them all and leaving them sprawled behind him. The Mexicans began to shout warnings to each other and pleas to their patron saint, *"¡Ay, Gerónimo! ¡Cuidado!"*

The Ndee didn't know what *Gerónimo* meant, but they took up the cry. He Who Yawns had infected them with his mad courage. The battle scattered and skirmishes broke out as men closed and grappled.

Morning Star, Loco, Broken Foot, and the other Warm Springs warriors used a gulley as cover and picked their targets from among the nearest soldiers. Morning Star began to recognize the individual Mexicans who darted across the broken ground like wraiths in the haze of blue smoke from their muskets.

Morning Star called to the men around him, running from one to the other and urging them on. The Mexicans began shouting, *"¡Vitorio!"* at him whenever he showed himself. The Spanish words for "victory" and for "shouting encouragement" were similar. Morning Star didn't know which one they meant, and he was too busy to care.

As the sun climbed toward the top of the sky, it hammmered them with heat. Ignoring the musket fire and the shouting, Morning Star crouched in the shade of a creosote bush and wet his dry lips with the last of the water from the cow's intestine he used as a canteen. The gunfire began to taper off as the soldiers ran out of ammunition.

He Who Yawns and two of his men had fired their arrows and broken their lances. Now they were fighting with knives and fists. When Swimmer bolted toward them, Morning Star shouted at him to come back, but he kept going.

Five soldiers, firing as they came, ran at He Who Yawns and his men. Two of the warriors fell, and He Who Yawns headed back for another spear. Swimmer turned and started running for the trees while a soldier, sword raised, raced to cut him off. Morning Star reached over his shoulder for an arrow and found none in his quiver. He grabbed his lance. Shouting, he ran toward Swimmer, but the soldier met him first. The blade sliced a shining arc that intersected with Swimmer's head and continued downward, splitting it neatly in two.

Morning Star kept going. While the soldier yanked his sword from Swimmer, Morning Star drove the point of the lance into his chest with such force that it came out the back. The soldier looked at him with mouth open and eyes wide.

Morning Star's moccasins slid in the puddle of blood mixed with the slippery gray substance leaking from Swimmer's skull. He regained his footing, planted the palm of his hand on the butt of the lance, and shoved. The skewered soldier toppled backwards, his arms and legs jerking wildly. The lance point projecting from his spine gave an arch to his back.

He Who Yawns pushed past Morning Star. He grabbed

the man's sword and waved it, looking for more enemies to kill. Mexicans lay scattered across the battlefield. The soldiers retrieved as many of the wounded as they could and melted off into the thick underbrush. The Ndee rushed to catch the horses they left behind and to take the weapons from the dead.

Morning Star looked down at the shattered wreckage that had been his wife's sister's husband. He wondered how he would transport him to a mountain crevice where he could give him a proper burial. He thought of the words he would use to tell his wife's sister that she would not see him again in this world.

Broken Foot came to stand next to him. "Three of our men dead. There will be much weeping when we return."

"A good leader does not waste lives." Morning Star was furious. If they had followed their usual tactic and lured the soldiers into an ambush, Swimmer would probably still be alive.

Morning Star went to cut agave stalks for a litter to carry the body. He felt tired. Like Swimmer and all the others, he had been eager to make the Mexicans pay for the slaughter at Janos, but he had discovered for himself what old Red Sleeves once had told him, the act of revenge rarely satisfied as much as the anticipation.

The long battle had invigorated He Who Yawns, even though a soldier's lance had sliced a gash on his face that made the right side of his mouth droop. Caked with dirt and blood, he began a dance around the bodies of the Mexicans, pointing at the ground here, stomping there, marking the places where he had fought and killed.

As the warriors gathered to watch they chanted, "Geronimo! Geronimo!"

He Who Yawns had acquired a new name.

Chapter 12

SHE WHO TROTS THEM OUT

Lozen led her brother's pony, Coyote, past the women gathered at the boulders called They See Them Off. She took up a position at the tail end of the line of boys waiting to greet the warriors. It was not the proper thing for any girl to do, much less one who would soon celebrate the four-day ritual transforming her into a woman.

Lozen's family was working day and night to prepare for her feast of White Painted Woman, and she regretted the embarrassment she was causing them. Her brother had left Coyote in her care, though. She wasn't going to relinquish him to some feckless youth whose only qualification for standing in this line was the penis in his breechclout.

When the youngest sentry had come pelting in on his pony that morning, the village had broken out in joy. The boys and old men keeping watch had spotted the war party a day's ride away. They could see that some of the men must have stolen ponies, but they couldn't tell who.

She Moves Like Water was so happy that she hadn't given Lozen much of an argument about Coyote. She and Corn Stalk had helped groom him. Coyote sported the family's best Mexican saddle decorated with leather fringes, silver *conchos,* and jingling tin cones. Lozen had unraveled a red cotton shawl to make fat tassels for the bridle.

Lozen and Stands Alone had ridden here together, but Stands Alone remained with the women, sitting on her horse with her chin at a defiant cant. A pair of shriveled ears hung on a thong around her neck. Everyone knew they had once belonged to the Mexican, El Gordo. They also believed that wearing the ears might lure his ghost back to haunt her, but she didn't agree.

"The Mexican black robes say there's a place where bad men go when they die," she had told Lozen. "They say horned devils with spears torment the spirits there." When she said it, she radiated the old grin that Lozen remembered from years ago. "I know El Gordo is there."

As soon as Skinny appeared on a small gray at the opening in the cliff, the women began vibrating their tongues against the roofs of their mouths to produce their high, ululating call. A few widows had been sampling the *tiswin* they'd made for the feast and the victory dance. They danced half-naked for the warriors, begging them for gifts. It was a vulgar way to behave, but no one interferred. They had lost their men, and they had to support themselves somehow. The other women disdained them for it, but they were glad they weren't in the same position.

Morning Star rode on a bay in the position of honor directly behind Skinny. Broken Foot came next, then Loco.

Talks A Lot ran from the rear where the apprentices were herding the stolen mules and cattle and caught hold of the bridle of the paint pony that Broken Foot rode. The waiting boys shouted to Morning Star, pleading with him to let them take his horse, but he reined the bay to a stop in front of Lozen. A small face peered from around behind him. Her black hair fell in a tangle across her big, fearful dark eyes.

Lozen did not think about where the girl came from or who her parents were or who might be mourning the loss of her. She belonged to The People now. She would be part of their family.

"Her name is María." Morning Star waited for Lozen to mount Coyote; then he swung the child over to sit behind her. She wrapped her arms around Lozen's waist and buried her face in her back.

Lozen tried to remember what little Spanish she knew. *"Está bien, niña."*

"She can sleep in the lodge with you and Stands Alone," Morning Star said.

Broken Foot called to Lozen. "The Mexicans named your brother Victorio before we killed them all. Skinny will announce it at the feast."

Victory. It was a good name.

Victorio dismounted and led Coyote and his new bay pony to where Corn Stalk danced with the women, and he handed the bay's reins to her. She knew what the gift meant. Her young husband had not come back.

"You must be strong, Sister," he said. "Your man died bravely. We gave him a warrior's burial. We must never speak his name again."

Corn Stalk pulled her blanket over her head and led the pony away. She Moves Like Water hurried to catch up with her. Soon, over the laughter and the shouting, came the sound of women wailing.

THE SUN WAS ABOUT TO RISE WHEN THE DANCING ENDED and people headed for their families' clusters of lodges. Lozen carried the captive, María. The child slept with her head resting on Lozen's shoulder and her arms and legs dangling.

She Moves Like Water led Victorio to the new arbor she and the women of her family had built. Stacks of goods filled it—sacks and parfleches, baskets and trays of food, piles of blankets, and two beautiful burden baskets decorated with fringe tipped with tin cones. She Moves Like Water unwrapped a cowhide and held up one of the doeskins folded inside it. Someone had tanned it so well that it draped across her hands like the softest cloth.

"He Makes Them Laugh brought five of these. He shot the deer through the eyes so he would leave no arrow holes or blemishes in the skin. His mother tanned them for Stands Alone's dress." She lifted a feed sack and shook it so he could hear the metallic rattle of the tin cans inside. "Squint Eyes' children found these at the diggers' camp to make jingles for the two dresses." She held up several pouches. "Cowrie shells and pollen for the blessing."

"The traders from Alamosa will come soon," said Morning Star. "We can trade the mules we took in Mexico, for corn and gifts. We can slaughter my share of the cattle and dry the meat for the feast."

Victorio was glad to lie down on the blankets. He and the others had traveled for three days and nights, dozing in their saddles. He closed his eyes, breathing in the familiar smells of home.

"People are saying that your sister is *di-yin*, a shaman," She Moves Like Water said.

Victorio grunted. He had detected the change in Lozen as soon as he saw her. When he left she had been uncertain of her gift of far-sight; but now that most of the women in the band had witnessed it, she believed it herself. He saw that certainty in the set of her mouth, the confident look in her eyes. Power did that for those who possessed it.

She Moves Like Water lifted her tunic over her head. She let her skirt fall around her ankles. She lay down next to Victorio, and he stroked her neck, shoulder, arm, hip, and thigh. He lost himself in the pleasure of her smooth curves. The longing for her consumed him, but he could not finish anything he might start here.

"Should I ask Corn Stalk to marry me?" he murmured.

When She Moves Like Water spoke, Morning Star could hear the relief in her voice that her sister would be cared for.

"I could use help gathering mesquite beans and digging roots."

Victorio sighed. He would be responsible for another person, but if he married his wife's sister, he wouldn't have to wait three years to enjoy a woman. And he wouldn't have to acquire a second mother-in-law. That was almost a bigger advantage than the first one.

AS PEOPLE VISITED RELATIVES IN DISTANT BANDS, THEY spread the word of the powers of Victorio's sister to see enemies. When Victorio and She Moves Like Water sent invitations for Lozen's *Da-i-dá*, the Ceremony of White

Painted Woman, everyone accepted. Everyone.

During *Da-i-da* the spirit of The People's original ancestor, Istún-e-glesh, White Painted Woman, entered the girl being honored. She gave her the power to bestow health, children, prosperity, and long life on those she blessed. For four days the candidate became White Painted Woman. How much more powerful that blessing would be coming from a *di-yin* to whom the spirits had given the gift of far-sight.

Cheis and the Tall Cliffs people had ridden from their territory to the west. Red Sleeves and his followers had come from the Santa Rita area. Long Neck brought his family and other Enemy People from their stronghold in the Sierra Madre. Even He Who Yawns, whom many now called Geronimo, made the trip with the In Front At The End People.

The guests set up their shelters along the river and on the surrounding hillsides. They went from camp to camp visiting friends and relatives. They laughed and talked long into the night. Horses grazed everywhere, and packs of boys stole rides when they weren't committing other mischief. They threw rocks at the girls and at each other. They snatched blackened slabs of ribs from the fires as they chased through the camps.

The Warm Springs women set up long arbors around the ceremonial ground. For days they peeled and sliced and chopped. Kettles of venison and mule stew hung over the fires. Breads of acorn, mescal, and cornmeal baked on flat rocks in the coals. Smoke and aromas blanketed the valley.

The men led in mules loaded with wood. They stacked a small mountain of it in the center of the dance ground. They piled more of it at the perimeter. Loco led the Gaan, the Mountain Dancers, into the nearby heights to prepare for their performance.

Songs, prayers, and the cackle of laughter drifted up from the sweat lodge under the cottonwoods as Broken Foot and his five helpers and drummers purified themselves. When they finished, they charged out naked and glistening and jumped into the cold river water. They spent the rest of the day making the sacred items for Lozen and Stands Alone.

As afternoon lengthened, people put on their finest clothes and gathered for *bi kehilze*, the Dressing. Broken Foot and his helpers laid out the musicians' drums and two large, shallow baskets of yellow pollen. They added the two sacred staffs, the turquoise prayer stones, the six eagle feathers, and the two drinking tubes and scratchers tied onto thongs. The sound of bells preceded Lozen and Stands Alone through the low door of their ceremonial lodge. A murmur rose from the crowd at the sight of them.

Grandmother and Her Eyes Open had washed the girls' hair with suds from the yucca plant, and it hung to the backs of their knees in lustrous cascades. A thick border of tin cones around the rectangular yokes of their doeskin blouses jingled each time they moved. The fringes at the shoulders fell to their wrists. Those along the skirt hems brushed their ankles. The tail of a black-tailed deer hung down the back of each dress. Beaded circles represented the sun, with long leather strips streaming from the center as its rays. Crescent moons and morning stars decorated the hems of skirt and top. The leather had been rubbed with ochre and pollen until it glowed a golden yellow.

The murmuring grew to a loud buzz, and Lozen faltered. She had thought she was ready. Grandmother and Her Eyes Open had spent the past month explaining the ritual, but no amount of instruction could have prepared Lozen for this. Never had she seen so many Ndee, and they were all staring at her. They expected her to heal their sick, straighten their deformities, and give them long life. For the next year, if the weather turned bad, they would blame her for it. If the corn crops failed or someone fell ill, they would hold her responsible. The combined force of their anticipation, their fears, and their hopes hit her like a gale wind.

Grandmother spoke behind her. "Stand on the deer hide. Hold your chin high." She gave Lozen a gentle push. Broken Foot held the two tall staffs painted with black, yellow, green, and white bands. He had decorated them with eagle feathers, turquoise stones, and tin cones.

"These canes were made of an acorn-bearing oak so that

you will have many children," he said. "The eagle feather will give you strength. The colors of the four directions mean that Life Giver will watch over you wherever you go."

Broken Foot explained the need for Lozen and Stands Alone to have endurance and patience for the long ceremony ahead. He admonished them to be virtuous so the blessings of White Painted Woman would have good effect. Finally he fastened the smaller eagle feathers to their shoulders with the small thongs sewn there. As he tied the large eagle plume onto the hair at the crown of Lozen's head, an eagle circled four times above them and flew off toward the mountains. The crowd gave a cry of delight. It was the best possible omen.

FOR DECADES MEXICAN TRADERS FROM THE VILLAGE OF Alamosa had hauled their cumbersome oxcarts along the rocky streambed and through the narrow opening in the cliff face. The Red Paint sentries had a special signal to advise everyone of their coming. Their arrival was always cause for celebration. The women flocked around them, craning to see what treasures they had brought. The children scrambled for the *chicle* and the pieces of cactus candy that they tossed from the rear of the carts. The little ones clambered aboard the sad-eyed oxen.

On their last visit, Victorio and She Moves Like Water had traded every tanned hide, basket, and horse they had except Coyote and two others. They had received a stack of goods in return, but they hadn't kept them long. They gave Broken Foot two of the remaining ponies. They added two tooled Mexican saddles and a stack of blankets.

In return for the presents, Broken Foot had agreed to sing the entire sixty-four-song cycle for Lozen's ceremony.

As Broken Foot ended the first four-song series, Lozen glanced at Stands Alone. She was marking off the songs by twisting a fringe on her tunic whenever his voice died away and he gathered himself to start the next song. Lozen wondered if she would have enough fringes.

Broken Foot's singing lasted until sundown when the dancing began. Lozen and Stands Alone danced continually, striking the ground with their staffs at each step. She Moves Like Water danced beside Lozen, and Corn Stalk accompanied Stands Alone.

After standing motionless all afternoon, Lozen's legs ached, but She Moves Like Water smiled encouragement at her. She danced so gracefully that Lozen couldn't shame her by stumbling or grimacing. Fortunately, this was only a half-night dance. When the full moon hung directly above them, Broken Foot and the drummers stopped.

Lozen and Stands Alone, Grandmother, and Her Eyes Open could sleep a few hours. At dawn the girls walked out onto the dance ground. On the hides laid out in front of them sat baskets of pollen and others holding cowrie shells, chicle, nuts, tin cones, and fruit symbolizing the gifts that White Painted Woman would give to her people.

For the rest of the morning the girls danced in a jingling of bells with She Moves Like Water and Corn Stalk next to them. Now and then Grandmother lifted Lozen's heavy fall of hair and wiped her neck and forehead. She let her sip water through the drinking tube. At midmorning, Grandmother motioned for Lozen to lie on her stomach on the hide, and she massaged her all over to make her vigorous and strong.

When Lozen stood up, she felt taller. Her legs no longer hurt. Her feet and hands, then her legs and arms tingled as the power of White Painted Woman surged through her.

At midday the dancing stopped, and people crowded closer. This was the climax of the ritual, and no one wanted to miss it. To the east Broken Foot set a basket containing sacred pollen and ocher, a deer-hoof rattle, an eagle feather, and a bundle of grama grass. Spectators lined the track.

Lozen looked down the narrow open space with dread. The welfare of her people depended on her four runs. What if she stumbled? What if she fell? What if she overturned the basket?

This was when Grandmother earned the title She Who

Trots Them Out. She pushed Lozen into the run and gave the high call as Lozen sprinted to the basket, circled it, and raced back. Broken Foot's assistant moved the basket closer, and Lozen ran three more times while the spectators shouted and the women added their cries to Grandmother's.

At the end of the fourth run Broken Foot sang in a voice almost too hoarse to hear.

White Painted Woman carries this girl
She carries her through long life
She carries her to all good things
She carries her to old age
She carries her to peaceful sleep

The crowd's excitement intensified as the Gaan dancers appeared with their tall, fan-shaped headdresses painted in the four sacred colors. They danced around the women through four more song cycles. Spectators began to shout when Loco in his guise as the Clown took a brush full of pollen dissolved in water and painted Lozen with it from her head to her feet. Lozen closed her eyes when the pollen crusted her lashes. When he finished, the Gaan danced away, and Grandmother wiped the pollen out of her eyes.

Her people's goodwill washed over Lozen. Tears ran down her cheeks, leaving tracks in the pollen. She felt as though she were rising off the earth and floating on the affection of those around her.

"It's almost done for her," they shouted. "The end is coming!" "She's beautiful! She brings us joy."

Broken Foot dipped the brush into the liquid pollen, and with flicks of his wrist, sprayed the crowd with it, turning so that the drops went in every direction. The din grew deafening.

Lozen picked up the deer hide on which she had been standing. She shook it to each direction, to send away any diseases that might harm her. Broken Foot poured one of the baskets of fruit and trinkets over her, and the children rushed forward, laughing and jostling to pick them up. Possessing something from the basket assured them that they would prosper for years to come.

When he had done the same for Stands Alone, Grandmother offered the basket of pollen to the four directions and took some of it on her fingers. She marked a stripe from cheek to cheek across the ridge of Lozen's nose and painted another stripe along the part in her hair. Lozen marked her the same way.

People formed a line that circled the perimeter of the dance ground and stretched off among the nearest shelters. As individuals reached the front of the line, Lozen and Stands Alone marked them with pollen. Mothers held their children up for their blessings. When He Steals Love approached Lozen, she tried to avoid his eyes, but he gave her a look of such longing that she almost dropped the basket of pollen in her confusion.

When the last person had received a blessing. Lozen and Stands Alone went to the tall tipi of four poles raised to Broken Foot's exact specifications. They passed between the food and gifts to be given away later and lay down on the thick bed of pine needles. Tonight Lozen and She Moves Like Water, Stands Alone, and Corn Stalk would dance with four of the Gaan dancers, circling in complex patterns half the night.

The Gaan dancers wore black masks. They painted their bodies gray with magical black designs. The sight of their tall crowns silhouetted against the orange sunset sky as they came down from their hiding places had always terrified Lozen. As a child, she had screamed when her grandmother held her up so they could thrust their wands at her to drive away evil spirits.

Now she knew who the men were inside those costumes. She also knew that her brother had had to use all his charm to persuade them to perform. If a man made a mistake in the ceremony, he could become ill or call evil down on everyone. If he didn't put the mask on with the proper gestures, he could go mad. The touch of a dancer who had been made up by a stronger shaman could paralyze him.

When the Gaan finished their performance, the social dances would begin. People would pair off and dance all night. This was the best of all possible nights to fall in love, and many would, but Lozen knew she wouldn't be one of them.

She didn't care. Her brother had promised her something better. If she could endure the training that the boys received, she could go with him on a raid for the horses they desperately needed to replace the ones the family had given away. She fell asleep exhausted and smiling. She knew she would never feel such ecstacy again, but she didn't care about that, either. To have experienced it once was enough.

PART TWO

1852

Apprentice

Coyote Makes Women Valuable

A long time ago, they say, Coyote saw a pretty woman. Coyote's not bashful like those boys over there. He's always wanting to have intercourse with women. They don't even have to be pretty, but this one was.

He smiled at her, and he joked with her, and he walked with her in the moonlight that shone through the branches of the cottonwoods by the river. He was about to put his penis inside her when he saw rows of sharp teeth in her vagina. So instead of his penis he poked a stick in there. Those teeth bit that stick in two with a loud crunch, and they gnawed the pieces into tiny little splinters.

So then Coyote put a rock in and broke the teeth right off. Because he did that, the woman's vagina became like it is today, without teeth.

The woman was happy about it. She said, "From now on men will desire me, and I'll be worth many horses and other good things."

That's why these days men give horses and blankets and saddles and other valuable gifts to a woman's family when they want to marry her.

I'm talking about fruit and flowers and other good things.

Chapter 13

GETTING A LEG UP

In the desert Rafe was used to light, heat, thirst, and his own inner imps playing tricks on him, but something here was amiss. Red whinnied. The four mules brayed and pitched their ears forward.

In their haste to get to California, the gold rushers had left behind the usual broken-down wagons, furniture, cast-iron stoves, trunks, and millstones. Clothes caught on the prickly pear or blew along the ground like wounded birds. In the distance, though, two rows of dark forms paralleled the rutted trail.

Coffee-colored Othello performed his mincing sidestep, rattling the traces in the process. His partner, the smaller, shifty-eyed Iago, tried to sit down. In front, Rosencrantz and Gildenstern each gave a kick, setting the iron chains on the whiffletree to jangling.

Rafe squinted into the glare of the morning sun. The shimmering waves of August heat caused the figures to undulate. As he drove closer he saw pairs of oxen and mules, horses and sheep facing each other across the trail, each pair fifteen or twenty feet away from the next one. They were all dead. Their blackened skin had shriveled around their parched bones and held them together. Someone had propped them up with limbs and rocks and boards. Rafe estimated that at least a hundred of them stood silent guard, and he realized that for the past few miles he hadn't seen any dead animals with the abandoned wagons.

Beef-on-the-hoof brought such a high price in California that driving them west could make a man rich, even if most of them died on the way. The ordeal of the trek killed thousands of dray animals, too. Whoever did this hadn't lacked material for their creation. Rafe wondered who the jokesters were and why they decided to haul the corpses into place. Were they blessed with a sense of the ridiculous? Was this their comment on the folly of mankind? More likely, Rafe thought, a couple fellows had gone mad with the heat.

The first animal in line was an ox with a desert wren perching in his eye socket. Flies still buzzed around the fresher bodies. The scene was eerie, unnerving. It was the sort of multitude that could make a man feel more than alone in the universe.

He had neared the end of the line when he saw a horse with a saddle still attached. Hanging from the saddle was a holster with a book inside. Rafe stopped the wagon and climbed down. The book looked almost new. *Romeo and Juliet*. He glanced around, half expecting this to be an extension of the joke of the mummified entourage.

He reached out a hand; then he drew it back. He could see no rock or plank scratched with the dread words, in various spellings, "Died of Asiatic cholera," but that didn't mean anything. No telling where this particular horse had expired or where his owner might be.

What if cholera clung somehow to the things its victims touched? What if it infected whomever touched those things next? After the war, Rafe had seen his first boss, an old army stager named Blue, die of it. Blue had vomited until the arteries in his forehead had burst. Rafe had watched in horror and fascination as the ruptures crept across Blue's face, like streams flowing under old ice.

Rafe had been relieved when Blue died. He suspected Blue had been, too. Rafe had heated an old army bayonet in the coals and burned the letters into the plank for Blue's grave marker. He had spelled the words right, too. The fact had given him some pride, him being so new to the magic of letters.

Cholera or not, this was Shakespeare. It was *Romeo and Juliet*. The officers of his brigade had favored the military plays, the Henrys, the Richards, and Macbeth, but Rafe harbored a secret passion for this most romantic of the Bard's tragedies. He gingerly lifted the holster's belt off the saddle horn and threw it onto the high seat. He climbed up next to it. As he drove away, he eyed it as though it might bite him.

By the time he reached the end of the line he had become so accustomed to the corpses that he jumped when he saw a horse moving on the trail ahead. He flicked the lines to speed the mules' saunter to a brisk walk. The man must have heard him coming, because he turned around and waited.

"Absalom!" For once the desert had coughed up a friend instead of an enemy.

Absalom shaded his eyes. "Rafe?" He waited until Rafe drove the team alongside him. "Did you ever see the like?" Absalom nodded at the boulevard of bones.

"Naw. And I reckoned I'd seen it all."

"Is there water near?" Absalom upturned his wooden canteen to show that it was empty.

Rafe passed him his canteen. "There's a spring not far from here."

Absalom wiped his face and neck with his bandana. "If I find a running stream, I shall do as the Indians at Yuma crossing."

Rafe knew he was supposed to ask what they did, but as happy as he was to see Absalom, he had trouble making conversation. Days alone made his voice rusty and strange in his ears. The heat here in the part of the New Mexico Territory known as Arizona had a different quality and intensity about it. It was like standing in front of the open door of a lime kiln. It left him dazed.

Absalom didn't need prompting. "When the temperature rises to a point where the devil himself begins to perspire, members of the Yuma tribe sit in the river up to their necks with mud on their heads. I was treated to the spectacle of a group of mud balls talking and laughing together."

"Apaches have been frisky in these parts. You shouldn't be traveling alone."

"I'm not alone now." Absalom grinned. "And neither are you."

"How is your man, Caesar?" Rafe figured the question would keep Absalom occupied and spare him the need to talk at all.

"That is a long story." Absalom glanced at the mass of cactus and snakeweed stretching to the distant peaks rising abruptly from the desert floor. "But I suppose I have time to tell it. Suffice it to say that the streets of California are not paved with gold. Nor does the average fellow come across it while digging a privy or washing his drawers in the stream. The rich veins have been claimed, and now men are killing each other over them. Most earn a pittance laboring dawn to dark at the stamping mills. Caesar decided he had had enough of grubbing in the dirt."

"What's he doing, then?"

Absalom smiled. "He's not exactly fleecing the miners, but he's shearing them. He bought a tent and a barber chair and a pair of shears. He's perfected a pomatum of lard, spermaceti . . ." He saw the noncomprehension in Rafe's eyes. "Spermaceti is a waxy substance from whales. Caesar orders it and elder-flower water from a high-toned San Francisco bordello where the ladies think he is just the bee's knees. He cooks it all up with brandy and oil of nutmeg and tells the yokels that if rubbed into the scalp, it will grow a bumper crop of hair on a bald knob. It's proven quite popular."

"And will it grow hair?"

Absalom shrugged. "At least it doesn't kill what's already there."

"We can stay at Don Angel's hacienda tonight," Rafe said. "He has a rancho in a canyon in yonder mountains."

"That would be fine as frog's hair. I've not slept in a bed in a week."

"Don Angel sets a good table, but I'd avoid the bed. It comes equiped with six-legged livestock. We can camp in the cottonwoods near the river and take turns keeping watch." Rafe opened the saddle holster and pulled out the book.

Absalom's grin widened. "I saw Miss Fanny Kemble herself perform Juliet."

"You never! Where?"

In the opera house in San Francisco. She put the brogan-and-canvas-trousered set into quite a fervor."

Rafe opened his mouth, then closed it. He wasn't ready to confess, even to Absalom, how much he longed to see Shakespeare acted on a real stage.

"I have something to show you, too." Absalom turned in the saddle, rummaged in the saddlebag, and pulled out a long package wrapped in a feed sack and tied with twine. "While in Tucson a few days ago I acquired the means of financing my return home and setting myself up in clover when I get there." He started undoing it. "I met a poor fellow quite down on his luck and mad to get to California. He sold me this priceless war relic for a song. I figure to sell it in San Antonio."

He held up a piece of pine carved in the shape of the lower half of a leg with leather straps on one end and a crude foot and misshapen lumps for toes on the other.

"What's that?"

"This . . . ," Absalom paused for effect, "is the wooden leg that belonged to General Santa Anna."

"If you paid a song for it, then you received fair value."

"You don't think it's the real goods?"

"If it's Santa Anna's leg, then it has more lives than the shifty old polecat himself. I've seen a dozen like it, all sworn to be the genuine article. A fellow from Illinois told me that the actual leg is on display at the state house in Springfield."

Absalom looked at it ruefully. "I reckon it would make a fine fire tonight."

"It would."

Rafe smiled, remembering when the American soldiers had looted Santa Anna's estate, *El Encierro*, after the battle of Vera Cruz. They had found the leg, left behind in a carriage abandoned in Santa Anna's flight. For weeks they had sung "The Leg I Left Behind Me," to the tune of "The Girl I Left Behind Me." Some of the verses were quite vulgar.

Rafe began singing them as they rode along. They would

have plenty of time for reading *Romeo and Juliet* aloud, and pleasure deferred was pleasure increased.

"I'M NOT YOUR FRIEND."

Victorio had stayed at the hunting camp in the mountains behind her, but she heard his words in her ears anyway. She stumbled on a tuft of snakeweed, regained her footing, and settled back into the lope that had brought her this far across the desert floor. She had managed not to swallow the water Broken Foot had given her at the start of the run. Holding it in her mouth would force her into the habit of breathing through her nose so her body would lose less moisture. She wanted to let the water trickle down her parched throat, though. She wanted it more than anything.

"My woman is not your friend," Victorio's voice murmured in her skull. "Broken Foot is not your friend."

The horizon tilted. The cacti danced. The dust-colored peak in front of her floated on air thick as corn gruel. The figures of the boys running ahead of her wavered in the rising waves of heat. Each boy looked as though he were scattering like cottonwood seeds in a breeze and coming together again.

"No one is your friend," Victorio told her. "After a battle, no one will come back for you. You must keep up or you will die."

As she and the boys had gathered for the run, Victorio had instructed her to ignore the others, but she couldn't help glancing at them. She wished at least one of them would stop, would fall, so she wouldn't feel so badly if she did, too. She wondered if the boys' muscles ached as much as hers did. She wondered if the air seared their lungs with each breath the way it did hers.

The boys had to do this, or people would call them lazy. Men would laugh at them. Women would not want to marry them. But Lozen didn't have to do it. Lozen wasn't even supposed to do it.

"Your legs are your friends," Victorio had told her. "They will carry you away from danger. Rub grease on them every day to feed them. Your brain is your friend. With it you can outsmart the enemy."

Lozen's feet hung like stones. The pain in her side was a knife blade twisting in her flesh. Lights flickered like fireflies in front of her. The straps of the pack she carried cut into her shoulders.

The air was cool back at Warm Springs. She could have been splashing with Stands Alone in the waters of the spring and gossiping with the women. She could have been helping Skinny tame the horses he had gotten from the comancheros, the Mexican traders.

Instead she wore a breechclout with a sweat-soaked, white cotton shirt belted over it. Victorio had brought the shirt back to her from Mexico, along with his new name and the child called María. After their great victory at Arizpe, he and Loco had raided a farm and taken the shirt, along with corn, beans, and the child. The others had wanted to kill the farmer, but Victorio said they had killed enough Mexicans. They had appeased the spirits of the dead at Janos.

Victorio said the farmer was María's brother. Victorio had taken the shirt and left him there, quaking among the stunted stalks of his third crop. Victorio didn't have to point out that Lozen couldn't train in only a breechclout as the boys did.

A sweat-soaked band of leather held back the loose black hair that reached beyond her waist. Lozen had rolled the tops of her old moccasins down. She carried an extra pair in the pack on her back. Stones inside weighted it, to make the run harder.

She glanced at Talks A Lot, Flies In His Stew, Ears So Big, and Chato. She wasn't gaining on them, but she wasn't falling behind, either. Victorio had trained her on the sly. He waked her before sunrise; then he went back to his blankets while she pelted up and down the mountain that overlooked the camp. On the coldest mornings he sent her to the river to break the ice and sit in it.

Talks A Lot and the three others reached the base of the peak rising abruptly from the desert floor and started up it. Lozen veered to the west. The narrow path started behind the bison-shaped boulder where Victorio had said it would. This was not so easy an ascent as the other one. When it became almost perpendicular, she grabbed the spiny bushes and hauled herself along.

The massive outcrop of limestone towered at the top where Victorio had said it would. A narrow defile ran between it and the side of the mountain. Victorio had studied her when he told her about it. "The boys are too big, but you're small enough to fit through it," he had said.

She put a hand on one of her small breasts, firm as cactus fruit under the shirt. She hoped they wouldn't grow any bigger. They were a nuisance already, getting in the way and attracting attention she'd rather not have.

She took off the pack, the shirt, and the breechlout. In the pack she found the yucca leaf tied with agave fiber. She opened it, dipped her fingers into the grease inside, and rubbed it over her body. Holding the pack and her clothes over her head, she turned sideways, sucked in her chest, and started inching through. In the middle of the opening she became so tightly wedged she feared she could go no farther.

She wondered how long Victorio would take to find her here and what he would have to do to pry her out. The prospect of his friends and the boys witnessing that served the purpose. She held the pack higher and shoved. She rubbed a patch of skin off her back, but she made it through. She put her clothes back on.

As she started along the ridge on the other side, she noticed a ranch in the small canyon below. The house was built around a courtyard in the usual manner, but the house didn't interest her. The corral behind it did. She could see that the corral's adobe wall stood high and thick. She watched the men of the hacienda drive at least twenty horses into it. Four men were required to swing the door closed behind the remuda as it milled inside. The door was made of huge oak planks, strapped with iron. Lozen watched one of the men pass an iron chain through rings sunk into the wood and fasten the ends with a padlock.

She gave a ghost of a smile, careful not to let any water

escape from her mouth. So this was why Victorio told her to take this route. She turned right and followed the path away from the canyon. When she reached the crest of the ridge, she took a roll of rawhide from her pack. She laid it out at the brink, sat on it, and slid down the talus slope. She hit the valley floor in a shower of gravel, picked up the tattered piece of rawhide, and started running.

She could see no one ahead of her. The boys would be gloating about now, thinking that she had quit. She would beat them all back to camp, and when she arrived, she would tell her brother how many horses were locked up in the corral and how many men guarded them. As for the corral's massive adobe walls, she already knew what to do about those.

Chapter 14

TO WITCH THE WORLD

The light of the rising moon didn't reach the rear of the hacienda's adobe-brick corral where Lozen crouched. She had rubbed sage into her hair and cotton shirt. When stealing horses, it helped to smell like a pasture.

Pastures had smells other than sage. She smeared horse manure on her cheeks and arms and legs. Victorio, Loco, and He Makes Them Laugh did the same.

She was amused by the image of He Steals Love doing this. He had asked Victorio if he could come on this expedition, but he had changed his mind when he heard that Lozen would be along. Victorio had reported the struggle in the young man's face when he approached Victorio at the hoop-and-pole field, and in a low voice took back his request to go. Victorio knew what he was thinking. On the one hand, he could spend days in Lozen's company. On the other hand, he would have to spend days in Lozen's company.

Since Lozen's feast last fall, he had been trying the usual ploys to get her attention. He had laid double rows of stones along the paths she took to the pasture, the river, and the cornfields, He hid nearby to see if she walked between them, but she walked around them instead. He had left a haunch of venison outside her lodge at night but had found it back at his door in the morning. He had hovered near her at all the dances, but she would not ask him to step with her.

As much as he desired her, the thought of going after horses with her dismayed him. Young men did not associate with young women, and He Steals Love could not break that most basic rule. That Lozen broke it all the time bewildered, bothered, and intrigued him. Also, the possibility that he might do something stupid terrified him.

Unmarried women were not supposed to spend time in the company of their brothers, either. She Moves Like Water had started to protest this latest breach of decorum but stopped. Dancing together at the ceremny of White Painted Woman had made her and Lozen so close they now called each other Sister, but even so, her pleadings with Lozen to stop going to the horse pasture every day had changed nothing. Protesting to Victorio about her training with the boys had been futile. So She Moves Like Water had given Lozen a bag of mescal meal cakes mixed with sumac berries and honey, and said, "May we live to see each other again."

Lozen had to put her head back to see the moonlight lying like a tarnished tinsel ribbon along the top of the wall. When she did, the eagle feather from the ceremony of White Painted Woman dangled from her hair, along with an amulet that Broken Foot had given her to protect her from snakes. Loco laced his fingers together and held his palms up so she could put a foot on them. She stepped from there onto Victorio's shoulders, then to his head. She grasped the top of the wall and hauled herself up, with the men pushing on the soles of her feet.

Even though the wall tapered from its base upward, the top was wide enough to accommodate her. She lay on her stomach and stretched her hand out to help He Makes Them Laugh. Then the two of them hauled up Loco, with Victorio pushing from below. When Loco reached the top, he held one end of Lozen's rope while she lowered herself into the corral. When her toes touched the ground, Loco, still on his stomach, pulled the rope up and dropped it down the outside of the wall for Victorio.

Inside the corral, Lozen paused to let the horses adjust to her presence. They whickered and crowded together at the other side of the enclosure, their ears pricked forward, eyes wide in the moonlight. Murmuring, Lozen walked toward them. She couldn't see their conformation or their color in the darkness, but she could almost sense their thoughts, their collective individualities that made up the personality of the herd.

Still talking softly she ran her hands over them as she moved among them. She checked the arch of their necks and line of their backs. She ran her hands over their withers, haunches, legs, and their hoofs. She pushed back their lips and felt their teeth.

As soon as she stroked the big mare's muscular withers, short back, and well-set hindquarters, she knew she was the one. She caressed her velvety muzzle and blew into her wide nostrils to mingle her breath with the horse's. She put a loop of her rope around the mare's lower jaw. She put her mouth near the mare's ear and whispered.

"You're mine now. We'll ride everywhere together. You'll run faster than the wind." She knew that what she said didn't matter. "You're the fastest, the strongest, the smartest, the bravest. No one will catch us."

The mare shoved her cheek against Lozen's chest and cocked her ear so that it lay cupped against her lips. She stood without moving while Lozen whispered to her. The two stayed that way while Loco and He Makes Them Laugh chose which horses they would ride. Victorio picked the remuda's leader, a big, long-necked stallion. Lozen remembered him from that day she had watched the horses driven into the corral. He was what the Mexicans called *de cria ligera,* of racing stock.

The three men sat with their backs against the wall where the shadows were deepest, draped their blankets over themselves, and fell asleep. Lozen joined them. Even if one of the hacienda's workers looked inside, the blankets would help them blend with the wall.

She looped the knotted end of the mare's rope over her wrist and settled in to wait. He Makes Them Laugh slid over to sit next to her, and Lozen put her fingers against his lips to keep him from doing something foolish, like speaking. The two of them had acted as apprentices on this scout. They had run errands, tended the fire, cooked, listened a lot, talked little, and ate whatever was left over. For the entire scout He

Makes Them Laugh had shadowed her, pleading with her to put in a good word for him with Stands Alone.

"Has a witch given her a charm to put a spell on me?" he would ask while he helped her haul wood. As she stirred the stew of dried venison and pinole, parched cornmeal, he would hold out an arm that was sinewy and strong. "Look at this." He would put on a doleful face. "I'm wasting away from love. You have to help your poor cousin, or else you must bury me." He looked so comical that she laughed and said she would do her best.

Lozen fell asleep almost under the mare's belly. She awoke when Victorio nudged her before the sun rose. The four of them draped their blankets across their shoulders and waited. In the milky predawn light Lozen could see that her mare was a blood bay with dark stockings, tail, and mane. She took off her moccasins and tied them together so she could sling them across the mare's neck. She wanted to make this first ride barefoot because she had someone to greet in her own way, and moccasins would hamper her.

At the sound of sleepy Spanish voices outside, Lozen took a small run and leaped onto the mare. The other three mounted and took up positions at the perimeter of the herd. Lozen put her hand over her mouth to stifle a laugh. The key grated in the iron lock. The chain rattled outside the big oaken door. As it swung open, Victorio galloped his midnight-blue stallion through it. Loco and He Makes Them Laugh flapped their blankets and yelled. Lozen trilled the women's call. The loose horses headed out after Victorio and the big black. Lozen felt the mare's muscles bunch under her, and she was ready when she reared. As the mare sprinted through the gate, Lozen caught a glimpse of the vaqueros' sleepy, astonished faces. She let the laugh loose then. The joy was too intense to contain.

With Victorio in the lead, the herd thundered toward the cottonwoods by the river and the wagon parked there. Absalom was washing his face in a basin of muddy water. Rafe had just set a soot-lacquered pot of water on the fire to boil. He was roasting coffee beans when he heard them coming.

He saw Don Angel's black stallion in the lead with a tall Apache on his back. He grabbed his rifle and leveled it, but there were too many other horses in the way for a clear shot. Then one of the thieves broke away and headed for him.

Rafe swiveled the rifle toward him. The horse veered suddenly, galloping parallel to the campsite, and so close Rafe could have tossed a stone underhand and hit her. The rider pulled his feet up under him, crouched, then stood on the mare's back, his bare soles comforming to the horse's lines; his long, brown legs flexing in rhythm with her stride. Rafe had seen Comanches and rambunctious Texans do the same thing, but it still impressed him.

As the mare pulled alongside, Rafe realized that the rider wasn't male. Lozen held the lead rope lightly in her left hand, and with her right she gave Rafe a military salute as sharp as any West Point second lieutenant. He had never seen such a look of joy and mischief.

"Capitán Pata Peluda," she shouted. *"¿Cómo estas?"*

Captain Hairy Foot. She remembered him. She must have known all along that he was camped here. She and those other red rogues had been watching him, just as they had been watching Don Angel, his vaqueros, his horses, and his Apache-proof corral.

When she had passed him, she dropped back into a sitting position; then she and the others splashed across the stream in the sandy arroyo. Rafe stared at her until she and Don Angel's remuda—every horse he owned, by the look of it—disappeared around the end of the canyon wall. He wanted, suddenly and with an astonishing intensity, to ride away with her. He wanted to feel at ease on every crag and in every cranny of this wild country. To live in the cool, shady canyons and cedar-fragrant mountain slopes while the white men struggled across the deserts. To take what one wanted with no fear of consequences. To disdain money and commerce and social constraints. To eat no one's drag dust.

" 'To turn and wind a fiery Pegasus,' " he recited aloud. " 'And witch the world with noble horsemanship.' "

"Henry the Fourth?" Absalom lowered his rifle.

"Henry the Fourth, Part One."

"Do you know that Apache?"

"Yep. She's the minx we saw that day we returned Pandora, Armijo's Apache slave." Rafe paused. "Armijo's dead, by the way."

"Do tell. What got him? Apoplexy? An irate husband? A cheated peon?"

"Apache steel. While he was shitting. I'd wager that Pandora did it."

"I reckon he's where he belongs to be," Absalom said.

The pungent odor of burning coffee beans sent Rafe back to the fire to rescue them. As he crushed them with the blade of his knife, he thought about that Apache child. What was her name? Lozen? Sprightly? She did keep appearing in his life; but then, for all its vastness, this territory didn't boast that many permanent residents, and only a few trails crossed it, not that Apaches stuck to the trails except to plunder them.

Rafe had discovered that some people had a way of crossing his path. Like Absalom here. They had some connection to him that reached beyond understanding. He wondered if he would see her again. And if so, under what circumstances.

"They got Don Angel's prize stud," Rafe said. "The Don has always bragged on his Apache-proof corral." He chuckled. "He'll be miffed." He shook his head. "The Apaches will not stop their thieving ways. In spite of all the powwows, palavers, and promises, they seem hell-bent to keep Mexico and the United States, and every other tribe out for their scalps."

"This horse trader I know," drawled Absalom, "was trying to pass off a skin-poor, spavined, hidebound gummer of a jade, with at least one other serious problem besides. The buyer watches the horse for a while, and then he turns to the trader and he says, 'Mister, this horse is blind. Look at how he keeps running into trees and fences.' The trader shifts his chaw from one side of his jaw to the other, and he says, 'Naw, he ain't. He just don't care.' "

Absalom squatted near the pan and with a beatific smile inhaled the coffee beans' aroma. "I reckon the Apaches are like that horse. They just don't care."

Chapter 15

AN EGG-SUCKING WEASEL

S omeone had painted *GARGLING OIL* and *PLANTATION BIT-TERS* on the cracked side of the sutler's store. The low-slung adobe building stood at the end of the row of them that made up the former Mexican presidio at the Santa Rita mines. Only a single company of American soldiers occupied the triangular adobe fort itself.

The store's thatched roof kept the sutler's wares from the worst of nature's elements, but not from the worst elements of humanity. Rafe had heard the rumors that the sutler himself, a pole-thin individual named Fletcher, might be counted among those worst elements. Fletcher wore trousers of black domestic, a high-collared linen shirt, and a sanctimonious expression. He quoted Scripture and, according to rumor, sold whiskey to the Apaches. Rafe knew that the whiskey was composed of grain alcohol for devilment, red pepper for kick, tobacco for color, and dead toads and urine for spite.

According to the peace treaty signed with the Boundary Commission, the Apaches were supposed to farm in exchange for land, tools, and rations until the crops came in. Red Sleeves had persuaded his people to give it a try, but Fletcher hired Mexicans to plant the land set aside for the Indians. He sold the crops, and Rafe had no doubt that he pocketed the profits.

That hardly mattered, since the government had not given the Apaches even a hoe. Fletcher skimmed the rations intended for his charges, too. Rafe had hauled the beef, flour, and beans, and he could see that considerable shrinkage had occurred by distribution day.

Rafe's concern about the thievery wasn't altruistic. He

didn't care that the Apaches weren't getting their full share of the dole, but riling them up with broken promises wasn't healthy. Rafe was tempted to go against his policy of let-live-and-live and report Fletcher, but he knew in his bones that no one would do anything about it.

Fletcher's store was the only one for a hundred miles, which was why Rafe and Absalom stood at the counter. They were paying for their gunpowder and bullets, salt, cornmeal, coffee, tobacco, and a few tins of meat and peaches when three young Apaches entered. Ignoring the stares from the clientele, the boys examined every shovel and button as if they had nothing else to occupy them. Absalom raised an eyebrow and Rafe shrugged.

He laid on the counter several segments of Mexican escudos and some American silver quarter dollars embellished with a bust of Liberty, who looked as though she would brook no nonsense. "You remember old Chief Red Sleeves . . . ," Rafe said.

"The one who looks like he should be standing in front of a cigar store?"

Rafe nodded. "His people have the run of the place."

"Damned gummint coddles them," Fletcher growled.

Absalom divided the purchases between two feed sacks. "What about the Apaches' raids on pack trains and wagons?"

"Red Sleeves still pretends he and his people are the best friends the white men ever had." Rafe threw the sack of cornmeal across his shoulder. "He claims the raids are the work of hotheads from the wild bands in Mexico." He gave a wry chuckle. "The country's crawling with Apaches from across the line."

"Why?" Absalom followed him out to the manure-strewn ruts that served as a street. Absalom was topped off as usual with questions.

"Apaches are shrewder than Philadelphia lawyers. They've savvied to the notion of the new border. They've moved north across it where the Mexican soldiers can't get at them. The whole breed is treacherous, but the ones from the Sierra Madre are the worst of the lot."

Rafe threw the sack of cornmeal across Red's back and tied it in place. As he and Absalom headed away from the post, they saw the crowd of Apaches waiting at the door of the agency office. They were a sorry sight, shabby and stoic and wrapped in tattered blankets. He had the feeling the blankets weren't so much for protection against the sharp-edged December wind as to make them feel invisible. They reminded him of a trained bear he had seen when he was a boy. The bear's handler had pulled the animal's claws and teeth and kept him on a short leash attached to a collar so tight he struggled for each breath.

Better that they're here, he told himself, than waiting in ambush along the road. But still, he couldn't shake off the memory of the scamp Lozen, standing on that bay mare and saluting him as she galloped past. He wanted to turn around to see if she was among the silent crowd, her blanket wrapped around her, her head bowed.

THE GREAT WESTERN'S LATEST EMPIRE OCCUPIED A FEW acres of creosote bush a mile from Fletcher's store. Her husband, Albert, had erected a building of unseasoned pine boards. If Albert's talents lay in carpentry, his interests rested elsewhere. The pine-board skeleton poked through a mottled skin of canvas, packing-crate planks, and sheets of zinc.

The board over the door announced that this was THE AMERICAN HOUSE. If it was anything like The Western's former establishment in El Paso, it served as beanery, bar, hotel, boardinghouse, gambling den, music hall, theater, laundry, barbershop, post office, and brothel. The Western didn't miss much in the way of opportunity. Rafe was surprised to see her still here, though. Western had a fondness for the army, and the thirty soldiers and one shavetail lieutenant left at the adobe fort hardly qualified as one.

Rafe and Absalom rode through the gate of Western's wagon yard. Rafe unloaded his supplies into his wagon. They walked to the American House where the keening of a love-savaged trio of musicians filtered out through the thin walls.

"Mexicans can 'suck melancholy from a song as a weasel sucks eggs,' " observed Absalom.

"*As You Like It,*" Rafe said. He and Absalom had lined out so much Shakespeare in their travels that the response was reflexive.

They would part company here. Rafe was going north to deliver planks and nails for the barracks the army was building at Socorro. Absalom was heading for El Paso with a load of hay. He had been paid in advance, and the money would get him as far as San Antonio.

Rafe was melancholy at the thought of Absalom leaving, but someone named Lila, with eyes like sunlight on sapphires and hair like corn silk, waited for him at home. In Rafe's opinion, Absalom possessed the two rarest luxuries of life: love and a clear conscience.

When they entered The American House, the musty odor of the walls' canvas lining almost choked Rafe. The smell always reminded him of his time in the army. Sometimes at night when he'd tried to sleep in his tent, the odor had seemed heavier than a dozen blankets smothering him. He thought it would steal his breath away, like a witch's cat.

The American House swarmed with humanity. A host of dogs waited, ever-hopeful, for beef to topple off one of the trays held aloft by the help. The staff consisted of Mexicans, blacks, a Seminole by the look of his turban, and even a Chinese. The clientele included miners, drifters, and card-sharps.

In the corner, the lovely Mexican woman whom Western called Mrs. Murphy dealt monte in a bubble of civil tranquility. He decided to join that game as soon as he had wet down the dust in his throat, the way Mexican women sprinkled water onto their dooryards on dry summer days. When the game ended, Western would provide him with a señorita who would come to his wagon. She would pretend to love him, at least for an hour or so, and he would love her for the same amount of time.

The musicians finished their mournful invoice of passion, lies, flashing eyes, and everlasting sorrow and went to the bar to restore their energy. The room filled with conversation and the cicada chirp of cards being shuffled.

Absalom and Rafe ordered a whiskey each. They leaned their backs against the rough lumber of the bar and surveyed the activity.

"I'm anticipating with delight a night on a bed," Absalom confided.

"Have you seen the sleeping arrangements?" Rafe nodded toward the cloth partition, pulled back to expose a row of cots placed about two feet apart.

Absalom shrugged. "The Great Western is a laundress. The sheets will be clean."

"But your bedmate may not be." Rafe let the whiskey burn to the core of his sadness at Absalom's departure and soothe it. "And he'll almost certainly harbor fleas."

"No matter. I sleep sound as a pig of lead."

The Great Western's voice rose over the general din. "Where are you going with that rooster?"

A dry-goods drummer with a shock of gray hair and a beard to match brought both wayward eyes to focus on her. "Madam, I must rise early, and I intend to use him to awaken me."

"No, you won't. Chickens attract panthers. Had one come through a window last month. Threw my shoe at him, and he made off with it."

Western walked over to Rafe and Absalom. She wore a pair of Colt six-shooters in the belt of her purple velvet skirt. The handles nestled under the generous overhang of bosom in its starched linen shirtwaist. The yellow cap of the Third Artillery perched on one side of her ebullient red hair.

"Mr. Collins, a pleasure to see you again."

"I see you're prospering, Mrs. Bowman."

"Busy as a flea in a tar bucket," she made a deprecatory wave at the bustle around her. "We're just temporary here. Now that the boundary commission's left we plan to up stakes and head west."

"Where?"

"The army's building a fort at the Yuma crossing. Albert

thinks the gold diggings will be good up on the Gila."

"Do you still have the bathing tub?" Rafe had been in a revery of suds for the past fifty miles.

"Some Bible salesman shot holes in the India rubber one. Said it was the work of the devil. I guess he never read his own wares or he would know that cleanliness is next to godliness. I have a horse trough out behind the kitchen. I'll tell Juanita to heat you some water."

"I'd appreciate that, ma'am."

"There'll be a supper set at eight and another at nine. Steak and poached eggs." Western leaned close to be heard over the whooping of a man who'd just come through the door. "Anything else you gentlemen need?"

Rafe gave her a wry smile. She winked in return.

"I have just the one for you," she said. "Her name's Migdalia." She turned to Absalom. "And you, sir?"

"Thank you kindly, ma'am, but I have a sweetheart."

"Then you are blessed." The whooping continued, punctuated by panther screams. "Rogers, pipe down or get out."

"You should stand me drinks. Western," Rogers whooped again, "I just whipped that old bastard Red Sleeves."

A cheer went up from the miners.

"What do you mean?" Western asked.

"He came into camp and pulled each of the boys aside, telling 'em real confidential like, that he knew where there was lots of gold in Sonora. Said he'd tell them where it was, but to keep it a secret from the others. The boys got to comparing their stories and realized he'd promised each of 'em the same thing. I said, 'The polecat plans to lure us out where his red scum can murder us. Let's administer a strapping to the old heathen.' So we tied him to a tree, and I whipped the billy bejeezes out of him. I don't reckon he'll bother us no more."

Western glared at him. "Did you kill him?"

"Naw. We let him go so's he can show the other lice and nits that we don't tolerate lying and horse thievery."

"Hellfire," Western muttered. "Those idiots will get us all kilt for certain."

Rafe shook his head as gloom set in. Despite the treaty with the Apaches, the odds on them killing the unwary were always good anyway. Rogers had just made them better.

ABSALOM STUCK IT OUT INSIDE LONGER THAN RAFE WOULD have thought. He didn't retreat from the cot at the American House until halfway between midnight and dawn. At least he waited until Migdalia left before he climbed into the wagon bed and started rustling around next to Rafe, fluffing up the empty feed sacks and scratching like a hound.

"You were right," he said.

"Don't bring them in here."

"The fleas were bad enough, but twenty men snoring make a racket that would wake the dead." He laid his blankets on top of the sacks. "That's not why I left, though."

Rafe resisted the urge to ask why he did leave. Absalom could talk all night, if given any encouragemnt. Or even if not given any encouragement.

"You missed all the commotion," he said.

Rafe grunted, half-asleep, and still adrift on a sensual cloud.

"That drummer with the rooster got drunk and started bothering the ladies." Absalom would never refer to a woman as a whore. That was one of many qualities Rafe admired in him. "I think the damsels slipped some sleeping potion into his drink. When he tumbled onto the other side of my cot to get busy knitting up 'the raveled sleeve of care,' they sneaked in, stripped him buck-naked, and shaved him, from ankle to scalplock. When he woke up, all hell broke loose among Samson and the assorted Delilahs."

Rafe chuckled and drifted off to sleep to the lullaby of Absalom talking about his Lila. The next morning he wasn't happy to see Rogers's boiled onion eyes staring through the rear opening of the wagon's cover.

"I'll be with you in a twinkling." Absalom pulled on his boots.

Rogers's eyes and the rough country of his face disappeared.

"What's he doing here?"

"He's going to El Paso, too. I said I'd travel with him."

"He's an egg-sucking weasel, Absalom."

"I can take care of myself. And you yourself have told me how dangerous the road is. Best to travel in company. Anyway, since they've found gold up at Pinos Altos, there's a lot of traffic. Prospectors are heading there in droves, Rogers says."

"Keep your money close."

"I have it strapped to me." Absalom reached under his shirt and patted his stomach. "When will you start for Socorro?"

"Tomorrow morning." Rafe would have left it at that, but he knew Absalom would ask why he wasn't leaving today. "I have to get a new tire on the left rear wheel before I load up. There's no sense attempting El Jornado del Muerto late in the day." Actually, Rafe would prefer not to travel the hundred-mile stretch of desert called The Day's Journey of the Dead Man at any time, but it couldn't be avoided.

Rafe climbed out of the wagon and went to see to the mules and his own plumbing. On the way, he passed Rogers's horse. He saw the tips of a bow and several arrows sticking from the blanket roll tied behind his saddle. Odd. Rogers didn't seem the sort to collect souvenirs.

Chapter 16

ASHES TO ASHES

L ozen stopped and climbed down from her mare.

"What is it?" Stands Alone leaned down from the pinto that Lozen had given her from her share of the stolen horses.

Lozen crouched to study the frayed mark of the broomed hoof on the horse's rear left leg. "This is Red Sleeves' pony, the smoke-colored one with the rabbit's ears."

"Why would he be here?"

"He sometimes camps in the canyon where Loco killed the bear. He says the yucca ripens there first, and he likes the roasted stalks. He usually brings his wives to do the roasting, though. And he usually stops to visit with Skinny and with Broken Foot."

"Maybe he's in trouble."

Those who knew Red Sleeves best had begun to worry about the old man's judgment. He seemed to think the Americans would keep their promises. It wasn't like him to embrace such foolish illusions.

They followed the tracks upstream. At the entrance to the canyon, they tied their ponies to a cedar and crawled through the bushes. They stopped when they could see the thatched lean-to.

Red Sleeves must have been bathing at the stream. He walked back naked and dripping, and neither Lozen nor Stands Alone dared let him know they were there. They stifled giggles at the sight of his member swinging from side to side and slapping against his bare thighs. Broken Foot gave Red Sleeves a sly look whenever he was present for the story of Coyote's big penis. The rumors were true.

As he drew closer, Lozen and Stands Alone could see diagonal red stripes on his legs. Then he turned, and they saw the raw, bloody gashes on his back. They heard the buzz of flies. Red Sleeves flicked at them with a bundle of grass and winced at the pain it caused.

He groaned as he limped around his camp gathering wood. Lozen had never seen him look so old and exhausted. Since before she could remember, he had been the Chiricahuas' ablest warrior and wisest counselor. Even Cheis came to him for advice.

Lozen crawled backwards, and Stands Alone followed. Stands Alone wanted to spend time with He Makes Them Laugh, and as his cross-cousin, Lozen could act as chaperon. They retrieved their horses and led them up the slope to the ledge where the boys kept watch.

He Makes Them Laugh, Chato, and Talks A Lot were observing the trail winding across the plain below. One end of it unraveled into the maze of alleys in Mesilla to the south. The other came to an abrupt halt at the new mines at Pinos Altos.

"We saw Red Sleeves," Lozen said.

"Where did you see him?" He Makes Them Laugh took the bag of dried mule meat and boiled mesquite beans that Stands Alone handed him and smiled his thanks.

"The Canyon Where The Bear Fought. He looks as though a bear attacked him."

"Then the story is true."

"I told you he would know what happened," said Stands Alone. "He knows everything."

He Makes Them Laugh pointed his chin at Talks A Lot and Chato. "We went to the lodge of the Pale Eyes trader who's been stealing food from Red Sleeves' people."

"A Mexican there told us that the diggers had caught The Old Man and whipped him," Talks A Lot said.

"Whipped him?"

"Like a mule," said He Makes Then Laugh. "They almost killed him. The Mexican said the Pale Eyes taunted him while they did it. They turned him loose, and no one has seen him since."

"Maybe he's waiting for the wounds to heal before he takes revenge." Chato was thinking about earning glory and a warrior's rank.

When Stands Alone gave the water jug to He Makes Them Laugh, she let her fingers rest on his for just a moment. He turned his head away, suddenly shy, which was not like him at all.

Talks A Lot nodded at the dust cloud growing in the west. "We've been waiting for them."

They watched a wagon and rider approach. They were passing below when the wagon's driver stopped and climbed down to relieve himself. The man on the horse rode up behind him and bashed him on the head with the butt of his carbine. Even from their ledge, Lozen and the others could see that it must have crushed his skull, but the murderer dismounted and stabbed his victim several times in the back, anyway. He cut away a circle of scalp and yanked it off. He threw the hair down and rolled a rock over it.

He pulled a wide belt from under the man's shirt, tugged off his boots, and took his weapons. He unhitched the two mules and tied their reins to his saddle horn. He fired several arrows into the wagon and a couple more into the corpse. Then he led the mules away from the trail and into the foothills to the south.

"He doesn't know how to use a bow very well," Chato remarked.

"When the enemy is dead, one doesn't have to," Lozen said.

"He wants the other Pale Eyes to think our people did it," said He Makes Them Laugh.

"But we don't take our enemies' hair." Stands Alone thought a moment. "Maybe he wants the other Pale Eyes to think Comanches did it."

"Why would two Pale Eyes be enemies?" Chato asked. The puzzling ways of white men provided a constant source of speculation.

"The dead one must have had something the live one wanted," Talks A Lot said. "They always want what others have."

The sun traveled its own trail while they watched a dust cloud grow in the south until it produced four men. Three of them kept watch while the fourth examined the body. Then they, too, rode away.

Lozen and the others continued to observe. No more riders appeared, but buzzards did. A single dark dot in the sky at the horizon grew until an eddy of them circled high over the body. Lozen led her mare down the trail. Stands Alone and the boys followed her. The Pale Eyes might have overlooked something useful. Pale Eyes threw away so many useful things.

When they arrived at the wagon, Chato began searching through the hay in case the Pale Eyes had hidden anything there. He Makes Them Laugh used a metal rod from the wagon to wrench off the iron rings. Talks A Lot untied the rope used to tie down the hay and coiled it.

A trio of buzzards had landed next to the corpse and stood in a huddle, discussing who would eat the eyes. Lozen threw rocks at them, and they rose in a flapping of wings. Absalom lay on his stomach, but his face was turned in profile, his cheek resting in the bloody dust, his eyes open.

Lozen recognized him. "He's the one who came to our camp with the black white man and Hairy Foot."

"The ones who helped me escape from El Gordo," Stands Alone added.

Talks A Lot kept a safe distance. No telling what any spirit might do, much less one murdered and a Pale Eyes besides. "Yesterday we saw Hairy Foot and this one at the lodge of the Pale Eyes trader."

"I have to take him to Hairy Foot." Stands Alone maneuvered her pony into position near the body and dismounted. "Help me lift him onto the horse."

"Have you become foolish?" The boys backed away. Ghost Owl might come at any moment to claim the soul—and take theirs while he was about it.

"He and the other two saved my life. I owe him a debt. I cannot let buzzards and ants and brother coyote eat him. Hairy Foot will know the proper Pale Eyes ceremonies."

"You don't owe anything to a dead white man," Chato said.

"He did me a favor. That makes him my brother. It's the custom, and you know it." Stands Alone turned to Lozen. "Will you ask your spirits for protection?"

"I don't have ghost magic." But she walked away and stood in silence, trying to remember the prayers Grandmother recited to keep ghosts from capturing the souls of the living.

Holding high a pinch of pollen, she prayed. "We trade this sacred dust to you to take the evil away from our sister and our brothers." She scattered the pollen to the four directions so that it would carry her prayer upward. She asked that the dead man's ghost be allowed to leave unhindered on its journey to wherever Pale Eyes went when they died.

She took ashes out of the bag hanging from her belt. Chanting the prayer Grandmother had taught her when she was very small, she rubbed some of them on Stand Alone's face and the backs of her hands. The boys both came forward to receive them, too. She rubbed more of them on the muzzle of Stand Alone's pony and on his back. Then she made a cross mark with pollen on the foreheads of Stand Alone, the boys, and on the horses, too.

He Makes Them Laugh and Talks A Lot caught hold of the dead man's arms. Lozen and Chato took his feet. Together they lifted him onto the pony's back. Lozen pulled Stands Alone up behind her on the mare. Leading the horse with Absalom's body lying facedown across its back, arms dangling on one side and legs on the other, they set off for the Pale Eyes' settlement.

RAFE SAW THEM APPROACHING BEFORE HE HAD RIDDEN three miles from the fort. He knew, without knowing how, that the corpse was Absalom. He drew his army-issue Hall carbine from its saddle boot, primed and loaded it, and laid it across his thighs.

He put the palm of one hand on the angular stiffness of the letter in the pocket of his old army coat. Not much more than an hour ago, four prospectors had come into the American House where Rafe had ordered a whiskey to fortify himself for the Jornada del Muerto. They had announced that they had found a man who had met the common death of the country, slaughtered by Apache marauders. One of them had held up the letter he had found in Absalom's pocket.

Absalom had written it to Lila. He must have planned to mail it in El Paso, where he could buy one of those newfangled postage stamps. Rafe understood how the officers must have felt when they had to draft condolence letters to the kin of those slain in the war with Mexico.

He had finished his whiskey while he debated with himself. The sensible self advised him to continue his journey north, write to Absalom's fiancée, and post the two letters in Socorro or Albuquerque. His mad self told him he had to recover Absalom's body and bury it, Apaches or no Apaches.

His mad self won. So here he was alone on the trail with four Apaches coming toward him. Maybe they had heard already about the whipping the miners gave Red Sleeves. Maybe they were coming to take revenge. They didn't have the look of a war party, but they didn't look like those wretched-looking Apaches he had seen at the agency, either.

The three boys rode ahead, and he realized they were the ones in the sutler's store the day before. Then he recognized the two women mounted on the same mare he had seen galloping away from Don Angel's Apache-proof corral. He had once again come face-to-face with that horse thief, Lozen, and the lovely assassin, Pandora, who collected ears and dispensed padlocks.

He felt a strange calm. He wanted to smile at the four of them as they rode so close that Red stretched his neck to nuzzle the mare's nose. He felt as though he knew them. He longed to talk to them. He had so many questions he wanted to ask. He could ask them in Spanish, but he didn't even have the words in English. Just an inchoate desire to find out more about them.

Lozen kicked her mare's sides until she was sitting almost thigh to thigh with Rafe, but facing in the opposite direction. He could clearly see the grains of pollen on her forehead and the ashes. She wore the clothes of an Apache woman today instead of the dirty cotton shirt and breechclout he had last seen on her. She had hiked the skirt well above the tops of her high moccasins. Rafe tried not to stare at the exposed brown thighs as muscular as any boy's.

Instead of letting her hair fall in a shaggy mass held back with a headband as he had last seen it, she wore it in a thick, double loop caught at the nape of her neck and tied vertically into a beaded oval of leather. Rafe knew that the hairdo meant she hadn't married yet. He wondered if one of the three sprigs accompanying her considered himself a suitor. He wouldn't have been surprised if all three of them did.

Behind the swag of hair that reached below her heavy eyebrows, he could see the roguish glint in her dark eyes. He got a good look at the strong line of her nose and the wild flare to her nostrils, the sensuous set of her full lips, their edges as gracefully defined as if chiseled by a sculptor.

My God, Rafe thought. She has sprouted into a beauty.

She took the pony's lead line from Pandora and passed it to Rafe. The touch of her fingers sent a single shiver and a herd of thoughts of a carnal variety racing through him.

"*Gracias,*" he said.

"*Por nada.*" She had acquired a woman's voice, low and husky.

He looked at the pony. Surely they didn't mean for him to have that, as well. He held up the lead line. "*¿Y el caballo?*"

"*Es suyo,*" Pandora answered him from behind Lozen's shoulder.

Without another word they wheeled their horses and rode away. As he watched them go, Rafe felt sure that Apaches had not killed Absalom. Certainly those four hadn't.

Rogers, he thought. Rogers did it.

He thought about what he would say when he buried his friend. The choice was obvious. "Good night, sweet prince, / And flights of angels sing thee to thy rest!"

Chapter 17

DEAD MAN'S JOURNEY

Rafe named the mule Othello because he was aristocratic, loyal, the color of very strong coffee, and prone to jealous snits at imagined slights. Othello's nigh-wheeler position was reserved for the strongest, smartest animal. At night Rafe preferred to ride him rather than occupy the wagon seat.

He had started to doze in Othello's saddle when a crack like a rifle shot jerked him upright. The noise came from just behind Othello's hindquarters. In the middle of the hundred-mile stretch of desolation known as the Jornada del Muerto, with dawn's hot breath almost on his neck, a spoke in the front wheel had snapped.

"Whoa, Rosie." Rafe pulled on the jerk line to the left lead mule, a compact and nervous sidestepper with a reproachful gaze and the name of Rosencrantz.

Rafe walked to the side of the wagon and ran his hands around the wheel until he found the broken spoke. The others were sound. He could keep going until light.

He felt hot breath tickling his ear. He reached up and cradled Red's velvety muzzle in the hollow of his neck and shoulder. Red nibbled his shirt, then his ear. Red was the reason Rafe dared to travel the Horn, as the Americans called the Jornada, alone. Red could throw dirt on any horse the Apaches could put up against him.

He climbed back aboard Othello and collected the jerk line. He raised up in the stirrups, cracked the whip, and gave a Comanche yell. The singletree chains jangled, and the wagon moved forward, the dry wood of its parts groaning as they rubbed together.

The thread of light at the horizon broadened to a ribbon

and diffused into a soft glow. It hardly seemed capable of creating the inferno that he knew the summer day would become. Rafe felt like a beetle crawling over that flat expanse. He imagined an Apache lookout perched on some outcrop in the mountains about five miles to the east. He would be squatting on a rock there, with his forearms on his bare thighs, smoking the first cigarillo of the day. Rafe imagined him spotting the beetle wagon with its paired feelers of mules, then calling to the others, and all of them starting out full of bustle and glee on their day's enterprise.

Don't borrow trouble, he thought. He always grazed the mules at sunup out here anyway, if no one was chasing him.

When the sky lightened enough to see the dark patch on Rosie's rump, he halted the team. He carried buckets of water to them from the keg in the back of the wagon and picketed them where they could graze. Red joined them.

Rafe took a stout piece of mesquite cut to the length he needed from inside the coffin in the wagon. He braced it under the axle and dug a shallow hole under the wheel. Next, he rifled through the spare spokes and wedges, the hammer, saw, adze, the coils of rope, and the box of nails, bolts, harping pins, cleats, and linchpins until he found the pry bar, pliers, and wooden mallet in the coffin.

He had won the pine box from an undertaker in a game of euchre. Rafe said it was the only possession that would come in handy whether he was dead or alive. The other teamsters thought him mad to tweak fate by carrying it. They had also mentioned that he was crazy to squander cargo space on tools and parts when wrecked wagons littered the countryside like so many abandoned good intentions. Rafe preferred to leave as little to chance as possible.

He had even paid a blacksmith in Santa Fe to fashion a metal rack and fasten it to the outside of the wagon bed at the rear. Rafe went back there now and lifted off the spare wheel that hung on it. The sight of it entertained the freighters so much that they had taken to calling him Fifth Wheel.

He rolled the wheel to the front of the wagon. He unlatched the removable section of the wooden cap that fit over the hub and pulled it out to expose the end of the axle and the iron linchpin. The broad head of the pin had broken off. He would have to take the entire cover off the hub so he could hammer it out.

He could lose his temper. He could curse luck, the world and the devil by sections and miles, then by yards, feet, and inches. Or he could be grateful that a spoke had broken and not the axletree. A less careful man would have tried to finish the trip with the broken spoke, but Rafe knew better.

Of course, those same less careful men were now bedded down in the wagon yard in Santa Fe, or with their snores, they were disturbing the sleep of the comely señoritas at Doña Rosa's. Not one of those careless men had agreed to come with him, even though the army offered six times the going rate. Given the fact that the Apaches had been making travel in the Jornada del Muerto a precarious propostition, it was cheap at the price.

Rogers had not taught Red Sleeves a lesson by whipping him. On the contrary, Red Sleeves and his marauders were now teaching even Rogers a lesson in rascality. The Apaches had vengeance down pat.

He hung the old wheel on the rack at the rear and was positioning the new one when Red whickered. Rafe saw the cloud of dust with more exasperation than fear. He had gotten out of the habit of fearing. He took his brass spyglass out of his saddlebag, but the dust obscured the riders' identity.

"I expect what we have here, Red, is not a fleet of deacons."

Rafe put his hand to his hat brim and studied the cloud. He tried to judge the number of men and horses that had raised it, and how soon he could expect them.

I'm like some Mesopotamian humbug, he thought, pretending to read omens in a swirl of smoke or in the quivering liver of a goat.

"I expect what we have here is a distilled extract of murder and inconvenience," he added aloud for Red's benefit.

He was angry about losing the cargo. He had always gotten his loads through. Except for the fat and sassy mule named Iago, he was sorry that the team would most likely end up in Apache stew pots. He was angrier then he wanted to admit at the prospect of losing the wagon. It had become his only home.

He unharnessed the mules and swatted his hat at them. "Git, you worthless sacks of sorry."

Iago took off immediately. Loyalty had never been one of his virtues. Rosie and Guildenstern, Lear and The Fool circled until Rafe threw rocks at them. They galloped off to turn, stand, and watch him from a distance. Othello stood his ground.

"Suit yourself," Rafe muttered.

He saddled Red, trying not to stare at the cloud. Whoever was raising it would be richer by a few crates of guns. They were the same .69-caliber smoothbore flintlocks the infantry had carried, with few modifications, since 1795. Those in charge in Washington City were supplying the soldiers with a gun designed for close combat with massed armies. Never mind that their present enemies never fought massed or close.

Rafe had suggested removing the firing mechanisms, but the colonel couldn't be bothered. He had taken offense at Rafe for advising him at all. If the mechanisms had been in a sack, Rafe could have disposed of them so the muskets would be useless in Apache hands.

He recapped his six-shooters and stuck two in his belt and two in his saddle holsters. He knotted the cords of his hat under his chin. He doubled a Mexican blanket, flung it over his shoulders, and tied it with a thong to deflect arrows. The Apaches didn't have many guns, but as of today that would change for this mob.

He could see that the dust cloud had shifted. The raiding party planned to head him off. If he could make it to the foothills, he knew a shortcut. The Apaches almost certainly knew about it, but they wouldn't expect him to.

He gathered the reins while Red danced from one foot to the other. Rafe vaulted into the saddle and grabbed the pommel. The seat of his trousers had hardly brushed saddle leather when Red gathered the almighty muscles of his shoulders and haunches into the fleshly equivalent of steel springs, tightly wound. Red's front hooves dug in so hard they left furrows deep enough to plant potatoes. He launched himself with a power and exuberance that made Rafe throw his head back and howl with joy.

As the wind blew the brim of his hat up and the desert floor flashed past, Rafe's only worry was whether Red would survive the run. He decided that when he reached the fort he would rub him down with soft straw. He would administer a dose of whiskey for Red and some for himself. He would wrap him in blankets and give him hay with raw beefsteak, diced. A bed of clean hay to sleep in, and Red would be fine in the morning.

If something unforeseen happened and he lost the race, Rafe would leave two bullets in his pistol for Red and for himself.

As Victorio rode, he admired the new musket riding across his thighs. It was a beautiful thing, with vines etched into the face plate and tendrils twining out along the barrel. A mountain lion prowled the brass lid of the patch box set in the burnished walnut stock. He wondered who had first thought of such an amazing thing. What Pale Eyes shaman had carved these pictures into it, and what spirits did they represent?

Loco rode a pony of the color brown that the Mexicans called *tostado*. Loco hummed to himself, a Bear song probably. The stranger behind him rode a big gray stallion. When the sun shone on the horse, the white hairs scattered through his coat made him glint like steel dust. The stranger had an old musket of his own with a winged metal snake engraved on the side.

Victorio, Loco, He Steals Love, and the three herd boys had killed no deer on this hunting trip, but they didn't care. They had taken twenty-four of these firesticks along with powder and bullets and five mules. They had found knives in Hairy Foot's wagon, as well as blankets, cloth, shovels, hoes, axes, and shiny copper kettles.

In a way, the miners at Pinos Altos had done them all a favor when they humiliated Red Sleeves. The old man had tried to keep the promises he made on the Pale Eyes' paper talk. He had tried to persuade the Red Paint warriors to stop stealing the Americans' horses and cattle and killing the owners when they objected.

In return the Pale Eyes had driven away the game. They attacked the women at harvest time and destroyed the winter food supply. Bluecoat patrols intercepted the warriors on their way back from Mexico and seized the stock they had stolen there. Now the diggers had sent Red Sleeves back on the war trail where he had excelled in the past. They had restored the natural order of life.

When Victorio reached the cleft in the wall of rock, he looked back. Talks A Lot, Flies In His Stew, and Ears So Big prodded the mules along at the rear of the procession. He Steals Love, wearing a coat of red dust, rode guard behind them.

Victorio didn't have to see He Steals Love's handsome face to know he looked morose. He hadn't wanted to come on this trip, and even the new musket had not cheered him. Jealousy prodded him like a pebble in his moccasin or a cactus spine in his breechclout.

He Steals Love was wondering if one of his rivals had won Lozen's affections while he was away. Since most of the eligible women in the village had flirted with him, being spurned was new to him. The experience had him confused and truculent.

Victorio had asked him to come along so Lozen could have a respite from his attentions. Victorio was saving He Steals Love from her, too. He shadowed her constantly, and that caused her to become irritable. An irritated Lozen was likely to play some prank that would make him even more miserable and a laughingstock, as well.

When Victorio asked him to join them on the hunt, He Steals Love had stared at him like a rabbit at a rattlesnake.

He couldn't turn down a chance to go with his beloved's older brother. Maybe Victorio would come to regard him as a friend. Maybe he would persuade his sister to behave sensibly and marry him.

On the other hand, one of those shameless coyotes who'd been courting Lozen might acquire love magic and bewitch her in his absence. He Steals Love would return with gifts, only to find that she'd moved in with Short Rope or Swimmer or that fool Poppy. The prospect had him in a seethe.

The shimmering summer day cooled and dimmed as Victorio guided Coyote into the defile and the walls closed around him. Half a day's ride from here the Bluecoats were mixing clay and water and straw like mud dauber wasps. They were perpetually repairing the cluster of adobe hovels they called a fort. Victorio laid his head back and looked up at the strip of sunlight far above him. It glittered like the shiny yellow trim decorating the Bluecoat soldiers' jackets. He held an arm out so that the tips of his fingers brushed the cool stone. This was a *fortaleza*.

When he thought about the valley on the other side, he could almost feel the cool air under the huge cottonwoods along the stream. He could almost hear the children's laughter as they splashed in the water. His people would feast and dance tonight to celebrate the plunder he brought. The men would hold council with the rider who came with them, the mysterious one they called Gray Ghost. People had been talking about Gray Ghost since a hunting party first sighted him a month ago. They discussed the possibility that he really was a ghost, or an omen. Maybe the men in council could discover more about him than Victorio had been able to.

Victorio wondered what Lozen had done in his absence to set the other women's tongues to flapping like loose pack ropes. What arguments would be brewing between her and She Moves Like Water over her refusal to behave like a young woman ready for marriage? What jokes had she played on the young men who courted her?

Lozen was waiting for him on the other side of the defile.

She was sitting in the shade of a cedar and teaching Maria to play the rock game. She tossed a small stone into the air while she picked up four more, one at a time, and set them on the knuckles of her other hand.

She stood and hiked her old deerskin skirt up under her belt. She lifted Maria onto the mare, took a short run, and leaped. Placing her hands on the mare's rump she vaulted onto her bare back just behind Maria. She reined the pony over to walk beside Victorio and Coyote. Her face lit up when she saw the musket. She reached out to stroke the barrel.

"We took twenty-four of these from Hairy Foot," Victorio said.

"Did you kill him?" The possibility bothered her.

"No."

"Was he riding my *colorado*?"

"Yes. He Steals Love chased him all day."

"That horse belongs to me, not to He Steals Love."

"He Steals Love lost that red horse at Dead Woman's Pass," said Loco. "Hairy Foot looked like a cactus with all those arrows sticking out of him. Maybe he has magic against bullets and arrows."

"He tied a blanket around his neck," Victorio added. "Its flapping knocked the arrows away."

"We should have burned the wagon," Loco grumbled.

"If we burned his wagon, how would Hairy Foot carry more things for us to take from him later?" Victorio and Loco had argued about this ever since they left the wagon standing as forlorn as a three-legged bison after the herd had moved on. Victorio leaned closer and lowered his voice. "I left pollen for Hairy Foot in the pouch you made for me, the one with the long fringe and the hawk feathers."

Stands Alone owed her freedom to Hairy Foot and his friends. Victorio felt some regret about harrying him, but it wasn't as though they had taken the goods from Hairy Foot himself. He was only carrying them for others. The pouch would give him something to think about. Victorio liked to give people something to think about, even Pale Eyes, who generally didn't seem to think at all.

Lozen handed Victorio a packet of corn husks tied with a twist of grass. Victorio unwrapped it and took one of the crisp piñon-meal cakes that were inside.

"The boys offered to help us women hoe the corn yesterday," Lozen said.

Victorio knew she meant her suitors, although Poppy, Short Rope, and Big Hand were not boys anymore. After the battle at Arizpe, the council had voted them all the rank of warrior, but Lozen still dismissed them with a wave of her hand.

"While Poppy was clearing the new cornfield he made a noise." Lozen pursed her lips, puffed out her cheeks, and blew three loud explosions of air. Stands Alone laughed so hard she had to sit down." Lozen grinned. "Poppy turned as red as *naletsoh*, his namesake. No one has seen him since, although his sister says he came prowling like a coatimundi around her fire looking for food after dark last night."

Victorio laughed, and he thought how boring life would be with a sister who was normal.

"Aren't you married yet?" Loco asked.

"None of those boys is ugly enough. I'm waiting for you to ask me." She raised her right hand in the sign that she was joking, with her palm forward, the first and second fingers up, and the thumb folded over the third and fourth.

"We brought someone back with us," said Victorio.

Lozen turned around and saw the gray stallion and his rider emerge at a trot from the opening in the cliff face. As the rider came closer, she could see that he looked like a red man, but he was wearing brown canvas trousers. Broad bands of silver around his upper arms gathered in the full sleeves of his calico shirt. He had on the type of hat the Pale Eyes wore, but a white plume curved over the edge of the wide brim and lay in a cloud on his shoulder. Sunlight glinted off a silver crescent that hung above the crimson sash across his chest. Even from here she could see that he was handsome. She stared, her lips slightly parted.

With a flick of his wrist Victorio caught a fly. It buzzed in his fist when he held it out to Lozen. She looked up, startled.

"It's easier to catch them this way," he said, "than to trap them in your mouth."

She leaned closer to him. "Is he Gray Ghost?" she murmured.

"Yes. You don't have to speak low. He can't understand you."

"How did you meet him?"

"Pale Eyes were chasing him along the canyon floor. We shouted to him and showed him the Tall Rock trail. We met him on the other side, and he consented to come with us."

"Who is he? Where does he come from? Who are his people?"

She wanted to ask, Is he married? Does he have a sweetheart?

"I don't know. He doesn't even speak Mexican, but he knows sign language. He says he comes from the east.

"His people live so far to the east," Loco added, "that the rising sun bakes their bread for them."

Victorio handed two of the cakes back to her. "Give him these." Lozen wanted to refuse, but she took them and rode toward Gray Ghost.

He had the high, strong cheekbones of her own people, but his face was thinner, his features more delicate, his skin a lighter brown. She guessed that he had seen about thirty harvests. His eyes were as gray as his horse. Each tendril of the white plume quivered and danced in the sunlight. The sun had faded the red cloth of his shirt to a pale pink. He wore moccasins of a type she had never seen before.

A roll of blankets rode behind his saddle. Fringed saddlebags hung on either side of the gray. He carried a musket in a saddle holster. From another leather case protruded the working end of a curved war club, a heavy wooden ball with a bear's tooth set in it.

He gestured "Greetings," in the silent language everyone knew.

She returned the sign and held out the mescal cakes. He accepted them with a smile that made her feel as if her insides were melting and flowing into her moccasins. She reined the mare around and urged her at a trot to where Victorio rode.

She felt as dizzy as if she had drunk a gourdful of tiswin. She felt as foolish as a child, but the longings that stirred in her weren't a child's. She wanted to laugh. She wanted to cry.

Love. This was what the women talked about when they wove baskets in the morning. It's what they joked and teased about as they gathered berries and tanned hides. It was terrible. She wondered if Grandmother or Broken Foot had a song that would cure it. And if they did, would she want to be cured?

Chapter 18

PLUNDERED

Lozen should have been excited about the muskets, but when Victorio distributed the plunder from Hairy Foot's wagon, she couldn't take her eyes off Gray Ghost. She stood in the gloom beyond the fire's light and pleaded silently with him to look her way. She asked the spirits to persuade him to come to her and stand by her here in the shadows.

She longed to hear him speak to her, even if she couldn't understand him, and even if she were too befuddled to answer him. She hadn't talked to anyone about the uproar going on behind her calm eyes, but she wanted to complain to She Moves Like Water and to Grandmother. Why had no one told her that love would make a fool of her?

Victorio opened the wooden box and began handing the firesticks to those with the most people dependent on them. Then he called the names of the fiercest fighters among the older warriors, and finally the younger men in order of their accomplishments.

Lozen was lost in a reverie of the dancing that would follow this. She thought of how men and women let their hands, their shoulders, their glances brush each other. The dancing was always suffused with desire, but it had never touched her before. Would she have the courage to ask Gray Ghost to dance?

She jumped when Stands Alone poked her. "Take the firestick."

"Firestick?"

Stands Alone gave her a shove, and Lozen stumbled into the fire's light. Victorio held the musket out to her and a pouch of bullets and another of powder. Her hands shook when she took them from him. Talks A Lot, Flies In His Stew, Chato, and the others would be angry that she got one and they didn't, but if anyone protested, she was too dazed to hear it. She walked away holding the heavy musket to her chest. The women crowded around to see it.

"She thinks she's too good for any man." Tall Girl observed. "She'll need that gun to hunt, or else she'll have to dance for the warriors and beg gifts from them."

She Moves Like Water glared at her. She was beginning to accept that fact that Victorio was right. The spirits had other plans for Lozen. Maybe she wouldn't find a man with whom she could have children and share her life. The possibility made She Moves Like Water sad.

THE NEXT TWO MONTHS WERE JOYOUS MISERY. GRAY GHOST moved into a lodge near She Moves Like Water's camp, and he spent most of his time with Victorio and the friends who gathered at his fire in the autumn evenings. Even Skinny joined them as often as not. Lozen was quick to offer to take them food and drink. Gray Ghost was polite, but he always treated her as nothing more than the younger sister of a friend.

As he learned The People's language, he could talk more about the troubles in the east. This night Red Sleeves was visiting, and Gray Ghost told his story again in words and gestures.

The Pale Eyes had overrun the land where his people had always lived, he said. They chopped down the trees. They killed the game or drove it away. They ripped into Mother Earth with big metal blades dragged by horse and mules. When they tired of chopping and digging, they set fire to the forests and the prairies, destroying what was left of the ancient hunting grounds.

Gray Ghost had watched his people die in agony, disfigured by diseases that no one had experienced before, and against which they had no medicine or magic. For more than a hundred years the Pale Eyes had made promises to his people, and they had broken all of them. Gray Ghost had decided to journey west in search of a refuge.

"To trust a Pale Eyes is like trusting a rattlesnake not to bite you," he said with a sad smile.

"There is one Pale Eyes I trust," said Red Sleeves. "His name is Tse'k. He's a good man." His heavy lids drooped over his sad, bulging eyes. His mouth sagged. "He promises us food if we live with him at the fort and plant corn and beans and squash. When winter comes and my joints feel like water freezing, I am going there with those of my people who are willing to follow me."

"When you did that before, the Pale Eyes agent robbed you," said Victorio. "He sold your warriors whiskey that made them fight with each other and beat their women." He didn't mention the beating that the diggers gave Red Sleeves. No one spoke of it in his presence.

"This one will not do that." Red Sleeves pulled a sigh up from his chest, like a man would draw a heavy bucket from a well. "I am tired. My bones ache. They have worn me down, those Pale Eyes, like water wearing away stone." He hunched over to prop his elbows on his bony knees and stare gloomily into the fire.

"There is no end to them," said Gray Ghost. "I have seen their cities teeming like ant heaps. I have been to Washington."

"Wah-sin-ton!" Victorio and the others came to attention. "The Pale Eyes always talk of Wah-sin-ton. Who is Wah-sin-ton?"

"It's the town where their Great Father lives. It covers more land than your canyon here. It has paths wider than two hoop-and-pole fields set side by side. It has stone lodges as big as the cliffs that surround us."

The men stirred and looked at each other. No one would call Gray Ghost a liar, but his stories stretched belief to the snapping point.

"It has more people than in all this country," he added.

"Maybe that's where they come from," said Skinny, "The way snakes breed by the hundreds under the same rock."

Lozen's cousin, He Makes Them Laugh, trotted up panting. "Twelve men on horseback are coming. And a wagon that looks like an arbor on wheels. They speak the Mexicans' language, but they aren't Mexicans."

He Makes Them Laugh was right. The wagon's cover was not curved like those of the Pale Eyes. It had a flat, red-and-white-striped top attached to four upright poles. The sides had been rolled up and tied in place. Thick red fringes jostled along the top edge of it as the wagon jolted along. Tassels and bright brass bells flounced and jangled at each corner. Four white geldings pulled it. They were handsome but thin. Broken Foot rode ahead of them.

People clustered around him asking questions, but he didn't know much. "We found them stranded and thirsty and led them to the nearest spring. I told them they could rest here until they're ready to travel on toward the sunset."

Everyone tried to see inside the wagon, but the twelve dusty men, dark-haired and dark-eyed, ringed it. They sat in their saddles with a ferocious ease, their muskets held upright with the stocks resting on their thighs. From under the wide flat brims of their black felt hats they watched like birds of prey.

The wagon's driver set a wooden box on the ground. An old woman, solid and formidable, took the driver's hand and stepped down. A much younger woman appeared behind her. She wore a long dress of a blue cloth that shimmered with streaks of purple and green in the sunlight. The bodice clung to her like a second skin and emphasized a waist that reminded Lozen of a wasp's. She laid one pale hand on the old woman's shoulder and lifted her skirts up past her tiny black shoes and slender ankles with the other. The skirts rustled as she descended.

When she pushed the fringed black shawl back, the murmuring rose in volume. She was beautiful. Perfect hair framed a perfect face with perfect features set perfectly in it. Lozen looked at Gray Ghost and almost cried out in despair. He was staring at her with the same dazed expression that came into Lozen's eyes whenever she saw him.

LOZEN THOUGHT SHE HAD KEPT HER PASSION SECRET, BUT Grandmother knew all along. When Grandmother was about Lozen's age, she had thought she would wither and perish because the boy she loved went to live with a Mescalero woman. Now Grandmother couldn't remember his name. She had married a man who had made her happy until the Hair Takers killed him at the Santa Rita mines, how along ago? Fifteen harvests?

Sometimes Grandmother wished she could travel back through the years the way she traveled across deserts and mountains and high, green valleys. She wished she could tell that unhappy child, herself, that all would be well. But she couldn't, not any more than she could tell Lozen that this ache would fade, and she would smile one day at her foolishness. Young people had the gift of certainty, and they were certain that no old person had ever felt the way they did.

Grandmother watched as the wagon and its passenger rumbled away in a clangor of brass bells. All anyone knew was that the young woman came from beyond the wide water to the east. She was headed for the land that bordered the endless water at the western rim of the world. Her father lived there, she said, and he had sent for her.

The stranger's wagon had arrived with twelve men as an escort, but it left with thirteen. Gray Ghost rode his big stallion alongside it, his possession in the new saddlebags that Lozen had given him, and his blankets tied behind the saddle. The children ran after the wagon, shouting and laughing. The women drifted off to their chores, and the men returned to their hoop-and-pole games.

Lozen and little María stood staring at the dust it left. María took Lozen's hand to comfort her. The child was learning to speak Apache, but she already knew the language that required no words. She called Lozen *shidee*, "my older sister," and she could sense her sorrow.

Grandmother, Her Eyes Open, and Grandmother's friend,

Turtle, watched Lozen as they ground corn and acorns into meal.

"She'll get over him." Her Eyes Open scraped the ground acorn meal into a shallow basket.

"Marrying a Mescalero or a White Mountain man is bad enough." Turtle had a narrow chin and a small hooked nose. Wrinkles around her close-set eyes made her look more like her namesake every year. "But to marry a man who doesn't speak your language would never do."

"At least if he scolds her," said Her Eyes Open, "she won't understand him."

"Love is more common than flies," said Grandmother. "And at least as bothersome."

"I don't see love bothering you these days, old woman." Turtle said.

"No, but the flies still like me well enough." Grandmother glanced up to see Lozen walk into camp. Her hair hung in a ragged line that ended above her shoulders.

"Who cut your hair?"

"I did."

"No man will want you with your hair like that." She Moves Like Water offered her a gourdful of stew, but Lozen waved it away.

"I will not marry, so it makes no difference."

"How will you live if you don't marry? If you don't have daughters, who will care for you when you grow old?"

Lozen turned to Victorio. "Brother, your woman has her sister now to help her, and her mother and María. I want to be your apprentice. I want to accompany you on the war trail."

"That's impossible." She Moves Like Water frowned at Victorio, in case he was inclined to agree with such a preposterous request. "Unmarried women don't go on the war trail with the men. You'll disgrace the family. People will ridicule you."

"My woman is right," Victorio said. "They will talk about you."

"They already talk about her," Corn Stalk put in quietly.

Everyone stared at her. She rarely spoke up in family discussions, much less disagreed. Maybe the nights she spent laughing softly in her lodge with Victorio had made her bold.

"They say she isn't like others," Corn Stalk went on. They say the spirits have blessed her with the power to heal, the magic to make horses follow her, the gift of far-sight. They don't expect the usual of her. I think they would be disappointed, maybe, if she behaved like other women."

STANDS ALONE LOOKED DOWN AT THE GIFT LEFT IN HER blankets. It was a gourd with big eyes and a grinning mouth carved and painted around the long, curved end that formed a nose. The pupils of the eyes looked inward at the nose and tufts of rabbit fur had been glued at the base of it. The artist had painted the tip of the nose with a spiderwork of veins that resembled those of a man's penis. Even with the eyes and mouth, Stands Alone could not mistake what it represented. Inside was a bag of cactus candy, the specialty of He Makes Them Laugh's mother.

Stands Alone collapsed in laughter onto the blankets. Lozen and Maria looked over at her from their bed. Stands Alone held up the gourd so they could see it. Maria giggled and Lozen smiled, even though she had thought she never would again.

"Did He Makes Them Laugh give it to you?" asked Maria.

"Who else?" Stands Alone raised up on one elbow and studied the gourd "What should I do?"

"That's for you to decide, Sister," said Lozen. "Do you love him?"

"I do, but he's so different from the others."

"Do you care that he's different?"

Stands Alone thought about that. "No. I don't care. He's a good hunter. He's a good man."

"Then do what your heart tells you to do." Lozen felt suddenly old. Now that she had experienced the power of love, she felt qualified to give advice about it. "Like magic, love is a gift from Yusen."

With a rustle of pine boughs, Lozen turned over on her side and faced the lodge's curved side. She could see the glow of the fire through the canvas covering that once had stretched over Hairy Foot's wagon. Maria cuddled against her back, but the touch only increased Lozen's longing for Gray Ghost.

Tears scalded tracks down her cheeks. She was still awake when Stands Alone gathered her blankets and tiptoed out. She must have decided to go to the lodge of He Makes Them Laugh. Tomorrow she would cook for him, and everyone would consider them married.

Her absence made Lozen feel even more bereft.

Chapter 19

A LIGHT DUSTING

An icy wind blew gaunt gray clouds across the December sky. It played tag with leaves and trash around the corners of the adobe huts called Fort Webster. The soldiers wore their greatcoats with the collars turned up and the flaps on their hats pulled down over their ears. At night, Apaches drifted through the fort as silently as the occasional gusts of snow. No one in the garrison went out after dark without his gun primed, loaded, and at half-cock.

Still, camping here was better than sleeping in the open, and Rafe had taken a liking to Dr. Michael Steck, the superintendent of New Mexico Territory. Rafe had found work as a driver for the government's freight wagons, too. The army had returned to protect the miners and ranchers. Rafe suspected that the miners riled the Apaches up on regular basis to keep the army around.

Rafe appreciated the irony of the fact that the army paid him to haul beef and corn to feed the Indians whose thefts and murders the soldiers had come here to stop. And why not feed them? Warfare hadn't worked. Bribery might—for a little while, anyway.

On this trip Rafe planned to bargain for some mules and harnesses and recover his wagon. A recent patrol had told him it was still sitting in the Jornada del Muerto. In the meantime, he was playing a game of two-handed euchre with Dr. Steck.

Steck watched as Rafe set the rest of the pack facedown on the table and turned over the top one. Steck studied the five cards in his hand. "Some of Red Sleeves' people put on an exhibition of horsemanship the last time they came in for rations," he said. "It was quite a performance."

Rafe said nothing, and Steck glanced at him over the cards. "The Apaches don't impress you?"

"They impress me, all right, but not their horse savvy."

"Ah, yes. You're familiar with Comanches, aren't you?"

"You know what they say. . . ." Rafe took one of his cards and placed it crosswise under the undealt pack.

"What do they say?"

"A white man will ride a mustang until he's winded. A Mexican will take him and ride him until he's dead. The Comanch will then ride him wherever he's going."

"That says more about their indifference to life than their man horsemanship."

"I thought the Comanch were about as indifferent to life as the human species could get, but that was before I made the acquaintance of the Apaches."

"Considering the insults and betrayals that Chief Red Sleeves has suffered, I would say he's shown considerable restraint."

"Then I reckon I'm not familiar with the definition of restraint."

"The miners raid their camps and attack their women and children. The soldiers confiscate horses that they obtain legally from Mexican traders."

Rafe let that delusion slide right on past, and Dr. Steck continued with the list of crimes and injustices against his wards.

"My predecessor, that rascal Fletcher, stole the docile Apaches' rations. He sold them whiskey. The government neglected to send them the tools they needed for agriculture."

"Docile Apaches. Now there's a notion."

"I firmly believe that many of the thefts and murders in this country are committed by our own criminal element, and blamed on the Apaches. I tell you, they have become quite tractable. I'm expecting them here for their rations at any time. Red Sleeves says the Warm Springs people will come in with him."

"Of course they will."

Steck looked at him quizzically. "What do you mean?"

"You're a good man, Michael." Rafe meant it. Dr. Michael Steck was moral, honest, kind, exacting, and resolute. He had taken on the superintendent's job with responsibilities that Job, Solomon, and Hercules would all decline if they had sense. He had done the job so well that even the Apaches liked him; and they didn't like anybody, as best Rafe could tell. But Steck was new here, and he had more to learn about his charges.

Dr. Steck waited for an answer to his question.

"What I mean is that winter is not a good time for raiding. They'll let the government feed them and give them blankets and kettles and knives and gewgaws for the next few months. When spring comes, they'll head south again, and we can all be grateful we're not Mexicans."

"I think you're wrong, Rafe. This time they will stay, and they will farm."

And that, Rafe thought, is like expecting a wolf to hoe beans. He changed the subject. "Have you heard of a man named Rogers?"

"The scoundrel who whipped Red Sleeves?"

"Among other transgressions."

"They say he went to harry the good folk of California. Good riddance to bad cess."

The door opened and let in the draft that had been waiting outside like a cat. A lieutenant, his face red from the icy wind, poked his head in. "They're here, Dr. Steck."

"Did Victorio and the Warm Springs people come, too?"

"I reckon. They all look alike to me." The head disappeared; then it popped back in. "Mr. Collins, the boys brought back your wagon. It's missing its cover and has a load of sand in it, but it looks none the worse for wear, considering. They took it to the wagon yard."

With Red trailing after him, Rafe accompanied Dr. Steck to the storehouse where the Apaches had gathered. The first detail he noticed was the absence of young men. He shook his head with a small, rueful smile. He wasn't surprised. The young ones hadn't waited until spring to raid into Mexico.

The second thing he noticed was how old and weary and harmless Red Sleeves looked. The wrinkles in his face had deepened to gullies that pulled the corners of his mouth down into a doleful pout. Rafe almost couldn't imagine him spreading death and desolation.

"Hairy Foot! My friend!"

Before Rafe could react, Red Sleeves engulfed him in a hug that compressed his rib cage and squeezed the breath out of him. Red Sleeves hadn't bathed lately—but then, who had? Rafe pulled away with the imprint on his cheek of the metal tweezers the chief wore on a cord around his neck. The chief conversed in Spanish.

"Give me *fósforos*, my good friend."

"I don't have any."

"And the stockings?"

"All gone."

Red Sleeves held up a bare foot, the sole of which looked like a very dirty tortoise shell. "Like my moccasins." He displayed a massive grin packed with teeth.

Rafe wondered, though, if his moccasins had really worn out, or if he was putting on a show of poverty for Dr. Steck. If he and his people were putting on a show, it was a damned good one. What were they buying with all those horses they'd stolen this fall? Maybe they ate them. Red Sleeves looked like he could eat a horse on any given day.

"Telescopio?" Red Sleeves asked hopefully.

"I was telling him about your telescope, Rafe." Dr. Steck beamed at the ragged crowd, and they beamed back at him. Rafe had never seen Apaches so pleased with a white man. They were good judges of human nature, after all.

Rafe pulled from his saddlebag the sack made from the sleeve of an old shirt. He took the telescope out and handed it over. Red Sleeves looked through it, exclaimed *"Enjuh!"* and passed it in turn to the young man whom Dr. Steck called Victorio. Victorio was tall for an Apache, about Rafe's height, and as muscular as any panther. He would have seemed taller if he hadn't been standing next to Red Sleeves.

Rafe remembered him from that time in John Cremony's tent at the Santa Rita mines, and at the shooting contest when the little horse thief got her name, Lozana. He realized that the last time he had seen the two of them, they were galloping away aboard a pair of Don Angel's prize horses.

Rafe surveyed the crowd and found Lozen standing with Pandora among the women at some distance away. He suppressed the urge to smile and wave. Lozen wore a blanket wrapped around her, but below it he saw the fringes of a skirt that hung around the ankles of her old moccasins. She no longer wore the maiden's hair or ornament. She must have married, maybe to that good-looking, strapping specimen who couldn't stop staring at her.

Victorio handed the glass to her. She aimed it at Rafe, and he stared back into its single eye for what seemed like a long time before she passed it around. All the women stared at him through it and giggled.

Rafe never expected to see the telescope again, but when it reappeared in his hands, he tried to feel Lozen's touch on it. He wished he could separate the warmth of her hands from all the others. What foolishness.

He watched the Apaches walk to where the army had assembled to oversee distribution of the beef and corn. As Lozen turned to go, Rafe saw that she wore a musket in a leather case whose strap rode across her back. A pair of white hawk feathers decorated the case, along with strings of beads and shells, and a small leather bag no doubt full of Apache hocus-pocus. He wondered if the gun was one of those stolen from his wagon. Several of the men had them, but she was the only woman with one.

He wanted to stride after her. He wanted to yell, "Hey, you, let me see that." He wanted to catch hold of her arm. He wanted to touch her. Instead he walked to the wagon yard with Red butting him playfully in the small of the back. He was startled to see his wagon and an old friend there.

"Othello."

The mule looked up as though he had seen Rafe a few

minutes earlier instead of almost five months. He looked thin, but otherwise he seemed in good spirits.

Rafe walked around the old Packard. He ran his hand along the familiar gouge taken from the side by a sharp boulder that had tumbled down a slope and barely missed destroying the wagon. He poked a finger into the splintered holes left by Apache arrows. He could remember what event had left each dent and scar and gash in it.

It would need work to make it serviceable again, but at least he had recovered it. Instead of returning home, home had come back to him. He stepped onto the hub and climbed inside. The lieutenant had been right about the sand.

He noticed several strands of fringe lying outside a heap of it in the corner. He brushed the sand away and uncovered a leather bag, beautifully beaded. One of the thieves must have dropped it. No one would leave such a piece of work behind on purpose.

He opened it and saw the heap of pollen inside, like a remnant of a golden summer's day. He started to empty it over the side, and then he stopped. He thought of his Navajo woman and the reverence she had had for pollen.

He shook some of it onto the driver's seat, and it glittered like powdered sunlight as it fell. He climbed down and sprinkled it on the axles and on the tongue. He scattered the last of it to the four directions as he had seen her do. He did it in memory of her, and—though he would never admit it—he did it in thanks to God for the return of his Packard. He also did it, maybe, for luck. When he finished, he put the copy of *Romeo and Juliet* into the pouch and stuck it into the back of his trousers. Then he went off to talk to the army's wainwright about the repairs to the wagon.

That night Rafe laid his bedroll next to the wagon with the saddle for a pillow. He rolled up in the blankets and tied Red's tether to his wrist. Even if he woke up with snow stacked on top of him, he would not leave Red alone with the Apaches camped nearby.

LOZEN MOVED, SILENT AS THE DRIFTING SNOWFLAKES, among the hulking forms of the adobe buildings. A door opened, and a rectangle of light fell out onto the snow. Loud voices spilled after it. Lozen slid into the deep shadow between the officers' lodge and the room where the Pale Eyes agent, Tse'k, conducted business. She pulled her blanket around her and pressed against the wall. She watched three Bluecoats walk past, silhouetted briefly in the strip of moonlight beyond the front corners of the buildings.

The door slammed shut, and the light blinked out. Lozen continued on to the wagon yard. She knew where everything was. They all did.

She also knew that the sentries paced opposite courses around the perimeter of the corral and the wagon yard. She knew when they would pass each other, and where. She left a bottle of whiskey there, as though some careless soldier had dropped it; then she settled into the darkness to wait. The whiskey had cost her a mule, but it would be worth the price. The sentries didn't let her down. She heard one of them give a low call to the others. She saw them look around, then slip off into the shadows.

She found Red near Hairy Foot's wagon. He eyed her warily in the full moon's light, but he didn't move. He didn't snort or whinny. She stared at him, sensing his plan.

No, she thought. "You can't fool me. As soon as I try to untie you, you'll wake Hairy Foot."

He could have done it now, but she had the feeling he was playing a game with her. He would let her get close, and then he would alert Hairy Foot. She made a loop in the horsehair rope she carried, so she would be ready to put it around his nose to guide him once she mounted.

She found his tether line. With fingers light as a moth's feelers, she followed it to the saddle and the sleeping form. It disappeared under Hairy Foot's blanket, tied, no doubt, to his wrist.

His saddlebags lay next to him. She probed them with her fingers. When she found the cloth-wrapped far-seeing glass she eased it out of the bag. She stuck it into the back of her belt under the blanket she wore like a poncho.

She crouched next to the sleeping figure and stared down at him. In the full moon's light, Hairy Foot's face in repose looked young and untroubled, although Lozen knew that he had had his share of troubles. He didn't appear to be the powerful *di-yin* that the warriors believed him. He was appealing in his defenselessness, not a powerful magician who repelled arrows and bullets as though they were horseflies.

She thought him handsome for a Pale Eyes. She couldn't see colors at night, but she knew his hair was the yellow of the sacred pollen. He had a strong mouth and a straight nose. His eyelashes were as pale as the moonlight. A snowflake drifted down onto them. Another landed on his brow, then several more fell onto his hair. Lozen felt an urge to brush them off, as she would do for a sleeping child.

What foolishness. The men would think her stupid if they could see her. But then, she would probably never have another chance to see a white man so close, at least not a live one.

She could cut the line without waking him, but this was more of a challenge. She took a deep breath. Whatever happened, the spirits would take care of her. Even if every Bluecoat in the fort arrived on the run, shooting as they came, she could escape them. She knew that for a certainty.

She lifted the edge of the blanket so slowly it seemed not to move at all. She folded it gently back on itself, exposing his wrist and the rope. She laid her slender fingertips on the knot, feeling the ridges and valleys, the intertwinings. It was a simple knot. She concentrated her attention on it.

She had teased out the first end of it when she felt a prickling at the nape of her neck. She glanced up and saw him staring at her. She dropped the knot, and—still at a crouch— she ran into the shadows under the wagon, then out the other side and away, dodging under the bellies of the sleeping mules.

Rafe lay still, frozen not by fear but by disbelief. Had she been real or a dream? He could still see her glossy black hair as it fell forward, embracing her oval face like a fanned pair

Chapter 20

FIDDLING AROUND WHILE THE PACKARD BURNS

Others might prefer the bustle of Santa Fe, but Rafe liked the village of Socorro, the adobe oasis at the northern end of the Jornada del Muerto. In English, *soccoro* meant "aid," or "relief," and Rafe was always relieved to reach it alive after a passage through the Horn. He usually went to the cantina called La Paloma. The Dove.

Mexicans made up most of The Dove's clientele, which also suited him. The farmers and muleteers, the shopkeepers, wood-hewers and artisans drank there. They got into their share of squabbles as the evening progressed, and they took aboard so much liquid cargo that they sloshed when they tottered outside to relieve themselves.

All in all, though, the Dove—like Soccoro itself—basked in a sense of contentment. Its people went about their business and their pleasure with the self-assurance that came from living in the place where they were "bred and buttered," as Absalom used to say. Maybe that was what attracted him, since a sense of belonging had always eluded him.

Tonight The Dove was crowded with more Americans than usual. Rafe sat in a corner at a table with one of the few chairs that could claim a back. He conferred with a bottle of the local brew witched from the agave plants that covered the desert for miles around. Between sips he watched the women who, with trays held high, slipped among the tables crowded close together.

The women were heartbreakingly beautiful. They all enchanted him, even the brazen ones whom he suspected would cheerfully lay him out with a stool and pick his pockets. He was always astonished that women persisted in being so completely unlike men, in spite of eons of association. Women's coexistence with men seemed to him the pairing of meadowlarks and tanyard dogs.

When Milagro, his favorite, glanced his way, he held up his empty glass. She crossed the smoky room with the slow sway of her hips that inspired him to drain the glasses faster so he could watch her amble toward him and away again. He especially liked watching her walk away. She was, as her name proclaimed, a miracle.

She smiled with her full, red lips and regarded him from somewhere far behind her sad eyes. "Another, Señor Rafael?"

"Yes, please, Señorita Milagro."

She swayed off, with his attention trailing after her like a hungry puppy. He jumped when someone cleared his throat in his ear. He turned to look up into a broad face with bulging red cheeks, a turned-up nose, and fox-colored side-whiskers. The man leaned down to make himself heard over the noise, and his face loomed too close. Rafe pushed his chair away from it.

"Would you be Mr. Rafe Collins?" the whiskers said.

"Not if I had my druthers." Rafe realized that he was already having trouble focusing—and the evening was young yet.

The man threw back his head and laughed so loudly that people turned to stare. "Oh, I see. You wouldn't be Rafe Collins if you had another option. Very good." He extended a hand the shape and size of a small shovel, and Rafe took it. It was calloused and strong. "My name is Ezekiel Smith. People call me Zeke." He pulled a stool from a nearby table. "Is it all right with you if I set?"

Rafe nodded.

"I'm looking for drivers."

"What's your cargo?"

Zeke winked. "Two legged cattle."

"People?"

"Passengers, mail, and a little freight."

"My wagon won't accommodate passengers."

"We won't be needing your wagon." Zeke raised a hand, and Milagro headed his way with a bottle of whiskey and a glass. "Have you heard of John Butterfield?"

"The same John Butterfield who thinks he can run a stage line from St. Louis to San Francisco?"

Zeke's eyes took on an evangelistic glow. "It will be one of the great achievements of the age." He made a grand sweep with his arm, and Rafe rescued the tequila bottle just before he knocked it off the table.

"Think of it. A stage line that spans the continent twice a week. We'll cover almost two thousand and five hundred miles in twenty-five days, traveling a route of stage stations located twenty miles apart." Zeke's eyes glowed. "Two hundred and fifty coaches are being built as we speak. And tank wagons and stage stations with corrals and smithies. We're hiring drivers, conductors, station keepers, blacksmiths, mechanics, hostlers, herders, wainwrights, wheelwrights. Only the best. Butterfield insists on it. His motto is, 'The mail must go through.' When we finish, there will be two thousand men and two hundred stations along the line."

Rafe shook his head, surprised yet again at how mankind's follies could surprise him. "Did anyone mention to Mr. Butterfield how happy he will make the Apaches?"

"I beg your pardon?"

"I mean, he will provide them with a reliable source of plunder."

"Oh, yes—that." Zeke dismissed them with a wave of his hand. "Chief Cochise himself has agreed to supply wood for the station at Doubtful Pass."

"He did?" Rafe was more than astonished, he was "dumbfounded," as Absalom used to say.

"I've talked with the chief. I believe him to be a man of his word."

Rafe sat back in his chair. He wasn't considering the job. He was thinking of John Butterfield and men like him. Men who dreamed large. Men who weren't content with a single old Packard wagon and a span of mules. He had a moment's regret that his own horizons were limited to those encircling the vastness of New Mexico and Arizona Territory.

"I thank you for the offer."

"Then you accept?"

"I decline."

"But why, man? Did I mention that the pay is good?"

"No, thank you."

"You must have a reason."

"I don't reckon I want to work for any man."

"I see." Ezekiel Smith rose with a sigh. "If you change your mind, I'll be staying at Doña Margarita's on the plaza."

Rafe nodded and watched him stride toward the door. Dreaming a thing and making it a reality were quite different. Rafe didn't know about Butterfield, but he suspected if any man could build stage stations in the middle of Apache country he would be Ezekiel Smith.

Rafe went back to his conference with the tequila bottle while American voices rose steadily from the other side of the room. Through the haze of tobacco smoke, he made out several miners and a few lieutenants from the United States Army. Rafe could tell by the miners' drawl that most of them came from the South: Alabama, Georgia, Louisiana, the Carolinas, maybe. He deduced by the lieutenants' stubborn reliance on reason that they were recent West Point graduates.

"What do you mean I have to pay to send a letter?" The miner was outraged.

"The government says so." The lieutenant settled back in his chair and crossed his arms on his stomach, probably to bring attention to the brass buttons that were his badge of authority here.

"What the hell kind of newfangled notion is that?" a second miner put in. "Person at t'other end always pays fer the letter."

"Not anymore."

"When did this happen?"

"Three years ago."

"It's tyranny!"

The lieutenant tried to explain. "People refuse to accept

their letters, and the post office loses money. Has to return them to the sender at government expense."

"I ain't never re-fused a letter in my lifetime," said a third miner.

"Jesus, Rufus, you ain't never got a letter in your lifetime."

"Iff'n I did, I sure as hell wouldn't refuse it."

"If you did get one, you couldn't read it."

"No matter. If someone took a notion to write me, I wouldn't say no to their efforts."

The first miner got back to the real issue. "It's another way for the politicians to bleed honest citizens in order to pay for their highfalutin ways."

Rafe almost laughed out loud. One could look a long time and not stumble across an honest citizen in New Mexico Territory. He'd have to search a lifetime to find one in Arizona, on the other side of Doubtful Pass, where, he was astonished to learn, Cochise would be hauling wood for white men. Wonders would never cease.

The aggrieved letter-writer expanded on his theme. "It's like that damned tariff. Why should we pay tariffs on Northern goods so the Yankee manufacturers can live high on the hog whilst we root in the mud? It's taxation without representation, that's whut it is. We'uns done alriddy fit that battle."

Here it comes, Rafe thought. He took his bottle and shoved his chair farther back into the corner. He tilted it so he could lean against the wall and watch the fight that would surely erupt.

He had heard this argument before. Individual words cut through the general shouting. "Sovereignty of the states." "The unrestrained will of the majority perpetrating injustice against the minority." And the one Rafe heard most often, "Ain't no damned Yankees gonna tell us what to do with our darkies."

Rafe stayed aloof until Shadrach Rogers walked through the door. Apparently San Francisco had spit him out again and he had landed here. The debate turned into a loud hum. Everyone else went out of focus. Rafe stood up and, concentrating on each step, walked straight for him. He swung his left fist in a fast arc that ended at Rogers' ear. It got his attention, but it didn't knock him down.

With a curse at his own incompetence, Rafe grabbed him by the throat and threw him to the ground. Women screamed. Men started swinging at each other. Tables toppled. Bottles and stools took wing like startled birds.

Rafe saw only the bulge of Roger's boiled onion eyes. He heard only the gargle of him struggling to suck air past the fingers locked around his throat. Then Rafe felt a blow to the back of his head, and everything went black.

He woke up in heaven, or close to it. A woman's warm, naked body lay on top of him. He grunted, put his arms around her, and discovered he didn't have any clothes on either. He threw all his concentration into opening his eyes and ignoring the drumbeat of pain behind them. In the darkness he could only make out the pale curve of the wagon's new canvas cover arching over him. He heard a fiddle in the distance. Apparently the fight had ended at The Dove, and the dancing had begun.

Milagro murmured in his ear, sending a current of excitement the length and breadth of him. "How do you feel?"

"Like I've been through an ore crusher."

She giggled and began kissing him slowly and lightly on his neck and shoulders and chest. She paused in her survey of his body to whisper with her lips brushing his. "I can make you feel better."

Pain still crashed against the backs of his eyeballs, but Rafe began to feel better anyway. Part of him began to feel very good. He rolled over so that Milagro was under him and returned the kisses she had left on him.

He lost himself so completely in pain and passion that he almost didn't hear Red whinny, but he smelled the lantern oil. He raised up on his elbows.

He heard a splash against the canvas cover and saw the flare of a lucifer through the cloth. A whooshing sound followed it and men's laughter. The canvas burst into flames that lit the inside of the wagon.

"¡Ay, Dios! Milagro scrambled for the rear opening as the fire roared through the canvas and caught the dry wood of the wagon's bed.

Rafe grabbed the pouch with his book in it, a blanket, and his faded blue army pants. The heat intensified until he thought his brains would bake in his skull. He tried to push Milagro through the opening, but a rope tangled around her ankle and held her fast. A spark lit her hair and he threw the blanket over it. She screamed and clawed at it, trying to see, while he fumbled with the rope. He freed her, picked her up, and threw her out the back of the wagon. She landed on her feet, staggered forward, fell, and rolled clear. He jumped down after her.

He untied Red from the picket line and led him away from the inferno. At a distance, the night was chill. He draped the blanket around Milagro's shoulders, and she clutched it to her, shivering. He pulled on his trousers. With a grim fascination they stood under the glittering sweep of a night sky spangled with jewels, and watched the dancing flames devour everything except the metal fittings.

"Who would do this?" Milagro asked.

"I think I know who."

Leading Red, Rafe walked with her to her small room facing the rear courtyard of La Paloma. Then he mounted and rode Red to a narrow street off the main plaza where Doña Margarita kept a boardinghouse. Maybe Zeke Smith was still awake. Maybe the job offer would still stand.

Tomorrow, Rafe thought, I will look for Shadrach Rogers.

Chapter 21

DUCK!

The word *party* had magical properties. It made men appear where a clear-eyed observer would have sworn none existed. Or maybe the possibility of free food and whiskey lured them out—although how the word had spread to them, Rafe couldn't guess. Men had trickled out of the lilac haze draping the hills around the new stage station about twenty miles west of Doubtful Pass. More of them had trooped out of the desert, their silhouettes shimmying to the sprightly dirge of heat.

Most of them led mules or burros burdened with prospecting gear. Hairy and tattered and filthy, they looked as though they had spent the winter under the same rocks they hoped would produce their fortunes. They gathered at the new station to attend a party in honor of the stage line's owner, John Butterfield.

When the coach and Mr. Butterfield failed to arrive, the prospectors started the party without him. Many had brought their own concoctions fermented of everything from the rock-hard, brown Mexican sugar to the sap of the maguey plant and the buds of the mescal. One claimed to have distilled rattlesnake venom into a potion that would grow hair on the soles of the feet, but Rafe preferred the brew of a rancher named John Ward. Ward's whiskey was the only attribute that Rafe or anyone else appreciated about him. Ward intended to charge Mr. Butterfield far more than the going rate for it. By ten o'clock, most of the revelers had forgotten who Mr. Butterfield was.

Near the new stone station stood a ranch house where ten years before Red Sleeves and his warriors had killed the ten people who had lived there. Since then, Red Sleeves had tried to abide by his promises to Dr. Michael Steck or at least to only raid south of the border, but his young men were a different matter. Stock still disappeared. The Apaches were the reason Butterfield's man, Ezekiel Smith, had asked Rafe to take this leg of the route. The pass was prime country for them.

John Ward gestured with his whiskey jar toward the ranch house. "I know fer a fack that a duck's done built a nest under that thar building."

John Ward knew a lot of facts, but in Rafe's experience, few of them assayed out as truth. Rafe finished off the tin mug of Ward's whiskey. The fumes swirled like jig music.

He waved the mug at the cactus and scrub. "There are no ducks for five hundred miles."

" 'Cept the one under that house." Ward spoke with the contained fury of a circuit lecturer after someone has over-handed a rotten cabbage at his head.

He was not a man to tolerate contradiction when he was sober, much less when he wasn't. He had no softness any-where about him, not in the taut skin stretched over his pink skull, or in the bumpy ridge of his nose, or in lips like a folded barlow knife, or in the plow blade of scapula bones that pushed against his shirt, woven appropriately enough from the fleece of a black sheep or two.

"Hell, they ain't no ducks under there," spoke up someone from the crowd around the kegs.

"I'll bet a silver dollar they is," responded another.

A clamor rose as people placed their wagers.

"Felix, git over here." Ward beckoned to a boy of ten or so.

Dirty red hair hung to the boy's shoulders, and a shock of it covered his left eye, which looked perpetually upward. Apaches had captured his Mexican mother and, in spite of his red hair, some said one of them had fathered Felix. When he and his mother escaped from them, Ward had taken them in, but the arrangement couldn't have been much of an improvement in Feliz's lot. *Feliz* meant "happy" in Spanish. Happy, Feliz was not.

A rawhide thong held up a pair of his stepfather's castoff breeches. The hems dragged through the dust around his bare feet. He approached as though expecting his stepfather to strike him as soon as he got within reach.

"Crawl under yon hacienda and fetch that thar duck."

"They's rattlesnakes and scorpions under thar." The boy stepped back, certain now that he would get hit. John Ward raised a hand to oblige him.

Rafe stepped between them. "Let's have a look see."

Torches held aloft, the crowd surged across the ranch yard, with one of Ward's whiskey kegs riding the crest. They gathered in a crescent around the front of the house. The corners of the building sat on boulders that raised it a couple of feet off the gravelly soil. The black strip of night encircling it at ground level gave the impression that scorpions and rattlesnakes were the least of the evils under it.

"Let's pry off a few of them thar clapboards and see if we kin find the duck," someone suggested.

A cheer went up. While most of the crowd revived their strength with drink, some went back to the stage station for tools. Changing off as they grew weary or thirsty, the men worked by torchlight. By two in the morning the heap of lumber that had been the house burned merrily, illuminating its own destruction. Five headless rattlesnakes hung over the hitching rail beside the banjo picker.

Most of the wrecking crew lay asleep or passed out around the dooryard. One dark corner of the house remained, and the men who were still standing stared at the dog.

"By jimminy," one of the miners said. "The duck's got fur."

With feet planted apart and back a-bristle, the dog defended the shelter she had found there. Rafe moved closer and crouched for a look. Even in the predawn light and the shadows under the corner, he could see that she was a sturdy bundle of grit and gristle. She was snub nosed, savage eyed, and dust colored. She snarled at Rafe.

Two puppies milled and squeaked between her legs. Rafe wondered how the mother had dissuaded the rattlers from eating her young. She and the snakes must have arrived at some sort of uneasy armistice under the house. Or maybe these two were the survivors of a larger litter.

Rafe didn't see Ward aim his old revolver. He jumped when the pistol went off in his ear and the mother fell. Her legs jerked as though chasing a rabbit in her dreams, and then she lay still while the puppies struggled to crawl out from under her.

Rafe rounded on Ward, but the man was quick. He grabbed one of the puppies by the neck and squeezed, shaking him to and fro. Rafe picked up the remaining animal. Ward threw the dead puppy onto the fire and reached for the one Rafe held. He saw the look on Rafe's face, thought better of the plan, and turned away, muttering.

Sober as a stone now, Rafe walked through the litter of sleeping men, broken fence rails, rotting horse tack, and tilting grave markers. He could sleep a few hours with the puppy on the cot in the back room of the stage station before the stage coach arrived in the morning.

Shouting and a pistol shot woke him. Apaches! He grabbed his new shotgun and ran outside, but instead of Indians, he found that it was raining baggage and blowing invective. A carpetbag plummeted toward him as though it were packed with cannonballs. A pickax followed and buried itself in the bag.

The first Concord coach of the Butterfield's Overland Mail Company had arrived. At least three hundred men jostled and argued around it while the hostlers struggled to hitch the new team in the confusion. Some men threw their bags and satchels onto the rack atop the coach, and others tossed them down again. They accompanied all of it with swearing that would make a mule driver feel outclassed.

Rafe walked closer to inspect the coach. It was a beauty. It was made of the finest hickory, springy and tough, with steel fittings and axles. It was dark red, with a yellow-and-brown-striped undercarriage. A painting laid down in oils on the lower panel of the door depicted the desert, with slants of sunlight illuminating saguaro cacti against a sunset sky and lilac mountains. Rafe peered inside at the russet-colored leather upholstery and side curtains.

He stooped to inspect the wide leather thoroughbraces, heavy straps woven through the steel stanchions of the undercarriage. They lifted the coach above the axles and gave it a comfortable swing. It looked like the perfect vehicle, and Rafe knew it would never do. It was durable, yes, but cumbersome and top-heavy. A careless driver would turtle it at the first arroyo. Though the necessity pained him, he would have to suggest that Mr. Butterfield employ something lighter.

The riot finally caught Rafe's attention. The station manager had only recently arrived from Connecticut and was no bigger than a minute. The miners' lice received more of their notice than he did.

"What's the problem?" Rafe shouted in his ear.

"They've heard of that strike north of Gila City. They're all in a fever to go there."

Rafe had heard the stories, too, of nuggets weighing five hundred pounds, of gold enough to ransom all the kings the world could produce. Rafe went back into the station. He took a packet of stale soda crackers and a tin of powdered milk from the storeroom. They would have to do for the puppy. He added them to the woolen shirt and socks, the linen drawers, and the coat stuffed into his rucksack. He put the dog on top of the coat, gave her a piece of jerked beef to chew, and slung the rucksack over his shoulder.

He loaded his shotgun and walked outside. He picked up eleven stones, put them in his pocket, and climbed onto the driver's high seat. The conductor, Toomey, pushed his hat back and settled in next to him with his own shotgun across his knees and his bugle in hand.

Perched above the fray, Rafe fired into the air. When he had everyone's attention, he heaved the rocks at the eleven men who looked least likely to cause trouble. His aim was as good as his judgment.

The chosen cursed him, but he said in a voice just loud enough for everyone to hear, "Those men are going. The rest of you stand back." When the rejects began objecting, Rafe aimed his revolver at them. "Mr. Butterfield said that nothing on God's earth must stop the United States mail, and I'll shoot any son of a bitch who delays it."

He returned the pistol to his belt. "While I throw the baggage off the left side, you eleven men hand your things up to Toomey on the right. If we aren't loaded by the time I finish Hamlet's speech, what's on the ground stays there."

Reciting "To be or not to be," he began heaving boxes and trunks overboard. Men dodged into the fall of luggage to retrieve their things. Rafe worked steadily in rhythm with the words of the soliloquy. He stowed the heavy canvas mailbags with something like reverence. He thought of all those letters scattering the breadth of the country with their tidings glad and sorrowful, official and intensely private. Carrying nails and lumber, corn and salt pork was a living. Delivering the mail was a calling.

He reached the last lines of the speech as he and Toomey pulled the oiled tarpaulin over the heap of trunks and lashed it down.

And enterprises of great pith and moment
With this regard their currents turn awry.
And lose the name of action.

He was so intent on his work that he didn't notice the silence that had fallen below him until he tightened the last knot and spoke the last word. He looked down to see the men staring up at him. Most surprising of all was that his audience now included a tall, handsome Apache and a shorter, stouter man who bore a resemblance to him.

Rafe recognized the tall Indian as Cochise. The other one was the chief's brother, Coyundado. In the distance stood three Apache women with mules piled high with mesquite branches. True to his word Cochise had delivered the firewood for which he had contracted.

The sight of him made Rafe feel better. He would be passing through Cochise's territory. He saluted Cochise, and the chief and his brother saluted back in crisp military fashion. They looked solemn as a brace of chickens on a roost, as Absalom used to say. Then the corners of Cochise's sinuous mouth twitched in a smile so fleeting and rare that Rafe assumed he was mistaken in thinking he saw it.

Well, he thought, I guess we do seem a mite peculiar to you, Chief.

He set the rucksack at his feet and rolled back the top of it so the puppy could see out. Rafe looked at the new day from the height of the driver's seat of this most amazing coach. A sense of exhilaration raised the hair on his arms and started his heart like a quarterhorse with a fast field behind him.

Rafe had always sworn he would never work for any man, but then Rogers burned his wagon and vanished again. Some said Rogers had heard Rafe was hunting him and had hightailed it for Mexico, as if the Mexicans didn't have troubles enough. In any case, he left Rafe little choice but to take this job.

If Rafe was going to work for any man, Butterfield was the one. Delivering the mail from Memphis to San Francisco twice a week safely and on time—that was a notion only a lunatic would promise. In less than a year, though, Butterfield's surveyors, engineers, and pick-and-shovel men had cleared roads, leveled riverbanks at fords, constructed bridges, sunk wells, and built stage stations. They had done it in blistering heat, under the threat of death by thirst and Indian attacks. Butterfield promised to get the mail through on time. Rafe intended to fulfill his part of the bargain.

He picked up the six reins, each held singly between his fingers, the three from the animals on the near side in his left hand, the offside ones in his right. As always, he felt the power of the horses surge along them, flow into his fingers and up his arms, spread into his chest, and then outward through his entire body.

"Git along there, boys." With a flick of his wrists he gave the reins a hard snap, and the coach lurched foward.

The men cheered, and Rafe wondered what Cochise was really up to.

Chapter 22

PASSED OVER

Broken Foot sat on a blanket in the shade, along with Victorio, Skinny, Loco, He Steals Love, and a few others. Broken Foot had just sent the apprentices off on a race to the top of a nearby peak and back. Talks A Lot would probably run himself half to death rather than allow Lozen to pass him. Loco had counted on that when he bet his piebald pony on him.

"Letting your sister come on this raid was a good idea." Broken Foot ripped a page from the Bible and rolled tobacco in it. He had stolen cattle from the same Mexican priest who had involuntarily supplied the Bible. He licked the edge of the paper to seal it into a cigarillo. "The boys are working twice as hard as usual."

"They're better behaved, too." Loco lifted the bear-ravaged lid of his right eye to see them more clearly as they scrambled up the rocky slope.

Broken Foot and Loco were right. When Talks A Lot, Flies In His Stew, Chato, and the others weren't bent double under loads of wood and toting two water jugs each, they were waiting to be sent on an errand. They didn't grumble about tending the fire or cooking or having to eat whatever was left after the men finished. They raced off across the desert or up a steep slope whenever ordered to. They were careful to use the special words reserved for the war trail. This was supposed to be a raid on the Bluecoats' horses and mules, but it could easily turn into a battle.

They listened attentively to Victorio's instructions. "Do not lie in the shade. Enemies will look for you there. Do not turn quickly to look back. That brings bad luck. Do not sleep until given permission."

Lozen had always competed with the boys, but now she was doing it where the men could watch and judge. She was amused to see the effect of that. The pain of Gray Ghost's departure eased like a healing wound as Lozen stared into the fire at night. The salve for it was the sound of the men's talk, and the privilege of hearing the stories they told only among themselves, in the language reserved for them. She had discovered a world that she never would have known if she had stayed with the women in camp.

She paced the boys in the races. She blew the first embers into flames in the morning. She rolled up in her blanket after everyone else had gone to sleep. She didn't speak unless spoken to. And worst of all, she cooked better than any of them.

None of that surprised Broken Foot. What did surprise him was that the boys didn't resent her as much as he had expected. They had known her a long time. They were used to her. They all wore amulets that she had made for them, charms to give them keener sight and make horses docile for them.

What the boys envied and resented was not that Lozen had invaded their world, but that the spirits had given her magic, and quantities of it. Worse, she used it with the dignity, generosity, and serenity of someone three times her age. If it occurred to them that that was the reason the spirits gave her such gifts, they didn't admit it.

BROKEN FOOT WAS WAITING AT DAWN WHEN THE ARROW-head of geese appeared at the horizon, their faint, rackety honks announcing the arrival of spring. Broken Foot thought their song the most awesome of all the sounds in the world. They were calling to him, inviting him to come north with them. He lifted his chin, spread his arms out from his sides, and imagined joining them in flight.

If he could fly, his shriveled leg wouldn't matter. If he

could fly, maybe the warriors would have voted him leader of the Warm Springs band yesterday after Skinny announced that he was giving up the position. Everyone agreed that Broken Foot was brave, experienced, and wise. They knew his Goose magic made him tireless and strong. They came to him for advice, for war medicine, for ceremonial sings, and for amulets. In spite of that, they chose a younger man, a handsomer, more vigorous man, one who drew people to him with the quiet force of his character. They chose Victorio.

Broken Foot loved Victorio as a son. He admired him as a warrior and respected him as a man. Broken Foot knew Victorio deserved the honor, but he had thought he himself had a chance in spite of his limp. The men of the Enemy People to the south had elected Long Neck as their leader, even though he stuttered so profoundly he had others speak in council for him. Crook Neck's head canted at an acute angle, but the Mescaleros to the north picked him to lead them. A crippled leg, though, that was different.

At least, Broken Foot thought with a grim smile, he had a reason for not being chosen. The warriors passed over Loco, too, and his only physical defect was his scarred face and his bear's temper. At Broken Foot's urging, Victorio had chosen Loco as his second, but Broken Foot knew that was small consolation for him.

In his cap covered with goose feathers, Broken Foot looked like a large, ungainly bird himself. He had increased the resemblance by painting a broad, black band across his cheeks, nose, and eyes, forehead and temples. He had painted the lower half of his face and his neck white following the curve of his jaw.

The annual flight of the geese always awed Broken Foot. Each spring they left from farther south than any of The People had traveled. They passed over this country and flew to a land where, Broken Foot had heard, the snow never melted, not even in the low country. In the fall, they reversed directions and did it again with their young trailing them. Many birds traveled with the seasons, but in Broken Foot's opinion, the geese were the most powerful flyers. As they soared overhead Broken Foot sang to them, asking them to share their stamina with him.

When their calls faded, he climbed down from the flat rock jutting out over the water. He limped to the cottonwood grove where the women were pulling the hide coverings off their lodges and folding them. They had banked the fires and stacked the bed frames. They were preparing for the annual trading trip to Alamosa.

He had to pass She Moves Like Water's camp to reach that of his wives, and Grandmother set a gourd of soup on a log for him. The last handful of acorn meal thickened it a little. Potatoes bobbed in it, and a few early onions. Grandmother went back to packing utensils and old blankets onto her pony. Lozen and María folded the hides from Grandmother's lodge. Six years of wind, rain, and hot sun had long since torn and rotted the canvas Victorio had taken from Hairy Foot's wagon in the Jornado del Muerto.

Corn Stalk and She Moves Like Water loaded the pouches of dried meat and bundles of tanned hides onto the family's last mule. Winter, the season of Ghost Face, had camped long and cold with them. Many of the Warm Spring horses and mules had ended up simmering in the rusting kettles or roasting over the cookfires. Few of them were left for trading, and more of the people would be making the trip to the Mexican town of Alamosa on foot. Still, everyone looked forward to the spring outing.

Victorio's child was eight now and looking more like her father every day. When she saw Broken Foot approaching with the limp that gave him a goose's rolling gait, she formed her friends into the geese's flying formation. With arms outspread, she led them toward him. Honking like a goose, she veered this way and that, and they followed her lead, imitating the flight of the birds.

Broken Foot craned his thin neck and jutted his bony chin. He crouched and snaked his head from side to side. He draped his blanket across his shoulders, grasped the corners, and fluttered them like gray wings. He rose to his full height.

He stretched the blanket out as far as it would go, flapped it, and hissed.

The children had played this game before. They screamed and scattered. Broken Foot chased them among the women. He hissed, flapped, and pretended to peck at them, and at the women, too. They laughed and swatted at him with whatever they were holding.

The sun hadn't been up long when the women hoisted their burden baskets and cradleboards onto their backs. Those who were riding put the cradles' straps over the pommels so they hung at their mounts' sides. From there the babies could stare wide-eyed at the passing scenery until the rhythm of the horses lulled them to sleep. Older children clambered in twos and threes and fours onto the backs of the family ponies. The herd boys chivvied the stock into place at the rear. The men took up positions along the flanks.

The column of horses, mules, and walkers started toward the opening in the cliff where the stream passed through. Usually Skinny led it, but now Victorio rode at the head with his family. If Loco was angry that the council had passed him over for the position of chief, he gave no hint of it. He closed his eyes and napped as he rode.

Stands Alone and He Makes Them Laugh joined Lozen, and soon they put her in better spirits. Loco and Broken Foot weren't the only ones passed over in council. The warriors had voted Talks A Lot, Ears So Big, Chato, and Flies In His Stew to the rank of warrior. Even though Lozen had served as an apprentice on seven horse-stealing expeditions, no one had suggested making her a warrior. She wasn't disappointed because she didn't expect it.

People came to her with problems. They called her by the affectionate name of Grandmother. Warm Springs men asked her to look for enemies before they headed out on raids. In Alamosa, the Mexicans would seek her help in breaking wild mustangs. They knew she could make a horse docile without harming it.

Lozen was glad to be included on horse-stealing expeditions now and then. That was privilege enough. Women had to be able to defend their families when the men were away. They learned to ride well and to shoot accurately; but now Lozen realized that She Moves Like Water was right. They did not become warriors.

Chapter 23

TOO MUCH OF NOT ENOUGH

The last day of December blew sleet like a swarm of ice arrows down the narrow canyon and into Rafe's face. The year 1860 wasn't leaving without a fight. Rafe pulled down his hat, shifted the collar of his faded army greatcoat up around his ears, and slouched lower on the seat of the light coach called a celerity. Slouching didn't make his high perch any warmer. The five passengers had lowered the canvas curtains over the open sides, and Rafe envied them that small protection.

One or more of the passengers must have brought a supply of whiskey, because the voices coming from inside the coach grew steadily louder and more contentious. Rafe sighed. They had looked a hard lot when they boarded.

The hardest of them was a barrel-chested, basset-eyed fop with drooping side-whiskers called Picadilly weepers framing his square jowls. He wore a plug-hat, patent-leather half-boots, and the newfangled arrangement of matching wool vest, coat, and trousers. Rafe pegged him for a troublemaker. He hadn't proved Rafe wrong.

None of the passengers had elected to ride on top of the coach today, but Rafe's dog did. She sat with her head up, a lacework of icicles dangling from her muzzle. He had named her Patch, short for Apache. He hoped she had a nose for her namesake, although today she would have to wait for the odors to melt to smell them. She probably couldn't even detect the cheap cologne that the guard, Toomey, wore. The aroma reminded Rafe of a dead possum rotting under a jasmine bush.

Toomey had gone the whole hog with the Butterfield look.

The same clothes he wore today hung in the window of every general merchandise store from Memphis to Tucson. The style's namesake had never gotten closer than Arkansas, but one couldn't fling a dead rooster in Tucson and not hit a John Butterfield.

Toomey had pulled the legs of his pantaloons down over the tops of the high leather boots, as Butterfield did. It was a style that defeated the boots' purpose in this thorny country, but vanity would win over practicality most of the time. In warmer weather Toomey wore Butterfield's calf-length yellow linen duster, silk cravat, and starched, white linen shirt. Now, however, he had on a coat made from a bison hide worn fur-side out. Rafe felt as though he were sitting next to the bison itself, though a bison would have smelled better, been more predictable, and more amusing company besides.

Butterfield's flat-crowned hat covered the bald spot that captured more of Toomey's cranial real estate each month. If Rafe ever needed a hat himself, he had only to ride along the route of the Butterfield stage and choose one. The trail was littered with them.

Toomey shouted over the wail of the wind. "Have you ever plugged an Apache woman, Collins?"

Rafe almost wished the man had kept himself occupied shooting at everything that moved, and some things that didn't. Toomey was partial to blasting small birds with his shotgun and shattering cacti into green mist.

Rafe shook his head and stared at the horses' rumps. The thought of bedding an Apache woman hadn't occurred to him. He had seen women of other tribes in the establishments he frequented, but he'd never known anyone to take an Apache except by force. From what he had observed, Apache women were surprisingly demure. Except for that minx of a horse thief, he amended. She was not like any Indian woman, or any woman of any race for that matter, but she was not what he would call flirtatious. He would as soon court an irate badger as woo her.

"I know they's standoffish as a rule," Toomey said, "but

I hear if you can get one liquored up, she'll teach your doodle to dance, and no mistake."

Doodle? Rafe almost laughed in spite of his sour mood. Did they call it a doodle in San Francisco, where Toomey came from? Did Toomey's fellow members of the Committee of Vigilance refer to their doodles?

To Rafe's relief, the canyon opened out, and sunlight warmed the wind's chill, although it still blew with enough rancor to keep him turtled inside his greatcoat. Maybe Rafe was trying to insulate himself from Toomey and the rising storm of passengers inside the coach. He knew that when Toomey got the bit in his mouth on the subject of women, he could neither be stopped nor turned, so the sight of half a dozen Apaches driving about twenty head of cattle cheered him up. They would distract Toomey. All Rafe had to do was make sure Toomey and his Henry rifle didn't start a war right here, right now.

The Apaches were approaching the trail at an angle and heading northeast. Toomey loaded the shotgun and his two pistols and put them at half-cock. His Henry stayed loaded all the time. As they came into range, Toomey raised the Henry and sighted on the man in the lead.

"Put that down," Rafe said.

"Between us we have enough pills to make them all mightily sick."

"Put it down but keep it handy."

Toomey set the rifle alongside the shotgun resting across his thighs. The game he enjoyed hunting more than anything else was the two-legged kind. He often bragged about bagging greasers and maybe murderers back in California. For variety, the members of the Committee of Vigilance hung some of the cuplrits, or innocent men. Whatever.

Rafe leaned out to the side. He had to shout several times before a hand pulled back the canvas curtain, and the plug hat and Picadilly weepers poked out and tilted to look up at him. The bulging eyes below the hat's brim and above the weepers had gone from shifty to unfocused.

"A party of Indians is approaching," Rafe said. "They

don't look to be on the warpath but keep your pieces ready. Do not fire unless I tell you to."

The man poked his pistols out anyway and began waving them. Rafe put all six reins in one hand and took the whip from its boot. He snapped it with a loud crack so that the tip grazed the man's hand. The plug hat withdrew abruptly, and Rafe shouted after him.

"Fire those without my say-so, and I shall make you wish you hadn't." He turned forward again. "If the 'Pache don't kill us all first," he muttered.

The Apaches made no effort to avoid the coach's path, or to interfere with it. Rafe halted the horses and watched the cattle and their rag-and-bone escort cross the trail about fifty feet ahead of him. They were dressed as usual except for one. A boy in homespun pantaloons and the rags of a shirt rode behind the leader. He turned to look at Rafe as he passed. If Rafe had had any doubts about his identity, the red hair hanging from beneath his old hat and the upward cast to his left eye would have dispelled them.

Rafe didn't believe in interfering with other people's business, but maybe the Indians had taken the boy against his will. Felix Ward wasn't worth saving for the benefit of civilized society any more than his stepfather, John Ward, was; but getting him away from his captors now might avoid a heap more trouble later. Rafe wasn't prepared to fight for the lad, but he would try to trade for him.

"Felix Ward," he called out. "Do you want to come with us?"

The boy glanced at him, and the sullen expression never changed. He looked away as though he had heard nothing. Rafe and Toomey watched the procession head off into the mountains.

"Cain't blame the boy for quitting John Ward's company," Toomey observed. "I knew Ward in California. The Committee cast him off for bad behavior."

Rafe chuckled at the notion. How low would a man have to sink to be rejected by the San Francisco Vigilance Committee? In any case, Felix Ward was well gone, and no one would miss him, least of all his not-quite-stepfather.

Rafe hadn't time to ponder the situation any further. The heat of Plug Hat's temper had brought the contention in the coach to a full boil. The canvas sides flew up, and men spilled out of them in a roil of fists and heels and oaths. Rafe was tempted to drive on and leave them, but he pulled the horses to a halt.

All he needed was for one of them to develop the "starts." The starts were the demented fits that frequently overcame passengers deprived for weeks of sleep and subjected to the fear of attacks by Comanches or Apaches. The fits usually occurred when a passenger did fall asleep, only to be wakened suddenly by noise or jostling.

Imagining himself to be under attack, the afflicted one lashed out at his fellow passengers. Rafe had also known them to jump down from the coach and hightail it off into the desert.

He decided then and there to drive for Butterfield only until he saved enough money to buy a wagon of his own. He would return to hauling freight. The salt pork and corn might harbor worms and weevils, but at least they were quiet.

RAFE'S LEG OF THE BUTTERFIELD ROUTE ENDED HERE AT the stone stage station at Siphon Canyon. The canyon was one of the many that formed the six-mile-long cleft dividing the Dos Cabezas and the Chiricahua mountains. Americans called the long defile Doubtful Pass. The Mexicans had named it Paso del Dado, the Pass of the Die. *Die* in this case meant the singular of dice. It carried the sense of risk, of chance, of taunting fate. What made it chancy were the Chiricahua Apaches who had preyed on travelers here for centuries.

Covered with alkali dust, Rafe took a bucket to the spring. He stripped in the bitter February cold, and sluiced water over himself, dancing to keep warm. He dried off with some sacking and dressed; then he slept on the bunk in the back room for a few hours. When he woke up, he had time on his hands.

The westbound stage wasn't due for two days.

He volunteered to help Jim Wallace deliver corn and salt beef to the troops bivouacked over the ridge and downslope from the station. Jim was the best driver Rafe had ever met. He was a soft-spoken sensible sort whose only noticeable point of pride was a large front tooth of gold. He had dark, wavy hair slicked back, and the lean, scarred body and hands of a man who had survived here for twenty years. He spoke a little Apache, and he often shared tobacco with Cochise. He was the one who had persuaded Cochise to supply wood for the station.

Rafe also came along because Wallace had mentioned that Cochise would be here. Cochise had become famous among Indians, Anglos, and Mexicans alike. People said that a look or a word from him could subdue the most fractious of his followers.

When Rafe and Wallace finished unloading the barrels at the cook tent, Patch set about clearing the area of rabbits while Rafe hunkered by the stream. He broke the thin crust of ice and scooped up the icy water. He looked glumly at the thirty or so tents set in neat rows. He should have been relieved to see the infantry arrive, but he wasn't.

In Rafe's opinion, the neighborhood went into a steep decline when Second Lt. George Bascom arrived. Rafe had disliked him the instant he strode into the station to introduce himself to Wallace. In Bascom's close-set blue eyes Rafe could see the cold fire of ambition, but no spark of intelligence. Wallace summed Bascom up when he observed, "The lieutenant's got too much of not enough."

Bascom had not the wit to distinguish shades of good and evil. For him the world was neatly divided between those who agreed with him and were right, and those who didn't and were wrong. Baby fat tautened his sleek, pink cheeks. He cultivated a wedge-shaped beard, maybe to disguise the fact that his Creator ran short on materials when He reached Bascom's chin. The lieutenant reminded Rafe of a salamander lurking in river grass. He started referring to him as The Newt.

The weather didn't lighten Rafe's mood. The ceiling of iron-gray clouds drooped with the weight of snow, making the sun's light look like dusk rather than early afternoon. The surrounding peaks seemed to press closer in menace.

Rafe assessed the ponies tethered outside Bascom's tent. They had Apache saddles and bridles with the usual oddments of feathers and claws and beading attached. Even though he knew Lozen's mare wouldn't likely be among them, he looked for her anyway. He wondered what mischief she was up to.

"I have a bad feeling about this soiree of Bascom's." Rafe climbed up to sit next to Wallace on the wagon seat.

"The chief brought his wife and a couple kids, his brother, and two nephews with him." Wallace handed Rafe a canteen of whiskey. The silky liquid warmed Rafe's throat as it went down. "He wouldn't be planning any trouble with his wife and little ones along."

"I'm not worried about Cochise." Rafe felt an unease stir just above his belt buckle. "What do you reckon Bascom's up to?"

"He says he and his men are passing through, and he wanted to visit with the chief. They've probably finished dinner and are drinking coffee right about now. I told Bascom that the chief's partial to coffee."

"Bascom's not the hospitable type."

Wallace shrugged. "John Ward's been raising holy Moses about the theft of his cattle and that kid. Maybe Ward wants the soldiers to fetch them, and Bascom thinks Cochise can help him do it."

"Ward doesn't care about that boy." Rafe's unease festered into foreboding.

"A kidnapping will set the army into action faster than a few missing steers. Hell, everybody around here has come up short in their steer inventory, thanks to the 'Pache and the Mex banditti. I imagine Ward's sorry they didn't kill Felix. That would have gotten the army's attention even faster."

"Cochise had nothing to do with any of it. I saw Felix

with the Indians who probably took the cattle. They were headed north, and they had on moccasins like those the White Mountain tribe wears. The boy didn't look kidnapped to me."

"Maybe you should tell Bascom that."

"Reckon I will." But Rafe could see that he was already too late. As though watching a runaway team careen toward a cliff's edge, he saw the fifty-four soldiers of Bascom's command load their rifles and take up positions around the tent. The soldiers tensed when they heard shouting from inside it.

"That shavetail is doing something stupid," Wallace said.

A knife blade appeared through the tent wall and glided downward. A large, brown hand gripping a tin coffee mug pushed through the opening. Cochise leaped out just behind the mug. He dodged through the astonished soldiers and sprinted into the creosote bushes behind the tent. He zig-zagged up the slope as though running fresh and well-hayed on a level straightaway. The soldiers opened fire, fifty rounds at least by Rafe's reckoning. Cochise, who must have been fifty years old, never slowed down. The last Rafe saw of him, he still gripped the mug.

"Hell-fire! You damned dunderheads!" With arms waving and eyes a-bulge, Bascom rushed out in a spray of spittal, oaths, and orders. "Hold these savages prisoner. Cochise'll return that boy or pay dearly. By God, I'll show the filthy heathen who's in charge."

Wallace swore steadily under his breath. In a workmanlike manner, he attributed to Bascom the same lineage and wished him the same fate as his most intractable mules.

Rafe blew out his breath in exasperation. The damned fool has dragged us all feet-first into the fire now, he thought.

Chapter 24

"SHE WALKS IN BEAUTY"

A high stone wall extended out from the stage station and enclosed the stalls where the horses were kept. Each stall had a loophole at the end of it, and Rafe, Jim Wallace, and the station's hostler peered through them at the Apaches outlined against the gunbarrel-gray sky at the crest of the hill.

Bascom's sergeant, John Mott, joined Rafe at his loophole. Mott was probably no more than thirty years old, about Rafe's age, but he looked ten years more than that. Years in the sun had tanned his face and hands to the texture of saddle leather. Squint lines radiated out from his pale gray eyes. Rafe was relieved to see him among Bascom's green troops.

Bascom expected an attack from Cochise, so he had moved his camp to just outside the walls. Rafe could have spit and almost hit the lieutenant's tent, the rip in its side sewn up with large, uneven stitches. It reminded Rafe of a wound that wouldn't heal any time soon.

Leave it to The Newt to locate his tipi the closest to the walls, Rafe thought.

Cochise and his men had appeared on the hill an hour or so ago. At the sight of them, Bascom and his command had crowded inside the gate. Now the station's yard teemed with soldiers and mules.

"The Newt looks pale as a bleached shirt, don't he?" said Wallace.

Neither Rafe nor Wallace worried about their immediate safety. They knew that no sane Apache would attack a fortified position, not even if they outnumbered the defenders, which in this case they certainly did. But they could not convince the lieutenant of that. He rushed around, giving his men one order, then changing his mind on the next pass, and issuing a conflicting one.

"The chief's carrying a white flag," Sergeant Mott called out. "He wants to parley."

With the white cloth flapping in the cold wind, Cochise and three of his men walked down the hill toward the station. They stopped just out of rifle range and waited. The sergeant took a large white handkerchief from the front of his tunic and tied it onto a guidon pole.

"The lieutenant must be shitting his breeches just about now," Jim Wallace observed to Rafe.

For a few moments Rafe thought Bascom would order his men to fire on Cochise and his delegation. Instead, he selected a corporal and two privates to go with him. He ignored Wallace, who spoke a little Apache, and Rafe and the sergeant, who were the only other ones with any knowledge of them. Rafe knew why. Bascom could not abide anyone who was more competent than he was. That narrowed his society to just about zero.

Sergeant Mott spoke to Bascom before he handed him the white flag. Bascom cut him off with a wave of his hand, turned, and stalked away.

"What did you say?" Wallace asked when the sergeant rejoined him and Rafe on the bench.

"I told him if he wants to avoid a war bloodier than he can imagine, he must release the hostages. I told him he can rely on Cochise to keep his word and work to get Felix Ward and the cattle back. Was I right about the chief keeping his word?"

Both Rafe and Jim Wallace nodded.

"Bascom said he would give them their freedom when the boy is restored." Sergeant Mott hitched up his belt and crossed his arms over his chest. "I reckon he thinks that even if Cochise didn't snatch the lad himself, he can make all them brunets jig to his tune."

"Shit," Wallace breathed softly. " 'Pache don't jig to nobody's tune but their own."

From the blacksmith shop where the Apache prisoners were locked up, Cochise's brother, Ox, began chanting in a high, loud voice. The soldiers crowded around the loopholes so they could watch the parley. Rafe, Wallace, the hostler, and Sergeant Mott had already selected holes with a view of Cochise's face. Bascom's face didn't matter. For all his gold braid and bluster, he was helpless as well as powerless, and Rafe knew it. Wallace knew it. The sergeant knew it. The hostler knew it. Cochise was the one who would decide whether they lived or died here. The irony was that Cochise's decision, and everyone's lives, depended on what Bascom said and did.

They could tell that the talks were going badly. Jim Wallace swore under his breath.

"I can't let him get us slaughtered." Wallace unbuckled the belt that held his holster.

"I'll come with you," Rafe said.

"I'll go, too." The hostler took the pistol from the back of his trouser belt and hung it by its lanyard on the peg with Wallace's.

Rafe added his Colt revolvers to them, but he didn't feel good about it. He studied the bushes and rocks and the shallow ravine that lay along the route to the hill. From here he could see almost to the bottom of the ravine. Nothing stirred there. Rafe remembered Wallace's advice about driving a stage. "When you see Apaches, be careful. When you don't see Apaches, be more careful."

The big iron hinges squealed as two soldiers pulled the doors ajar. Rafe scratched Patch's ears and told her to wait for him. She sat with her ears cocked, eyes intent until the closing gate blocked her sight of him.

Rafe, Jim, and the hostler started across the broken ground. They had passed the midpoint when nine half-naked warriors appeared over the rim of the ravine. They alarmed Rafe, but they didn't surprise him. He should have known the Apaches had performed their invisibility act. He whirled and sprinted toward the high stone wall that seemed to have moved itself considerably farther away since he left it.

Bullets whined past him from at least three directions. He heard Jim Wallace shout for help. Rafe didn't slow down. If the Apaches had gotten Wallace, Rafe knew he could be of no use without his pistols.

He had almost reached the wall when the lead ball hit him like the flat of a hand shoving against his left shoulder blade. The force of it knocked him off balance. He tripped on a rock and pitched forward. He felt the grittiness of the sand against his cheek and in his mouth, but no pain from his back, only a spreading numbness. He got halfway to his feet again when Bascom pelted past and knocked him down. Neither he nor the three soldiers with him offered to help.

Rafe lay with eyes closed, the stones pressing into his cheek, and prepared to attempt verticality again. When a pair of hands grabbed him under the arms, he tried to fight them off. He wondered how he could kill himself before the Apaches did it in their own, leisurely way.

Then he saw the iron tips of Sergeant Mott's boots at nose level. He felt Patch licking his face. The sergeant hauled him to his feet and half supported him, half dragged him toward the gate.

He saw the hostler make a run at the far end of the stone wall and scramble up it. A soldier's head and shoulders popped up at the top of the wall, fired straight down into his face, and then disappeared. The hostler fell backwards and lay still. Rafe, Patch, and Sergeant Mott slipped through the gates before the soldiers slid the big bolt home.

"Jim Wallace?" he asked.

"The hostiles got him," Mott said.

Rafe swayed, leaned his back against the wall, realized that the contact hurt, a lot, and slid down it, anyway. His last thought, before he went unconscious from loss of blood, was bitter disappointment that the Apaches hadn't killed George Bascom.

SHE WORE ONLY A BREECHCLOUT AND MOONLIGHT. LIKE war paint, the moon's silvery glow outlined the straight ridge of her nose and the curves of her high cheekbones. It lay in an arch across the top of each taut, upturned breast. Her hair floated in a midnight forest around her. Rafe ached to wander into that wilderness and never come out.

"Lozen." He didn't know if he said it aloud or not. He did know that he was naked, unarmed, and defenseless, and he didn't care.

"She walks in beauty. . . ." He was surprised he remembered the poem. He couldn't remember from which army officer he had learned it or who had written it. "She walks in beauty like the night / Of cloudless climes and starry skies; / And all that's best of dark and bright / Meet in her aspect and her eyes."

She smiled like a desert sunrise, bright and lovely, but with the certainty of misery and devilment to come, and more heat than a man could bear. He walked toward her, unable to stop himself even if he'd wanted to. She put a hand to her waist and the breechclout fell away.

Dear Lord, he thought, she's more beautiful than any woman has a right to be.

He walked into the fortress of her arms and into the fragrance of smoke and sage and horses. He cupped her breasts in his palms, lowered his head and kissed them. She pulled him to her, and he put his arms around her. He kissed her neck and shoulder. Passion so addled him that the boundaries of his body vanished. He could not have said where her skin and his touched. His skin became her skin. When he kissed her, his mouth melded with her soft, full one. His bones became hers, his desire hers.

When he entered her, her muscles tightened around him as though she held him in her strong hand, and squeezed with a slow, tantalizing rhythm. He thought the heat inside her would sear him. He thought the exaltation that flooded him would drain the life out of him. Then he stopped thinking.

With unconcern, he saw her big knife flash in the moonlight. He felt the flat of its tip a cold triangle under his ear. He tilted his head back to expose his neck to her.

The old Navajo song, *Yeibichai*, the "Prayer of the Night Chant," echoed in his head.

May it be beautiful before me.
May it be beautiful behind me.
May it be beautiful below me.
May it be beautiful above me.
May it be beautiful all around me.
In beauty it is finished.

He felt the blade slice like a caress across his throat while she smiled at him, bewitching, beguiling. He died and climaxed at the same time in a spate of warm blood and hot semen. Death was worth it.

With a grunt he woke up, heart pounding and body drenched in sweat despite the cold air. The cot's blankets twisted around him in a clammy knot. His arm and shoulder throbbed with an ache that penetrated his bones. His cock throbbed, too, but it was already slumping from the perpendicular. He lay shaken and panting from the dream.

"She walks in beauty like the night. . . ." He had dreamed of Lozen before, but never like this. He looked around in the pale light. He remembered that he was in the storeroom next to the station manager's office. Lieutenant Bascom had established his quarters in the office, and Rafe could hear him and Sergeant Mott arguing there. Rafe could hear mules braying outside, too. From the pitch of their complaints he could tell what was bothering them.

He tried to say, "The mules need water," but his own mouth was dry as dust and all that came out was "water." It didn't matter. No one could have heard him over the argument, anyway.

"That misguided fool, Michael Steck, has coddled the savages." Bascom's shouting reminded Rafe of the mules' braying. "With the connivance of the government, he's made pets of them while they murder and plunder at will. It's time to teach them a lesson."

The sergeant spoke too low for Rafe to hear everything

he said, but "Damn fool," and "West Point jackass" did filter through the thin planks of the wall.

"Corporal," Bascom shrieked, "Arrest this man for insubordination."

Moments later the door of Rafe's room slammed open, and four soldiers propelled John Mott through it. They locked manacles on his wrists and ankles and fastened the long chains to a beam overhead.

They left, and the sergeant looked Rafe up and down. "Son, you've got the hoofmarks of the nightmare all over you."

"I feel like I've been rode hard and put away wet, all right." Rafe wondered if he had said anything aloud while he dreamed of Lozen, but he was too embarrassed to ask. He glanced toward the wall that separated them from Bascom. "What happened?"

"Cochise brought your friend Wallace to trade for his kin. Led him on a rope like a mule to that hill outside. He looked unharmed."

"Bascom won't trade for him?"

"Nope. The chief is being remarkably patient, though."

"He wants his family back."

"I reckon. This morning he left a note on the hill."

"What did it say?"

"Don't know. Bascom won't let anyone retrieve it." The sergeant managed to unhook the canteen from his belt with both manacled hands, and in a rattle of chains he slid it across the floor. Rafe hung off the edge of the cot and almost fell into an eddy of his own frailty. He snagged the canteen by its lanyard. It hadn't much water left in it.

"Water's rationed." The sergeant leaned his head against the wall. "I had to dig the bullet out of your withers with a spade," he added in a wry tone. "The lead ball had spread, of course. You didn't like it much."

"I remember."

"You were a might feverish afterward, from the putrefaction. I put some maggots in the wound. They cleaned it out."

Mott gave Rafe a sideways look as wry as his tone. "We have a generous supply of maggots."

"I thank you." Then he remembered the mules braying and what Mott had said. "Rationing water? How long has it been?"

"Three days."

Rafe remembered that the spring was almost a third of a mile away, at the head of that ravine where the Apaches jumped him. He raised himself on his elbows, sat up, and slung the sergeant's canteen over his good shoulder. He managed to swing his legs off the edge of the cot and teeter there, as though perched over an abyss. He waited for the room to stop jigging before he stood up, ignoring the pain in his shoulder which the sergeant had wrapped in the red sash from a dress uniform.

Using the three-foot-long handle of his whip as a cane, he walked outside and through the press of men and filth. The westbound stage had arrived while Rafe was unconscious, adding a driver, conductor, and seven disgruntled but supremely fortunate people to the tally. The mules still brayed in the corral. Patch trotted anxiously next to him as though determined to prevent any more evil from happening to him.

A soldier stood aside so Rafe could look through the loophole in Red's stall. The boy didn't look more than fifteen. He reminded Rafe of himself when he joined the army, a lifetime ago, it seemed.

The lad's thin wrists outran the cuffs of his rumpled tunic by at least three inches. His yellow hair slanted across his left eye. Hard calluses paved the palms of his hands, but he hadn't been in the army long enough to have acquired them here. Plow handles must have laid them down. Rafe wondered if the lad would live to return to that plow and the rich Mississippi delta soil it churned through, or if he would die here.

The hostler's body still lay face up where it had fallen, eyes bulging toward the leaden sky. A light snow sifted like powdered sugar over it.

"The lieutenant won't let us send a detail out to bury him," the soldier said. "I been throwin' rocks at the crows to keep 'em from eatin' his eyes. An' I fed your dog and horse whilst you was asleep."

"That's kind of you, son." Rafe looked out at the hill and the tall stake planted at the crest of it. He considered the wall's heavy wooden gate, the big iron bolt, and the arm bandaged against his side.

"Open the gate for me," he said.

"Cain't, sir. Lieutenant Bascom's orders."

"Give me your canteen, then, and as many others as you can gather."

The soldier returned with fifteen or so, and Rafe slung them over his good shoulder. He braced the base of his left palm against the bolt and pushed, leaning his body into it. He shoved against the gate with his left shoulder. Lights exploded in front of his eyes, but he pushed the gate open enough to squeeze through. Patch came after him. Behind him he could hear Cochise's brother Coyundado start his serenade again.

He climbed the hill, feeling the stare of Apache eyes from the rocky aeries that surrounded the station. He untied the folded paper from the stick. The message had been written on the back of an invoice for bowler hats, brogans, and Dr. Kilmer's Cough Remedy. He recognized Jim Wallace's neat hand, but the words were Cochise's.

"I have three other white men now, besides the one called Wallace," it began. "Treat my people well, and I will do the same by yours. Cochise."

Three others. Rafe wondered who they might be. The express rider? Some luckless travelers? Freighters?

From the hill he walked to the spring and filled the canteens. He gave the sergeant's to Patch to carry by the cord. She trotted behind him with her head up so it wouldn't hit the ground.

By the time Rafe reached the gate, the canteens felt as though they weighed fifty pounds each, but he was almost hopeful. Surely now that the stakes had been raised by three more lives, Bascom would relent.

He delivered Sergeant Mott's canteen to him and knocked on the lieutenant's door. He started into the persuasion he had rehearsed, but he knew before he had waded in ankle-deep that he would fail. He could tell by the panicky look in Bascom's eyes and the stubborn set of his thin lips. The man would not relent. His fragile opinion of his own abilities would not let him do anything that could be interpreted as retreating.

Rafe's hands shook with rage as he handed over the note. He wanted to strangle him. He wanted to watch his round, mantis eyes pop from his head. He wanted to hear Old Man Death rattle and wheeze and cackle in Bascom's throat.

He thought of trying to find Cochise in that deadly maze of rocks and peaks where he had his stronghold and bargain for the lives of Wallace and the other three men. He knew he could do nothing, though, so long as Bascom held Cochise's family. He imagined the leisurely, agonizing death the four men faced. He wanted to curse Bascom to eternal damnation. He wanted to rant at heaven over the surplus of boneheadedness that God had added to His ultimate creation, Man.

Chapter 25

WOMEN'S WORK

Geronimo rode in front with Victorio and Loco. Lozen came behind them with Broken Foot and Red Sleeves. Talks A Lot, He Steals Love, and the other young warriors and apprentices followed. They had climbed all morning toward the towers of fawn-colored rock that flanked the narrow defile leading to Cheis's stronghold. They leaned into the cold wind whining through the cliffs, outcrops, and heaps of avalanche rubble.

Geronimo was discussing the group of The People who had acquired the Spanish name Tontos, Foolish Ones, or *Bini-e-dinéh*, People Without Minds. Geronimo now spent most of his time with his sister's husband, Long Neck, leader of the Enemy People. He seemed unconcerned about the low esteem the Chiricahua had for his adopted band. The Enemy People clawed out a living in Mexico's Sierra Madre, a territory even less charitable than that of the Chiricahuas. Everyone looked down on the People Without Minds, but the Chiricahuas generally considered the Enemy People to be inferior, too.

Geronimo talked loudly, so the apprentices could hear. "Those *Bini-e-dinéh*, those People Without Minds, they're so ignorant, they eat coyotes, snakes, even fish. If one of them ever invites you boys to eat with him, sniff the pot first. You never know what he might feed you. You could grow all smelly and spotted like a fish."

Geronimo was jollier than Lozen had ever seen him. He was the only jolly one. Everyone else rode grim-faced, in spite of his stories and jokes, in spite of the prospect of mules for the taking.

Geronimo had brought the news that the American soldiers had betrayed the sacred trust of hospitality. They had invited Cheis to a meal, and they had captured not only his nephews and his brother Ox, but his wife and children, too. The Blue-coat chief would have held Cheis prisoner if he had been slower with his knife and his feet. Word had spread like a grass fire through the Chiricahuas country. Already people referred to the incident as Cut the Tent.

"Why won't the Bluecoat let the captives go?" Victorio asked.

Geronimo grimaced, although with him a grimace was hard to distinguish from his usual expression. "I went with Cheis when he held council with the Bluecoat chief," he said. "The Bluecoat is frightened. He's afraid of seeming a fool in front of his men, and so he's acting like a bigger fool. I think the Pale Eyes are People Without Minds, too."

"And all for that red-haired, crazy-eyed, no-good coyote of a boy," said Loco. "It was a good day for the White Mountain people when his mother escaped from them years ago and took him with her. Now they've stolen him back."

"How many mules do the Bluecoats have?" Talks A Lot led the conversation back to the most important point.

"Fifty-six, if the Bluecoats haven't eaten them or they haven't died of thirst," Geronimo said. "The only water they have is stored in one of those big, wooden pots." He made a circle of his arms to indicate a barrel. "Even if the Pale Eyes sip like lizards, that pot has been dry for at least a day."

Red Sleeves slumped in his saddle, his face trenched from care and weariness. Cheis's wife was Red Sleeves' daughter. Her children were the Old Man's grandchildren. The news of their capture seemed to have hardened Red Sleeves' spirit like an insect gall on a scrub oak leaf.

"The Pale Eyes are very troublesome people," he said sadly.

They stopped on a ridge and looked down. The four wag-ons in the rutted road below were the reason for Geronimo's good humor. Buzzards wandered among the ruins and sat on the blackened wheels. The men of Cheis's band had tied the nine Mexicans' wrists to the wheels before setting the wagons on fire. The heat had cooked their flesh until it fell away from the bones, and then it had charred the bones.

"We took the three white men to trade for Cheis's family," Geronimo said. "The Bluecoats don't care about Mexicans, so we amused ourselves with them." Geronimo grinned. Nothing made him happier than dead Mexicans, and the more horribly they died, the happier he was.

Victorio forbade torturing enemies. He and Lozen left the others joking about Geronimo's cooking talents and how best to prepare Mexicans. They walked to the nearby pile of rocks deposited by Ndee grateful to have come to the top of that long climb. Lozen added a piece of shale to the altar. She scattered pollen to the four directions and then onto the pile of stones.

She was praying for success with the raid on the Bluecoats' mules when she heard the familiar sighing in her head. She felt the sucking sensation in her chest, as though the wind that gusted around her had formed a vortex that drew away her breath.

She turned until she faced the southwest. She trembled as the dread washed through her like a flood through a narrow canyon. When it passed, she stood drained and shaking. Each time the spirit spoke to her the feeling became more intense. She opened her eyes and found the men staring silently at her. The group had grown. Cheis and several of his warriors had come to meet them.

"Have the Pale Eyes sent your family back to you?" she asked him.

"No." Cheis had always maintained a dignified calm, but now he looked about to explode with hatred and rage.

"Where are the enemies coming from?" Victorio asked.

She pointed her chin toward the southwest.

"Did the spirits tell you how many?"

"Many, I think, but they're far away."

"My wife's cousin was hunting," said Cheis. "He saw seventy Bluecoats with three Ndee prisoners. He thinks the Ndee are Coyoteros. The Bluecoats are on foot, but they should arrive by midday tomorrow." He looked down at the wreckage below. "The Bluecoat chief took our men from their families. I didn't stop those men's women from killing the Pale Eyes we captured from those wagons. They killed the white man from the stone house, too, and left the bodies where the Bluecoats will find them on their way here."

"The Bluecoats will make war on us," said Victorio.

"Let them."

BY THE WAN LIGHT OF THE SETTING MOON LOZEN LAY ON her stomach near the spring. She could feel the ground's chill through her doeskin shirt and breechclout and on her bare thighs, but the scrub oaks that hid her from sight also provided some shelter from the cold wind. Victorio had held her chin steady while he painted a broad, reddish-brown stripe of deer blood mixed with mescal paste across her cheeks and the ridge of her nose. The horizontal stripe matched his own and those of the men who rode with him. It also confused the familiar contours of her face so that it would blend with the light and shadows of the desert.

Lozen had wondered if Victorio could hear her heart pounding while he did it. The expedition for army mules had turned into something much more significant and dangerous. She had expected to be sent home, but the men had voted to allow her to come with them.

Lozen rubbed dust into her hair. She broke leafy twigs from the scrub oak and stuck them into her headband. She draped her faded blanket over her back and legs, rested her chin on her crossed hands, and vanished into the landscape. In less time than it took a nearby spider to wrap up the fly thrashing in her web, the rest of Victorio's men turned into stones and earth and bushes as magically as she had.

Cheis wasn't interested in mules. He wanted to lure the Bluecoats out so he could kill them and rescue his family. If he could not do it this morning, all would be lost. He did not have enough men to take on these soldiers combined with the ones who would be arriving soon.

Through the branches of the scrub oaks, Lozen could see the spring's rock-lined basin. She could hear the desperation in the mules' distant braying. The Pale Eyes would have to water them soon, or their corpses would start piling up behind that wall. But the Pale Eyes operated on assumptions and beliefs that were incomprehensible to reasonable people, so she and the spider waited.

The sun had risen when the whistle of a hawk signaled that the Pale Eyes were opening the gate. Lozen stayed relaxed. Before she and the others took the mules, they would let them drink enough to slake their thirst, but not enough make them bloated and slow. They had to be in shape for the long trip to Mexico.

She could feel the vibrations of hooves through the ground pressed against her stomach. The braying grew louder and more frantic. The hawk whistled twice more. Only two men were driving the mules, and the spring was out of rifle range for the soldiers at the stone house. This would be easy.

At the sentry's last, long, mournful hawk call, she stood up and tucked her blanket into the back of her belt. Already she could hear the shouts of Victorio's men and the *pop-pop-pop* of their muskets firing over the mules' heads to spook them. Giving her high, eerie cry, Lozen ran to join the warriors converging on the spring.

The mules didn't stampede as they were supposed to. Most didn't even raise their heads from the water. Lozen flapped her blanket, but as Broken Foot often said, a mule was more stubborn than Her Eyes Open, his wife, on her worst day.

With shouts and snapping blankets, cudgels and gunfire, the men drove individual animals away, only to have them wheel and dodge back to the water. Lozen was running toward the milling throng of swaying rumps and sharp hooves when she saw the big roan approach at a gallop. Hairy Foot was heading back to the stone wall with his dog racing beside him.

Lozen stood between him and safety. She picked up four stones, and as she trotted along, she knotted each one in a corner of the blanket. Then she ran at an angle intersecting the roan's course.

He saw her coming, but her war paint had changed her so completely that she detected no light of recognition in his eyes. She saw no fear either, just a determination to get where he was going. As he approached she sprinted to cut him off. With the dog snapping at her heels she ran parallel to the roan's forequarters and tossed the blanket. The weighted corners sent it soaring above his head. It settled like a large bird on a branch. The horse stopped short, throwing his rider over his neck.

Hardly breaking stride, Lozen vaulted into the saddle. She tucked her blanket into her belt, grabbed the reins, and kicked the horse's sides. Hairy Foot picked himself up and ran for the wall. She felt a twinge of regret at setting him afoot among men who would do their best to kill him, but it passed. Life was hard and death was easy, but if anyone could outrun death, Hairy Foot could.

Without bothering to put her feet in stirrups that were set too long for her anyway, she galloped away. She tugged Hairy Foot's carbine from its saddle boot and waved it over her head with a shout of joy. She glanced over her shoulder to see if Victorio had witnessed her triumph. The roan swerved. Lozen turned in time to see the tree limb rush toward her, but not in time to dodge it. The branch hit her across the chest and knocked her heels over head in a somersault along the horse's rump.

She landed on her stomach, bounced, and skidded, still clutching the rifle. Gulping to suck air into her lungs, she watched the roan, stirrups flapping, prance up to Hairy Foot. Hairy Foot climbed back aboard, and he and his dog reached the gate safely. She heard the iron bolt slam shut.

Aching and bleeding from abrasions on her arms, knees, and cheek, she limped to where the men were rounding up the mules. She hoped no one had seen her fall. If someone had, everyone would hear about it.

She had a rifle, though. As for the horse, he was still hers.

Possession had only been delayed. She felt sure she would see him and Hairy Foot again.

"COLLINS, COME OVER HERE." DR. IRWIN BECKONED TO Rafe.

Lieutenant Bascom walked away from Irwin, and his hasty breakfast came up faster than it went down. Rafe could hear the remains of cold beans and biscuit splattering onto the hardpan of the desert floor.

Rafe winced as he eased out of the saddle. The fall from his horse at the spring had reopened the bullet wound in his back. He didn't relish seeing what Irwin wanted him to look at, so he used the wound as an excuse to take his time.

He limped slowly toward Bascom and Dr. Bernard Irwin, the post surgeon from Fort Buchanan. Irwin had arrived with seventy soldiers and three captive Coyotero Apache cattle thieves six days before, just in time to be too late to save the mules. Knowing Cochise, Rafe had a feeling that wasn't a coincidence.

Rafe had been more than glad to see the soldiers. Thirst had swelled his tongue until he felt as though he were sucking on a saddle horn. Added to that inconvenience was the blight of life with Bascom. Rafe and Sergeant Mott had tried to convince the lieutenant that Apaches couldn't send for reinforcements the way the U.S. Army could. Hence they would not attack stone walls, and they would not take on overwhelming odds, but the lieutenant had swung from bravado to gibbering terror and back again several times between every sunup and sundown.

As the days dragged on, stretched out by boredom and fear, the soldiers had commenced quarreling. Those from the North argued with the fervently secessionist Southerners. Their political discussions ended in brawls as often as not. By the time the infantry from Fort Buchanan arrived, Rafe had been ready to whistle to his dog, saddle Red, and load his pistols and Jim Wallace's fine new slant-breech Sharps rifle. He had been ready to ride through the gate to take his chances with Cochise and his minions.

He discovered that Dr. Irwin was cut from the same cloth as Bascom, but at least Irwin had allowed Lieutenant Moore to take his men on a three-day scout. They had returned yesterday to announce that they had found only old tracks and hastily abandoned camps. They said the Apaches had left for parts unknown, but Rafe didn't believe that. People believed that the Apaches had no feeling for friends or kin, but Rafe felt sure Cochise wouldn't abandon his family.

Now the soldiers were headed for Fort Buchanan, seventy miles away. They had stopped when they came to the abandoned campsite. Rafe walked to the clearing sheltered by the canopy of four huge oaks, their limbs as parallel to the ground as ridgepoles. Three bodies lay strewn like so much litter in a shallow gully. Irwin and Bascom were standing over the fourth near the cold remains of a campfire.

"Can you say who this is?" Bascom's face had turned as gray as last night's ashes.

Rafe looked down at the wreckage of flesh and bones and entrails that once had been some mother's son. His stomach wanted to add his breakfast to Bascom's, but he only hawked and spit out the bile that rose in his throat.

The Apaches had staked the man spread-eagle on his back. They had stripped the body and cut off various appendages. His abdomen had been ripped open and charred areas covered his chest. Gaping holes left by lances had obliterated his features. Rafe took a deep breath and crouched for a closer look. The sun glinted on a gold tooth in the bloody hole that had been a mouth.

"It's Jim Wallace."

"What kind of men could do this?" Irwin asked.

"This is woman's work," Rafe said. "Probably they were kin of the people we're holding."

"Well, let's see justice done and then get moving." Irwin polished the dusty toes of his boots on his trouser legs. He swiveled on his heels and strode toward the six men, the boy, and the woman holding a baby in a sling on her hip.

They were all tied in a line and guarded by a dozen men with rifles.

"Lieutenant, assign a detail to bury these poor bastards. We'll need a second one to hang the prisoners, two men to a tree. We'll hoist them so high the wolves can't get them. We'll leave them here as a lesson to any thieving, bloodthirsty savage who passes."

Rafe knew that was a bad idea. It would only make matters worse, although he didn't see how they could get any worse. Even so, the sight of Wallace made his gut writhe with fury, revulsion, and disillusionment. He had thought Cochise honorable, and he had been wrong. Cochise had allowed this to happen to the man he had called friend.

The torture had a significance lost on Irwin and Bascom. The Apaches believed that their victims would have to pass to the other world as they had died. They had damned Wallace to spend eternity deformed.

And damn the Apaches for it, Rafe thought.

Soldiers began untying the ropes that held the canvas-shrouded crates and sacks in the wagon.

"You speak some Spanish, Collins," Irwin said. "Explain to these bucks that they're to be executed for the death of those men."

Rafe pointed out the obvious. "But they didn't kill them."

"Just tell them."

"What about the woman and the two kids?"

Irwin looked about to snarl at Rafe for pestering him with questions; then he remembered that Rafe wasn't an enlisted man. "My inclination is to squash the nits with the lice, but Lieutenant Bascom advises turning them loose. He seems eager to be rid of them. He didn't want to hang Cheis's three bucks, either, but I convinced him it was the right thing to do."

Rafe wanted to observe that if Bascom had come to his senses ten days earlier about the woman, the children, and the three bucks, none of this would have happened. He walked over to the six Apache men who watched the proceedings as if they had far less importance than a card game or a new horse. Then, joking and laughing, the soldiers tied knots in the ends of the ropes to weight them. One stood on the wagon seat and threw the first rope over a high limb. The prisoners became more intent.

Another soldier led the wagon's team forward so the man on the seat could heave the second rope five feet farther along the limb. Then he led the team to the next tree. Behind him two men began tying nooses in the dangling ends.

"They're going to kill you," Rafe said.

Coyundado stepped forward from the group. He was shorter than Cochise, and he had coarser features, but he was as muscular. To Rafe, he radiated a nonchalant menace that was remarkable even among people for whom menace was second nature.

"¿De garrote?" Coyundado put a hand to his neck, above the necklace of silver conchos. Will they strangle us?

"Sí."

"Tiranos," he said.

Rafe turned to Irwin and Bascom. "They want you to shoot them."

"What do they care?"

"Vanity. If they die hung in a noose, they'll have to spend eternity with their necks stretched."

"Their necks are the least of their worries in eternity. I will not grant depraved thieves and murderers the honor of a firing squad."

Rafe translated the decision, although the men undoubtedly had guessed what it was.

"Entonces, danos pulque."

"They want whiskey," Rafe said.

"This isn't a goddamned tavern." Irwin motioned to the soldiers to finish the arrangements.

"No importa." Coyundado hands were tied behind his back, but he shook his head, as though dismissing death like a bothersome fly. "I killed two Mexicans recently," he said in Spanish. "I am satisfied."

The soldiers unhitched seven horses from the wagon teams. The six Apaches' hands were tied, so the soldiers helped them mount. They positioned each horse under a noose. The seventh soldier mounted and arranged the nooses over their necks and tied the other end to their saddle horns. As he did it, he looked not at all sure they wouldn't find a way to kill him even while trussed up.

The young soldier jumped visibly when he reached Coyundado, who began to chant in a loud, steady voice. Rafe would have sworn Coyundado did it as much to scare the lad as to celebrate his own death. Apaches did like their little jokes.

The older of the two boys looked to be about ten or twelve years old. He stood as silent and expressionless as his mother and the child riding in a sling at her hip. They stayed that way when the soldiers lashed the horses with their quirts. The animals bolted, cutting Coyundado's song short and hauling the prisoners up until the tops of their heads hit the limb bringing the horses to an abrupt halt. The men swung and kicked so hard they bumped into each other. When the last one had stopped twitching, the soldiers tied the other ends of the ropes around the oaks' trunks.

The sergeant untied the woman and gave her a shove between the shoulder blades. Rafe watched her and her son walk away without turning back. He wondered if she would be capable of torturing a man the way Wallace had been tortured. He was pretty sure she would. He wondered how she would find her husband, if indeed Cochise and his men had gone to Mexico.

Well, that wasn't his problem. His problem was to make it back to Fort Buchanan alive with this bunch of greenhorns. That should keep all of them occupied for the duration of the trip. Then he would try to stay alive each day after that, just as he always had.

Chapter 26

THE GIFT

If Cheis was going to drive out the Pale Eyes, his warriors would need weapons, ammunition, and provisions. Mexico was where they had always gotten them. Victorio and his men came with Cheis to trade the horses and cattle they had stolen on their way south.

The *comanchero* pushed his fingers up under the conical crown of his sombrero, knocking the wide brim askew enough for Lozen to see one eye black as a midnight abyss, if she had bothered to look. Profound contemplation settled onto his pock-cratered face as he scratched through the tangles of his hair and waited for Lozen to select a string of beads. He harvested a louse and popped it into his mouth.

Lozen chose the string of red glass beads and added them to the pile laid out on top of two folded wool blankets—a pouch of lead balls, and another of gunpowder, three looking glasses, ten yards of calico, a sack of corn, and a knife. She handed over the lead lines of the mules. She began packing her new possessions in the rawhide pouches that hung behind the mare's saddle.

If the trader thought it odd that a young Apache woman would be on a raid, he gave no sign of it. The new mules had his attention, anyway. They had developed a sudden and contrary fondness for Lozen, and they didn't want to leave her. The *comanchero* hauled them toward the milling herd of army mules taken from the stage station.

The trader's nine companions were short of stature and principles, but long on guile and nerve. They were dealing, after all, with people who had been killing Mexicans for three centuries. They were mostly Tarahumara Indians. Luxuriant black mustaches draped the lower halves of their faces and the sombreros threw the upper halves in shadow, which was just as well. Their eyes wouldn't instill confidence. Their trousers and short jackets were the color of the desert dust.

Cheis and Victorio had no trouble finding them. They had only to follow the broken cottonwood axletrees discarded from the traders' lumbering two-wheeled carts. When in place, the ungreased axletrees sounded like the din a double-bass horse fiddle would make if the double-bass horse fiddle were being castrated. The carts had wheels sawn from the trunks of oak trees. They required six oxen to pull them when loaded.

They could never make the climb up the zigzag trail into the sharp-sided mountains where Long Neck and his people lived. The traders had arrived at Long Neck's usual meeting place with pack mules that were as raffish, unkempt, and ungovernable as they were. They looked like foothills of goods plodding along on hooves so frayed they resembled their masters' mustaches.

When the leader of the *comancheros* finished his trade with Lozen, he turned to Victorio. He spoke a mix of Spanish, Apache, and sign language. "Jefe, we have a present for you."

His men hauled on a rope, the other end of which was looped around Shadrach Rogers's neck. Rogers's wrists were tied behind his back, and a twisted length of sacking hobbled his ankles. He struggled, sobbed, and pleaded, although no one understood what he was saying.

The *comanchero* made an offhand wave in his direction. "This coyote is a Hair Taker. I think maybe he scalped some of your people. He killed an old man and old woman of our people, after they fed him and gave him shelter. We were going to hang him upside down until he died, but"—the trader shrugged in a gesture of magnanimity—"we thought maybe our good friend Victorio would like to have him."

"He was at the diggers' village ten years ago," Lozen murmured to her brother. "I took the cartridge belt from him while he was drunk."

"I remember him," said Victorio. "He was apprentice to the *pesh-chidin*, the ghost of the iron."

"He was a bad man then," Lozen said. "And he's a bad man now."

Victorio took the rope and passed it to Chato and Talks A Lot. A dark, wet stain spread across the front of Rogers's already filthy trousers. The *comanchero* beamed. He looked as though he would like to stay around to see what a crew of drunken Apaches did to a Hair Taker. It would be an entertaining show, but not a prudent move.

Some of the Chiricahuas were already upending the bottles of pulque they had gotten from the traders and were letting the contents gurgle down their throats. The *comancheros* knew better than to stay around while the liquor worked its devilment. Cracking their whips and shouting the most scurrilous of oaths, they clattered around the first fold in the trail, leaving behind a cloud of dust and the phantom braying of the mules.

Victorio and Lozen walked away so they would not see what the young men did to the Hair Taker. They could still hear his screams, though, so they mounted and rode until the cries were no louder than the raucous calls of the chachalaca birds.

"What did Long Neck say to Cheis's proposal to drive out the Pale Eyes?" Lozen asked.

"He says his quarrel is with the Mexicans, not the Pale Eyes, but he'll listen to what we have to say."

"Will you hold council at Long Neck's village?"

"No. Cheis knows he'll need more help from the spirits than usual. He wants to go to the holiest place to discuss it."

"The Canyon With No End?" Lozen had heard about it all her life, and all her life she'd wondered if she'd ever see it. The Mexicans called it Barranca de Cobre, Copper Canyon.

Victorio smiled. "It's a hole big enough to put the world in."

———

WHITE CLOUDS SWIRLED IN THE AZURE SKY AS LOZEN walked to the edge of the precipice. She stood with the toes of her moccasins hanging over the edge of the world. She looked down at a land so far below that she thought if she dived forward she would fall until the sun set.

Lush green forests covered the broad valley. Mist as white as the clouds floated over the silver ribbon of a river that snaked along the valley floor. Long Neck's people called the Sierra Madre the Blue Mountains. Lozen could see why. In the distance the deep green of the forest cover shifted to aqua, then to a dark blue against the sky that rose from behind them. The size, the beauty, the grandeur, the richness of it stunned her. She felt as small as the ant crawling up her moccasin.

Victorio said this wasn't the Underworld, the Happy Country, but maybe he was wrong. Maybe she was standing at the opening where the dead went. All the spirits who had gone on their last journeys since Old Man Coyote let Death out of the sack could live comfortably in this valley and the thousands of others leading out from it. She imagined the ghosts hunting and gambling, making love, feasting, dancing, laughing, and telling stories. She imagined her mother and her father there, never cold, hungry, frightened, sad, or in pain.

She walked along the cliff until she came to a narrow canyon branching off from it. She followed the eastern rim of it until long past time for the midday meal back at the encampment. The twists and turns, the wind-sculpted rocks drew her on. She had almost reached the place where the canyon narrowed to a cleft when night's shadows began to pool among the rocks and trees below. She unrolled her blanket and sat cross-legged on it at the edge. She could throw a rock and hit the entrance to a cave just below the rim on the other side.

She watched the sun slip behind the mountains. She watched the sky take fire and the clouds turn the brilliant hues of desert flowers after a spring freshet. She watched the color flow down the sides of the canyon and into the stream below, until the water glowed deep pink.

Bit by bit night stole the canyon away from the day. The shadows met and blended until she could no longer make out the forms of the rocks. She sat all night listening to the rustle of animals going about their business and the calls of cougars and wolves and coyotes, the night songs of birds.

The next day and the following night she left the blanket only to relieve herself. She was aware of hunger and thirst, weariness, and the icy night wind, but they didn't seem important. She didn't think about Victorio, either, or the council that he and Cheis, Red Sleeves, Loco, Broken Foot, Long Neck, and others were holding. Victorio was used to her wandering off in search of advice from the spirits.

The third night she began hearing voices. She saw movements at the periphery of her sight. Coyote came. With his head cocked and his tongue lolling, he watched her for a long time. He told her the story of the time he shit on a rock, and it chased him until he apologized and cleaned it off. His story made her laugh, but she kept a wary eye on him. One could never tell what Coyote might do.

Later that night the stones, sculpted by the elements into grotesque shapes, moved in the moonlight and whispered to her. Her own spirit helpers visited her, too. The last one swirled like a mist between the two rims of the canyon. Its message vibrated in the bones of her skull.

"To know the strength of your enemies, watch the cave. To know where they will come from, watch the cave." Three more times the spirit repeated its advice.

On the fourth morning, as soon as Lozen could see the darker splotch of the cave opening against the pale face of the cliff, she stared at it. The sun hadn't risen over the top of the cliff yet when she heard the beat of drums like those of the Bluecoat soldiers.

Gusts riffled the wisps of hair that had pulled loose from her braid and curled around her face. A rumbling grew louder and then became the rhythmic tromp of the clumsy boots the Bluecoats wore. She saw the first rank of them, six across, appear in the cave entrance. Their shouldered rifles rose like spikes above them. Another line followed them, then a third, a fourth, and a fifth. The apparitions wore identical blue jackets and trousers. Under the stubby brims of their tall black hats, their faces were pale disks, without eyes, noses, mouths, anything that would distinguish them one from the other. They marched into the air in front of the cave and vanished, but more followed, rank after rank of them. The walking soldiers were interspersed with companies on horseback.

Lozen watched them until the sun started its journey down the slope of the sky. Finally the last of them vanished into the same nothingness that had swallowed the others. The drums stopped. The sound of hooves and boots ceased. Silence rang in her ears like a gun barrel struck against the big metal cylinders the miners abandoned in their journeys through The People's country.

She stood up slowly, but sparks exploded in front of her eyes, anyway, and dizziness caused her to sway. She wrapped her blanket around her waist and started off at a trot. Night arrived at the encampment before she did. Long Neck and his people had come in her absence. Long Neck's wives' Mexican slaves were clearing away the remains of the feast scattered about on hides and blankets. Lozen heard laughter from the big fire near their lodges in the center of the camp.

Red Sleeves sat on Long Neck's left side and Cheis on his right. Victorio, Loco, Broken Foot, and Geronimo sat beside them in the places of secondary honor. The other men took places according to rank, with the apprentices behind them. The women and children sat or stood at the rear.

Lozen spread her blanket next to Cheis's wife, Dos-teh-seh, who was nursing her youngest boy, the one they called Mischievous. She handed Lozen a gourd of water and a piece of dark, crisp bread. The Mexican traders' wives made the bread from toasted cornmeal ground four times on successively finer stones. It had a rich, smoky taste, crunchy outside and a little softer inside. Lozen ate it slowly to get her stomach used to the idea of eating after four days without food.

Dos-teh-seh had had no trouble finding Cheis when the Bluecoats let her and her sons go. Cheis and his men had watched the execution of Ox and the others from an overlooking crag. The fact that Cheis could not risk the lives of his men to save his brother and nephews added to the anger that consumed him.

Cheis was no longer the man who had laughed and joked with Lozen. Rage had darkened his spirit. People avoided contact with him. He had always found time to play with the children, but now they dared not go near him. Lozen caught a glimpse of his face silhouetted against the fire's light. She could see that not even Broken Foot's jokes and stories would bring a smile to it. That would be like trying to make the wind-carved rocks in the canyon smile.

When Broken Foot stood up, the new gold chains he had gotten from the traders glittered in the fire's light. He had fastened them with thread through the holes in his earlobes, and they dangled past his shoulders.

"I'm going to tell a very funny story," he said.

One of the youngest warriors and a woman about his age stood up. Those around them laughed and reached up to tug at their clothes as they left. They were sweethearts, and they were heeding Broken Foot's hint. A very funny story was certain to be too embarrassing to hear in the presence of one's new love. Broken Foot waited until they had disappeared into the darkness, in opposite directions.

"This is a story of Old Man Coyote. You must only tell stories of Snake and Old Ugly Buttocks the Bear in the winter, the time of Ghost Face. Snake and Ugly Buttocks hibernate then, so you won't make them mad, talking about them. And when you finish a story about them, you must trick them by saying you were talking about fruit and flowers and other good things." He thumped a sleeping child on the head to wake him, then steered a meandering course back to the fire.

"Long time ago, they say, Coyote was watching the young Prairie Dog Women play the stave game. They were pretty, those Prairie Dog Women, and Coyote wanted the prettiest one. Coyote is always after pretty women. Some men are still that way because he showed them how."

Everyone laughed. They knew which men he meant.

"Coyote said to Gopher, 'See that Prairie Dog Woman sitting there? She won't have anything to do with me, so I'm asking you a favor. Tunnel over there and make a hole right up under where she's sitting.' The Gopher, he said, 'All right, I'll do it.' And he began to dig. You could see the earth humping up where he went. Then he dug under the Prairie Dog Woman. Coyote went into the tunnel and looked up that hole and saw another little hole. His penis grew as hard as a log. He pushed that penis through the hole to make love to her. The Prairie Dog Woman felt something bumping against her. She looked down and saw Coyote's penis jumping up and down like a rabbit trying to get out of a deep hole.

"Prairie Dog Woman picked up a big rock, and she dropped it on his penis. 'Make love to this,' she said. Then she and the other Prairie Dog Women laughed and ran away." Broken Foot added the usual disclaimer. "I'm talking about flowers and cactus fruit."

Broken Foot's stories would go on until dawn, but about midnight exhaustion overcame Lozen. She curled up on her blanket. She pulled the end over her so Broken Foot wouldn't see her there and thump her on the head or tickle her to wake her. She fell into a dreamless sleep.

When she woke up, she felt as though her bones and muscles had turned to mescal paste. She poked her head out, eyes still closed, and yawned.

"The turtle is emerging from her shell," Victorio said.

Victorio, Broken Foot, Talks A Lot, and Loco sat smoking their cigarillos. They looked as though they had been waiting for her to wake up. The rest of the meeting ground was empty. The men sat with their backs to the sun, and Lozen narrowed her eyes to see them.

"She must have gotten turtle magic," Broken Foot said. "She looks like a turtle now with her eyes all squinty."

Lozen wrapped the blanket around her. She felt a weariness in her bones, as though her encounter with the spirits had drained the strength and will from her. She didn't want to tell Broken Foot and her brother what she had seen. No one would believe her when she told them from which direction the Bluecoats had come.

"The council will start soon," Broken Foot said. "You should attend."

"What use would I be?"

"You can tell us what you saw while you were gone."

With her blanket still cocooned around her, she sat across from him and Broken Foot. "I saw Bluecoats."

"How many?"

"More than I could count. They passed by all day, row after row of them. Some of them walked and some rode horses. They were not headed here, though. I think they're coming to our country."

"They have to march through the pass near the stone house where we stole the mules."

"And where you didn't steal the big red horse," Broken Foot added.

Victorio rolled another cigarette. "We can wait for them and kill them there."

"These Bluecoats came from the west, and they marched east, into the rising sun."

"The west, my daughter?" Broken Foot had been absentmindedly rubbing his lame ankle, and he looked up in surprise.

Someone in the group nearby laughed. Lozen could hear them murmuring some jest. They would add this preposterous tale to the story of her falling off the big roan. She sighed. Sometimes the spirits' gifts were burdensome.

"Yes. From the west."

She could tell that Broken Foot and even Victorio were skeptical. She couldn't help that, though. She had seen what she had seen, whether anyone believed her or not. These enemies did not come from the east like all the other Pale Eyes did.

They came from the west.

Chapter 27

THE DIVORCE

Bill's estate looked like a castle built by lunatic elves. It always reminded Rafe of the old bedtime story about the three little pigs and the big, bad wolf, only this house was built of sticks and straw and iron. The iron boiler rose like a rusty donjon from a welter of bowlegged arbors, sway-backed tents with shreds of canvas fluttering like banners in the fitful wind. There were huts of spavined mesquite limbs, scrap lumber, and mangy grass thatch. Open-front shelters put the *lean* in lean-to.

Silver seekers had expended enormous amounts of money and labor getting the boiler this far a few years earlier, and then they had abandoned it. The bones of the twelve oxen who had died hauling it lay heaped not far away. It stood ten feet tall and eight feet in diameter. It was a formidable patchwork of square plates riveted together, with iron reinforcements where the pressure valves, pipes, tubes, and fittings would have connected. There it loomed, like a stray lighthouse, in the desert country between Tubac and Tucson.

Bill's salvage flowed outward from it—grindstones, a pianoforte genuflecting on two broken front legs, and a small herd of Franklin stoves with lizards, snakes, pocket mice, cotton rats, and ground squirrels nesting in them. Bill had steamer trunks, wagon parts, picture frames with the gold leaf peeling off, old wheels, harnesses, hames, singletrees— all of them scavanged from the litter left by the gold rushers. Rafe thought it safe to say that anything that came into Bill's possession never left it.

Now, in mid-May, squash and gourd vines were well on their way to covering it all in a lumpy green carpet. Bill did keep a small area clear for a garden. The only plants he grew there were more varieties of chile peppers than Rafe had seen in all his years.

A palisade of flowering ocatillo cactus ten feet high threaded through the sprawl in no particular plan that Rafe could see. Bill had a name for each hut, jacal, tent, and bower. Rafe didn't know what half the words meant, but he could locate the portico and piazza, the vestibule, conservatory, office, library (though Bill couldn't read), great hall, salon, pantry, forge, scullery, boudoir, and refectory.

The refectory consisted of a brush arbor next to an array of fire pits, circular stone hearths, and iron rods with slabs of wild pigs' ribs perpetually charring over glowing goals. Rafe deduced that refectory meant eating place because that was where Bill always carried the iron stew pot, its outer surface shiny black with soot and grease. He set it on a wagon's tailgate laid horizontally across two barrels, and the men dipped their gourd spoons into it and ate standing up.

The pot's contents varied each time Rafe visited, but he suspected that it never ran completely dry. The chiles provided the one constant. Bill added new ingredients as he dug them from the ground, ran them into the ground, lured, shot, garroted, bushwhacked, or snared them. This evening Rafe detected snake, jackrabbit, and he was pretty sure that the foot floating in the broth in his spoon had once belonged to a rat, possibly a former inhabitant of one of the potbellied stoves.

They lowered the level on this edition of the stew and retired to the "veranda," the arbor next to the door Bill had gotten a blacksmith to cut into the boiler and then set in place with the hinges inside. Rafe sat in the big rocker, his favorite of Bill's many chairs, and Patch lay by his feet. Red had finished his bucket of corn, and he watched with interest while Rafe drew the book out of its bag.

Bill occupied a buggy seat with a whip still standing upright in the boot on the left side. His thin legs and moccasin-clad feet splayed in front of him. He laid his head back so the smoke from his cigarillo wreathed his lumpy nose like clouds about a mountain peak.

Rafe read aloud from *Romeo and Juliet* each time he stopped here. He could have recited it from memory, but Bill preferred being read to. Both Bill and Red listened intently now as Rafe read the sorrowful scene in the crypt where the two young lovers died. Bill's eyes were closed, but his lips moved, silently forming the words. Through the years of Rafe's visits, Bill had memorized all the lines and the stage directions and the asides.

" 'For never was a story of more woe / than this of Juliet and her Romeo.' " Rafe closed the book gently. Men had offered him as much for this book as they had for Red.

Bill snuffled and wiped his eyes on his sleeve, as though to get the sweat out of them. Rafe slipped the book into the pouch of soft leather smoked to the color of tupelo honey to make it waterproof. He folded down the long neck of it and tied it with its rawhide thong. Some woman had chewed this leather to a supple softness. Her hands had fringed and beaded the pouch and sewn cowrie shells and bits of turquoise onto it. He sometimes wondered whose hands they had been and what had happened to her.

More than two years had passed since he had scattered the pollen from this bag onto his old Packard, but traces of it still collected in the bottom corners of the pouch. It worked its way inside the book, too, and sometimes fell in a golden shower like fairy dust when Rafe opened its pages. It seemed fitting to him, that Shakespeare should be connected to pagan magic, though *Romeo and Juliet* contained no Caliban, no Puck, no Bottom or Titania.

He stuck the book into his trousers at the back. He rocked slowly in the chair and thought about Titania the fairy queen, dressed in gossamer and spider webs. Titania, a midsummer night's dream, indeed. He felt a pang of regret that he had no woman to love, to hold, to cherish.

"Women," Bill said.

With his eyes still closed, Rafe waited for him to expand on the subject. Bill had never disclosed anything about his past, and Rafe was curious to see what the jug of whiskey he had brought might jog loose, like mud off a wagon axle.

"They bring you to grief every time," Bill confided.

They sat in silence while Bill rolled another cigarillo of the tobacco Rafe had brought. "I had me a honest woman once't," he said. "When I was a rich man in Californy."

Rafe tried to imagine Bill a married man, and a rich one at that, but couldn't.

"Then one day she ups and says she wants a dee-vorce. She got her a Philadelphia lawyer, and he tells her she must have half of everything we owned. So I give it to her." He chuckled. "I pulled her dresses out of the wardrobe, and I cut every one of them in half with this hyar blade." He held up a bowie knife as long as his knotty forearm, the steel edge honed thin as paper. "I ripped my pantaloons down the middle, and my waistcoat, shirts, and coats."

The most amazing thing to Rafe about Bill's story was that he once had owned more than one suit of clothes. A waistcoat? Rafe tied to conjure up the image of Bill in a waistcoat.

Bill winked at Rafe. "You've heard of cuttin' a rug? Well, sir, when I finished with the duds, I did cut the rug. I broke up the stove and all the pots and pans and put the fragments in two equal heaps. I took an ax and commenced to divide every piece of furniture in two, and every lamp and faldeerol, while she danced around screaming like someone was jab-bin' her with her own hat pin." He sighed with contentment. "She followed me outside, still hollerin' like a stuck pig, and whilst I was trying to figure how to split the house in two with that ax, the police arrived to quell the riot."

Silence followed while Bill relived the joy that true justice can bring, as opposed to the courtroom variety. "And now here I am. Happy as if I had good sense."

"Have the Apache bothered you lately?"

"Naw. Cochise and his merry band, they think I'm crazy, and they believe crazy people are holy. Besides, once't the 'Pache stole my horse and mule, I hadn't nothin' left they wanted. They used to pay social calls now and then, and we'd share smokes and a tipple or two, but now when I sees 'em, I goes inside and bolts the door." He leaned back and knocked on the iron plating with his knuckles. They made a dull ringing that persisted, like the sound of a hummingbird's wings. "Gets a might hot in there in summertime, though."

"That's why they call them boilers."

Rafe rocked, the motion soothing, like being in a cradle, while he, Bill, Red, and Patch watched the sun set in a silence as comfortable as an old pair of moccasins. When night fell good and hard and dense, Rafe would saddle up, whistle for Patch, and ride on. He did most of his traveling at night. Safer that way.

"Everything has its point, don't you know. Even Apaches." Bill broke the surface of the silence. "Men, now, the Good Lord put them on earth to eat, drink, and stay awake a leetle while at night." He sank back into the silence and let it close comfortably over his head.

"And women?" Rafe asked finally.

"Women, they was a-made to cook the vittles, brew the booze, and help the men stay awake at night." Bill winked at Rafe.

They saw the dust cloud coming from the north. Bill primed and loaded his musket, and Rafe capped his Sharps and laid it across his knees. The riders wouldn't arrive for a while, but the weight of the carbine was a comfort, anyway.

Darkness arrived about the same time the six soldiers did. John Mott, the sergeant that Rafe had met at the beleaguered stage station a year before, was in charge of the company. While his men watered the horses at Bill's well, he dipped out a ladleful of stew. He sank into a ladder-backed chair, put his boots on a keg, and tilted the chair's front legs up.

"The rebels fired on United States soldiers at Fort Sumter last month," he said.

"Where's Fort Sumter?" Rafe asked.

"On an island off Charleston. South Carolina. War has been declared."

"I could smell this divorce coming," Bill said. "Which is

more than I could say for my own. I reckon they mean to cleave the country in two, don't they?"

"The army will stop the secessionists in a few weeks." Mott sounded certain of it.

Rafe didn't comment, but he doubted that. He knew Southerners. They didn't understand the meaning of defeat. You could cut them off at the knees, and they'd fight you from the ground, their teeth set like a badger's in your ankles.

When Mott's men had eaten and filled their canteens, they mounted. Mott called back over his shoulder. "The rebels have elected Jefferson Davis as president of their government."

Rafe listened to their hoofbeats fade in the darkness. "Jeff Davis." He grunted. "Too bad the rebels didn't make him general. The war would end soon then."

"You know 'im?"

"Heard of him. After his Mississippi Rifles won the day at the Battle of Buena Vista, they say Jeff took on airs. Considered he had a head for strategy, when what he has is luck and pluck."

"So you're for the Yanks, and you from Texas?"

Rafe thought about it. His answer surprised him. "Maybe so."

Rafe realized that the army won out with him over Texas. But then, the army had done more for him than Texas ever had. Besides, Southerners as a species annoyed him. Their main goal in life was to prove that they could whip anything that moved, and some things that didn't. He could imagine the arrogance that had led Davis and the others to start a war with a foe many times stronger and better equiped and trained, with far more resources.

"Makes no never mind to me what they do." Bill said.

Rafe knew how he felt. The squabbles of ambitious men in cravats, striped trousers, and patent leather pumps seemed remote, irrelevant. Renegade Mexicans, murderous Americans, implacable Apaches, and the desert itself were already slaughtering honest and dishonest folk alike here on a regular basis.

Then the realization hit him.

"Oh, shit," he murmured.

Bill looked at him, one furry eyebrow arched.

"Oh, shit," Rafe breathed again.

IN SPITE OF A STORM THAT SENT JAGGED BLADES OF LIGHT-
ning slashing into the ground and thunder booming like
heavy artillery, Rafe found the fort in the uproar he expected.
He tied Red in front of the stable, shook the excess rain from
the brim of his hat, and with Patch at his heels, wove off to
find the captain.

The captain glanced up from the account book lying open
on the desk in the quartermaster's tent. "You heard the
news?"

Rafe nodded, though the captain had returned his attention
to trying to make out the quartermaster sergeant's scrawl.

"Some of the Southern soldiers have already deserted us
here."

"What will happen now?"

"We've received orders to pull out. They need us at the
front."

"The front?" Rafe had fought alongside hundreds of
Southerners in the war with Mexico. He tried to imagine
fighting against them. He wondered if the government might
call him up, force him to fight, too.

"The latest dispatch just arrived." The captain held up the
rumpled paper. "We're to burn everything and march east by
the first week in July."

"The Apaches will slaughter people like cattle."

The captain shrugged. "I have to follow orders." He
looked up at Rafe. "Come with us, Collins. You've not contracted gold fever like those other fools. Leave this godfor-
saken territory to the savages. The Apaches deserve it, if you
ask me."

The thought had never occurred to Rafe. For a few moments he considered it. Maybe Fanny Kemble was touring
the Unites States doing readings of Shakespeare. Rafe had

seen a lithograph of her in an old copy of Frank Leslie's magazine, worn tissue-thin by the hands through which it had passed. The picture was ghostlike, but he could see that she was beautiful. He tried to imagine sitting in an ornate theater, with cherubim painted on the ceiling, and women with plumes in their hats, listening to Miss Kemble's voice.

He shook his head. "I reckon I'll stay."

"Better the evil you know, I suppose."

Rafe realized there was a distinct possibility that the army might conscript him into the fighting if he went east. Besides, he might as well go to the moon as cross the Mississippi. He had heard the stories of what the east was like. Crowded. Smelly. Noisy. Nowhere to stretch your arms or your soul. A man couldn't howl at the moon there, if he'd a mind to.

The captain considered this country a wasteland, but Rafe disagreed. He realized that somewhere along the treacherous, hot, dusty road, he had come to love it. He couldn't divorce it now.

Chapter 28

TUCSON, TUBAC, TUMACACORI, AND TO HELL

The Bluecoats were leaving. Broken Foot wasn't surprised. He glanced over at Victorio and Lozen, then back at the fort in the broad bowl of a valley below. "All that lightning worked magic for us."

"The Bluecoats have lots of iron." Victorio couldn't believe what he was seeing. "Iron thwarts lightning's power."

"I'm telling you, brother, my prayers to lightning have driven the Pale Eyes away."

Red Sleeves had no trouble believing that the spirits, Lightning or otherwise, had answered everyone's prayers. He held his arms out at his sides with his palms up. He tilted his slab of a chin so the hot sun beat down onto his face. With his eyes closed, he started to dance. He hopped on one huge, flat foot and then the other, waving his arms and circling in place. He looked like a vulture trying to get into the air after eating too much of a dead mule.

Lozen lay on her stomach next to Victorio while he studied the Bluecoats through Hairy Foot's far-seeing tube. Broken Foot lay nearby, with Geronimo next to him, and the rest of the raiding party was hidden across the ridgeline. The Bluecoats' collection of wooden buildings in Doubtful Pass controlled access to the only spring for a day's journey in either direction. They hindered the Chiricahuas' travel between Cheis's stronghold to the west of the fort and the Red Paints' country to the east.

They hadn't kept Cheis's Tall Cliffs men and the Red Paint warriors from stealing the army's horses and mules. They had attacked supply trains and sniped at patrols, but the Bluecoats had taken their toll, too. Companies of them rode into the mountains and harried The People. No one could sleep in peace.

Now they were leaving. They gathered on the parade ground and formed their ritual lines, angular and precise. The drivers pulled their loaded wagons up in formation behind them. The few head of stock that the Chiricahuas hadn't stolen made a pitiful showing at the rear.

Soldiers walked from building to building with torches. They reached up and touched the flames to the roofs whose shingles were dry as punk. The fires spread quickly. Lozen could hear the distant crackling, like insects in rotten wood.

"The day must not be hot enough for them." Victorio passed the telescope to Broken Foot.

"Maybe they're planning to have a feast before they leave." Broken Foot peered through the tube. "Maybe they're going to toss those few sorry mules onto the flames to roast."

"We killed Mexicans without their help." Geronimo's thin lips warped into a smile. "Now we can kill them without their interference."

Behind them, Red Sleeves, still dancing, started chanting a victory song. The Chiricahuas had driven away the Bluecoats. This country would be theirs again. Red Sleeves had made excuse after excuse not to go to the talks that would force him to surrender his people's land. Now he would have to endure no more of Tse'k cajoling him to pick up the writing stick and make an *X* mark on the Pale Eyes' talking leaves.

Red Sleeves feared those pale, angular, whispering leaves more than thunder, lightning, Ghost Owl, or as many guns as the Bluecoats could level at him. The paper derived its power from a magical place called Wah-sin-ton, or maybe a powerful *di-yin* named Wah-sin-ton. Whatever it was, it had the power to take his country from him, to drive his people from their homes.

A tardy soldier, hoisting his rucksack onto his back, ran to fill the last empty spot in the ranks. The bugle gave its cry, and the drums started a cadence so compelling that Lozen's feet twitched in time to it. The mounted Bluecoats left first, and the walking soldiers followed. The wagons started in the squealing of axles; then the drovers whistled and shouted to get the cattle and mules moving into the cloud of dust.

Lozen realized that they were marching from west to east, as she had seen in her vision, but this was not how she had interpreted it. She braced herself for the ridicule. Victorio, Broken Foot, Loco, and He Steals Love said nothing, but not Geronimo.

He looked at Victorio with a satisfied smile. "Perhaps your sister is not so wise as she thinks."

Victorio ignored Geronimo as a wolf would ignore a hound pup. Lozen could hear the others start in, though. They pointed with their noses at the retreating army.

"It's just as *nantan*'s sister said," they chortled. "The Bluecoats are marching from west to east."

They had a lot more to say, and Lozen remembered what Broken Foot had told her more than once. "A seer has much more difficulty holding on to his reputation than acquiring it."

"Don't pay any attention to them." Victorio said. "You saw correctly, but we interpreted your vision wrong."

Lozen stared at the men, wagons, and animals disappearing into their own dust. She hadn't misunderstood the vision. This was not what she had seen. This was not what it meant.

BATS TRAVELED SWIFTLY, AND THEY WERE GOOD AT CLINGing. People who rode well were believed to have bat magic. People said Lozen had it herself. She suspected that the tall Pale Eyes named Hairy Foot had Bat magic, but she started calling him *Ch'banne*, Bat, for another reason.

She knew his big red stallion's hoofmarks as well as the footprints of each member of her family. On her trips with Victorio she often found them on the trail in the morning, where they had not been the night before. To avoid Cheis's war parties, he had become a night creature, like Skunk, Ring-tail, or Owl. Like Bat.

Victorio and some of his people had been visiting Cheis, and now he, Lozen, and few others were enjoying the freedom to roam unhindered. If they came across a supply of ammunition or some cattle, so much the better. Cheis's people had plundered the country so thoroughly, though, that cattle were scarce.

This morning the sun had caught Hairy Foot just north of the old Mexican church called Tumacacori. He was far from a cave or outlying rancho, or wherever he holed up when daylight caught him between destinations. Talks A Lot, Ears So Big, Chato, and He Steals Love were jubilant. They all wanted Hairy Foot's horse.

Kicking their heels into their ponies' sides, they slid down the slope in a shower of talus, hit the valley floor running, and galloped after him, trailing their war cry. Lozen followed them. Victorio and Broken Foot knew better than to waste their time. They had chased that big red chimera before.

Lozen had no illusions of catching Hairy Foot. She only wanted to pull ahead of the men and get between them and their quarry so they couldn't kill him. She was riding a gray gelding that she had recently stolen from a hacienda. He had good wind and strong legs, and he had almost paralleled Chato when he raised his musket and fired.

Hairy Foot jerked; then he regained his seat and his horse leaped forward. Steals Love nocked an arrow and raised his bow. Lozen wanted to shout at him, to tell him not to kill this yellow-hair. This one should not die like a deer on the run. But warriors did not tell others what to do. The men might refuse to consider her a warrior, but she would give them no reason to think of her as a meddling female.

He Steals Love's arrow sank into Hairy Foot's back, but he didn't fall. He pulled away from them with the arrow still stuck in him, bobbing behind him. It looked as though it were waving at them in the silly way white people flapped their hands in farewell.

Talks A Lot turned his smoke-colored pony around to ride alongside Lozen. "You're right about that one," he said. "He's hard to kill."

RAFE SLOWED RED TO A WALK WHEN HE SAW THAT HIS pursuers had given up. He reached behind him and tugged at the arrow. The arrowhead came out attached to the shaft only because it hadn't penetrated his body. The Apaches fastened the points with deer sinew that stayed taut as long as it was dry. Once wet with blood, the cord loosened and left the head inside to work more mischief when the shaft was pulled out. Often the Apaches coated the arrowhead with poison.

He tugged his shirttail out of his trousers and took the beaded pouch from where it rode at the small of his back. It now had two holes in it, a round one and a triangular tear. He took out the book inside.

When he opened it, pollen fell out, staining his fingers yellow. He leafed back, separating the pages stuck together by the passage of the ball. He found the flattened piece of lead in Act V, punctuating the line, "The time and my intents are savage-wild, / More fierce and more inexorable far / Than empty tigers or the roaring sea." The bottom of the ball was wedged into the back cover, dimpling it.

He pried it out and tossed it in the palm of his hand. He started to throw it away but put it into his coat pocket as a keepsake. He murmured thanks to the Almighty that the Apache who fired it had been either careless or frugal when he measured his powder. If this bullet had had a few grains more force behind it, it would have torn through the slender volume and severed his spine.

He let Red blow while he waited for Patch to catch up with him. The dog bustled out of the brush, sniffing every rock and bush as she came. She stood in front of Red with her muzzle raised. Red lowered his head so he could touch noses with her in their usual greeting.

Rafe pulled his coat closer in the chill February wind and started out again. Patch coursed ahead of him, casting here and there. She alerted Rafe whenever Apaches were near, and she knew how to avoid them when they arrived.

He turned in at the ranch where he often stopped, but he found the roof of the main house burned, and the front wall battered in. Broken furniture, torn mattresses, and pottery shards filled the courtyard. The naked bodies of the two men who had lived here lay sprawled behind an upturned oak table splintered with bullet holes.

"Dear God," Rafe breathed.

Lances jutted up from the corpses. A pitchfork had been sunk to the base of the tines in the chest of one of them. Rafe wanted to bury them, but he had to reach Tubac, and the Apaches might return at any time.

He checked the stone-lined cistern in the center of the court. At least nothing dead floated in it. He let Red drink. He found a copper pot among the debris, filled it, and set it down for Patch. Then he filled the canteens hanging behind his saddle like two clusters of big wooden grapes.

Behind the canteens rode the leather mailbags. They weren't very full these days, but though he delivered less he charged more, so it evened out. Carrying messages, mail, and small loads was making Rafe a rather wealthy man, if he lived long enough to spend it. Few men would leave the safety of Tubac's walls not far to the north of here. Tucson was the only other settlement in the part of New Mexico Territory called Arizona. Below Tubac was the deserted mission of Tumacacori. Tucson, Tubac, Tumacacori, and to hell, was how people described this road, but hell started well north of the border with Mexico these days. Rafe figured the devil was expanding his territory as much as the Apaches were.

Rafe always collected his fees in advance. There was too much likelihood that the receiver would be dead when he arrived or the sender would be dead when he returned. He might be killed himself, of course, but that was a chance he and his employers would have to take.

This rancho had been the last inhabited place on the road between Tumacacori and Tubac, and now Cochise's men had destroyed it. With despondency weighing heavy, Rafe started out again, past the bones of dead cattle, burned wagons, abandoned houses, and ranches. In the past year something new had been added to the landscape. Canted, sun-bleached boards stuck vertically into the ground marked the graves of those caught by marauders of one race or another. Rafe felt as though he were riding through a vast graveyard.

"Bascom." Rafe said it aloud. He had taken to talking to himself just to hear the sound of a voice in the middle of so much desolation. Red's ears flicked back to listen. "That damned, arrogant shavetail lieutenant. He set this butchery in motion, Red, and it may be the death of us all."

He thought of Cochise looking up at him while he loaded baggage on top of the stagecoach and recited Hamlet's soliloquy. He remembered the slight smile of amusement Cochise had given him. He had a face that made you look twice at it. It was a wise face, a reasonable face. Not the face of an implacable murderer.

An eye for an eye. The Apaches operated on that old biblical principle. They just didn't care whose eye it was, nor did they keep a strict accounting. For them the dictum was a thousand eyes for an eye.

Rafe knew better than to turn off at the road to the silver mine. He had gone there a fortnight ago to deliver a message from Don Esteban Ochoa, a merchant in Tucson who always paid him more than he asked. *"Para suerte,"* Ochoa would say with a smile when he handed him the extra coins. "For luck."

Rafe had found the mine's American manager with a steel rock-drill through his chest. Bullets had perforated the two German employees. One of the Germans still lay on his cot, wrapped in his blankets, as though to use it as a shield against the bullets.

Apaches hadn't wrought that particular carnage. Rafe had found no lances, no arrows, and no Mexican corpses. Apaches would never have let the Mexican workers escape. He had studied the trampled ground around the American's body, circling outward until he found the print of a sandal. The rope sole swirled in a pattern peculiar to Agua Zarca in Sonora, just over the border from the Tumacacori mission.

He guessed it was the work of the gang of Mexican roughs who had added their malevolence to the general evil plaguing the country. Once the army left, they had hustled across the border like bargain hunters to a fire sale. They probably had recruited their countrymen working at the silver mine. They had slaughtered the American and the two Germans and taken what silver had been smelted into bars.

Rafe could tell that Apaches had been there since the massacre. He recognized the prints of their unshod ponies. Also they had chipped off hardened pieces of slag from the smelter furnace to use as bullets. The slag contained sulfur and arsenic as well as copper and lead. The wounds they created always became hideously infected. Rafe believed the Apaches knew that. For people without advanced industry of their own, they were swift to take advantage of any that came their way.

He reached Tubac safely, but he stayed only until nightfall. When the United States soldiers decamped in July, they had burned all the supplies. They had heard that Col. John Baylor was on his way from San Antonio with a horde of Texans, and they didn't want anything useful to fall into rebel hands. Rumor had it that Baylor had announced a plan to lure the Apaches with promises of treaties and presents, then exterminate the men and sell the women and children as slaves to cover the expense of his campaign. Rafe didn't want to cross trails with him.

Whether Baylor was on his way or not didn't really matter. The Mexican banditti to the south of Tubac and the Apaches to the east made survival there difficult enough. The twenty men holed up behind the settlement's adobe walls had decided to sneak out after dark and make a dash for Tucson thirty miles north.

Rafe said he had things to do and let them leave first. If any Apaches were awake tonight, the thunder of eighty hooves would get their attention. He dozed, sitting with his back against the inside of the west-facing adobe wall, trying to extract the last of the afternoon sun's warmth from it.

When the men were long gone and the full moon had risen, he saddled Red and whistled for Patch.

Rafe rode all night. The sun had yet to make an appearance, but the desert was awash in pale light when Rafe approached Bill's rambling estate. A breeze blew the odor of roasting meat toward him. His stomach rumbled, and his mouth watered in anticipation of the barbecued pig's ribs he would share with the old man for breakfast. The chili-laced sauce that Bill slathered on the meat would keep Rafe awake for the rest of the ride to Tucson. Then he saw Patch's hackles rise. He loaded his Sharp's and capped it.

As he drew closer, he saw that most of Bill's arbors and huts had collapsed into charred ruins. Apaches, most likely, had dismantled Bill's handiwork and stacked the wood against the base of the boiler. From the size of the heap of ashes there, Rafe could see that the fire they started must have made a hellish inferno even in the February cold.

He leaned on the pommel and stared at the door Bill had cut into the side of the boiler. From the various openings for fittings issued a stench of burnt, rotting flesh that almost overpowered him. Rafe wanted to ride away, but he dismounted and tried to open the door. He was relieved that Bill had bolted it from the inside. He rattled it.

"Bill, you old fool, I can't even bury your sorry carcass." He stepped back and surveyed the boiler. "Although you couldn't have done better for a crypt," he added. "It'll be standing till the Next Coming."

He took off his hat, breathing as shallowly as possible to avoid the smell. He tried not to imagine what Bill's last hour on earth had been like.

"You made me laugh, Bill. A man can't ask better than that from a friend." He bowed his head and recited the words he had heard so often in his life. " 'We therefore commit his body to the ground; earth to earth, ashes to ashes, dust to dust; in sure and certain hope of the resurrection to eternal life.' "

In Bill's case, he thought, the ashes part is surely appropriate.

A gust stirred up the ashes heaped against the boiler and blew them in an eddy around his legs. He remembered the ashes he had seen smeared on Lozen's face and Pandora's when they returned Absalom's body to him. His Navajo wife had told him many years ago that Apaches believed the ashes kept away ghosts. The odd notion struck him that these ashes belonged to Bill, even though he knew Bill's remains were inside the boiler. Or at least he assumed they were. Something in there was stinking up the countryside.

As more ashes blew toward him, he felt a sudden certainty that Bill's ghost was clutching at him, trying to get him to stay, to visit, maybe read a little *Romeo and Juliet* to him. Rafe clamped his hat back on his head and tightened the cord under his chin. He shifted the book at the small of his back into a more comfortable position and backed with respectful haste toward Red.

Chapter 29

SOUTHERN DISCOMFORT

Tucson had always been a rough-and-tumble town, but after the army left to quell the Southern rebellion in the east, it took on the desperate air of what the Bible called the Last Days. That being the case, Rafe wasn't surprised to find a celebration in progress when he rode through the main gate of the adobe wall that encircled it.

Makeshift bunting of cedar and juniper branches basted the rows of adobe houses together. Confederate flags flapped in the February wind. They'd been crudely sewn from bandanas, old army coats, and flour sacks. Most of the town's inhabitants whooped and hollered on the main street. Some of the men raised considerable dust jigging to a banjo that was playing either "Skip to My Lou" or "The Old Oaken Bucket," but Rafe couldn't tell which.

"They must be expecting a shipment of southern comfort," Rafe observed to Red. Red flicked his ears in agreement.

This southern comfort wouldn't be the sipping kind, though. It would have arms, legs, bad teeth, and a worse attitude. Soldiers of the Confederacy, what Rafe thought of as the rebel rabble, were on the way.

The sensible people had fled the territory. Those left were mostly Southerners, and the Southerners were mostly outlaws. The citizens of Tucson had always been strongly secessionist. Even if they weren't, they would welcome armed white men of any persuasion.

Rafe headed for the main plaza and the latest edition of Sarah Bowman's American House. A man standing on a crate near the door had drawn a small crowd. He pointed at

Rafe with a finger that seemed to have more than the required number of knuckles.

"Beware the serpent on the sideboard," he roared. "Shun the demon rum."

His audience raised high their bottles and mugs of home-made whiskey, and gave him three lusty huzzahs. Rafe glanced at him with a sudden, brief hope. Rum? Had The Great Western procured rum?

"The inhabitants of this yar earth have transgressed, my brethren. They have broken the everlasting covenant with their Maker." The prophet raised a dejected-looking Bible and shook it. "It says right here in Isaiah, chapter twenty-four, verse six. 'Therefore hath the curse devoured the earth, and they that dwell therein are desolate: therefore the inhabitants of the earth are burned, and few men left.' "

"You got that right, old son," Rafe muttered. He thought of the ashes blowing around the base of Bill's boiler and the canting wooden grave markers standing silent watch over the trail.

He handed Red's reins to the American House's hostler and stood in front of the notice tacked to the door. He had read it before, but he read it again, maybe hoping the news had changed since the last time. It was a torn, yellowed sheet from a newspaper seven months old. The article told of Union losses at a place called Bull Run in July of 1861. Untrained rebel forces, under the general who'd earned the nickname "Stonewall" Jackson there, had checked the Union soldiers' advance and then driven them back. The Federal retreat to Washington City had turned into a rout.

Rafe shook his head and went inside with Patch at his heels. Patch raised the hair along her back and growled at the dogs already in residence. They moved aside politely to let her pass. For once, the place was fairly quiet.

The only good to enter Tucson in the last seven months had been The Great Western. She had left Fort Yuma with the army when it pulled out, but she'd braked her old Stu-debaker wagon here. She had told Rafe then that this was as far east as she cared to go. Her Albert figured he'd be in place to stake claim to the abandoned silver mines when the dustup ended.

And besides, from what she had heard, the east was in turmoil, too, with brothers killing brothers in numbers that made the Apaches look like pikers. She had winked at Rafe and observed that at least the Apaches hadn't gotten ahold of cannon yet. "God help us when they do," Rafe had answered.

Now Western emerged from the kitchen, her yellow cap of the Third Artillery perched at the usual angle atop a heap of red hair. "No, Rafe," she shouted jovially. "We ain't got no rum, despite what Old Hellfire outside says. People been asking fer it ever since he started his sermon this morning."

She gave Rafe a hug that squeezed the breath out of him. The two pistols in her belt pressed into him painfully, but her bounteous breasts did, too, and he didn't complain. She held him out at arm's length and looked at him, her bottle-glass-green eyes bright with tears; then she pulled him against her again. She didn't say that she feared he had been killed, thus reducing by half her complement of friends outside her immediate household. She was an old soldier. Soldiers didn't talk about death. That was for amateurs.

Rafe sighed and closed his eyes, luxuriating in the comfort, warmth, and muscular softness of her, wrapped in arms like a pliant fortress of flesh. He was almost as tall as she was, but to be held by a woman her size made him feel like a child again. When she released him, she raised a hand and gestured toward the bar where Paz, the beautiful fifteen-year-old daughter of her Mexican friend, Mrs. Murphy, held court. Paz reached for the bottle she kept out of sight of the riffraff. Rafe knew his credit was good. Western kept his money for him in the strongbox hidden in the dirt floor beneath her bed.

He collected the bottle of bourbon and two glasses and took them to the table in the corner where Señor Esteban Ochoa sat. Don Esteban stood and extended a slender hand. His large dark eyes lit up, making him even handsomer and more aristocratic, if that were possible.

"Señor Rafael, I give thanks to God that He has brought

you back safely." He spoke better English than anyone else in town. Only a trace of an accent, his straight, black hair, dark eyes, and honey-colored complexion gave him away as Mexican.

Don Esteban reminded Rafe of the fact that there were men who wore grace and elegance as easily as others wore their skin. Rafe was always grateful to Don Esteban for that, for it was easy to forget, given the general quality of the citizenry of Arizona. Don Esteban, Mrs. Murphy, Western, and her swarm of adopted children—they gave him reason to believe humanity still had hope.

Don Esteban bowed to Western and Mrs. Murphy and pulled out a chair for each of them. They now had a quorum of the Union sympathizers in Tucson. Western held on her lap one of the orphans she had recently adopted, a doe-eyed Mexican boy three or four years of age. Another one, slightly older, wrestled with Patch on the dirt floor.

"Who are they expecting out there?" Rafe poured boubon into a glass and set it in front of Don Esteban. "Are the rebs coming?"

"They are already here." Don Esteban nodded thanks for the bourbon. "Under the command of a Captain Sherod Hunter."

"I've met him." Rafe poured himself a drink "Can't say it was a pleasure."

"He arrived yesterday with a hundred worthless wretches who call themselves the Confederate Arizona Volunteers," added Western.

"Where are they?"

"Most of them have gone to ground in the saloons. I told them their custom warn't welcome here."

Mrs. Murphy spoke, her husky Spanish accent mixed with Texas, Tennessee, and Ireland. "Captain Hunter told Don Esteban he had to take an oath of loyalty to the rebels or leave town."

"The captain was quite civil about it," said Ochoa. "Apologetic, even."

"Sherod Hunter has a lot to apologize for," Rafe muttered.

"He said he had heard I was a Union sympathizer, but he hoped that I would see that the Union was a thing of the past. He asked that I take the oath of allegiance to the Confederacy so that he would not have to confiscate my property and turn me out."

"What did you tell him?"

"That I owed everything to the Government of the United States and that I could not betray it."

"When do you have to leave?"

"Tonight. Captain Hunter will allow me a horse and a pair of saddlebags with whatever I can carry, plus a rifle and twenty rounds of ammunition."

"Twenty rounds of ammunition!" Western exploded. "Why didn't he just stand you up in front of a firing squad and be done with it?"

"Where will you go?" asked Rafe.

"Mesilla."

"By yourself? That's at the nether end of three hundred miles of Apache territory."

Ochoa shrugged. "God looks after children and fools."

"Crossing the border into Sonora would be closer. Besides, Mesilla is in the hands of John Baylor and his secesh rabble."

That Baylor had taken southern New Mexico rankled Rafe. He was mortified to the marrow by the buffoonery of the United States Army there. The chief buffoon was Maj. Isaac Lynde, who surrendered his five hundred men to Baylor's three hundred hairy Texans-on-a-tear. It hadn't helped the Union cause when many of the United States soldiers filled their canteens with whiskey for the hard retreat across the mountains from Arizona. They hadn't arrived in fighting trim.

"I have business contacts in Mesilla." Don Esteban's smile shifted into irony. "And the people in charge there do not know me."

He did not have to add that the people in charge were Anglos, and Texans to boot, and to them one Mexican looked very much like another.

"I'll go with you," Rafe said. "I know that country."

New Mexico. The lovely hoyden named Lozen seemed to be always on the roam there. Rafe had a brief but vivid memory of waking up in Fort Buchanan's wagon yard and seeing her face hovering over him like some wild sprite from one of Shakespeare's fantasies. He remembered the look of elusive chagrin that passed over her face when she realized she had failed once again to steal his horse. The thought only now occurred to him that she could easily have slit his throat while he slept and taken Red, but she hadn't.

Now he would be returning to the forested high country she no doubt thought of as home. He wondered if he would see her again. He wondered if she had lived through all this bloodshed.

Maybe New Mexico wasn't such a bad idea after all. Warfare raged there and lots of it, but at least so many soldiers in blue uniforms and gray ones meant the Apaches were keeping their heads down.

Don Esteban smiled. "You will be the archangel Rafael, sent by God to guide Tobit." Don Esteban leaned down to rub Patch's ears. "That Rafael had a dog, too."

"Who was Tobit?"

"It's an ancient tale from the Apocrypha. I'll tell it to you as we ride."

"Will you and your people come with us, Western?" Rafe had to ask, although he knew that Western would be all right here. No one ever troubled her, at least not more than once.

"No, but I thank you kindly for inquiring. I figure the United States Army will rout this rabble, and Albert and I will return to Fort Yuma with them quicker'n an earthquake wakes weasels."

"Why do you want to go back to Yuma?"

"It has its charms."

Rafe had carried a load of flour and bacon to Fort Yuma once, and he hadn't noticed any charms whatsoever. He hadn't even stayed long enough to impoverish the officers in a high-stakes game of whist.

"A soldier died there," Western said.

Chapter 30

LIGHTNING DANCES ALL AROUND

Morning was the time to weave baskets. Not even the grandmothers could say why, but that was the way it had always been. This morning was a particularly fine one. The women brought their children and their bundles of withes to the cottonwoods by the stream. They spread blankets and shared the food they had brought. They fed whatever child happened to toddle to them on legs just getting accustomed to walking.

Corn Stalk hung Wah-sin-ton's cradleboard from a low limb. The baby stared at the feathers and bird vertebrae strung along the canopy and dancing in the breeze. Other mothers leaned their cradles against the tree trunks or hung them so that they dangled like oversize fruit.

Some of the babies slept. Some watched the birds sing and squabble on nearby limbs. The little girls set down their miniature cradles and buckskin dolls. They began building a brush shelter by the stream and preparing a feast of twigs, acorns, and mud cakes. The stream rushed past, chuckling at the small boys who chased beside it, following the bark boats they had made. The sky shimmered as blue as the flowers of the wild flax. The trees and bushes and grasses glowed in vibrant green splashed with sunlight.

Lozen helped Daughter tie withes together to form the basket's frame while Stands Alone, Maria, She Moves Like Water, and the others set out their materials. Shallow baskets held the red bark of the yucca root and the black fruit of the devil's claw to work into designs. Stacks of mulberry withes to be used for the vertical framework were left whole. With teeth and fingernails the women split into thirds those that would form the horizontal rows. They scraped out the piths with the points of their knives.

Most of the women were making the wide-mouthed burden baskets for the coming harvest. The harvest would be dangerous, though. Cheis and his warriors had driven most of the Pale Eyes east across Doubtful Pass and into this country. They had divided into the Bluecoats and the Graycoats, and they swarmed everywhere, carrying their war with them.

Everyone speculated about why the Pale Eyes had gone to war, but not even Red Sleeves or Cheis or Victorio could explain it. The Bluecoats and the Graycoats were too busy killing each other to hunt the Ndee, but both sorts of soldiers fired on them whenever they saw them. The women had to gather what food they could, even if it meant staying higher in the mountains where fewer plants grew. Food supplies were so low that the men were talking of a raid into Mexico. Talks A Lot and several of his friends had already gone on one, their first alone.

The long withes nodded and whispered over the women's heads as they twined the split strands in and out among the vertical ones. Stands Alone was so large with the child inside her that she had to work at arm's length. Broken Foot's second wife, a young Mescalero woman named *Nteele*, Wide, pointed with her chin at Stands Alone.

"Looks like that one is about to push out a pony." She patted her own stomach. "I think I'm going to produce a bison."

"I hear when you Mescaleros drink *tiswin*, you sneak off to do something with the bison," said She Moves Like Water. "I hear that the bison over there, they look like Mescaleros."

Wide threw back her head and laughed. She was round and solid as a cactus fruit. She had a merry laugh and twinkling eyes. Broken Foot had brought her to live with him and his first wife a year ago. She was not a Chiricahua, but people liked her, anyway. They joked about her accent, though, and the strange words she used. They remarked about the odd shape of her moccasins. Some of the women called her Kiowa because her people's lands bordered those of that tribe. She took it with good humor, and she gave as good as she got.

"Kiowa," said She Moves Like Water, "that old man of yours must rub his thing with mescal paste, so it's plenty stiff."

"That old man of mine, he has the strength of two young ones," said Wide. "He's pretty good for a Chiricahua."

Wide pushed herself to her feet, bottom first, and lowered that bottom next to Lozen on the blanket. She took out a large packet of tin cones and another of cowrie shells and nodded toward Daughter.

"Maybe your niece would like these on the dress for her feast. I also have two fine skins I can give you for it."

"These would look pretty on a dress." Lozen let them stay on the blanket. She wanted to know what was expected in return.

"Will you make the little one's cradleboard for me?"

"Grandmother is the best at making them."

"I want you to make it. My people talk of your power."

Lozen looked at her in surprise. Women still asked her for herbs to cure whatever ailed them, but since the soldiers had retreated toward the east, everyone seemed to think most of her powers had left her. Spirits were fickle and apt to change allegiances with little notice.

"My people say good comes from whatever you touch," Wide added.

Lozen had helped Grandmother make many cradles, but she had never completed one herself, or sung the prayers that would grant its occupant long life.

"Grandmother gave me her song," Lozen said.

"Then you'll do it for me?"

"I'll ask the spirits, and give you my answer tomorrow."

A gnat flew into Wah-sin-ton's eye, and he began to cry. Daughter retrieved him and carried him to Lozen's blanket. She caught a bee, split it, and held it to his lips to taste the sweetness inside.

"Aunt," she said, "When I have a baby, will you make the cradle?"

"You have to run four times first." Lozen knew that She Moves Like Water was already thinking about whom to ask to sponsor her daughter in the ceremony of White Painted Woman.

"And you must learn how to cook and sew better than you do now," She Moves Like Water added. "No man wants a woman who lies around in the sun all day like a lizard."

How was it possible that the tiny child had become a woman, Lozen wondered. Where had the time flown? The years were like Broken Foot's geese, heading off to some unknown destination. She put her hand against her own stomach, as flat as any boy's. She felt sad not because she had no husband or children, but because she did not want them. She thought of the words her grandmother sang while making a cradle.

Good, like long life it goes.
With White Water circling under it, it is made.
With White Shell curved above it, it is made.
Lightning dances all around it, they say.
With Lightning it is fastened across.
Its strings are made of rainbows, they say.
Black Water makes a blanket to rest on.
White Water makes a blanket to rest on.
Sun rumbles inside it, they say.
Good, like long life the cradle is made.

As Wah-sin-ton now is wrapped in the good things of the world, so I once was, Lozen thought.

She had never tried to imagine herself as an infant in a cradleboard on her mother's back. Once, a blanket of White Water had kept her warm, White Shell had shaded her, the zigzag lacing of Lightning down the front had held her secure. Thongs of rainbows had tied the parts of her cradle together. Sun had kept her company, rumbling and ruminating in the rabbit fur blanket with her.

Several of the ten- and eleven-year-old boys skidded to a

stop in front of Lozen. Burns His Finger delivered the message. "Your brother wants you to come."

Lozen didn't ask why. She would find out soon enough. "Niece, take these things to my lodge."

Lozen didn't hurry. She didn't want to seem disconcerted, but she was. Victorio didn't usually send for her in the middle of the day. The women must have wondered about it, too. They gathered their work and their children, and hurried after her.

Lozen found the men at the council ring. Most of the band had assembled there already, and others hurried in.

Victorio stood up as she approached. "Sister, these men have something to report."

Talks A Lot directed his message to Victorio. "*Nantan,* we saw two thousand soldiers with three hundred and fifty horses and five hundred mules. They were three days' travel on the other side of the pass."

"How did they get to the other side of the pass without our seeing them?" Victorio asked.

Talks a Lot looked squarely at Lozen. "They marched from the west, just as your sister described."

The crowd murmured. That was impossible. How could soldiers come from the west? Lozen felt elation and fear. Her vision had been right about the Bluecoats, and that meant peril for them all.

"That's not possible," Geronimo growled.

"Do you say I deceive?" Talks A Lot rounded on him. "Or do you think I'm so foolish I don't know east from west?"

Geronimo waved his hand. "The sun rises in the east and so do Bluecoats."

"Not these Bluecoats." Talks A Lot knew that losing his temper in council would mark him as immature, so he held it in check. "We talked with Cheis. He knows about the soldiers. He saw a group of them on a scout, and he smoked with their leader. The Bluecoat told Cheis the soldiers' plan."

Talks A Lot paused. He knew what he had to say next would cause a stir. "The Bluecoat soldiers are going to march on foot through the pass to the Red Paints' country when the moon is full again. They plan to kill all the Pale Eyes Graycoats. Cheis wants the Red Paint warriors to join his men and ambush them in the pass. He sent messengers to hold council with Red Sleeves and with Long Neck."

Victorio didn't have to think about that long. "The plan is a good one. In a month the sun will be hot enough to cook a bird's egg on a flat rock. The soldiers must march a day and a half across the desert without a spring or a stream."

"That's what Cheis says." In his eagerness, Talks A Lot almost spoke before Victorio had finished. He looked chagrined, but Victorio waved him on. "We can hide above the spring at the pass. When the Pale Eyes get there, they'll be tired and thirsty. We can kill them all."

Victorio could see the eagerness in his men's faces. This was a plan that could not fail.

"We have to prepare. We'll collect the lead the Pale Eyes left at the mines when they fled east. We'll trade with the *comancheros* for powder. We'll soak cowhides in the stream to make shoes for the horses. We'll butcher our mules, and the women will dry the meat to take with us. We'll make war medicine."

"We have talked among ourselves, *Nantan*," Talks A Lot said. "All of us want your sister to come with us when we fight the Bluecoats. Cheis also asks that she come. He says that *nantan*'s sister is a *di-yin* with great power."

That was little consolation for Lozen. For longer than anyone could remember, Mexicans had attacked from the south and Navajos from the north. Yavapai, Pimas, and Papagos raided from the west. Bluecoats always marched from the east. Now the Pale Eyes soldiers could spring from anywhere. Like lighting.

Lozen thought of the cradle song. "Lighting dances all around it." The words had always comforted to her, but now they turned ominous.

PART THREE
1862

Shaman

Coyote and Dog Argue

Some dogs were going along in the woods. A coyote saw them, and he said, "Why don't you dogs come stay with us in the mountains. We're happy here. We live free among the trees and the cold clear streams. We eat deer and all kinds of good things."

The dogs said, "We live with some people, and they give us meat and a warm, dry place to sleep. They're all the time saying to us, 'You dogs, we love you.' "

The coyote said, "But up in these hills we hear you crying down below when those people whip you."

"If we don't obey our masters, they have to whip us sometimes."

"A whipping is a whipping," said Coyote.

"But you have many enemies out here in the woods. Down below, we don't have to dodge anyone the way you do. When it snows, you get cold while we stay warm. Sometimes you don't have enough to eat. We don't think we should live in the woods with you."

Coyote watched the dogs trot off down the mountain. "Still," he said to himself, "A whipping is a whipping." And he went away.

I'm talking about fruits and flowers and all sorts of good things.

Chapter 31

EXPENSIVE GIFTS

Grandmother was chanting her morning song so softly that it did not carry beyond the cluster of lodges and arbors of She Moves Like Water and Corn Stalk's camp. Lozen could see her sitting cross-legged at the doorway of her lodge built between a sandstone boulder and a walnut tree. Grandmother said the rock would shield her lodge from the wind. It would absorb the sun's rays on clear winter days and share its warmth with her. The walnut tree would shade her in the summer and deliver nuts to her in the fall. All she had to do, she said, was make sure the tree's gifts didn't hit her on the head. Gifts were like that, liable to hit the recipient on the head when she wasn't looking.

A few women gathered wood, fetched water, and blew the banked embers of their cookfires into flames. If they saw Lozen, they would tell her about their illnesses and misfortunes. They would solicit her advice on conjugal matters about which she knew little. They would ask her to hold a sing for them and give them medicine and charms. Usually she listened patiently, but she had something important to do today.

At the family's storage arbor she picked up her saddle, newest saddle blanket, and best bridle. Carrying the saddle on her hip with the blanket and bridle draped over it, she climbed to where she often greeted the day, and she said her morning prayers as the sun rose.

She circled the hoop-and-pole field where Talks A Lot and Chato were sweeping away debris. Battle with the Bluecoats might be imminent, but that wouldn't stop the men and the boys from spending most of the day here. Lozen cut across a shallow wash and heard a man's voice and a laugh from the thicket that filled the upper end of it. She was pretty sure the speakers were Maria and Ears So Big. Lozen smiled to herself. So that was why Ears So Big had been showing up at mealtimes and offering to help with the chores.

As Lozen approached the horse meadow, she saw the three children. Their mothers had probably sent them to gather sticks for the fire, but instead they were doing what Lozen had done when she was five or six. They had cornered Skinny's old gray warhorse. One boy held the gray's nose while the second one set a bare foot on the jutting angle of the pony's back knee. As he scrambled to climb aboard, the girl put her shoulder under him and lifted. He hauled himself up until he was lying on his stomach across the horse's back with his feet flailing. He righted himself, leaned down, and pulled her up. Then the two of them helped the other boy join them. They drummed their heels on the gray's sides and shouted. The pony moved as far as a thicker stand of grass.

Lozen walked through grass that brushed her thighs. Her new mare and old Coyote headed toward her at a trot, and the others followed, worried that they might miss something tasty, or at least mildly entertaining. The children whooped and bounced as the gray lurched into a canter to catch up with the herd.

The horses gathered around Lozen, and she stroked them. She crooked her arm under the jaw of Victorio's black stallion and slipped the bridle over his nose. He was the fastest and biggest the family owned. Only the best they had would do for the favor she was about to ask. She saddled the black and tied on the saddlebags. She slung the carbine case's strap over her shoulder and mounted.

Broken Foot's wives' camp was tucked into the crook of a sandstone outcrop near the river. Standing apart from them was the arthritic cedar that Broken Foot called Uncle. Broken Foot liked to spread his blankets between the exposed roots. He said that Uncle whispered stories to him when he slept there.

When Lozen was younger, she would stand with her arms

wrapped as far around Uncle's rough trunk as they would go. She would press her ear against the cedar, listening for whispers. She thought she heard them, but they might have been wind sighing through Uncle's branches.

She rode to the arbor where Wide and Her Eyes Open were slicing venison and hanging it on racks to dry. Since the birth of her daughter, Wide's breasts had outgrown her doeskin top, and she wore a blanket like a poncho while she sewed a bigger one. At the hoop-and-pole field, Broken Foot liked to grumble that he would have to trade for a couple of bison hides to get enough leather to cover her. "She'll keep me warm this winter though," he would say. Victorio had looked solemnly at him. "We'll have to send a search party for you, old friend. We will have to roll her off you, and pull out your flattened body."

Her Eyes Open handed Lozen a warm mescal cake. "He's expecting you, Daughter."

Wide nodded toward the dark-eyed child staring at her from her new cradleboard. "My daughter has learned to catch the blue stone you hung from the cradle. She goes after it more often than the other charms. Wouldn't you say that's a good sign, Cradlemaker?"

"My grandmother says that's a very good sign. She says your daughter will be a great beauty."

Lozen turned the horse upriver. She didn't tell Wide that Grandmother had also said, "That child will cause her family trouble."

Her Eyes Open had said Broken Foot was expecting her. That was good. Lozen had to time this right. Before his morning prayers, Broken Foot usually limped off downriver to find a good place to defecate. He sometimes walked a long way in search of the best spot, one where he wouldn't be disturbed.

Lozen dismounted and led the black to where Broken Foot sat cross-legged on his favorite shelf of rock jutting out over the stream. His long, wrinkled legs and arms looked like driftwood washed up there. This was where he came to greet each new day, enjoy a cigarillo, and see the sun along on its journey. Smoke issued from his narrow nostrils and spiraled past his nose.

He turned to look at her, his face as long and narrow as a horse's. His upper lip was so thin that it seemed folded in above the lower one. His lower lip protruded full and dark red as a ripe cactus fruit. He had a habit, when he was deep in thought, of chewing on his lower lip as though it really were a cactus fruit.

He stared at her for such a long time that she began to fidget.

"My brother hopes you have use for this pony and saddle, and for the blankets and tobacco he sends you." Lozen tethered the black to a cottonwood where he could crop the grass. She put the tobacco pouch onto the rock, along with the carbine. Parting with the rifle pained her, but small gifts would not do today.

"You and your brother trained that black horse well."

Broken Foot took out a pinch of tobacco. He picked up a leaf from the stack next to him and trailed tobacco along its length. He took a smoldering shred of juniper bark and lit the cigarillo. He watched the smoke rise as though he had never seen such a thing before.

Lozen waited, but he seemed to have forgotten her. Maybe her lessons would start later. Maybe he had changed his mind. Maybe he didn't want to teach her at all. And maybe, now that the time had come, maybe she didn't want to learn.

Becoming a *di-yin* was an arduous, time-devouring process for the teacher and for the student. It was ruinously expensive besides. Years were required to learn the hundreds of songs, the prayers, and the rituals necessary to keep on good terms with the world of spirits. If Broken Foot didn't want to start down that long trail, life would be much simpler. Relieved, Lozen turned to leave.

"Where are you going in such a hurry?"

"I have to weave baskets for the harvest and scrape deer hides for Daughter's feast dress."

"Sit."

She climbed onto the rock and drew her heels up under

her skirt. She wrapped her arms around her legs, rested her chin on her knees, and watched the stream hustle over the rocks. As the silence lengthened, she began to hear voices in the splash and chatter of the water. She was trying to make out what they were saying when Broken Foot spoke.

"Are those the deer hides He Steals Love brought for you?" His voice jerked her back to the rock and the business at hand.

"He brought them for Daughter's feast."

"He brought them for you. He pretended they were for Daughter."

"He asked nothing from me in return."

"He still wants to marry you." He turned to look at her. "He's a good fighter, and handsome besides. You can marry and be a *di-yin*, too, you know."

"I'm too old to marry."

"You were born the year of the Hair Takers' Death Feast. That means you've seen twenty-five harvests. That's not so old."

Lozen changed the subject. "Where do the geese go?"

"When I was a boy, the old men told me that the geese start their journey far to the north. They each carry twelve pieces of bread and they fly south for twelve days. When they've eaten the bread, they stop."

"Who bakes the bread for them?"

Broken Foot chuckled. "I never thought to ask the old men that." He drew in another lungful of smoke, closed his eyes, and let it out slowly. He blew smoke in each of the four directions.

"The places of our land speak to us," he said. "They tell us to act sensibly. They tell us not to make mistakes." He gestured to the water, the mountains, earth, and sky, the trees, and the buzzards circling. "Power saturates the world. All things have power, some more than others. Sometimes spirit beings give us some of their power. Sometimes, if we ask correctly, we can get power from them."

"Are the rocks alive, too?"

Broken Foot looked around at the high cliffs rimming the

valley, the boulders heaped at their base, and at the towering formations of sandstone. "Some of them."

"When I was a child, the tall rocks seemed like sentinels to me," Lozen said. "Like warriors protecting us all."

"That's what they are. You will protect our people, too, all of them. We will need all the protectors we can train. The young men think we can defeat the Bluecoats forever at Doubtful Pass, but I'm not so sure. We will have troubled times ahead, I think."

"I don't feel strong enough to protect everyone."

"The old ones, the grandmothers and grandfathers, watch all the children from the time they're born. They know what each is capable of. This one will be a great warrior. That one will prefer to stay home by the fire. This one will make people laugh. That one will cause sadness to his family. That one will chase women. The other will run away from a battle. They've been watching you for years. They're not surprised that the spirits have spoken to you."

"Sometimes I wish they hadn't"

"We have all wished that from time to time." He chuckled. "I prayed and fasted and asked for my power, but your spirit chose you. If you accept the responsibility, you must know how to approach that spirit and any others you encounter. You have to be able to appease your spirit and keep it happy, or it will turn on you. They can be spiteful."

"I don't think I'm ready."

"No one is ever ready." Broken Foot gave a rueful little smile. "The association between a *di-yin* and his power is like a marriage. It's different for each person, but it will last all your life, unless something goes wrong. And like a marriage, the union is not always peaceful. Sometimes it becomes strained, and the spirit gets angry with you, or you with it.

"You can refuse the gift, but you must choose now. You shouldn't start, then decide you want to quit."

Broken Foot smoked in silence while Sister weighed dread, excitement, pride, fear, awe, and uncertainty to see which was dominant. "I want to learn," she said finally.

"*Enjuh!* Good." He took a breath and started. "Remember that you do not merely pray. You are prayer. When you eat, that is prayer. When you dance, you're praying. When you sleep, when you chew hides to soften them, when you defecate, you're praying. But there are some prayers that can call the spirits and persuade them to help you."

He started to chant the prayer he recited each morning to greet the day. When he reached the end of the first line, he stopped. The words were different from those used every day. Lozen repeated them. He sang it again and she repeated it again. Then a third and a fourth time. When he thought she imitated the pronunciation, the timing, and the intonation well enough, he chanted the second line.

Lozen remembered sitting at a curing ceremony for her father. She and her family had sung the chorus of the *diyin*'s songs. The sing had gone on all night, and Lozen had fallen asleep to be poked awake by Grandmother's elbow in her side. She remembered trying not to sway as she stood for hours and days during the ceremony of White Painted Woman when Broken Foot sang cycle after cyle of four songs each. Thinking about it now, another emotion joined the dread, awe, fear, excitement, and uncertainty.

Boredom.

Chapter 32

MOVING HEAVEN AND EARTH

The women of The Great Western's household referred to her oversize bedstead as El Cielo. They called it "Heaven" because across its mahogany head-, foot-, and side boards, its Navajo maker had carved and painted, at Western's request, a fandango of cherubim in a gaudy cantina of clouds. On the stout legs supporting heaven, the Navajo had carved the four chiefs of the Insect People who were the first inhabitants of earth—Water Monster, Blue Heron, Frog, and White Mountain Thunder.

Four of Western's mustachioed muchachos tilted the bedstead to maneuver it through the door from the inner room. Once they cleared the opening, Western danced alongside, waving her arms and shouting, "*Tengan cuidado, tengan cuidado.* "Have a care, have a care." When they dropped it, she loosed a string of oaths in Spanish that made even Rafe blush. Ignoring her, the muchachos picked up the bed and headed for the front door. They seemed to consider her just the largest obstacle among many.

Western and her household had cleaned up the rubble from a hellacious going-away party the night before. Judging by the number of broken bottles, abandoned boots, pieces of torn clothing, and the still-unconscious revelers swept out with the cigarillo stubs, it must have been quite a fandango.

Now they were packing to move back to Fort Yuma. Rafe had seen armies break camp with less hullabaloo. The thick adobe walls resonated with shouts and orders in English and Spanish. Women and children ran back and forth. They dropped things, and occasionally, when circumstances warranted, they threw things.

Rafe felt disoriented by all the activity. Traveling alone at night made him think of himself as the only human being left in an indifferent universe. The solitude of those long night rides still rang like a knell in his bones.

He had arrived here before dawn as usual, as the last conscious celebrants staggered, singing, into the night. He had fallen onto the narrow bed in a small room off the rear courtyard. Still in darkness, he had risen to consciousness when Dulce, his favorite of Western's women, slid naked under the sheet and curled against him. She said nothing, but he recognized the scent and the feel of her.

The delirium her touch loosed in him was more intense than any that alcohol could create. The two of them had made a slow, langorous love that seemed more dream than reality. When they finished, he had fallen headfirst down the well of sleep.

He had waked after dawn to find Dulce so long gone that the covers no longer held her warmth. He had gotten up, washed in the horse trough, checked on Red, and with Patch at his heels, he had wandered into the kitchen. With stale tortillas, he had scooped the residue of cold beans from a pot and shared them with Patch while the kitchen staff stuffed utensils into sacks.

Rafe had returned to Tucson after four months of freighting supplies for the Union troops in New Mexico Territory. The only good news to come from there was that George Bascom had been killed at the battle of Valverde. Unfortunately the Rebs also were killing a lot of Union soldiers who had less to answer to heaven for than Bascom.

Rafe knew it was time to leave New Mexico when recruiting sergeants started eyeing him wolfishly. Besides, he'd heard that federal troops from California had retaken Fort Yuma and were headed for Tucson. He arrived to find that the Rebs had decamped and the Union soldiers had occupied the town a few days before.

Now he was trying not to think about how much he would miss Western and the assortment of humanity she referred to as her family. Rafe sipped the whiskey Dulce set in front of him as she rushed by, and he savored the frisson caused by her hot breath stirring the hair above his ears. To keep his mind from how much he would miss her and Western, he read the latest edition of the *Tucson Times* slowly from front to back, and then from back to front.

The editor usually included a column of instructions on some useful subject or other—how to shoe a horse, or build a flutter mill, or rive shingles. This week he offered his readers advice on how to kill Apaches. He suggested mixing brown sugar with strychnine and pressing it into cakes. One could wrap the cakes in cloth bags and tie them to the saddle. "When pursued by the red vermin," he wrote, "cut the sacks loose and return in an hour or so to collect a crop of hair from the corpses." He added a postscript, "The method works equally well on Navajos, coyotes, and rats."

Western approached, curly strands of damp red hair clinging to her forehead. She pushed them away with the back of her hand.

Rafe rose politely, and while he was up, he put his own hand on the back of the chair. "Do you need to load these?"

"No." Western sat down. "A gent has offered to take the whole kit and caboodle. He wanted to buy my girls, too. I said they go with me, if they want to."

Rafe thought about asking Dulce to stay with him. He tried to imagine living on a small rancho with her. He would plant corn and raise some cattle. She would keep his clothes clean and neatly patched, and his belly full of tortillas, beans, and chiles. If he married her, he would have to stay with her, to protect her from the Apache raids. He would have to look at the same view every day. He knew he couldn't do it. He knew he would only break her heart.

Western broke into his reverie. She gestured to the people still scurrying past her. "What was it Poor Richard said in his almanac, 'A few moves are as bad as a fire'?"

Rafe chuckled. "You could stay." That would solve the problem really. Dulce would be waiting for him here whenever he returned from his wanderings.

"My Albert is certain that the diggings near Fort Yuma will produce gold and silver in quantity."

Rafe couldn't bring himself to tell her that he had seen her Albert in Mesilla in convoy with the young widowed wife of a miner. Albert seemed to have been consoling the widow very effectively.

Rafe handed Western a piece of paper, creamy-colored, stiff as parchment, folded in thirds, and sealed with a circle of red wax. "Don Esteban sent you this."

Sarah stowed the letter in the waist of her skirt, next to her pistols. "I thank you kindly, Rafe. Is the don doing well?"

"Very well." Rafe knew Sarah would ask Mrs. Murphy to read the letter to her later. Rafe would never embarrass her by offering to read it, thereby letting slip that he knew she couldn't do so herself.

Sarah leaned forward and lowered her voice. "We're leaving the strongbox till last. Bring your saddlebags 'round back after sundown, and we'll transfer your money." She crossed her arms, as though about to offer him the deal of a lifetime. "Of course, I can give you fifty thousand dollars in paper money for those double eagles of yours. The paper'd be easier to carry."

"That would be Confederate currency, would it not?"

Western gave him a green-eyed grin. "Guaranteed theft-proof."

"That's the only thing guaranteed about them. I hear that since the Rebs left, people have been using their paper money in the privies." Rafe let the whiskey burn down his throat. "What do you hear about the general in charge of the California troops?" Rafe figured Western would know. News stopped here first, even official army dispatches.

"James Carleton? I met him at the market shortly after the troops arrived." Her smile soured a bit. "He's thin as a windlestraw, pale as a peeled turnip, and as gloomy as if his mother had just died owing him two dollars." She glanced toward the door. "Speak of the devil."

The tall officer took off his hat and peered into the dimness of the American House's interior. "Mrs. Bowman, good day to you." He looked distinctly uncomfortable at being here, and he wasted no time on amenities. "Perhaps you could tell me where I might find a Mr. Rafe Collins." He had the pinched accent of someone from the spare, cold northern states—Maine, maybe, or Massachusetts.

"You might find him sitting here with me, General. Won't you join us?" Sarah produced a bottle and set it on the table.

"I do not touch spiritous drink, Mrs. Bowman. 'Nor thieves, nor coveters, nor drunkards, nor revilers shall inherit the kingdom of God,' " he intoned.

"I suppose," said Western. "But there you have Jesus turning all that water into wine at the wedding. Don't you reckon he inherited the kingdom?"

Carleton pretended he didn't hear her. Standing as though on parade, he turned his gray eyes to Rafe. Rafe had seen musket balls with more mercy in them.

A George Bascom departs this mortal coil, he thought, and a James Carleton arrives. God does have a sense of continuity.

"Mr. Collins, you have been recommended as a scout and a driver who knows the Overland Trail better than anyone in the Territory.

Rafe glanced at Western. She shook her head.

"Twarn't me, Rafe. Though it's true, no one knows the trails like you do." She smiled up at General Carleton, obviously amused by his discomfort at being in her den of iniquity. "Apache arrows bounce off Rafe Collins like pebbles off an India-rubber bathing apparatus."

Talk of bathing apparatuses turned General Carleton's face as scarlet as the trim on his starched uniform. "Captain Cremony said I should try to find you, Mr. Collins, if you were still alive."

"Would that be the John Cremony who served on the Boundary Commission back in '50, '51?" Rafe asked

"It would. He's in charge of my cavalry troops."

"You would have to hire me and my rig. I plan to buy a wagon today and a team of mules." Though, to tell the truth, Rafe had no idea where he'd find enough mules to make up a span, unless he bargained with the Apaches, who'd stolen most of them in the territory.

"Then we will pay you as an independent contractor. Captain Cremony will put you on the rolls."

In his years in the army, Rafe had met plenty of Carleton's ilk. If the word *martinet* hadn't been coined to fit him, then he had been created to define the word. He was the sort who mistook bluster for the aura of command. Carleton raised two fingers and touched the air where the brim of his hat would be if he were wearing it. He turned on his polished heels and left.

"He fair bristles with dispproval, don't he?" observed Western. "He's a God-fearing man and an Apache-hating man."

"Most men hate Apaches. Even the Apaches hate each other."

"Not like this one, Rafe." Western stared at the door through which Carleton had just hurried, knocking aside a couple of muchachos in his flight. "Not like this one."

RAFE WAS MORE AT HOME IN WAGON YARDS THAN ANY-where else. He felt a muted joy and an intense satisfaction in the beauty, practicality, and toughness of wagons. He liked to put a hand on them, to feel the rough wood of their frames and the cold iron of their fittings.

Apache and Mexican bandits had put an end to freight hauling. These wagons had been parked a long time. Their condition hadn't improved any in the four months Rafe had been away. Grass and bushes grew between the spokes. Canvas rotted on their ashwood hoops.

The one Rafe wanted stood in the same place he had last seen it. It was an old Wilson wagon, the sort the government used during the recent war against the Mormons. The iron fittings had rusted and would have to be replaced, but even in this dry climate, the wooden body did not have to be wedged to make it fit tightly. Its makers had used oak for the framing, gum for the hubs, hickory for the axletrees, and poplar for the siding. He could find no knots or soft spots.

"If you's fixin' to buy her, Marse Rafe, you's made a good choice."

Rafe whirled around. "Caesar!" He held out his hand, and with no hesitation Caesar's huge fingers enveloped it. His grip was strong and sure, and Rafe could find nothing of a slave in it. Caesar's haunting hazel eyes looked directly into his.

"I's sure glad to see you, Marse Rafe. I thought those Apaches might have caught up with you. Then I saw Red over yonder at the stable, and I knew they hadn't."

"It hasn't been for lack of trying." Rafe and Caesar walked around the wagon, studying it from every angle.

"When you buy this here wagon," Caesar said, "I could help you fix it up. I's learned a thing or two about 'em."

Rafe lifted the mildewed canvas and looked inside while he searched for the best words to break sad news to Caesar. "Are you driving for the army?"

"Yes, sir, thanks to you, sir." Caesar slid him a sideways smile. "All that training you gave Marse Absalom and me came in handy."

"How is Carleton to work for?"

Caesar shrugged. "I stays out of his way. He surely hates Apaches, though."

Rafe found it odd that two people would mention a fact that applied to so many. "Does he hate them more than most?"

"Yes, sir, he does."

Rafe knew he couldn't avoid the subject any longer. "I saw Absalom when he rode through on his way back."

"Did you now?" Caesar's face lit up. "I was thinking of going east once't the Yanks have whipped the Rebs. Helping out on the farm with him and Miss Lila. I 'spect the slaves will all be freed then and he'll need a hand."

"He was killed."

"Apaches?" Caesar squatted, sat back on his heels with his elbows resting on his knees, and pretended to study the broken rear wheel.

Rafe leaned against the wagon bed, glanced sideways, and saw a glitter of grief in Ceasar's eyes. "I don't think so," he said gently. "Remember Pandora?"

"I do." Caesar pretended to wipe his brow on his arm.

"She and that little horse thief they call Lozen brought his body to me, must've been ten years ago at least."

" 'The quality of mercy is not strained,' " Caesar said.

Rafe knew Caesar was referring to Absalom, and he wasn't surprised that he could quote Shakespeare. He had heard Absalom and Rafe recite the Band for hours, for days, for weeks on the trail.

" 'It droppeth as the gentle rain from heaven,' " Rafe added.

" 'It blesseth him that gives and him that takes.' "

"He was a good man," Rafe said. "Merciful and just."

"Yes, sir, he was that. Do you know where he's lying?"

"I buried him under a cottonwood on a pretty hill near a stream in the mountains not far from Pinos Altos. Lots of sunlight in winter and shade in summer. Birds singing all year round. It's a place I'd like to spend eternity, if I had a choice."

"General Carleton reckons to use the infantry to secure the spring at Doubtful Pass. Then the wagons will follow with the cavalry as escort. He plans to build a supply depot at the Pass. Once't the army has dug in its heels there, I'd like to find Marse Absalom's grave."

"I'll take you to it, but the Apaches might have other plans for that spring at the pass. It's a proper place for an ambush."

Paso del Dado, the Pass of Chance. Cochise had made the name more fitting than ever in its long history.

Caesar rose and beckoned. Rafe followed him to where canvas shrouded two humped shapes. They had a familiar profile, but Rafe hadn't seen any like them since he left the army in 1848.

"Morning, Private Teal," Caesar said to the soldier on guard.

Private Teal touched the brim of his hat. He had the face of a boy. He reminded Rafe of a thousand others.

"May I show Mr. Collins the twins?" Caesar asked.

"Be my guest."

Caesar pulled back one of the canvas covers.

"Howitzers," Rafe said.

"I reckon these will give the hostiles something to chew on," Private Teal said.

Rafe nodded toward the plaza and the long adobe building that still had The American House's sign over the doorway.

"I would bet my liver that The Great Western has saved out a bottle or two," Rafe said to Caesar. "I'm buying."

Caesar hesitated. "I don't want to cause no trouble for you, Marse Rafe, sir. They's a lot of Southerners in this town."

Rafe winked. "Not as many as there used to be."

As the two of them walked toward The American House, Caesar said in a low voice, "Marse Rafe, Absalom was my brother."

"I know," said Rafe.

Chapter 33

UNDER FIRE

A gaudy parade of lightning and thunder marched through the pass. Lozen, Victorio, and the Warm Springs men stacked their weapons at the back of the sandstone overhang and waited out the storm there. While the rain cascaded off the ledge above, the men pretended they didn't fear the sickness that lightning and thunder could cause.

He Makes Them Laugh sat on his heels apart from the others. He rested his elbows on his thighs and watched the river of mud thrashing by on its way downslope. Lozen crouched next to him and shouted over the racket of the water and the thunder.

"Have you decided to become a warrior at last, Cousin?"

"No." His eyes were sad, and Lozen realized she had never seen him that way. "Courage is the fear of being thought a coward," he said. "But I don't have even that much courage. I'm too much of a coward to care what people think of me."

Lozen knew that wasn't true. He didn't lack courage. She waited. He would tell her what was on his mind, or he wouldn't. The rain stopped, and water dripped from the ledge overhead. The thunder growled off like a mountain lion leaving a carcass after it had eaten its fill.

"I'm here because of the child that my woman carries."

He held his hand out, as though he could touch the tawny undulations of the plain far below. It seemed to go on forever, but they both knew that beyond it rose tree-covered mountains laced with clear streams. Birds sang there in cool glens.

Lozen knew what He Makes Them Laugh was thinking. The Bluecoats wanted to take all this from them. They had hounded Red Sleeves and his people to abandon the land and live on the tiny portion of it that the Pale Eyes left them. What had begun as a contest over horses, mules, and cattle had become a battle for their country, and for survival.

He Makes Them Laugh was right. A father couldn't let the land be taken from his child.

THE AIR HERE ON THE RIDGE WAS HEAVY WITH DUST AND held no trace of the storm that had roared through the day before. The parched ground had soaked up most of the rain-water that didn't run off into the washes. The summer sun had evaporated what little stood in puddles. It had heated the rocks until they burned Lozen's palms.

She dug the toes of her moccasins into the gravelly soil and heaved the boulder up the slope. Perspiration soaked the back of the blue shirt. It darkened a band at her waist where her cartridge belt cinched the cloth against her body. Another stain spread outward from the strap of her arrow quiver.

The shirt had been part of a supply train's captured load. Chato had given it and a Mexican saddle to her in exchange for a war amulet she had made and prayed over for him. The shirt was a fine one, but Lozen envied the men. They wore only moccasins, headbands, breechclouts, war cords, amulets, and bandoliers with their war caps tucked in them.

Lozen had tied her hair at her nape, but it lay wet and heavy on her neck. She wiped her face with her forearm and continued pushing the rock toward the ridgeline above her.

"Put it here." Victorio pointed to an opening in the low walls his men were building along the crest of the ridge. He poked his arm through the loopholes to make sure they would accomodate a gun barrel. On the other side of the narrow canyon Cheis's warriors were doing the same. Red Sleeves' men were making redoubts on the adjacent hilltop.

Talks A Lot and Chato helped Lozen lift the rock into place. All of them were filthy and bruised. Their hands bled. Talks A Lot spit on the rock, and the drops sizzled and vanished. He grinned at her.

"We could bake mescal cakes on these."

It was like him to waste the moisture he should have conserved. The boys and young men admired him for his bravado. If a bear had confronted him, Talks A Lot would have spit in his eye.

"I'm glad we don't live in stone houses like the Pale Eyes do," grunted Chato. "This would be a lot of work for the women."

"Why do we need a wall?" Talks A Lot grumbled. "We'll kill all the soldiers before they get this far."

Lozen didn't say anything. He knew the answer; wise warriors always planned for contingencies. The Bluecoats must not be allowed to reach the spring cascading into a green cleft below them.

Lozen ran her tongue over her dry lips. She remembered the times she and her friends had scooped up handfuls of the cold water after a long day of traveling. When they reached it, they were halfway between their country and that of Cheis's Tall Cliffs People. After today she could drink from it whenever she wanted. When the buzzards circled overhead, and the crows and coyotes gathered to feast on the dead soldiers, this country would belong to the Chiricahua again.

When the men finished the barricades, Lozen headed for the highest point of the pass. Many of the warriors followed her in case her spirits had something important to say. Below her, among the ribs and crevasses of the two converging ranges, threaded the trail that crossed the stony beds of washes, ran through steep-sided canyons, along the edges of ravines, and around rockfalls. It traversed narrow valleys and climbed talus slopes. This was the trail the soldiers would take.

Lozen could feel the rocks like live embers through the soles of her moccasins. The Pale Eyes walking soldiers must be suffering inside all those clothes. Blood must be filling their stiff shoes.

She circled slowly, and when she faced west, the rumbling started. She felt the familiar tingle in her fingers; but now she experienced a new sensation. In the darkness behind her closed eyelids she saw fire falling from the sky. She heard men shouting in terror, but which men were they?

"I saw a rain of fire." The image shook her.

"You saw the bullets from our guns falling on the Bluecoats," said Victorio. "We have three men for every one of theirs. We cannot lose this battle."

Of course he was right. The scouts had counted only sixty-two walking soldiers and six horse soldiers approaching. Half a day behind them ambled 240 cows and forty-five men with the wagons.

Victorio looked out over the land below. "The Bluecoats were born of women just as we were. They can be killed. When they enter the pass tomorrow, we'll kill them all." He held his musket over his head and shook it. Lozen felt confidence surge through the men like flood water down a wash.

Red Sleeves and his fifty warriors angled over to join them. His men had trouble keeping up with his long-legged strides. Now and then he turned to run backward and joke with them. As he loped along, the turkey feathers sticking out all over his war cap quivered. Red Sleeves had made his medicine and given his warriors a rousing speech. He had drunk the *tiswin* that his third wife had sent with him. He was going to kill Pale Eyes. He was a happy man.

"My brother," he shouted to Victorio, "My men and I are going to ride ahead and scout for those Bluecoats."

If Victorio didn't approve of Red Sleeves leaving his position, he could not say so. Red Sleeves wasn't asking for his approval or permission.

About midnight the spectral clank of a chain and a heavy tread caused Patch to growl and bristle. Rafe laid a hand on her back as he and Caesar watched the ghost walk into the fire's light. The ghost's left arm supported the blanket, bridle, and Ringgold saddle he carried on his shoulder. In his right hand he held a cavalry saber and scabbard near the middle so that it swung forward and back in counterpoint to his stride. The iron rings hitting the scabbard created the sound of a chain rattling. He looked tired for reasons other than the fact that it was the middle of the night.

"Lordy," Caesar breathed.

Rafe knew what he meant. John Teal was supposed to be dead. The sergeant said he had seen Teal's horse go down. The sergeant's other men, riding double, had barely made it back to the wagon train's camp. The Apaches had shot three horses out from under them.

"I'll fetch the sergeant." Caesar hurried off into the darkness.

John Teal let the saddle and bridle slide down his arm to the ground. Rafe held out his canteen, but Teal gave him a quizzical look. Water was more precious now than gold or silver.

"Drink your fill," Rafe said. "We'll reach the spring tomorrow."

"Mebbe." Still holding the saber, he tilted the canteen up. "First drink I've had in over twenty-four hours," Teal said. "Did the others make it through?"

"They did," said Rafe.

"Did they tell you what happened?"

"They said the Apaches let them march into the pass, then opened fire on the rear guard."

"They poured lead and arrows down on us for hours, and we couldn't even find a target. The captain, he sent out skirmishers, and we fought our way to the old stone stage station. We had shelter but no water. Marching forty miles and then fighting six hours with but one cup of coffee each, we was about used up, I can tell you. Had to keep fighting, though. If we couldn't reach the spring, we was dead anyway."

"What about the howitzers?"

"By the time we got 'em unpacked from the mules and assembled, dark was nippin' at our heels. Then one of the pieces overturned, and the hostiles' fire drove the other crew to shelter."

The sergeant strode up, tucking his uniform blouse into his trousers and buttoning his jacket. "Good God, man. What happened?"

Teal lowered himself onto a log. "The 'Pache put a bullet through my horse's hindquarters."

"We thought you was a goner."

"They was armed with single-shot muskets and my breechloader kept 'em from making a run at me. About sunset my ammunition give out. I decided that if they was going to kill me anyways I'd make the second-to-last bullet count. I picked out the biggest one, a giant of a fellow with an exploded chicken on his head."

"An exploded chicken?" Maynard asked.

"Feathers sticking out all over. Put me in mind of the time my oldest brother got ahold of a sizable firecracker. He tied it to one of the hens and lit it. Our ma gave him such a whuppin'."

"Did you hit him?" Rafe thought he knew who that big Apache was. He thought of Red Sleeves cadging tobacco and lucifers whenever he ran across him. He thought of the mistreatment Red Sleeves had had at the hands of the miners at Pinos Altos. Even so, he couldn't work up any sorry that the man might be dead.

"My ball hit him in the chest, and his friends dragged him off. I heard them riding away, so I unbuckled my spurs, collected my gear, and hightailed it."

"We know the lay of the land now," the sergeant said. "Tomorrow we'll get those howitzers working. Henry Shrapnel's exploding case shot will make Cochise regret that his mother introduced him to the light of day."

HE STEALS LOVE SNORED SOFTLY AT THE OTHER END OF the stone breastwork from Lozen. Talks A Lot and Flies In His Stew moved at a crouch to where she lay in her blanket. She couldn't see their faces or hands in the moon's pale light, but she knew that powder burns blackened them, just as they did her own. Firing the musket all afternoon had created a thirst that the few sips left in her water pouch could not satisfy. It wrapped her tongue like a blanket. It lodged in her throat like a thistle.

During the battle she had used her water to cool the carbine's lock and barrel, but the water sizzled and evaporated as soon as it hit the metal. As she primed, loaded, and fired, warfare became as methodical as stacking stones, and much hotter than that. Even in the night's chill, she could remember the gun's heat. Firing it had been like handling live coals.

She sat up with her blanket around her, and she and Talks A Lot and Flies In His Stew leaned their backs against the wall.

"A Bluecoat shot the Old Man in the chest," Talks A Lot murmured.

Lozen felt a chill in her bones. Red Sleeves had led his people since before she was born. Her brother, Skinny, Cheis, Loco, even Long Neck down in Mexico, they all depended on his wisdom and advice.

"Where is he?" she asked.

"His men are taking him to the Pale Eyes medicine man in Janos."

"All his men?"

"Yes. They left already." Talks A Lot paused. "The Bluecoats' wagons arrived at the stone house a while ago. The scouts say they were easy to track. They only had to follow the trail of dead horses and mules, but the wagons made it here, anyway."

They all knew that those wagons must surely carry bullets and powder to resupply the Bluecoats. Lozen also knew that Talks A Lot had no ammunition or arrows left. He had thrown rocks at the Bluecoats, and when that failed to stop one of them, he had attacked him with his knife. The men were calling him Kaytennay, He Fights Without Arrows.

Almost everyone was out of ammunition, and most of them had few arrows left. No one had thought that killing the Bluecoats would require so many bullets.

Victorio returned from conferring with Cheis. He sat next to Lozen with his knees drawn up and his arms wrapped around them. Lozen fell asleep leaning against the wall, with Victorio softly chanting his war song. Before dawn, she awoke to the echoing call of the Bluecoats' metal horns and drums and their small metal flutes.

This song had no words, but the Bluecoats greeted each day as faithfully with it as she and Victorio, Broken Foot, and Grandmother did with their morning songs. She had heard it often after a night spent watching the fort's corral and sentries. With all their rituals of bugle song and formations and walking in step in strange patterns on their dance ground, Lozen assumed the Bluecoats must be religious, but what a strange religion it was.

Leaning on the top of the rock breastwork, Lozen and Victorio watched the morning brighten along the mountain peaks. Rocks and bushes materialized from the gloom. Broken Foot limped downslope to join them. He looked up at the cloudless sky, wet a finger in his mouth, and held it up into the wind. "A good day to fight," he said.

The bugles sounded again, and the soldiers flowed in their neat ranks from the gates in the stage station's wall. In the center of the column soldiers pushed a pair of small, two-wheeled wagons, each with an iron tube mounted on it.

Chato, Ears So Big, Flies In His Stew, He Makes Them Laugh, and Talks A Lot, the one they now called Fights Without Arrows, ran at a crouch to where Lozen knelt at the wall.

"These boys want to be near your Power." He Makes Them Laugh grinned at her.

Chato scowled. "We can see better from here."

"Make sure every shot hits the man you aim at," Broken Foot said.

Today they would finish what they had started. When they ran out of arrows, they would fight with their knives, with their lances, with rocks, with their hands.

The soldiers stopped long before they came into musket range, though. They unloaded the wooden chests from the horses. They bustled around the two small wagons like ants around a dead catepillar. Heads appeared above the breastworks as the warriors watched them.

"They're getting balls as big as loaves of Mexican bread

from those boxes." Victorio handed the telescope to Broken Foot. "The tubes on the wagons must be a new sort of firestick."

"Two guns with big bullets." Fights Without Arrows gave a scornful snort. "What use are two guns, even big ones, against so many of us?"

The Bluecoats stepped away from the left wagon. Flames shot from the mouth of the tube. The rumble that followed it was loud even at this distance. Lozen and the others watched the ball make a whistling arc against the blue sky. The warriors in its path moved away from it. A second one followed from the other wagon.

"Those balls will be easy to dodge," Fights Without Arrows said.

Then the shot exploded with a roar. Glowing fragments of lead and iron streaked outward, shattering rocks and sending them on their own deadly trajectories. The second one did the same. The Bluecoats pushed the wagons closer and fired two more shells. They advanced again and fired to the left, to the right, and down the center. Shells burst one after the other over the breastworks, raining fire down on them. The din drowned out the warriors' cries.

Men sprinted up the mountains, zigzagging as they ran. Lozen climbed onto the wall and stood silhouetted against the sky, transfixed by the power of the Pale Eyes' magic. This was what her vision had shown her.

She was more curious than afraid. How did the Pale Eyes do this? What spirits gave them thunder and lightning encased in balls of metal? How did the spirits teach them to deliver death so well?

She scanned the rocky slope above her and saw Victorio coming back. Why was he returning? He had told her time and again that in battle she would be on her own. Everyone must scatter to make pursuit more difficult.

He shouted as he slid down the slope, but his words were lost in the explosions, the pop of gunfire, and the clatter of rocks pelting past her. He pointed upward, and she saw the ball shrieking toward her.

She sprinted away, grasping branches to pull herself along. Victorio leaped and hit her with such force that the fall knocked the wind from her. He threw himself across her. Pressed against the rocky ground by his weight, she gasped for breath. The world exploded with a crash that deafened her. A hail of metal clattered around her. Flying chips of rock stung her legs and arms. Dust choked her. Her ears rang.

She felt the warm, slow flow of blood down her arm and for the first time panic shook her. If the Bluecoats had murdered her brother, she would run at them. She would kill as many as she could with her knife and her bare hands until they finished her.

Then Victorio pushed himself to his feet, and Lozen stood, too. A long gash had opened his left arm from his shoulder to his elbow. More blood ran from a diagonal cut across his thigh. Lozen put an arm around his waist, and the two of them scrambled down the far side of the ridge. The din of the big guns stilled suddenly. Lozen heard the shouts of the Bluecoats coming closer.

Chapter 34

AN ULTIMATUM FOR DESSERT

Dr. Thomas Overland did not expect Apaches to knock before entering. No one in Janos did. But Apaches had never shown an interest in rustling his leather bag of medical instruments, so he also didn't expect fifty-three of them to push open the street door and walk into his small examining room. The door was made of fourteen-inch-thick oak planks banded with iron, but Dr. Overland never locked it.

Dr. Overland's wife, Doña Elena, was serving him coffee and milk custard in the kitchen beyond the arched doorway at the rear of the examining room. His three daughters were arguing about whose turn it was to pump water to clean the supper dishes. The maid was in the examining room dusting the framed paintings of Jesus, the Virgin Mary, and St. Jude, the patron of desperate causes. She ran screaming through the kitchen when the front room filled with dusty warriors, a bristle of bows, arrows, war clubs, lances, knives, and muskets, cracked traces of war paint, plenty of menace, and flies. As more of them crowded in, the ones in front pushed into the kitchen and ranged along the walls.

The daughters bolted after the maid. Doña Elena came to stand behind her husband's chair. He was fluent in Spanish, so he did not need her to translate, but she put a hand on his shoulder to let him know that if they were to die today, they would die together.

Dr. Overland thought there was a chance he and his family wouldn't die. The reason occupied the litter made of blankets and agave stalks that four of the men carried in. Its occupant must be as important as he was big for them to have toted him all this way.

A lad who couldn't have been much more than eighteen ran his lance horizontally along the table and swept the earthenware dishes and serving bowls onto the hardpacked dirt of the floor. He gave a wave of his hand and the four men lifted the litter onto the table, where the patient lay like a main course in front of Dr. Overland. The doctor fanned away the flies.

The patient raised himself on one elbow and barked something at his men. Half of them trotted away, probably to keep watch in the street. Dr. Overland was observant, even in adverse circumstances. He noticed that the young man looked chagrined, probably because he hadn't thought to assign a watch.

"The American Bluecoats shot Red Sleeves, my father," the boy said in Spanish. "Heal him or we will kill everyone in Janos." He didn't have to say that they would start with the present company. "We will kill even the chickens and those ugly little dogs that have no hair."

So this was the famous Red Sleeves. Dr. Overland lifted the blanket, and the stench of the chest wound hit him like the flat of a hand. The hole crawled with maggots, but at least the worms had eaten some of the putrefying flesh.

"Mi amor," the doctor said to his wife, "Bring my bag."

Doña Elena slid through the door, trying to put as much distance as she could between herself and their visitors. She returned with the leather bag.

Red Sleeves shivered, and Dr. Overland gently laid the blanket back over him. Doña Elena hurried to put the kettle on the fire. She went behind the big adobe-brick stove, stepped out of her petticoat, and began tearing it into strips.

Dr. Overland washed his hands. *"Traigame dos botellas de la medicina especial,"* he called to his daughters peering in from outside. He added in English so the Apaches wouldn't understand him, "Don't let them see where we keep it."

The oldest daughter returned with two bottles of brandy. Dr. Overland gave one to Red Sleeves. The son supported his father in a half-reclining position and held the bottle so

he could drink. For a sick man, Red Sleeves didn't take long
to drain it. He looked hopefully at the second bottle, but Dr.
Overland shook his head.

"That's for sterilizing the wound, Chief. For killing the
bad spirits," he said. *"Para matar a los espíritus malos."*

"Espíritus santos para matar espíritus malos. Holy spirits
to kill evil ones." The old man lay back down and smiled
beatifically up at the doctor. *"Tu eres muy buen amigo."* He
closed his eyes and began to snore like a bison in a mud
wallow.

With his forceps, the doctor picked out worms a few at a
time. When he realized that would take too long, he scooped
up wriggling masses of them with his hand and threw them
into a wooden bucket of table scraps intended for the family
pig. As he pushed his hand deeper into Red Sleeves' chest
in search of more of the maggots, he prayed.

THE SCORES OF BUZZARDS TOOK FLIGHT, THEIR WINGS
cracking loud as a volley of gunfire. Crows hissed at Rafe
like an audience displeased with the villain in a melodrama.
Even in the December chill, the stench of rotting flesh hung
as heavy as artillery smoke.

Caesar pulled his bandana up to cover his nose and mouth.
Standing on a low rise upwind and at a distance, he surveyed
the body stripped naked and staked out facedown across a
stout yucca plant. The spiked leaves had pushed through him
to protrude from his back.

"It ain't human to do a man that-a-way." The bandana
muffled Caesar's deep voice.

Rafe didn't say anything, but he disagreed with Caesar.
This was terribly human. An act of kindness would have
suprised him more than brutality. Besides, what animal could
have thought up such torture?

The charred shape of another man hung head-down from
a blackened soapberry tree. The Apaches had set the dead
tree on fire, and Rafe had no doubt that they had watched
him roast alive, starting with his head. He could imagine

them making jests and cackling at his agony. The other men had been luckier. Lances, bullets, and arrows had sent them to whatever reward or punishment awaited them. From the way body parts were scattered, Rafe figured coyotes had dined here, too.

"Been dead a couple weeks," he said.

"Do you know them?" Caesar asked.

"Hard to say, but I recognize the clothes on some of them." The men Rafe knew usually wore the same canvas trousers, flannel shirts, and baggy wool coats year in and year out. Rafe had come to recognize the nuances of each man's set of them.

Rafe continued to walk among the bodies. Those who had died on their backs stared up at him from empty sockets. He had the feeling they were pleading with him to find their eyes and put them back where they belonged. Rogers wasn't among them.

"They're miners from the Santa Rita, bound for Tucson, I would wager. The Apaches probably hid in that wash we just crossed."

"More of Cochise's devilment?"

"This side of the pass is Red Sleeves' country. He has a particular want of affection for the miners at Santa Rita and Pinos Altos."

"Maybe John Teal's bullet killed Red Sleeves."

Rafe started to say that the old buzzard would probably bury them all, but it was too grim and too likely a prophecy. He didn't want to lend it encouragement by voicing it.

"Shouldn't we give them a proper burial?" Caesar asked.

"The soldiers can do it when they get here."

Caesar looked grateful to be excused from the task of burying close to a ton of decaying flesh in rocky soil. He took off his hat and bowed his head. Rafe waited until he finished praying.

As they turned to walk to where Red and Caesar's big bay gelding cropped the dry grass and Patch lay in a puddle of sunlight, they saw the line of mounted men round a bend in the trail. They led a string of mules, heavily loaded. They weren't Apaches, but Caesar and Rafe readied their guns anyway. As they drew closer, he saw that a company of Carleton's soldiers rode with them.

"Howdy." The civilian in the lead glanced at the untidy litter of corpses, as though he had seen plenty such before.

He had intense blue eyes. His white cascade of a beard reached the middle buttons on his coat of bison fur. He would have loomed large even without the coat. With it, he made Rafe feel like David exchanging amenities with Goliath.

"How do you do?" Rafe said.

"Still got my hair on my head." The stranger took off his hat and released the wild white thatch of it to spring out around his head in defiance of the rule of the hat's crown.

"So do they." Caesar said dryly, and he nodded toward the bodies.

The man looked only mildly surprised that a Negro would be so impertinent to a white man, and Rafe put a mental mark on the credit side of his ledger.

"The name's Walker, Joseph Reddeford Walker." He gestured behind him with the hat before he jammed it back over his unruly hair. "Me and the boys are on a jaunt looking for wealth beyond the dreams of avarice." He grinned. The man had a way about him.

Rafe had heard of Joseph Walker. The word was that he'd spent thirty of his sixty-five years on the frontier. Gossip also said that he had struck a deal with General Carleton. He could do anything he wanted, and Carleton wouldn't interfere, so long as the general got a cut of whatever discoveries Walker made. Walker's company of forty men reminded Rafe of John Glanton's scalp-hunters. He would have bet Red that their number included the usual thieves, murderers, trappers, miners, and Confederate deserters. From somewhere in his past Rafe found an image of Ali Baba and the Forty Thieves and hung it on Walker and his associates.

"We've ridden clear across the country to California, but the rich veins have played out there, so we're of a mind to do some prospecting in this neck of the woods. We have a plan to thwart any mischief the Apaches might hatch."

Rafe couldn't stop himself from asking. "What plan might that be?"

"We intend to kidnap one of their high muck-a-mucks and hold him hostage until we're safely through the territory."

"God go with you."

"We've taken care of ourselves through four thousand miles of wilderness and savages out for our hair. God knows He needn't concern Hisself with us."

Caesar and Rafe swung into their saddles and watched the party rumble off.

"I reckon that means God can spend more of his time looking out for us," said Casesar. "Do you think the scheme will work?

"Look how it worked for Lieutenant Bascom."

Rafe had other doubts about the plan. General Carleton was quite specific in his orders concerning Apaches. Rafe had read them.

The campaign against Red Sleeves' band of Apaches must be a vigorous one, and the punishment of that band of murderers and others must be thorough and sharp.

If Walker did manage to capture a chief, would the army let him live long enough to serve as a hostage?

"Your brother's grave isn't far from here."

"Shouldn't we wait for the soldiers to arrive and give us an escort."

"No. We can be back before they finish with this burial detail." Rafe saw the hesitation in Caesar's hazel eyes. He gave a sparse smile that had little of humor in it. "Don't waste your last bullet," he added.

" 'I have hope to live, and am prepared to die,' " Caesar recited, with a hint of a smile. *"Measure for Measure."*

"I don't know that one."

From inside his patched and faded cotton shirt, Caesar retrieved a packet wrapped in oiled cloth. He laid back the corners of the cloth to reveal red velvet. He opened that, too, and held out the book inside. "The ladies at the house where I lived threw a good-bye shindig when I left. They knew I liked the Bard, so they gave me this. I was going to give it to Absalom."

Rafe opened it and leafed through it.

"Page fifty-one," Caesar said.

Rafe read from where Caesar left off. " 'Be absolute for death; either death or life / Shall thereby be the sweeter.' " He closed it and held it out, but Caesar shook his head.

"You take it." He looked down, suddenly shy. "Maybe we could recite from it the way you and Absalom used to do."

"That we can. That we can." But what Rafe really wanted to hear was the account of how Caesar had fared all those years, living in a brothel. "Did you enjoy that farewell fete the ladies threw for you?"

Oh, yessir." Caesar's grin grew impossibly wide. "I do believe San Francisco is still talking about it. I can't remember the last day of it, but the ladies told me I had a good time."

LOZEN AND STANDS ALONE LAY ON THEIR STOMACHS ON the ledge and looked over the edge of it. Both had their bows and arrows on their backs. They had left their long pieces in camp because they saw no sense in carrying heavy weapons for which they had no ammunition.

They watched the two men lead their horses to the oval-shaped mound on the low rise by the river. Hairy Foot's dog followed along. Dogs were bad luck, but this one didn't seem to have brought Hairy Foot bad luck. Maybe the dog was his helping spirit.

The men stood at the foot of the mound, took off their hats, and lowered their heads. Were they praying? Lozen knew that under that mound was the corpse that she and Stands Alone had brought to Hairy Foot long ago. What drew the two men here? Why would they stand on top of a dead man's bones in the country of their enemies, risking danger from both the dead and the living? Were they seeking help from the spirits?

"The black white man is back." Stands Alone recognized Caesar as soon as he took off his hat.

Lozen gave a small grunt of agreement. She was still trying to understand what brought these men here. They must have had some strong connection, the two living men and the dead one.

"Why do you follow Hairy Foot?" Stands Alone murmured.

"I want his red horse."

"You have horses. And besides, Hairy Foot's horse is old now."

"He's still better than any I have. And soon we'll have to kill the few ponies we have left to feed everyone."

Lozen herself wondered why she watched Hairy Foot whenever she found him. She wondered why she listened for word of him from returning scouting parties. And when the men boasted that they would be the ones to kill him, why did the idea of his death bother her? She wondered why she dreamed of him sometimes. Was he trying to tell her something?

"For a white man, he has strong magic," she said at last.

"How do you know?"

"Everyone's trying to kill him, but he's still alive."

Chapter 35

THE BEST LAID SCHEMES

A frigid wind raked the exposed lookout post. Lozen shrugged off the cowhide and stood up. She opened the blanket and let the cold wind buffet her. She tried to do what her brother had taught her. She tried to imagine herself as an icicle, a friend to cold, to snow, to ice. The wind cut like knives, though, and she decided it was no friend of hers.

She wrapped the blanket back around her. Snow covered the valley floor below and the mountains all around. Light from the rising sun gilded the tops of the higher peaks. They were more beautiful than the gold rocks that the Pale Eyes sought. In the darkness of the coldest winter she had always known that this country would feed, protect, and teach her people. Now she couldn't be sure. The reason for that was slogging through the drifted snow of the valley below her.

Red Sleeves led twenty-three men toward Pinos Altos, the mines that her people called Where They Whipped Him. He had returned from Janos wearing the Mexican hat, trousers, and shirt that the American doctor there had given him. Red Sleeves was determined to talk to the diggers and Bluecoats who had recently come to the abandoned mining camp.

The Pale Eyes had sent a Mexican to tell him that they wanted peace. They said that if he would come in alone and unarmed, they would guarantee him safe conduct. They would give him blankets, flour, and beef for his people. Only Red Sleeves believed the Pale Eyes' promises.

"Maybe we have displeased Life Giver," he said. "Why else would he give the Pale Eyes such powerful medicine. They can shoot wagons at us now."

Those exploding wagons at Doubtful Pass had demoralized everyone. The warriors had planned to kill all the wasps, but instead they had stirred up the nest. Bluecoats swarmed everywhere. A cloud of despair had settled over the Chiricahuas, over the Red Paints and the Tall Cliffs People alike.

Even Red Sleeves' oldest friend, Skinny, could not convince him to stay away from Pinos Altos. Red Sleeves said he could not listen to the hungry cries of the children anymore. His *muy amigo*, the American medicine man in Janos, said he should do whatever was necessary to make peace, and Red Sleeves agreed with him.

Lozen heard the rustle of the stunted juniper behind her and turned to see He Steals Love using its trunk to pull himself up over the ridge of rock. Lozen was sure that he wanted to be alone with her, but he also worried that people would gossip. Lozen knew that people had stopped gossiping about her. No one wanted to offend her. They might need her to sing over an ill relative someday, or calm a wild horse, or make a cradle or a war amulet.

"Share my lodge, Lozen." He spoke in a rush. "I will bring you horses and mules loaded with goods from Mexico."

"Life Giver has shown me another path."

"Life Giver does not intend that you live alone, without a husband, without children."

He Steals Love annoyed her the most when he tried to tell her what Life Giver intended for her, but she changed the subject rather than argue with him. He Steals Love should be used to her changing the subject. It always signaled that the discussion about matrimony had ended.

She gave him the mirrored glass the sentries used to signal each other. "Watch Disgruntled and He Runs." She pointed her chin toward the ledge below. Two boys sat with their legs dangling over the edge of it. "If they fall asleep, throw a rock at them."

"Do you think the Old Man will return?" He Steals Love called after her.

She stared at the dark, wavery line of men straggling across the vast bowl of snow. "He always returns."

THE BIG PALE EYES HAD HAIR AND A BEARD ALMOST AS white as the cloth he carried tied to the end of a stick. Red Sleeves waited patiently while White Hair conferred in Spanish with the warriors who had come with him. He watched his men ride away to wait for him at the old campsite called Leaves Shaking. The forty Pale Eyes reined their horses in around him. He supposed they wanted to be in position to head him off should he decide to bolt.

He had no intention of running, though. He rode his pony at a walk behind the white-haired one who was almost as tall as he was. The Pale Eyes' *nantan* looked like Ghost Face, like winter itself with his ice-blue eyes and hair and beard as white and unpredictable as blown snow.

Red Sleeves knew he was more likely to die today than live to see the sun rise. He felt sad at the thought of not seeing another morning sky. The bright colors of dawn always reminded him of the bright paper bunting at the fiestas in Janos. He thought of dawn as a time when the sun threw a party for the new day.

Red Sleeves could think of no alternative to making peace. Not for himself. The young men could go on fighting, but he was too old. He was too tired.

The days of glory were gone for him. The Bluecoats with their exploding wagons had made sure of that. He probably would never come home triumphant from a battle again. And if he did, he would know the triumph was temporary. The women who used to sing greetings now wailed out their grief instead. He heard their cries in his dreams. He felt saddest for the young ones. What sort of world would they inhabit?

He had thought this all out. If the Pale Eyes did surprise him and keep their promise, then his coming here would save the lives of his people. He would take them the presents the Pale Eyes promised him. The women would sing and dance, and he would hear laughter again. If he died, maybe his son Mangas would step out from his father's shadow and become a great leader. The worst that could happen would be that the Americans killed him and sent his spirit to the Happy Place.

Lulled by the sway of his pony and the unintelligible hum of the Pale Eyes' talk, he wondered what sex was like in the Happy Place. Was the sensation of entering a woman better there? He hadn't been able to satisfy his wives, or himself, since he returned from Janos. In that respect, death and the spirit life after it would be an improvement.

He could play hoop-and-pole every day. Maybe he could win back the brindle pony he lost to Chief Juan José before the Hair Takers killed the old man at the Death Feast so long ago.

Maybe the chief had already lost the pony to someone else. Being careful not to think of anyone's name, Red Sleeves amused himself by remembering the list of friends and family who had left for the Happy Place, and speculated as to who might now be in possession of the brindle pony. He smiled to himself. He didn't know why the animal had appealed to him, something about the slightly loco look in his eyes.

He hoped that no one called his name after he died. He would be glad to leave the sorrow that his life had become. If death released him from his pain and his responsibilities and his shame, he did not want anyone trying to coax his spirit back.

SAD AND PERPLEXED, GRAND AND COMICAL. THAT WAS HOW Red Sleeves looked to Rafe as he rode in on a pony so small that the old man's bare feet almost brushed the snow. Night had fallen, and the frigid wind had gotten even colder. In spite of that, Red Sleeves had on only a red-and-white-checked cotton shirt and blue overalls of jeans cloth with the legs cut off, exposing knees and calves as knobby and scarred as cedar stumps. A straw hat perched on top of his huge head with a cord tied under his receding chin to hold it in place. Once Colonel West took custody of him, and

Joseph Walker and his men rode away, Red Sleeves towered over everyone around him.

He brightened when he saw Rafe. *"Mi amigo. ¿Como estás?"*

Colonel West stepped between them and nodded to the two guards. With bayonets fixed on their muskets, they motioned Red Sleeves toward the fire. One of them tossed him a blanket.

"Make certain he does not escape." West enunciated the words very carefully. "Not under any circumstances. Is that clear?"

"Yes, sir." The guards grinned. "If'n he tries to escape, should we shoot his red arse?"

"Certainly."

As the men marched Red Sleeves away, Rafe walked over to West. He didn't much care what happened to Red Sleeves. He knew that if the old hypocrite hadn't been responsible for the death and destruction on this side of Doubtful Pass in the past ten years, he hadn't done much to stop it. But he knew that what West intended would mean more trouble.

"Colonel, the Chiricahuas will never surrender if you kill the old man."

"This isn't any business of yours, Collins. I have my orders from General Carleton."

As Rafe headed for the wagon where Caesar watched the horses and mules, he passed the guards' post. Red Sleeves had rolled himself up in his blanket by the fire there. His bare legs and feet stuck out of the end of the bedroll, and he was snoring. The old man had gumption, Rafe had to give him that.

Rafe went to sleep thinking about the events that had led to this, as surely as a lighted fuse would set off dynamite. They started with Bascom, of course, but the situation would have gotten out of hand anyway. Old Red Sleeves was no saint. And even if he had been, he couldn't stop his young men from rustling cattle and horses any more that Carleton could control the thievery and rascality among civilians and soldiers alike in his jursidiction.

The moon stood at midnight when Rafe got up to take the pressure off his plumbing. He was about to crawl back into the warm cocoon of his blankets when he heard Red Sleeves shout in Spanish. "I am not a child to be played with." Six shots followed. Caesar sat up and grabbed the pistol under his saddle.

"The old man is dead," Rafe said.

"Red Sleeves?"

"Yep." Rafe started to crawl back into his bedroll.

The deed was done. They would have to survive the consequences. Then curiosity got the better of him. Hunched against the cold, he walked to the fire. Patch followed him. The two guards stood looking down at Red Sleeves' body. By the fire's light, Rafe could see raw burns on the old man's legs. They were in the shape of bayonet blades. The soles of his feet were charred. The guards must have applied a lot of heat to have an effect on those calluses.

One of the guards looked at Rafe, then spit a stream of tobacco not far from where Red Sleeves' lay. "The old snake tried to escape."

"He's still wrapped in his blanket."

"Are you calling me a liar?"

"Yes."

The guard spit again, just missing the toe of Rafe's boot. A lieutenant arrived and prodded the body with the barrel of his musket.

"Let him lie. He'll not rot between now and sunup."

"Hell." One of the guards laughed. "In this cold he ain't gonna rot till April."

Rafe went back to bed. He wondered how long the Apaches would take to find out their chief was dead, and to learn that the white men had hoodwinked them again. Not that they hadn't done their fair share of hoodwinking over the years. He fell asleep grateful that they weren't likely to know about it yet. When they found out, there would be hell to pay.

At first light, Rafe and Caesar went to toast their outsides at the cook's fire and scald their insides with some of the toxic brew he called coffee. The man who had walked sentry duty the night before stared morosely into his tin mug while steam embraced his head. He was one of Walker's men, and probably nettled that his party's guarantee of safe conduct had been rendered null and void during the night. The teeth he had knocked out of Red Sleeves' jaw as souvenirs didn't cheer him much.

Soldiers had gathered around the body, and one of them left the group and double-timed toward the cookfire. He was a spindly young specimen that Rafe thought the army should have thrown back, but probably kept because its war with the Confederacy had left it short on cannon fodder.

"I need your knife, Cookie." The soldier snatched the butcher knife from the cook's hand and ran off.

He returned a short time later holding aloft a bloody rag of skin with a hank of coarse black hair attached. "Got me a keepsake, boys. I got me the big chief's scalp." He tried to hand the bloody blade back to the cook who waved it away.

"Damnation! Wash the infernal thing off."

The soldier rinsed the hair with water from his canteen and sat down to begin stretching it onto a hoop. When the others finished stripping the body of anything that could be kept as a trinket, they picked it up, still in the blanket, and threw it into a shallow gulley.

Rafe and Caesar spent the day making repairs to the harness and shoeing the mules. That night Rafe lay in his blankets and listened to the coyotes quarrel over the largesse in the gully. He woke up the next morning with a sense of relief that bordered on giddiness. Maybe West and Carleton were right. With Red Sleeves dead, maybe the situation would improve.

He wasn't surprised to see the soldiers assembling at their camp a few hundred yards away. Colonel West wasn't the sort to let grass grow under his feet. The sentry wandered over to watch Rafe and Caesar load the coffin of tools and spare wagon parts back into the wagon box. He still looked morose.

"Guess what Colonel West is claiming," he said.

"That Red Sleeves rushed the guards, and they shot him in self-defense." Rafe slipped the bridle over Othello's head.

"That's right. He also says the army captured the old man in a bloody battle."

Rafe remembered Joseph's Walker's plan to use Red Sleeves to get them safely through Doubtful Pass. What was it that Scottish poet said about the best laid plans? Rafe grinned at Conners.

"And now your hostage is about as useful to you as a three-legged mule."

"You're just right all around this morning, Collins."

"You could prop him up and tie him on his horse," said Rafe, looking deadly solemn. "Maybe you could fool his men long enough to get through the pass."

"We might, if'n the chief had a head."

"What?"

"Surgeon Sturgeon cut it off." Like everyone else, the sentry enjoyed saying the surgeon's name.

Rafe and Caesar found Sturgeon watching the kettle boil. Red Sleeves' face looked up at Rafe from the roiling water, like some monstrous practical joke. The cook was not happy with the use of his kettle, but Dr. Sturgeon seemed pleased with his prize.

"I plan to send the skull to O. S. Fowler, the eminent phrenologist," he said. "I would venture to say that he has never seen a specimen of such herculean proportions."

"What is a friend-ologist, suh?" Caesar, too, could not stop staring into the big black kettle. He was disoriented by Red Sleeves's head in a place where a hunk of salt pork should be. He expected to see onions and potatoes bobbing around it.

The doctor looked pleased to be asked. "Phrenology is the study of human behavior as it relates to areas of the skull. By measuring irregularities on the surface of a person's head, the bumps and hollows, a skilled practitioner can predict the development of such traits as combativeness, amativeness, philoprogenitiveness . . ."

In spite of his misgivings, Rafe smiled to himself. He didn't know the meaning of *amativeness* or *philoprogenitiveness,* but he was familiar with phrenology. During the war, he had overheard the officers' discussions of the subject. He remembered a captain quoting John Quincy Adams, something to the effect that he did not see how two phrenologists could look each other in the face without laughing.

When the Apaches get wind of this, Rafe thought, all hell will break loose, but when it does, how will anyone be able to distinguish it from the present situation?

Rafe, Caesar, and Dr. Sturgeon watched the soldiers prepare to march out. One of them carried a white flag.

"What're they up to?" But Rafe could guess. It was the only sensible thing to do, given the circumstances.

"He's going to use the white flag to get close to the men who are waiting for Red Sleeves, then bushwhack them." The doctor verified Rafe's suspicions. "General Carleton has a surefire plan to annihilate Apaches and Navajos. He'll lure them into coming in for talks and presents. Those who surrender he will move to a reserve somewhere far from civilized society. He says he will subjugate them or destroy them. He's enlisted Kit Carson to take hostilities to any who resist."

Rafe had only met Carson once, in a card game in Santa Fe, but he knew his reputation. Carson was the man for the job. Even so, the words "surefire plan," roused Rafe's old friend, foreboding. He wondered why no one else seemed to notice that a plan based on massacring groups of Apaches who came in to talk peace could not convince the others to surrender.

If they did agree to go to a reservation, forcing the Navajos and the Apaches to live together would never work. They had warred against each other for centuries. Kit Carson might be able to subdue them, but even he could not persuade them to get along.

Rafe wondered if the army made special efforts to promote stupidity in its officers, or did promotion to higher rank engender it?

Chapter 36

HOLDING UP THE SKY

The two miners stood in the doorway of the tent that served as the officers' mess. Rafe had seen them earlier at the sutler's store, buying strychnine. They had held it up and announced. "Gonna mix this with cornmeal and use it to bait some red-bellied rats, boys." The boys had cheered.

Now the more bearlike of the two held a shilling shocker, a small book of the sort that sold for one bit, about twelve and a half cents. On the cover, a yellow-maned giant in a fringed leather shirt wrestled with a snarling Indian wearing a Comanche's bison-horn headdress and brandishing a Sioux tomahawk. A cluster of blond scalps dangled like a line of fish from the Indian's belt.

The title read, *Kit Carson Battles the Apache Menace*. The book's current owner stared at the man sitting at the table with Rafe and Caesar. Then he studied the cover again. He and his companion, who bore a striking resemblance to a ferret, held a whispered conference that carried to the back of the tent.

"I tell you he is," said the ferret.

"He ain't," said the bear.

"Ask him."

"I hain't makin' no dad-blamed fool of myse'f."

Finally, they sauntered to the barrel that served Rafe, Caesar, and Col. Kit Carson as a table.

" 'Scuse me, mister." Ferret fixed his attention on Carson. "A feller tole me you was at the scrape with those 'Paches over yonder on Turkey Creek."

"I was."

Ferret flashed an I-told-you-so look at Bear. "And how many of the red rascals did ya kill thar?"

"Nary a one."

"How come?"

"I mizzled."

"Mizzled?" asked Bear.

"Mizzled sartin."

"He departed suddenly," Ferret translated. "With nor muss nor fuss," he added.

"You ran away?" Bear claim-jumped the I-told-you-so look.

"Hell, yes," said Kit Carson. "They was a chance of red gallinippers lookin' fierce as two cents, so I skeedaddled."

"And was Colonel Kit Carson there?"

"I won't lie to you. He war."

"Cracky!" Bear lit up. "Is he as all-fired brave as they say?"

"I h'yar tell he is some punkins."

The two men waited for the stories. Everyone who knew Kit Carson had stories, but Kit continued sawing at a chunk of beef with his bowie knife and seemed disinclined to elaborate.

Ferret glanced at Bear. "Reckon we won't occupy any more of your time, mister."

"Good day to you, then," mumbled Kit around the mouthful of beef.

The two left with Bear singing, " 'My partner, he laid down and died. I had no blankets, so I took his hide.' "

Rafe figured they would have been more disappointed if they'd learned that this really was Kit Carson. Carson was small and compact, maybe a few years past fifty. He had sunken cheeks, a drooping mustache, and thin, graying hair retreating from the bulge of his broad forehead. He had a bookish look, but he couldn't write, and he couldn't read the outlandish stories printed about him.

"Then that story about you killing ten Apaches ain't true, Marse Kit?" asked Caesar.

Carson shook his head. "I jist told the 'Pache how the

world was wagging and that the jig was up. They held a caucus and voted to adjourn the proceedings."

Rafe had heard a different account from a man who'd been there. Even adjusting for the usual windage of exaggeration, it was a thriller. Fifty or sixty Apaches had approached Kit and seventeen militamen. They were yelling like banshees and flaunting their weapons when Kit walked out in front of his party.

The witness said Carson had seemed to elevate and expand. His eyes took fire. He drew a line in the dirt with the toe of his shoe and, in Apache, invited them to cross it and die. They declined.

Carson was affable and talkative until the conversation turned to his own exploits. Those he dismissed with the wave of a hand as slender as a woman's. As Col. Carson's guests at the mess, Caesar and Rafe had joined him in disposing of bubble-and-squeak, a heap of boiled beef, cabbage, and potatoes. Caesar and Rafe had just arrived with the supply train, and they were avoiding the chaos of distribution day on the reservation here at Bosque Redondo.

Kit Carson had a lot on his mind, so he added two glasses of whiskey to the menu. Maybe he had a lot on his conscience, too. Kit Carson was a conundrum. He was honest, fair, and good-natured. He admired and sympathized with Indians, but he fought them anyway, and he did it more effectively than anyone else. A conscience was an inconvenience for any soldier, but it was a lethal liability for an Indian fighter.

Rafe felt a nipping at the heels of his own conscience when he thought of the paltry amount of corn and beef that he and the other freighters had hauled in. That wasn't his fault, but he still felt guilt by association with a government that would starve the people it had promised to feed. He knew there would not be nearly enough to provide for the eight thousand Navajos that Kit Carson had recently brought to join the five hundred Mescalero Apaches here.

The sound of voices grew outside. Mescaleros and Navajos were gathering at the building where the rations and blankets were distributed, and where Dr. Michael Steck had set up a temporary office. The general hum was punctuated by shouts in the Apache and Navajo dialects, and in Spanish and English as soldiers tried to restore order.

"A reg'lar pandemonium of breech-rags and red bellies, hain't it?" Kit sighed and drained the last of the whiskey.

Caesar headed for the wagon yard. Rafe and Kit waded into the resentment and anger. Outnumbered, the Mescaleros stood on a slope a hundred yards away while the Navajos crowded around the door of Dr. Steck's office. The two groups traded insults and accusations of thievery, murder, abduction, slander, depravity, and, worst of all in their view, mendacity.

Under General Carleton's orders, Carson had waged war on the Navajos through the summer and fall of 1864, but he had disobeyed the general's directive to kill every Indian he found. The general held with the common aphorism that nits made lice, but Carson hadn't fallen into the habit of murdering women and children. Instead, he burned the Navajos' orchards and fields and slaughtered their sheep and cattle. By winter, destitute, frozen, and starving, they had surrendered. Scores of Navajos had died on that terrible march through the bitter winter. Regret kindled in Kit's eyes whenever the subject came up.

For all that, they had learned that Carson kept his word, which was something no other white man except Dr. Steck would do. They believed he would try to help them as best he could. They were right, but their current affliction was beyond his ability to remedy.

When the Confederate troops fled the territory, they left behind three soldiers with smallpox. All three died, but not before they spread the disease to the Union army. The army spread it to the Navajos.

Now many of them carried their sick kin on makeshift litters. They called out *"Ka'-san, Ka'-san,"* and pleaded with him to help them. With sorrow in his gray eyes, Kit pushed through the crowd. He was finding that the burden of peace could be as heavy as war.

The hideous sores that covered the sick Navajos' faces repulsed and frightened Rafe, and he followed close on Carson's heels when he went inside. They stood in the cheerful heat of the cast-iron sibley stove while Dr. Steck and General Carleton carried on their argument as though they were alone.

"There was no need for you to come here," Carleton thundered.

"I wanted to see the inhuman conditions for myself."

"I am seeing to their welfare. I have sent to Santa Fe for a teacher to school them."

"The Navajos need medicine, not someone to teach them the ABC's."

"The Navajos have contracted smallpox from the soldiers because their women fornicate with them."

"No matter what the cause, hundreds are dying, and many of them are innocent children."

"I've taken care of the problem."

Dr. Steck looked hopeful. Maybe Carleton had included the cowpox vaccine in this current shipment. "How?"

"I sent orders for them to throw the corpses into the river."

"But the Apaches are camped downstream from them."

"The Apaches should have thought of that when they were stealing everything on four hooves."

"The Mescaleros have been the least troublesome of the Apache tribe. They were poised at the brink of starvation. They ate whatever stock they stole." Steck was heating to a cherry-red state of eloquence on the subject. "If all the Indians were Spartans, they could not bear up against the relentless tide of gold seekers. The white man has disrupted their ancient means of subsistence."

"You know very well that their ancient means of subsistence has always been thievery. 'For the thief should make full restitution; if he have nothing, then he shall be sold for his theft.' Exodus, chapter twenty-two, verse three."

Kit raised one eyebrow and glanced at Rafe. They both knew about the shady deals Carelton had been hatching with men like Joseph Reddeford Walker and his crowd. If they weren't outright thievery, they were close enough. Rafe reck-oned Carleton could never be sold as punishment for any thefts though. Not even those who agreed with his policies would give two cents for the man himself.

Carleton turned to Rafe and Kit. "Unload the provisions quickly." He started for the door. "Dr. Steck is going back to Santa Fe with you."

THE RAIDING PARTY DIDN'T HAVE TO FIND A WIDE CLEFT IN which to bury Skinny's remains. A narrow one accomodated him. Fights Without Arrows, Flies In His Stew, Ears So Big, Chato, and the others wrapped him in his blanket. They low-ered his slender frame, his weapons, and all his belongings into the crack in the basalt.

The rancher and his vaqueros had put up more of a fight for his horses than the warriors expected. A bullet had made a neat hole above the ridge of Skinny's nose. The bullet's exit from the back of his skull had not been so neat.

Fights Without Arrows delivered the news to Skinny's wives. The smoke from his burning lodge and possessions lingered like a pall over the village. The wailing went on for days.

Victorio had depended on Skinny's advice. Now he couldn't even talk with Red Sleeves about the troubles be-setting their people. Red Sleeves and his men had gone to Pinos Altos more than two years ago, and they had not come back. His son, Mangas, was leading his band in the absence of a better candidate.

Mangas was good-natured and strong, but he lacked the boldness and cunning of Red Sleeves. Mangas visited often at Victorio's fire, brooding about the disappearance of his father. Many of his people had sought shelter with relatives in Victorio's and Loco's villages. They were hungry, cold, and disheartened.

The world had always harbored dangers for The People, but it had become more perilous than even the oldest ones could remember. A gang of Pale Eyes had attacked Loco's village while its inhabitants slept, and had killed mostly women and children. They had taken scalps. They had knocked out their victims' teeth and sliced off body parts. Mexican traders from Alamosa said the Pale Eyes didn't even collect a bounty for the hair. They took it as souvenirs.

The Warm Springs people depended on Lozen's powers to warn them of approaching enemies, but they still lived like hunted creatures. No longer could they enjoy a big blaze and storytelling in the open air. Now twenty or so of them huddled close to the small fire built in a cave. Lozen sat between Grandmother and Daughter, and she held three-year-old Wah-sin-ton on her lap. She rested her chin on his head, closed her eyes, and listened.

He Makes Them Laugh had invited them here. He knew that second to food, laughter was the best remedy for hunger. Tonight he wore his favorite headdress, a skunk's pelt with the tail hanging down the back of his neck and the stuffed head perched over his forehead. Stands Alone had sewn on two black seeds as eyes. Sometimes when speaking, He Makes Them Laugh would barely move his lips. He had convinced the younger children that the skunk could talk.

"Coyote was going along . . ." He began with the familiar phrase and the children came to attention. Stories about Trickster Coyote always made them laugh. "He came to a tall, dead pine tree, reaching up into the sky. A fat lizard sat on the trunk. Coyote looked up at him and said, 'I only eat fat. Come down here so I can gobble you up.'

"Lizard said, 'Old Man, the sky is about to fall on us. I have to hold up this tree because it's supporting the sky.'

" 'I don't believe you.' Coyote put his two front paws as high on the tree trunk as he could, but he couldn't reach Lizard. 'Look up,' said Lizard. 'You'll see what I mean.'

"Coyote leaned his head back on his shoulders. He stared up at the top of that tree, and it seemed to sway and rotate in the wind. The clouds moving past the top of that tree made Coyote dizzy. They convinced him that the sky really was about to fall on them.

" 'I'm getting tired and can't hold the tree up much

longer,' said Lizard. 'Catch on and hold it while I fetch my children to help us.' Coyote grabbed that tree trunk, and he held on with all his strength. Lizard scampered down and ran away.

"Coyote held that tree all night while sleet fell on him and icicles formed on his nose. In the morning his muscles ached so badly he couldn't hold on anymore. He let go of the tree and ran to a hollow place in the rocks. He waited for the sky to fall, but it stayed where it had always been. Coyote realized that Lizard had tricked him.

" 'Worthless Coyote!' he grumbled. 'Son of a Coyote! You never will have any sense.' Angry and hungry, cold and wet, he headed off to wherever he was going." He Makes Them Laugh paused before he added, "I'm talking about flowers and fruit and other good things."

He Makes Them Laugh started another Coyote story, progressing through them in the usual order, and Lozen sank into an anxious revery. She felt like Coyote, holding up the sky, straining until her muscles ached. How much more weighted down must Victorio feel as every day people arrived asking him for shelter, food, and advice.

The world had gone so far awry that the sky falling no longer seemed far-fetched. For instance, how could someone as big as Red Sleeves vanish? Where were those who had gone with him to hold council at the diggers' village two years ago? Had the Pale Eyes killed them? Had they decided to visit Long Neck in Mexico and been detained there for some reason? Had they set out on a horse-stealing expedition south to the wide water because the stock in northern Mexico had been depleted by warriors desperate to feed their families?

If Red Sleeves and his men were dead, then their names must never be spoken again. Their wives must marry other men who could bring meat for the family kettle. If the missing ones lived, then they could be discussed. For a few men to fail to return from a raid was common enough, but not all of them. Never all of them.

Parties of warriors had gone out looking for them. Once

Victorio had approached Bluecoats under a white flag, to talk peace and ask about Red Sleeves, but the soldiers had opened fire on him.

The mystery tormented everyone. Whispers of witchcraft circulated through the villages. Suspicion roosted like crows among the arbors and lodges. It circled like vultures over the dance grounds and the hoop-and-pole fields. People became wary of their own friends and relatives. They watched each other, looking for signs of evil magic. Many came to Lozen, asking her for protection against witches and spells.

He Makes Them Laugh started the last tale as the sun was about to rise. He had just finished when Chato and Fights Without Arrows appeared. People moved closer to hear whatever message they brought.

"Many Mescalero relatives and friends of Broken Foot's second wife have come," Chato said. "They bring news of Red Sleeves."

"The Bluecoats lured him to their camp with promises of peace and gifts for his people," Fights Without Arrows said. "Then they killed him. They ambushed those who waited for him and killed all of them."

A murmur rippled through the crowd.

"There is more." He waited for the talking to stop. "The Bluecoats cut off the Old Man's head. They boiled the flesh from it."

A woman screamed. People drew their blankets over their heads and moaned with horror and grief. Lozen sat stunned.

Death was inevitable, and Red Sleeves had lived a long life. But to be condemned to spend eternity headless, that was worse than death. That was worse than the Pimas, who dropped heavy rocks onto the faces of their slain enemies so their loved ones would not be able to recognize them in the afterlife.

Fights Without Arrows crouched next to Lozen. He opened a saddlebag so she could see the calico, tobacco pouch, and Broken Foot's best saddle blanket inside.

"Grandmother," Fights Without Arrows murmured. "Broken Foot knows these are insignificant gifts, but he asks that you bring your curing herbs, your wand, and your healing stones to his second wife's camp."

"Is someone ill?" Lozen wondered why Broken Foot, her teacher, would be asking her to hold a sing when he was more qualified.

"He doesn't know."

"He doesn't know?"

"You must see for yourself." Fights Without Arrows stood up. "He asks that you hurry. Chato and I are going to Red Sleeves' village to tell them what happened."

Quietly, so as not to disturb Grandmother, Lozen collected her medicine and hurried through the gray light of dawn to Wide's camp.

Wide's relatives had walked for two days and three nights from the reservation at Bosque Redondo. Exhausted, they wrapped themselves in blankets, hides, and rags, and slept. Some had stacked their few belongings in an attempt to block the cold wind.

Broken Foot limped to meet her. He clutched his curing wand so tightly that pale half-moons formed at his knuckles.

"What is it?" she asked.

"I don't know. I think the Bluecoats put a spell on my second wife's cousin's small son. They are powerful witches, those Bluecoats. They cursed the Navajos. They gave them a sickness that covers them with running sores. The Navajos threw corpses full of maggots in the river near the Mescaleros' camp. Many of my wife's people got sick, but I don't think that caused this boy's condition."

Broken Foot looked wearily around at the sleeping relatives for whom he would now be responsible. "I've seen patients suffering from bear sickness, coyote sickness, the effects of lightning, thunder, witchcraft, and snakes, but I've never seen anything like this."

A PALE STREAM OF MORNING SUNLIGHT ENTERED THE LODGE door. When it flowed over the child, he cried out in agony. His arms jerked and his fingers became rigid claws. His legs contracted with such force that his knees struck his chin, snapping his teeth closed on his tongue. Blood dribbled from the corners of his mouth, but his jaws had clamped so tightly together that Broken Foot could not pry them open. The sound of the child's gurgling filled the shelter as the blood backed into his throat and trickled from his nose.

With trembling hands Lozen fumbled at the cords of her medicine bag. She spilled some of the pollen, and she was so shaken she couldn't remember the first song of the healing cycle. But the songs would not have helped anyway. A convulsion shook the boy. His eyes rolled up in their sockets, and he went limp.

His mother began to wail. The aunts and uncles and cousins took up the cry. The keening spread through the camp. It made Lozen's head ache and jumbled her thoughts. She went outside with Broken Foot.

"What's happening to us, Uncle?"

"We have strayed from the path. We must ask Life Giver to send us a sign so we can find the correct way again."

The boy's father stood off to one side, staring at nothing. Lozen put a gentle hand on his shoulder.

"My brother, did your child eat anything unusual on the way here?"

"He found three sacks of pinole by the trail, but his mother told him not to eat any of it."

"Where are his belongings?"

The father pointed his chin at a feed sack lying by the door. Lozen crouched beside it and searched through the contents. Underneath his rolled up shirt and a small pair of moccasins, she found the pinole. One of the pouches was half empty. She poured some of the parched corn into her hand and sniffed it. She held it up for Broken Foot to smell.

"Something's wrong with it," he said.

Lozen emptied it onto a woven tray and carried it to her shelter.

Grandmother was waiting for her. "What happened?"

"Wide's cousin's child died."

Grandmother glanced at the tray of parched corn. "Where did the pinole come from?"

"Someone left it by the trail, Pale Eyes probably. It might be poisoned. Maybe it killed the boy."

That night Lozen left the tray out when everyone went to sleep. She wasn't surprised to find three dead rats in it the next morning.

Chapter 37

SEEING RED

Just because horse-stealing was necessary didn't mean it couldn't be fun. Lozen felt the usual mix of excitement, glee, serenity, and power, and a hint of fear. She lay on her stomach and watched the Bluecoats through the far-seeing tube. This was the new fort the Bluecoats had built at Doubtful Pass. Lozen looked for the guns on wheels that had killed so many warriors, but she didn't see any.

The helter-skelter of wooden lodges amused her. Any Mexican peasant knew he should build a wall around his village to fend off attacks, but the Bluecoats were either too stupid or too lazy to bother. They had merely picketed the horses.

The sliver of a moon was well on its way along before Lozen heard Victorio's quail call. She ripped up a bundle of grass and stuffed it down her shirt. She added branches of the pungent bush the Mexicans called *hediondilla,* "little stinker." She stuck more of the bush into her headband, into the tops of her moccasins, and under her belt. That should throw the dogs off her scent.

She eased slowly downslope. She lay behind a yucca plant downwind of the pasture and watched the twin glows of the sentries' cigarillos approach. Talking in low voices, they strolled past, their muskets dangling in the crooks of their arms. When they were out of sight, Lozen slipped in among the horses. Some of them moved away nervously, but none whinnied or tried to rear. That was why Victorio had sent her in first.

She found the bell mare, stroked her, whispered in her ear, and gave her the grass from her shirt. She left six horses tied securely so they couldn't bolt when Victorio and the others stampeded the herd. The men would cut those lines themselves and ride the horses away. She retied the lines on the others with slip knots.

She had time before dawn arrived, so she glided to the wagons parked behind the fort. The sentries and several teamsters were engrossed in a game of cards. A lantern threw their shadows up the adobe wall of the saddlery. Gliding through Bluecoats' villages while they slept was one of Lozen's favorite pastimes. It made her feel invisible. She ghosted past the men and slipped in among the wagons.

She climbed into a couple of them and felt around. The sacks and barrels contained cornmeal and bacon by the smell of them. The wagon held enough food to feed her people through the hungry time of early spring, and she wished she could drive it away. In the third wagon she found a cartridge belt and a powder horn.

She slung the powder horn across her shoulder and buckled the cartridge belt at her waist. She fastened it in the last hole, but it still rode low on her hips. Maybe Broken Foot's song to bring ammunition was going to work as well for her as it did for him.

She was about to cut the mules' tethers when she saw the big red horse. She was surprised that Hairy Foot had left his roan unguarded. She regarded him solemnly in the stars' light. He stared at her just as solemnly.

You're playing with me, she thought. If I try to catch you, you'll cause a commotion.

He looked so docile, though, that she began to think perhaps her powers had grown strong enough for her to steal him. She stroked his soft muzzle. The stars reflected in his big eyes gleamed like sparks.

You're a trickster, she told him silently.

She ran a hand up his muzzle, then along his neck. He didn't back away from her. Her heart bagan to beat faster. This was the night he would become hers.

Then she felt his teeth clamp onto her shoulder. He bit her hard enough to send a tingling sensation into her fingers, but not enough to break the skin. He could have drawn blood if he'd wanted.

I understand, she thought. You are his horse. His spirit is stronger than mine.

He would not be hers tonight. She unfastened the amulet she had braided into her hair to make her run faster. She had tied together the pair of hummingbird's wings and skull and the piece of blue stone with deer sinew, and she had sung over it.

Maybe this would help Hairy Foot and his horse outrun death. The young men of her band were determined to prove themselves by killing him and taking his horse as a prize. Lozen separated out some hairs in Red's mane and used them to tie the amulet in place.

She cut the mules' tether lines; then she snaked on her stomach back to the nearby pickets and waited for the sentries to pass again. When they did, she gave the nightjar's call. Yelling and flapping their blankets, Victorio and the others charged in among the horses.

Lozen gathered the lead line of the bell mare and jumped onto her, relishing the twitch and flex of the mare's muscles against her thighs. She heard the sentries' shouts and the pop of gunfire as she rode toward the hills with the mare's bell clanging wildly. The other horses followed the bell, and Victorio and his men brought up the rear, chivvying strays back into the herd.

As the bullets whizzed past her, Lozen vibrated her tongue against the roof of her mouth in the high, triumphal cry. Dawn splashed pink across the dark sky, and the mare moved effortlessly under her. If she and the men could avoid patrols and get the herd safely home, her family could contact the Mexican traders in Alamosa. They could use their share of horses to obtain goods for Daughter's ceremony of White Painted Woman.

Everyone needed the ceremony. In celebrating Daughter's entry into womanhood, they would remember how important they all were to Life Giver. They would know that as long as they had women like Daughter, The People would continue.

The difficulty now lay in avoiding attacks from the miners and the Bluecoats. The soldiers had fired on every group who had approached them to ask for a peace council. The miners shot at everyone, regardless of their sex, age, or intent. As Lozen rode into the new day with the army's herd behind her, a plan occurred to her.

"So I MANAGED TO STAY AHEAD OF THE APACHES, AND picked them off until my last cartridge was gone." While he talked, Capt. John Cremony shuffled the deck and dealt hands to Rafe, Caesar, and the young lieutenant. "Then I headed up a canyon, and I'll be doggonned if it didn't end in a sheer wall. I was trapped like a rat with a dozen Apaches closing in on me, whooping louder'n so many banshees. And me without so much as a penknife or a tooth-picker to defend myself."

He paused to study his cards. The silence lengthened. Finally the lieutenant asked, "What happened?"

Cremony looked up, nonchalant. "Why, they killed me. Damn them, sir, they killed me."

Rafe never tired of seeing the chagrin on the faces of John Cremony's latest audience. Cremony was in a good mood for someone exiled to Fort Bowie, ninety miles from what passed for civilization. Cremony confided in Rafe that he was damned relieved to put a hundred miles between him and General Carleton. He pronounced Carleton the most unscrupulously ambitious and exclusively selfish man of Cremony's acquaintance. Rafe didn't dispute that.

"I was at the battle of Pittsburg Landing," the lieutenant said

"Shiloh?" asked John Cremony.

"That's what they call it. Almost twenty thousand on both sides killed or wounded." The lieutenant rearranged his cards. "Shortly after the battle we boys were feeling pretty used up and dejected, even though ole General Grant saved the day, and we pushed the Rebs back. I was on advance picket line on a moonlit night, and the Rebs had a post not more than a hundred yards away. We shot at each other till we tired of it; then we swapped newspapers, coffee, and tobacco. We'd set them out in the middle of the ground for the other side to fetch.

"A Reb corporal walked right into our camp, sat on a log, and asked if anyone knew how to play poker. Well, I guess we did. He pulled out a deck of cards and a few of us sat down. Pretty soon another Reb came over, and another, until blue and gray together squatted around watching the play.

"They were absorbed in the game, when a man on a horse rode up. 'By crimminy,' I cried. 'It's General Grant.' "

The lieutenant paused, and Rafe, Caesar, and John Cremony leaned forward. "What did the general do?"

"We all stood up, looking like whipped schoolboys, and saluted. Grant eyed us stern as a sphinx. He took the cigar from between his teeth, and he asked the Reb corporal. 'Who's ahead?' 'Why we are,' said the corporal. 'Those chumps you brought down here can't play poker a little bit. But they can fight, General.' 'Have to sometimes,' said Grant. And he rode away."

Rafe thought about those twenty thousand men dead and wounded in one battle. It made the dustup at Doubtful Pass seem like small potatoes.

"I hear that General Grant says he knows but two songs," said Caesar, " 'Yankee Doodle' and the other one."

They all chuckled, and then Cremony went back to letting off steam about Carleton.

"At Bosque Redondo the Navajos and the Apaches were killing each other over a pint of whiskey or a spavined mule or a patch of corn. They were dying of flux from the water and the smallpox that the Rebs left behind, so what does Carleton do?"

"He opens a school," said Rafe.

"He opens a damned school. You can imagine how successful that was."

"Why wasn't it?" asked the lieutenant.

Cremony gave him a pitying look, as though condoling him for having been in the privy when intelligence was handed out.

"Their chief explained it to me."

"What did he say?" Rafe looked up, interested.

Cremony leaned back in his chair, stared at the ceiling, and took a few puffs on his cigar while he remembered the exact words, translating them from Spanish to English as he went.

" 'You say that because you learned from books, you can build all those big houses. Now, let me tell you what we think. You begin when you are little to work hard at learning so you can learn to do all those wonderous things. And after you get to be men, the real work of life begins for you. You build the houses, the ships, the towns. And then you die and leave them all behind. We call that slavery.' "

"He's right," said Rafe. "The Apaches don't need to work."

"That's what the chief said. He said they were free as air. He said the Mexicans and others work for them. What they cannot get from the Mexicans . . ."

"And the American ranchers and farmers and miners," added the lieutenant.

". . . What they cannot get from others, then the river, the woods, the mountains, and the plains provide. He said, 'We will not send our children to your schools to become slaves like yourselves.' "

Rafe finished the story. "So, the chief packed up everyone, lock, stock, and moccasins, and lit out." Rafe poked his stockinged feet farther under Patch's stomach. Her solid body and thick fur provided a bone-soaking warmth in the December chill.

Cremony laughed. "I wish I could have seen the look on Carleton's face when he discovered that five hundred Mescaleros had decamped in the night."

Rafe chuckled himself. A sizable pile of chits lay on the table in front of him. A few glasses of more than middling brandy sloshed inside him. It gave the rough-walled room a soft glow and a sensuous shimmy. Best of all, he held a handful of cards that looked to be winners. Rafe felt expansive, lucky, and—temporarily at least—blessed.

He should have known better.

When the shouts and the gunfire sounded, Cremony and the lieutenant were fast, but not so fast as Rafe and Caesar. They dodged among the soldiers pouring out of the barracks, pulling up their braces, and priming and loading their new percussion-lock Springfields.

With Patch ahead of him, Rafe raced toward the wagon yard. As the rocks and thorns destroyed his latest pair of bison wool socks, he cursed himself for taking his boots off. He cursed himself for not tying Red at the door, although an Apache could steal him from there as easily as anywhere else, if Red would allow it. He cursed himself for almost believing the sergeant when he said the Apaches had a superstition about this place and would never attack it.

Caesar reached the wagon yard first. "Othello and Desdemona are here," he called. "The other two are gone. I'll check the wagon."

Rafe let his breath out in a rush when he saw Red silhouetted against the pink sky. He knew that chasing the raiding party by himself wouldn't accomplish anything, so he didn't bother to saddle up.

He limped up to Red. He rubbed his muzzle and squeezed his ears, something Red liked more than anything else. Red put his face against Rafe's chest and pushed. Rafe ran a hand down his neck and felt an object in the mane. It was tied into the hairs, not merely entangled with them, as though snagged by accident. He cut it free and studied it in the pale light.

"What have you been up to, old man?"

Red didn't answer.

It was an amulet, that was certain. That an Apache had made it was also certain. That it had belonged to Lozen was most certain of all. But did she intend it for a good purpose or an evil one?

The amulet lay as light as spider webs in the broad palm of his hand. He touched the tiny skull and stroked the feathers with his scarred fingertips. He couldn't say why, but he felt sure she had left it to bring him and Red good luck.

Chapter 38

POKING AT A POSSUM

Tall Girl held out a folded blanket with a pouch of tobacco and a fringed bag balanced on top. She lost her own balance, and Lozen caught the things she carried before they hit the ground.

"Help me, Grandmother," Tall Girl mumbled. Her eyes held that blank look that Lozen abhorred. No matter that The People had eaten their meager winter supplies and that few berries or seeds were ripe now. Tall Girl had managed to hoard enough mescal to ferment into the thick gray beverage called *tiswin*.

"Is someone sick?"

Tall Girl only turned and wobbled away. Lozen handed the presents to Daughter and started off after her.

"Will you come to the dance?" Daughter called after her.

"If I can."

Lozen heard the baby screaming before she reached Tall Girl's lodge. She must have given the child *tiswin* again.

Tall Girl herself fell asleep, but Lozen sang all day and into the night while the baby's two grandmothers and her own chanted, *"Yu, yu, yu, yom."* With explosive, gutteral chants of *"ha, ha, ha,"* Lozen marked the baby on the forehead, lips, chin, and chest with pollen. Hissing, she rubbed the carved snake over the child's body. Finally she shouted, *"Ugashe.* Be gone," and threw the stick into the fire.

As she chanted and rubbed the child's contorted limbs and neck, she fell into a trance. She didn't hear the distant pulse of the dance drums or even the two grandmothers singing nearby. She forgot that the men she had ridden with were dancing the story of their raid on the fort. She didn't hear the laughter when He Makes Them Laugh did his parody of a victory dance over a bedraggled chicken he had found.

As dawn approached, more people joined the grandmothers, until fifteen or twenty swayed in rhythm to the chanting. Corn Stalk, Maria, even Stands Alone added their voices. When the sun rose, the baby seemed exhausted by the struggle. Lozen despaired. Her legs ached from being folded under her all night. She wanted, more than anything, to sleep. Instead, she prayed one more time to Life Giver.

When she finished, she looked down and saw that the baby had quieted. His breathing steadied; his muscles relaxed. Lozen thanked Life Giver; then she shook Tall Girl awake.

"Do not ever give your children *tiswin*."

Tall Girl looked frightened, as if Lozen would put a spell on her if she disobeyed. "Yes, Grandmother."

Lozen and her own grandmother walked back among the sleepy dancers who talked quietly and yawned as they dispersed to their camps.

"Do you feel as though you've been in another country?" Grandmother asked.

"Yes." Lozen recognized everyone around her, but they seemed unfamiliar. She always felt this way after a sing.

"When we sing for someone," said Grandmother, "Life Giver takes us to the place where spirits dwell."

Lozen wanted to roll up in her blanket and sleep the day away. Instead she found the family waiting for her. When Corn Stalk's and She Moves Like Water's mother arrived, Victorio walked away to sit at a distance with his back to her. The subject under discussion was Daughter's feast.

"Her Eyes Open has agreed to be her sponsor," She Moves Like Water said. "Will you accompany her in the dancing, Sister?" she asked Lozen.

"Yes."

With that settled, they discussed whom they would ask to drum, to sing, and to officiate. They took inventory of what goods they still needed as gifts, and how much the new horses would bring. The most troublesome problem was how to avoid the Bluecoats during the months they prepared for the ceremony and for the days they held it.

"We can agree to go to the place the Bluecoats have set aside for us," said Corn Stalk. "We'll be safe from attacks."

"No." She Moves Like Water was adamant. "You've heard Wide's relatives talk about that place. We will all grow sick and disfigured and die, like the Mescaleros."

She Moves Like Water's mother picked up the moccasins she was mending and headed for her own fire. Victorio dipped a gourd into the rabbit stew and joined the women. Most men disdained women's company, but he welcomed their opinions. They looked at problems in a different way than the men did.

There was a larger issue than holding Daughter's ceremony without fear of attack. The Bluecoats demanded that all The People move to places set aside for them, to live under the army's supervision.

"We have always moved about this country as we pleased," Victorio said. "Now the Bluecoats try to tell us where we can live and hunt."

"Why can't our set-aside place be right here?" asked Lozen. "We can ask Tse'k to let us stay. The fort is only a day's ride away. The Bluecoats can hand out the food and gifts there. We can use our share for the feast and the ceremony."

Victorio smiled to himself. None of the men had suggested that. Maybe they all believed it was far too reasonable a solution for the Pale Eyes to accept. If they did think that, they were probably right.

"The Pale Eyes won't talk peace," Victorio said. "They shoot at everyone who comes near them."

"That's right," She Moves Like Water added. "Remember what the Bluecoat *nantan* said."

The Mescalero refugees had told them about General Carleton's orders to his soldiers. "Kill all the men found off the reservation, regardless of what they're doing. Capture the women and children." He seemed to be the only one who didn't recognize the absurdity of demanding that The People go to the reservations, and then shooting them when they tried to do so. Lozen had nicknamed Carleton Bidaa Digiz, Cross-Eyed, because he looked no farther than the end of his own nose.

"The Pale Eyes, Tse'k, has been like a father to us," said Lozen. "He does not lie. He treats us fairly." He treated them so fairly, in fact, that they had nicknamed him Ba'ch'othlii, He Can Be Trusted.

"We don't know where he is," said Victorio.

"We can ask Hairy Foot to deliver a message to him."

Victorio grunted. Maybe she was right. Maybe Hairy Foot would help them. He was as honest as Tse'k. "How will we find him?"

"I know the trail he uses. I can wait for him."

"It's too dangerous." Alarm gave a ragged, insistent tone to She Moves Like Water's voice.

Lozen had become too valuable to the Warm Springs people, to all the Red Paints, to take such a risk. Besides that, She Moves Like Water knew that Victorio would go with his sister. Victorio called Lozen his right hand. They went everywhere together.

"I will go with you," Victorio said.

"You should stay here, Brother." Lozen didn't say what they all were thinking.

What if the Bluecoats captured Victorio? What if they cut off his head and boiled it? Since the horrific fate of Red Sleeves, many people came to believe that the Bluecoats ate the people they took captive. Lozen could be walking into a terrible trap.

"Maria can come with me to talk Mexican to Hairy Foot," she said. "He understands our language a little, too."

Victorio didn't think the plan would work, but if anyone could get word to Tse'k, Lozen could.

AT TWILIGHT, RAFE, CAESAR, AND THE OTHER TEAMSTERS circled the wagons of the supply train. They strung lines between the wheels and tied the horses to them. They tethered the draft animals in place at the wagon tongues. While some cooked, others played cards and swapped stories. Patch lay with her hindquarters to the wheel and bared her teeth at any hound who looked remotely enamored of her.

The dozen men of the army escort pitched their tents and picketed their horses among the piñon trees. They stacked their rifles against the tree and hung their bridles, powder horns, and knapsacks from the branches. Civilians and soldiers took turns standing watch, although some of the civilians grumbled about it.

They didn't mind standing watch—they just didn't like the company. The men of the 125th Infantry were black, and the sight of former slaves in United States Army uniforms was repugnant to the Southerners in the train. Caesar rode with the soldiers when he could, finding men who had lived near his father's plantation and listening for news of the war.

Rafe poured hot water from the kettle into a tin basin, set it on an upturned crate, and rinsed out his second shirt and his spare pair of socks. As he worked, he watched Caesar perform supper. He wasn't the only one. The lieutenant, the sergeant, the other drivers, and the cattle drover drifted over. The lieutenant brought venison he had shot, and Caesar fired up another skillet.

The lieutenant had haunted their camp all the way from Santa Fe. Rafe was amused by the spectacle of a white officer almost on his knees before a black man, trying to recruit him for the regiment. In a troop of former field hands, Caesar was a gold strike. He could read, write, and cipher. He was stronger than two average men, and he knew the country. The lieutenant had promised him a sergeant's stripes and the princely sum of fifteen dollars a month, the two extra dollars to come out of the lieutenant's own pay.

Rafe had twitched an eyebrow when Caesar politely refused. Caesar caught the look and he explained later. Well, he didn't exactly explain. He had only asked Rafe, "Would you join the army again?"

Rafe had laughed. No, he wouldn't.

Caesar had spent a lot of time at army posts. He had seen

the men sweating in the August heat to make adobe bricks for barracks that would let in the rain and the wind. He had watched them chopping and hauling thousands of cords of wood. He had observed that it wasn't so different from slavery. Neither were the brutal punishments that some officers inflicted for minor offenses.

In the settlements and forts, Caesar added *Marse* to the front of every white man's name and *suh* after it. He rarely spoke unless asked a question; but on the trail a transformation came over him. He spun yarns about San Francisco. He recited fables starring that trickster, Bre'r Rabbit. When he wasn't talking, he sang. Tonight it was an old Southern field hands' song.

" 'Love, it am a killin' thing,' " he sang. " 'Beauty am a blossom, but if you want yo' finger bit, just poke it at a possum.' "

As they traveled, he would pick up limbs and throw them into the "possum belly," a hide slung under the wagon. By the time they stopped for the night, he had enough for a bonfire. He tied a rolled bandana around his head to keep the perspiration from his eyes. As he worked, he wiped his hands on half a feed sack stuck into his belt.

A gooseberry and currant cobbler bubbled in the dented dutch oven. A pot of peeled bulrush stems, lamb's quarter, and pigweed came to a hesitant simmer. He wrapped the sacking around the handle and pulled the pot off the flames so its contents would only parboil. While he was at it, he added a chunk of brown sugar and some of the vinegar he and Rafe used to clean their weapons.

Rafe had shot a javelina, and Caesar had threaded the boar's ribs onto a spit. Now and then he used a new axle-greasing brush to baste the ribs with a lethal blend of ground chiles, onions, wild garlic, strong black coffee, and whiskey. He called the results House Afire.

The skillet occupied the center ring. Fist-size chunks of boar meat sizzled in grease along with spring onions and wintered-over carrots and potatoes. Like a fencer, Caesar turned sideways to the fire. He held his right hand out to one side as though for balance and used his left hand to tip and shake the frying pan while the grease sizzled like fireworks.

He strewed a handful of chopped red chiles over the ingredients, added some salt, and tossed them. He put in more grease, a blizzard of flour, and a little water, and stirred the roux into a thick gravy.

"Boy, where did you learn to cook like that?" the lieutenant asked.

Caesar winked. "Why, suh . . ." His drawl thickened, his stock of words shrank. He became deferential, the way a chameleon took on the colors of his surroundings. "My mammy done taught me, suh."

Rafe knew that was only partly true. Caesar was too shrewd to admit that he had added *parboil, puree,* and *roux* to his vocabulary when he lived and worked in the bordello in San Francisco. Caesar claimed that the French cook there could produce a savory soup from an old pair of boots.

Being known as a black man who had consorted with white women, even ones of easy virtue, would get him into deadly trouble here. He was so discreet about his private life anyway that only Rafe knew about the quiet Mexican woman named Mercedes who welcomed him whenever he went to Socorro, or vivacious Concepción who did his laundry and more in Tucson, or Pilar in Tubac who had learned to cook greens and fatback.

After dinner Rafe scrubbed the pots with river sand while Caesar fed and watered the mules and horses. The two of them were looking forward to reading from their latest find, *Twelfth Night,* while the soldiers, teamsters, and drovers gathered to listen. The men formed a remarkably well-behaved audience considering they were so heavily armed that they clanked whenever they scratched or coughed, which was frequently.

Caesar let Rafe do the reading. A black man who could read became known as uppity, which was not healthy. They settled into their canvas chairs near the fire's light, and Rafe began with Duke Orsino's first line, " 'If music be the food of love, play on, / Give me an excess of it. . . .' "

Red's head went up, and his ears pricked forward. Patch growled, then barked, and all the dogs chimed in. A chorale of coyotes sang descant in the hills. The men scattered for cover in a clicking of breech bolts that sounded like a swarm of metal crickets.

They all waited on point like so many spaniels. Finally, the camp dogs grew bored and went back to sniffing each other instead of the wind. Rafe had dowsed the fire at the first alarm, which made reading out of the question. He rolled up in his blankets with his head on his saddle. He was floating so far out on the calm waters of sleep that at first he thought the woman's voice was a dream. A woman's voice here would more likely be a dream than reality anyway.

"Hóla, Capitán. Capitán Pata Peluda."

A chill ran through Rafe. The stir in his stomach wasn't butterflies, but more like beetles. The dogs started again. The lieutenant, his Springfield waving vaguely in the direction of the voice, hustled over to him. He wasn't desert-smart, but at least he had the sense to know who was.

"Who the hell is that?"

Rafe started to say, "An old friend," but he realized that would be taken in all the wrong ways. The men already called him a nigger-lover. They would add Injun-lover.

Injun lover.

Don't wander into that wasteland, son, he admonished himself. Aloud he said, "Someone who wants to parley, I reckon."

"I'll tell the men to saddle up, and we'll see to this."

"If it's a ruse, then they want you and your command to chase the decoy so they can attack the wagons while you're gone." Rafe knew the lieutenant was green, and not the brightest candle in the mineshaft. He was the one who had swallowed John Cremony's old chestnut about being killed by Apaches.

"Keep a close eye on Red," Rafe said. "My man and I will go out and see what they want. If you hear gunfire, send Sergeant Mott and a few men after us."

He'd found that acting as though the matter were settled

usually helped new officers make up their minds to do the sensible thing. He put on his hat, touching the hummingbird amulet on the hat band for good luck. He stuck his knife into his boot, loaded his pistols, and set them at half cock. Caesar did the same.

Rafe pulled a burning branch from the fire. He knew better than to insult Lozen by calling her name.

"Yo vengo," he called. "I'm coming."

"Abajo el álamo grande al lado del rio," came the answer.

"She wants to meet us under the big cottonwood by the river." From habit Rafe translated for Caesar, although Caesar had learned a lot of Spanish from Mercedes, Concepción, Pilar, and who knew whom else. He probably understood more than Rafe did.

"Who is she?" Caesar asked.

"I'd wager she's the hoyden who's been trying to steal Red."

Patch maintained a low growl in the back of her throat. Rafe didn't have to see her to know that the fur stood up like the spikes of a teasel along the ridge of her back. Rafe knew how she felt. The fur at the back of his own neck was stirring.

Lozen's voice sent shivers all through him, mostly generated by fear, but not completely. What did she want of him? What if this were a trick? What if he were poking at a possum and risking Caesar's life in the doing of it?

His blood drummed in his ears as he waited for the piercing warble of attacking Apaches. He listened for the whine of the arrows. Then he heard the steady crunch of Caesar's boots and sensed the quiet, rock-steady strength of him.

Caesar was brave, yes, but that was nothing special out here. Caesar woke up every day knowing that he might be singled out for insult or injury by some brute or other who had nothing close to his education, strength, and grace. That took fortitude of a special kind.

Rafe reached up and touched the amulet again. He felt the bit of blue stone, the hummingbird wings, and the skull that was smaller than the nail on his littlest finger. They calmed him. The person he was walking toward through the darkness had given it to him. The fear left him, and he was relieved that once again he had kept quiet through it and had not made a fool of himself.

The torch burned quickly, but a few more bundles of flaming grass took them to the cottonwood. Rafe saw two shadowy figures standing under it. Once again the scamp had eluded the sentries.

"¿Qué quiere?" he asked. "What do you want?"

He waited while Lozen held a whispered conversation with her companion, a Mexican captive maybe. Finally she spoke in halting Spanish aided by whispered prompts.

"My brother, the one they call Victorio, he wants to talk to Tse'k."

"Does your brother desire to live in peace?"

"Yes, if our people can stay in our own country."

"You mean a reservation at Warm Springs?"

"Reservation?" Lozen consulted with her companion. *"Si,"* she said. *"Reservación. Bina'nest'thl'oo,"* she added.

"Been a nest loo?"

Lozen laughed, a soft ripple of sound. *"Bina'nest'thl'oo."* She repeated it as though instructing him in the correct pronunciation. "It means *r*." She paused, searching for the words in Spanish. " 'A fence goes around them.' "

"Where does your brother want to meet Dr. Steck?" asked Rafe.

"He will wait in the willow grove in the small canyon east of Alamosa."

"When?" Rafe wanted to ask Lozen if she would be waiting there, too.

"A month from now. At the time of the new moon."

"I'll talk to Dr. Steck."

"Enjuh," she said.

Rafe knew that meant "good," and that she probably considered the parley to be over.

Caesar touched his arm. "Ask her about Pandora."

Rafe obliged. "Is the captive well?"

"She lives still."

She lives still. Rafe supposed that was as much as one needed to know in these perilous times. He realized he finally had the opportunity he'd wished for from time to time. He stood face-to-face with an Apache who would talk to him without trying to kill him. But he couldn't think of anything to say, except maybe to ask if she and her people had eaten the horses they stole from the fort a month ago. And if she still had his telescope.

"Are your people suffering?" The question sounded ridiculous to him. Of course they were, but that they might be hadn't occurred to him before. Apaches served up suffering, they didn't partake of it themselves.

She held up a fist, palm inward, with only the little finger extended skyward. "We carry our lives on our fingernails." She said it without emotion or bitterness, though it was a bitter thing.

While he pondered that, Lozen and her companion disappeared. One moment he could see them standing there, outlined in a pale glow of starlight, and the next, they were gone. They reminded him of the very ghosts Apaches feared so much.

"What do y'all s'pose she meant?" Caesar asked. " 'We carry our lives on our fingernails.' "

"I don't know."

Rafe did know. He just couldn't explain it.

Chapter 39

DAVID AND GOLIATH

Rafe found Dr. Steck slumped behind his desk in Santa Fe. He was responding to the latest fiat from General Carleton, and he wasn't in a good mood. He slid the glasses to the end of his thin nose and looked over them, brightening when he saw Rafe. He lit up when Rafe told him that Victorio had asked to meet with him and arrange to live in peace on the land his people already occupied.

He was humming to himself when he set out on horseback with Rafe and Caesar the next morning. They read *Twelfth Night* aloud, passing the book among them as they rode.

"I like this play the best," Casesar said.

"Why is that?" asked Dr. Steck.

" 'Cause Sebastian, the brother Viola thought was drowned, he turned up live and kickin' in the end."

"Do you have a brother?"

"I did. He's gone on to the Lord, though."

"We only have the brothers and sisters that God allotted to us," Dr. Steck said, "but there is no limit on friends."

Friends, Rafe thought, are rarer than hen's teeth in this country. He was grateful to have found one in Caesar.

Twelfth Night occupied them for most of the ninety-mile trip to Bosque Redondo, but General Carleton was not happy to see them.

"I forbid it!" Carleton pounded the desk top so hard the quill pens, ink well, and account book did a little jig. "As far as the Indians are concerned, I am the sole authority in New Mexico."

Dr. Steck tried to slip reason sideways into the tirade. "Victorio's proposal to live on a reserve in his own country is a sensible one. I'm sure he and I and the other Chiricahua Apaches can reach an amicable arrangement."

"You will have nothing to do with them. One of my officers will parley with Victorio. He will give him and his tribe two choices. They can submit to the authority of the United States Army and go peaceably to Bosque Redondo, or they will be hunted down and killed."

"That's monstrous!"

"You will leave immediately," Carleton's eyes bulged. "If you return here, I shall have a detail of soldiers escort you away."

Michael Steck rested one hand on the table, leaned into Carleton's fury, and pointed a finger at the general's nose. "You are a madman," he said in a low, calm voice. "You are a hypocritical, greedy, cruel, stupid, short-sighted megalomaniac."

Megalomaniac. Rafe had never heard the word, but he liked it. He thought the maniac part particularly suited Carleton.

RAFE MET CAESAR AT THE OUTSKIRTS OF ALAMOSA BEFORE dawn and they headed southwest. Caesar rode his dapple-gray gelding, the only horse around who stood as tall as Red. Caesar gave Rafe a quizzical look.

"Are ya'll sure you want to ride that hoss into the lion's den?"

Rafe flashed him a sardonic smile. "If an Apache steals Red, it will be over my dead body and Red's, too, I reckon."

Out of habit, Rafe looked for Patch. Some mongrel with more charm than the rest had gotten past her curt refusals. She gave birth to four puppies last night. When Rafe left the tiny inn on one of Alamosa's side streets this morning, the innkeeper's children were staring raptly into the box they had lined with straw as a nest for them.

Rafe didn't ask Caesar where he had slept. Caesar wasn't welcome in places where Anglos predominated. Rafe would insist that his friend and partner be allowed to stay where he did, and ugly scenes ensued. More than once both of them had stalked out of a hotel or boarding house and unfurled their blankets under a tree. Caesar usually found his own accommodations. He had a knack for finding accommodating accommodations.

They led two mules loaded with the gifts that Dr. Steck had asked them to buy in Alamosa's market. Steck hadn't said so, but Rafe assumed the gifts were an apology for the treatment Victorio and his men had received from Inspector General Davis, Carleton's envoy. Davis had delivered Carleton's ultimatum, and Victorio, being no man's fool, had refused to take his people to Bosque Redondo. He and his warriors had ridden up into the mountains, and no one had seen anything of them since.

Rafe knew the officer Carleton had sent. Afterward, Rafe had seen him in the officers' mess. He had raised his glass of brandy in a toast, "Death to the Apaches, and peace and prosperity to this land!"

Rafe had to admit that he was right. If all Anglos had been like Dr. Steck, coexistence might have been possible, but Rafe was amazed to have met even one man like him. There would be no peace or prosperity while Apaches and Americans tried to occupy the same space. Steck talked about the need to preserve this "interesting" people, as he called the Apaches, but he wasn't trying to earn a living running cattle or prospecting for gold or hauling freight.

Rafe and Caesar followed the small river, climbing steadily. It chortled past them as though tickled by the tips of the willow branches brushing it. A gentle night rain had washed the dust off the rocks, trees, and bushes, and now the sun was polishing them. Birds sang as if strife hadn't been invented. It was a lovely day to go courting death.

"Now how is it you know where Victorio and his people pitch camp?" Rafe asked Caesar.

"Josefa, she say the folks in Alamosa have trucked with the Warm Springs 'Paches since her gran'mammy was a sprat."

"Josefa? You mean you have a woman cached in Alamosa, too?"

"I reckon I catched her, all right." Caesar gave him a sample of the smile that beguiled women of all ages.

"Did Josefa say why the Apaches never attack Alamosa?"

"She say they always treats 'em fair. They ain't never bushwacked 'em, cheated 'em, sold 'em bad whiskey, nor stolen they women."

"Are only saints allowed to live in that town?"

"Naw, but if you had rattlesnakes residin' in your back forty and you knew they was too clever for you to kill 'em, wouldn't you treat 'em with respect?"

"I would."

"Do ya'll s'pose the Apaches'll shoot us first or say, 'Howdy do'?" Caesar asked.

"Too late to worry about that now."

Around the middle of the afternoon the stream seemed to disappear into a wall of basalt towering a hundred feet into the clear blue sky. They dismounted and made themselves comfortable under the walnut tree that Josefa said was the customary meeting place. They heard the high whistling keen of a hawk, but they didn't see any birds circling overhead. The hawk's cry always sounded mournful to Rafe, but now it sent shivers along his spine. He was pretty sure no hawk had made it.

"How long did Josefa say we should wait here?"

Caesar scanned the top of the cliff. "Long as it takes,"

It took a few hours. When the sun was about to insert itself between the sky and the top of the cliff, Caesar said, "Mebbe this is the wrong place. Mebbe they's waiting under another walnut tree."

"They've got to put on their best bib and tucker. And we're probably a goodly distance from their bivouack."

"What is a tucker anyways?"

"Damned if I know. Something to do with female attire, I think."

Red's ears pitched forward. Caesar's hand went to the butt of the old breech-loading flintlock in the saddle boot. At least fifty Apaches rode toward them. They had put on their best bibs and tuckers, all right, but they hadn't painted the red stripe across their faces. That was a good sign. They were armed, though. Besides their usual cutlery, many of them carried old Mexican flintlocks. A few had the Spencer repeating rifles and the Smith carbines used by Union troops in the late war of the rebellion.

Victorio rode in front. He did not look like a harried fugitive or one of the ragtag beggars waiting for rations at the agency. None of them did. He wore a fringed leather hunting shirt stained white with clay and decorated with silver disks, tin cones, and beadwork. The lower parts of his tall moccasins were solidly beaded around the turned-up, red-painted strips of rawhide at the toes.

Rafe was surprised to see Cochise riding next to him, and he thought about how many men would like to have had him in their gunsights. On the other side of Cochise was a tall, ferocious-looking individual on a coffee-colored pony. The stranger was almost the same color as the pony, darker than any Apache Rafe had ever seen, and much heavier. He carried over two hundred pounds, and all of them solid meat.

He fit Kit Carson's description of Juh, Long Neck, the most elusive and bloodthirsty killer in the whole tribe of them. Carson pronounced the name Whoa, or rather Wh-Wh-Whoa because of the man's stammer. "Wolf mean," Carson called him. "Wolf mean with b'ar and painter thrown in. Old Wh-Wh-Whoa is wrath walking upright."

On Victorio's left rode Lozen and an old man wearing a cap of hawk feathers and long gold chains dangling from his earlobes.

His name is Nanay, Rafe thought, but they call him Broken Foot.

Rafe was struck by how much Lozen and her brother resembled each other, and how handsome they both were. Lozen rode a bay mare with black feet. Rafe remembered the bay mare she had stolen from Don Angel at least thirteen years ago. He almost smiled at the memory. She had looked so brash and rafish in a boy's breechclout and shirt that day.

She reminded him of Shakespeare's Viola, both of them jumping the fence men put around their sex. Lozen was still doing it. She must be older than twenty-five by now, with no sign of a husband, and here she was, riding with the men.

Rafe tried not to stare at her, but that was difficult. She struck such a contrast with the warriors in their breechclouts and blankets, their headdresses of fur, feathers, bones, and antlers, and their motley assortment of Apache, Mexican, and Anglo attire, with the addition of army jackets, some with bullet holes neatly patched.

Strings of beads hung from Lozen's earlobes. Necklaces of beads and shells formed a collar around her neck. She wore a magnificent doeskin skirt and tunic, intricately beaded and stained a golden yellow with cattail pollen, probably.

The hoyden still prevailed, though. To accommodate the saddle, she had hiked the skirt up on her strong brown thighs. The long fringes on the tunic swayed gracefully as she moved in rhythm with her horse. The hundreds of tin cones around the tunic's square yoke jingled merrily.

Her long hair flowed across her shoulders like black water over smooth river rocks. The ends lay mingled with the fringes on her thighs. Her hair was clean and soft. Rafe wouldn't have expected that. What did Apaches use for soap, anyway? He tried to imagine the women washing their hair while the United States Army hounded them and gangs of drunken miners roamed the countryside on scalp hunts. Sparks glinted where the sun glanced off stray locks. Wisps curled like black swan's down around her face.

You're not here to admire Victorio's sister, Rafe thought. He figured that showing any interest at all in a man's sister could get him killed. At least it could in Texas where he grew up. Lozen looked at him as though she had never seen him. He returned the indifference.

Victorio dismounted, and as he and Rafe approached each other, a woman from the rear of the group rode up. She was dressed like an Apache, but she looked Mexican.

Before Rafe could say anything, Victorio put his arms around him and drew him into an embrace. Rafe fought the reflex to stiffen and recoil. Men didn't hug each other where he came from.

"I bring greetings from Dr. Steck," Rafe said in Spanish.

The Mexican woman translated from Spanish to Apache, then back again. Rafe recognized her voice as the one he had heard with Lozen under the cottonwood by the river that night a few months ago.

"Where is Father Tse'k?" asked Victorio. "The sight of him would make our hearts glad."

"General Carleton is the *nantan* for this territory. He forbids Father Steck to meet with you."

"Kal'ton." Lozen stared at the end of her nose, bringing her dark irises close together. "Bidaa Digiz."

The men laughed, and Rafe smiled. He could guess why she called Carleton cross-eyed. He was incapable of seeing anything beyond his own limited view of the world.

"Father Steck sends you these presents to show his friendship and respect for you," said Rafe. "He asks me to tell you that he regrets the decision of *nantan* Carleton. He will try to convince him to let you stay at Warm Springs."

"We do not need the permission of Kal'ton to stay where we have always lived," Victorio said. "We do not tell Kal'ton that he must take his wives and children and leave his home."

A young man dismounted and walked toward them. He was small and wiry, and Rafe had the feeling he could run for days over rough country, but then he would have said the same for any of them. What set this one apart was his headdress, a skunk pelt with the head, the tail, the four legs, and some of the aroma still in place.

He tilted his chin down and waggled the skunk's head so it seemed to be the one talking. "Tell me, Hairy Foot," the skunk said, "does Kal'-ton have a wife and children?"

"Yes, I think he does." Rafe felt like a fool talking to a dead animal, but the rest of the party seemed to enjoy the joke. And to tell the truth, the effect of a skunk talking in Apache was comical.

"And where do they live?"

"A month's journey to the east of here."

"They must be very happy, then. They do not have to talk to Old Man Cross-eyed." The young man took the reins of the mules and led them back to his horse through the laughter of his companions.

Rafe expected the meeting to end then. The Apaches had the presents and Dr. Steck's regrets. "Do you want me to carry a message to Father Steck?"

"You will come with us," said Victorio.

The side of beef mounted on the coffee-colored pony grunted. He looked as though he had a bone to pick with Victorio's decision to lead two Pale Eyes to his village, and that the bone was stuck in his throat. His face contorted as he struggled to speak. Victorio glowered at him.

Kit Carson said old Whoa had a stammer. Carson also said he roosted in the Sierra Madre a hundred miles south of the Mexican border. If so, that didn't stop him from raiding southern Arizona and New Mexico Territories. Rafe wondered what brought him this far north. From the look that passed between him and Victorio, Rafe would have bet it wasn't brotherly love.

Victorio gave an impatient wave of his hand and made a curt reply. Then he gestured to Lozen, who handed Caesar a wide strip of sacking.

"So you can't see the route," the Mexican woman explained.

Caesar looked at Rafe, and Rafe nodded. Caesar folded the sacking and tied it tightly around his eyes. When Lozen handed a strip of cloth to Rafe, she looked up at the amulet on his hatband and smiled. Rafe fought the urge to reach out and touch her hair.

As he was getting ready to tie on the blindfold, he saw her ride forward and take Red's reins. Red balked.

"It's okay, partner." Rafe reached forward and rubbed Red's ears.

Rafe sank into a reverie, lulled by the conversations around him. He hadn't noticed before, but the men spoke in low, gentle tones. He heard none of the shouting and hardness of the white men's talk. He listened in vain, though, for Lozen's voice.

He was about to doze off when he heard Skunk Head talking at his elbow and Maria translating. Apparently Skunk Head had decided to entertain the two Pale Eyes.

"Old Man Coyote was going along," Skunk Head recited, "and he saw a white man with a herd of fat sheep. Coyote said, 'What pretty animals. Can I herd them for you?' The white man said, 'No, I've heard you're a bad fellow.' But Coyote begged until finally the white man said, 'All right, but see that big mud puddle over there. Don't let the sheep get in there. It's pretty deep.'

"The white man went off home, and Coyote killed those sheep and ate them. Then he stuck the heads and the tails in the mud puddle. He called to the white man, 'Hey, your sheep are stuck in the mud. Come quick.' The white man ran out, and he saw the heads and the tails. 'Run to my house and tell my wives to give you a shovel,' he said.

"Coyote, he ran to the house, and he said to the white man's wives, 'Your husband told me to have intercourse with you.' "

Rafe heard Caesar chuckle. The Apaches guffawed.

"The wives said, 'We don't believe you. He wouldn't say that.' Coyote, he went to the door and he shouted, 'Your wives won't do what you say.' The white man got angry, and he yelled, 'Tell them to hurry up!' 'See there,' said Coyote. 'What did I tell you?' So the women had intercourse with Coyote. When he finished, he went away laughing."

Skunk Head went away, too, chuckling to himself, and the conversations started up again. After a while Caesar started a spiritual that the field hands sang while chopping cotton.

O David,
Yes! Yes!
My little David,
Yes! Yes!
And he killed Goliath,
Yes! Yes!

Yes, he killed Goliath,
Yes! Yes!

When Caesar paused between verses, Rafe realized that
conversation had ceased. He considered telling Caesar to
stop. The Apaches might think he was making "bad juju,"
as Caesar called it. But no one protested. No one stuck a
lance into either of them. The song was a long one to begin
with, and Caesar made up more verses as he went along.

Oh, Daniel,
Yes! Yes!
Poor ole Daniel,
Yes! Yes!
Daniel in the lion's den,
Yes! Yes!
Safe in the lion's den,
Yes! Yes!

The silence between the verses began to seem reverential.
The repetitive words must have sounded like a shaman's
medicine song to the Apaches. Come to think of it, Rafe
mused, it was a medicine song. Caesar was asking God to
keep him as safe as Daniel in the lion's den.

David and Goliath. It was an appropriate theme, given the
state of hostilities. Since the United States Army would be
Goliath in this contest, Rafe hoped the outcome would differ
from the biblical one.

Chapter 40

KINFOLK

Caught in the night behind his blindfold and lulled by the surefooted gait of Red under him, Rafe dozed off. He woke with a start to the high, wailing women's call that pumped fear through his veins. He almost yanked off the blindfold and pulled his pistols from the saddle holsters.

"You may look now," said the Mexican woman.

Lozen handed him the reins, and when Rafe's eyes adjusted to the light of the full moon, he thought he was dreaming. As the procession rode through the rows of boys and women and into the village, he saw cookfires illuminating the hillsides all around. The size of the encampment made him reconsider just who was Goliath and who was David.

Rafe estimated that several thousand people had turned out to greet them. Dr. Steck's presents wouldn't go far with this mob, but they seemed overjoyed to see the mules and their loads, anyway. The women danced, sidestepping in time to a chant that sounded to Rafe like a thousand cats with their tails caught in vises. The children swarmed around the procession. Boys led the Apaches' horses away, but Rafe and Caesar declined all offers to take theirs. Rafe didn't feel like testing the dictum that Apaches wouldn't steal from guests.

Caesar rode up beside Rafe. "They sure ain't layin' low, is they? Don't they savvy that Ole Cross-Eyes Carleton means to root 'em out, wheat and weed?"

"They savvy." But Rafe himself was at a loss to understand the carefree mood and the huge number of people.

The singing, dancing crowd of women led them to an open space where they had laid out blankets and hides. Victorio gestured for them to sit on his right side. Rafe took that as a high honor because he could tell the other leaders had been seated by rank on Victorio's left. Cochise sat next to him, then Red Sleeves' son, Mangas, and Whoa, with Broken Foot beside him, and the scar-faced one Rafe knew as Loco. Lozen sat behind her brother. From much farther along in the ranking of warriors glowered a square-jawed, beetle-browed, droop-mouthed, thin-lipped visage that Rafe had caught glimpses of at Santa Rita.

Caesar saw him, too. "Is that Geronimo?" he murmured.

"I think so. He must be taking a holiday from murdering Mexicans."

Whoa and Geronimo present in the same location. Rafe imagined Kit Carson looking at him from across a tableful of beer bottles and saying, "Those two will present you with a complete invoice of rascality."

"Con permiso." The young Mexican woman knelt behind Rafe and Caesar. "I will translate," she said in Spanish.

"What is your name?"

"María. María Mendez."

Rafe realized that he and Caesar were about to be included in a council. It began with more oratory than a congressional filibuster. Even Whoa gave a speech, or rather he muttered it to Geronimo, who delivered it.

Victorio finally arrived at the point. "Tell Father Tse'k that his children, the Ndee, long to see his face again and welcome him at our fires. Tell him that our women can no longer gather food to eat. Our children are hungry. Mothers weep for their dead sons. Wives weep for their husbands. Tell Father Tse'k that we want peace."

"But you will not take your people to Bosque Redondo."

"No, we will not live with the Navajos at that place."

Nanay, the one called Broken Foot, stood up. He waved an arm to include the surrounding countryside. "This land speaks to us," he said. "It teaches us how to behave correctly. It keeps wickedness away."

Cochise rose next. "If we leave our land, the young ones will forget the names of the places here. Those who forget the names, forget what the names mean; they forget what happened there. When we cease to know the meaning of the land, we no longer know who we are."

Rafe wondered how he would explain all that and realized he needn't even try. Dr. Steck would understand it, but he could do nothing. No one else would have the slightest interest.

"I'll tell him, but I do not think Carleton will change his mind."

"Life Giver decides who will eat well and who will not. Life Giver decides who will live and who will die. Life Giver decides who will go and who will stay."

After the council, the women served a feast; then Victorio distributed the gifts of blankets and knives, the pots and beads. Rafe noticed that most of the first recipients were women, widows he assumed. He was impressed by how self-assured Victorio was, and by the fact that no one grumbled about their share.

When all that was finished, the dancing started. The crowd milled in and out of the light thrown across the ground by the huge fire. They greeted friends. They chatted and laughed, at ease with each other and at home in a situation that felt totally alien to Rafe. Rafe and Caesar stood with the men, aware that they were being scrutinized by the women in particular. Rafe watched for glimpses of Lozen in the crowd, and he knew Caesar was looking for Pandora. Then Skunk Head appeared and held a conference with María.

She turned to Rafe and Caesar. "The one they call He Makes Them Laugh wants to give these to the black Pale Eyes."

He Makes Them Laugh carried a pair of tall moccasins, covered with beadwork. He started talking, and María had to speak fast to keep up.

"I told my woman when she cut these out four years ago that they were so big she could use them to carry the baby in. She said they would fit the black Pale Eyes and that some day she would give them to him." He Makes Them Laugh handed them to Caesar.

"Don't say, thank you," Rafe muttered.

"Why not?"

"Not polite. Say you'll wear them a long time, or something like that."

Caesar took off his hat. He held it to his chest with one hand while he accepted the moccasins with the other.

"Tell your woman these are very beautiful."

"She says to tell you she named our son Ch'inayihi'dili," said He Makes Them Laugh. "It means Sets Him Free."

"I'd surely like to meet him."

He Makes Them Laugh and María held another conference; then he sent a boy off with a message. Stands Alone arrived soon after with her five-year-old son walking behind her.

"Don't talk to her directly," warned Rafe. "No matter what white people might think, Apache women are as chaste as Desdemona."

Caesar crouched down and held out a penknife with a deer horn handle. The child stared fixedly at it while Caesar demonstrated how to open it. He held the blade so the haft pointed toward Sets Him Free.

"Please tell him it's a present for him," said Caesar.

Maria obliged.

The child ran forward, snatched the knife, and retreated to his mother's skirt. Caesar laughed so heartily everyone turned to look.

"Tell him I'm gonna call him Charlie."

Stands Alone bent down and whispered something to her son. He walked out to stand in front of her.

"Shida'a," he said.

"Shida'a means uncle," said María.

"Uncle," Caesar beamed at Rafe, "I gots me some kinfolks."

A second boy joined Charlie Sets Him Free. María said he was Victorio's son by his second wife and his name was Washington. Before long the two of them were riding on Caesar's shoulders. Before the dancing ended, they had fallen asleep in his lap.

By the time Victorio announced the last dance, Rafe was

dozing, too. Then he felt a tap on his shoulder. Lozen walked away from him and onto the dance ground where couples were gathering. Rafe wanted to decline the invitation, but he had seen what happened to men and boys who did. Broken Foot and Loco seemed to be in charge of the dance, and they dragged the reluctant ones out to face their partners.

Rafe joined Lozen so that they stood a pace away from each other. At least he wouldn't have to touch her. The step was simple enough, and he'd been watching them do it all night. Together they swung back and forth, she taking five steps forward and he backwards, and then reversing so that he advanced on her.

The singing, the drumming, the crackle of the leaping fire, Lozen facing him; her strong, lovely face now in shadow, now lit, all seemed like a dream, except that he would never have dreamed of doing this. The throb of the drums and the sway of bodies around him mesmerized him. He drifted away from his reality to a world more fantastical than he could have imagined.

When the drums and the singing stopped, he and Lozen walked toward the crowd standing around the dance ground. She spoke to him in Spanish, though she looked straight ahead and she hardly moved her mouth. Maybe she didn't want people to see her talking to a Pale Eyes.

"*¿Donde está su perra?* Where is your dog?"

"*Tiene niños.* She has little ones."

"Dogs are useful," Lozen said. "They have far-sight. They can warn of enemies."

"I will bring you a puppy."

"*Enjuh*, good," she said. She looked slantwise up at him, a mischievous smile playing across her full lips. She knew he was ignorant of the customs. "The man is supposed to pay the woman for dancing with her."

All Rafe had in his pockets was lint, except for a shiny copper penny. He held it on the palm of his hand so the engraved likeness of the Indian faced up.

Lozen's smile was radiant, though Rafe knew she had no use for a coin as currency. She took it and slipped it into the small pouch hanging at her waist. She reached out a hand and touched the leather pouch that he had found in his old wagon years ago, and in which he kept whichever of Shakespeare's works he was reading. Her smile turned a little sly, and he knew for sure, finally, who had made it.

Without saying anything more, she put her arm through that of an old woman with a ringtail's elfin face and flared ears. The two of them walked off into the assembling dawn.

Her grandmother, Rafe thought. The old one is probably Lozen's grandmother.

Lozen had a family. She had a life far different from anything in Rafe's experience, and yet similar, too. Rafe had had a grandmother, until the Comanches, frugal with their arrows, clubbed her to death.

Victorio took Rafe and Caesar to a brush-covered shelter at his wife's camp. Someone had put down two heaps of fragrant cedar branches inside. Rafe and Caesar picketed their horses at the entrance. The camp grew quiet except for occasional coughs and snores and the brief fussing of a baby. Rafe slept more soundly than he would have thought possible, being in the den of the lion and all. He left his boots on, though.

When the sound of women's laughter woke them, the sun had already risen. Charlie Sets Him Free and Wah-sin-ton stood in the doorway.

As soon as Caesar stirred, the boys shouted, "*Shida'a.*" They ran in, jumped on him, and started bouncing on his chest.

Caesar spoke in gusts as his new relations jolted the wind out of him. "What's the word for *nephew,* Rafe?"

"I think it's *shik'a'a.*"

Rafe left them wrestling in the tangle of the blankets and stepped outside. The first thing he noticed was that both Red and the gray were munching on piles of grass that someone had left for them. The second thing he noticed was that the valley was on fire, or at least it appeared to be. Smoke hovered over everything. It came from the cookfires scattered along the river and across the surrounding hills as far as the eye could see.

The rancheria covered much more area than he had thought, and all of it was in a ferment. In spite of the fact that they had spent most of the night dancing, women and girls swarmed in and out of Victorio's wives' arbors and the cookfires scattered around them. Rafe saw Lozen and her grandmother and Pandora sorting, chopping, peeling, skinning, and gutting with the rest. A second arbor contained baskets and trays of food and trinkets. Leather pouches bulged with goods. So much for Victorio's claim that his people were poor.

Other women hurried to and fro with loaded burden baskets and water jugs. Some bent at the waist under heaps of firewood. The young children collected kindling and carried small water jugs, or they chased each other around, more excited and frenetic than the day before. An army of small boys rubbed down the hundreds of ponies and led them to better grass. A group of girls sang and danced where the boys would be sure to see them.

Victorio, Loco, and fifteen or twenty men were clearing rocks and pebbles from the dance ground, then sweeping it with bundles of brush. Some of them laid a foothill of wood for a fire and dragged in four thirty-foot-long saplings that seemed to have some special purpose. Steam rose from a hut by the river, and Rafe heard the muted chant of male voices from inside it.

Caesar came out, hoisted the boys onto his shoulders, and stood next to Rafe. He was wearing his new moccasins with his wool trousers tucked into the high tops. Rafe felt a twinge of envy.

"Looks like they's fixin' to throw a hoedown," Caesar said.

"I don't know what to make of it, pardner."

María arrived with a cradleboard on her back.

"Look at this." Caesar walked around Maria to admire the baby.

María half turned so Rafe could see the wide-eyed child

staring at him from under a shock of black hair.

"Boy or girl?" Rafe asked.

"She is a girl."

María had brought them a gourd of stew, a sotol stalk for a spoon, and an explanation. Victorio's daughter was to participate in the ceremony of becoming a woman, she said. People had come from all over the Apacheria for it. The celebration would go on for days. It was the most sacred of their rituals. The Pale Eyes would have to leave.

As they were saddling the horses, Victorio and his number-one wife approached them. At least Rafe assumed she was his number-one-wife. She had taken charge of distributing the gifts to the women the night before. She held out a rawhide saddle pouch with painted designs on the carrying straps and long fringes. The tin cones on the ends of the fringes jingled when Rafe took it.

"This will be very useful." Rafe tried to think of something he could give in return, but last night he had divided out all his tobacco. He had not packed clothes, and what he had was old and shabby.

"Give her my darnin' kit," Caesar murmured.

When Rafe opened Caesar's saddlebag to look for it, he noted that nothing had disappeared in the night. He retrieved the leather packet that contained a small quilted sack with two steel needles, heavy black cotton thread wound around a peeled stick, a few wooden buttons, and a packet of straight pins. The name ELLIE was embroidered on the sack.

"I can't take this, Caesar," he said. "It belonged to your mother, didn't it?"

"She'd be proud."

Rafe hesitated.

"Go on. Shake a leg. They wants us out o' here so's they can get on with the fandango."

Rafe handed the sewing kit to Victorio. "For your daughter, in honor of her special day."

Victorio passed it to his wife, who gave the slightest of smiles, then turned and went back to work. Victorio shook their hands the way he had seen Pale Eyes do. María continued translating.

"*Nantan* says, 'May we live to see each other again, my brothers.' "

"God keep you," said Caesar.

As they mounted, Victorio handed Rafe a war club. The round stone head was encased in a cow's tail which had been wet, slid over a stout oak handle, allowed to shrink in place, and tightly wrapped with sinew. A flexible section of hide was left between handle and the stone so the head moved freely. The design allowed it to deliver a skull-crushing blow without breaking off. A loop through the butt of the handle fit over Rafe's wrist. Rafe took the Green River knife and sheath from his belt and gave it to Victorio, who smiled his gratitude.

Rafe and Caesar put on the blindfolds again. This time a few young boys escorted them away. Caesar started singing to himself as soon as they were out of sight of the rancheria, and Rafe smiled.

Rafe realized that Caesar had had kinfolk even before Sets Him Free called him "Uncle" yesterday. Rafe himself had come to think of Caesar as a brother. He knew he would fight to the death for him, and that was no idle proposition. He knew that Caesar would do the same for him.

Chapter 41

AMONG THE WILD MEN

"They're mean people." Grandmother folded the blankets as though she were wrestling them into submission. "How will you find Long Neck's wild men?" she muttered as she stuffed the blankets into the saddlebag. "They live like coyotes, just anyplace."

This was the third time she had asked the question this morning, but Victorio answered it again. He knew she was upset by his decision to move south and take with him whomever would follow. He knew that fear had run off her smiling disposition and left this quarrelsome one in its place.

"Geronimo says Long Neck will leave a sign for us at the Place Where Rocks Are Stacked Up," he said.

"Who's Geronimo?"

"He Who Yawns."

"He Who Yawns! He's a coyote, that one. He persuades the young men to hunt Mexicans with him all the time. He's gotten many of them killed. He and Long Neck don't care how much we suffer because of their wild ways."

"He Who Yawns knows the trail south better than anyone."

"You don't like Long Neck." Grandmother returned to the subject at hand. "Nobody likes him."

"I'm not going to take my blankets to his lodge and marry him." Victorio tried to make her smile, but she wasn't having it.

"Long Neck's people eat wild pigs," she said. "And pigs eat snakes. You are what you eat. That's why the Enemy People act like snakes. If you live among them, your daughter will marry one of those wild coyotes."

"I'm going to marry Short Rope." Daughter looked up from the moccasin she was mending and gave Grandmother something else to fuss about.

"Short Rope's not even a warrior yet."

"The men voted him warrior rank after the last raid."

"You had your feast only two moons ago. You're too young to marry. You have a lot to learn about being a wife." With her gnarled fingers Grandmother struggled to tie the saddlebag's laces. Victorio wanted to help her, but she didn't like to be reminded that she needed help.

"Your son will learn bad habits," Grandmother scolded him. "He'll forget the proper way to behave."

"When we find a good camping place, we'll come back for you and the other old ones. You can teach him the correct way."

Victorio had told her that, too, but often these days she forgot what people said. She would stop in the middle of a healing sing, confused about what song came next. She had seen more than eighty harvests, so he shouldn't have been surprised, but she had always seemed unchanged and unchanging, able to go on forever.

As Victorio watched her carry her belongings to the mule, he realized how frail she had become while he was preoccupied with the troubles the Pale Eyes were causing. Streaks of white mingled with the gray in her long hair. Her wrists looked brittle as salt bush twigs. Her skin had a translucent quality, as though if she stood in front of the fire the light would shine through her, silhouetting the curved branches of her ribs.

While Corn Stalk held the mule, Daughter kneed him in the stomach to make him expel his breath so she could pull the hempen cinch as tight as possible. It held the Mexican-style packsaddle, a flat leather pouch stuffed with straw. Grandmother tried to fasten the broad strap that went around the mule's rump, but her gnarled fingers couldn't maintain a grip and pull, too. She let Daughter tighten it for her, to keep the load from slipping forward on steep inclines. She also let Daughter tie the saddlebag in place. Daughter and Lozen were the only ones she allowed to help her, maybe because they had both done it since they were young and she considered them her apprentices.

The Warm Springs women had already stored grindstones, baskets of food, blankets, and water jugs near the cave where the old ones would live. Corn Stalk smoothed over the fire pit, and She Moves Like Water carried the bed-frame poles to the dance ground where people were stacking them. They could not leave the village the way it was when they lived here because if they did, whatever happened here would affect them wherever they were. If enemies attacked here, they would be attacked. If a bear left feces in the old site, they would become sick.

Victorio was relieved to see the mother of She Moves Like Water and Corn Stalk stop at the usual place near a boulder and stand with her back to them. He had an excuse now to end this discussion and leave so She Who Has Become Old could say good-bye to Grandmother.

Victorio joined the men gathering at the dance ground. They had a lot to talk about. His people had become prey here in their own country. They had to plan the route south carefully. They would discuss which tanks and springs and seeps to camp at, and where to find the caves with supplies hidden on earlier journeys. They would decide who would ride ahead looking for enemy sign, who would guard the rear, and who would take up flanking positions. Until they crossed the invisible line between the Pale Eyes and the Mexicans, they would have to travel at night using the Fixed Star as a guide. They would have to risk Ghost Owl's rapacious appetite for souls.

Lozen returned from the pasture leading her mare and Victorio's war pony. Grandmother met her with more objections.

"Granddaughter, ask Hairy Foot to send word to Father Tse'k that we want to stay here."

"The Pale Eyes *nantan*, Cross-Eyes, won't agree to it." Lozen knew why her grandmother was in such a state. Lozen was afraid, too, and furious that the Pale Eyes had made this necessary. "Loco went to ask the Bluecoats for a peace council one month ago. Don't you remember? While he and his men were away, Pale Eyes attacked when everyone slept. They killed twenty-three of his people. When we find a safer place for the women and children, we will try again to make peace."

Grumbling at Life Giver for creating Pale Eyes, Grandmother helped Lozen cut rawhide covers for her mare's hooves and tied them in place. The men had debated leaving the horses behind. Horses made noise. Horses had to eat. They left tracks easy enough for even Pale Eyes to follow. The men in council decided to start out with them, though. They could turn the ponies loose or kill them if they became a liability.

In the afternoon, with their belongings piled onto the backs of their ponies, people began gathering in the center of the village. Usually this would be a happy time. Usually the women would be heading for the low country where they gathered mescal buds, and baked and dried them to make meal for the coming year. This time they didn't know when they would return. This time they were leaving the country where they had always lived, the place that White Painted Woman had given them, the place where The People first walked the earth.

The old ones' relatives helped carry their parents' and grandparents' belongings to the cave in the cliff. Fourteen-year-old Disgruntled and Burns His Finger, and thirteen-year-old Big Hand joined them. Victorio had assigned them the duty of keeping watch over the old ones. The responsibility carried great honor, but none of the boys wanted it. To make it more appealing, Victorio had given them carbines and cartridge belts with ten precious bullets in each of them. For days they had struck straddle-legged, scowling poses, the belts low on their hips, the guns held with careless bravado.

He Makes Them Laugh's grandparents refused to leave their lodge. They said if they were going to die, they'd just as soon do it in the comfort of their home. The boys helped the three sick women mount three old ponies that hadn't ended up in the stew pots yet. Lozen led Victorio's pony to a flat rock so Grandmother and her old friend Turtle could climb onto him.

Grandmother knew why her son had left his favorite horse behind. Coyote was too old for the rigors of the war trail. Grandmother and the others could ride him if they needed to, and if necessary, he would provide meat for them.

They rode as far up the slope as they could and dismounted. Big Hand led the ponies to the upper pasture, and Lozen and the other two boys carried the ones who couldn't climb to the cave. Then she helped Grandmother and Turtle. Grandmother had to stop often, and Lozen waited with her arm around her waist. When they reached the ledge, Grandmother sat on a rock to rest, and Lozen pulled away the stones that hid the entrance to the nearby cache of food and belongings. Everyone except those who were ill gathered brush to make beds. They ate dried mule meat and parched corn with berries.

When they had settled in, they embraced the children and grandchildren. They murmured, "May we live to see each other again," and "I will pray to Life Giver each day that He keep you safe." They watched their families start down the slope, single-file, but Lozen stayed behind.

By nightfall Lozen and the old ones had turned the cave into a comfortable shelter with a small fire built in a rear corner so the light wouldn't be visible from below. With a weary sigh Grandmother lay down in the darkness near Turtle and pulled the blanket over her. Lozen sat at the mouth of the cave, looking out over the cliffs and outcrops sculpted into wraithlike shapes by wind and rain, moonlight and shadow. Since Lozen was old enough to understand the words, Grandmother and the other old ones had told her the names of each one of them and the stories that went with the names.

The old ones talked softly back and forth in the cave behind her until fatigue caught up with them. One by one their voices stilled. A large shadow swooped almost at eye level beyond the ledge, and the owl gave his spectral "hoo, hoo,

hoo." In fear of Ghost Owl, Lozen backed into the cave and crawled under the blanket with Grandmother.

"You should go with the others," Grandmother said. "They need your far-sight."

"I'll catch up with them tomorrow. I know if enemies are around, so I can travel in the day while the rest are hiding at the Place Where The Widows Stopped To Cry."

"Do you know why it's called that?"

Lozen thought for a long time about what her grandmother wanted her to see when she asked that question.

"Holes In The Earth," she said finally. It was the name of the Santa Rita mine where, thirty years ago, the white men and Mexicans had invited the Red Paints to a feast and then killed and scalped Grandmother's husband and daughter, Lozen's mother. At Holes In The Earth Grandmother became one of the widows who stopped to cry on their flight back to Warm Springs.

By speaking with names, by identifying the places where the events happened, Grandmother took Lozen and the others there. The stories of those places reminded them that The People had been through bad times before. At the Death Feast they had suffered from the treachery of Pale Eyes they had thought were their friends. They had lost loved ones, but they had survived. Life had continued.

Turtle said, "They dug mescal buds again."

Another long silence, then a second voice said softly from the darkness in the cave, "They watched their children dance."

"Pleasantness all around," spoke up a third.

"Good things all around," said another.

No one else spoke, but Lozen could feel the mood in the cave shift, lighten. Grandmother had let people visit those places. They had stood there and looked at them. They had heard what the land told them about endurance and the heal- ing effects of time.

Lozen cupped her chest against her grandmother's knobby back and put her arm around her, pulling her close. The night air was frigid, and the cave was dank. Grandmother had so little flesh and fat left on her bones that she felt the cold more than she used to. Lozen put her cheek against Grandmother's hair and closed her eyes.

She Moves Like Water had confided to her that she feared they would not find Grandmother alive when they returned. Lozen didn't believe that, though. When she came back for her, Grandmother would flash that sly ringtail smile. She would hug Lozen and tell her stories of what had happened while she was away, just as she had always done.

Chapter 42

FEEDING THE HAND THAT BITES

Rafe and Caesar dismounted to stretch their legs under the old cottonwood. While Caesar watered the pack mule, Rafe lifted the puppies out of the burden basket hanging in front of his stirrup and set them down in the grass. Patch came over to sniff, lick, and inspect them.

Rafe would miss them on the ride back, but they were presents for Caesar's nephews, Charlie Sets Him Free and Wah-sin-ton, and one for Lozen if she wanted him. Rafe had knitted tiny socks for Maria's baby, and he and Caesar had brought presents for the adults, too.

Lozen's comment about wanting a dog had surprised Rafe. He knew her people had always regarded dogs with a superstitious fear, but the Mescaleros living at the Bosque Redondo reservation had started keeping them as pets, or at least they tolerated the soldiers' strays.

Rafe and Caesar scooped the cold water over their heads and threw handfuls of it at each other. The bloated storm clouds advancing from the west seemed to push the July heat ahead of them and made drawing breath a labor. Rafe and Caesar lay in the grass with their hands clasped behind their heads and waited for the sentries' hawk whistle signaling their arrival. The horses grazed, and the three puppies played until they grew tired and fell asleep. Rafe sighed in contentment.

He and Caesar had had little time to lie about and do nothing. The government had shifted territorial offices to California, which left the departments of New Mexico and Arizona in disarray. Army posts were established and abandoned, expanded, reduced, relocated, and renamed. Rafe and

Caesar kept busy freighting construction materials. They hauled lime from Mesilla, lumber from Pinos Altos, and charcoal from Santa Rita. Rafe hated the idea of dying while defending a wagonload of lime, but the pay was good.

One of the new posts was Fort Bascom. In the sort of irony lost on the army, the starched-collars in Washington named it after George Bascom, the lieutenant who had bungled negotiations with Cochise about ten years earlier and started the warfare that consumed them all still.

Maybe it's fitting, Rafe thought. Bascom had been responsible for providing a living for thousands of soldiers, and in many cases, a dying.

Bureaucratic idiocy, the egregious thievery of the rations contractors at Bosque Redondo, and George Carleton's irrational arrogance had finally worn down Dr. Steck. He had resigned in disgust. He should have waited. The Department of the Army had relieved Carleton of duty, although his departure hadn't helped the situation. A succession of generals squabbled and dithered while roving packs of Apaches continued to raid the army and civilians alike.

"It's ironic," Rafe mused.

"What is?" asked Caesar.

"Don't most of the white men in this territory make their living supplying the army?"

"They do."

"If the Apaches are exterminated, the army marches away, and the good citizens are left with their hands in an empty till."

"You means white folk hereabouts want the Injun troubles to go on, so's they can keep makin' money off the gum'ment?"

"Exactly. But here's the irony. With the army scouring the mountains for Apaches, you'd think they'd make themselves scarce."

Caesar laughed. "Nosiree-bob. They hovers around the forts and the roads like so many turkey buzzards. They stole six mules, 'leven horses, and three oxen from down to Fort Cummins' just last week."

"Yep. The Apaches have become as dependent on the army as the hooligans roosting in the saloons."

"I reckon you could say the gum'ment's feedin' the hand that bites it."

Rafe chuckled. "You could say that."

The two of them read aloud for a while, passing the book back and forth, while dark clouds encroached on the blue sky, setting the cottonwoods' leaves to fluttering in the wind. By midafternoon they had heard nothing that sounded like an Apache signal. No one had come for them, and the first drops had started to fall.

"Let's go." Rafe set the puppies back in the basket.

Rafe and Caesar put on the gutta-percha ponchos they always carried in July and August, the rainy season. Rafe's was big enough to form a tent that covered the saddlebags and the puppies. Caesar's was the same size, but it barely covered him.

"We goin' back to Alamosa?"

"Nope. We came to deliver Dr. Steck's last presents to Victorio and his people, and we're going to see that they get them."

"How do you expect to find them? We was blindfolded last trip."

"I'll follow my ears."

"Your ears?"

"Remember how we splashed through that stream for quite a ways?"

"Yeah, but where is it?"

"You're looking at it."

Caesar stared at the stream, then up at the cliff a mile or so away. "You mean they rode us in a big circle and brung us back to it?"

"I'd say so. I think your new brother-in-law, He Makes Them Laugh, told us stories to distract us from listening to what was going on." Rafe didn't know whether to be insulted or amused that the Apaches thought so little of his intelligence. "Did you notice the echo we heard part of the way, as though we were going through a narrow canyon?"

"You think they's a way through that wall?"

"Like the Mexicans, I half believe that Apaches can make themselves invisible, but I doubt they can walk through solid rock."

"The Lord parted the Red Sea for Moses." Caesar grinned at him. "Maybe He can part that there cliff for us."

Neither of them spoke about the possibility that they wouldn't be welcomed as friends on the other side. A crash of thunder opened the fandango. Rain poured down as though someone had slid back a sluice gate.

EVEN THOUGH THE LOUD SPLATTER OF RAIN OBSCURED ANY signals the sentries might give, Lozen knew something was wrong when no one came to meet them. Fights Without Arrows, Chato, He Steals Love, Flies In His Stew, Ears So Big, and He Makes Them Laugh knew it, too. They dismounted, and the apprentices took the horses' reins. They all waited in silence while Lozen closed her eyes and prayed to Life Giver to tell her if enemies were near. When she finished, she made the sign for no.

The rain abated. A few more wind-driven sprays hit them; then the storm grumbled off over the mountain, leaving the trees to drip. Fights Without Arrows used gestures to divide the group and send individuals in different directions.

Lozen and He Makes Them Laugh crawled across the meadow where the ponies usually grazed. Before they reached the edge of the village, gusts carried the odor of wet ashes and charred wood, and the sound of a dog barking. Then they saw the burned arbors and the blackened heaps of Stands Alone's lodges in the gloom under the tarnished gray sky. Two horses, a mule, and two men shrouded in glistening black ponchos stood in the mud in the middle of Stands Alone's camp. The dog barked furiously in the direction of Fights In A Line and Chato, who were approaching from upwind. The men faced the same way, with their hands held out at their sides to show they were empty. Lozen and He

Makes Them Laugh couldn't see their faces, but they recognized the horses.

"Hairy Foot and Uncle," He Makes Them Laugh murmured. "Chato will shoot them."

As though to verify that, they heard the solid *ka-thunk* of a bolt sliding home. Lozen could tell by the sound that it was Chato's shiny new rifle, the one he called Many Shots. Hairy Foot and Uncle must have heard it, too, but they didn't move to defend themselves or flee.

Lozen stood up and walked into the open to show Chato and the others that she didn't consider the Pale Eyes a threat. He Makes Them Laugh splashed after her through the puddles that were shrinking as the water soaked into the earth.

The dog whirled on them. Hackles raised, head lowered, she started toward them at a stiff-legged gait. The two men turned around, and Lozen saw grief in their eyes, and relief at the sight of her instead of someone more likely to murder them. She did not detect guilt or fear or deception.

Hairy Foot said something to the dog. She sat down, her ears laid against her head, her lips drawn back to expose sharp teeth in a snarl. Hairy Foot slowly drew the poncho off over his head and threw it aside. He untied the bandana from around his neck and wiped the sweat from his face with it, although Lozen thought he might be wiping away tears, too.

"No lo hicimos," he said. "We didn't do it."

"Yo se," said Lozen. "I know."

Fights Without Arrows, Chato, and the others advanced across the dance ground, converging on them with rifles leveled and arrows nocked.

"They led the Bluecoats here." Chato aimed his Winchester at Rafe's face. "We will kill them slowly by fire, as befits Pale Eyes witches."

"You will not harm them." Lozen moved to stand in front of him. "They're brothers to Stands Alone."

He Makes Them Laugh ignored them all and ran to his grandparents' camp. When he began to howl in mourning, Patch threw her head back and joined in. Lozen started at a headlong run toward the trail to the cave. Now that the rain had stopped, the vultures had begun to weave their circles in the sky above the cliff.

She sprinted up the steep slope, grabbing rocks and bushes to pull herself along faster. She leaped a boulder that had rolled onto the path and almost landed on the outstretched hand of Disgruntled. Someone had scalped him. Nearby lay Victorio's pony, Coyote.

She pleaded and bargained with Life Giver as she scrambled upward, oblivious of the scrapes, cuts, and bruises the rocks and brambles left on her hands, arms and legs. The stench hit her as she cleared the top of the ledge. The sun broke through the clouds and shone into the cave, lighting up the bodies that lay sprawled across the floor. Most of them had bloody wounds on the crowns of their heads.

Lozen scooped ashes from the firepit and scattered them on the bodies as she moved among them. She found her grandmother with her friend Turtle. The two of them lay in each other's arms as though they had fallen asleep, except that they, too, had been scalped. Lozen sat at Grandmother's side and rocked back and forth, trying to contain her grief, but the effort was futile. She lifted her face toward the sky beyond the cave's ceiling, closed her eyes, and wailed.

RAFE TRIED TO FOLLOW LOZEN AND THE OTHERS, BUT THEY soon disappeared around the second bend in the path. He was left to scramble up as best he could. He hadn't gotten far when he heard the keening cry. Lozen had found something terrible. He wondered whom the marauders had killed. Her mother, her father? Her grandmother? Caesar's new family?

Not long after, male voices joined Lozen's in wailing their grief. They startled Rafe. He would not have thought Apache men capable of so much emotion.

He had almost reached the top when Chato came back. He stood in Rafe's path, with one foot set on a boulder and his forearm resting on his thigh. He glared down at Rafe and spoke in Spanish.

"Grandmother Lozen says not to kill you. She says, 'Hairy Foot, go away. Go away, pronto.' "

Rafe turned and started down the slope, leaning back to counter the pull of gravity while the angle of descent jammed his toes into the ends of his boots. The hair on the back of his neck stirred. He didn't think Chato would waste a bullet on him. He would probably sneak up on him and bash his skull in with that serviceable-looking war club dangling from his belt.

Rafe let his breath out in a gust of relief when he made it to the bottom of the trail. He found Caesar with He Makes them Laugh. They had wrapped two bodies in blankets and tied them across the mule's back. The mule's original load of gifts sat stacked in the center of the dance ground with Caesar's gutta-percha poncho covering it.

"These are my brother-in-law's grandparents." Caesar nodded toward the bodies. "I reckon the riffraff that set up shop near the fort kilt them. My brother here says they must've kilt the 'ole folks in the cave up yonder, too. He says Lozen's grandmother is up there."

"We have to leave."

"I'm gonna help bury his people."

"If they find us here when they get back, they'll kill us."

He Makes Them Laugh listened intently, trying to understand the strange words.

Caesar nodded toward He Makes Them Laugh. "He's family. I can't leave him to do this alone." Caesar collected his gray's reins and the mule's.

When He Makes Them Laugh saw that Caesar intended to stay with him, he yanked the reins away fom him.

"*Vaya.*" He waved toward the trail back to the cliff wall. "*¡Vaya!*" He drew a hand across his throat, the sign for quick death in any language.

Rafe felt in his pocket and pulled out the tiny socks he had knitted. He handed them to He Makes Them Laugh.

"*Para la niña de María Mendez,*" he said.

The puppies would have to go back with him. This was not the time to leave a present of something the Apaches considered bad luck.

He Makes Them Laugh took the socks and stuffed them into the top of his moccasin. He turned abruptly and led the mule away.

Chapter 43

TREACHEROUS WRETCHES

Rafe paused at the door of the quartermaster sergeant's office. As angry as he was, he knew he would enjoy this anyway. Sometimes he could almost believe that God had a sense of humor.

He knocked, then opened the door and walked in without waiting for an invitation. As he expected, the owner of the Belly-Up Ranch and his weasel of a foreman were doing business with the supply sergeant. Or at least they thought they were. Rafe was about to change their plans.

"Hello, Collins." The sergeant looked up from the beef contract spread out in triplicate on the desk in front of him.

"The cattle the government ordered from Mesilla are here," Rafe said. "My men are driving them into the pen."

"How many head?"

"As many as you ordered."

"Thirty?"

"Have I ever come up short on the count?"

"No, but there's always the first time. Apaches hit a supply train heading for Fort Cummings. Drove off the horses and mules."

When Belly-Up and his man registered the fact that Rafe was delivering all the cattle, they didn't disappoint him. Surprise, anger, guilt, and chagrin went chasing across the mendacious bad-lands of their faces. The sergeant was a smooth one, though. His gaze never wavered. He might have been innocent, but Rafe doubted it. That was why Rafe didn't make any accusations. As with most army supply contracts, he couldn't be sure who was in cahoots with whom.

Rafe took the invoice from his coat pocket, laid it on the

desk, and bent over to smooth it out. While he was at it he read, upside down, the amount and the date written on Belly-Up's contract.

Eleven steers to be delivered tomorrow. What a coincidence. Eleven was the number of stolen animals that Rafe and Caesar had tracked to the Belly-Up Ranch. They had arrived as the two thieves were driving the stock into the corral. A few shots had sent the pair galloping off into the scrub oak. The Mexican vaqueros said that the Belly-Up's *patron* and his *segundo* had gone to the fort. Rafe and Caesar had driven the steers back to the herd and headed for the fort themselves.

That sort of swindle had happened to others, but never to Rafe. He was more than furious. He was embarrassed that the thieves had gotten the drop on his two Mexican herders and made off with the cattle.

Even so, he was grinning when he left the sergeant's office and met Caesar coming from the stock pen with his gray and Red. Rafe patted the chest of his coat to indicate that the payment for the cattle was in the wallet inside it.

Caesar grinned back. They were headed for Central City to spend the money. They had heard that the town's amateur theater troupe would perform soliloquys from Shakespeare's plays. Caesar had never seen Shakespeare's words delivered from a stage, and he'd been talking about it all day, even while they tracked the stolen cattle and had a galloping gun battle with the thieves.

"Mistuh Red was wooing that paint mare of the cap'n's," he said.

"Red's too old for wooing, and he's overdue for retirement. Next time we have business in Arizona I'll take him to Camp Grant. The blacksmith there has agreed to let him frolic in the tall grass, even if the old boy can't fire his artillery anymore."

Red had lived almost twenty arduous years. He was still game, but he had earned a rest. Rafe had been putting off the decision for a long time. He couldn't bear to think of riding anywhere without Red under him.

"I wish I'd seen the look on ole Belly-Up Hardin's face when you sashayed in with the invoice for those cows," Caesar said.

"It was some entertainment."

"You reckon the supply sergeant was in on it?"

"Most likely."

They rode in a comfortable silence for a mile or two before Caesar spoke again.

"The colored troops got into a row with the officers whilst we was gone," Caesar said. "It turned right squally."

Caesar gathered the latest news while Rafe collected the pay for whatever they were hauling. Caesar was usually more successful at his task than Rafe. Money had a way of vanishing in the short distance between the government strongbox and Rafe's outstretched hand.

More than once he had carried Victorio's war club into the quartermaster sergeant's office. He merely laid it on the desk. Rafe made no threats with it, nor did he glance at it, but it was a disturbing artifact even for seasoned campaigners like the sergeants. It obviously had one purpose only. With its flexible head, it would never serve to hammer in tent pegs or nails. It was designed to crush a man's skull, clear and simple.

More disturbing was the question of how Rafe had obtained it. Had he taken it from a dead Apache, or had a living Apache given it to him? Either way, he was a man to reckon with, and the sergeants always found the money they owed him.

"The colored soldiers said they'd kill anything in shoulder boards," Caesar went on.

"The food's bad enough to cause a mutiny."

" 'T'warn't the victuals. The lieutenant says his new colored maid stole his wife's brooch-pin. The colonel, he says she has to leave the fort. The soldiers say she didn't take the brooch, and even if she did, the colonel might as well put a gun to her head and shoot her his own self as turn her out alone in Apache country."

"Do you know her?"

"Naw. She come on the mail stage whilst we was to Mesilla. The soldiers say she belongs to the lieutenant's family back in Louisiana." Caesar corrected himself. "She used to belong to 'em. Don't nobody own nobody no more. Mistuh Lincoln saw to that, God rest his soul."

Well, nobody owns anybody officially, anyway, thought Rafe, not since General Lee handed over his sword and ended the Southern rebellion more than four years ago. Four years. Had that much time passed? Had it been two years since he last saw Lozen in the ruins of her village, with dead grandparents scattered about?

The time seemed much briefer than that because he still heard her grief-stricken wail in his dreams. It was a cry of such sorrow distilled to its essence that it would not let go of him. He would wake up with his heart pounding and realize that a coyote had howled, and he had made it part of the dream of her.

He wondered where she and the others had gone. They had vanished as though they had never existed.

Rafe had a bit of news of his own. "The sergeant said the colored troops will be leaving in a couple months," he said. "Their enlistment is up."

"They been here three years already?"

"Yep."

A figure on the trail ahead shimmered in the late-August heat. She carried a sack on her back, and at first Rafe assumed she was a Mexican woman going to the market on the outskirts of Central City, five miles away. She was tall, though, and she walked down the middle of the road, which wasn't like a Mexican. It wasn't like a Negro, either, but as Rafe drew closer he saw that where perspiration washed away the dust on the woman's bare feet and calves, the skin underneath was the rich, vibrant brown of molasses.

"Mus' be Mattie Martin," Caesar said.

"The maid?"

"I 'spect so."

She wore a red bandana on her head with the four ends tied at the base of her skull, leaving exposed a neck long and gracefuly curved. She had on a calico dress that had started out blue but had faded to streaks of gray. She set down the sack and turned to watch them approach, her hand up to shade her eyes.

Rafe saw why the lieutenant had gone to the trouble and expense of bringing her from Louisiana. He understood why the black soldiers had rioted over her mistreatment. And he suspected that the source of the lieutenant's wife's anger was not a stolen brooch.

Mattie Martin looked as though God, in a fit of remorse, had tried to make up in beauty for the sorrow and hardship the color of her skin—flawless as that skin was—would cause her. *Ripe* was the word that came to mind when Rafe looked at her. Full, succulent mouth. Large, bright eyes. A broad sweep of a nose with flaring nostrils. And breasts—well, the breasts definitely looked just fine under the dress that draped her slender body with an artless grace. The slight loft of her chin gave her a look that was wary, combative, and imperious.

No doubt Caesar intended to play Galahad again. He had a knack for finding damsels in distress, even when damsels of any sort were in short supply and those who existed seemed able to take care of themselves. Rafe didn't have to be a mind reader to know that his friend had been struck by an arrow, though this one came from the bow of a bare-arsed cherub named Eros. Rafe figured he could be smitten by Miss Mattie Martin himself.

Caesar reined the gray to a stop. "Good day, ma'am." He tipped his hat. "My name is Caesar Jones, and this here's my associate, Mistuh Raphael Collins."

"Pleased t'meet you ge'men, I's sure." She flowed into a curtsey. "I's Mattie Martin."

"Miz Martin, may we offer you a ride to town?" Caesar asked.

"I'd thank you kindly for it."

While Caesar tied her sack of belongings on top of his bedroll, Rafe offered Mattie his canteen. She looked at it as though she didn't believe a white man would do her any kindness. After a pause, she reached for it, took a long drink, and returned it.

Caesar pulled her up behind him, and she put tentative hands on his waist. As the three of them rode toward the mismatched cluster of mud-and-straw hovels and makeshift shebangs called Central City, Rafe felt happier than he could remember being since the death of the Navajo woman he called Dream Weaver. He knew with a fair certainty that he would never find another woman to bring him the contentment that she had, but he could enjoy the thought that his friend might.

SHAKESPEARE COULD NOT COMPETE WITH MATTIE MARTIN, but Rafe figured the Bard wouldn't want to. The author of *Romeo and Juliet* would understand the urgency of love. Instead of coming to the performance, Caesar took Mattie to an inn where he knew the owner was looking for a maid and a cook. He said he would be along shortly, but Rafe doubted that.

Bushrod Franklin's saloon was the location of the performance because Bushrod was a shrewd business man, because it was the largest building in town, and because it contained a billiard table. The billiard table was the key to the enterprise.

The entire population seemed to have gathered there. Rafe had to turn sideways to work his way through the noisy crowd. He reached a far corner of the rough-timbered room, climbed onto a crate, caught hold of the rafter, and swung himself up onto it. The effort winded him. He didn't know the exact date of his birthday, but he was pretty sure he was going to be thirty-nine years old soon.

The view of the billiard table was worth the effort. The actors had laid pine boards across it to form a platform. Putting the stage on top of the billiard table not only made it more visible, but it also raised it off a floor awash in tobacco juice.

Rafe recognized the saw marks on the planks. They came

from the mill at Pinos Altos, and they were part of a government shipment he and Caesar had freighted in so the soldiers could build their barracks. He wondered why he and Caesar had bothered to unload it at the fort since the supply sergeant was going to sell it to the merchants in town, anyway.

Rafe had been present at the last drama involving this particular billiard table. Someone had shot a miner in a falling out over one of Bushrod's doxies. The town's barber had laid the man out on the table to see what he could do. The patrons crowded around to watch, and the betting began, twenty dollars that the patient would die, twenty that he wouldn't. They watched with rapt attention, and whenever he coughed up blood, those who had bet on his mortality cheered while the others booed. The cheering and booing reversed when he rallied. In the end, the barber lost the twenty dollars he had bet on his own skill.

Today, though, the men expected to see a "leg show," women in tights, or at least a view up the skirts of the two female members of the troupe. They were hoping for a long view, maybe as far as the lace hems of the pantalettes, but the lower portion of the calves would suffice. They would even settle for ankles clad in lisle stockings.

Most of them had primed themselves with whiskey, and they were growing restless. Rafe could tell that they were almost ready to start throwing the old eggs they had brought for any actor whose performance didn't meet their standards. Bushrod Franklin mounted the packing crate steps and held up his arms for silence. He never got it, but the uproar diminished enough for people to hear him if he shouted.

"Ladies and gentlemen, as you know, the purpose of this evening's performance is to raise funds to outfit that brave company of Indian fighters, the Bear Creek Rangers, led by our own James Halloran. We are gratified to know that these intrepid men do not think it worth the effort to take murderous redskins as prisoners."

A cheer went up, and Halloran leaped onto the stage brandishing his rifle in one hand and a long hank of hair in the other. Rafe knew Halloran. He had eyes the color of stale beer, breath like a singed cow horn, and a tanyard cur's sort of courage. If the Bear Creek Rangers and their ilk had any advantage in hunting Apaches, it was that they considered no act too low and dastardly to commit. If they did engage the Apaches, stopping the Bear Creek Rangers would be like stopping a rabid badger.

"The only way to rid our country of the treacherous wretches," Halloran shouted, "is to make them bite the dust wherever we find them."

The noise of the huzzahs made Rafe's ears ring and set the candles in the saloon's wagon-wheel chandeliers to guttering. When the men had hollered themselves hoarse, Halloran went on.

"When we return from our scout, every lady who subscribed with a donation to tonight's show will receive an Apache scalp to make a fall for her coif."

Rafe wondered where Halloran had palmed the word *coif*. Probably from the fop who led the acting troupe. In any case, the women would have to be content with falls of gray hair, because the only Indians the rangers seemed to kill were old people.

He wondered if these were the men who had murdered Lozen's grandmother and the other old folks two years ago. Probably not. They had only recently mustered in, and the span of their attention wasn't great. A few days of discomfort on the mountain trails, and they would return to Central City's saloons to replenish their emptied whiskey kegs and boast about their exploits.

Caesar had found out that someone in Alamosa had told a drunken mob just like this one where to find the rancheria of Victorio's people. Rafe didn't blame them. They thought that the Warm Spring Apaches had gone south to Mexico, and the mob had threatened to kill them all and burn the town if they didn't tell. Quite likely they would have done it, since the people of Alamosa were mostly Mexicans and didn't count for anything to the Americans.

The leader of the acting troupe climbed onto the stage to

a chorus of hoots and catcalls. He wore knitted red hose with the holes darned in black thread. Over them he had on the puffed-out sort of short breeches that looked like a toadstool sprouting from around his waist, with his skinny legs as the stem. Yellowed lace cascaded from the neck of a blue velvet doublet trimmed with tarnished tinsel. He carried a skull, which meant he was taking the role of Hamlet.

Rafe leaned forward, holding on to the rafter's brace for support. He was about to hear his favorite soliloquy. Love or not, he wished Caesar could be here.

The Apaches regarded writing with a mixture of awe and disbelief. For Rafe the written word was magical, like electromagnetism or steam power or passion. He and the Apaches had something in common in that respect.

Hamlet finished and the red-haired Mrs. Dougan was giving a stirring performance of Lady Macbeth's speech, wringing her hands and crying to the rafters, when shots rang out in the street. The saloon emptied, in spite of the fact that Mrs. Dougan had shapelier ankles than the audience had dared to expect. Irish ankles, someone had observed, best served for tethering tent flies and beating surly mules.

Rafe dropped from the rafter and joined the surge out the door. At least thirty Apaches charged down Central City's main street, driving horses, mules, and oxen ahead of them. Most of the horses' reins were only looped over the saloons' hitching rails. The Apaches knew that. The frightened horses reared and yanked loose; then they took off running.

Rafe watched one young Apache leap from his pony onto Red's back and pull the rein loose from the rail. Rafe walked out into the street where he could have an unobstructed view. Red cantered off while his rider settled down to enjoy his prize.

As soon as Red sensed that his rider had relaxed his guard, he gave the warrior a view of the landscape from a surprising height and angle. He leaped up and sideways, then did a turnabout in midair. He continued to whirl, exchanging his withers for his hindquarters with the speed and agility of a ballet dancer. He finished the performance by kicking his rear hooves so high, so hard, that he looked as though he were standing on his nose.

The Apache took graceful flight and landed on his stomach. With arms outstretched, he tobogganed under the hooves of an oncoming horse, who reared, sliding his rider back onto his rump. He recovered, humped back into place, and pulled the downed man up behind him. They all thundered off with yips and whoops, exuberant good spirits, and belly laughs that rattled the flimsy facades of the buildings.

Red sauntered back and butted his head into Rafe's chest, as though asking if he'd enjoyed the joke. Rafe put an arm around his neck. He leaned his cheek against him, and the hairs of Red's mane tickled his nose. He rubbed Red's ears and laughed softly.

Chapter 44

TAKING HEARTS

No one would ever accuse a mescal plant of being deferential. Still, in a country where the pads of prickly pear latched on to the noses of hungry horses, where the finger-length thorns of the devil's-claw seeds hooked into the skin of passers-by, and mobs of cockleburs hitched rides on moccasins, clothes, and hair, the mescal was not the worst. It didn't go looking for trouble like the cholla cactus that fired balls of stinging spines, and it had a benevolent streak. The water trapped in its leaves sustained life on days like this when the ground cracked like badly fired pottery and the world shriveled and crumbled to dust.

If trouble came its way, the mescal plant could defend itself. Leaves like fat, green spearheads radiated from its center. Each blade had a double row of thorns along its edges, with a thumb-size spike at the end. It would not let anyone take its heart without a fight, and its heart was what Lozen wanted.

The mescal plants here in Long Neck's country were bigger than those she was used to. The thick red flower stalk at the center of this one was four times taller than she was. When Lozen jabbed her piñon limb into the center of the bush, a rattlesnake as long as she was slithered out the other side and into the brush.

"It was a year ago," she murmured, to confuse the evil spirits that the snake possessed.

She lay on her stomach, pressed a leaf downward, and with her drinking tube, sucked the water that collected at the bottom of it. It was hot and musty, and she spit out the ants and beetles in it.

Lozen was used to heat, but here in northern Mexico it burned like the side of a hatchet blade held in the flames. She plaited her damp hair into a thick braid that hung to the backs of her thighs and tucked the end of it into her belt. She placed her foot between the two rows of thorns at the base of a leaf. She pressed it and several more down and cut through the leaves close to their bases. When she had cleared the way to the bone-white bud of the flower stalk, she wedged the sharpened end of her piñon limb under it and pounded the butt of it with the side of her hatchet. Stands Alone and Maria came to help.

Stands Alone and María's two youngest sons, He Throws It and Darts Around, were almost five years old. They chased the eddies of wind that raised spirals of dust and zigzagged across the ground before vanishing. When they tired of that, they stalked sparrows and cactus wrens, mice, ground squirrels, and pack rats. They caught beetles and let them grab their earlobes with their pincers and dangle as earrings.

"Look out for snakes," María called to them. "They have powerful magic. Do not shoot them or touch them. If you happen across one, say, 'Grandfather, I do not want to see you, so stay out of my way.' "

Daughter arrived with her baby girl in the cradleboard that Lozen had made. "Her Eyes Open said to tell you we have enough mescal."

Lozen leaned on her stick and surveyed the broad slope where the mescal grew. Little Eagles was the season of flowers. Patches of blue, purple, orange, red, and white were woven into the yellow blanket of poppies. The blossoms of the palo verde flowed like a golden waterfall into a ravine.

Lozen, Stands Alone, María, and Daughter finished cutting the bud out. It was so big that Lozen could hardly wrap her arms around it, but she put it and the others into burden baskets and lashed them onto the pony. They called to the two boys, who raced to the packhorse and started the process of clambering aboard. Lozen and Daughter rode double with the little one's cradle hanging from the saddle horn.

They followed the other women down the sweep of country that flowed off into the desert and away. They rode along a deep ravine filled with clouds of the tiny, fragrant yellow flowers of the white-thorn bush. They threaded through a thicket of ocatillo cactus and passed the prickly pear and stunted mesquites.

The Warm Springs women had set up camp in a grove of junipers. They had stacked the woven trays they would use for drying the baked mescal. They had hung the water jugs and the babies' cradles from branches to catch stray breezes. They had built their brush-covered lean-tos against the trunks. They had laid stones in circles for their cook fires and spread hides in the shade for the toddlers to play on.

The women enjoyed being on their own. They could build their shelters close together, and at night they could call conversations back and forth. They could tell whatever stories they wanted and laugh as loudly as they pleased.

The young girls explored the new site, looking for colored seeds to string into necklaces. They built miniature lodges and improvised grinding stones. They made cooking utensils of acorns for their dolls.

The boys were a different matter. The women needed someone to keep watch for enemies while they worked. They had had to cajole the boys with promises of new moccasins and shirts. Even then, the only ones who would agree were those like nine-year-old Sets Him Free and Wah-sin-ton, who were too young to go on raids as apprentices.

At fourteen, He Bends Over was the oldest. He came along because Knot's thirteen-year-old daughter, Mouse, had addled him until he didn't seem able to function unless he could sight on her the way a night traveler followed the Fixed Star. The women knew it, and they took advantage of him. With oblique glances at his beloved to see if she was noticing, he carried the heaviest burdens and did the hardest work. The women praised his strength and his good looks while the shy object of his passion pretended to ignore him.

Her Eyes Open had sized up the heaps of buds and figured they would need at least two pits. The women loosened the hardpan with bayonets, saber blades, and sharpened sticks.

They dug with the scapula bones of oxen or with rusty shovels. They handed baskets of dirt to others to dump in a heap nearby. The small girls carried the rocks away, but left the larger ones so the women could use them to line the bottom of the pit.

They worked until they had two chest-deep holes as long as two women. Before dawn the next morning, they built fires on top of the stones. When the flames burned down to a bed of coals, they laid on the mescal buds, turning their faces aside to protect them from the searing heat. Then they covered the pits with a layer of grass.

With a forked stick, Lozen held a mescal stalk upright in the center while the women tossed rocks around it to hold it erect. They shoveled dirt on top to keep in the heat and steam. Tomorrow, Her Eyes Open would pull out the stalk to see if the bottom of it was cooked and the mescal buds ready.

While the mescal baked, they collected yucca leaves and wove more drying trays. Lozen took Daughter to look for the plants she would use as remedies. As they walked through the undergrowth, Lozen told Daughter what she had heard countless times before.

"When Life Giver created the world, he gave a purpose to all the plants." She pulled up a bush with small purple flowers. She broke off the root, brushed the dirt from it, and shared it with Daughter. It had a sweet taste. "If you boil the stems, the liquid is good for colds and coughs. It will cure stomachaches and pains in your muscles." She crouched next to a vine with yellow flowers and leaves that looked like a hand.

"That's called Five Fingers," Daughter said. "It eases toothache and sore throat. It cures ague and fluxes."

When they had filled their bag and were walking back to camp, Daughter asked, "Grandmother, will we go home again?"

"Yes." Lozen stared north. "We always go home."

"*Nkah le*." murmured Daughter. "Let it be so."

"Holes In The Earth." Lozen pronounced the name for the Santa Rita mines exactly so that the young ones would know the right way to say it. To speak of the Earth carelessly was to show disrespect. After a long pause she said, "The Place Where The Widows Stopped To Cry." She rode in silence for a while, then added, "Flat Rocks Stacked Up."

The return trip from where the mescal grew to the Warm Spring people's encampment near Long Neck's village took most of a day. Lozen passed the time naming the places between the high plateau where they had spent the last four years and their home country to the north. She did not care if anyone heard her. This was her journey. The rest could come along it they wanted. Some of the women and children paid attention. Others rode at the back of the procession, where they could talk. Each time Lozen paused, those who listened remembered what had happened there, and how it had looked the last time they saw it. In their minds, they made the journey home.

At dusk, they reached the sheer walls of the flat-topped mountain. As they rode along its base toward the single trail leading up to Long Neck's stronghold, Lozen neared the end of her own journey, the places close to where they had always lived. By now, most of the women and even the children were listening.

"*Dzil ndeez*," she said. "Tall Mountain."

They imagined the lavender peak outlined against the glow of the eastern sky at dawn. It was the first sight to greet them when they went outside their lodges at Warm Spring each morning.

"Shinale. My Grandfather." That was name of the sacred spring. At its origin the warm trickle of water seemed insignificant, but it filled a basin in the rock and overflowed into the larger one below it, into the pool they called The Eye.

When Lozen said, "Bidaa', the Eye," a collective sigh went up, like a soft, sad wind. The women remembered bath-

ing in The Eye's warm water in the winter. Someone sniffled.
Another blew her nose.

From The Eye, water ran into the stream that had carved
a slot in the high bluffs, giving an easily guarded access to
the outside world.

"*T'iis bidaayu tu li ne*. Cottonwood tree, around it, water,
it flows, the one." By now the words had become a chant, a
medicine song to heal aching hearts.

With the names, Lozen took them into the valley and
showed them the stream that flowed through it all year. She
showed them the lodges scattered in the shade of tall trees.
She let them see the sleek ponies grazing on the grama grass.

Many were crying quietly now, but when she said, "The
Place Of The Grandparents," they began to sob. All had been
related to at least one of the old people murdered in the cave
overlooking their village.

As they neared the path to the top of the mountain, Wah-
sin-ton and Sets Him Free joined them. They carried strings
of quail and ground squirrels. He Bends Over waited for
them all to pass, and he reined his horse to parallel Mouse
near the end of the line.

She Moves Like Water led the procession. She turned in
the saddle and called back, "The Water, It Is Deep There."

The women laughed. By invoking that place name, she
could have some fun with love-befuddled He Bends Over
without criticizing him or naming him directly. She Moves
Like Water went on to tell the story so the children could
learn from it. It was about boys who let their attention wander and who suffered because of it.

"At The Water, It Is Deep There, at that very place, some
boys are staying cool in the summertime." She Moves Like
Water used the present tense, as though this were a historical
tale, but it was about Lozen, before people called her Aunt
or Grandmother or even Lozen.

I am so old, I have become history, Lozen thought. The
idea made her smile.

"Along comes a girl named Sister," She Moves Like Water said. "This girl is like Coyote, always playing pranks.

She sees those boys sitting in the water there. She sees their clothes piled up under the cottonwood tree. She sees a wasp's nest hanging from the limb that stretches out over the stream.

"She sneaks up on those boys. When they wade out of the water, she uses her sling to throw a rock and hit the place where the nest is fastened to the tree. It falls on them. Some of the boys run back into the water, and the wasps buzz around their heads. Some run for their clothes, but the wasps cover them like a blanket. Those boys are jumping around and yelling. They're doing the Wasp Dance.

"Sister laughs at them. Then just like Coyote, she goes along. It happened at The Water, It Is Deep There, at that very place."

Everyone laughed and looked at Lozen. She had been Wah-sin-ton's age when she dropped the wasp nest on Fights Without Arrows, Ears So Big, Flies In His Stew, and their friends. Even now, sometimes the women would make buzzing noises while they pretended to be busy at their chores. The men knew what they meant by it.

She Moves Like Water reached the place where the trail took a turn upward. The people of Long Neck's village called the area at the bottom of the trail the Rubbish Heap. The hair stirred at the nape of Lozen's neck when she passed through it. Bones and bits of leather and metal littered the place. They were the remains of Mexican soldiers who had tried to attack over the years.

Lozen could feel their spirits clinging to their sand-scoured bones. She sensed their hatred and their fear. She heard their cries when Long Neck's men pushed the boulders down onto them, but the other women were not bothered by them. They laughed and shouted back and forth along the line. The ponies' hooves clattered on the rocks, and their loads swayed as they lunged up the steep trail.

Her Eyes Open kicked her pony up alongside Lozen. She turned in her saddle to watch the parade winding away below them. "This is the way it was in the old days," she said, "before we had to fear every shadow and crack of a twig."

She Moves Like Water dropped back to ride next to

Lozen, too. She cut off a chunk of the baked mescal and handed it to her. "Listen, Sister, when your brother returns, let's tell him we want to go home."

Lozen ripped off a piece with her teeth and started to work on it, like chewing hemp rope dipped in molasses. "Maybe he's convinced the Bluecoats to let us live at Warm Springs," she said.

That was what he and some of the young men had ridden north to do. They had been gone a long time, though, and everyone was worried.

"Even if he can't convince the Pale Eyes to let us live in peace, we should still go home."

"We're better off running like lizards and hiding in caves in our own country than staying here," added Her Eyes Open.

"*Gunku*, that's true," said Daughter.

"Long Neck brings many good things when he returns from scouts," Corn Stalk said. "Here, we sleep quietly at night."

She was right about that. The plateau was a two-day ride across. It had forests, streams, grass, and game. Long Neck could raid in Sonora and sell the stolen stock to the people in Chihuahua. He could strike north across the border and then ride back south where the American soldiers could not chase him.

She Moves Like Water lowered her voice. She had her own name for Long Neck. "Old Ugly Buttocks has a bear's temper. I do not like it here. Sister, talk to your brother. He listens to you."

LOZEN CAME HOME EXHAUSTED FROM THE FOUR-DAY SING for Long Neck's ailing wife. She ate a few mouthfuls of stew, drank from the water jug, and fell headlong into sleep. She woke to the wailing of women.

"Sister." She Moves Like Water called in to her. "Long Neck returned from the war trail, but many of his men did not."

"What happened?" Lozen pulled on her moccasins.

"The warriors attacked a Pale Eyes wagon train. They found bottles and thought it was whiskey, but maybe it was a Pale Eyes trick to poison them. Many of them got sick."

Corn Stalk looked up from her grindstone. "Maybe the bottles did have whiskey in them. The men got drunk and fell into cactus."

"Their wives have spent all day picking the thorns out of them." The niece of She Moves Like Water and Corn Stalk was a new addition. Her husband had been shot while on a raid with Long Neck. The women in the family built a lodge for her near theirs, and she moved in. No one thought Victorio would object. She was good-natured and hardworking. She was Daughter's age and had a laugh like a meadowlark's song.

"Long Neck wants you to come to council," said She Moves Like Water.

When Lozen arrived at the council ground, Long Neck gave her a small nod of his head. They had been waiting for her, which surprised her. Maybe this was Long Neck's way of acknowledging that her medicine had made his wife stronger than she had been in two months.

Lozen sat at the rear with the women, but attending a council without her brother seemed strange. She felt even stranger sitting among people who weren't Chiricahuas. Many of Long Neck's warriors came from the Mescalero, the Coyotero, the White Mountain people, and even the People Without Minds. Some of them had sought refuge from attacks by the Bluecoats, and some were fleeing punishment from wrongs they had committed among their own people.

The main topic was the new Bluecoat lieutenant. Many had lost relatives in his attacks on their villages. He was thin and sandy-haired, quick, furtive, and relentless. The warriors called him Weasel.

Weasels attacked prey several times their size, and when they smelled blood, they even ate injured siblings. The men admitted that the Bluecoat weasel probably didn't eat his own family, but he would go anywhere in search of his prey.

Once his blood was up, he killed every Apache he could find, young or old, male or female.

For a long time the men discussed how to stop Weasel. Finally Long Neck asked if Victorio's sister had anything to say.

"We can steal the boxes of silver disks that come from the east in wagons," she said.

"*Zhaali?* Money? What do we want with that?" Long Neck looked irritated at such a foolish suggestion.

A Mescalero said, "We can use the disks in Janos to buy horses and cloth and corn."

"The comancheros will take them for ammunition and guns," added a Coyotero.

Long Neck snorted. "We know what a horse is worth." His words became more halting as he grew more agitated. "We know what a blanket is worth, or a basket of pinole or a bundle of hides. Who among you knows the value of the silver disks?"

No one spoke.

"They will cheat us." Long Neck glowered at Lozen.

"We do not have to use the coins."

"Then why should we steal them?"

"The Bluecoat soldiers fight because they receive those disks instead of a share of plunder."

"That's so." Almost everyone had been at a fort on payday. They had seen the effect the silver disks had on the Bluecoats.

"Without the silver disks, the soldiers will not fight."

Long Neck's leg started to jiggle while he pondered the plan. It was a sign that he was perturbed. "I don't like that idea. We will hunt this lieutenant down and kill him our own way."

Lozen wanted to say that this lieutenant was smart. Catching him off guard would not be easy. She wanted to say that too many men had already died fighting the old way. She wanted to say that the spirits had told her to seek peace with the Pale Eyes, but she didn't. Long Neck rarely accepted any opinion other than his own, much less that of a woman.

She returned to camp to find that Victorio was sitting at his usual place by the fire. She Moves Like Water, Corn Stalk, Third Wife, and Daughter hovered nearby, as though they were on invisible tethers. Wah-sin-ton sat with his elbow on Victorio's knee, to make sure he didn't go anywhere anytime soon.

"If we camp close to the fort near Warm Spring," Victorio said, "the Pale Eyes agent promises we will be safe. He will give us food and blankets. He is only waiting for consent from the Great Father in Wah-sin-ton to grant us the land that is already ours."

She Moves Like Water put her hand on his shoulder. "Sister, we're going home."

Chapter 45

EARLY BIRDS

Rafe sometimes wondered why Arizona Territory seemed hotter and dustier than New Mexico Territory, even though they sat side by side. This was late April 1871. The sun had not yet cleared the mountain peaks, but already the heat would melt hell's hinges. Patch lay panting in the shade of Joseph Felmer's wagon. Red munched hay in Felmer's corral. The chestnut gelding that Rafe intended to ride when he left Red here stood saddled and grazing.

Felmer pumped the pedal on his grindstone to get the heavy wheel spinning. He angled Rafe's long blade against it and sparks flew, prickling Rafe's bare forearm like insect nips.

"The heat makes early birds of us all, don't it?" Felmer spoke mining-camp English with a hint of a German accent. He tested the edge with his thumb and made quick touches with it against the wheel to even it out.

Felmer knew horses, and he was good with them. He had river-bottom land waist-high with succulent grass, and he was willing to let an old retired warhorse eat as much of it as he wanted. Rafe figured if anyone could prevent the Apaches from stealing Red, Joseph Felmer could.

He had married a woman of the small band of Aravaipa Apaches, and he spoke the language fluently. Felmer called his wife Mary. She spoke only kitchen-English, but she could cook a savory pot roast with potatoes and carrots stewing in its juices. And she had taken to the rest of white ways as Rafe had never seen an Apache woman do. He was always startled by the sight of her in corseted bodice and an excess of skirts and petticoats, her glossy black hair heaped up and secured with tortoiseshell combs.

When she rode away early yesterday morning, she left some cold roast behind for last night's supper. She had gone to visit her uncle, old Chief Eskiminzin, and her other relatives at their camp three miles on the other side of the army post.

Whenever Rafe's work brought him to Arizona and to the tumbledown, wretched collection of huts called Camp Grant, he stayed with Joe and Mary Felmer. He liked to sit at the kitchen table, with the aromas of a woman's cooking soaking into his clothes. He liked to listen to her and Joe conversing in the low, throaty, musical language of her tribe. To him, people speaking Apache or Navajo always sounded as though they were sharing secrets.

Mary Felmer reminded Rafe of his Navajo woman and the life they had shared. She made him wonder if he could ever find someone like his woman or like Mary. He thought fleetingly of Lozen, but dismissed the notion. The Warm Springs people were Chiricahuas, and the Chiricahuas were not like the peaceful Aravaipas. Even if they had been, Lozen was not one to put on a ruffled apron and bustle about in the kitchen. Come to think of it, he wouldn't want her to.

Still, if everyone had Felmer's generous attitude, the situation here would improve vastly. Maybe then Lozen would ride with him. She knew all about horses, that was certain, and probably mules, too. He had no doubt that what she didn't know she could learn faster than an owl could blink. He indulged in a brief reverie of her sharing the trail with him. A partner. A lover. A friend. He shook his head to clear it of such foolishness.

Rafe helped Joe heave the portable forge onto the wagon. He climbed aboard and took the anvil and smithing tools that Felmer handed up to him. Joe was headed for Camp Grant and his weekly stint of shoeing. Lt. Howard Cushing and the men of the Third Cavalry gave Felmer a lot of work. If Cushing wasn't returning from a scout against the Apaches, he was preparing for one.

Mary called Joe Felmer by the name Apaches gave black-smiths, *pesh-chidin*, ghost or spirit or devil of the iron, but that was just the latest of his identities. He did have a devilish look. He was tall and gaunt, with black hair, a single black eyebrow hovering like a storm cloud above his keel of a nose, and a luxuriant mustache. His dark eyes had a fire at their centers as intense as any he stoked in his forge.

He told a different story whenever the subject of his past came up. Rafe knew he was German, but he claimed at various times to being a Russian, a Pole, a Turk, a Polynesian, and a Theosophist. Where the latter was concerned, he said he was a personal friend of Helena Petrovna Blavatsky. Madame Blavatsky had received her Theophisitic notions from a cluster of Oriental mystagogues who had staked claim to a more elevated tract of real estate than the rest of mortality. Felmer had tried to explain it all to Rafe, who found it fascinating but irrelevant.

Joe levered his long legs onto the high wagon seat. Rafe checked the cinch on the chestnut and swung into the saddle. Red had been restless, but now he started galloping from one end of the corral to the other. As Joe and Rafe started down the rutted track toward the main trail, Red let out a series of shrill whinnies. Patch whined and ran back and forth between the corral and the wagon. Even the chestnut neighed in sympathy.

"Sounds like a rally of widders and orphans," said Felmer.

"I've left him behind before."

"Yep, but you never meant it to be permanent before."

Rafe knew he was right. He didn't know how they did it, but Red—and Patch, too—always seemed to sense his intentions. Red trotted to the far side of the corral, and Rafe could see that he was about to make a run at the fence. He was far too old for that nonsense.

Rafe held up his hands and shouted "Whoa! Hold on, old man." He went back and opened the gate so Red could join them. Red touched noses with Patch; then he trotted alongside the chestnut as though it had all been a stupid mistake and he forgave Rafe for it.

Rafe nodded at the dejected mule who stood at the corral fence with drooping head and an adoring swarm of flies mining the sores on his back.

"Is that the critter you bought from condemned army stock?"

"He is. I call him Lazarus."

The men at the fort had told Rafe about it. They thought Felmer's senses must have taken leave of him. Rafe was not in the habit of asking questions, but he had to ask this one. "Why?"

"Fer bait. The 'Pache is hungry nowadays and on the scout fer anyting edible. I figure they'll come into my alfalfy field atter 'im, and then the joke's on them."

"I thought the Apaches around here were tame," Rafe said.

"Mary's people are, but you know Apaches. They tend to stray into other folks' pastures. The trail to the reservation passes near here."

"How's that going, Lieutenant Whitman's unofficial reserve for the Aravaipas?"

"Better than anyone expected. Old Eskiminzin and a few hundred of my woman's people came in askin' for peace and plenty. They's plantin' corn and squashes along the river bottom where they always did afore the troubles. Whitman is payin' them to cut hay for the army stock. He even convinced the ranchers hereabouts to hire the men to help mit the barley crop."

"Did he ever get authorization to feed them?"

"Naw. Hell, he sends dispatches to department headquarters in Los Angeles every week. He don't get no reply." Felmer spit a stream of tobacco. "He's a good 'un, Whitman is. Honest. Treats the 'Paches fair."

"They don't have anything good to say about him in Tucson or Prescott."

Rafe was aces at understatement. The Prescott newspaper, *Arizona Citizen*, wrote that Lt. Royal Whitman was a scoundrel and a drunkard and a slave to vice. They said he only wanted to gather the Apaches at Camp Grant because he had an unnatural sexual attraction to "dusky maidens."

Halfway to the fort, Rafe and Joe passed the spindly poles and crossbar marking the entrance to the ranch of Hugh Kennedy and Newton Israel. Prickly pear, mesquite, and clumps of coarse grass were taking over the wagon ruts that passed through it and off into an astonishing glory of spring flowers.

"Did anyone find out which Apaches killed Kennedy and Israel?"

"I tink it was old Whoa and his bucks and maybe Geronimo. They was headin' for Mexico, at any rate."

Rafe knew the story of the raid on the wagon train. He'd heard Felmer's description of the goods strewn everywhere and of Newton Israel's naked corpse punctured with lance and arrow wounds, his skull smashed in. The Apaches had cut out Israel's heart and a small piece of his scalp and thrown them onto the body.

Felmer expanded on the subject, maybe because he had had time to think about it. "When we found them, the buzzards hadn't gotten to old Newt's eyes yet, and he had a tranquil look, doncha know. Never saw the like."

"And Kennedy?"

"We found him alive. Thought he would make it, but he said, 'No, boys, it's all up mit me. I'm a goner.' He was right."

Rafe was tempted to ask a question that had occurred to him more than once: Was it worthwhile to pay so dearly for so little that was good? But he knew that was a stupid question. It must be, because he and Joe Felmer were both here and not somewhere else.

"I hear the Apaches stole a case of patent medicine."

"Dr. Worme's Gesundheit Bitters." Felmer pronounced that with a double-barrelled, waterproof, wrought-iron German accent. "They got powerful drunk on it, too. When Lieutenant Cushing lit out after them, I went along to track fer 'im. We could see that the bucks had staggered all over the landscape, homing in on cactus like they was chickens going to roost. Falling full-out into 'em, too. Must've been quite a sight."

About seven o'clock Rafe and Felmer reached the fort,

named Grant after the current president of the country. The flag hung limp from the stubby pole. Dogs quarreled over the scraps of shade. They found Lt. Royal Emerson Whitman at breakfast in the officers' mess. As he ate his eggs, ham, and biscuits, he complained about the lack of response from his superiors in Los Angeles. Rafe had a good idea why the brass was being evasive. The idea of assembling and feeding another batch of Apaches was very unpopular with the civilians here in Arizona. If the effort worked, headquarters could take the credit. If it failed, Whitman would suffer the salvo of criticism.

A runner knocked and hustled in, panting for breath.

"Sir, a mob from Tucson has drawn Sharps and Spencer rifles from Governor Safford's stores. They set out in this direction."

"How many?" Whitman stood up so fast his chair crashed to the floor behind him.

"About a hundred Papagos, forty-eight Mexicans, and six whites."

"Oh, Lord," breathed Whitman. "Oh, Lord."

RAFE SEARCHED FOR THE INFANT'S LEGS AMID THE SCATtered debris of baskets, blankets, clothing, and lifeless bodies. He felt he could not bury the child until he found his legs. He spotted them next to a burning lodge, picked them up, and laid them carefully so they joined the places where they had been severed.

All the lodges were on fire, but the smoke did not obscure the devastation; it only made it more hellish. The Tucson mob must have arrived as the earliest birds were tuning up, and before the Aravaipas woke. Bodies lay sprawled everywhere, almost all of them women and children. The men must have gone off hunting or had taken cover to defend their families.

The Papagos had clubbed and knifed their victims, taking care to smash their faces so they would have to spend eternity that way. They had mutilated them in other ways also, whatever struck their sense of whimsy. They had clubbed the dogs, too, a lot of dogs.

Felmer's wife lay on her back with her skirts up over her face, her legs spread. Ashen-faced and silent, Joe Felmer gently pulled the skirt and petticoats down and arranged them. Her face had been smashed and Felmer laid his jacket over it. He wrapped her in his blanket and lifted her as he would a sleeping child. He carried her to his horse and laid her across it. Oblivious of everyone, he led the horse away.

Lieutenant Whitman, his eyes red from weeping, handed Rafe a shovel. He took a bandana from inside his jacket and blew his nose as he walked away to supervise the troops with burial detail. He ordered the soldiers to carry the bodies to the dance ground in the center of the village and line them up, a routine they had learned, no doubt, from the slaughters at Gettysburg, Antietam, and Atlanta. Rafe stopped them.

He pointed out that the men could dig the graves now, but if the bodies were allowed to lie where they had fallen, relatives could identify them more easily. If Eskiminzin and his people didn't return by the next day, they could bury the corpses before the stench became overpowering. Of the 125 corpses, only eight were men.

Lt. Howard Bass Cushing arrived with a company of soldiers. Sgt. John Mott rode with him, and Rafe was glad to see him. He'd known Mott for over ten years, since that imbroglio with Lieutnant Bascom and Cochise.

Howard Cushing had been in the territories for only a year, but he had covered a lot of ground and killed a lot of Apaches in that time. He and his three brothers had earned an impressive record during the late war of rebellion, but the other three hadn't lived to crow about it. Cushing had packed his kit and come west to continue doing what he did best: killing the enemy, whomever he might be. His superiors had given him vague orders to attack Apaches wherever he found them and Cushing was eager to oblige.

Cushing put Rafe in mind of the relay races soldiers held when off duty. Men would space themselves out along the course so they could snatch the baton from the flagging runner who started before them. The army was like that, beginning with Bascom. Or maybe the line went back a couple hundred years to that first high-toned Spaniard rattling through the desert in his suit of armor like a loosely packed case of tinned sardines on horseback. The Spaniards, after all, had been the first to enslave the Apaches and start the whole chain of events in motion. The lineage of military demagogues passed through Bascom, Carleton, and now Cushing. They were the men for the job, if killing Apaches was the answer.

Cushing was four or five inches shorter than Rafe's five feet, eleven inches. He was lean and sinewy, and with his sleeves rolled up, Rafe could see the veins standing out on his arms and hands. He was slightly stoop-shouldered and restless as a ferret. He had sandy hair and eyes like smoky quartz.

Rafe heard Lieutenant Whitman ask him if he and his men had come to help bury the dead.

"I kill them," Cushing said. "I don't bury them." He gestured to the wagon loaded with water, food, ammunition, blankets, and medical supplies. "We're heading east to hunt Mescaleros."

Whitman shrugged and went back to digging.

"I heard the blacksmith's here," Cushing said. "I want him to look at the mounts' shoes."

"They killed his wife. He took her home to bury her."

Cushing shook his head. "A white man's got no business setting up house with a squaw."

Royal Whitman didn't turn to look as Cushing strode back to his big black horse and ordered his men to mount.

Rafe could see that digging graves would occupy most of the day. He helped throughout the morning, and then he took his leave. He had heard that Victorio and the Warm Springs band had returned from Mexico and had set up camp near Fort Craig in New Mexico.

Rafe could see from the devastation around him that the army was not providing protection for the Apaches who came in peacefully. Rafe decided to leave his wagon at Joe

Felmer's ranch and ride east. He would pick up Caesar at Central City, and the two of them could warn Victorio to be careful.

He decided to keep Red with him. Red had emphatically stated his feelings about retirement. Besides, Rafe could switch off between Red and the chestnut and cover ground faster. He had made that trip so many times, he knew the shortest routes, the narrow, steep, God-help-us trails that Cushing's supply wagon couldn't maneuver. If he started well before sunup, he could cross Doubtful Pass before Cushing arrived there. The traveling would be more bearable before sunup, too.

Honest labor, desperate rescues, and brutal slaughter. In Arizona they were all best conducted early, before the kiln of a sun sapped breath, nerve, muscle, and thought.

Chapter 46

IN THE BAG

Lozen stopped pouring the chunks of piñon resin into the kettle and listened to the whinnies coming from the pasture. "Your gray is after my mare again, Sister."

"Maybe he won't misfire this time." Stands Alone added sticks to the blaze under the kettle.

The horses weren't the only restless ones. From the river came the doleful notes of a flute. It sounded as though it were going through that awkward stage when a boy's voice changed pitch without warning.

The young man playing it must have learned from one of the men of the western bands during the stay in Mexico. Flutes made the Chiricahua uneasy. They were connected with love magic. Love magic could go awry and cause sickness and insanity, but this flute was being played too badly to pose much danger.

"He'd better have other arrows in his quiver," Third Wife said, "because that flute will not bring down his prey."

The women leaned forward to avoid the pack of small boys careening past, waving wooden spears and rifles. The boys could imitate the lever action of a Winchester and the report of a rolling block Remington as perfectly as they could a quail or a sharp-shinned hawk. No one wanted to be a Bluecoat, so they wrestled for it. The Bluecoats always died, but they did it with enthusiasm. They whirled, staggered, fell, groaned, got up. They fell again, writhed, bucked, and sprawled full-out. The others rushed in to finish them with their lances.

Stands Alone's six-year-old son, Darts Around, and María's boy, He Throws It, fired at each other from behind lodges and tanning frames, rocks, bushes, drying racks, and the women. The women ignored them. Smearing the woven jugs with piñon pitch was a tedious process, so Lozen and her friends made a social occasion of it.

Stands Alone poured the warm resin into her jug. She added a hot rock and tilted the jug to spread the pitch evenly. Other women were smearing it on the outside, using a stick wrapped with buckskin. Some worked in red ochre for decoration.

They were still waiting for word from Washington that this land was theirs permanently. In the meantime, they were happy to be able to sleep through the night, and to see their children run and shout again. The agent at the fort provided food and blankets. The men occasionally raided into Mexico, but they spent most of their time playing hoop-and-pole. Some of the women weren't happy about having them around so much, but they all felt safer.

Stands Alone called to her son, Darts Around, to bring more wood, but he pretended not to hear her. Maybe he had become rebellious because his father refused to go on the war trail and the boys made fun of him. Whatever the reason, he stole meat from the drying rack. He took a family pony without permission, rode it into a gopher hole, and broke its leg. Something must be done about him. Stands Alone glanced toward the hoop-and-pole ground and smiled.

Loco was on his way. He had painted white circles around his disfigured eye and mouth. He wore a straw wig, and he carried a feed sack. Growling like a bear, he chased Darts Around, who dived into his parents' lodge and burrowed under the blankets. Loco dragged him out feetfirst while the women laughed until their sides ached.

Loco lifted Darts Around up by an ankle and tried to lower him headfirst into the sack, but Darts Around grabbed the edges. Her Eyes Open pried his fingers loose so Loco could slide the sack up over him. He slung it over his shoulder with Darts Around screaming and thrashing, and then sneezing.

"Listen!" Loco growled. "Listen, boy, if you do not behave as you should, I will carry you to the Mountain Spirits."

The wriggling stopped, but the sneezing continued.

"The Mountain Spirits will tie you up and eat you, piece by piece." Loco pinched the closest bulge in the sack. "Will you behave as a Red Paint should?"

The reply was muffled, "I will."

"*Enjuh.* Good."

Loco dumped the sack onto the ground, and Darts Around crawled out, shaken, mortified, and covered with dust. Loco turned to the other boys peeking from behind the lodges.

"This will happen to all of you who disobey your parents. If you don't listen to them, you could be killed by enemies. Or you could cause the death of others."

Loco stamped his feet and lumbered off. He passed Long Neck without a greeting. Loco counseled peace with the Pale Eyes, which meant that he and Long Neck did not agree. But because of Loco's Bear power, even Long Neck did not try to bully him.

Long Neck and Geronimo had come to Warm Springs to recruit men to go after the Bluecoat lieutenant known as Weasel. The Warm Springs men gathered at Victorio's fire to talk about it.

"I will wait here for a message from the Great Father in Wah-sin-ton," said Victorio. "I have given my word that I will keep the peace."

Long Neck's leg started jiggling, a sign that he was angry. He started telling a story, in his halting way. "Long ago, they say, at the Place called Three Peaks Together, the People Without Minds were camped near some soldiers. They thought the soldiers were their friends, but one day the soldiers started killing them. Instead of fighting or running away, the People Without Minds held a council. They asked each other, 'Why are the soldiers shooting us?'

"By the time they decided to run away, most of them were dead. It happened just so, at the place called Three Peaks Together."

Everyone knew what he was saying. Eskiminzin was a fool to trust the Pale Eyes, and he had grown careless besides. The old man's sentries were asleep when the Papagos, Mexicans, and Americans attacked before dawn. Eskiminzin did not keep watch. He did not walk around his camp at all hours. He did not tell the young ones to sleep with one eye open and with their weapons in their hands.

"I have a plan," said Long Neck. "My men and I attacked the Bluecoats' wagon and caried away the box of metal disks they value so much. Taking their money will stir them up like hornets. My woman will lead them into the canyon called Where They Trap Horses. We will wait for them there."

Lozen remembered whose plan that had been originally, but she said nothing. There was no point in losing her temper at Long Neck. He was as Life Giver made him. To get angry with him would be like railing at a mountain gale or a roaring flood.

Long Neck scowled and studied the ground, reluctant to bring up his men's request. "The warriors ask that the sister of the Warm Springs *nantan* go with them to fight Weasel."

Lozen answered for herself. "I have prayed long and often about this. My spirits have told me to keep peace with the Pale Eyes. I will not put my people's lives in danger to go with you."

Long Neck acted as though he hadn't heard her. "We see now where a man gets his womanly ways."

The skin paled along Victorio's jaw as he clenched his teeth. Long Neck was his guest here, and one treated guests with courtesy. "The soldiers attack those who attack them," he said. "We do not attack them, so they cause us no harm."

Everyone knew he was implying that the raids of those like Long Neck and Geronimo brought retaliation against any Apache not directly under the army's protection.

"Than you and Eskiminzin are brothers." Long Neck dismissed him as though he, too, were a careless old man who would allow his people to be slaughtered by those he was fool enough to trust. "Cheis will go with us. He is a warrior who's not afraid to fight."

Lozen spoke up. "They say, long ago, that Coyote was

very hungry, and he came upon a tip beetle. That beetle was standing right up on his head, the way tip beetles do.

" 'I'm someone who eats only fat,' said Coyote. 'And I'm going to eat you.'

"The beetle, still standing on his head, said, 'Be quiet, old man. I'm listening to what they're saying under the ground.'

" 'Tell me what they're saying then, because when you finish, I'm going to eat you.'

" 'They're talking down there. They're saying that they're going to come up here. They're going to catch a certain person who shit on that rock, and they're going to kill him.'

"That scared Coyote because he was the one who had dirtied the rock. He said, 'I forgot something. I'll be back.' But he didn't return."

The men laughed. Lozen had eased the tension, but everyone got the point. Whether tip beetle heard someone talking underground or whether he made up the story to scare Coyote didn't matter. Only fools ignored the voices of their spirits and disobeyed their commands.

The other, subtler implication was that shitting where one shouldn't, or raiding where one shouldn't, could get one in trouble.

SMOKE FROM THE GRASS FIRE SMUDGED THE BLUE SKY OF early May, but it did not obscure the footprints in the moist sand in the arroyo. The footprints weren't a mystery. For miles, the soldiers had been following the woman who made them.

"She's heading up the canyon." Lt. Howard Bass Cushing beckoned to thirteen of the sixteen privates in the company. "These men and I will trail her. Sergeant Mott, you and Collins, Green, Pierce, and Fichter cover the rear."

"The tracks are too clear, sir," said John Mott.

"What do you mean?"

"The squaw set her feet down heavy. She avoided places where the prints won't show. Looks like she wants us to follow her."

"More likely she doesn't know we're here. She's being careless."

"Apaches aren't careless." Rafe knew that disagreeing with Cushing wouldn't change his mind, but he had to try.

Cushing rounded on him, the steel predominating in his gray-blue eyes. "I suppose the bucks who attacked that wagon train and drank all that tonic and got falling-down drunk weren't careless." He charged his Remington revolvers and capped them, lecturing all the while. "I don't believe all that superstitious mumbo jumbo about the Apaches, Collins. They aren't magic. They can't make themselves invisible. They don't know everything. They don't see everything. They're human, like everyone else. They make mistakes."

Cushing waved his hand, the signal to move out, and the men followed him on horseback up the arroyo. While Mott and the three privates waited, Rafe made sure the pack mules were well tethered and their loads secure. The situation might get busy before long.

"You brought the old warhorse." Mott nodded at Red.

"Yep." Rafe knew he shouldn't have, but his young chestnut gelding had thrown a shoe. The real reason was that Red would not allow Rafe to go a scout without him.

"And your hound?"

"She's getting deaf as a dog iron. I left her with the sutler."

When Patch saw Rafe filling his two cartridge belts, she had started her dance, rocking from one front paw to the other. When he rolled spare paper cartridges, and packets of coffee, bread, and bacon into his blanket, she had started leaping in place and barking. Rafe had taken her to the sutler's store and tossed scraps of jerked beef and biscuit crumbs onto the floor. When he sneaked out, she was inhaling every last bit, and the loungers in the store were making much of her.

Rafe and John Mott studied the high rock walls toward which Lieutenant Cushing and the other thirteen men were riding, spread out across the narrow canyon.

"This might be a hunting party, John. War parties don't usually take women with them." Still, something made the hair stir at the back of Rafe's neck. They'd seen no other Apache sign. No sign meant a person should be more careful than usual.

Rafe, Mott, and the three privates spurred their horses forward at a walk and spread out. They scanned the steep sides of the canyon for signs of life and of death.

"Too bad we ain't got the sons of bitches who stole the payroll," Mott said in a low voice. "That was a low-down, dirty trick. The troops would have kicked the traces by now if anyone but Cushing were in charge." He spit. "I never did see such a devil-take-the-hindmost scrapper as the lieutenant."

Rafe kept his peace on the subject of Cushing and stared at the thorny landscape until his eyes watered.

"If I were an Apache, I'd set up an ambuscade in that canyon," said Mott. "That dry gulch is a sack waiting to close around us."

As though on cue, rifle fire reverberated across the canyon. Where no Apache had been, dozens appeared. Cushing and his troops retreated and joined Mott and Rafe to form a line, firing as they fell back.

The Apaches advanced down the slope, keeping a formation rather than scattering, and Rafe noticed the big man on a small brown pony at the ridgeline. With his lance, he was directing the movements of his men. Even at that distance Rafe recognized Whoa.

The soldiers' fire drove the Apaches back, and Cushing shouted the command to advance. Rafe started to protest, but Mott beat him to it.

"Sir, we will be crossing open ground when the hostiles have the cover and outnumber us. Do you think it's prudent to go farther?"

Cushing squinted up at the hills and the retreating Apaches. "We've routed them."

"Maybe they want us to think that," said Rafe.

Cushing eyed him coldly. "I'm in command here, Collins, and may I remind you that you are merely a civilian."

Rafe wanted to say that being merely a civilian, he would

go back to his mules, who, on their most obdurate days, had more sense than Cushing. But he could see that if anyone was going to escape this canyon alive, they would need every man. He and the others left the horses with two of the privates and went forward on foot.

They had advanced about twenty yards when the slopes erupted Apaches. Far more of them were hiding there than had originally shown themselves, and every rock and bush sprouted one. They swarmed down, firing as they came. During the fight they shouted, "Come get us, you white sons of bitches," in passably good English.

Rafe and John Mott retreated together, reloading and firing as they went. They had almost reached the mouth of the canyon when they heard Cushing cry out, "Sergeant, I am killed. Take me out."

Rafe and Mott ran back to him. They each grabbed an arm and, holding their rifles in their other hands, they dragged him toward the horses. A bullet grazed Rafe's sleeve and hit Cushing in the head, but Mott and Rafe continued to haul his lifeless body along with them.

Each of them knew that if they were him, they would not want to be abandoned to this enemy. They couldn't bear to think of other soldiers finding them and looking at them in horror and disgust, the way they had reacted to the sight of Apache victims. It wasn't a reasonable dread, this anxiety about their corpses. Their souls would have decamped, just as the lieutenant's had, leaving their bodies behind like so much discarded bivouac litter, but they both had thought about it.

Mott glanced back. The first of the warriors had closed to less than two hundred feet behind them. "Time to save our hides."

They dropped Cushing, and Mott took his pistols and Sharps. They slung their carbines across their backs and sprinted for the horses. Bullets whined around them, and the nearest Apaches ran across the broken ground as though it were a level cinder track.

Rafe had seen them run footraces. He had no illusions that

he could outpace them. He only hoped he could reach Red before they caught him. He vowed that if Red could save his arse one more time, he would find him a pasture of sweet grass with a pretty filly to dote on him.

He heard the rhythmic sigh of moccasins coming up behind him, but he dared not look back. If he stumbled, he was caught, and if he were only killed outright, that would be the good news.

He whistled. Red broke the tether and started for Rafe at a gallop. Rafe could feel the warrior's presence behind him now, like a wind pushing against his back. He could smell the rank odor of the man's sweat mingling with his own, which didn't smell so good, either. He could hear the rasp of breathing which made him think he at least was giving him a run for his money. It wasn't any kind of consolation.

He felt his hat jerked off his head. The slight tug pulled him off balance. He stumbled, then sprawled full-length, and the Apache, unable to stop, leaped over him. Rafe lifted his stubbled cheek off the ground in time to see his pursuer skid to a halt.

Rafe had never seen anything with such preternatural clarity. The Apache stood as though frozen in time and bathed in light, knife in one hand, Rafe's hat in the other. He wore only moccasins and a breechclout of unbleached muslin draped over a rawhide thong. Rafe could count the stitches in his moccasins and see the individual threads in the muslin.

Red reared and caught the man on the head with a hoof. He fell, a long gash opened across his forehead, eye, and cheek. Red came down on him with his front legs; then he reared up and did it again. Rafe got his feet under him and grabbed the Apache's rifle. When he settled into the saddle, Red was already in motion.

Rafe heard two shots. Red faltered, gathered himself, and plunged on. Rafe saw the next bullet cut across Red's neck, severing his spine. Red lurched, then collapsed, and Rafe jumped clear. Rafe stretched out alongside Red, using his body as a shield. He no longer heard the gunfire and the shouting.

He always carried small lumps of coarse brown sugar in his pocket, and he pulled out the last one and held it in front of Red's muzzle. Red took it between his teeth, but his throat muscles would no longer work below the wound in his neck. Red licked Rafe's hand instead.

With his free hand Rafe stroked the velvet of Red's muzzle. He scratched his nose, then rubbed and pulled his ears, the way Red liked. He murmured to Red as he reached along his leg and pulled his knife from the sheath tied above his boot.

With his bandana he wiped the tears from his eyes. He did not want to bungle this because he couldn't see. At least the blacksmith, Felmer, had given his knife a fine edge.

Still talking, Rafe placed the blade at one side of Red's neck. Red sighed, as though in thanks or acceptance. Rafe drove the big knife in as far as the hilt and pulled it toward him. It was hard work cutting through hide, muscle, and sinew, but he managed to sever the windpipe. As blood poured out and the breath rattled in Red's throat, Rafe put an arm around his neck and his face against his chest. He was listening so intently to the burble of blood from the gash, the rale of wind through the severed windpipe, and the last desperate heave of Red's gallant heart that he didn't hear the hoofbeats.

"Rafe, move out" John Mott pulled Cushing's big stallion to a halt, showering Rafe with dirt. "The damned ammunition mule won't budge. You're the only one he'll heed." Mott led a piebald with a chunk taken out of his ear. "Are you hit?" He handed the piebald's reins to Rafe.

Rafe looked down at his blood-soaked shirt. "No. No. I reckon not." In a daze, he took the reins and mounted.

"The hostiles have pulled back," he said. "Maybe we can flank them and recover the bodies. Kilmartin, Fichter, and I will cover the pack train's retreat. We need you to handle those damned mules."

"The Apaches haven't pulled back. They're planning to cut us off where the trail passes through the foothills."

"If we retreat across the river, we'll put the swamp at the

headwaters between us. It's longer, but it should throw them off." Mott put a finger to his hat brim. "Sorry about your horse." Then he galloped away.

When he was gone, Rafe saluted Red. He could hardly speak around the stone of grief in his throat. "So long, old friend."

Chapter 47

PROMISES, PROMISES

The day was mild for November. Rafe whistled "The Battle Hymn of the Republic" as he rode. His chestnut gelding was in a good mood, too. Rafe had found him this morning with a length of tether rope. The chestnut had made large circles with his neck and head, flinging the rope round and round. Rafe could see no purpose to it except high spirits. If the critter developed a sense of humor, Rafe figured he would have to give him a name sooner or later.

Patch's granddaughter ranged through the scrub and cactus, ever alert for the threat of jackrabbits and quail. The three of them had made it through the pass in one piece. That was cause for celebration.

Anglos had begun referring to the break in the mountains between southern Arizona and New Mexico as Apache Pass, but Rafe still thought of it as Doubtful. Either name fit. Apaches were the ones who made it doubtful, Cochise and his Chiricahuas, with the able assistance of Whoa and Geronimo and their merry band.

Rafe was in Victorio's territory now, and he relaxed a little. Victorio had kept his word. The Warm Springs people had remained at peace. Rafe looked forward to seeing them again. Maybe Lozen would be there this time.

She had been away six months ago when he had gone to tell them about the slaughter of Eskiminzin's people and to warn them about Cushing. Caesar had inquired about her among his Apache kinfolk, and He Makes Them Laugh had said she had gone to see someone. Finally he admitted she was conferring with her spirits. He said that her people called her Grandmother, and that they thought of her as *di-yin,* a shaman, a very holy woman.

A holy woman. The more chances Rafe had to see her and talk to her, the more unapproachable she seemed.

Rafe found Mattie Jones cutting Caesar's hair in the door-yard of their one-room adobe house on the outskirts of Central City. Two of Patch's great-grandchildren were tussling around Caesar's feet. A pig rooted in a dusty pen. Chickens bustled around. A horse and a mule munched hay in a corral of mesquite limbs.

Next to the corral a truck garden had gone mostly to autumn seed, but cabbages still flourished. Beyond the corral lay a field of dry corn stalks and the remains of the bean and squash plants that had grown up alongside them. Another field had been planted in cotton. Rafe would have thought Mattie never wanted to see cotton again, but there it was.

Caesar sat on a stool reading a newspaper while Mattie brandished a pair of shears manufactured with sheep in mind. She had to stand back and extend her arms to make room for the bulge of her stomach. She wore a .41 caliber Butterfield Army Model revolver in a holster on her hip. She had to use the last hole in Caesar's belt, and she wore it slung under the overhang of her belly, but in less pregnant circumstances the holster and its contents would have suited her. Mattie had never lacked an air of confidence, but now there was a feeling of calm mixed with it.

Caesar threw his arms around Rafe, and Rafe hugged him back, though the act embarrassed him. An embrace would not have occurred to either of them before they'd started spending time among the Apaches.

Caesar nodded at the chestnut. "So you put Red to pasture?"

"Killed at Bear Springs." The words stuck in Rafe's throat still. He coughed to cover the break in his voice.

"Then you were with Cushing when Whoa got him."

"I was."

Mattie tugged Caesar's jacket so he would sit back down. She regarded Rafe with suspicion and some hostility. Rafe knew she was thinking that he had come to lure Caesar away and get him killed. She was right about the first part, anyway.

Rafe took from his saddlebag a package wrapped in clean sacking and tied with cord and handed it to her. She untied it and drew in her breath at the sight of the red woolen shawl with long fringes of the sort the Mexican women wore.

"There's something inside," Rafe said.

She unfolded the shawl to expose the tiny pair of blue stockings, a cap, and mittens, knitted from an old wool army uniform jacket that Rafe had painstakingly unraveled. Rafe didn't mention that the owner of the jacket had died at Bear Springs. Some would consider it an evil omen, but Rafe looked at it as new life from the rags of death.

Mattie smiled at Rafe with her luminous dark eyes. She picked them up in hands as large and calloused as a man's, but with long, graceful fingers. She held them so Caesar could see them.

"That's mighty nice of you, Rafe," said Caesar.

"A pleasure."

"Can you learn me to do this, Marse Collins?"

Rafe thought that she would have learned to knit in the big house, but then he realized that the mistress must have kept her as a field hand. She would not have allowed anyone as beautiful as Mattie to be close to her husband and son, the lieutenant who brought her out here.

"I reckon I can," he said " 'Tain't hard."

Rafe gave Caesar a stack of the Prescott *Miner*. The earliest one, dated April 1871, lay on top. In jubilant fourteen-point type the headline read, EIGHT BUCK INDIANS KILLED. And in smaller print, 117 SQUAWS AND PAPOOSES CAPTURED.

Caesar leafed through the papers, reading aloud, while with a currycomb, Mattie raised the tight curls so she could see where they were uneven. She trimmed the ones that stuck out and brushed the loose hair off his shoulders with snaps of her apron. When she finished, Caesar stood up and offered Rafe the stool, but Rafe preferred to stand.

"I'll put water on for coffee." Mattie carried the shawl and the baby clothes inside. Rafe took advantage of her absence to get to the main reason for his visit.

Before he could, the chestnut reached his head over the top of the gate and pulled the bolt. The gate swung open, and he trotted after Rafe.

"Look at that!" Caesar said.

"He learned it from Red." He glanced at Caesar. "Are you finding steady work?"

"This and that," Caesar said. "I works at the mines, hauls freight for the gum'ment."

"Caesar, the army finally sent the man for the job."

"Killing Apaches, you mean?"

"Making peace with them."

"I guess you'd be referring to General Crook."

"He's a wonder." Rafe had never met any officer like Crook. "Something must have infected the stiff-dickies in Washington with horse sense. They sent a sane, competent general. He yanked the flagpole from Los Angeles and brought it back to Tucson where it belongs."

"By the looks of those new boots, I'd say you signed on as a scout."

"A mule skinner. Crook's too smart to trundle supply wagons around the country. He's depending on mules. He's asked me a thousand questions about them. He's recruited a bunch of scouts, too; men who really know the country. You should think about joining us. The pay is good, and the enlistment is only for six months."

Rafe didn't say what was really on his mind. He and Caesar could ride together again. Without Caesar and without Red, he had been feeling lonelier than usual in this lonely life.

"I can't leave Mattie, what with the child and all. I gave her my word I'd keep close to home."

That was the answer Rafe had expected. "I'd say the same thing if I were in your boots." He wanted to suggest that Caesar bring Mattie with him to Cook's headquarters at Camp Grant, but of all the filthy, flea-ridden, squalid posts in the territory, it had to be the worst. The soldiers assigned there called it the Old Rookery. Besides, Mattie had made a home here, and she wasn't in condition to travel.

"What you boys hatchin'?" Mattie came outside carrying a blue-and-white china plate with fat chunks of corn bread on it.

She held the plate out so Rafe could take a piece. She let her fingers linger on the plate, as though unable to believe such a beautiful object belonged to her.

"Rafe says General Crook is looking for men to scout for him."

Mattie's eyes narrowed.

"I tole him I wasn't going nowhere."

"Praise the Lord." Mattie smiled, gracious in victory. "Rafe Collins, that yaller hair of yours looks like a hayfield in a windstorm." She pointed to the stool. "Sit."

Rafe's eyelids drooped as she combed the worst of the tangles from the thick mop of hair whose ends brushed the shoulders of his red flannel shirt. He felt an acute attack of elation at the touch of her fingers separating out a section, cutting it, and then moving on. Making love with a woman was the greatest gift bestowed on man, but this and home cooking vied for second place.

"I'm going to visit Victorio and his people as long as I'm on this side of the Pass."

"They's gone," said Caesar.

"Where?"

"The gum'ment moved 'em to the Tulerosa Valley."

"That's a hundred miles north of here."

"People 'round here decided the Warm Springs land was too good to waste on savages," said Mattie. "Now what did the gum'ment do with that land, Caesar?"

"They declared it public domain."

"And Victorio went peacefully?" Rafe remembered what Victorio and the others had said about the country where they lived: "When we forget the names of the places, when we cease to know what happened here, we no longer know who we are."

"Yeah, and he's the one who kept things peaceful around

here. Now that he's gone, I's expectin' the riffraff to come tricklin' on over the pass from Arizona." Caesar put a hand on his rifle. "My brother-in-law says Victorio would rather take his chances with the Bluecoats than live with Whoa again. He says Whoa is one mean coyote."

"Then you've seen Pandora and your nephew?"

"Yep. I took 'em some blankets and corn. They was raggedy looking, Rafe, all of 'em. And hungry. You could see it in their eyes. The Tulerosa is north of here and colder. They won't have a chance to plant anything before winter sets in."

"The army will take care of them."

"The gum'ment promised them a thousand blankets and plenty of beef and corn, but I ain't seen none of it, and I'm the one who freights the goods."

"At least on the Tulerosa there aren't many whites to bother them."

"Not yet," said Caesar.

THE TATTERED COVERING OF THE DOMED LODGE DIDN'T stop the icy wind. It hardly slowed it down. Lozen tried to scoop snow higher onto it to provide some protection, but her hands were so numb she could hardly grip the board she was using as a shovel. Her People had suffered hard times before, but they had never been forced to stand still for them. In winter they could move to the sheltered valleys or go to Mexico.

She went inside to continue to sing and make medicine for Third Wife. Corn Stalk and She Moves Like Water lay on each side of Third Wife, sharing the heat from their bodies. Third Wife shivered so violently the other two had to hold her to keep her from rolling off the mattress of pine branches. Lozen fed the last few sticks into the small fire in the middle of the lodge.

Food might have helped Third Wife, but the cook pots were empty. The promised beef hadn't arrived. Instead, the agent had given them pig meat in small metal containers.

Each container had the picture of a devil painted in red on it. Lozen's people had recoiled in horror at *itsi chidin*, devil meat. They knew then that the Pale Eyes were trying to poison them or witch them. Lozen and Broken Foot had had to hold a four-day sing to rid the camp of the sorcery.

The agent gave out blankets, too, but they were flimsy things, thin and full of holes where the moths had eaten them. When Broken Foot saw them, he commented that at least the insects were getting enough to eat. Third Wife's new baby boy lay with Daughter and the other children in a pile under some of those blankets. Stands Alone and Maria kept watch, huddled together under a blanket that they shared. The rest of the blankets were wrapped around Third Wife, and still she shivered.

Third Wife had had a hard time delivering the child. They all knew the trip here had caused it. A woman was not supposed to ride on horses or in wagons after the fifth month, but she had had to endure the trek across the mountains, five days in a jolting army wagon. No one was surprised that the baby became wedged in the birth tunnel. Third Wife had struggled for a day and a half before Daughter could finally pull the child free, wash him, and wrap him in rabbit skins.

Third Wife stopped shivering. She looked up at Lozen, her eyes sunken in the purple hollows around them. Lozen could see her spirit leaving as surely as if she were watching Third Wife ride away on her little buckskin mare. The light went out in those laughing eyes.

The women began wailing their grief. Lozen walked outside, the thin soles of her moccasins munching in the new-fallen snow. In a fury, she faced into the howling wind. The noise of it sounded like the spirits laughing. She had something to say to the spirits.

"If you will not help me," she shouted into the storm, "then do not talk to me anymore. Don't come around here if you're only going to do what you want."

She crouched with her head down and her arms around her knees. She thought about promises made. Her brother had promised to take care of his people. If he left here he would have to abandon many of them because they were too sick or weak to travel. He could not bring himself to do that. He hoped the Pale Eyes would keep their promises.

Lozen knew they wouldn't. The Great Father in Washington had promised that Warm Springs would belong to her people for as long as the mountains stood and the rivers flowed; then they had taken it. They had promised Lozen's people they would give them the things they needed, but they had not.

The Pale Eyes belonged to a rich and powerful nation. They ate beef and soft bread. They rode big horses and wore warm coats when the cold wind blew. As rich as they were, they could not spare food and blankets for those they had made homeless and destitute.

Promises. Lozen thought of the promise she had made to her capricious and crotchety spirits. She had said she would keep the peace with the Pale Eyes for the good of all her people, but the bad behavior of the Pale Eyes and her own spirits made that promise hard to keep.

Chapter 48

SLINGS AND ARROWS

As the light snow drifted around her, Lozen stood near the pool where the other women were bathing. Steam rose from the surface of it. She pulled off her moccasins. She put her bead necklaces and her small bag of pollen inside them. Holding her blanket in front of her with one hand, she struggled out of her dusty tunic and skirt.

She slid into the pool, leaving the blanket on the ledge. Stands Alone, She Moves Like Water, Corn Stalk, Maria, Her Eyes Open, and Daughter sat with their heads leaning against the wall of dark gray basalt. Lozen joined them and let her legs float in front of her. She watched her breath mingle with the steam rising off the water. She felt as light as the snowflakes falling on her hair.

Whenever she bathed in the hot waters of the spring she knew the past year here wasn't a dream. She was truly home. After that terrible time at Tulerosa, the Pale Eyes had finally kept their promise. They had given the Warm Springs country back to them. They also distributed blankets, beef, and corn at the agency half a day's ride away. Lozen's people were beginning to think they might recover from the terrible losses of the past ten years of warfare.

Lozen closed her eyes and felt the snowflakes tangling in her eyelashes. The snow had come early, but it wasn't a heavy one. The women had worked all morning harvesting corn. The thick ears filled the baskets and overflowed in heaps in the arbors.

Broken Foot's second wife, Wide, arrived and stripped. Unlike most Ndee women, she wasn't shy about her body, and she didn't ease into anything. She gathered herself to leap.

"Avalanche," announced Lozen.

"Avalanche and flood," added She Moves Like Water.

"Avalanche, flood, and earthquake," said Corn Stalk.

Wide jumped, tucking in her elbows and pulling her legs up to form a tight, round projectile. She landed with a force that sent water sloshing over the lower rim and into the stream below. She came up sputtering and flinging her long black hair back and forth.

While they talked about the old days, they washed each other's hair with suds made from the pounded roots of the yucca. As the shadows lengthened, they climbed out and dressed. They sat with their feet dangling in the water and draped their hair over their arms to dry. They were almost ready to start for home when Wide's eleven-year-old daughter, Denzhonne, Very Pretty, galloped up on her mother's pony.

Wide frowned. She had told her daughter not to ride the horse until the sore on his back healed, but Very Pretty had a habit of doing what she wanted. Lozen tried to sympathize with Wide, but she remembered being the same way.

Very Pretty called to Lozen. "Grandmother, Hairy Foot is here, and Uncle and Uncle's woman and son. They brought a man who has a box that captures people and makes them small."

The women hurried to the field to collect the baskets of corn. The boys were supposed to be chasing off the crows with their bows and their slings, but the lure of Pale Eyes visitors was too strong to resist. Lozen lingered. Seeing the crops flourish, knowing her people would have corn and beans for the winter, reassured her. The Red Paints had always grown some corn, but for many years their lives had been too unsettled to plant or harvest.

She turned to see Hairy Foot sitting on his big chestnut under the walnut tree. She held out her arms at her sides and grinned at him, inviting him to admire the corn plants. Then she ran to catch up with the other women.

THE SMALL WAGON HAD "SIERRA SAM'S STEREOPTICON EX-
TRAVAGANZA" painted on its wooden side. The finer print
proclaimed that the wagon's owner could produce PAPER
PRINTS, AMBROTYPES, STEREO VIEWS, AND CABINET CARDS OF
BREATHTAKING CLARITY AND SCOPE. Sam used the wagon's
white canvas cover as a backdrop for his lantern slide show.
He intended to coax Victorio and his people to pose for pho-
tographs. He told Rafe and Caesar that the suckers in the east
would cough up cash for them.

The black burnsides and beard bordering Sam's solid jaw
looked like an extension of the top hat he wore at a rakish
angle. The hem of his wool coat came halfway to the knees
of his dust-colored canvas trousers. If photography hadn't
been invented, Sam would have been a snake-oil salesman,
and a good one, too.

His assistant was Carlos, an Apache boy of about fourteen.
Sam had found him living as a slave among the Pimas a
couple years ago, had bought him from them, and become
his guardian. Carlos's hair was neatly clipped. He wore trousers, shirt, and jacket, lace-up shoes, and a wool porkpie hat.
Everyone watched him set up the big projector on its three
spindly legs as though they expected a procession of tiny
people to emerge from it at any moment.

As usual, He Makes Them Laugh set to work embarrassing Rafe while they all waited for the show to begin. How
many wives did Rafe have? When he shit, what color was
it? He had heard that white men's shit was red with white
stripes. With owl-like solemnity, he told Rafe that the women
wanted to know how big his penis was.

Mattie stood with the women, although she kept a nervous
eye on her son, Abraham Lincoln Raphael Jones. All afternoon the two-year-old had bobbed, laughing, from one
woman to another while each observed that he was the hand-
somest, strongest boy they had ever seen. People gave him
presents and fed him fingerfuls of the sweet paste made from
dried juniper berries pounded and mixed with fat.

He ended up with Lozen. As darkness fell, she balanced him on her hip while she chatted with Stands Alone, and Rafe shot glances at her. She had looked so carefree in the cornfield that afternoon, smiling with arms held wide embracing the world. He had never cared about photography, but he wished he could have a picture of her like that.

She was dressed like the other women, and she had the air of someone who had carried a child on her hip countless times before. She did not look like a powerful medicine woman. She did not look like the rogue who rode with the men, stole horses and telescopes, and neglected to get married and have children of her own.

Then she did what Rafe had a feeling no other Apache woman would. She walked over to stand next to him, so close he could smell the fragrance of her hair, like new-mown grass. She bounced Linc on her hip and smiled up at Rafe as though he were an old friend, which, in a manner of speaking, he supposed he was.

"Tomorrow," she said in Spanish, "I will give Uncle's son a name, and we will cut his hair."

"Uncle will be pleased." Rafe said.

He Makes Them Laugh bent down so he was eye-to-eye with Linc.

"Grandmother will cut your hair short all over, Boy." He rested the back of his wrist above his forehead so his fingers jutted out like a quail's crest. "She'll leave strands in front so you'll look like a quail." He mesmerized Linc by imitating the quail's song, from the moaning *uweea* to the high, sharp cries of *spik, spik,* to soft chuckles and a selection of noises in between.

This is all very heartwarming, Rafe thought, but he had seen Geronimo in the crowd. Geronimo's depredations had made his name well known on both sides of the border. Rafe had also noticed the hundreds of horses and mules grazing. A lot of them had the look of army stock. Rafe almost believed Victorio when he said his men were not stealing army horses, but Geronimo was a different matter.

RAFE HAD MET MEN WHO SEEMED UNFAMILIAR WITH THE
notion of fear, but Tom Jeffords was that and something else.
He had a quiet certainty about him, the belief that if he did
the right thing, the decent thing, no harm would come to
him. With their eye for the obvious, the Apaches had named
him Red Beard. He stood an inch shorter than Rafe and carried more meat on him, but he was about the same age,
somewhere on the far side of forty. He had powerful hands
and an old stager's squint.

Rafe had known him when the two of them drove the
stages. Now he was the superintendent of mails between
Tucson and Fort Bowie at what was called Apache Pass.
Even after the governor appointed him superintendent, Jeffords often carried the mail himself on account of attrition
among his men due to what he called Cochise fever.

As interpreter on this trip, Jeffords had brought along a
wisp of an Apache from Cibicu Creek to the north. He was
a pale man. He often stared off into space, and Rafe wondered what he was thinking. Of late, he had taken to calling
himself Noch-ay-del-klinne, Dreamer.

As the three of them rode up into the melee of boulders
that made Cochise's aerie about as accessible to outsiders as
the moon, Rafe asked Jeffords how he had come to befriend
the old chief. He'd heard stories, and he figured none of them
was exactly true.

"The chief's bucks kept sniping at the boys when they
were carrying the mail," Jeffords said. "Killed a few too
many of 'em. I knew I'd never find the old man in this
malpais, but I wandered up this way until his scouts intercepted me. They took me to him."

That was a much tamer version than any Rafe had heard.
For almost fifteen years, ever since Lieutenant Bascom hung
Cochise's kin, no white man had seen him up close and lived
to brag about it. The way Rafe heard it, Cochise's men had
a discussion of just how to dispose of Jeffords, but he had
been so cool in the teeth of it, they had decided to take him

to the chief instead. The two had become fast friends.

"I'll tell you, Rafe, until General Crook showed up, Cochise was the most impressive human being I'd ever met."

"Too bad they transferred Crook out."

Jeffords shrugged. "Grant wanted to give his peace commission a chance." He chuckled. "The head of that commission tried to talk Cochise into going to Washington to see President Grant. The old man said 'No, thank you very kindly.' He said a few officers sometimes kept their word, but the Great Father never did."

Grant's peace commission had cut short General Crook's campaigns against the Apaches. The Americans in Arizona did not approve. The editor of the *Arizona Miner* called the head of the commission "a cold-blooded scoundrel," "a red-handed assassin," and for good measure, "a treacherous, black-hearted dog." Maybe the editor didn't know that the man riding with Rafe was the one responsible for the dastardly act of making peace between the red man and the white one.

Jeffords had gotten Cochise to promise to stop raiding on the condition that the government put Jeffords in charge of a reservation that included Cochise's vast territory. Cochise also demanded that Jeffords have authority over the military in southeast Arizona, and that his word was law. Jeffords treated the Apaches so fairly that for four years, since 1871, trouble had been sporadic. What thefts and killings occurred were the work of rengades of various nationalities roving back and forth across the border, Geronimo being the most notable.

Rafe and Jeffords rode all morning until they reached a high plateau carpeted with lush grass. Cedars, oaks, and pines covered the slopes. A stream ran almost deep enough to float a canoe.

They found Cochise smoking among the exposed roots of an oak. The spot comanded a view a hundred miles in every direction. He could see the Chiricahua Mountains all around, the Dragoon Mountains to the west, and wild, magnificent country in between. The grandeur of it caused Rafe to catch his breath.

As best Rafe could tell, Cochise's worldly estate consisted of a few buckskins, blankets, and a water jar hung from a limb so evaporation would cool the contents. A shallow basket held dried mescal and jerked beef. Coffee brewed in a small tin pail. His bow and arrows, knives, Winchester rifle, saddle, and bridle were near at hand.

"Oh, lord," breathed Jeffords. "He don't look good."

Deep hollows exaggerated the bony ridges of Cochise's face. Rafe figured he must be seventy at least. He was obviously ill, but he sat straight as a gun barrel. A spot of vermilion paint graced each cheek. Pain haunted his dark eyes, but they still gleamed with intelligence. Even the editor of the *Arizona Miner* had written of him that he "looks to be a man who means what he says."

He was thinner than Rafe remembered him, but muscular. When he adjusted his blanket, Rafe saw the scars on his bare chest. He recognized the puckers of bullet holes, the graveled expanse where buckshot still lodged under the skin, the raised welts left by knife blades, and even a ragged scar of the sort an arrow would make.

Cochise's two sons, Taza and Naiche, his two daughters, and three wives watched from their cluster of lodges and cookfires. Taza was the oldest, and he looked as though he were trying to act like someone who could walk in his father's moccasins. Rafe thought that unlikely. Napoleon would have a tough time following Cochise's act.

Cochise fed sticks into his small fire and adjusted the pail on its three flat stones. He was as gracious a host as any officer in his quarters. The men rolled cigarettes while the coffee brewed. They smoked and stared out at the view.

"You know, old friend," said Jeffords. "The army surgeon can remove that thing growing in you."

"Life Giver sent this evil to me." Cochise put a hand on the bulge below his stomach. "You once told me that the evil which one knows is better than the evil one does not."

He gave a wry smile. "The Pale Eyes medicine men sometimes cut more than is necessary."

Rafe and Tom knew what he meant. An army surgeon had treated a young Chiricahua with an infected foot. He had amputated the boy's leg at the torso and boasted afterward that he had made sure one less Apache would trouble anyone.

Cochise spoke to Rafe, and Dreamer translated. "He says many years ago he saw you loading goods onto the stage. He said you chanted a prayer that tamed the wild Pale Eyes there. He wants to know what that prayer was."

Rafe searched his memory. He didn't think of himself as the praying kind. Then he remembered that first run of the Butterfield Southern Overland stage when he had recited Hamlet's speech as he loaded the trunks and bags. Cochise had stood in the crowd, and apparently he had wondered about it ever since. How could Rafe explain Hamlet's soliloquy in Apache?

He waded in. "The words were written by a great storyteller. He lived many years ago, about the same time the Spaniards came to your country. Pale Eyes still remember his words."

Cochise leaned forward, a rapt expression in his pain-filled eyes. "Was he a black robe, a holy man, a *di-yin*?"

"No, he was just a storyteller."

Rafe started to recite, using as many Apache words as he could, and Spanish, and asking Dreamer and Jeffords for help.

To be, or not to be: that is the question.
Whether 'tis nobler in the mind to suffer
The slings and arrows of outrageous fortune,

Cochise held up a hand. "The storyteller was a Pale Eyes?"

"Yes."

"And did his people use slings and arrows, as we do?"

"Yes."

"That is very interesting." Cochise permitted himself to lean against the oak. He motioned for Rafe to continue.

Or to take arms against a sea of troubles,
And by opposing end them? To die; to sleep;
No more; and by a sleep to say we end
The heartache and the thousand natural shocks
That flesh is heir to. 'Tis a consummation
Devoutly to be wish'd. To die; to sleep;
To sleep? Perchance to dream! Ay, there's the rub;
For in that sleep of death what dreams may come . . .

"Your storyteller speaks of dreams and death. He speaks of a heart that aches and a thousand hardships." He smiled. "He was wise for a white man." He waved for Rafe to go on.

As Rafe continued, he had to agree with Cochise.

For who would bear the whips and scorns of time,
The oppressor's wrong, the proud man's contumely,
The pangs of dispriz'd love, the law's delay. . . .

Shakespeare could have written this speech for Cochise, for a people, a place, and a tragic unfolding of events of which he could not have dreamed, asleep or awake. Cochise was right. Shakespeare was savvy.

Rafe realized that he was a praying man after all, given the right circumstances. He didn't like to bother the Lord for trivial needs, but now, Rafe asked God not to let Cochise die while he and Tom Jeffords were there. Jeffords said that Cochise's people believed someone had either poisoned the old chief or put a spell on him. In either case, all members of the pale-eyed race were the prime suspects. Rafe knew the Apache cure for sorcery. They hung the witch upside down from a tree, lit a fire under him, and watched him roast from the brains up.

He thought about the relative peace that Jeffords and Cochise had been able to maintain in this trackless wilderness set aside for the Chiricahuas. The agreement was one of gentlemen with nothing on paper, not that paper counted for anything with the government. What would happen when Cochise died?

Chapter 49

HEAD COUNT

After Cochise's death in June of 1874, the United States government's Indian concentration policy went awry. Instead of collecting most of the Apaches at the San Carlos reserve, it attracted all their flies. At least that's the way the situation seemed to John Clum when he stepped out of the hovel where he had spent his first night. He looked out from under the wide brim of his soft felt hat at the grisly souvenirs in the middle of the agency's assembly area.

The month was August. At seven o'clock in the morning, the thermometer refused to recant its declaration of 110 degrees, even though Clum had rapped briskly on the glass. The flies didn't mind the heat. What appealed to them more than the infirmary's dysentery patients, the quartermaster's casks of rancid pork, and the overflowing privies, were the seven severed heads that greeted Clum when he stepped outside. The flies were concentrating around them with the sort of enthusiasm the government envisioned for the Apaches.

Clum assumed the rotting remains belonged to the Apache outlaws who had attacked and killed the passengers on a stage passing through the Chiricahuas' reserve a couple hundred miles to the south. Clum knew that the army had tracked and shot the murderers two weeks ago, which would explain the heads' unsavory state.

Until Clum saw them, he had been preoccupied with the heat, and with the centipedes, spiders, snakes, and scorpions that inhabited the mud-chinked log shed that the post's commander, Major Babcock, had assigned as his quarters. He had awakened with a fist-size tarantula ankling up his chest to hold a stare-down with him. He suspected that the vermin-infested hut and the welcoming committee of decayed heads were Major Babcock's way of letting him know who was in charge here.

Clum had news for the major.

John Philip Clum was not quite twenty-three years old, not quite five feet six inches tall, and not quite 125 pounds. He had the confidence of a man twice his age and the strength of one twice his weight. He was arrogant, aggressive, cocksure, and cantankerous. He was honest, able, smart, and fearless. And when in high dudgeon he could write letters that would singe the bristles off a badlands boar.

Major Babcock was in for a tussle.

RAFE WASN'T USED TO HEARING THIS MUCH GAITY BETWEEN paydays at a fort, and he could see no sign of ardent spirits. It wasn't natural. The lamplight shining through the pale canvas of the soldiers' tents was normal enough, but the laughter was louder, more carefree. From beyond the lines of tents came drumming, singing, and hands clapping in a bewitching cadence.

As Rafe led his chestnut throught the bivouack, he could see through the open tent flaps the soldiers with their jackets unbuttoned, and their sleeves rolled up. They were playing cards, rolling cigarettes, cleaning their guns, polishing their boots. They were doing everything that soldiers did except drink whiskey and start fights. The other disorienting aspect of the men of the Ninth Cavalry was that they were shades of brown, from beige to ebony, with ebony predominating.

Rafe followed the sound of celebration and found Caesar standing at the rear of the crowd spilling out of an arbor walled with brush on three sides. The Ninth had arrived in New Mexico only a few weeks ago, and this was the first time Rafe had seen Caesar in his uniform. His sky-blue trousers were tucked precisely into knee-high boots polished till they shone like obsidian. The brass spurs glowed.

The trousers and the dark blue jacket were spotless,

starched, and ironed with precise creases. The yellow stripe on each leg and the yellow piping around the collar identified Caesar as cavalry. The big gold chevrons on his sleeve proclaimed him a First Sergeant. The forage cap with the crumpled, low crown, and the stiff leather bill sat forward at precisely the correct angle. Rafe imagined that with the dress uniform's white plume in the cap, Caesar would resemble his namesake.

Rafe leaned close so Caesar could hear him over the noise. "I thought you despised army life, Sergeant Jones."

Caesar turned and grinned at him. "This is the cavalry, Rafe. This ain't just soldierin', it's horse-soldierin'. And they treats my family well here."

Rafe had a hard time keeping his boots from falling under the spell of the drums. He shifted from one foot to the other in time with the beat. "Is this a special meeting?" he asked.

"No, they does it just about every night. They calls it a shout."

The drummers stood to one side, beating out the complex rhythms on kegs and crates, on tin pots, canteens, and a mule's jawbone. A dozen or more men moved in a circle in the center of the *ramada*. Some danced, some whirled, others rocked side to side or trembled, while spectators shouted encouragement.

Another man joined Rafe and Caesar, and the three of them started toward the long adobe building where the sergeants lived with their families.

"Rafe, I wants you to meet Sergeant George Carson. Sergeant Carson, this here is my friend, Mistuh Rafe Collins. Mistuh Collins and I go back a long ways."

"Pleased to make your acquaintance, suh."

George Carson was as tall as Caesar and much thicker through the middle. At first glance a stranger would notice his exaggerated features, his wide, flat nose and swollen lips, and his field hand's grammar, but Rafe knew to look into his eyes. He could see the quiet competence. He saw curiosity and a thirst for knowledge, too. A good sergeant was more valuable to a company of soldiers than a good captain, and the army usually did better at selecting them.

They met Colonel and Mrs. Hatch coming from the officers' mess with their daughter Bessie trailing behind. Mrs. Hatch was tall and rawboned, cinched into a palisade of iron corset stays. Cascades of lace foamed up around her sturdy jaw. Her hair was pinned up so tightly under her hat that it pulled the skin taut over her cheekbones. She had to stop in mid-harangue so the colonel could salute the sergeants, and she was not happy about it. The dusty hem of her long skirt quivered with the motion of the foot tapping under it.

Colonel Hatch was taller than average, five feet ten inches, but he looked small next to the two sergeants. He was slender, with a snug, military bearing. He had an abrupt span of a nose, thin lips, and a heavy black mustache. The soldiers, true to tradition, called him The Old Man, but he was a year younger than Rafe. Rafe noticed streaks of gray at Hatch's temples, and he wondered if he had them too. He tried to remember when last he saw himself in a mirror.

Hatch gave a crisp salute. "And are you being treated well here, men?"

"Yas, suh," said Carson. "But we be ready to go to work, suh. Don' t'ink we should lie 'round camp eatin' up the pervisions."

Hatch laughed. "You'll be going out on scout in a week or so, as soon as the recruits arrive. We're at half strength now."

"Yas, suh, but we's ready to go wiffout 'em."

Hatch smiled. "Yes, I know you are."

Hatch walked away, and his wife took up where she left off. Rafe heard Hatch say, "My god, Hattie, let me run the post, will you?"

Carson stopped at his quarters a few doors down from Caesar's. When Caesar opened the door to his own place the room looked inviting in the lamplight. Something aromatic bubbled in the iron pot hanging over the flames in the fireplace. A rag rug covered part of the dirt floor. A trunk, a pine washstand, a bedstead with a quilt, and a table with four stools filled the space. The room was on the end of the row, so there was a side window trimmed with a calico curtain. Caesar's army-issue McClellan saddle rested on a wooden stand in the far corner. The bridles and other tack, the quirt and spurs hung from pegs above it, as did Caesar's saber, spare uniform blouse, and trousers.

Linc was almost four now. Shouting "Uncle," he threw himself at Rafe. He took Rafe's hand and dragged him around the room to show him his collection of spiders, scorpions, and beetles housed in jars and meat tins on the shelf. He had on his Apache moccasins, and he wore his bow and quiver of arrows across his back. Linc's uncle, He Makes Them Laugh, had probably made them for him.

"Chile, be still." Mattie rolled her eyes at Rafe. "I swear them Apaches done put a juju on him and turned him into a wild Indian. He wants to sleep with them arrows."

They heard a knock, and Sergeant Carson came in with his wife. Rebecca Carson was tidy, plump, and gracious. She was one of those women who could emerge from a hurricane with every hair in place. She set a bowl of early greens and ham hocks on the table next to the skillet of corn bread and the pot of boiled chicken and dumplings with carrots, onions, and potatoes.

As they ate, they talked about the raids of Whoa and Geronimo and the other renegades hiding out in the Chiricahua's reserve. Caesar listed the ranchers who had lost cattle, horses, and lives. Geronimo and his boys had been busy.

"I hear that John Clum intends to bring all the Apaches to San Carlos," said Rafe.

"Where's that?" asked Sergeant Carson.

"About seventy miles north of Tucson. He brought fifteen hundred Apaches from the reserve on the Verde River. Next he convinced the Coyoteros, the White Mountain people, and Eskiminzin's Aravaipas to come. I hear he counts the men every day and the entire mob of them on Saturdays."

Like a miser his coins, Rafe added to himself.

"Maybe he thinks the tame Injuns will set a good example for the wild ones," said Carson.

Caesar chuckled. "Iff'n he thinks that, he don't know Apaches."

"How many 'Paches you suppose is still runnin' loose down in the Chiricahuas Mountains?" asked Carson.

"God only knows," said Rafe. "And most likely He's estimating."

"When you gonna take a rib, Mistuh Rafe?" teased Mattie.

"Looking around this room, I would say all the good ribs are taken."

"Mus' be a woman somewhere for a fine man like you." Rebecca Carson's voice was soft and warm, a loving voice. Sergeant Carson was a lucky man, and so was Caesar.

Caesar decided to distract the women. When they got onto the subject of marriage, he called them the hallooing hounds of love. He took a primer and slates from a box under the bed. The primer's cover and pages had been worn to the texture of the softest cloth. He and Mattie, George and Rebecca gathered in the light of the oil lamp.

George smiled at Rafe. "I has to be able to write the morning reports for my men, how many are out sick, and how many absent."

"Spellin' am a good word for it," said Mattie softly. "It's a mighty spell, readin.' "

The lamp's wick was starting to flicker and die when they heard the bugle playing "Taps." Everyone grew quiet.

Rafe had never heard it played like this. It tugged at his heart with its melancholy air. Unfamiliar grace notes in a minor key gave it an infinite sadness and hope.

"That man shore can tease magic from a horn," said Mattie. "He could bring down the walls of Jericho if he set his mind to it."

Chapter 50

ROUNDUP

Lozen tried cooing like a dove to the big brindle bull, but she didn't fool him. He could see that she looked nothing like a dove. She didn't smell like one, either. He was irate and chagrined that she had sneaked up on him while he cavorted on his back in the mud, singing to himself, his lanky shanks churning the hot air.

He lurched up out of the wallow and gave four grunts and a snort. His horns looked wide enough to hang one of those Mexican hammocks between them. His crusted muzzle, pulled by the counterweight of his horns, swung from side to side like a snake's. Strings of saliva whipped back and forth.

He plowed the earth with his left horn, then with his right. With a bellow, he charged Lozen and tried to rip out her horse's entrails. The gray sidestepped and seemed not to take the discourtesy personally. Lozen decided to leave the bull to breed with the cows that she and the men didn't manage to round up. She'd gotten his attention now, though.

The pony fled up the canyon with the brindle's breath singeing the far end of his tail. Lozen turned the horse sharply, and he leaped like a goat up the rocky slope. The bull's momentum carried him past and into the cloud of green-and-yellow-striped grasshoppers and the turkeys that chased them. The grasshoppers soared above the grass, and the turkeys rose in a great flapping of wings. Lozen headed into a small side canyon in search of livestock hiding in the scrubby growth of creosote bush and cactus.

She had come to Cheis's country with Victorio, Fights Without Arrows, Broken Foot, Chato, Flies In His Stew, He

Steals Love, and He Makes Them Laugh. The usual complement of herd boys included fifteen-year-old Wah-sin-ton and Sets Him Free. These animals were what the Mexicans called *ladinos*, crafty and wild.

Cheis's men had driven them here years ago. The Tall Cliffs People had let them multiply so they could hunt them when they needed meat. After a witch put the evil into Cheis's belly and killed him, the band's council voted his son Taza *nantan*. Cheis had trained Taza for the position, but Taza was not the leader his father was.

Then in early summer, John Clum, whom The People called Hat, Soft And Floppy, arrived with fifty-six White Mountain Apache police. He said the Tall Cliffs People's land no longer belonged to them. He said that too many bad men lurked there. He persuaded Taza to take three hundred of the band north to San Carlos with him. Over four hundred others chose to go to Mexico with Long Neck and Geronimo. About two hundred headed east to live on their own or join Victorio's and Loco's bands. They were the ones who had told Victorio about the wild cattle.

The Pale Eyes agent at the Warm Springs agency cut beef rations. The snowy season of Ghost Face was on the way. Victorio's people needed more than the few cattle they could butcher here and carry back in the hides. Victorio and Broken Foot had decided to drive them to the camp where the women were gathering piñon nuts. They could slaughter them there and dry the meat.

Lozen had gone on enough raids to know how to drive stock, how to head them, how to turn them, when to crowd them, and when to give them room. By late afternoon, though, she and her horse were lathered, lacerated, winded, and irritated. She and the others decided to start back to camp with what they had. On the way, they met Long Neck, Geronimo, and their men headed south with a herd of cavalry horses.

Victorio shared tobacco with them. "Do you have guns?" he asked. "And bullets and powder?"

"We don't need powder anymore." Long Neck gestured,

and a Mexican rode forward with a shiny new carbine.

Victorio hefted it. It was lighter than the old ones. He worked the lever, listening to the action of the bolt and the hammer, watching the smooth, interconnecting slide of it parts. He handed it to Lozen, who levered it, raised it, and looked down the two sights.

"I'll give you four cows for it," Victorio said.

"Six."

"Six then."

"Come with us, and get your own guns," Long Neck said.

"Not today."

Geronimo smiled his parody of good humor. "The Americans will keep cutting the beef issue until you agree to go into the San Carlos corral with Taza and the rest of the tame ones. You'll have to live with those White Mountain coyotes."

Victorio followed his usual policy of ignoring him. He gestured to the herd boys to cut six cows from the herd. Then he and Lozen and the others rode away without looking back.

CAESAR RODE WITH FOURTEEN MEN OF THE NINTH CAValry and the lieutenant, plus ten White Mountain scouts on foot, their captain, Joe Felmer, and the rancher whose cattle they were hunting. The scouts had no trouble finding the cattle's prints. The track was well trampled.

Dust covered the men, the horses, the pack mules, and the equipment. It settled in Caesar's eyes, his ears, his nose, his throat. It clung in the two-weeks' growth of beard. Only a few sips of water remained in each canteen. Over the long summer, the soldiers had learned to survive in a land determind to kill them. They had always had endurance, but Caesar was proud to see them develop resourcefulness.

In the search for renegade Apaches, they had forded rivers, climbed mountains, slid down talus slopes, crossed barren expanses, and threaded their way along narrow ledges. The Apaches had used their old method of dividing their raiding parties when pursued, then dividing again and again and scattering so the soldiers could never chase them all.

Caesar had no illusions. Some of the raiders were bad men, but many were only trying to feed their families. He thought of the cornfields the soldiers had destroyed. The loss of their crops only made the Apaches more apt to raid.

The lieutenant waved him forward. Felmer and the scouts had found a large camp of women and children, and the cattle were there.

The rancher shifted the twig he was chewing to the corner of his mouth. "I hear tell they's a big camp in these parts where the 'Pache been taking stolen stock. I reckon we done found it."

"We'll ride in fast," said the lieutenant. "Aim for the men, but if anyone else takes a bead on you, shoot him. Round up the women and children to hold for transport to San Carlos."

Night had almost fallen by the time they neared the camp and the lieutenant shouted "Charge." When they passed the outermost lodges, the soldiers began to whoop. Caesar wasn't sure who let off the first shot, but his men fired at will, until they realized that no one was shooting back. The camp was deserted. In their headlong career, they overturned trays of piñon nuts. The horses knocked over racks of drying meat, too. There were a lot of racks. Caesar smelled a piece of the meat. Beef. He was ready to bet they wouldn't find any cattle on the hoof here.

The horses had scattered embers from the cookfires and ignited arbors and lodges. By their light men picked up souvenirs—bows and arrows, leather pouches, a few tin pots. They milled about; then they drove off a colt and a sorebacked mare, the only horses they found.

HE MAKES THEM LAUGH WAS AS RESPONSIBLE FOR SAVING everyone as Lozen was. He had invited them all to hear stories, so when Lozen heard the roaring in her ears, they could get the women and children to safety quickly.

At dusk the next day, when Lozen could assure them that

the Bluecoats had ridden far away, they returned to see what they could salvage. Victorio was taut with rage as he walked through the ruins, trying to comfort and reassure those who chose to walk the path of peace with him. When they asked why the Bluecoats had attacked them Victorio had no answer, but Lozen knew he blamed Geronimo and Long Neck as much at the Bluecoats.

JOHN CLUM WAS ON A TEAR AGAIN. HIS SHOUTS CARRIED to where the 110 men of his Apache police force had set up camp. Eight companies of the Ninth Cavalry were supposed to have been waiting here at Fort Bowie.

"What do you mean they aren't here? Where in the goddamned hell are the unreliable sons of bitches?"

Dead Shot glanced toward the commandant's office; then he went back to sewing a new sole on his moccasin. "Take cover," he said solemnly in Apache. "Turkey Gobbler is dragging his wings again."

Rafe laughed at the image of that whiffet, Clum, posturing to make himself look larger. He realized, with a start, that he had understood what Dead Shot had said. Dead Shot realized it too. He and Dreamer, Little One, Flattened Penis, Skippy, and Big Mouth beamed at Rafe as though he were a dimwitted child who had just learned a clever trick.

Clum had asked Rafe to take charge of the mule train on this expedition, and Rafe had almost refused. Weeks of heat, thirst, hardship, bother, and sphincter-constricting peril he could abide, but not in John Clum's company. In the past three years, John Clum had protested just about every order, directive, suggestion, and memorandum that the army or the Department of the Interior had sent him. Yet here he was, setting out to follow the government's latest whim telegraphed to him March 20, 1877, a month ago. He was to arrest renegade Apaches. He was to seize stolen horses and restore property to its rightful owners. He was to march the renegades to San Carlos and hold them until they could be tried for murder and robbery.

The idea was foolhardy to the point of insanity, but Clum was enthusiastic about it. Rafe could agree, for once, with the *Arizona Miner*'s editor when he wrote, "The brass and impudence of this young bombast is perfectly ridiculous." But Rafe was between jobs, and, since they would be going to the Warm Springs agency, he might see Lozen.

Once he got to know Clum, Rafe could understand why the Apaches on his police force put up with him. He was charming when he wanted to be. He was honest, courageous, and a demon for hard work. People admired him or hated him, but they were never indifferent on the subject.

Rafe thought of Geronimo whose smile reminded him of Caligula watching lions eat Christians. He remembered Whoa, as imperious on his little brown pony as any Roman caesar.

God knows, Rafe thought, the Apaches are used to arrogant leaders.

The best part of the trip had been getting to know the White Mountain Apache police. Rafe liked to sit at their fires, sharing tobacco and listening to them tell stories, the point of which seemed to be to poke fun at each other. Tonight they were mending their moccasins, cleaning their new breechloading Springfields, and rolling powder and lead balls into squares of paper, then twisting the ends closed to make cartridges. They did all of it with a sort of ferocious domesticity.

Dreamer took from the fire a sharpened green stick threaded with chunks of sizzling venison and handed it to Rafe. Rafe started to blow on it to cool it enough to eat, but the men all grunted in disapproval.

"If you blow on the meat," said Dreamer, "you'll blow the deer away."

While Rafe waited for the venison to cool, he asked the question that had bothered him the entire trip.

"Why do they call that one Flattened Penis?"

Dreamer shrugged, a gesture he'd picked up in his travels. "I don't know. It's just a name."

The talk meandered on, a discussion mostly of the trouble

that Geronimo, Whoa, and the wild Chiricahuas had brought down on everyone. Little One opined that it was fine for the leaders and the young men to go off raiding, but the women and children and old people suffered.

Big Mouth summed up their feelings about the renegades. "We're done with them," he said. "We'll catch them all and lock them up."

"Mba'tsose indee tsokonen," Dead Shot added. "Those Chiricahua people are coyotes."

Rafe was about to head for his cot when Dead Shot started a story. "Long time ago, so they say, Coyote saw some Prairie Dog Women sitting in a circle playing the stave game."

Flattened Penis stood up abruptly and walked away. Rafe snapped to attention. He had figured out that the Apaches' stories were often parables intended to teach some lesson. He had started catching enough of their language to know it was as subtle and enigmatic as any oriental mystic's. He might learn the words, but he would never understand the assumptions and beliefs behind them.

Flattened Penis's abrupt retreat made Rafe think he might get a clue about how the man earned his name. He also realized that Dead Shot had heard his question to Dreamer and had been waiting for a chance to address it. One could not expect immediate answers from Apaches, or even decipherable ones, but the answers came nevertheless if one were patient. They were like the newfangled telegraph with its code of short and long clicks. One had to study them to know what they meant.

Dead Shot told how Coyote convinced gopher to dig a hole up under the prettiest Prairie Dog Woman so he could wiggle in there and poke his thing up into her. But when she felt it, she took a big rock and smashed it. "Make love to this," she said. The men thought the story was side-clutchingly funny.

Rafe wondered if the point of the fable was that Flattened Penis had tried to woo the wrong woman and had suffered for it. If that was the case, he was still suffering for it.

Rafe chuckled to himself. The Apaches' other name for

John Clum was Hat, Soft And Floppy. He was lucky they didn't call him Penis, Soft And Floppy.

GERONIMO WAS ENJOYING A GOURDFUL OF VENISON AND mesquite bean stew and admiring the view at the camp of his half brother, Fun. The view consisted of Broken Foot's fourteen-year-old daughter, Very Pretty, who was visiting Fun's wife. Very Pretty sent Geronimo looks across the cookfire like arrows shot into his heart, the points deeply embedded, shafts vibrating, feathers quivering.

The messenger found Geronimo there at dusk. He said that Hat, Soft And Floppy had come to Warm Springs with only his pet Indians. He said that Hat, Soft And Floppy commanded Geronimo and his most important men to come to a council at the agency the next day.

When the messenger left Geronimo announced he would fight them rather than talk, but Fun proposed a better idea.

THE WARM SPRINGS AGENCY SAT ON A FLAT, DUSTY SHELF of land with hills sweeping up and away from it on all sides. When Geronimo, Fun, his younger brother Eyelash, Old Fatty, Ponce, and the others arrived, the first light of day hadn't even considered making an appearance.

Although no one was around to see them, all the warriors had put on their best beaded moccasins. They wore their feathered war caps and war cords with the amulets dangling from them. They had painted their faces. This would be a foray for plunder, not a council. It would be a joke on Hat, Soft And Floppy.

Geronimo and thirty others strode across the moonlit parade ground, the breeze fluttering the feathers in their caps. They had tied the tin cones so they wouldn't jingle. The only sound was the sough of high leather moccasins brushing against each other, the soft pad of soles, and a faint wheezing from Old Fatty.

Geronimo and his men gathered in front of the commissary. Eyelash poured oil on the rusty hinges of the wide double doors so they wouldn't squeak. Fun wrapped a blanket around the bolt so it wouldn't rattle. Geronimo smiled to himself. He would take what he wanted and be gone before the Pale Eyes knew what had happened.

Fun and Eyelash pulled the doors open, and the men crowded around. From the building's black maw they heard the clicking of more rifle hammers than they could count. They backed out of the doorway and into the moonlight misting across the parade ground. A hundred of Hat, Soft And Floppy's White Mountain coyotes poured out, rifles leveled. They surrounded Geronimo's men at a brisk trot.

"Hold 'em, boys," said Rafe.

He shouted for Clum and then turned his attention to the lively situation on the parade ground. Some of Geronimo's men looked ready to shoot, some looked ready to run, and some looked ready to do both. It reminded Rafe of the time, as a kid, he had trapped a very large rat in the root cellar. He could hear the rat scurrying around, but he didn't know what to do with him.

Damn, but Clum was lucky. The scourge of two countries and a couple hundred thousand square miles had walked into his trap, although it wasn't supposed to have happened this way. Clum had planned to lure Geronimo and his men in for talks and signal the police hidden in the commissary across from agency headquarters.

Clum rushed out onto the porch, tucking in his shirt and pulling on his hat. The hat's wide brim undulated in gentle curves like the surrounding hills. Clum probably intended it to make him look taller, but it had the opposite effect.

He didn't waste time. "If you will listen to my words with good ears," he shouted, "no serious harm will be done to you."

Geronimo managed to laugh and scowl and expand his chest at the same time. He was at least as good at dragging his wings as Clum.

"If you speak wisely no harm will be done to you," he shouted back.

Clum ignored that. "You and your men are to report to the blacksmith shop."

Geronimo's fingers tightened on his Winchester. He knew what the blacksmith meant. He had seen renegade Bluecoats chained like wild mules and locked in a room for long periods of time. His first thought was to start shooting and kill this little upstart, but he realized how badly his people were outmanned and outgunned.

He relaxed. *"Enjuh,"* he said.

No skilled warrior threw his life away when he could live to take revenge later. And Geronimo would have revenge; that was as certain as the sun that was about to rise.

He stood at ease while the police collected his weapons. They marched him and his men to the smithy where the blacksmith riveted shackles to their wrists and ankles. From there the guards directed them to the corral, a large pen of thorny mesquite limbs laid horizontally between pairs of uprights.

"No somos mulas," Geronimo muttered. *"No somos ganado.* We are not mules. We are not cattle." With their chains rattling, he and the others walked into the corral.

On the agency porch, John Clum folded his arms and struck the pose that Rafe had seen so often. For once, Clum had reason to be smug.

"This will put a check on those rascals' depredations." His grin had satisfaction stamped all over it. "Today I'll call in Victorio and Loco and tell them that they and their people must come to San Carlos, too. We'll leave as soon as the cavalry gets here."

"But they're not renegades. They've kept the peace."

"My orders have been changed. I'm now to take all the Warm Springs people back with us, whether they're raiding or not."

He was probably telling the truth about the new orders. That was just the sort of double-dealing policy the Department of the Interior would dream up. It suited John Clum, though. He was determined to concentrate the Apaches not on a series of reservations—feeding stations, as the government called them—but on one. His.

"The Warm Springs people have planted their fields. The corn is already waist high." Rafe remembered the look of joy on Lozen's face as she stood, arms outstretched, inviting him to admire the crop.

Clum gave that impatient wave of his hand. "We'll provide corn for them. A contractor in Central City has offered to buy the crop when it's ripe. I can use the money to get some of the things the Warm Springs people will need."

Rafe shook his head and walked away. Thieving crows were always a problem when corn was ripening, but now those fields would be picked clean by vultures in frock coats.

Chapter 51

UNITED, WE FALL

"The Americans have more copper cartridges than grains of sand in the desert." Dead Shot scooped up a handful of sand and let it sift through his fingers.

The grains sparkled like powdered copper in the fire's light. As though in a trance, Lozen watched them fall. So did the others in her family.

"I feel as you all do," Dead Shot said, "I do not want to see any more of our people killed. We have to learn to exist with the Pale Eyes as we exist with winter storms, with rattlesnakes, with drought."

"I went to Wah-sin-ton." Dreamer spoke from the shadows. He had gone east with Hat, Soft And Floppy, and he still wore the silver medallion that President Grant had given him.

He had been so quiet they had almost forgotten he was there. He was used to being called a liar when he told these stories, but he had to tell them, anyway. To keep quiet would be the same as not warning them of a terrible flood rushing toward them.

"The Pale Eyes have lodges of stone as big as a mesa, as tall as a cliff. More people live there than you have seen in your life. I rode in an iron wagon that does not need a horse to pull it. Men put black rocks in it, and it breathes fire and smoke. It makes as much noise as an avalanche, and it rushes along faster than a horse can run."

"We have heard of those things," said Victorio. "We have eyes. We can see that Life Giver has granted the Pale Eye great power. We must find a way to live in the same country with them."

"It is impossible to resist them." Loco hunched in the shadows as though trying to gather night around him. His scars blended with the deep creases in his face, and he looked old, drained of ambition.

They sat in silence for a while. They were all tired and disheartened. They had spent most of the day in council discussing the ultimatum that Hat, Soft And Floppy had given them. The talk had been contentious.

Victorio had ended it by saying, "Each must do what he thinks is best. My family and I are going to San Carlos. If we do not like it there, we will come back."

Hat, Soft And Floppy had said he wanted to know how many would be making the trip, so they had taken a count: 324 people had decided to leave with Victorio and Lozen. Almost as many voted to go to Mexico with Long Neck. And 110 of Geronimo's band would travel with Victorio's people. Broken Foot had his own plans.

When Dreamer and Dead Shot saw Broken Foot approaching, they stood up and melted into the darkness. They knew how he felt about them. He had remarked that those who betrayed their own should be hunted down. The old man didn't intend to go to Mexico, but for once he sided with Long Neck. He could not believe that Victorio would meekly follow that strutting Pale Eyes turkey gobbler, Hat, Soft And Floppy.

Broken Foot, Her Eyes Open, and Wide led their horses into the fire's light. Pouches and baskets of their belongings hung from the horses' saddles and were piled across their hindquarters. Fights Without Arrows came, too. In the shadows at the edge of the fire's light, Wah-sin-ton and Sets Him Free sat on their ponies and held the lines of a pair of mules loaded with weapons and ammunition. Wah-sin-ton would hide the weapons in a nearby cave so Victorio could retrieve them if he decided to leave San Carlos and return to Warm Springs.

Very Pretty stood sullen and silent off to one side. She wanted to stay with Geronimo, and she was furious that her parents insisted she come with them. Wide was just as furious. "That *Bedonkohe* Coyote has put a spell on my daughter," she would mutter.

A month ago Broken Foot had asked Lozen to hold a sing to try to restore Wide's good humor, but it hadn't had much effect. Wide had been happy to see Geronimo in chains. She thought maybe that would discourage Very Pretty, but it hadn't.

Broken Foot solemnly pretended to count them all like Hat, Soft And Floppy did. Then he pretended to forget where he was and counted them again. Each time he arrived at a different number. He did a good imitation, but no one laughed.

Broken Foot and the families who chose to go with him were headed for the Mescalero reservation on the Tulerosa River. He planned to camp with Wide's family there.

"Are you leaving now?" Victorio asked.

"Yes. We want to be far away by the time the Bluecoats get here." Broken Foot lowered himself onto a log and sat with his knees almost in the fire. He had seen seventy harvests, and he seemed to be growing in reverse, getting shorter as time passed. His joints, though, had become bigger each year. They pained him constantly, but he would never admit it. The heat felt good on them.

"We'll take the old ones to the agency and get ration tickets for them," he said. "The young men and the horses will stay in the valley across the mountain so they can come and go whenever they want. We'll register their wives and families with the older men who are left." He winked. "The Pale Eyes will think we old farts have a lot of stamina, to keep so many wives."

"Come with us, brother," said Her Eyes Open.

"Many of our young men have gone to raid with Long Neck." Victorio's voice was tired. "And many have died there. Their women and children and old ones have no one to bring them meat and hides. Their children cry with hunger. Hat, Soft And Floppy says he will care for the women and the old ones."

"They'll feed us on the Tulerosa."

"Hat, Soft And Floppy says all those Mescaleros will have to move to San Carlos soon. I do not want the old ones to have to make two such long, hard trips."

She Moves Like Water didn't try to keep the bitterness out of her voice. "Hat, Soft And Floppy says he intends to unite our people—the White Mountain bands, the San Carlos, the Tontos, the Aravaipas, the Coyoteros, the Cibicu, the Chiricahua, the Red Paints, even Long Neck and his Enemy People."

"That's not possible," said Fights Without Arrows. "The people over there hate us. And we hate them."

"Grandmother," Wide asked Lozen, "What do you think?"

Lozen looked up, her face shadowed in the fire's light. "If I were alone," she said softly, "I would ride south to Mexico. But there is no worse lot than to live without family. Our people depend on us. We cannot abandon them now. My brother is my heart, my right arm. I will go wherever he goes."

"They say that at San Carlos the flies eat the eyes out of the horses in the summertime," said Fights Without Arrows.

"If we cannot live there, we'll leave," Victorio said.

Broken Foot got up, limped to his pony, and tightened the cinch. He and his people made their good-byes, going to each person and murmuring. "May we live to see each other again." Wah-sin-ton dismounted and embraced his father. He turned, mounted, and rode away with Sets Him Free, Broken Foot, and the others.

CAESAR AND THE MEN OF THE NINTH RODE IN FRONT OF the long line of people on foot and on horseback. Rafe and the Apache police brought up the rear. Caesar had recommended that Clum take the Apaches around Central City, but he had refused. Caesar understood why. Clum had the hated Geronimo and five of his henchmen in chains in a wagon, and more than four hundred Apaches straggling behind him. He would want to make a show of them.

The image of rounding the people up that morning and

driving them from their village haunted Caesar. Women and children had cried and clung to those who refused to go. They had run to get a few last things from their lodges. They had put the sick on the ponies or rigged litters to carry them. The old people hobbled on foot carrying baskets and bundles. The soldiers had burned the lodges behind them, to discourage them from changing their minds.

Maybe Clum didn't know what the reactions of the citizens of Central City would be—or maybe he didn't care. No matter. Caesar called back to his men to sit straight in their saddles and to look straight ahead. All of them knew what to expect. Most of the white folks in Central City were Southerners, and they hated everyone equally—the Apache police, the Apache prisoners, the black soldiers, and their white officers, most of whom were from the North.

"Whatever anyone says or does," he told them, "do not make a reply. Do not look to the left or to the right."

The jeers started as soon as they passed the first building at the end of the main street. Women gathered in small clumps at a safe distance. Men poured out of the saloons, boardinghouses, and mercantiles. "The gum'ment's put uniforms on a bunch of niggers."

The white officers didn't fare any better. People shouted, "Damned Yankees," "Nigger-lovers," and worse at them.

Caesar heard the jeers turn to curses when they saw the wagon with Geronimo and the other Apache leaders. Caesar knew that they would not content themselves with words. They would throw dirt, dung, rocks, vegetables, whatever came to hand.

Caesar wanted to turn and look. He wanted to ride alongside Stands Alone and He Makes Them Laugh and their two boys. He wanted to protect them, to shield them from the humiliation, but he could not.

Life is hard, he thought. Life is just too damned hard.

THE ROAD TO SAN CARLOS LED THROUGH THE MOUNTAINS. Freezing temperatures at night and burning sun in the day did not make the trip easier. John Clum counted heads every evening, and every evening the count went down. In the morning a body usually needed burial, and sometimes more than one. Also men slipped away in the darkness, leaving the rest, stone-faced, to continue the march.

Rafe tried to help an old man carrying a burden basket with his crippled wife in it. The man had cut holes in the basket for her legs. He had crossed rivers with her on his back and clambered over rocks and deadfalls. Rafe managed to convince him to let him carry her up one of the steepest slopes, but he hovered behind, worried that Rafe would drop her. He refused to let anyone take her from him again.

At the start of the journey, Victorio's family gave their horses to those who needed them more. They kept one for She Who Has Become Old, the mother of She Moves Like Water and Corn Stalk, but the pony had died soon after they left. Corn Stalk and She Moves Like Water took turns helping their mother along the roughest parts of the trail.

Lozen carried the cradleboard of Daughter's baby boy so Daughter could walk for a while unburdened. Daughter was also trying to distract Pretty Mouth, whose incessant complaints made their good-natured husband, Mangas, even more dejected. Mangas' friends suggested that he beat Pretty Mouth, but Mangas knew better than to try it. Pretty Mouth would turn on him like a rattler and cause him more embarrassment.

Daughter's seven-year-old daughter, Beside Her, led her sister who whimpered as she stumbled along, trying to keep up. Lozen knelt so she could put her hands on the child's small shoulders.

"Do not cry," she said gently. "Do not complain. Do not falter. Show the Pale Eyes that The People are not weak."

Lozen told stories and encouraged the weakest until her voice grew hoarse. Rafe figured that by the time they arrived, she would have walked much more than twice the distance because she went from one end of the line to the other, many times a day.

Rafe rode up from the rear where the Apache police

walked. He dismounted, and with flourishes that sent each laughing child in a swooping arc, he lifted Little Sister and Beside Her into his saddle. Without asking permission he took the cradleboard's tumpline from Lozen's forehead and hung it on the pommel.

"I found a place for She Who Becomes Old in the supply wagon," he said.

Lozen smiled her thanks. She Moves Like Water's mother had been growing weaker and coughing constantly. Rafe wondered if she would reach San Carlos.

He Makes Them Laugh took advantage of Rafe's arrival to start up where he'd left off the night before. He cheered the children by making up stories about Rafe. "Hairy Foot eats rocks and scorpions and cactus spines," he told them. "He has twenty-three wives and a hundred children. His penis is so big that at night he drapes a canvas over it like a tent so all his children can sleep under its shelter."

Lozen could hear the stories, too, and Rafe felt his cheeks grow hot with embarrassment. He had almost decided to retreat back to the rear of the column when He Makes Them Laugh wandered off to annoy Hat, Soft And Floppy. Rafe had a feeling that he intended to distract the agent from his lectures to Victorio.

Clum had dogged Victorio for most of the trip. He talked about the advantages of the Warm Springs people uniting with their northern Apache brothers to form one strong, progressive, civilized nation. He outlined his plans for an Apache court at San Carlos with Victorio as one of the judges. Victorio kept his face neutral, but Rafe could imagine what he was thinking. Clum wanted to make Victorio a jailer in his own prison, and Victorio was plenty smart enough to know it.

"Where is the big red horse?" Lozen asked.

"Killed," he said.

They walked in a silence accented by the sound of the chestnut's hoofbeats behind them and the two girls chattering together on his back. Rafe thought of Dead Shot, the White Mountain scout. He had taken a shine to one of the young

Warm Springs women. He had been sharing his food with her and she accepted it, which, as Rafe understood the custom, meant she had taken a shine to him, too.

She and Dead Shot were supposed to be enemies, but Rafe had seen the looks they gave each other. He wondered if he himself might ever see that look in Lozen's eyes. He could make simple conversation in her language now, but simple conversation with a woman who enchanted him was as hard to carry on in Apache as it was in English or Spanish.

Rafe knew how to say, "I love you," *Shil danohshoo*. The words meant. "With me, you are nice." He knew they would stick in his throat if he ever tried to say them, but he couldn't help wondering what she would answer if he told her that. He wondered what her reaction would be if he asked her to marry him, to be his companion for life.

Lozen opened her medicine bag and took out the Indian-head penny that Rafe had given her. She looked pensive as she rubbed her thumb across the woman's face, feeling the raised lines of her feather headdress. She held it up so he could see it. Grains of pollen clung to it and to her fingers.

"Dreamer says these marks can talk," she said.

Rafe looked at the single word engraved there. "Yes, they can."

"What do the marks say?"

"Liberty," Rafe answered.

Chapter 52

THE DEVIL MADE HER DO IT

In June of 1877, Cheis's youngest son, Naiche, stood outside John Clum's door. Naiche was seventeen. He had not received his warrior status yet. His name meant Mischievous and it fit him.

He was a handsome boy. Some said he was handsomer than Cheis, but no one had ever taken him seriously, least of all his father. As he came each morning to stand motionless in the full glare of the sun while the agency routine bustled around him, he had acquired dignity.

Everyone knew why he stood there. He was waiting for Hat, Soft And Floppy to tell him what had happened to his older brother, Taza. John Clum took Taza and nineteen other young men east with him to put on an exhibition of dance at the Centennial Exposition in Philadelphia. From there they went to Washington. The other men came back, but Taza did not. Everyone believed the Pale Eyes had poisoned him just as they'd poisoned his father, Cheis. When Clum repeatedly refused Naiche's request to talk to him, the young man took up his vigil.

Victorio and the other Warm Springs men were hauling dirt, water, and straw to make adobe bricks for more buildings, so Lozen and her niece and sisters waited for the family's rations. The line that started at the window where the food was distributed stretched the length of the office and warehouse and snaked around the corner. Three thousand people from various Apache subtribes had gathered for the sugar, coffee, cornmeal, and that white powdery flour that stuck to their fingers when they mixed it with water. Quarrels would almost certainly break out as tempers and old animosities flared up.

Heat battered them like clubs. The air teemed with flies that crawled over the eyes of the infants in the cradleboards. Smaller children were assigned to wave them away, but the flies plagued them, too, landing on the mosquito bites that the little ones had scratched raw and bleeding. Lozen heard coughing up and down the line.

They all wanted to receive their sacks of food and leave before twilight, when the mosquitoes arrived like a black fog. People fed green branches onto the fires then and sat in the smoke. Lozen spent a lot of time singing at the bedsides of those racked with malaria. Sometimes they got well. Sometimes they didn't.

The land assigned to the Warm Springs people was called The Flats. No trees grew there. No mountains offered cool, shaded canyons with streams flowing through them. Most nights when Lozen's family gathered at the fire they talked about leaving, but they knew that if they abandoned the old ones here, they might not be able to come back for them for a long time.

Lozen had never seen her brother so uncertain, so distraught. The longer they stayed, the harder it was to leave because there were fewer able-bodied people and more of those who would have to be left behind. Victorio confessed to Lozen that he made the wrong decision. They should have gone with Broken Foot. Victorio was waiting for the young men to return from raiding. They would bring supplies to feed the women and children when they all fled this place. The wait became more difficult each day.

Victorio felt as though he'd dug himself into a pit. The more he tried to free himself, the more sand fell in on him. Lozen saw him suffocating with doubt and worry. She remembered how enraged and humiliated Cheis had looked in the years after the white men betrayed him and hung his relatives up by ropes. Victorio had the same look.

No one could see how the situation could get worse, and then it did. At the end of June, John Clum resigned in a blizzard of insults and accusations. Maybe he was angry because his superiors would not increase his salary in spite of the fact that he had assembled more than 4,500 Apaches here.

Maybe he was mortified that his prize exhibits—Geronimo, Ponce, and Old Fatty—had slithered off into the night not long after he gave in to Eskiminzin's threats of a mutiny and had the blacksmith remove their shackles. Maybe he was coming to realize the magnitude of his responsibility. Maybe the wailing of the women got on his nerves when he finally told Naiche that his brother had died of pneumonia in Wahsin-ton and been buried with a fine ceremony.

Maybe he was angry because his work here had not gained him the acclaim he thought he deserved. Maybe he was frustrated because nothing he could do would ever turn San Carlos into the tranquil Eden he envisioned. His charges all spoke the same language, and still the enterprise was a tower of Babel. Maybe the mosquitoes and the heat got to him, and the tarantulas, the scorpions, and the rattlers that moved into his new quarters before he did. And so he left.

The man who replaced him made everyone appreciate Hat, Soft And Floppy. At least Clum had been honest. Soon after Henry Hart took over, shipments of tools, blankets, and food began to disappear. The weekly quota of flour lasted only three days. Coffee and sugar were cut by fifty percent. Hart issued hundreds of passes to the women to go looking for wild food, but they didn't find much.

Mines and sawmills sprang up inside the reservation borders. White ranchers started timbering and grazing their cattle there. Mormons settled on adjoining land. They diverted the river, destroying the irrigation systems that the Apaches had constructed with their bare hands. Some of the Warm Springs men went to the mines to look for work. Many of them bought whiskey there, and some were killed in ensuing fights.

One sweltering night late in August of 1878, Hairy Foot appeared in the cloud of mosquito-repelling smoke belching from the fire of green wood. He dipped his tin cup into the pot of stew. He sat with Victorio and Mangas and He Makes Them Laugh. Lozen stood where she could watch him.

Even given the fact that Hairy Foot must have strong magic, Lozen couldn't explain the odd sensation in her chest whenever she saw him. She felt as though his spirit were tugging at hers. She recognized him as one of those rare individuals who stood outside the boundaries of race and nationality, of language and beliefs. She also sensed what other women knew about Rafe, that he loved them not for what he could get from them, but for who they were.

He gave out the coffee and tobacco he had brought, and the blankets. He distributed lengths of bright calico to each of the women and penny whistles to the children. They started blowing into them with all their might, but they stopped when they saw him reach into his pocket again. He took out a small, horseshoe-shaped metal object with a thin projection in the middle.

He put it between his lips, vibrated the center piece with his finger, and blew a frisky tune that sounded as though he had a mouthful of cicadas. Lozen tapped out the rhythm with a stick on the stew pot, and Daughter's children danced to it. Two-year-old Charlie Mangas stomped and whirled with a ferocity that made everyone laugh. Lozen had the feeling Hairy Foot knew that the music and the laughter were the best present he could bring them.

Rafe played several more tunes before he put the mouth harp away, and the children curled up on the new blankets laid out where the smoke would roll over them. Rafe spoke his stumbling Apache in the low, diffident tones of the people around him. He had known for a long time that Apache, like its close relative Navajo, had to be the most difficult form of communication ever invented. Any white man who thought the Apaches were a simple, primitive people had never tried to learn their language.

"They say that you are not receiving as much issue corn as you used to. They say you do not see as much coffee, sugar, or beef, either."

"*Gunku,*" Victorio said. "That's true."

"And the flour is mostly chaff," said Rafe.

"Gunku!" She Moves Like Water agreed emphatically.

They all leaned forward to listen as Rafe told them about the Tucson Ring. A group of businessmen there connived with Harry Hart, the new agent, to sell the goods to the mining camps and the local merchants. They used the talking wires to communicate with Hart. A corrupt government inspector was altering the reports to cover the thefts.

"In English, *Harry* is another name for *chidin*, the devil," he said.

"He is well named," said Victorio.

"Dreamer told me that in English your name is Hairy," added Lozen.

"Do you think I'm a devil?"

"Lashi." She smiled. "Maybe."

"Harry Hart switches the good flour for the bad grown around here. He has men unload the inferior goods to distribute to you. Then they drive the wagons to a ranch to the south. The bad men meet them there and collect the better merchandise."

Rafe had seen the shipment's invoice, and he told them what was on it—food, clothing, blankets, knives, axes, shoes, cloth, even a case of lucifers packed in small boxes of a hundred each. He told them what route the wagons would take and when they would be passing. He described the best place to hide along the way. He mentioned that White Mountain men would be driving. Harry Hart was so greedy he would rather order the people being robbed to deliver the goods than pay outsiders.

When Rafe left, Victorio and Lozen looked at each other with a grim sort of glee. They understood Hairy Foot's unspoken message as easily as Harry Hart read the decoded, staccato language of the talking wires.

RAFE ARRIVED EARLY AT THE PLACE HE HAD DESCRIBED AS superb for an ambush. He led the string of four army mules he had borrowed. He had won the use of them playing cards with the captain of the small garrison at San Carlos. The captain knew Rafe was up to something, but he was so disgusted with Harry Hart he didn't care. Rafe knew he could have used his own wagon team, but they were used to pulling, not packing. Mules were creatures of custom, and he didn't want to risk delays trying to turn them into pack animals.

Rafe found Victorio, Mangas, He Makes Them Laugh, and a couple spavined, sore-backed mules standing around the telegraph pole. The mules were grazing. The men were gazing skyward. Lozen, dressed in breechclout, moccasins, and belted army shirt, perched with her legs wrapped around the top of the pole. She cut the wire with her knife.

"My heart is glad to see you, Hairy Foot," she called to him.

She eased down the pole, leaping the last ten feet to land lightly. Rafe noticed that she was wearing a necklace made from the spent casings of copper cartridges. She led one of the mules to where the wire dragged the ground. She jumped onto his back and stood up so she could cut off as much of the iron wire as she could reach.

She held up the coil of it. "We can string beads on this and make bracelets for the feast of Broken Foot's daughter."

The thought occurred to Rafe that Broken Foot and his lovely, petulant daughter had gone to live with the Mescaleros on the Tulerosa reserve a couple hundred miles away, but he knew that Lozen knew that. Distance seemed to mean little to Apaches.

Rafe assessed the single weapon they had among them, Victorio's Winchester. "Are you going to rob the wagon train with one gun?"

"We will shame the White Mountain drivers," said Victorio. "They know that they're doing wrong, but I think maybe they aren't men enough to defy Da'ighaazha Chidin, Hairy Devil."

Rafe knew they meant the Indian agent, Harry Hart, but this wasn't the time to explain the difference between *Harry* and *Hairy.* Or *Hart* and *heart,* for that matter. "Do you have cartridges for the carbine?"

"No." Victorio's smile was equal parts resignation and devil-may-care.

They picketed the mules out of sight and took up positions in the rocks near the trail. Lozen sprinkled dust over Rafe and showed him how to make himself part of the landscape. As he lay near her, he tried to ignore the itches that tormented his nose, his ear, his right shoulder, left side, leg, foot, and most places in between, but he couldn't have gotten the grin off his face if his life had depended on it. He had never, in all his reveries on those long rides between towns and forts, imagined he would be lurking on this side of an Apache ambush.

When the wagons appeared, Rafe walked to the middle of the trail. He thought about pulling his bandana up to hide the lower part of his face, but that seemed ridiculous. He did feel like a highwayman, holding up his right hand and cradling his Sharps in the crook of his left arm. The first wagon jolted to a stop, as did the one that followed it. Victorio, Lozen, Mangas, and He Makes Them Laugh appeared from their hiding places. The drivers must have known they were going to be robbed, but the presence of a Pale Eyes made the transaction seem official.

Rafe recognized the driver of the first wagon. "Big Mouth, how is your family?"

Big Mouth answered warily. "My family is good, Hairy Foot, but my wife's mother is sick. Maybe the *di-yin* will come to our camp and sing for her." He pointed his chin at Lozen.

Lozen gave him a look that indicated she would consider it.

"Leave the wagons here," said Victorio. "We will not hurt you."

The drivers climbed down and started back on foot. Their moccasins sent up puffs of dust with each step. Victorio had served as a magistrate on John Clum's tribal court. He understood a little bit about the white men's system of justice.

He called after them. "If someone speaks against Hairy Foot in the Pale Eyes' council, that man will regret it." As for himself, he knew he would get into trouble, but he didn't care. He surveyed the wagons, goods, and animals stalled in the middle of the road. "We must move these before someone comes."

"We can drive them to that arroyo." Rafe looked up and down the empty road. "No one will see us there, and we can choose what's useful and unload and repack. You should take only what's rightfully yours and leave the wagon mules here.

"Enjuh," said Victorio.

"Do you know how to drive a wagon and mule team?"

"No."

"We can learn," said Lozen.

"I'm sure you can."

Rafe assigned He Makes Them Laugh the job of leading the mules. Victorio and Mangas were to take the second wagon, and he would manage the first one. Lozen could come along with him. He showed Victorio where the brake was, told him how to hold the reins and what to do with them, and gave him a quick lesson in cracking a whip. He expected to handle the first team himself, but when he climbed aboard, Lozen was sitting in the driver's seat with the reins in her hands.

He shook his head in exasperation, reluctant to waste more time teaching her. As it turned out, it took precious little time. Lozen set the mules in motion as if she had been staging all her life.

"So, Chidin Alch'ise, Little Devil . . ." She looked over at him. "How do you like being a wild Apache renegade?"

He threw his head back and laughed. The two of them joked and chuckled all the way to the transfer point in the arroyo. Rafe couldn't remember when he had felt this happy.

WHEN HARRY HART CALLED RAFE INTO HIS OFFICE A FEW days later, he didn't have to guess what the topic of conversation would be. Hart's tantrum made John Clum's look like tempests in a coffee pot. He screamed at Rafe that he would never work for the government again.

"And when I prove that you are responsible for the theft of government goods, I will see that you rot in jail."

Rafe smiled and laid Victorio's gift, the war club, on the desk. Hart gave it the look Rafe had come to expect and anticipate with pleasure. He stared at it as though it were a rattlesnake. He grew pale around his dingy collar.

"If any more wagons lose their way and wander into your Tucson friends' clutches . . ." Rafe gave him a wolf's grin. "There will be hell to pay."

Rafe walked out, still wolfish about the gills. Hart's threats didn't bother him. In the past thirty years, he had outlasted scores of army officers, governors, commissioners, Indian agents, and bureaucrats of indeterminate stripe. He would outlast this one, too. As for Victorio and Lozen, now that they had supplies, only one lack prevented them from bolting like a spooked team with the bit in their teeth. They needed horses.

The White Mountain people had plenty of them grazing loose. Dead Shot and the boys had told Rafe that Lozen's nickname was Tlii-yin'iihne, She Steals Horses. Taking her neighbors' mounts would be a cakewalk for her.

Rafe decided to keep his chestnut with him even when he visited the privy.

Chapter 53

OUT OF THE POT AND INTO THE LINE OF FIRE

When Victorio and Lozen came back from a council, they found Broken Foot smoking a cigarillo and warming his swollen joints at the fire. He wore a shiny tin pot upside down on his head, a sharp, new ax stuck into the back of his belt, and a happy smile. When he stood up, his knees and ankles cracked like distant rifle fire.

"*Ha'anakah*, you are come." Victorio and Lozen embraced him.

"Where are the young men?" asked Victorio.

"They've camped among the tall pines to the east." Broken Foot corrected himself. "Some of them are waiting there. The others have come here to see their sweethearts, their wives, their children. Right now, Brother, your son is probably whispering through the back wall of Maria's daughter's lodge. He'll be here soon."

They knew that everyone would be here soon. They would come for the distribution of the stolen issue goods stacked under She Moves Like Water's arbor. Broken Foot lifted the canvas that covered the bounty and peered under it.

"Have you been on a raid to Mexico?" he asked.

"No. Just as far as the road to Tucson."

"The road to Tucson is more convenient than Mexico." Broken Foot looked pleased and relieved that the man he called Brother had not turned into a cringing dog trotting after the Pale Eyes, like his old friend, Loco. Broken Foot sat down and turned up the heat on his knees again.

"You have been on a raid yourself, Uncle." Lozen tapped on the tin pot.

"No." Broken Foot adjusted the pot at a steadier angle.

"We took these from a wagonload of things that the agent was delivering to his friends instead of to us."

"Then the situation at the Tulerosa isn't any better than here."

"It's not good, but I think it's better than here. The Mescaleros are easier to get along with than the White Mountain people." He rolled a cigarillo. "Your son has brought you many things from Mexico. One more raid, and the council will consider voting him warrior rank." Broken Foot didn't point out that the boy had served his apprenticeship with men other than his own father. "You've trained him well. He'll be a good fighter and a leader."

Lozen held out the coil of iron wire. "This is for your daughter's feast."

"We have decided to hold her feast at Warm Springs, even if we have to fight every Pale Eyes in the country." Broken Foot took the pot off his head, put the wire inside it, and set it back on his head. "The young men have hidden supplies and weapons in the usual places along the trail south. Come with us, brother."

"Did you bring extra horses?" asked Victorio.

"We stole some, but the army chased us and took them back. We have only what we're riding."

"I went to Big Mouth's camp to talk to his wife about a sing for her mother." said Lozen. "The White Mountain people have at least two hundred ponies. They'll be easy to take. The boys can go with me."

She was happy at the prospect of stealing horses again with her old friends, Fights Without Arrows, Chato, and Flies In His Stew.

THEY HAD HAD TO LEAVE THE OLDEST AND THE FEEBLEST people behind, but over three hundred women and children and sixty warriors left San Carlos under cover of darkness. Lozen rode up and down the line, encouraging the weaker ones, looking for stragglers, and urging people not to lag.

When morning came, Lozen's spirits sent her a warning.

She joined Victorio and Broken Foot at the head of the column.

"Can you tell how many are coming?" Victorio asked.

"A lot."

Fights Without Arrows, Flies In His Stew, and Chato returned from their scout and confirmed it.

"At least two hundred are following us," said Fights Without Arrows. "We saw Bluecoats. We saw the Pale Eyes' White Mountain scouts. We saw white men from the country all around here. They must have left this morning before light."

"Too bad we can't go back and raid that country," said Chato. "No one is left there to protect the stock."

"Most of the White Mountain men are on foot, but they're trotting along like Old Man Coyote."

"Those White Mountain men are mad about all the horses we took from them." The smile filled the deepest crevasses of Broken Foot's face. "I bet they feel pretty foolish."

Lozen leaned sideways on her piebald pony so she could murmur to her brother. "They expect us to head for Mexico. If the women and children break into small groups and turn east into the mountains, Fights Without Arrows, Chato, Flies In His Stew, and I will cover their tracks."

"The rest of us men can keep riding south to leave a trail," said Victorio. "When we come to Ash Creek, we'll scatter, double back, and meet you at Three Flat Rocks."

The plan worked for a while. For ten days they kept to the high ground and evaded their pursuers. As the band's animals gave out, the young men swooped down on the ranches in the valleys and stole more.

The local ranger company gave up about two days into the chase. The other civilians drifted off to protect their own livestock. After a week, the soldiers returned to San Carlos for supplies. The White Mountain men and the police, with Dead Shot as their leader, kept going. Dead Shot and the others could follow tracks through rough country, and the White Mountain men wanted their horses back.

They caught up with Victorio's people and pinned them

against a sheer cliff. Victorio's warriors and Lozen kept up a covering fire, but the women and children had nowhere to go. The White Mountain scouts captured several of them and rounded up the horses.

Then Lozen and the others saw Dead Shot raise his rifle and signal the White Mountain men to leave with the captives and the horses. They had gotten what they'd come for, and they'd just as soon Victorio and his people didn't return to San Carlos. In his own way, Dead Shot was letting them know he understood why they were going, and maybe he even wished them well.

On foot, the Warm Springs people traveled east and south for hundreds of miles through the mountains. They crossed lava beds and broken buttes, peaks, and canyons until they reached the country they knew so well. Then came the hard part, living through the deep snows and freezing cold of winter with few horses, their food supply exhausted, and hunted by every Pale Eyes for a hundred miles around.

IN MARCH 1878 LT. CHARLES MERRITT WAS STARTLED TO see Victorio and twenty-two warriors ride in to the fort that once had been the Warm Springs agency. They were ragged and emaciated, and their ponies looked as though they could drop dead on the spot. Lieutenant Merritt called for an interpreter and beckoned Victorio into his office. He set a chair near the stove for him, but Victorio stood with his blanket wrapped around him.

"We're willing to surrender," he said, "if you'll let us stay here. We want to bring our old ones home, but we would rather die than go back to San Carlos."

Merritt thought about it. The army and the irate citizenry had been chasing this man all over two territories, and now here he was, standing in the office, making a very reasonable request.

"You have my sympathy. I know this is your home country." He offered Victorio a cigar, but he waved it away. "You can stay until I receive orders telling me what to do. If you and your people make no trouble, I'll supply you with food."

"We will cause no trouble."

Merritt believed him. While he and his superior, Colonel Hatch, waited to hear from Washington, Merritt arranged for the old ones at San Carlos to be sent by wagons to Warm Springs. He managed to have an agent assigned to the post to distribute food and blankets. The new agent was rigid and arrogant. Neither Lieutenant Merritt nor Victorio liked him, but at least he did his job with a fair degree of honesty.

Given the wrangling between the Indian Bureau and the War Department in Washington, Merritt realized he might never hear from them. For once, their inefficiency might have a good effect. Victorio's people lived quietly through the summer and fall. They farmed their old fields. They stole no horses or cattle. They did nothing to molest the settlers crowding in around them, and even became friends with some of them. None of that was good enough.

LOZEN AND HER SISTERS LOOKED OVER THE HEAPS OF PIÑON nuts, berries, and cactus fruit. The harvest had been good. Ears of corn lay in colorful heaps in all the arbors. They would have enough food this winter.

Victorio and fifteen of his men galloped across the dance ground. Victorio gave a hawk's shrill whistle to signal the boys to bring in the rest of the horses. The men scattered to their families' camps. Victorio leaped off his pony before he had stopped. Lozen had never seen such a wild look in his eyes.

She grabbed the carbine that Wah-sin-ton had given her, and her pouch of cartridges. She Moves Like Water, Corn Stalk, Stands Alone, and María prepared for flight. Daughter called the children.

Victorio talked fast as he stuffed food, ammunition, his fire drill, extra rawhide rope, and spare moccasins into a saddle pouch. "The Pale Eyes judge and sheriff from Central City are at the Fort. Dead Shot says they plan to arrest me.

The agent says the Bluecoats will take us all back to San Carlos."

"They will not put chains on you and lock you up like they did Geronimo." Lozen was ready to kill anyone who tried.

"We won't go back to San Carlos," said She Moves Like Water.

"That's what I told them." Victorio tied the blankets behind his saddle. "I did what I have wanted to do for a long time. I pulled the agent's beard so hard he couldn't straighten his neck afterward. I would rather have killed him."

Daughter carried her youngest son in a cradleboard. The rest of her young ones gathered around her. Besides her own, she and Corn Stalk were caring for several orphans. "What about the children?"

"Go with the Bluecoats. They'll feed you all until we can come for you." Victorio followed She Moves Like Water to the lodge. "You must stay here."

"I'm coming with you."

"Dead Shot says the Bluecoats have orders to shoot any of us men and boys they see. They will not give us a chance to surrender. If you are with us, they will kill you, too."

She Moves Like Water reached up to touch his cheek. "I will not go anywhere without you."

She hugged Corn Stalk, Daughter, and the children. Each of them murmured, "May we live to see each other again."

SOLDIERS AND SCOUTS OF THE NINTH CAVALRY CAUGHT UP with Victorio and his sixty warriors in the Black Mountains. All around them, snake-tongues of lightning flicked at the horizon and thunder rumbled. Dodging bullets, Victorio, Lozen, Wah-sin-ton, and the others dismounted and scattered up the slope, taking cover and firing as they went. When Victorio ran out of cartridges for his Winchester, he handed it to She Moves Like Water and took from her the old musket she had primed and loaded.

They reached the series of ledges as a frigid wind roared

through and a bolt of lightning struck a mesquite tree on a nearby promontory. The detonation of thunder left their ears ringing, and the first huge drops of rain began exploding around them.

They knew these mountains well. The heap of boulders behind them had an opening at ground level. They could slither through it before the Bluecoats knew they had gone. Once on the other side they could disperse into the creases and folds of the mountains. Victorio motioned for the men to go on while he and Wah-sin-ton and Lozen kept up a steady fire to draw the soldiers' attention and keep their heads down. He shouted over the thunder and gunfire for She Moves Like Water to go with the men, but she took his empty musket and went on loading.

A bullet struck a nearby rock and shattered it. A chunk of it hit She Moves Like Water's hand and sent the sack of bullets flying. She crawled out along the ledge to reach for it, and another bullet hit her in the head. She pitched sideways, with her legs over the cliff's rim, and began to slide down, the wind whipping her long hair across her face.

"Mother!" Wah-sin-ton screamed.

Victorio scrambled toward her. He made a desperate grab and caught one blowing corner of the blanket she had draped across her shoulders. He pulled on it, but it came loose. Her arms dragged along the ground, pulled backward by the weight of her body. Victorio's fingers grazed hers as she disappeared over the edge.

Lozen crawled to him. "Come away," she shouted into the wind. "You can do nothing here."

She saw the bewilderment and the disbelief in his eyes. He slid on his stomach toward the rim of the cliff, maybe to convince himself that she was really dead and not clinging to a tree root or some rocks just below the edge. Lozen knew that her sister had been dead before she fell. She held on to Victorio's moccasin with both hands.

"Her spirit is gone," Lozen screamed. "Come away now!"

Still on his hands and knees, Victorio wailed his grief and loss and rage. When the echoes of it died, Wah-sin-ton took his father's arm and pulled him away. As though in a trance, Victorio followed them through the opening in the rocks.

On the exposed slope on the other side, the icy wind blew the torrents of rain slantwise at them. Sleet and hailstones pelted them while thunder exploded one peal after the other. Lightning-struck trees crashed around them. The thunder and lightning frightened Lozen, but she was grateful for the rain. Even the Ndee scouts could not track them through this.

They found a large boulder with a huge cedar fallen at a slant across it. Tangled with it were tree roots, trunks, and branches weathered to a silvery gray. They crawled under its shelter and pressed against the boulder. Lozen chanted to keep Thunder from hurting them.

Continue in a good way;
Be kind as you pass through;
Do not frighten these poor people.
My Grandfather, let it be well.
Don't frighten us, your people.

Wah-sin-ton moved forward at a crouch and stared out at the storm. The blowing rain washed the tears from his cheeks. Lozen put her arms around Victorio. He leaned his head against her chest and sobbed for a long time. When the rain slowed, he went out to stand with his arms up. The wind blew his wet hair and his breechclout around him.

"No more peace," he shouted. "For as long as I live there will be war."

PART FOUR
1878

Warrior

Coyote and Walking Rock

Long time ago, so they say, Coyote was walking around. He came to some other coyotes sitting near a big rock.

"You'd better show this rock respect," they said. "It's alive."

"Don't be silly," Coyote said. "Rocks aren't alive."

"It can move fast, so you'd better be careful."

"You fools don't know anything." And Coyote, he jumped up onto that rock and he defecated on it. He jumped back down and he laughed.

"See, I told you so."

He started on his journey again, but that rock rolled after him. Coyote was surprised, but he said, "I'm faster than you are."

He started to trot along, but the rock rolled faster. When Coyote looked back over his shoulder, there it was, coming after him.

Coyote said, "I'll show you how fast I can go."

He ran as fast as he could, but the rock kept up with him. It rolled faster and faster, until it was right behind him.

Coyote got scared, and he dived down into a hole to hide. The rock rolled over the entrance to the hole and trapped Coyote inside. He tried to talk his way out, but that rock wouldn't move.

Finally Coyote said, "I'm sorry I soiled you. Let me go, and I'll clean you off."

The rock rolled away from the entrance to the hole, and Coyote came out and cleaned the feces off the rock. When he finished, the rock rolled back to where it had been, and Coyote continued his journey.

I'm talking about fruit and flowers, and all good things.

Chapter 54

IT'S HARD TO KICK AGAINST THE PRICKS

Rafe caught the end of the mule's lead line as it whipped past, and he planted his heels. Caesar and another soldier grabbed the rope and held on while the shrieking wind lashed snow into their faces. They pulled until the veins stood out on their arms and necks, but the mule continued to slide down the icy slope, dragging them with him.

When he lost his footing and rolled, Rafe shouted for the men to let go. The pack lines broke, strewing food and equipment into the drifts of snow. His descent ended against a boulder.

The lieutenant peered out from under the oilskin slicker tented over his hat. "Collect what you can salvage, Sergeant, and distribute the load among the troops." He looked down at the thrashing, braying mule. "Don't waste a bullet on him."

For the next three days they limped toward the army post at Warm Springs. Most of the horses and mules that hadn't died had gone lame. The black soldiers, Southerners all, shivered under their blankets as they walked through an assortment of rain, sleet, and snow, the one constant being wind. Rafe had never seen such weather, and this was only the first of December.

Icicles hung from the wide brims of the hats the soldiers had bought to replace their useless forage caps. Those on foot had shoes in tatters, or none at all. They left bloody prints in the snow, but no one complained. Even after weeks in the field with them, Rafe still found their endurance and optimism astonishing. He said so to Casesar.

"The Bible says it's hard to kick against the pricks," Caesar answered. "Acts, chapter nine, verse five. I reckon that means no sense the oxen complaining about the goad."

"This ain't so bad, suh." Private Ben Simpson carried the brand of his former master on the back of his hand. "Back befo' the sesesh war, my massa, he got in a heap o' trouble for killin' a white man, an' he drove all us slaves to Texas. I wuz just a sprat then. It wuz snowin' sumpin' powerful, but massa, he wouldn't give us no shoes. Wouldn't even 'low us to wrap our feets wit' sacks. My mammy's feet, they gots all bloody, and her legs swoll up. Massa he shot her, an' kicked her whilst she lay dyin.' He said, 'Damn a nigger what cain't stand nothin.' " Simpson shook his head. "Naw, this ain't so bad."

You can never know a man, Rafe thought, until you've been on a hard scout with him.

This scout qualified as hard. For a month they had followed a trail of dead ranchers, dead travelers, dead mail carriers, dead sheepherders, and their equally dead flocks. They had found houses burned and corrals emptied of horses and cattle. The newfangled telegraph wires hummed. Troops converged to try to head Victorio off before he reached the Mexican border. Neither Rafe nor Caesar were optimistic about their success.

"Shoulda known it would come to this pass," said Caesar as he and Rafe rode along, their heads down to shield their faces from the ice needles of sleet. "Shoulda known I'd have to hunt my own kinfolk 'fore it was all over."

"Victorio has to be stopped."

"You reckon we'll have to kill him?"

"Doesn't look like he's coming in hat in hand this time."

Caesar fell silent. He was still haunted by the memory of the woman falling over the cliff almost two months earlier, and the wail of grief that followed her. Caesar and Rafe had been horrified to find the body of She Moves Like Water. With the lieutenant chivvying them to move along, they had lowered her into a cleft. They had taken off their hats, in spite of the pelting rain, while Caesar said a prayer for her. Rafe reined his chestnut close so he wouldn't have to shout. "We had no way to know she was his woman, or any woman for that matter."

"I think my bullet might have killed her, Rafe."

"No. Dead Shot was the one who hit her."

"Do you think so?"

"I'm sure of it. I don't think he knew who she was, either."

"I reckon when we see Victorio," Caesar said, "we can tell him where she's buried."

If we see Victorio, Rafe thought.

So far they hadn't caught a glimpse of him. Lozen was almost certainly with him, and maybe what He Makes Them Laugh said about her was true. He Makes Them Laugh said the spirits had given her the power to heal, to gentle horses, to steal ammunition, and to sense enemies.

Rafe wondered if she now considered him an enemy. He wondered if she was as cold as he was. She certainly didn't have the shelter of an adobe room to look forward to, with a clay fireplace in the corner, a stack of fragrant mesquite wood, and a cot with a heap of dry blankets.

"There it is." Caesar pointed to the low, dark bulk of buildings.

"Thank God," Rafe murmured into the wind.

"I hope Cap'n Hooker is off on scout," said Caesar.

"That makes two of us."

Capt. Ambrose Hooker, the commander of Company E at Warm Springs, was infuriating. He was dangerous. He was insane.

Someone, Rafe thought, should shoot him. He had considered doing it himself.

"Rafe, someone's got to stop Captain Hooker. He's trying to get his men kilt."

"I know he's crazy, and he's incompetent. . . ."

"I didn't say he's going to get them kilt. I said he's trying to get them kilt."

"What do you mean?"

"He acts like Victorio ain't chewing up the countryside and spittin' out the bones. He grazes the livestock a couple miles from the fort, like he was inviting the Apaches to steal 'em. He only allows the sentries to carry unloaded pistols, and he won't let them saddle their mounts."

Rafe knew Caesar didn't lie, and he didn't confuse his facts, either. Still, he had a hard time believing even Captain Hooker would send his men out on herd duty with no ammunition and no way to control their horses if they had to escape.

"I'll talk to the officers I play cards with. I'll ask them to complain about Hooker. God knows, my letters to Hatch haven't helped."

When they reached the Fort, Capt. Ambrose Hooker wasn't on scout. He strode into the stable while Rafe was in a corner stall rubbing down the chestnut. A soldier was shoveling out the place, and Hooker lashed at him with his quirt.

"I never saw a nigger could do anything right." He aimed a kick at him, then several more.

The man held the shovel up to ward off the blows, and that enraged Hooker further.

"I will kick out every goddamned tooth in your black head."

"Hey," Rafe threw down the sacking he was using to dry off his horse and left the stall. "What are you doing?"

"I'm teaching this brute the difference between a soldier and a field nigger."

"Stop it." Rafe grabbed the quirt.

"Get out of my way, you contemptible puppy."

"Stop it, or I'll flog you with your own crop." Rafe motioned for the private to leave. He obliged.

"A nigger has as much business to be a soldier as a cur to be a saint." Hooker panted with rage. He had the same look in his eyes that Rafe had once seen in a bull that had eaten loco weed. "I'll be glad when the Apaches kill every one of those damned coons."

Rafe left him to swear and rant, and walked to his quarters to write another letter to Colonel Hatch.

Slander, discord, reprimands, suspensions in rank, assaults, and court-martials littered Captain Hooker's career. Only recently a superior officer threw him into prison for beating a black sergeant after Hooker had tied him in a squatting position with a pole passed under his knees. Colonel Hatch, faced with Victorio's outbreak and a shortage of officers, ordered Hooker freed from jail.

Rafe had disliked more than a few men in his life, but not since Shadrach Rogers had he loathed one as much as Ambrose Hooker.

RAIN PELTED THE WOMEN AS THE SOLDIERS HELPED THE children and the old ones out of the wagon. They watched in silence, their faces as unreadable as masks, as Caesar and the other men put their shoulders against the wagon's tailgate and the mud-covered wheels. When the driver cracked his whip, the mules heaved against their harnesses, and Caesar pushed until he grew dizzy. The wheels churned a foot or two through the mire and stopped.

The caravan consisted of four supply vehicles and twelve wagons for transporting the women, children, and old people left behind when Victorio and his warriors bolted from Warm Springs and went on their rampage. Each wagon would have to be hauled through this bog and then wrestled up the slope of the pass and down the other side. Even the oldest would have to walk much of the way. The trail was a morass of loose rocks and icy mud, and they had covered only a quarter of the four hundred mountainous miles to San Carlos. To make matters worse, Capt. Ambrose Hooker had been assigned to this detail.

The sensible plan would have been to wait until spring to transfer the band, but the army and the Interior Department thought they could hold the families hostage at San Carlos. They thought they would be able to bargain with Victorio for them.

Caesar was glad that his Apache family had left with Victorio. They would be on the run now, but at least they weren't suffering this misery. He missed the tomfoolery of He Makes Them Laugh, though. He hadn't seen his nephew,

Sets Him Free, in a long time, either. The boy must be close to seventeen now.

Caesar walked along the line and stopped at the fifth wagon back. Victorio's grown daughter and second wife, Corn Stalk, her mother, and several small children rode in it. Their clothes hung in tatters on their thin frames. The wind and rain had shredded the canvas covering, and they huddled together, trying to conserve the heat from their bodies and share it.

Every day he had tried to talk to them, using Spanish and a little Apache, but they only stared past him. Now, though, Corn Stalk caught his eye. She and her mother sat with their arms around six-year-old Istee, Victorio's youngest son. The boy shivered convulsively.

"Hisdlii," Corn Stalk said. "He is cold. *Kaa sitii,* he is sick."

His grandmother took the scrap of blanket from her shoulders and wrapped it around the child. *"Nohwich'odiih, Shida'a,"* she said. "You help us, Uncle."

Caesar untied the army-issue blanket from behind his saddle and handed it to them. He thought no more about it until that evening when he was sitting as close to the sputtering fire as he could get, and wishing he had the blanket. Captain Hooker roared into the bivouack area, his face as red as raw beef. Flecks of saliva collected in the corners of his mouth.

"Who gave military property to the Indians?" He held Caesar's blanket up and shook it.

Dread clenched Caesar's heart. "They was cold, sir."

"I'll have you brought up on charges, you uppity, damned dog. I'll have you branded, bucked, and cashiered. See if I don't."

THE YOUNG SOLDIER PULLED OPEN THE HEAVY OAK DOOR and let spring sunlight into the room dug into the side of the hill. The cell formed the basement for the adobe building that served as the post's guardroom. The guards in the room above had a cast-iron sibley stove for heat, but little of that warmth seeped below. Rafe had brought Caesar blankets, underflannels, a couple of wool shirts, and a greatcoat. Caesar had slept in all of them on the bare ground.

A narrow window near the ceiling had iron bars. The room's only furniture was a pail in one corner to serve as a privy. Caesar and his three cellmates wore shackles around their ankles.

The guard stood watch while Mattie and Rafe went in with the two children. Three-year-old Ellie Liberty ran to Caesar, who picked her up and hugged her. Then holding her with one arm, he knelt to encircle seven-year-old Linc with the other.

"We gots the corn and squash and beans in the ground," said Mattie. "Rafe done the plowin', and Lib and I scattered the seed. Linc keeps the blackbirds away." She ran her finger through Caesar's wild curls. "You needs a barberin'."

"You can give me one soon." He didn't tell her that when the afternoon was over, he wouldn't need a haircut.

"Thas' right. Rafe tells me you kin come home with us today."

"Yes, I can." Caesar looked at Rafe. "I'll be glad to be out of this army, brother. I don't want to be shooting at my own family."

"If I can find Victorio, I'll try to convince him to surrender."

"I reckon the gum'ment pushed that man as far as they's goin' to. I don't think he's gonna lay down his rifle and bow his head."

They talked until they heard the bugler play "Assembly."

"Mattie," Rafe held out a quarter dollar. "Here's two bits for the children to spend at the sutler's store." He gave her a long look. "Why don't you let them nose around there a while."

"Say, 'Thank you kindly, Uncle Rafe,' " said Mattie.

"And when you're done, Mattie, take the wagon and meet us down the trail, at the creek." Rafe chose that place because Mattie could drive there from the sutler's store without passing the parade ground.

Mattie put a hand on the back of each child's head and pushed them gently toward the door. She turned to give Rafe an anxious look.

"He'll be all right, Mattie."

When they had gone, Caesar said, "Mattie says you brought them vittles and other necessaries. She says without you, they would've had a hard time of it this winter."

Rafe shrugged. "I only would have lost the money at Flossie's poker table in Central City."

"You heard what happened to the men guarding the horses?"

"Victorio and his men shot all five of them and the three herders. They took off with forty-six head."

The Apaches had stripped the bodies, but they hadn't mutilated the men. It solidified Rafe's conviction that Victorio would be an adversary the likes of which the army had not seen so far. And to tell the truth, Rafe couldn't blame him for going on the warpath. Victorio was kicking against the pricks, all right.

He thought of something he had read once, "Revenge is a kind of wild justice." Victorio's justice would be of the wildest sort.

"I tole you Hooker would get those men killed."

"Yes, you did. Their deaths might be enough to convince Colonel Hatch to bring him up on charges. They're starting an investigation."

They heard the tread of boots. Now that the time had come, panic flashed through Caesar's eyes.

"The child was sick, Rafe. I had to give him that blanket."

"Any decent man would have done the same." Rafe didn't tell him that Corn Stalk and her mother had died at San Carlos over that terrible, freezing winter. Caesar had enough sorrow and regret to deal with today. Rafe put his hands on his friend's shoulders and looked into his hazel eyes.

"Now, listen, *shik'isn,* my brother. What they do will be difficult, but it will be short. And no matter what they say, or what they do, when it's over, you can go home to your family and your farm with a clear conscience. You know that, don't you?"

"Yes, I know it."

"Mattie and the children will not see it, but I'll be close by. Remember that most of the men will be on your side. And once a board of inquiry proves that Hooker's incompetence killed those sentries, they'll do the right thing. They will do to him what he's doing to you. You can take consolation in that."

The six soldiers of the guard arrived. Caesar, his ankle chains clanking, walked out surrounded by them. Hooker had assembled every soldier who wasn't in the field, about eighty in all. Rafe was relieved to see the blacksmith absent. Hatch had been as good as his word about forbidding Hooker to have Caesar branded. Hatch knew that branding a black man in front of soldiers who had been former slaves would almost certainly cause them to mutiny.

When the escort reached the front of the formation, Captain Hooker motioned for the color sergeant to unlock the shackles. Caesar knelt, and the barber began shaving his head. Rafe could hear the scrape of the dry blade across his skull. The tight curls coiled over the barber's hand and fell away.

When he finished, Caesar stood up so Hooker could rip the yellow sergeant's stripes from his sleeve and the brass buttons off the jacket. Mattie had sewn them on well. After yanking and tugging at them while Caesar stood stonefaced and unmoving, Hooker took out his knife. Snickers broke out in the ranks, and Hooker's face grew red.

From the rear a man called out, "Give the cap'n a bobtail and see how he likes it."

"Son of a bitch," someone else muttered.

Caesar turned his head and gave them a sergeant major's look.

The bugle, fife, and drum struck up "Rogue's March." The six soldiers of the guard marched Caesar up and down between the ranks until he reached the last one. Rafe was waiting for him with a saddled horse at the edge of the parade ground. Caesar mounted, and the two of them rode away.

Chapter 55

A MULE NAMED MALARIA

Lozen, Victorio, and Broken Foot looked down at the five men in the canyon below. They had wrapped their braids with colored yarn and rabbit fur. They wore leather leggings and low moccasins, but the rest of their outfits was a mix of Mexican and Anglo shirts, vests, and jackets. One had on a black silk stovepipe hat, and another a bowler.

They sat their gaunt ponies with haughty grace. While they waited for the signal that they had been spotted, they tore pages from a book and rolled tobacco in them. One of them dismounted to start a small blaze with his fire drill and dried moss. The others leaned down from their ponies and lit their cigarillos. One opened a faded pink parasol and held it up to shade himself.

"They aren't Ndee," said Broken Foot.

"Comanche." Victorio motioned for Wah-sin-ton and Sets Him Free to ride down and escort them to the camp.

Broken Foot chuckled. "They must have taken a wrong turn at the Rio Bravo."

"Go to sleep with Lipans and you wake up with Comanches," said Lozen.

Broken Foot laughed out loud, and Victorio chuckled. Some of the Ndee who called themselves Lipans had come to Victorio and asked to join his band. The Lipans lived in the country adjoining Comanche territory to the east, and they were rarely friendly with the Red Paints. They weren't on good terms with the Comanches, either, but maybe they realized that they had an enemy more dangerous than each other.

Maybe the Lipans told the Comanches about Victorio's

war on the Pale Eyes. Maybe the Comanches heard about it from the soldiers at Fort Sill, where the army had resettled them. If these men were some of those who had refused to go to Oklahoma Territory, maybe the *comancheros* had told them of Victorio's war. However they learned about him, they did what the army and its scouts couldn't. They found him.

So did a lot of others. All spring and summer men had arrived and offered to fight. They came on foot and on horseback. Some brought their families. Sometimes they led a pony loaded with belongings. Sometimes they carried only weapons and survival gear.

The Mescaleros, the Tall Cliffs Chiricahuas, and Mangas' Santa Rita Red Paints had always been Victorio's allies, but the Warm Springs band now included White Mountain men, and warriors of the Cibicu, Aravaipa, Coyotero, Jicarilla, and Tonto bands. A few In Back At The Front People had joined him, and some of Long Neck's Enemy People.

All of them agreed that the Ndee had not seen a leader of Victorio's abilities since the death of Cheis. Some said he was a better tactician that Cheis and wilier than old Red Sleeves. They whispered that the powerful far-sight of Victorio's shadow, the warrior Lozen, made it impossible for enemies to sneak up on him. Many believed that his success was due in some part to his sister's wise counsel, too.

Victorio had the same words for all of them.

"I can offer you death," he told them. "I can give you separation from your families. I can promise you hardship, grief, suffering, and war. All that you will receive in return is the honor of dying for your people, and the pride in being men who do not surrender."

RAFE NAMED THE YOUNG MULE MALARIA BECAUSE THE lop-eared, evil-eyed beast kept coming back to plague him. He should have died of thirst, or a dose of lead, or the epizootic disease that had cut down the herd in the spring. He should have been bitten by a rattlesnake or eaten by Apaches,

yet here he was, eager to irritate. Rafe had roached his mane
and shaved his tail, leaving only a tassel of hair on the end,
to warn soldiers and packers to watch out for him.

The other mules in the baggage train would find their place
in line each morning and stand patiently next to their stack
of goods. Malaria was a different kettle of fish. He would
shoehorn himself into the line, setting off indignant complaints. Once led to his proper place, he sidestepped and
bucked when the Mexican *arrieros*, the muleteers, tried to
tie on his load. After the cargo was secured and covered with
the straw mat, he often decided to lie down and roll.

Rafe and his men had finally gotten Malaria loaded. With
cries of *"Arre, arre, borricones,"* they chivvied the mules
into line behind the bell mare and the fifty men of the Ninth
Cavalry. Even now, five months after Caesar had been
drummed out of the army, Rafe still listened for his deep
voice chiding his men to straighten up, to look like soldiers,
to make him proud. His men missed him, too. They would
drift to Rafe's campfire at night to ask about him and to tell
stories about him.

Somewhere toward the front of the column, Pvt. Benjamin
Simpson began playing his banjo. The cascade of notes reminded Rafe of a mountain stream. It was a relief from the
shrill of insects and the August heat shimmering in waves
from the dusty rocks. Private Simpson had played his banjo
on one hard scout after another as the man in charge, Maj.
Albert Morrow, hounded Victorio and his band across the
baddest lands New Mexico had to offer. He had played
through cold weather and hot, through battles and boredom,
through storms and drought, through too much water and
none at all.

Soldiers from Arizona and New Mexico had cut off Victorio's routes to San Carlos and Mexico, so he had holed up
in the Black Mountains forty miles northeast of Central City.
Colonel Hatch said the Black Mountains made the lava beds
of northern California look like a lawn. Hatch understated
the case. When God finished his six-day construction project,
he dumped here everything that was too jagged, too poison-

ous, and too thorny for the rest of creation. Victorio, however, knew these mountains as well as the brightwork on his
Model 1873 Winchester.

The rifle fire started as soon as the last of the mules entered
the canyon.

He's done it again, thought Rafe.

Victorio had suckered even the army's Apache scouts. He
had led Major Morrow and the Ninth into another trap. Rafe
couldn't see anyone among the rockfalls and ledges and the
huge clumps of cactus. The gunshots seemed to come from
the canyon walls themselves.

"God damn him to hell." And that was just the beginning
of Major Morrow's oaths.

Morrow was a chubby-cheeked, mild-eyed, dapper man
with a dash of thinning hair slicked across the promontory
of his forehead. His swab of a mustache followed the curves
of his round chin, almost meeting under the middle of it. He
looked as though he would be more at home behind a dry
goods counter, but if he had been a clerk, no customer could
have left the store without buying something. Morrow was
persistent.

After nine months of being shot at by Victorio, he was
taking this affray personally. While his men dismounted and
found cover, Morrow ran to where Rafe was kneeling behind
a creosote bush. The rifle fire reverberated off the canyon
walls until no one could tell from which direction the shots
were coming.

"Collins, keep an eye on Gatewood," he shouted.

"Yes, sir."

Lt. Charles Gatewood usually rode at the head of the column so his Apache scouts could report to him first. Rafe set
off to find him. When Rafe met Gatewood a few months
ago, he wouldn't have bet that the twenty-six-year-old would
live long enough for the Apaches to kill him. Yet here he
was.

Some persistent illness whittled away at Charles Gatewood. It left him narrower than the average fence rail and
so fragile that he looked as though a strong gust would snap

him in two. He had huge, luminous eyes set in deep hollows
the color of bruises. His nose dominated his gaunt face like
an ax blade jutting from a parsnip root. His Apache scouts
called him Beak, and they had developed a fervent loyalty
to him. That told Rafe more about him than any official
report. Apaches could tell the cut of a man's cloth almost at
first sight.

As Rafe scuttled along looking for Gatewood, he scanned
the walls of the canyon. He tried to estimate Victorio's
strength from the gunshots. As far as he could tell, the total
number of warriors seemed to have doubled from the first
encounter last spring. Victorio must be attracting every renegade in the territories and Mexico, too.

Rafe found Charles Gatewood crouched in front of a boulder, but facing it, as though he were using it for cover. Rafe
ducked behind it and popped up to look over it. He startled
Gatewood so badly he almost toppled over backwards.

"Lieutenant." Rafe cupped his hands around his mouth and
shouted. "You are on the wrong side of that rock."

Gatewood, his expression awash in chagrin, dodged
around to sit next to Rafe. He leaned his back against the
rock and balanced his Springfield across his knees.

"Good Lord, Collins, everyone's firing every which way.
I think you're the only sane one in the bunch."

Something caught Gatewood's eye, and he came to attention. He took aim at an Apache running full-tilt along a low
ridge with two more following him. Rafe put a hand on the
barrel and pushed it down.

"That's Dead Shot, Dreamer, and Felix Ward." Rafe corrected himself, "I mean Mickey Free."

"How can you tell from here?"

Rafe shrugged. He couldn't have said how himself.

The sound of gunfire eased off as men reloaded. Rafe and
Gatewood saw Sgt. Dead Shot beckon to the men behind
him and heard his booming voice. "Goddamn," he bellowed.
"*Muy bueno!* Come on."

The Apache Scouts were wilder and warier than the Pimas
and Navajos, but they were more reliable, more courageous

and daring. The only rotten apple in the bunch was Felix Ward.

The boy responsible for Cochise declaring war on Arizona Territory twenty years ago had returned like a copper-haired bad penny. He had been living with the White Mountain band all this time. He had changed his name to Mickey Free for reasons known only to him. He still wore his greasy hair draped over his bad eye, though, and he was still lazy and sullen. He still looked like he wanted to take the world in his teeth and give it a good shaking.

The need to conserve ammunition allowed a man a surprising amount of time to think while bullets whined around him. Rafe thought about Dead Shot's young wife, the Warm Springs woman he had met on the first trek to San Carlos with Victorio and his people. She and Dead Shot had wasted no time. She carried one infant in a cradleboard, and in another six months or so she would need a second cradle. Rafe wondered how she felt about her husband drawing a salary to track her people and kill them if necessary.

Love, he thought, is like the mule, Malaria, indifferent to the rules of others.

The firing started up again when Victorio's men saw the scouts. During the lulls, they howled down at them like coyotes and barked like dogs. The meaning was clear. "You are the Pale Eyes' tame curs," they said. "You are as deceitful as Old Man Coyote."

The contest became personal for them. The scouts and Victorio's men shouted taunts in Spanish, Apache, and passable English. Victorio's crew favored, "Come get us, you sum-bitches." The only time Rafe saw the enemy was when they leaped into the open, turned their backs, bent over, and flipped up their breechclouts. A spate of gunfire followed as the soldiers tried to hit the neat, round targets.

The fighting went on all day, and it was as confused and cacaphonous a melee as Rafe had ever seen. By late afternoon Rafe could tell by the spurts of flame that Victorio's men were moving downslope and fanning out toward the Ninth's rear.

Rafe found Major Morrow with his fingers on the neck of

his fallen first sergeant, the man who had taken Caesar's place. Morrow took the time to close the dead man's eyes.

"Major," Rafe shouted. "Victorio's going to flank us."

"Bring up an ammunition mule. We'll distribute the cartridges and withdraw with the baggage train."

Rafe ran to the side canyon where he had left the mules. He skidded to a stop about twenty yards short of them. Two of his men lay sprawled in the dirt. Lozen sat on the bell mare, and she leveled her army-issue Spencer at him. If he hadn't known her, he would have mistaken her for a warrior, but even so, he almost didn't recognize her behind the band of red paint that covered the upper part of her face.

He saw other details with preternatural clarity. She wore high moccasins; a long, doeskin breechclout, and a faded blue army shirt cinched at the waist with a wide leather strap. A coil of braided rawhide rope, a knife in its sheath, and various leather drawstring sacks hung from the belt. The strap of the food pouch at her left hip ran diagonally between her breasts and emphasized them, though that was certainly not her intent.

She wore a cap of hawk feathers. She had gathered her hair into a thick black braid that reached past her waist. Amulets of bones and feathers, turquoise pebbles, and slivers of lightning-struck wood were tied in her hair and dangled from the cord across her chest.

The sight of her took his breath away, and not from fear, either. He had never encountered a woman like this, and he knew he never would again. She radiated a power, a majesty that he had felt only once before, when he spent an afternoon with Cochise.

She also disoriented him. He had assumed she would be hiding with the other women. At most he imagined her loading the men's guns for them. He never expected to see her in war paint.

She raised the gun barrel until it pointed straight up. She wheeled the mare, kicked her sides, and rode away with the mare's bell clanging. The mules trotted after her, all except Malaria. He whirled and made a beeline for Rafe. Rafe grabbed his lead rope in case the mule should change his mind and go off gallivanting. All he carried were tents and trenching tools. Rafe suspected the Ninth would not defeat Victorio with trenching tools.

Rafe had always known Lozen was a thief, but now he realized she was much worse than that. She had almost certainly killed one or both of the Mexican muleteers, both of them good men, men with families. She could have killed him, too, but she hadn't. Still, he couldn't let her make off with the supplies and the ammunition.

Rafe raised his Sharps and fixed her in the sight. She did not try to dodge, and she did not look back. He knew what she was saying. You are my friend. I know you will not kill me.

He increased the pressure against the trigger, feeling the crook of his finger interlock with the smooth curve of the metal. He took a deep breath. He gave himself a stern but brief lecture on duty and the folly of holding with the hare while running with the hounds.

He lowered the carbine.

Chapter 56

WE RUN LIKE LIZARDS

Mothers and grandmothers rode with the infants' cradle-boards slung from the saddle horns. Their older children sat behind them, sleeping with their cheeks against their backs, their arms dangling. The ropes that tied them to their mothers' waists kept them from tumbling off. Her Eyes Open's five-year-old grandnephew, Torres, sat behind her, and his baby sister's cradleboard hung alongside. Her Eyes Open and Lozen traveled up and down the weary line, waking the women who dozed so they wouldn't fall off their horses and take the children with them.

For months Victorio and Broken Foot's bands had barely kept ahead of the soldiers. They had beaten the Bluecoats at every turn, but the warfare had taken a toll. The old life, as unsettled as it might have appeared, seemed idyllic to Lozen. They had all been together then, instead of bereft of their very young and their very old. They had not been able to rescue the members of their band still at San Carlos, and the sense of loss never left them.

For generations they had built their lodges under the cottonwoods by the stream at Warm Springs. Now they never camped near water, and they avoided the shelter of trees and warm valleys. They built their tiny daytime fires among the boulders and in the high crevices. At night they made no fires at all, no matter how cold the wind. They laid out their ragged blankets on the bare heights or in caves. Lozen remembered winter nights when everyone gathered around a big fire and listened to stories until the sun rose. Those days were the stuff of legends themselves now, as distant as the tales of Giant Monster, Child Of The Water, and White Painted Woman.

The Comanches in the band suggested fleeing east into their country. From there they could swing south to Mexico rather than run the gauntlet of Bluecoats guarding all the routes here. The country to the east was more barren and provided less cover. The People had not cached food or supplies there, but Victorio agreed to try it.

For the journey the women had cut the tin cones off the fringes of their clothes so that the bells would not alert the Bluecoats. They were all hungry, thirsty, exhausted, and pursued, but they were alive, and they were free. No one complained, but they had to find water before the horses gave out.

The young men reported the army's scouts nearby, although the soldiers themselves must be many miles behind them. The nearest spring lay in an exposed position, and the band dared not stop there. They would drop down on it from above.

The trail to the broad ledge above it was so narrow that everyone dismounted before starting up it. Victorio walked along the line to make sure each small child was secured by a rope to an adult. Then he and Lozen headed the procession on foot while the other men led the horses at the rear. Lozen turned to watch the children and the mothers with their cumbersome cradleboards and water jugs. In some places the trail had crumbled away, and they would have to jump the gaps. If one of the adults fell, no one could do anything about it.

When they all had reached the top, Lozen lay on her stomach and wriggled out over the edge. She spidered down the cliff face, finding cracks and niches for her fingers and toes. She had always been strong, but a year on the run, fighting alongside the men, had hardened and defined every muscle. She had always been fast, too, but now she could overtake a deer on an uphill slope and not breathe hard.

While she waited at the spring for the women to lower the water jugs, she watched a lizard materialize from the coarse sand at her feet. Its speckled scales blended almost perfectly with its surroundings. It scurried between two boulders and vanished. Broken Foot often said they all lived like lizards these days, running and hiding among the rocks. Lozen reminded him that in the old stories, Lizard was clever enough to save his life by convincing Coyote that the sky was about to fall. Lizard also helped Child Of The Water battle the Giant Monsters back at the beginning of the world. Lizards could survive heat and cold, flood and drought. Resembling a lizard was not so bad.

She had filled the last water jug and sent it up when Fights Without Arrows signaled her that someone was coming. He and Victorio hauled her up while she fended off with her feet. From a distance she looked as though she were bounding like a deer up the perpendicular cliff.

Lozen, Victorio, Fights Without Arrows, Chato, and Broken Foot lay on their stomachs at the edge. They watched as the three Ndee, looking for tracks, approached across the plain below.

"The Bluecoats' dogs," muttered Fights Without Arrows.

When men of the Ndee had first agreed to scout for the Bluecoats ten years ago, they had enlisted to fight against their old enemies, the Pimas and the Navajos. They had adventures while the others languished on the reservations. Their monthly allotment of the Pale Eyes' metal disks meant little, but their people did envy them their freedom. They admired their shiny new rifles and their plentiful supply of ammunition. Now, they were leading Bluecoats to their own.

"I had no warning of enemies approaching." Lozen wondered if she knew them. She wished she had the far-seeing glass she had taken from Hairy Foot so many years ago, but it had long since broken.

"The spirits must be confused by this," said Broken Foot. "How can our own people be enemies?"

Fights Without Arrows glared down at the three men. "Those coyotes are the worst kind of enemies."

"I recognize them." Victorio couldn't keep the bitterness from his voice. "They're Chiricahuas. They're Nantan Chihuahua's people."

Each of the scouts drank while the other two kept watch, but they didn't look up. By the time they finished, Fights Without Arrows could not hold his rage any longer. He stood and leveled his Winchester at them.

"You betray your brothers for the Pale Eyes' metal," he shouted. "We'll reward you with plenty of metal. We'll make you so heavy with metal you won't be able to trot after your Pale Eyes masters."

The three scouts looked up; then they whirled and ran. Fights Without Arrows took aim at them.

"Do not shoot them, brother," Lozen murmured.

He glared at her, incensed that she would tell him what to do.

"Let them go," said Victorio. "They are few, and they aren't shooting at us."

Fights Without Arrows looked at Broken Foot, sure he would agree that they should be killed.

"Let them go," Broken Foot said.

"That was a stupid thing to do." Chato turned on Fights Without Arrows. "Now they know where we are, and they'll tell the Bluecoats."

"One with no sense at all should not call another stupid."

Chato threw down his rifle and lunged at him. Victorio stepped between them and put a hand on Chato's chest. "We have no time for childish fights."

Victorio turned and walked toward where his people waited. They would have to flee for their lives again, but he couldn't blame Fights Without Arrows for losing his temper.

ANOTHER HORSE COLLAPSED IN THE SCORCHING SAND. THE soldier who had been leading him unbuckled the cinch and wrestled off the saddle, bridle, and saddlebags. He threw them over his shoulder and staggered on through the cloud of alkalai dust.

The lava rocks had torn up the men's knee-high boots. The soldiers had stuffed their worn-out boots with scraps of leather, sacking, and blankets. The hot sand seeped into the holes, and poured in over the tops of the high boots. It grated like sandpaper on their raw blisters.

No one talked. Even Private Simpson's banjo had nothing to say. Each man set himself to the labor of picking one foot up, levering it forward, setting it down in a place likely to do the least damage to it, shifting the body's weight over it, and starting the process again.

The only good part of this scout was that Caesar had come along as a civilian to help Rafe with the mule train. He had confessed that he still hoped he and Dead Shot could convince Victorio to surrender. Neither Rafe nor Dead Shot thought that likely.

Dead Shot put it best. "That Victorio, he one smart sumbitch."

Now Dead Shot slowed his pace so Rafe and Caesar could catch up with him. "Tank, plenty close." He pointed his chin at the peak ahead, skirted about with lava outcrops and boulders.

"Will it have water?" Rafe couldn't imagine water anymore, except for the odorous, alkali sludge in his canteen.

"Sure 'nough fine water."

Dead Shot pulled a flat packet from one of his sacks and unwrapped the oiled paper and the cloth. With a shy smile he held up the small photograph on a copper plate stored in a leather frame with a hinged lid and a clasp.

The sunlight glinting across the silver coating of the old-fashioned daguerrotype gave the images an ethereal quality. Depending on what angle Rafe held the frame, the subjects faded in and out of view. The photographer had posed Dead Shot, his young Warm Springs wife, and their two small sons with the usual props—a barrel cactus, some striped Mexican blankets, and earthenware pots.

The baby, all eyes and button nose and bristly spikes of black hair, was laced into the cradleboard leaning against his seated mother's skirt. He looked startled by the whole enterprise. The young woman, in a calico dress, had her hands folded in her lap. With her head tilted slightly down, she looked up at the camera.

Dead Shot sat with his sturdy legs spread and his hands resting on his knees. The two-year-old leaned against his father's side, with his elbow set on Dead Shot's thigh and his head resting in the palm of his hand. The child had crossed his ankles jauntily.

Dead Shot had on his best checked gingham shirt. He wore a length of the same gingham wrapped around his head, the ends twisted and tied in a knot in the center of his forehead. He had tucked his cotton duck trousers into his high moccasins, and he wore a breechclout over them. The barrel of his Springfield rifle rested against his thigh. He stared straight out at Rafe with that direct, honest gaze of his.

The photograph had cost almost a month's salary. After his wife and children, it was his most precious possession. He was obviously waiting for some comment.

"*Ba'oidii,*" Rafe said. "*Ba'oidii zho*. Handsome. Very handsome."

Dead Shot grinned. He wrapped the photograph back up and stowed it in his pouch. He turned his attention to the country around him. What he saw, or rather, what he didn't see, puzzled him.

"Horse, him too damned quiet," he said. "Mule, him too damned quiet."

"What do you mean?" asked Rafe.

He went back to his own language. "The horses, they should smell the water in that tank now. They should be saying to themselves, 'Hey, I'm plenty thirsty. What are we waiting for? Let's go!' "

Rafe and Caesar exchanged a glance. Neither wanted to suggest that it had dried up. The possibility was unthinkable. Some of the soldiers were muttering to themselves, the first signs of the madness that thirst could trigger.

The scouts led the rush for the tank. The soldiers staggered after them. Lieutenant Gatewood caught up with Rafe, who could not manage more than a slow jog. They saw Major Morrow standing on the tank's rock rim. He waved his pistols to keep the men from reaching it.

Rafe smelled the stench before he saw the coyote floating

in what was otherwise a clear pool of water. Its rotting intestines floated out from the gash in its belly. Human feces bobbed around it. The meaning was clear to anyone who knew anything about the Apache sense of humor.

Desperate with thirst, men tried to veer around Morrow. He fired shots over their heads, but some of them reached the water and started drinking.

"I thought the Apaches had a superstition about killing coyotes."

"Killing a coyote is bad medicine," said Dead Shot, "but if they find a dead one they can do that." He nodded toward the gutted animal. "A man with coyote power could do it. Geronimo, he has coyote magic, but he'd have to make medicine afterwards to chase away the bad spirits."

Rafe put a hand on the chestnut's neck to steady himself. Pain pounded behind his eyes. His tongue had acquired the texture and tautness of a horsehair sofa. It made talking and swallowing an arduous and unsettling task.

Shouting, one of the soldiers set a zigzag course into the desert. Sergeant Carson ran after him and tackled him. Two other men helped subdue him, but they had to tie his hands and feet and carry him back. Rafe gave Carson the reins of his chestnut so they could load the man onto him.

"We have to go back," said Morrow.

Rafe wanted to cry with relief. He wanted to turn on his heels and start north immediately. He wanted to throttle Gatewood when he protested.

"We can't stop now. Dead Shot says we're almost up with them."

"The men are played out," said Morrow. "We have to go back to that last well or we'll all perish."

"Parker took seventy of his scouts into the field," said Gatewood. "We can rendezvous with them and keep on Victorio's track."

"Us red fellows," said Dead Shot. "We catch 'em."

Morrow looked at him in surprise. "Where's the next water?"

"Mebbe a day." Dead Shot pointed his chin toward the south.

"How will you survive?"

"We find water." Dead Shot poked a squat barrel cactus with the muzzle of his Springfield. "Little bit here, little bit there."

"Keep things stirred up then, until my troops recover."

Gatewood looked over at Rafe. "Are you with us, Collins?"

Rafe wanted to say no. He wanted to say. "Hell no." He wanted to say it more than anything, except maybe, "Howdy, ma'am. Give me a double shot of whiskey," to the pigeon-plump señora who ran his favorite cantina in Central City. The words stuck in his mouth, maybe stalled behind that overstuffed tongue. Maybe saying no was too damned much trouble. Maybe it was too damned humiliating.

Damn Gatewood, anyway. Why did he have to be such a dead-game gent? He was so frail, he wouldn't make a support for pole beans. What's more, waiting for him back at the fort was a lovely, willowy rib of steel, a bride named Georgia. He had no business going on with a bunch of wild, madcap Apaches.

Furthermore, he had the gall to be stoic about it. Once, when they were crossing a particularly pernicious stretch of desert, he had turned to Rafe with that bootjack face of his, "If you cannot put up with a certain amount of thirst, heat, and fatigue from nature, then it's best to stay at home."

The Apaches were bred to this country. They trained harder for it than Rafe could imagine. Still, he couldn't walk away and prove them superior to him. He couldn't let the scouts think that only one white man could keep up with the red ones, and that one white man wasn't him.

Wearily he nodded.

"I'm coming, too," said Caesar.

"What about your family?"

"Lieutenant Gatewood's missus has taken a fondness for the chi'run. An' Mattie's cooking up fatback and collard greens for the officers' mess. They'll take care of her till I gets back."

Rafe, Caesar, and Charles Gatewood hoisted their rucksacks onto their backs. They set out with the scouts, all of them on foot, with Dead Shot and Gatewood leading the way.

Gatewood nodded to the scorched, rocky country ahead and the devastated column of men straggling off in the opposite direction. "The damned shame is that all this could have been prevented."

Rafe wanted to tell Gatewood that he was the first officer he had ever heard admit that in thirty years, but he didn't have the energy.

"They try to shift these people around like so many marbles in a game of taws," Gatewood went on. "If only we had someone in authority who kept his word and made his decisions stick." He sighed. "Think of the lives saved, the untold misery averted."

They walked in silence for a time; then Caesar asked, "Sergeant Dead Shot, where's Dreamer?"

Dead Shot grinned at him and made the sign of the cross, like a priest blessing them all. "He gone Black Robes' house in Santa Fe. Mebbe forget how to be Red Man."

"Dreamer is studying Catholicism with the priests in Santa Fe?"

"You bet."

Adversity, friendship, Rafe thought. They could make men agree. Religion, he wasn't so sure about. Still, what harm could come from Dreamer becoming a Catholic?

Chapter 57

RIFLE'S WIFE

Lozen never let her carbine out of reach. She ate with it across her knees. She slept with it next to her. Stands Alone called it *shiyi*, my sister's husband. Other people called Lozen Ilti Bi'aa. Rifle's Wife.

Lozen stood *shiyi* against the trunk of a juniper while she cut a pad off a prickly pear cactus and singed the thorns from it in the tiny fire. Around her, people glided from the darkness, guided to the meeting place by the fragrance of the flowers of the acacia trees massed in the arroyo. They searched for missing children and other family members.

Lozen's spirits had not warned her of the Apache army scouts' approach. She was as surprised as everyone else when they started shooting into the camp at dawn the day before. Lozen and the warriors returned fire to cover the escape of the women and children.

Now some of the survivors went to the Rio Bravo for water. Those who were too tired to walk that far dug holes in the arroyo and waited for water to seep into them. They soaked cloths in the moisture and gave them to the children to suck on. Many lay down in the sand, still warm from the day's late summer sun, and fell asleep.

Lozen unwound the bloody strip of calico from around Victorio's thigh and removed the cactus pad she had put over the hole. When the bullet hit him yesterday, the world had gone dim before Lozen's eyes. In a rage she had screamed at the scouts that they would never see his body. Their Pale Eyes masters would not cut his head off as they had done to Red Sleeves. They would not slice off pieces of him to keep as trinkets.

She and Wah-sin-ton had lowered him on ropes down a precipice to make their escape. Now she held the burning brand up and gently probed the swollen, purple skin of his leg.

"The flesh is firm. No flies have laid eggs there." She placed the raw side of freshly split cactus pad onto the wound and tied it in place with her headband.

She sat next to him in the sand. Broken Foot, Fights Without Arrows, Chato, He Makes Them Laugh, and a few other men joined them. Broken Foot's five-year-old grandson, Torres, hovered nearby, and Victorio beckoned to him. He put a hand on Torres's head.

"From now on this boy will have a new name. We will call him Kaywaykla, His Enemies Lie Dead In Heaps." Victorio smiled down at Kaywaykla. "May the name bring you victories and honor, my son."

Victorio lowered himself back down. The warriors laughed when Kaywaykla squeezed in between Victorio and his grandfather, Broken Foot.

After Broken Foot blew tobacco smoke to the four directions and prayed to Life Giver, he spoke.

"Many of my second wife's people will be going to the place the Pale Eyes set aside for them."

Victorio grunted. The Mescaleros weren't the first to drift away once the Bluecoats and their scouts began outmaneuvering them now and then. People had thought the Bluecoats were a foolish lot, easily beaten, but they were wrong. The soldiers were smarter and more tenacious than anyone had anticipated.

Time and again Victorio's men approached water holes and found them surrounded by Bluecoats. Time and again the band had to move stealthily past without drinking. The constant pursuit was wearing away at them. Victorio's people were thirsty, ragged, and low on ammunition. Now the Mescaleros' departure left him with less than a hundred warriors.

"We will wait until we're sure everyone who survived has found us. Then we'll cross the river and ride into Mexico." Victorio didn't know that the Mexican government was of-

fering a reward of three thousand dollars for killing him.
Knowing wouldn't have made any difference. He had had a
price on his head before. "We'll steal horses on our way
south and trade them for ammunition."

Broken Foot's second wife's niece should have gone north
with her Mescalero people, but she had not. She was in no
condition for a flight through the sand-and-lava deserts of
northern Mexico, either. She had married Sets Him Free and
would soon give birth to his child.

"I'll stay behind and help Wide's niece with the child."
Lozen said. "After I take them them back to Mescalero, I'll
find you."

Only Lozen, and maybe Broken Foot, saw the shadow of
uncertainty cross Victorio's face. Only the two of them knew
how much he depended on his sister.

"You can meet us at Long Neck's village," Victorio said.

Wah-sin-ton frowned. "What about our people still at San
Carlos?"

Victorio nodded toward the weary folk sleeping wherever
they could. "The Pale Eyes' scouts killed more than twenty
yesterday. They pursue the rest of us like the dogs they are.
The old ones, the sick ones, the new mothers, the very
young, they cannot endure this life."

"I'm going to San Carlos." Wah-sin-ton glowered at his
father, angry that he would desert his own people. "On the
way, I'll steal as much as I can to take to those we left there."

Wah-sin-ton proposed to ride into the country of the enemy. It was as foolish as crawling into a den of rattlesnakes,
but Lozen understood why he was determined to do it. Wah-
sin-ton missed his sweetheart, Maria's daughter. Lozen also
knew that some of the young men would go with him, those
who longed to see their own sweethearts or their wives, those
who yearned to hold their children again.

ALMOST THREE HUNDRED PEOPLE LINED UP AT THE EDGE
of the river. Rain in the mountains to the north had swollen

it and made it live up to its name, Bravo, Wild. It ran fast and deep between its high banks.

While Sets Him Free took Niece aside to say good-bye, others gathered to make their farewells to Lozen. They were frightened that she was leaving. They depended on her farsight to protect them. Victorio waited until they all had finished.

For a year and a half Lozen and Victorio had not been out of each other's company for more than a day or two. Neither of them did anything of importance without consulting the other.

"May we live to see each other again," he said.

"May we live to see each other again, my brother."

Lozen felt a thrumming in the bones of her skull. She stood back to listen. She turned until she faced west. The hum was faint.

"Soldiers?" Victorio asked.

"They're still far away."

"Get the women and children across the river. Tell Her Eyes Open she is in charge until we return. Broken Foot has instructed the boys to follow her orders. They'll ride rear guard."

Victorio ran for the horse that He Throws It held for him. He and the warriors rode to intercept the troops.

At the river, the women sang the prayer for a safe crossing and made their shrill cry. They tossed bits of turquoise into the river to calm it, but no one attempted the deep current. Her Eyes Open, with her grandnephew, Kaywaykla, perched in front of her, tried to ride her little claycolored gelding down the steep bank and into the rushing river, but he balked.

Holding her carbine over her head, Lozen rode her big black horse toward the river. The long column of riders parted to let her through. The black hesitated before he plunged into the water. She turned his head upstream, and he started swimming.

Her Eyes Open followed. Those on foot held on to the ponies' tails and let them pull them across. Soon horses were lunging through the shallows on the other side and up the embankment where they shook water off in sprays. While people wrung out their clothing and blankets, Lozen delivered Victorio's orders to Her Eyes Open. Then she turned and headed back across the river. She found Niece holding her belly with both hands. She had the look of panic in her eyes that Lozen had seen so often in young mothers.

"Are the pains coming close together?"

"Yes."

Lozen rode upstream with her to a thicket under an outcrop of granite. The roaring in her ears had become a nuisance, but now she felt the enemy coming from the east. A second band of Pale Eyes must be on the way. She helped Niece dismount and flapped her blanket to drive the two horses away.

Niece lay on her side and wriggled into the thicket. Lozen swept away their tracks and crawled after her. The two of them crouched in a cleft of the rock. Niece put her hands over her mouth to muffle the sound of her panting as the contractions racked her.

The soldiers thundered by so close that the impact of their horses' hooves brought dirt and small rocks down on Lozen and Niece. When Lozen was sure they had gone, she helped Niece to an overhang surrounded by vines and bushes near the river's bank.

Lozen spread out the blanket, and Niece knelt on it with her knees apart. She braced her hands against the rock wall. While Lozen massaged Niece's stomach, Niece tried to push the baby out. When the baby's head appeared, Lozen eased him onto the blanket. She cut the cord with her knife and knotted the end. She tore off a piece of her own blanket to wrap around him and carried him to the river to wash him.

Lozen threw pollen to each of the four directions; then she held up the child and chanted prayers for his well-being. When she finished she handed the baby to Niece so she could nurse him. She washed out the blanket that Niece had knelt on and threw it over a bush to dry. She wrapped the afterbirth and the umbilical cord in a scrap of cloth and found a mes-

quite tree to hang it in. The mesquite renewed itself each
year. It bore fruit that sustained them, just as the child would
renew his people and sustain them.

Lozen sat on the riverbank and took stock of their situation. She and Niece had a three-day supply of parched corn
and dried venison between them. They could gather food on
their way, but Niece needed more than cactus fruits and berries if she was to feed her baby.

Lozen scouted along the river until she found a cattle trail.
She lay out on a flat boulder overlooking it. When the long-
horns came to drink, she picked out the fattest one. As the
cow passed under her, she leaped onto her back. She gripped
the longhorn's sides with her knees and put an arm around
her neck. The cow bucked and twisted, but Lozen drove her
knife through the cow's ear and into her brain.

She cut out the stomach to carry water in; then she skinned
off part of the hide and put as much meat into it as she and
Niece could cure. While the strips of beef hung on the bushes
in the hot sun, Niece and Lozen flensed the hide and tanned
it as best they could. When it dried, they used pieces of it
to resole their moccasins. Crooning the proper songs and
prayers, Lozen made a crude cradleboard of willow shoots,
the blanket, and thongs cut from the hide.

Lozen sat cross-legged in front of Niece, watching her
nurse the child in the shade of a palo verde. "I saw some
Mexican soldiers camped downstream. I'll swim across and
steal one of their horses."

Niece tried not to look frightened. "How long will you be
gone?"

"I should be back by the morning. They cannot chase me
across to this side of the river."

Lozen cupped the baby's tiny shoulder in her hand. With
her other hand she stroked Niece's hair. Then she set the
carbine, the ammunition, and her supply of food with Niece's
few belongings. *Shiyi,* her husband the carbine, was the possession most difficult for her to leave behind.

"If something happens to me, take the gun and walk northeast. Keep the rising sun on your right."

Chapter 58

REUNIONS

A day's ride from the three high hills known as Tres Castillos, Fights Without Arrows led one group of men off to scout for ammunition. Chato took another party to hunt for meat. Victorio and Broken Foot divided the remaining fifty-three warriors between them.

The three hundred women and children waited until Victorio and his men cantered past to take up positions as the front guard. Broken Foot and his group lagged behind to scout at the rear. Her Eyes Open reined her horse, gray as the cold autumn morning itself, into line at the end of the column. Her niece, Wise Woman, and Kaywaykla's nine-year-old cousin Siki, pulled their mounts in front of her. Kaywaykla's sister rode in her cradleboard on Wise Woman's back.

Broken Foot had hung his necklace of deers' shinbones from the cradle's canopy. From his seat behind his grandmother's back, Kaywaykla could hear the bones rattling cheerfully. He burrowed under the blanket draped across Her Eyes Open's shoulders. He fell asleep, lulled by the rocking of the horse and the familiar, smoky scent of his grandmother.

As the sun was setting, the procession rounded a knoll and Kaywaykla saw why Victorio had chosen to camp here. A bench of level land along the side of the mountain overlooked a grassy plain and a lake. The men had dismounted, and the herd boys were leading the horses to water.

People left the procession as they saw places to camp. Her Eyes Open rode uphill to a sheltered spot among boulders. She unsaddled her horse and started gathering wood. Wise

Woman bathed her daughter, wrapped her in a shawl, and laid her on the blanket. Cousin Siki had hung the water jugs from her saddle pommel and started toward the lake when gunfire sounded from the surrounding slopes. Mothers and children screamed for each other.

Her Eyes Open ran against the current of people fleeing the valley. *"Nakaiye!"* she shouted after Siki. "Mexicans!"

Wise Woman lifted Kaywaykla onto the mule, but when she tried to mount with the baby, the mule balked. He lunged and sidestepped while Kaywaykla clung to the saddle. Wise Woman put the baby on the blanket and tried to calm him.

A Mescalero man ran toward her. "Ride toward the mountain," he shouted.

"Get my baby." Wise Woman managed to mount the mule.

She held out her arms for the child, but the man scooped her up and kept running. When Wise Woman saw that he didn't intend to bring the child back to her, she turned the mule uphill. She stopped on the bench of land, and she and Kaywaykla looked back toward the lake.

Darkness was falling there in the shadows of the mountains, and the flashes from the rifles of Victorio and his men were scattered and infrequent. They had used up almost all their ammunition. Kaywaykla heard the rumble of shod hooves on the trail below. The Mexican soldiers were riding to cut off escape.

Wise Woman dismounted and lifted Kaywaykla off. She struck the mule and sent him galloping away; then she and Kaywaykla began climbing. She squeezed into a narrow cleft between two rocks and called to Kaywaykla, but he hesitated. Rattlesnakes hid in crevices like that. Wise Woman grabbed him and pulled him in to sit in front of her, their feet barely inside the opening. Kaywaykla could feel his mother's heart pounding against this back.

A soldier dismounted nearby and leaned his rifle against the rock. Kaywaykla could see him silhouetted against the darkening sky as he smoked a cigarillo. After what seemed forever, he dropped the butt almost at Kaywaykla's feet, ground it out with his boot, and moved on.

Wise Woman and Kaywaykla started creeping up the slope again. Below them came sporadic shots, and the sound of hooves galloping back and forth. The Mexicans were hunting down survivors.

"A narrow arroyo cuts across this bench," Wise Woman murmured in his ear. We must crawl along it to the bushes at the far end. From there we can reach the high ground. If the moonlight comes before we reach the other end, the soldiers will be able to see us."

On the way, they found Tall Girl and her granddaughter. "It's too late," Tall Girl whispered. "The soldiers are everywhere."

"We have to try," whispered Wise Woman. "Kaywaykla will go first."

"Keep low," Wise Woman whispered to Kaywaykla. "When you hear something, stop and lie flat."

Kaywaykla slithered into the dry ditch and started to crawl. Rocks bruised and cut his knees, and cactus thorns stuck in his hands, but he kept moving. He heard voices and the snort of a horse and knew the animal had smelled him. He dropped and waited. The drumbeat of his heart seemed loud enough to vibrate the ground under him, to shake the rocks around him.

He found the bushes at the far end of the arroyo and hid under them. A puddle of moonlight spread along the edge of the bench they had just crossed. Soon it would flood into the arroyo, making anyone in it plainly visible.

Kaywaykla searched for his mother but could find no sign of her. Panic washed over him like the cold moonlight soon would. Maybe everyone he knew and loved was dead.

The older boys had told him that the Mexicans liked to roast small children on spits and eat them. They had been clear and detailed in their description of it. Kaywaykla's lips trembled. Tears stung his eyes and burned his cheeks.

He almost cried out when he saw something move and recognized his mother. On their way uphill, they stopped and looked down. The valley and the hillsides below swarmed with soldiers, a thousand of them at least. A huge fire danced by the lake, its light reflected on the water. They could see silhouettes of people passing in front of it.

Almost as bright as day, the moon lit the narrow plain and the arroyo that cut through it. They could see that the ditch was empty.

"Where are Tall Girl and her granddaughter?" Kaywaykla whispered.

"They did not try to cross. Now it's too late. They can't make it." Wise Woman paused. "Nobody can."

VICTORIO SAW SETS HIM FREE leap from a boulder onto the back of the first of the soldiers pursuing him. He slit the man's throat, but fell under the onslaught of the others.

He Makes Them Laugh had been running just behind Victorio. Screaming with rage and holding his empty Winchester by the barrel, he charged the mob around his son. Victorio didn't stop to see if he killed any of them before they stabbed him with their lances.

Blood ran from Victorio's bullet wounds and the loss of so much of it made him dizzy. Doggedly he tried to find a passage through the cordon of cavalry, but each time riders turned him back. Slowly their advance forced him against a wall of rocks. Clucking and yipping, they shouted his name. They called him *amigo,* and they cajoled him to surrender.

By now Victorio had learned of the reward the Mexican government had offered to anyone who killed him. He watched the men riding toward him, and a smile played across his face. He would take from them the only advantage he could. None of them would collect that reward.

He held the haft of his knife in both hands, the point aimed at his heart. He sang his Enemies-Against song.

Right in the middle of this place
I am calling on the earth and the sky.
The black sky will enfold me and protect me.
The earth will enfold me and protect me.

He pulled the knife toward him with all the strength he could muster. When he fell forward, the weight of his body drove the blade in as far as the hilt. Light exploded around him. He felt himself spiraling upward like an eagle, soaring above the carnage. A sense of peace, of comfort flowed through him. He would put his arms around his beloved wives and his mother, his grandmother, and the grandfather the Hair Takers had slaughtered. He would hold his baby son and hear his laugh.

He would not have to be hungry or cold or exhausted ever again. He would not have to fight anyone ever again.

AFTER ALMOST TWO MONTHS ON THE TRAIL, LOZEN DELIV-ered Niece and her infant to the reservation at Mescalero. Feeling as heavy as lead, she sat by the family fire while Niece's family chattered and hugged their lost child again and again. They handed Niece's baby from mother to aunt to cousin to grandmother and back again.

Loco was visiting from San Carlos, and he came to see Lozen. He wore a breechclout, but over it he had on a rumpled black coat missing two buttons so that it parted over his outcrop of a stomach. The coat's sleeves stopped short of his thick wrists. A small black bowler hat perched on top of his big head. He had punched a hole on either side of the crown, passed a thong through them, and tied them under his chin to hold the hat in place. His scarred eyelid still drooped, giving him a woebegone look under the hat's rolled brim. His eyes glittered with tears as he put his arms around her.

She poked his stomach. "Old Horse," she said. "Grazing in the Pale Eyes' pasture is making you too fat for the war trail."

"I have given up war, my daughter. War is for the young ones. You and I and your brother, we are no longer young." He sat heavily next to her. "Come to San Carlos and live with us. The Pale Eyes aren't so bad there. The agent gives us corn and beef every week, and he doesn't steal too much."

"Niece's people said the Bluecoats attacked your people."

Loco's eyes saddened, though Lozen would have thought he could hardly look sadder than he already did. "We had camped near the agency. We were waiting to collect our rations when the Bluecoats rode through shooting. They killed thirty of our people, mostly the women and the little ones. Later they said they made a mistake. They were looking for renegades."

"Were they punished?"

"The Bluecoat *nantan* himself came to our council and apologized, but he punished no one." Loco sighed. "Also, soldiers killed your nephew in the Black Mountains. They said he was a renegade, that he intended to steal away his people from San Carlos."

Brave, impetuous Wah-sin-ton, Lozen thought. He wanted to see his love. He wanted to bring her food and cloth, blankets and horses. Would the Bluecoats murder all her family, felling them one by one, as the boys took crows out of the sky with their slingshots?

Loco talked of the old times until the day's first light glowed along the tops of the mountains. Finally he called for a sleepy boy to bring his pony. He mounted slowly, like an old man. He rode away at a walk. When he had gone, Lozen went off by herself to cry out her grief for Wah-sin-ton.

Lozen stayed at Mescalero long enough to name the new baby and preside at the ceremony of cutting her hair and piercing her ears. When she left, Niece's people gave her government-issue corn and dried beef in fringed parfleches. She tied the parfleches onto the big, gray, cavalry mount she had taken from a lone Bluecoat she had ambushed in a narrow canyon. He was the first man she had killed with a knife. He was much easier to kill than the longhorn at the Rio Bravo.

She took the soldier's saddle, bridle, and saddle blanket. She added his new trapdoor Springfield, full cartridge belt, and pouch of bullets to her arsenal. She took his thick wool blanket, his wool shirt and coat, and most valuable of all, his canteen. She cut the yellow stripe off his trousers and used it to tie her hair at the nape of her neck. When she started back toward Mexico, she was outfitted better than she had been in years.

Without Niece and her child along, Lozen could travel faster and take greater risks. She did not have to worry that the baby might cry when enemies were near. She missed them, though. She had never spent this much time alone.

Day after day she and the gray traveled southwest through the mountains. They followed dry streambeds, the horse's shod hooves clattering on the rocks. On steep inclines the gray lowered his head and started sliding. While dirt and rocks pelted past him, he floundered down the slope sitting on his haunches. After climbing steadily with no view but rocks and cactus and stiff brown clumps of grass, the gray would heave himself up onto the spine of a ridge, and Lozen would look out at the world spread before her, vast and intimate.

As she approached the Florida Mountains just north of the border, she began to see sign of troops. She started riding at night, ignoring the dread of Ghost Owl. She and the gray were walking in the bright moonlight just below a long ridgeline when she felt a wave of fear and a sharp pain in her chest. She looked up to see Victorio standing in the trail ahead of her.

He looked young. He had on the white fringed buckskin shirt and breechclout he had worn at her feast of White Painted Woman so many years ago. Lozen's horse snorted. He tossed his head and sidestepped, and she reined him to a stop. She knew she should be frightened, too, but how could she fear her brother?

"Take care of them," Victorio said.

"I will."

He vanished, and she knew there was no sense saying, "May we live to see each other again."

Chapter 59

AID AND COMFORT

Almost at sunset, Lozen found the tracks and heard rifle fire. She hobbled her horse in a meadow where thirteen others grazed. She tried to joke with the five apprentice boys who were playing cards there. They only answered, "Yes, Grandmother," and "No, Grandmother," in low, respectful voices, but they did tell her who was in the raiding party.

She followed the noise of the guns to a ledge overlooking the Pale Eyes' wagon road. In years past, she and the young men had watched the trail from here, and they had taken a lot of plunder. Chato had done the same today. Three wagons were charred, but the fire had died. Chato must have attacked them this morning.

Chato and eight or nine warriors had fanned out across the slope below the ledge, taking cover behind boulders. Lozen recognized Burns His Finger and Geronimo's half brothers Fun, Eyelash, and Little Parrot, but she didn't know the others. The men were shooting at a dead horse. Now and then the horse fired back. The dead horse's aim was better, and the warriors were keeping their heads down.

Lozen ran at a crouch and knelt on one knee beside Chato. He didn't seem surprised to see her, and he made no comment about the ashes she had smeared on her face. With so many dead these days, a lot of people wore ashes to ward off restless spirits. Lozen loved her brother, but she didn't want him visiting her again and delaying his last journey. The ashes would keep him away.

"Hairy Foot," Fun called out in Spanish. "You're a brave man. Join us. We'll make you a chief."

"I'll make you buzzard bait, you son of a bitch," Rafe shouted in the same language.

"Hairy Foot is down there?"

"Old Man Hard-To-Kill himself." Chato grinned at her, but his smiles had never had joy in them. "He must be a witch to have gotten away from us all these years. When he uses all his bullets, we'll hang him up and build a fire under his nose to burn the bad spells."

"Stop shooting at him."

Chato glared at her. "The yellow-hair might be your friend, Grandmother, but he's not mine." He nodded toward his companions. "He's not theirs."

Holding her Springfield over her head, Lozen left the shelter of the rock and walked down the slope toward the horse. Halfway there, she turned around. She set the butt of the carbine on the ground and grasped the barrel near the muzzle as she looked up at the war party.

"Fun . . ." She called his name, giving great weight to her request. A person could not refuse someone who did that. "This man has helped my people. I owe him a debt. I ask you not to kill him."

She didn't expect a reply. She raised her rifle over her head again and continued walking toward the dead horse.

"*Shilah,* brother," she called in Apache, "that's a smelly fort you have. Soon the buzzards and the ants will eat your walls."

"Grandmother?" Rafe's eyes appeared above the bullet-riddled carcass that was beginning to bloat and stink in the heat of the day. He raised his head a little higher so she could see he was grinning at her. "Those boys must have let their guns get dirty and pitted as usual. They don't have range or accuracy."

Lozen walked around the horse and crouched beside him. His arm was covered with dirt and dried blood. She could see from the hole next to him that he had buried his shattered elbow in the ground to staunch the flow from it.

She held her canteen out to him. Rafe didn't comment on the fact that it was army issue. He took only a few sips.

"Drink all of it," she said, "but slowly."

"Only have two cartridges left," he muttered in English. "Planned to use the last one on myself." He shook his new Winchester rifle, rattling the sling rings. "A problem with a long piece like this. Was trying to figure out how to use my toe to pull the trigger, but I'm an old fart and not that limber anymore."

"Come with me." Lozen felt a rush of affection for him, and comradeship. She wanted to hug him in a warrior's greeting.

She realized she felt more at ease with Hairy Foot than with Chato these days. She realized, too, that he was no longer the young man he had been when she first tried to steal his big red horse many years ago. He and she had grown old together. They had grown old together, and apart.

He struggled to stand, pulling himself up on the Winchester, and Lozen saw that a bullet had passed through his thigh, too. He had stuffed his bandana into that hole, but it fell away, and the bleeding started again. She tied the bandana around the top of his thigh to slow the loss. Supporting most of his weight, she walked him toward a distant arroyo choked with mesquite trees, palo verde, cactus, and catclaw. He probably had been heading for it when Chato and his men shot the horse out from under him.

Lozen glanced up. The hillside was empty. Chato and Fun and the boys must have left, but Pale Eyes used this road often. She was now in more danger than Hairy Foot was. The thicket would be a good place to hide. She could hobble her horse there. He could eat the mesquite beans and graze on the grass at the upper end of the wash.

When they reached it, Rafe collapsed. She could see that he would be unconscious for a while. She sliced away his trouser leg around the wound. She cut a cactus pad, split it, and bound it in place with the yellow trim from the dead soldier's trousers.

Rafe's lips had a blue tint to them, and he shivered. The sun was almost down. Already the night's chill was creeping up on them, but another cause of his trembling was the loss of all that warm blood. She retrieved his blanket roll from the back of the dead horse and unwrapped her own blanket from around her waist. She laid his on the ground and moved him gently onto it. She draped hers over him and tucked in the edges so the cold couldn't slither in like a rattlesnake.

She went to collect her horse and medicine bag. She had seen a pack rat's nest in the meadow where she left the gray. The mound was almost as high as her waist and probably full of piñon nuts. If the herd boys hadn't plundered it, she could collect the nuts.

RAFE LAY ON HIS UNWOUNDED SIDE WITH HIS KNEES DRAWN up and his arms pressed against his chest. Whenever he swam near the surface of consciousness, he heard Lozen singing. Her voice was quiet and rhythmic, hypnotic and unending, but the blackness he floated in was bitterly cold. He dreamed he was submerged in an ice-covered river. He wanted to strike out for shore, but he couldn't move his frozen arms and legs. His own quaking waked him.

Lozen slid under the blanket to lie along his back. She bent her legs to fit into the folds of his. She put her arm around him and pulled him close until her breasts pressed against him. He was surprised to feel her shivering, too. He had half believed the stories about Apaches being oblivious of cold, heat, pain, death, and sorrow.

His shivering lessened, and so did hers. He laid his good arm along hers, holding on to her forearm with his hand. It felt as muscular as a man's. He fell asleep with her breath warm on his neck, her aroma of smoke and horses in his nostrils.

When he woke up, the sun was beginning to burn off the chill, but he kept the blankets wrapped tight around him. The only parts of him that didn't ache suffered stabbing pains. He looked under the blanket and saw that Lozen had splinted his elbow with yucca stalks and wrapped it in the calico cloth she used as a headband.

Lozen sat cross-legged nearby. Her hair fell in two dark

curves around her face as she bent over her fire drill. The line from a song the Irish soldiers sang ran through Rafe's head. "Her dark hair would weave a snare that I would some-day rue."

She twirled the juniper stick between her palms so the drill's blunt point created friction in the notch cut in a flat piece of sotol stalk. A thread of smoke rose from it, and she fed in bits of dry moss and blew on it gently. At the first bloom of a flame, she added pine needles, twigs, and then mesquite branches.

She poured water into the cornmeal on the tin plate of Rafe's mess kit and mixed it with her fingers into a sticky dough. She patted it into thin cakes and set them on a flat stone in the fire to bake.

She was dressed as a warrior, and the muscles stood out in well-defined curves on her legs. In any war party she would look like just another handsome Apache boy. The soldiers would not notice the few strands of gray in her hair.

"How do you feel?" she asked in Apache.

"Like a herd of mustangs stampeded over top of me, then wheeled around and made another pass."

"You slept a night and a day and another night."

"No wonder I'm ready to drink a river and eat my dead horse down to the hooves and the tail."

She handed him the canteen. He shook it.

"Where did the water come from?" His voice sounded odd to him, as though his tongue were a rusty bolt sliding back and forth in an even rustier breechblock.

Lozen nodded toward a hole in the arroyo's sandy bed. She took his bandana from the bottom of it. She had rinsed it out earlier and let the water seep into it again. She held it up, raised her chin, opened her mouth, and squeezed the water into it.

"Give me your gun," he said.

She handed it to him, and he inspected the breech. It was fouled, as he expected. He had never seen an Indian who kept his piece clean. He took the emery paper, oiled rag, and prick from his kit, and cleaned it. He handed it back to her, and she gave him a yucca leaf heaped with piñon nuts and another of grapes, chokecherries, and mulberries.

While he ate, she unwrapped the bandage from his leg and inspected the wound. She laid a freshly split nopal on it and tied it back up. He tried not wince at the touch of her fingers on his bare skin.

Next, she broke off the big thorn on the end of an agave leaf and pulled it so that several long strands of fiber came attached to it. Sitting cross-legged, she sewed up a tear in Rafe's blanket. As if mesmerized, Rafe watched her casual skill in the simple details that were the basis of life.

He wanted to ask where she had been, why she was alone, where she was headed, but he knew that would be a mistake. She might think he was trying to find out her people's location and numbers. He hoped that she knew he wouldn't betray her to the army, but he didn't want to give her any cause to wonder.

"I have to go," she said, "But I'll leave you my horse."

"What will you do for a mount?"

"I'll steal one." The corners of her full lips twitched, and mischief lurked in her eyes. "I think you are not so good at stealing horses. You'd better take mine."

When he sat up, a groan escaped him. Trying not to jar his leg or elbow, he slid closer to her.

"Stay here."

She looked at him in surprise. "I can't."

He put a hand on hers. "Stay with me." Rafe couldn't believe the words came out of his mouth, but like wild horses cut loose, he could not call them back. She didn't move her hand, though. For a moment that thrilled and terrified him, he thought she might agree to it.

"I have to find my people," she said quietly.

"I'll go with you."

"You can't."

"If they surrender, the army will take care of them. We could be together then."

"They won't surrender."

"You can't fight all of Mexico and the United States."

"Yes, we can."

"You must know you can't win."

"We have already lost. We are *indeh*."

"*Indeh?* Dead men?"

"The Pale Eyes killed us years ago." She looked at him sadly, but without self-pity. "My people are ghosts. We live. We talk. We walk around on the earth, but we are dead." She stood up. "The wagon road is well traveled. Someone will come along soon."

She helped him to his feet, but he didn't let go of her once he was standing, nor did she pull away.

"If you came with me, I would try every day to make you happy," he whispered.

Lozen stood motionless, like a restive pony listening to someone with horse-magic croon in her ear. She had traveled, camped, suffered, and gone into battle with men. She knew more about them than most women ever would. She knew their strength, their loyalty, their humor, bravery, and stoicism. She knew their arrogance, their vanity, their cruelty, and their weakness. But other than the unspoken love of her brother, she had never known a man's tenderness.

She let Rafe put his good arm around her and pull her to him. She laid her head against his chest. She felt as though she would melt under the caress of his hand moving up her back, stroking her neck, rubbing the base of her skull, then tangling his fingers in her hair, tugging it gently at the roots. She closed her eyes and allowed herself this small comfort in a harsh world.

"I could never live as a white person." She looked up at him. "I could never live among them."

"I know." He smoothed back her hair, though it sprang out away from her face as soon as he lifted his hand.

He bent to kiss her, but she turned her head. He realized that kissing was not her people's custom. He put his face into the wildness of her hair instead. Reluctantly, he let her go. Longing, regret, and loneliness engulfed him, as deep an ache as that of his wounds.

Lozen saddled the gray and tied Rafe's blanket roll behind

it. She supported his weight while he put his foot into the stirrup; then she boosted him up. He winced as he swung his bad leg over the horse's back. Lozen walked around to the other side and put that foot into the stirrup.

He looked into her upturned face. He reached down and touched the tips of his fingers to her full lips, as though to pass to her whatever small portion of magic he might possess. Her mouth moved in the slightest of smiles under his touch. She understood.

"May we live to see each other again," he said.

"May we live to see each other again."

He watched her start south at a lope, her cartridge belt slung low on her slender hips. Her blanket roll, her clean trapdoor Springfield, and her bow and arrows hung between her shoulders. Her flat pouch of food and supplies rode at the small of her back.

She was setting out to look for her people in Mexico, a journey of three hundred miles or more across the worst terrain God ever created. She went knowing that anyone she met would try to kill her on sight.

We are dead already. We are ghosts.

"May we live to see each other again, Grandmother," Rafe murmured.

Chapter 60

BELIEVING IS SEEING

Lozen knew they couldn't all be dead. When her brother's spirit appeared on the trail, he had told her to take care of her people. He wouldn't ask her to protect bones and ghosts. But as she rode from one meeting place to the other, she began to doubt her vision.

She began to believe that her worst fears had come true. She was alone in the world. The realization frightened her to the marrow. She dismounted and led her stolen Mexican pony at a walk through the old campsite in the willow grove. She could find no sign that anyone had occupied it recently. The reins quivered in her trembling hands.

"Grandmother!"

She whirled and leveled her carbine at the figure silhouetted at the crest of the low ridge. She watched him slide down the steep incline in a shower of gravel and larger rocks. When Fights Without Arrows reached the bottom, he and Lozen walked into a warriors' embrace.

"*Enjuh,*" he said. It is good.

It is very good, Lozen thought.

He said he had come here to look for survivors. He and Lozen sat by the river, and he told her of the slaughter at Tres Castillos. He could not use any of the dead ones' names, but she knew whom he meant.

"I was hunting for ammunition when the attack happened. We stole plenty, but we were too late. When I found *Nantan* Broken Foot afterward, he asked me to take a few men and see to the dead."

"Broken Foot lives?"

Fights Without Arrows flashed her the boyish smile she

remembered from their childhood. It was like sunlight on a mirror. "Who could kill that old man?"

"And how many others live?"

His smile vanished as he listed the few survivors. "We found almost seventy dead. We sang over them. The Mexicans killed all the boys over nine years of age. They scalped everyone. They burned many of the bodies."

"And my brother?"

"Enemies lay dead around him. He had driven his own knife into his heart. There were no crevasses, so we piled rocks on top of him."

"What does Broken Foot plan to do?"

"He'll take revenge." The smile returned. "He's sent messengers north, asking men to join him." Fights Without Arrows paused. All his life he had haunted Her Eyes Open's camp, listening to Broken Foot and his wife banter and tease. He had basked in the good humor that hung about the place like the fragrant smoke from the cook fire. Her Eyes Open was as dear to him as his own mother.

"Broken Foot's first wife did not return," he said. "We think she and her niece were captured."

They both knew what that meant. Mexicans considered the older women useless as slaves. They usually killed them.

SOMEONE HAD TO PUSH UP ON ARTHRITIC, CRIPPLED, OLD Broken Foot's wrinkled posterior whenever he climbed onto his pony, but once in the saddle, he could ride the roughest country for days without stopping. He could make any Pale Eyes who crossed his path sorry for it.

He never spoke his first wife's name. He showed his grief in a more practical way. He and Lozen performed the gun ceremony so that their weapons would not jam. They sang to make their followers impervious to bullets. They prayed over the ammunition that Fights Without Arrows had brought.

Lozen joined Broken Foot and his army of forty warriors and more than a hundred dependents. She fought alongside him as he swept through southern New Mexico. He did more than take revenge. He proved that neither the Mexicans nor the Americans could kill the fighting spirit of the Ndee. "If you believe you can do something," he told his people, "then it will be done."

In a month and a half, living off the land and what they could plunder, he and his people rode over a thousand miles. They did it with more than a thousand cavalry troops and two hundred civilians in pursuit. They fought a dozen skirmishes and won most of them. They didn't keep count of their enemy dead the way the Pale Eyes did, but they killed about fifty soldiers, ranchers, miners, mule drivers, and sheepherders, and they wounded twice that number. They burned ranches and slaughtered stock. They stole more than two hundred horses.

Whenever the exhausted men of the Ninth Cavalry managed to catch up with them, they scattered into the mountains. If the army pressed too close, they crossed into Mexico where the Bluecoats couldn't follow. They suffered casualties, but not many. Everyone knew that was because of Broken Foot's canniness and Lozen's gift of far-sight

"If Grandmother had been at Tres Castillos," they said, "the Mexicans would never have killed her brother and the others."

Now Broken Foot, Lozen, and their people were moving north again, into Arizona. They circled to the west, away from the usual trails, and headed toward a place called Cibicu, two days' ride above San Carlos. The Mescaleros had told them about the former army scout, Dreamer, and the medicine dance he held there.

Dreamer had the power to drive out the Pale Eyes and return the country to them, the Mescaleros said. He said he could bring back his people's three greatest leaders, Red Sleeves, Cheis, and Victorio.

That was a frightening prospect. No one had ever tried to call back a spirit that had left its body. The Mescaleros said Dreamer wasn't promising to bring back a ghost, though. He would restore life to the men themselves.

Everyone talked about it long into the night. Would the dead men want to leave the Happy Place? Would the desperate need of their people pull them back into this conflict? Broken Foot and his people had to see for themselves.

CIBICU CREEK RAN THROUGH AN AVENUE OF TREES IN A broad, green valley dotted with meadows, cornfields, and peach orchards. Fires flickered in the darkness of the surrounding hillsides where thousands of people camped. On a level area near Dreamer's camp, the shuffle of the dancers' moccasins had worn the earth bare and packed it down. Hundreds of people formed a huge wheel with the lines radiating like spokes from the center where Dreamer prayed with his arms up. The dancers moved backward and forward in rhythm with the drums while Dreamer sprinkled them with pollen from his basket.

Lozen had drunk from one of the gourds of *tiswin* being passed around, but that was not why she had the sensation of flying. Dreamer could send his power out to his people. He could increase what they returned to him. As Lozen danced, she experienced the tingle and heat of energy flowing through her. She felt as though she were hovering and looking down at the largest gathering of Ndee that had ever happened.

Dreamer's quiet manner and peaceful words had convinced them to set aside old animosities. White Mountain and San Carlos people, Tontos, Coyoteros, and Lipans mingled with Chiricahua and Mescalero, Nednhi and Bedonkohe. Army scouts and members of the San Carlos Apache police danced with the people they had hunted.

Hope possessed those who had come here exhausted, starving, and numb with grief. A medicine man of unparalleled magic would rid their country of the Pale Eyes. He would restore the world to the one they remembered, the one they told their children about.

Lozen soared among dreams and visions of her own. Joy

and sorrow swept through her in waves. Tears rolled down her cheeks, but she could not stop laughing.

When the sky began to pale along the mountain peaks, Dreamer brought his arms down and the drums stopped. The silence reverberated in Lozen's skull. Her heart pounded, and the hair stirred on her arms and the back of her neck.

Dreamer was so small that when he strode though the lines of dancers, Lozen could only tell where he was by the people who moved away, clearing a path for him. In silence, they trailed him toward a hillside swathed in ground fog. He motioned for them to stay where they were and beckoned for Broken Foot, Lozen, Loco, Cochise's son Naiche, and Red Sleeves' son Mangas to follow him to the foot of the slope.

Dreamer raised his arms and began chanting to Life Giver. Lozen's stomach churned with fear and longing. What if he could bring her brother back to her? What if he couldn't?

Something took shape in the fog toward the top of the slope. The shadowy figures of Red Sleeves and Cheis rose slowly from the ground. Horses appeared, too, their heads first, then their necks, withers, and front legs. Victorio's head and broad shoulders emerged from the fog. Lozen shook with joy and reached out for him.

The three men rose as far as their waists. The horses cleared the ground to their hindquarters. Then they all began to sink back. Lozen cried out in anguish as the mist and the earth closed over them.

"Come back," Lozen whispered. "Come back."

WHEN RAFE AND THE SCOUTS ARRIVED TO ARREST Dreamer, he sat eating stew under his wife's brush arbor as though oblivious of the menace around him. He was as slender as a child, and so pale he could almost be mistaken for a white man. He looked up at his captors with an expression so mild that the word *Gethsemane* came to Rafe.

Dreamer's followers were not so meek. When the lieutenant ordered the scouts to hurry Dreamer along, outrage rippled though the hundred or more watching from a hillside.

The party moved out with Lt. Tom Cruse and his Apache scouts surrounding Dreamer. Dreamer's wife and son followed, and the soldiers guarded the rear. The Apaches trailed them.

Painted warriors emerged from every side canyon along the way. Rafe estimated seven or eight hundred of them were following Dreamer and his escort. He held his loaded rifle across his thighs and breathed a prayer to the Almighty. He was surprised when he arrived at the army's campsite without having to pull the trigger.

The soldiers waiting there had lit their cook fires and pitched their tents as though they were on a routine bivouac. They watered and fed the horses, and stacked arms. They made a circle of the pack saddles and the supplies, and Dreamer's guards ushered him into it. His wife laid their few belongings under a cottonwood close by and began gathering brush for shelter and a fire. His son led the horses to graze.

Rafe found the captain sitting in front of his tent while his orderly cooked his dinner. He was in a cocky mood.

"Do you think it wise to stack arms with the hostiles so close?" Rafe asked.

The captain laughed. "Don't fret, Collins. This outing is all bleat and no fleece."

"This outing is not over yet."

The colonel strode toward them. "Lieutenant Cruse says things looked pretty scaly to him back on the trail."

"*Scaly*, sir?" The captain raised one eyebrow.

"Yes. Scaly. He says on the way here a number of painted Indians joined the belligerants." The colonel waved his arm toward a group of them emerging from the dense brush and crossing the creek. "Clear them out of there, Captain. We can't have them skulking about."

"Yes, sir."

"Colonel . . ." Rafe started to suggest he send out ten or twenty men rather than one, but thought better of it. When the captain headed toward the creek, Rafe went looking for cover. He didn't get far.

The captain shouted at the warriors as though they were

bothersome children. "*Ugashe*, go away." He waved his hand at them.

Rafe didn't see who fired first, but the captain went down. Through a hail of bullets, soldiers ran for their carbines. Rafe dived behind the barricade of saddles and supplies surrounding Dreamer. He knew that saving Dreamer would not stop the fighting, but killing him would make bad matters much worse.

Soldiers killed Dreamer's wife when she tried to reach him. They shot his son as he brought Dreamer's horse to him. Dreamer crawled toward them. Rafe saw two of the guards aim their Springfields at him.

"No!" Rafe ran at a crouch along the barricade.

Bullets thudded into the padded packsaddles and pinged into the boxes of canned peaches, spilling the fragrant juice. The two men fired, and Dreamer went down. He got back on his hands and knees and continued to crawl toward his wife, until a soldier dispatched him with an ax.

Rafe heard yipping and the thunder of hooves. The Apaches were stealing the stock. He dodged toward the meadow where the ammunition mules grazed, still loaded. One more idiocy to add to Colonel Carr's inventory.

Rafe had almost reached it when Apaches began shooting at him from the trees. He saw Lozen bent low against her paint's neck. Flapping her blanket, she rode straight through the cross fire of American and Apache bullets. The soldiers were surrounded and outnumbered. Rafe knew that if Lozen got away with those ammunition mules, he and the others were dead men.

He couldn't bring himself to shoot her, so he aimed for her horse. Maybe Lozen had magic against bullets, too. Rafe was a good shot, but she galloped away with the mules running ahead of her.

She had stolen three or four thousand rounds of ammunition, enough to keep her people supplied for a long siege. She had taken more than enough to finish off every man here, but when darkness fell, the Apaches stopped shooting and vanished. Rafe stood in the ringing silence and thanked God.

Rafe stood between the chestnut and the pack mule as they drank noisily from the creek. Without thinking, he fell into a habit he had developed. He stared across the creek, south toward Mexico.

Don't worry about her, he thought. She's hard to kill.

He tugged at the mule, but the animal spread his feet and prepared to resist until the creek froze over. Rafe had named him Lawyer because he objected to everything. He didn't want to dally even this close to Fort Apache. Safety was a dubious commodity since so many Apaches bolted from Cibicu almost six months ago.

Roving gangs of them had raided ranches, mines, and even small towns until reinforemcents arrived from New Mexico and California. The renegades had surrendered in droves then, but not the Chiricahuas. They headed for Mexico, creating their usual havoc along the way. Rafe assumed that Lozen went with them.

Rafe couldn't shake the melancholy that haunted him. The day before, the troops and scouts at Fort Apache had watched Sgt. Dead Shot and two other scouts hung for mutiny, desertion, and murder in the fight at Cibicu. Rafe had his doubts that Dead Shot had turned on the Americans. The battle had been too confusing to know exactly what had happened, but Rafe imagined himself in the scout's moccasins. If Dead Shot had been enticed by Dreamer's promises of redemption and resurrection, Rafe couldn't blame him.

As Dead Shot stood with the noose around his neck, he had looked at Rafe before he fixed his eyes on his family. Rafe thought he saw regret and sorrow behind Dead Shot's stoic expression, and maybe even fear. Rafe looked away as the horse was driven out from under the man he had called friend.

The amount of time between when a noose tightened and when a hanged man's legs stopped jigging was a short one in the vast span of creation, but it always seemed an eternity to Rafe. He used the time to wonder what would happen to

Dead Shot's two young sons. The Apaches were becoming a tribe of orphans.

Rafe lured the mule from the water with a tasty thistle and headed for the scouts' encampment with food and blankets for the hanged men's families. He was only giving them what should have been theirs to begin with. He had had to buy the corn and blankets from one of the thieves operating out of Tucson, and an unctuous son of a bitch he was, too. He hadn't even bothered to paint over the government's stamp on the crates.

The Indian agent and his cronies ran what everyone called the Indian Ring. Rafe knew he couldn't do anything about it. The network of thievery had become so pervasive that an Apache war club set down on an agent's desk would serve no purpose.

When Rafe saw the body dangling from a big oak, he thought some hunter had hung up a deer carcass to drain it of blood. As he rode closer, he saw that it wasn't a deer. In the light wind, Dead Shot's wife turned slowly on the end of the rope. The young woman had not known how to tie a proper noose, and so she must have strangled slowly rather than dying more quickly of a broken neck. Rafe had could hardly believe she would hang herself. She had chosen to die as her husband had so they would spend eternity together with stretched and deformed necks.

Chapter 61

A HUNTING EXPEDITION

Most people thought Gen. George Crook was crazy. Rafe thought he was the sanest man the army had produced. Crook had added ten years since Rafe first met him, but otherwise he hadn't changed. He was fifty-three years old, tall, strong, and broad shouldered. He didn't drink alcohol, coffee, or tea. He didn't smoke, he didn't swear, and he didn't care about notoriety. He parted his long whiskers in the middle and combed them outward so that they looked as though he were facing into a gale even when no leaf stirred.

On a scout, Crook rode his old mule, Apache, at the front of the column, not matter how perilous the circumstances. Because he always wore a brown canvas suit, the scouts had nicknamed him *ba'cho delitsoge*, Tan Wolf. On the trail they liked to ride with him, and in camp they clustered around his tent. Rafe realized that they had, in their own way, elected him their chief.

The scouts were the reason people thought Crook was mad. When Geronimo kidnapped Loco and six hundred of his followers from San Carlos and headed for Mexico, Crook started after him with forty-two soldiers and two hundred Apaches. He allowed the scouts to ride horses for the first time ever, and he issued them headbands of red cloth to distinguish them from the hostiles. Just about everyone predicted they would turn on the army as they had at Dreamer's ghost dance at Cibicu Creek.

Now the scouts stood in formation for *Nantan* Tan Wolf's speech. Crook had named one of them Moses when he had first recruited him ten years ago, and Sergeant Moses had served the army faithfully ever since. With Mickey Free translating, Crook turned to him.

"Sergeant Moses, do you think we will catch the Chiricahua in Mexico?"

"No, sir."

"Why not?"

"They can hide like coyotes and smell danger a long way off."

"We are going to keep after those Chiricahuas until we catch them all. We wear the President's clothes, and we eat his grub. He wants us to catch them, and so we will." Crook held up a sheet of vellum. "I have signed a paper so that even if I get killed, the President will know what you all did for him. No matter if I live or die, the President will reward you for your service."

Crook had obtained permission from Mexican authorities for his men to cross the border in pursuit of Geronimo's renegades, but no one knew what to expect. The general had sent out Apache scouts as spies, but as he wrote in his report, "the Mexicans were having a revolution that week." So many Mexican soldiers and partisans were running around that the scouts were lucky to return with their scalps intact.

Each man could take what he wore, a blanket, and forty rounds of ammunition. The mules carried extra ammunition and rations for sixty days. Crook put Rafe in charge of the pack train and mule drivers.

Rafe felt uneasy crossing the border. He remembered the war there as if it had happened last month instead of thirty years ago. He couldn't imagine being in Mexico and not having Mexican soldiers shooting at him. He also knew what kind of country they'd face and the difficulty of finding Geronimo and his men. All the mountains in Arizona could fit into the Sierra Madres.

The soldiers and scouts rode down the sweltering San Bernardino Valley. They passed the mouth of Guadelupe Canyon and the stream that marked the boundary. They reined their horses up just north of it.

Crook stood in his stirrups. "We're on our own now,

boys," he shouted. "If we succeed, we will most likely solve the Apache problem."

"And if we fail, General?" asked Rafe.

"The politicians will trim my comb."

Crook flicked Apache's reins and led his little army into Mexico. The rough country swallowed them up as though they had never existed.

"AMERICANS DON'T CROSS THE LINE," SAID FIGHTS WITHOUT ARROWS.

"These do," said Lozen.

He and Lozen, Broken Foot, Geronimo, and forty warriors looked down from the ridge at the Apache army scouts occupying their camp. The Chiricahua women there had hung up white flags to tell the warriors not to shoot, but Fights Without Arrows and the others fired off taunts and insults. The scouts shouted back.

The soldiers themselves had camped downstream at a broad bend of the Bavispe River. Lozen and the others took turns watching them from the heights. Within a couple days, *Nantan* Tan Wolf himself rewarded their patience.

As Crook rode Apache through the tall grass, he held his shotgun ready and watched for quail to start up. Instead of quail, Geronimo and his men rose out of the grass. The hunter had become the hunted. If he was frightened, Crook gave no indication.

"Let's kill him now," said Fun.

"No." Geronimo took the general's rifle and the string of quail he had shot. "We're almost out of cartridges. We can't risk a fight." He turned to Lozen. "Grandmother, go to the Bluecoats' camp. Tell them I want that red-haired coyote, Lop-Eye, to explain my words to Tan Wolf."

Lozen took off her headband and let her hair fall loose around her shoulders. She rubbed dirt into her face and wrapped her blanket around her waist so the Bluecoats would not see that she was wearing a breechclout instead of a skirt. When she shuffled into camp, the soldiers ignored her. She saw Rafe, but she gave no sign that she recognized him, and he did the same. The soldiers had heard about her. She was safer if she was invisible, just another squaw come to beg.

Lozen searched until she found Mickey Free. No one liked or trusted him, but his Apache was fluent even if he had never bothered to learn Spanish tenses. In English, he only remembered how to swear and ask for tobacco and whiskey.

After much discussion, General Crook convinced Geronimo and his men to come with him to his camp for talks. When they rode in with Crook, the general looked as though getting captured by Geronimo's men had been part of his plan.

After days of discussion, Crook convinced Geronimo to bring his people to the reservation at Fort Apache, fifty miles northeast of San Carlos. Crook's two hundred scouts were a happy lot. They had proved themselves to Tan Wolf, and in the bargain, they had made a good start winning at cards everything the Chiricahuas owned.

Crook took back with him fifty-two warriors and 273 women and children, most of them on foot. The women held up branches of cottonwood leaves against the searing sun. Geronimo stayed behind.

He said his own people had scattered in fear of the soldiers. He needed time to gather them. He didn't mention that he had something else in mind. Lozen had made a suggestion, and for once Geronimo listened, but carrying it out would take time.

Eight months passed, but in that period Geronimo, Lozen, and the rest of their warriors stole 350 head of cattle from the Mexicans. Lozen's plan was to breed them like the Pale Eyes did, except that the herd would belong to everyone in common, as was their custom. They weren't going to trust the San Carlos agent to feed their people. The Indian agents' idea of an adequate diet for them was starvation rations supplemented with donated hymn books and sermons. Lozen wryly observed in council that the hymn books were not good to eat, no matter how the women cooked them.

Whenever the Pale Eyes met in council, they talked themselves red-faced about the Ndee becoming self-sufficient. They were not amused when the Ndee leaders pointed out that before the Americans arrived they had been quite self-sufficient. With this cattle, the Chiricahua could take care of themselves on the white men's terms.

Geronimo became edgier as he approached the border. Lozen understood why. Seven years ago, Hat, Soft and Floppy had put chains on him, humiliated him, and locked him in a small room. Would the Pale Eyes do it again, in spite of Tan Wolf's promises? Would they hang him and his men as they had Dead Shot? Would they sell the women and children into slavery? Lozen decided that if they tried to chain her she would kill herself with her knife the way her brother had.

GENERAL CROOK SENT LT. BRITTON DAVIS, CHIEF OF Scouts Al Sieber, and Company B of the Apache scouts to wait at the border for Geronimo. Davis was born in Brownsville, Texas, and he had the drawl to prove it. He needed to prove it from time to time. He was not the tall, weedy sort that Texas soil usually produced. He was not yet aware that the scouts had nicknamed him Fat Boy, but he would probably be amused when he found out.

Davis was a year old when the Civil War broke out twenty-four years ago. His maverick father had led a regiment of Unionists throughout the conflict and left the United States Army with the rank of brigadier general. That made his son Britton an oddity, a Texan who had graduated from West Point and did not cherish a gut-deep grudge against the damned Yankees.

Army life was a lark for Britt Davis. He was as resourceful and resilient as the leanest Texan, and smarter and more good-natured than most. He thought that leading a company of Apache scouts was the best sort of adventure. He was fair luminous with the prospect of escorting Geronimo and his band of brigands to San Carlos, and then to Fort Apache where they would live.

As the weeks dragged by, Davis wondered if Geronimo, the old jilt, intended to leave him at the altar as he had so many others, but he didn't complain. He fished for river trout, and he hunted quail, pronghorns, and wild pigs. He gave his prey to José María Soto, whom he dubbed "the cook from dreamland."

He discussed literature with a Yankee in a sack coat and a low-crowned wideawake hat clamped down on a bald spot shiny as a peeled onion. The Yankee claimed to be writing a novel about the Apaches. When he was out of earshot, Al Sieber allowed as how, like all writers, he was so lazy he had to lean against a tree to break wind.

In December Cochise's son Mischievous brought a dozen warriors and twice as many women and children. Davis escorted them to San Carlos, and no one could accuse him of dillydallying. He kept them off the main trails and still managed to move them along at forty or fifty miles a day. They covered the 175 miles in less than five days. He made the trip north again with Mangas and Chato and fifty or sixty of their people, then returned to the border camp to wait.

Finally, in February of 1886, a patrol sighted Geronimo's band. The women, children, and old folks outnumbered the fifteen or sixteen warriors four to one, and they were all well mounted. Geronimo was not happy to see a protective escort of the army's scouts, a third of whom were now Chiricahuas. Mickey Free translated his complaints.

"We made peace with the Pale Eyes." Geronimo's glower made it clear why he had a reputation as a bad piece of business. "Why should we need protection from them?"

Davis chose his words carefully. He did not want to stampede the old desperado back across the border. "There are bad white men just as there are bad Indians," he said. "They might drink too much whiskey and start trouble."

"If they attack us, we can take care of ourselves."

"If they see me with you, they will know you are at peace. You will not have to risk the lives of your women and your children."

Geronimo took his time thinking about that. Gradually the

scowl lines smoothed out some, making him look slightly less murderous.

"We are brothers." Geronimo shook Davis's hand. "From now until forever."

"And what is that?" Davis nodded to the cloud of dust behind them.

"*Ganado*. We will camp here while they graze."

Ganado. Cattle. With a herd of cattle, they could travel only twelve or fifteen miles a day. Cows had to graze. They needed lots of water. They had to stay on the beaten trails. They would be impossible to hide.

Dear God, Davis thought. What am I to do?

Chapter 62

A VERY PRACTICAL JOKE

Britt Davis watched the two pasty-faced individuals stride back through the gate in the adobe wall. Their city shoes clattered across the wooden porch. The heavy oak door of the ranch house slammed behind them.

One of the men claimed to be a United States Marshal and the other an American Collector of Customs from Nogales, just across the border. At first, Davis thought maybe one of his Mexican packers had smuggled something, but the case was much worse than that. They ordered Davis to arrest Geronimo and his warriors and take them to Tucson to stand trial for murder. While he was at it, he was to confiscate the contraband stock.

Davis protested that he could not do that without orders from General Crook. The marshal replied that in the morning he would subpoena Lieutenant Davis, his Mexican mule packers, Al Sieber, and the five cowboys here at Sulphur Springs Ranch. If Davis refused to help him, he would raise a *posse comitatus* of every man in nearby Willcox.

Davis analyzed the fix he was in. Making a run for it was out of the question. For miles the prairie lay flatter than that porch floor on the ranch house. The brush was no higher than a jackrabbit's ears.

The five cowboys had watched as Geronimo's people made camp in the shelter of the four-foot-high adobe wall surrounding the house. With much braying and shouting, the packers had settled their mules about fifty yards away. The scouts had chosen to bivouac just beyond them. Geronimo's herd boys had driven the cattle off a half mile where the grass was better. Britt Davis had just pitched his own tent and was anticipating the rapture of one of the cook's meals when the two city slickers arrived and ruined his appetite.

Fort Bowie was thirty miles to the east, too far to send for help tonight. As a show of good faith, Britt had allowed Geronimo and his men to keep their weapons. If they got wind of this, they would draw down on the escort or break for the border and maybe take the scouts with them. Many of the scouts, were relatives of Geronimo's people. They had come along to accompany them to the reservation, not the gallows.

Davis could obey the marshal, start an uprising, and die with the other Pale Eyes here on the ranch. If he succeeded in arresting Geronimo, he would fail in his duty to General Crook and the army would cashier him. If he defied the marshal, he would find a posse on his trail. If he escaped a lynching, he would face federal court and jail.

Britt almost cried with relief when he saw a tail of dust in the direction of Fort Bowie. The cavalry was coming, or at least one cavalryman. If the soldier was the man Davis thought he was, he would suffice. Now Britt had a plan. He was almost grinning when Lt. Bo Blake rode up and leaped off his horse. Bo could have just dismounted, but leaping was more his style.

"I'm damned glad to see you, Bo! With the Pandora's box I find myself in, I forgot I sent the courier to tell you I'd be here." Davis grabbed his hand and pumped it. Blake didn't just look the part of the ideal soldier, he fit the bill, too.

Bo lifted off his saddle and blanket, his saddlebags and rifle. He handed his horse's reins to the Apache lad who appeared. Davis was not surprised that Blake didn't give the boy even a suspicious glance. If Davis trusted him, then Bo did, too. In the morning, Bo would get his horse back watered, rubbed down, fussed over, well fed, and most likely with an amulet entwined like a charmed burr in his mane or tail.

Bo turned to Britt. "What's the trouble?"

The cook brought enough venison stew, corn bread, and

gravy for both. While they ate, Davis explained the dilemma and his solution.

"You graduated from West Point a year ahead of me, Bo."

"Yes, I did."

"That makes you my superior officer."

"Yes, it does."

"You can order me to stay here under the marshal's orders. Then you and the pack train, the scouts, and Geronimo's flock and stock can hightail it while the marshal, the customs man, and the cowboys are asleep."

Davis knew that meant Blake would have to exceed his leave, but he was desperate. Bo Blake was Irish to the core and always game for a scrap or a joke, but he wasn't stupid.

"Good Lord!" He looked around at the layout. "You propose to pack up and move a bellowing mule train out from under those cowboys' noses, not to mention all these people and cows and horses? There ain't a snowflake's chance in hell we could get out of here without a fight."

Davis waited. A fight had never stopped Bo Blake before, but he had one more question.

"Can you convince Geronimo to sneak away, what with him spoiling for a tussle and so fretted up about his footsore cows and all?"

"I figure if I stick by the Apaches, they'll stick by me."

Blake smiled. "Then I'm in the game."

"Speak of the devil." Davis nodded toward the marshal and the customs man heading their way. Did they intend to subpoena Blake, too?

To Davis's relief they only wanted to gloat. That Yankee writer at Britt's camp on the border, they said, had been their lookout. He had reported on the earlier groups of Apaches, but Britt had spirited them north before they could catch him. These slow-moving cattle, though, they made him a sitting duck.

"This is dry country, boys." Bo held up a quart bottle of Scotch whiskey. "What do you say to wetting the whistle?"

"I don't say no." The marshal held out his cup.

Britt and Bo made sure the two men drank most of the whiskey.

With a grin, Blake watched them teeter off to the ranch house a couple of hours later. "Geronimo could scalp them tonight, and they wouldn't wake up for it," he said.

Britt checked his pocket watch. Only ten o'clock and everyone was asleep. Frogs croaked at the springs. The lead mule's bell jingled now and then when he shook his head. Somewhere among the sleeping Apaches, a child coughed. Britt walked through the gate and stood between the two families who had bedded down on either side of it. His heart sank when he saw that the marshal had dragged his blankets out onto the porch not more than six feet away from them and was snoring like two grizzlies quarreling over a trout.

Davis went back to his tent, called in Sergeant Moses of the scouts, and told him his plan. Moses asked for no explanation. If the lieutenant needed it done, Moses would see that it was.

Davis then sent for Geronimo. While he waited, he rehearsed his story. He would have to mangle the truth if they were to get out of this alive.

LOZEN LOADED HER RIFLE. FROM THE DARKNESS AROUND her, she heard the men doing the same. She filled her two cartridge belts; then she and the others followed Geronimo to Fat Boy's tent. Thirty or so of the scouts fell in behind them. Everyone expected trouble. Fat Boy wouldn't call for Geronimo at this time of night to chat.

The scouts and the warriors formed a ring around Geronimo, Sergeant Moses, Mickey Free, Fat Boy, and the Bluecoat lieutenant who had just arrived. Lozen felt the tension resonating among them all.

Fat Boy said the two white men were government officials. They came here to collect a thousand dollars fee for the cows Geronimo had brought over the border. If Geronimo didn't pay it, they would take the cattle to Tucson. Fat Boy proposed that Geronimo and his people leave now. His Bluecoat brother would go with them while Fat Boy stayed behind to throw the officials off the trail in the morning.

Lozen could see that Geronimo was furious. She dared not say anything, but she tried to will him to listen to the Bluecoat.

Fat Boy has honest, laughing eyes, she wanted to tell him. *He wants to do what is best for us.*

"No!" Geronimo spat out the word as if it tasted bad. "You promised that the cows could rest and graze. Let those men try to take them in the morning." In his agitation he shifted his Winchester from arm to arm. "Why have you called me from my blankets for such a trivial thing?"

He was about to stalk away, but Sergeant Moses started firing words at him like bullets.

"You talk foolishness, like one of the People With No Minds." Sergeant Moses had always hated Geronimo. Lozen could tell he was enjoying this. "The young Bluecoat *nantan* is a brave man. He's an honest man. He is risking his life and his standing among his people for you, and you behave like an ungrateful child."

Moses waved his arm to include the country around them and the serrated rim of mountains in the distance. "All these places, they teach us, 'Don't make mistakes. Act sensibly.' If you don't listen to what they say, you will get into trouble."

The sergeant had a lot more to say, and he ignored Geronimo's attempts to interrupt him. Lozen could see Geronimo wither under his attack. When the sergeant paused for breath, Fat Boy spoke.

"Maybe Geronimo is afraid his people cannot sneak away without waking those two white men and the cowboys."

At first Lozen was as offended as Geronimo. Then she realized what Fat Boy was up to. It might work. Geronimo was shrewd, but he was also vain and oddly gullible.

Geronimo put his foot into the snare. "My people can leave you where you're standing and you would not know it."

Fat Boy's face eased into the mischievous smile that had

charmed Lozen the first time she saw it. "What a joke it would be," he said. "If those men woke up in the morning to find that all the Indians and all the cattle, all the mules and all the ponies had gone."

Geronimo continued scowling, but Lozen had learned to read his rockslide of a face as easily as she read tracks in wet sand. The idea of playing a joke on the Pale Eyes appealed to him.

Lozen felt the tension drain out through her feet, into the ground and away. What replaced it was the excitement and the joy she always felt when about to steal horses from under the noses of Bluecoats. Now they would steal themselves away.

THE SUN HAD BEEN UP MORE THAN AN HOUR WHEN THE marshal and the customs man, suffering from the evening's excess and wearing only their long johns, scrambled up a ladder to the flat roof of the ranch house. Cursing, they scanned the horizon with their field glasses. The land between the house and the seam connecting earth and sky was flat and empty except for two salient features. Davis sat on the empty wooden cracker box that the cook had left for him, and he held the mule's bridle.

The two men climbed down, went inside to dress, and then stalked to where Britt sat.

"Where are those Indians?"

"They're gone."

"Can't I see they're gone? I want to know where they are gone."

"I don't know." Davis shrugged. "Lieutenant Blake is my superior. He took command, ordered me to remain in obedience to your subpoena, and left with the outfit ten hours ago. By now they're forty miles from here. They could've headed in any direction."

"You are lying."

"Maybe so, but you can't prove it."

The marshal and the customs man conferred.

"I guess we're beat," said the marshal. "We might as well go home."

"If you have no further need of me, I'll return to my post at San Carlos."

"You can go to hell, and I wish you a happy journey." But the marshal reached out his hand and grasped Davis's. "It was a mighty slick trick, Lieutenant. I would never have believed it if I hadn't seen it."

The two men walked back to the ranch house where the cowboys were grinning at them over the adobe wall.

Chapter 63

HAY-WEIGH ROBBERY

The Bluecoat lieutenant called Fat Boy set Squint Eyes' bundle of dried grass on the scale's platform and cut the vine holding it together. When the bundle fell open, a large rock rolled from the center of it. Fat Boy tossed it among the other stones, mesquite limbs, and wads of wet grass he had found in the hay that afternoon.

Squint Eyes screwed up her wrinkled face and screamed at him. *"Hijo de puta."* Son of a whore.

At sixty, Squint Eyes was as brown and withered as the grass, but her indignation was fresh and full of juice. *"Vaya al diablo, Gordito."* Next she turned on the scout who caught her with her foot on the scale. "Goddam, no-good, sumbitch!"

The Apache language didn't include profanity beyond the enigmatic epithet, "Knife and Awl," so Squint Eyes and the other women had learned it from the mule packers, both American and Mexican. When Squint Eyes ran out of Spanish expletives, she reloaded with English.

While Fat Boy weighed their bundles, the older women joked with the scouts assigned to hay detail, and the younger ones flirted. The scouts were desirable. They had new rifles, handsome blue shirts, an air of importance, and accounts at the trader's store.

The army had agreed to pay the women a penny a pound for the hay, but they had become adept at badgering the lieutenant into giving them more. They refused dull nickels, accepting only shiny silver dimes, quarters, and half dollars. They had learned that they got more when they insisted he round the sum to the highest dime instead of a nickel.

Lozen and Stands Alone stood next to their bundles of grass. Lozen felt shabby in her leather skirt and tunic, dirty and stained. Stands Alone's clothes were as bad. The Chiricahua women who'd come to Fort Apache months earlier wore ankle-length skirts of flowered calico. Their blouses were decorated with ribbons, wide ruffles, and belts of silver conchos. They wore many strands of colored glass beads. Brass hawk bells jingled on the fringes of their moccasins.

The sun was setting by the time Lozen's and Stands Alone's turns came. With a grunt, Chato tossed Lozen's bundle onto the platform. Chato now wore the thick red-cloth headband and the dark blue shirt of a scout. Fat Boy had promoted him to sergeant, but he had acquired the worst sort of general's attitude.

Fat Boy opened Lozen's bundle and seemed surprised to find no surprises in it. He handed her a quarter and a dime, the first she'd owned. She stopped to stare at them. They were perfectly round with the images of eagles and people subtly raised on their surfaces. If she made a hole at the edge of each, she could hang them from her earlobes.

Chato shoved her away from the scale. She turned to look at him with an expression that was not quite neutral, not quite harmless, and not at all docile. She saw fear flicker in his eyes. Maybe he was remembering her magical powers and the harm she might do him.

Niece saw the fear, too. She whispered as they walked away, "Be careful of him, Grandmother. He makes up stories about people. If he gets mad at you, he might say you're a witch."

"He's the one to be careful. Lies gnaw at the liar's own soul."

Niece, Lozen, and Stands Alone followed the happy crowd of women to the Fort Apache mercantile. The trader, George Wratten, left his door open long after sundown. He was an honest man, and he spoke Apache fluently. His store had become the gathering place for the Chiricahuas. Lozen always looked for Hairy Foot there, but the scouts had mentioned that he worked mostly around San Carlos.

Lozen wandered the narrow aisles in a daze. She inhaled the aroma from the coffee and tobacco. She touched the smooth, cool sides of the canned goods. She draped the chintzes and calicos across her hand, marveling at how light and colorful they were. She studied the beads and ribbons, the knives, axes, hawk bells, and tinware.

She picked up a mirror, caught the lantern's glow with it, and flashed it onto the wall. She tilted her hand to make the butterfly of light leap and flutter. Her first thought was that she could use the mirror for signaling on war scouts, but then she remembered that her people were done with fighting.

Still, it might be useful for signaling even in time of peace. She studied the two coins lying on her palm. The big disk and the little one gave her no clue about their worth. How could she judge the value of something so useless?

LOCO WANTED TO SEND A TELEGRAM. RAFE WAS IN THE telegraph office at the San Carlos agency when the old man came in. He was dressed in his rusty-black coat and baggy trousers tucked into his moccasins. His drooping eyelid and scarred face looked particularly odd under the bowler hat. The white people at the fort thought him comical, but Rafe knew better. The Apaches didn't elect comical old men as their leaders.

Loco was happy to see Rafe. Surrounding him in a garland of smiles, he enlisted him to interpret the message he wanted to send over *pesh bi yalt*, Iron, It Talks. Loco intended his talk for a chief of the Pimas who, he heard, had made threats against him. His message was brief. If the Pima *nantan* showed his face anywhere around here, Loco and his men would make him wish he hadn't. "Me lickee him damnsight," was how he put it.

When Rafe left the office, the telegraph operator was trying to explain the concept of payment to Loco. Loco understood, of course, but he pretended not to. Rafe could see his point. Why should he pay to talk? Next, Loco must reason the Pale Eyes would charge him a fee for the air he breathed.

Al Sieber angled over from the stable and joined Rafe. "I hear tell that Crook took Geronimo's cattle. He plans to sell them and pay back the Mexican owners."

"Sounds fair."

"He ain't going to replace them."

"Why not?"

"The Indian Bureau insists the Apaches farm."

"Why?"

"Maybe the local ranchers didn't cotton to competition from the Apaches for government contracts," said Sieber, "and they put a bug in the Indian Commissioner's ear."

"The Chiricahua men were willing to herd cattle. Now what will they do?"

"They won't farm. That's women's work."

Rafe thought of the bruises he had seen on some of those women. They hadn't gotten them farming. With no work and no game to hunt, there was nothing for the men to do but get drunk, pick fights, beat their wives, and brood. Apache men excelled at those enterprises.

BROKEN FOOT PAUSED IN THE MIDDLE OF THE STORY ABOUT how Old Man Coyote offered to teach the other coyotes to lie in exchange for a white mule, a saddle, and silver-mounted bridle. He saw the wagon bumping toward them in the full moon's light, and he hurried the tale to its conclusion. He had just said, "I'm talking about fruit and other good things," when the wagon pulled up. Fat Boy drove the team.

Chato and Mickey Free climbed out. They walked to the fire as though they were old friends of the folk there, but no one liked them. Broken Foot's niece, Wise Woman, detested them.

"Those two could teach the coyotes to lie," she murmured to Lozen.

Everyone knew Chato and Mickey Free had told Lieutenant Davis that Fights Without Arrows was plotting an uprising. Fat Boy had ordered the scouts to arrest him. A jury of

White Mountain men had tried him and sent him to the prison on the rock in the middle of the great water.

They made other mischief, too. They told Geronimo that the Pale Eyes planned to hang him and the other renegades, or send them to that island of rocks to live forever in chains. Chato would draw his finger across his throat, and Mickey Free would open wide his off-kilter eyes and pretend to be strangling in a noose. The Chiricahuas were angry at Fat Boy for arresting Fights Without Arrows, but no one blamed him for believing Chato and Mickey Free. Those two could fool Old Man Coyote.

Fat Boy helped his four passengers climb down. Their clothes hung in tatters, and their feet were bare. Lozen almost shouted with joy when she saw them, Her Eyes Open and Kaywaykla's fourteen-year-old cousin, Siki, had returned.

While Mickey Free translated, Fat Boy said the four women had walked twelve hundred miles in search of their people. It made his heart glad to see them reunited with their families. The Father in Washington was happy to hear that his Chiricahua children were following the road of peace.

He said that when Fights Without Arrows returned from prison in five years, he would see what progress his people had made. He would see that sobriety and hard work had made them all prosper. Lozen mused that if Fat Boy thought stealing horses wasn't hard work, he didn't know what hard work was.

When Fat Boy, Mickey Free, and Chato had rumbled off into the night, people laughed and cried and hugged each other. Broken Foot put his arms around his wife and sobbed. Finally, Her Eyes Open told her story.

"They took us all the way to Mexico City," she said. "They sold us to a man who grew yucca and made pulque. Because I was old, I cleaned their house. Granddaughter and the other two worked in the fields.

"We pretended to believe what the Black Robes taught so our masters would trust us. In winter I stole a knife for myself and a blanket for each of us. One evening we got per-

mission to go to the Mexicans' god-house by ourselves.
Instead, we walked away.

"The cactus fruit ripened as we headed north, and we ate
it. One night while we were sleeping, a mountain lion attacked her." Her Eyes Open glanced toward the figure huddled in the cave of her blanket. "He bit into her shoulder and
tried to drag her away. My granddaughter and Young
Woman beat at the lion with rocks. I stabbed him until he
died. When we lit a fire, we saw that the lion had clawed
off her face."

The woman under the blanket pushed it back to expose
the scarred and twisted mask of her face. Everyone groaned
at the sight of her.

"I put the skin back and held it in place with thongs. I
rubbed the lion's saliva on the wounds to help them heal. In
the morning, I bound cactus pads against them. We found a
cave where our people hid supplies. We walked some more
until the Bluecoats found us and brought us here. Now we
are with you, and our hearts are happy."

Lozen was happy, too, but she wondered for how long.
She thought of the uneasiness that Chato's and Mickey
Free's lies were causing. She thought of her old friend,
Fights Without Arrows, on that faraway rock in the middle
of the water. She thought of Geronimo's fear that the Pale
Eyes would hang him. She thought of the men who were
drinking *tiswin* and quarreling with each other and with their
women. Fat Boy had arrested some of them for drunkenness
and for beating their wives. The arrests made the men angry
and afraid.

Life could not go on this way much longer.

THE POUNDING ON THE DOOR INCREASED BY A FACTOR OF A
hundred the throbbing in Al Sieber's skull. The Chief of
Scouts wanted to kill whomever was responsible, but it
would require too much effort. The iron latch rattled with
the force being applied to it.

What the goddam hell time of day was it, anyway?

Sieber pushed himself to a sitting position and swung his legs over the edge of the cot. When he muttered, "Stop that, you son of a bitch," the words shrieked in his ears. Maybe he shouldn't have had that last bottle of whiskey the night before.

He opened the door a crack and put his arm across his eyes to keep the sun from driving spikes into them. Through a roil of nausea, he saw the newly minted captain, fresh from the wrong side of the Mississippi. The captain waved a paper in Sieber's face.

"What the hell is that?"

"A telegram."

"Nobody sends me telegrams." Sieber started to ease the door shut. Now was not the time to be slamming doors.

"It's not for you."

"Then why the goddam hell did you bring it?" Maybe he would slam the door, and the devil take it.

"It's from Lieutenant Britton Davis at Fort Apache. He sent it to General Crook, but the general isn't here."

"Of course he's not here. These are my goddamn diggings, not his, you shavetail mule's arse."

"I mean the general's not on the post, so the telegraph operator brought it to me."

Sieber squinted at the paper, trying to make the milling letters form into ranks and come to attention. The lieutenant could see he was having trouble and so he read it aloud.

" 'Chiricahuas refuse to quit inbibing spiritous drink—stop—They refuse to quit beating their women—stop—Insurrection possible—stop—Please advise—stop.' "

Seiber didn't know what *insurrection* meant, but he was familiar with "spiritous drink."

"Ain't nothing but a *tiswin* drunk." He dismissed the telegram with a wave of his hand. "Pay it no mind. Davis will handle it."

He fell back onto his cot and started snoring as soon as his head hit the saddlebag he used for a pillow. The captain dutifully returned to his office, filed the telegram away, and forgot about it.

THE MERCURY HIT 125 DEGREES AND CRACKED THE GLASS of Britt Davis's thermometer. With a sideways flick of his wrist, he tossed it away. It traveled two feet up, two feet out, and three thousand feet down. He did not watch its fall. The trail was less than three feet wide here, and the view from the edge of it made him dizzy. Making himself dizzy was not a good plan.

The packers raised a shout at the rear of the column. Another mule must have fallen over the side. Chato and the forty scouts had already scampered up the mountain and disappeared over the ridge. With awe and envy, Davis had watched them go. He was still impressed by their strength, agility, and reckless courage. General Crook was right. They were the tigers of the human species.

Al Sieber shouted, "Look out below."

Britt Davis pulled his horse up against the rock wall. The loaf-size rock that Sieber had dislodged came bounding at him as though launched from a catapult. It hit the ground a rat's length, not counting the tail, from Britt's feet, ricocheted to one side, and went over the edge. Britt continued toiling up the trail.

All summer Geronimo's band had led the soldiers and scouts down one side of the Sierra Madres and up the other. Davis thanked God every day for Chato and the other scouts, because maps were only useful as tinder here. The men's sweat-soaked clothes hung in shreds. Davis's wardrobe had been reduced to overalls, undershirt, and the brim of his felt hat. A third of their animals had perished. The remaining mules' and horses' heads drooped until the sharp rocks abraded their lips.

Worst of all, Davis was dogged by the thought that this was all his fault. When General Crook sent no reply to his telegram four months ago, he should have sent another. Or he should have gone to see the general. Instead he had sat tight and hoped the Geronimo's Chiricahuas would settle down and start farming the way Loco and his people had.

With no word from Tan Wolf, Geronimo became convinced that the Bluecoats planned to arrest and hang him. So off he went again with forty-two warriors and a hundred women and children. They cut the telegraph wires, splicing them with thongs so the breaks were almost impossible to find. Then they scattered into the mountains. Chief Chihuahua's crowd headed east, and Geronimo's went south.

Geronimo's bunch knew that the Mexican ammunition wouldn't fit their Springfields and Winchesters, so they attacked the camp at the border. They killed seven soldiers and made off with a plentiful supply of cartridges. Chihuahua's trail through New Mexico had been bloodier. Britt had heard about the ranch family massacred near Central City. The soldiers had found the three-year-old daughter alive but hanging from a meat hook forced through the back of her head. She died soon after they took her down.

All in all, Davis's conscience was the heaviest piece of equipment he carried. He clambered up the last quarter mile and reached what would have seemed like the roof of the world if he hadn't already stood on hundreds of ridges like it. Stretching to the horizon were the same desolate ranks of mountains—barren, abrupt, and brooding—that he had seen for the past two months. The same array of bony ridges and yawning abysses filled the spaces between them.

The scouts were smoking cigarillos in the shade of their horses. Al Sieber had pulled his hat over his eyes. Compared to Sieber, Davis looked natty in his overalls and undershirt. Sieber wore cotton flannel drawers, an old blue blouse, and the torn brim of a felt hat. He looked asleep, but he spoke when he heard Davis approach.

"The boys have lost them. Old Gerry must have sent a few of his men ahead with spare horses to throw us off while the rest doubled back and dodged across that rocky piece of ground a few miles behind us."

Davis wished the scouts had discovered that before the column had followed them up here, but he didn't blame them. Chato and his men were the best in the tracking business, but chasing Geronimo's crowd was like trying to catch

Chapter 64

SHOULD AULD ACQUAINTANCE...

Kaywaykla's friend, Henry, was half a hand taller and at least seventy years older than he was, but the two went everywhere together. The Henry was the ancient flintlock musket that Lozen had given him. Kaywaykla polished the brass eagle on the Henry until he could use it to reflect the sun's rays as a signal when he stood sentry duty.

Almost every boy over the age of nine had a rifle. They wore two cartridge belts on their hips. They made hundreds of arrow points from the hoops of the Bluecoats' discarded water barrels. They rolled the tops of their high moccasins low on thin legs shiny with grease rubbed in to make them run faster. They stalked through the village, scowling like wolf cubs from under their shaggy bangs.

After his old Henry musket, Kaywaykla's next-best friend was Santiago McKinn. McKinn's mother was Mexican, and his father was a Pale Eyes. Six months ago Geronimo had killed his older brother, but he had stolen Santiago and the horses the two boys were herding.

The freckle-faced, pale-haired captive boy had taken to the Chiricahua life as though he had been with them from birth. Lozen thought of him as misplaced in a Pale Eyes family, like a catbird fledgling in a kingbird's nest. Whenever she looked at Santiago's sun-yellow hair, brown eyes, and deeply tanned face, she thought maybe this was what her son would have looked like, if she had said yes to Hairy Foot's proposal and gone with him.

Lozen dreamed of Hairy Foot often. Sometimes she dreamed he was chasing her, trying to kill her. Sometimes she dreamed that he was holding her in his arms as he once had. She felt his hand on her neck then, and his heart beating in time with hers. She woke with tears stinging her eyes.

The longing for his touch evaporated with the urgencies of each new day, and the struggle to survive until sunset. She didn't like the longing, anyway. So many loved ones had been killed. Why should she mourn one man who still lived, and who was *nzaadge goliini,* an outsider at that?

Lozen had made her Enemies-Against medicine for this raid, and now she was packing the things she would need. She and the warriors would be traveling north in search of cartridges and revenge, and they had a long way to go. This was the beginning of Ghost Face. The weather would be cold before they returned to Mexico. Kaywaykla and Santiago tried once more to persuade her to let them serve as her apprentices and take care of her horses on the war trail.

"Your duty is to protect the women and children," she said. "You must do whatever you have to to stay alive. We old ones will die one day, and you will carry on the fight."

Lozen finished tying her blanket roll to the back of the saddle. The boys stood one on each side of her horse's head so they could lead him to where the men were gathering.

"Remember this," Lozen said. "People who have easy lives are weak. Hardship is our friend. It makes us strong."

Lozen, Broken Foot, Geronimo, and eight others raided all the way to Fort Apache. They attacked at night and killed twelve White Mountain people within sight of the fort. They rode twelve hundred miles, lost one man, killed thirty-eight, and stole 250 horses and mules. Newspapers clamored for Gen. George Crook's head. His superior, Gen. Philip Sheridan, decided the time had come to transfer Crook and assign another soldier the job of taming the tigers.

Gen. Nelson Miles arrived tall, lean, erect, starched, pressed, and barking orders. Like General Crook, he also made one of his first acts a tour of San Carlos and Fort Apache. Unlike General Crook, he didn't talk to the leaders except to lecture them. He returned disgusted with what he saw as their drunken, squalid ways.

He dismissed most of the Apache scouts from service. He

said the cavalry could work more effectively alone, which proved to Rafe that the man was an idiot as well as an ingrate. Al Sieber knew Miles, and he didn't think as highly of him as Rafe did.

"Miles breaks into a powerful rash whenever he brushes up against a whiff of danger." Sieber pulled a silver coin from the pocket of his denim trousers, flipped it into the air, and caught it. "I'll bet you a dollar he gets no closer to the border than Tucson."

Rafe knew better than to take the bet. The Apache scouts had already dubbed Miles Always Too Late To Fight. They were never wrong.

Miles fired off a series of memos critical of General Crook. He hatched a plan that would eliminate the scouts loyal to Crook and would solve the entire Apache problem, too. Machiavelli would have admired it.

CHATO SAT BACK IN THE RED-PLUSH SEAT AND WATCHED the Kansas wheat fields unroll as the train, snorting and belching smoke and cinders, rushed toward the setting sun. Chato was a happy man. He and Mickey Free and a eight fellow scouts had traveled all the way to Washington. The president had shaken their hands. He had thanked them for their service to the United States. In a solemn ceremony, he had hung large silver medals around their necks on shiny red ribbons.

Chato knew that his people would call him a liar when he told them what he had seen, but he didn't care. The Pale Eyes had raised him far above the rest of his people living in their crude huts on the reservations or roaming Mexico like wild animals.

The train lurched to a halt at the Fort Leavenworth station. Soldiers came aboard and commanded the scouts off, by order of the new Bluecoat *nantan*, General Miles. They escorted them to a cell and locked them in. Confused, Chato and the others waited for an explanation. They received it on the way to prison at the fort in Saint Augustine, Florida.

Behind its six-foot-thick stone walls they would have twenty-seven years to think about the gratitude of the government.

BROKEN FOOT LIFTED THE LOOP OF HIS WAR CORD FROM across his chest and laid it over a leather satchel worn thin with handling. The cap of goose feathers inside looked like it had a serious case of the molt. He had performed a long ceremony over them, apologizing to them for letting them leave his possession. He had begged them not to be angry with him, and not to harm his family. He had shrieked five times; then both he and Her Eyes Open had hissed like snakes.

Now, Her Eyes Open cried softly while he waved his hands, asking the sky to swallow him up. He patted one shoulder and then the other with the palm of his right hand. He placed both hands over his heart and sang a song asking the spirits to bless the cord and the hat's new owner. He held them up and blew a breath in each of the four directions. Finally, he said, "*Yalan,* good-bye," five times. With tears glittering in his eyes, he handed the sacred items to Lozen.

"I have taught you the songs and ceremonies for these, Daughter. May they protect you."

Kaywaykla and Santiago McKinn helped Broken Foot onto his horse. Once settled in the saddle, he grinned at Lozen, but the smile resembled his former one as much as he resembled his young self.

"I have no use for war medicine anymore." He picked up the reins in gnarled hands that trembled constantly.

Her Eyes Open sat on her little paint and watched while the rest of Broken Foot's small band mounted. Kaywaykla and Santiago McKinn ran to Lozen and threw their arms around her. "May we live to see each other again, Grandmother."

"My sons, take care of Grandfather and Grandmother." Lozen was sorry to see both of the boys go. There had been so few children in the band even before Broken Foot decided to leave.

Broken Foot rode down the twisting trail leading from the high plateau to the desert floor. Her Eyes Open, six other women, and a few young ones rode with him. Almost a month ago Chihuahua and seventy-six of his people had headed north to surrender at Fort Bowie. The departures left behind Lozen, Geronimo, fifteen other warriors, twelve women, and six children, including two infants.

Lozen could only guess how many men were pursuing them. She and the others had discussed it, more to entertain themselves than for any strategic reasons. They estimated that their enemies numbered about five thousand Bluecoats, three thousand Mexican troops, and at least a thousand American ranchers, miners, farmers, and townsmen. They could assume that everyone they met would be against them.

Nine thousand men chasing seventeen Ndee warriors. The odds made Lozen proud. Beating the Pale Eyes was out of the question. All they could do was survive as long as possible and then take as many of their enemies with them as they could when the time came to die.

Lozen watched Broken Foot's small procession round a bend in the trail; then she climbed to the top of an outcrop and looked around at the mountains marching to meet the rim of the sky. From here the land looked empty of life. Lozen wondered if she and her little band were the last Ndee free of the Pale Eyes' yokes and nooses and fences.

The sun glowed with heat as intense as the charcoal fires of the Pale Eyes *pesh-chidin,* the spirits of the iron. She had scorch marks on her hands from the hot barrel of her rifle. Hunger caused her stomach to cramp. Her muscles ached.

A fierce elation swept through her, anyway. No matter how hungry or cold or hot she was, no matter how exhausted or sore or despairing, she was free. She could roam the wide world with no one to tell her where to camp or how to act. When her band wanted to see their families, they could sneak back onto the reservation for a visit. Maybe they could convince some of their people to come away with them again.

Lozen took pinches of pollen from her pouch and let it blow to the four directions. When she reached inside for more to rub on her forehead, she found the copper penny in the bottom of the sack. It was bright from the many times she had rubbed its surface while she wondered where Hairy Foot was and what he was doing.

She knew that Hairy Foot's intentions had been good when he gave the coin to her, but it had proved worthless as an amulet. The marks that said LIBERTY were another Pale Eyes lie. She threw the coin out into the hot summer air. It glinted in the sun, spinning as it fell toward the valley far below.

The elation left as suddenly as it had arrived. With a stone-heavy heart, she walked back down to the brush shelters of their camp, most of which were empty now. The cook fires would be lonely tonight.

FUR BRISTLED IN RIDGES ALONG GAUNT BACKS OF THE MEX-icans' dogs when Lozen and Stands Alone rode into the dust-coated collection of thatched huts and crumbling adobe houses called Fronteras. The women stopped grinding corn and patting out tortillas and stared. The children scattered into the houses. The men watched through narrowed eyes.

Lozen could sense the Mexicans' hatred and fear as easily as she could smell the corn, beans, and chiles cooking. Lozen's stomach growled. In the past three days, she had eaten a few handfuls of berries, some wild potatoes, and tornillo beans.

All summer they had done what Geronimo enjoyed most, they had killed Mexicans and stolen their possessions. In the process, they had used up their ammunition, and they headed north toward Arizona again where they could steal more. Before they reached the border, the children's gaunt faces had convinced Lozen to ride to Fronteras in search of sup-plies. Stands Alone had volunteered to come with her.

Both of them knew they hadn't much chance of leaving the village alive, but Lozen remembered what her brother said. "When one does not fear death, courage is easy." Lozen could have added to that wisdom. "When one is dealing with Mexicans, lying is easy."

She and Stands Alone were not surprised when soldiers locked them in a storage room hazy with dried grain chaff. When the mayor came, Lozen convinced him that Geronimo was willing to talk peace. She intimated that negotiating the surrender of Geronimo would enhance his esteem. As a show of his good faith, she said, he should send Geronimo presents of corn, beans, and dried beef, blankets, cloth, and knives.

Now Lozen and Stands Alone were leading three ponies loaded with supplies, including ten bottles of mescal. Lozen planned to throw most of those away, but she had to calculate the number of bottles she kept. If she didn't bring any whiskey, the men would become even surlier than they had been after their supply ran out. With too much of it, they would become dangerous to themselves and others in the band.

When Lozen and Stands Alone passed the last raving dog, she let out a sigh that was as much contentment as relief. The children would eat.

She couldn't see the *capitán* of Fronteras' small garrison requesting two hundred reinforcements wait for the Apache peace delegation. She couldn't see the mayor telegraphing Arizona to tell the new General Gringo that Geronimo was not two hundred miles south as everyone had assumed. Lozen did know that the Mexicans intended to throw a party when Geronimo's men came to Fronteras, and then to make a game attempt to murder them. The Mexicans' intentions didn't matter, because Geronimo had intentions of his own. His intentions did not include talking peace with Mexicans.

GERONIMO'S FOURTEEN-YEAR-OLD NEPHEW, KANSEAH, took sentry duty seriously. He did not sleep. He did not play cards with the one friend he had left. He peered through the army field glasses at the two men approaching across the valley floor. He gave a hawk's whistle to signal Geronimo and the others.

When Geronimo arrived with a few of his men, he took

the glasses from Kanseah and studied the riders.

"They're the Pale Eyes' dogs, Martine and Kayitah." Geronimo handed glasses to the warrior named Yanozha. "I have bullets for them."

"Kayitah is my wife's cousin," said Yanozha. "If you lift your rifle, I will kill you." He climbed onto a rock and waved at them. "Come up here," he shouted. "No one will hurt you."

When Martine and Kayitah arrived, they found Lozen and the other warriors waiting to hear what they had to say.

Kayitah began. "All of you are my friends, and some of you are my relatives. I don't want you to get killed."

Geronimo interrupted. "We do the killing."

Kayitah held his temper. No one expected courtesy from Geronimo. "The Bluecoat named Beak waits for you at Shady Canyon near the Bavispe River. He offers you peace."

"We are done talking with Bluecoats."

"He brings you presents, too." Kayitah knew that would bring Geronimo in, if nothing else would, but he gave them other reasons. "You people have no chance. You eat your meals running. At night you cannot rest. You listen for a stick breaking or a rock rolling down the mountain. Even the high cliff is your enemy. At night when you dodge around, you might fall off that cliff." Then he told them one more fact that they already knew. "You have no friends in the world."

WHILE RAFE WAITED FOR THE COFFEE TO BOIL, THE CANYON to sprout Apaches, and hell to freeze over, he thought about the lunacy of the situation. Any sane man would have refused this assignment. Lt. Charles "Beak" Gatewood was still sane after ten years of chasing Apaches, yet here he sat waiting to make a deal with the most mendacious, murderous mortal to claim the rank of human being, or maybe brevet human being.

Gatewood's presence was more remarkable because he looked too spindly to stand upright in a breeze, and unlike

Britt Davis, he didn't trust Indians. In fact, Rafe thought, if Davis hadn't quit the army to oversee a Mexican rancho, he would probably be here instead of Gatewood. Rafe would've enjoyed Davis's company more. The scouts might call Gatewood Beak, but Rafe's personal nickname for him was Bleak. He was as honest as Davis, and that counted when dealing with Apaches.

General Miles had ordered Gatewood to take twenty-five soldiers with him. Rafe knew that was another of General Always Too Late To Fight's bad ideas. Geronimo would never come in to talk if a lot of Bluecoats were loitering about. Rafe and Beak were relieved that the border outposts could spare only ten men. Now Rafe wished those fifteen extra soldiers had come along. He figured they would have given the Apaches someone else to shoot at.

Rafe and Gatewood, the interpreter George Wratten, and the Apache scout Martine ate their breakfast of corn pone and coffee. Martine had returned the day before with word that Geronimo would come for talks today. Geronimo had kept Kayitah as a hostage.

General Miles must have had a change of head about the usefulness of the Apache scouts. The rumor was that he had offered Martine and Kayitah seventy thousand dollars each if they persuaded Geronimo to surrender. That would buy a considerable amount of loyalty and enthusiasm from a white man, but it was meaningless to an Apache. All they wanted was some land on Turkey Creek near Fort Apache, where they could live with their families. Miles had promised them that, too. Hell, Miles would have promised them the moon and stars to get Geronimo in his clutches.

Since the money didn't mean anything to them, the scouts might be plotting an ambush with Geronimo's crowd. Kayitah was related by marriage to one of Geronimo's men, and he was friends with most of the rest. Maybe he hadn't stayed behind as a hostage, but as an ally. A plot hardly seemed necessary, though. The men of the small detachment were sitting ducks.

The morning advanced while Rafe, Beak, Wratten, and

Martine played whist in the shade of the walnut tree. Gatewood had just decided Geronimo was going to stand them up when a figure rose from the grass a few hundred yards away. Another appeared to the west and one to the east.

As the three Apaches walked toward them, two more popped up.

"How long you reckon they been there?" asked Beak.

"Probably since before sunup," said Rafe.

"Then I guess they'd've killed us already if they'd a mind to."

Rafe grunted. He was too busy counting heads to make conversation. His fingers twitched to reach for his carbine. When the last warrior appeared, Rafe totaled only fifteen plus Geronimo. Was this the fabled Chiricahua force that had beleaguered the armies of two countries for more than a year?

Rafe did not see Lozen among them. The scouts said that the Chiricahuas kept her out of sight, assuming the Pale Eyes wouldn't understand her unique position. They thought the Americans would judge her a loose woman. They were probably right.

The men stood out of rifle range while Geronimo and Mischievous walked to the camp under the trees. Mischievous was as tall and handsome as his father, Cochise. He was the buffalo-nickel image of a chief. Geronimo's face would have looked more at home on a pirate's flag than a coin. Even in the August heat, he wore a dusty, rumpled, black coat over his breechclout, faded cotton shirt, and cartridge belt. He had knotted one red bandana around his head and another at his neck.

Geronimo laid his Winchester on the ground, but his men kept their weapons. George Wratten stood by to interpret. Geronimo shook Gatewood's hand. The old man's smile reminded Rafe of the cheeky papier-mâché skulls the Mexicans made for their Day of the Dead festivals.

"Greetings, my old friend." Geronimo was positively jovial. The Pale Eyes were holding council with him on his ground, on his terms, and giving him presents, too. "What's the matter with you, Long Nose? Your legs look like a coyote's. Did you get skinny chasing us?"

"I'm glad you've come." Gatewood and Geronimo made themselves comfortable on two saddles laid across fallen logs. While George Wratten gave away the dried horse meat and other delicacies, Rafe handed out tobacco and papers.

Soon the warriors were smoking and laughing among themselves. Rafe knew what they were thinking. They would agree to meander north in the fall, visit with their families, and live on goverment rations through the winter. In spring, when life on the reservation ceased to suit them, they would take off again.

They're happy as butcher's dogs now, Rafe thought, but wait until they hear what General Miles has done with their people.

Before Rafe, Wratten, and Gatewood left Fort Apache, Miles had told them his plan. He would inform the Apaches on the reservations that the president of the United States wanted to see them and shake their hands. Then he would load them all, even the Apache scouts and those who had cooperated through thin and thinner, onto trains bound for Florida.

Arizona and New Mexico Territories would not be bothered by them again. Rafe was certain that Miles would not be bothered by his conscience, either. When it came to mendacity, Miles was a match for Geronimo. Gatewood was bothered by the scheme, but he knew he had to persuade Geronimo to surrender or the killing would never end.

Gatewood shot straight to the point. "Surrender, and you will be sent to join the rest of your people in Florida."

"Are all of our people gone?" Geronimo looked more than stunned. He looked poleaxed.

"Every man, woman, and child."

As Lozen walked between the two lines of jeering Bluecoats, she wanted to cover her ears. She didn't care about the soldiers' taunts, but the army band's bugle, trumpets, clarinet, fife, banjo, harmonica, drums, and tuba hurt her ears. A thousand braying mules could not have made such a racket.

She did not know that the song was "Auld Lang Syne," so she did not understand why the soldiers were laughing. She chanted her medicine song softly. It calmed her, but she had no faith that it would help her. Broken Foot always said that medicine worked only if one had a positive attitude. That was not possible here.

Lozen walked with Stands Alone at the rear of the column of fifteen men. She felt the brief, spider-touch of Stands Alone's fingers on her hand, a plea for reassurance. Behind them trudged the fourteen other women and two children.

Nantan Always Too Late To Fight had promised Martine and Kayitah land along Turkey Creek, but here they were, waiting to be loaded onto the train along with the people they had betrayed. Lozen found some satisfaction in the certainty that her people would make them suffer for their treachery.

Lozen glanced at Geronimo's cousin, Little Parrot. When he heard that *Nantan* Always Too Late to Fight had sent his family to that dark place called Florida, he had said he could not go on fighting, knowing he would never see them again. Others had defected, too. Geronimo and Lozen both knew then that this struggle was over and another one was beginning.

At the end of the blue tunnel of soldiers chuffed the huge iron monster that would carry them in its belly to a living death. No one had been to Florida before. People thought of it as the Death Journey that spirits made, but they would be making it while they still lived.

When fire and smoke roared from the engine, children cried and women screamed and hid their faces. Lozen flinched, but she kept walking. She chanted her Enemies-Against song.

I am of the sun.
I see from a height.

I see in every direction.
I call on earth and sky to show me.

For the past thirty years she had expected to die in battle,
and maybe she would have a chance to yet. When *nantan*
Always Too Late To Fight said Lozen's band would see their
families, most people assumed he meant they would see each
other in the Land of Death. Everyone thought the white people intended to take them only a short way in this snorting,
iron wagon. Then they would kill them.

George Wratten was coming with them as interpreter.
Even Lozen trusted him. Even she believed he was a friend,
but if the entire nation of Pale Eyes was determined to kill
them, what could he do?

Lozen knew what she could do. The soldiers had searched
all of them, but they had not found the thin knife she had
hidden in the thick, knee-length braid that was tucked into
her belt. If the white people attacked, she would kill as many
of them as she could, and then she would kill herself.

The last of the warriors climbed into the coach car. Lozen
put a hand on the rail and a moccasined foot on the bottom
step.

"*Shiwoye,* Grandmother."

Lozen looked back and saw Hairy Foot dodge through the
shouting mob of soldiers. He ran toward her. She turned
away, mounted the stairs, and walked into the monster's
belly.

The women and children boarded. Soldiers closed the
doors and locked them. The whistle shrieked. The train
chugged into life and crept forward.

Rafe walked alongside it in the shower of cinders and soot,
and tried to catch a glimpse of her through the windows. As
the train picked up speed, he stopped and watched it dwindle
into the distance.

"*Yalan, Shiwoye,*" he murmured. "Good-bye, Grandmother."

Epilogue

GHOST WARRIORS

Not all Pale Eyes wished Geronimo's people ill. Kinder ones protested the conditions at Fort Pickens in the malarial swamps of Pensacola, Florida. After six months they prevailed. The government transferred Geronimo's small band to Mount Vernon barracks, a sixty-year-old army post in Alabama. The buildings occupied a rise of land, but they, too, were surrounded by swamps. The forest grew so thick around it that the Ndee men climbed trees to catch glimpses of the sky.

General Nelson Always Too Late To Fight Miles had told them that they would see their families in five days, but eight months passed before they were reunited. George Wratten stayed with them as interpreter. Dr. Walter Reed served as their physician. They had need of him.

The Ndee tried to hide their children, but the authorities found them and took them away. They sent them to the Indian school in Carlisle, Pennsylvania, to be turned into law-abiding, God-fearing citizens. Kaywaykla, the child Victorio named His Enemies Lie In Heaps, was the youngest of the Chiricahuas to attend.

Lozen went with the parents when they greeted the train bringing the young ones back for holidays. They discovered to their horror that many of the children were stricken with consumption. It was a disease that they had never known. It was also a death sentence because neither their *di-yin* nor the Pale Eyes could cure it. A popular remedy with the Pale Eyes was a poisonous hallucinogen called lachnanthes mixed with alcohol, strychnine, chloroform, and morphine. Other Pale Eyes recommended the fumes from a cow barn or a syrup containing ground-up millipedes. The People declined them all.

The children coughed. They grew thin and spit up blood. Distraught parents begged Lozen to rid the young ones of the worms that caused the sickness. Lozen ground up the root they called *narrow* and steeped it in a watertight basket with four hot stones to heat the water. She performed the traditional rituals with pollen before she gave it to her patients, but the medicine had little effect.

She had to acknowledge that her spirits had deserted her, and her medicine was useless. Whenever one of her young patients died, Lozen felt as though a part of her went with the child. She grew thin from anxiety and sorrow and lack of sleep. No one was surprised when she caught the disease herself.

Stands Alone, Niece, and Her Eyes Open sat by her side while Broken Foot worked to make her better. The entire band stood outside and sang the choruses of the healing songs. Lozen heard it all, but she felt a strange mix of detachment, disorientation, and relief. She was supposed to be the healer, not the patient, but being a patient had its advantages. She did not have to feel responsible if the medicine failed.

When Ghost Owl came for her, she closed her eyes, smiled, and greeted him as an old friend. He and she had a long journey to make together, and she was eager to start. She did not stay to see her people carry her body far into the woods and bury her where no Pale Eyes would ever find her. She did not hear the wailing that went on for weeks. She was free at last to ride with her brother across every mountain and valley of the land she cherished.

Those who revere her memory know she still rides there.